LORI FOSTER

THE MCKENZIES OF
RIDGE TRAIL

Published by
Mills & Boon
An imprint of Harlequin Enterprises (Australia) Pty Limited (ABN 47 001 180 918), a subsidiary of HarperCollins Publishers Australia Pty Limited (ABN 36 009 913 517)
Level 19, 201 Elizabeth Street
SYDNEY NSW 2000
AUSTRALIA

MIX
Paper | Supporting
responsible forestry
FSC
www.fsc.org
FSC® C001695

Printed and bound in Australia by McPherson's Printing Group

CONTENTS

Also available from Lori Foster

No Holding Back

Very special thanks to army ranger master sergeant Shayne Laflin for answering the million and one questions I had on army rangers.

To amazing author Pamela Clare, and wonderful reader Kim Potts, thank you for sharing info on the Colorado landscape, highways, the front range and small towns along the Rockies.

I also want to share my heartfelt gratitude and deep respect to all who serve in our armed forces, and the families who love and support them.

And to the special police task forces fighting daily against human trafficking and forced labor, thank you. I know you see things no one should have to, and that your job is incredibly difficult on so many levels. Thank you for still doing it. You're making the world a better place.

Any and all errors, either on Colorado, rangers or task forces, are entirely my own!

CHAPTER ONE

SHIVERS RACKED HER body as she watched him drink. Curled in the corner, waiting, dreading the inevitable—even breathing was difficult with so much fear crowding in around her. She wanted to cry but knew it wouldn't help. She wanted to let in the hysteria, but she hadn't quite accepted her fate...not yet.

She couldn't.

Outside the room, two other men stood guard. They'd told her she'd be forced to do this up to ten times a night, and she wasn't sure she'd even survive this first time.

She wanted to go home.

She wanted to curl up and die.

Mostly she wanted to fight—but how?

Amused by her fear, the man watched her while tossing back another shot. He enjoyed her terror—and that amplified everything she felt.

What to do, what to do, what to do?

Her gaze frantically searched the second-story room. One small window, opened to let in a breeze, led to a sheer drop onto a gravel lot. Would she survive going out that window? At the moment, did it really matter?

The man stood near the door. He'd slid a metal bar into place, locking her in, ensuring she couldn't get past him. But also ensuring no one else could get in. Not until he'd finished.

He'd paid for two hours but now didn't seem in any rush to get started.

To the right of the door, a tiny table held a bottle of whiskey and a single glass. To the left, an empty wooden coat tree stood as a place for him to hang his clothes.

A bare mattress on a small bed occupied a wall.

Nothing else.

Only her fear, the reality, the terror, her hatred, the cruelty... *her will to survive.*

When his loose lips stretched into a smug grin, she braced herself—and noticed that he stumbled a little as he stepped toward her.

Her heart punched painfully. Slowly, she slid up the wall to her feet. An invisible fist squeezed her throat, but she sidled sideways, toward that barred door.

Toward the little table.

From the hallway, loud music played. Whatever happened in this room, they didn't want to be bothered with it.

She kept her gaze locked on his, her hands clammy with sweat, so afraid that her limbs felt sluggish.

"Thinking to run?" he asked, his grin widening with anticipation.

"I... I was hoping I could have a drink, too?"

"You want to numb yourself? No, I don't think so."

He wanted her afraid. He wanted her to feel every awful second of this degradation. With a lot of effort, she tamped down the need to vomit and managed to ask, "Then...should I pour you another?"

Snorting, he propped a shoulder to the wall. "Want to get me drunk, huh? Sure, go ahead and try it, but you'll see, I know how to hold my liquor." Tipping his head, he narrowed his eyes and the grin turned into a sneer. "Alcohol makes me mean."

Refusing to dwell on that possibility, she forced a nod, reaching for the bottle anyway, letting him see how badly she trembled. She filled the small glass, then lifted it...while keeping the bottle in her other hand.

The obnoxious brute paid no attention; he focused on watching her quake as she came to him, the glass held out as a feeble offering.

Instead of taking it, he caught her wrist in a painful grip, jerking her toward him, laughing as she cried out.

She swung the bottle with all her might.

STERLING JERKED AWAKE with a start, her heart racing and her throat aching with the need to scream.

She didn't. She never did—no matter what. Silence kept her safer than a scream ever could.

In just seconds, she absorbed the low light of the bar, the ancient rock and roll playing on the jukebox, the clamor of a few dozen voices talking low to one another.

God. She swallowed heavily, looking around at the familiar sights. Her gaze landed on the bartender.

He watched her. *Always.*

Nothing got by that man.

He could pretend to be an average guy, he could wear the trappings of a simple bar owner, but she knew better. He hid something, maybe something as monumental as her own secrets, but she wouldn't ask. The Tipsy Wolverine bar was her haven from the road. She could sleep in her truck, and sometimes did, but she didn't truly rest.

Here, in the little Podunk bar in the small mountain town of Ridge Trail, Colorado, she knew no one would bother her.

Because of *him*.

Again her eyes sought him out. She guessed him at six feet five. *Really* big, but solid head to toes. Posture erect. Awareness keen. He wore his glossy dark hair neatly trimmed, precisely styled... but it was those piercing blue eyes that really caught and held her attention.

His gaze had veered away from her, but that didn't make him unaware. Sterling pegged him as ex-military, or maybe something deadlier. He was too damn physically fit to be anyone ordinary.

Her nostrils flared a little as she looked him over. In the seedy area of town where locals slumped in their seats and laughed too loudly, he was always...mannered. Contained. Professional but not in the way of a suited businessman.

More like a guy who knew he could handle himself in any situation. A guy who easily kicked ass, took names and did so without a scratch. Those thick shoulders... Studying his body left a funny warmth in Sterling's stomach, sending her interested gaze to his pronounced biceps, watching the fluid bunch and flex of them with the smallest movement. His pullover shirt fit his wide chest perfectly, showing sculpted pecs and, letting her attention drift downward, a flat, firm middle.

Lord, the man was put together fine. Add in a lean jaw, a strong but straight nose, and those cool blue eyes fringed by dark lashes, and she assumed he broke hearts on a daily basis.

Not *her* heart. She wasn't susceptible to that kind of stuff. She could take in the exceptional view and stay detached. *She could.*

Only...this time she had to really concentrate to make it true.

His gaze locked to hers, catching her perusal, and his firm lips quirked in a small "you're not immune" smile.

It made her mouth go dry.

He couldn't know that, could he? Yet he looked as if he'd just read her every admiring thought.

Feeling oddly exposed, she held up her glass, realized it was still full and hastily mouthed, "Coffee?"

With a nod, he moved away to a service counter behind the bar. Less than half a minute later, he strode over in his casual yet confident way with a steaming cup.

He knew how she took it, with one sugar and a splash of creamer. He knew because he missed nothing. Ever.

Setting it before her, he asked, "Done with this?" indicating the shot she'd ordered—and hadn't touched.

Usually, to justify her lengthy naps, she bought a couple of drinks. This time, exhausted to the bone, she hadn't lasted long enough.

"Thanks." Sterling sipped her coffee.

That he didn't move away set her heart tripping. Defiant, she glanced up and caught a slight frown carved from what appeared to be concern. She was good at reading people—except for him. Most of the time she didn't know what he was thinking, and she didn't like that.

Suspicion prickled. "What?"

Heavy lashes lowering, he thought a moment before meeting her gaze again. "I'm worried that anything I say might put you off."

Sterling stiffened with accusation. "What do you have to say?"

"Such a lethal tone," he teased—as if they knew each other well. "You don't have to order drinks just to be in here. You want a place to kick up your feet—"

Abruptly, she dropped her feet from the seat of the chair across from her. She unconsciously braced herself—to act, to react, to protect herself if necessary.

"Or to rest without being disturbed," he continued, ignoring her tension. "You're always welcome." As if he knew her innate worry, as if he could see her automatic response to his nearness, he took a step back. "No questions asked, and no drink order necessary."

Before she could come up with a reply, he walked away.

For twenty minutes, Sterling remained, but he didn't look at her again.

Not until she walked out. He watched her then. Hell yeah, he did. She felt his gaze burning over her like a physical touch. Like *interest*. It left her with heightened awareness.

Of him.

Damn, damn, damn.

CADE WANTED TO kick his own ass.

She'd been coming into the bar for months now. She hadn't yet given her name, but he knew it all the same. He made a point of knowing everyone in the bar, whether they were important to his operation or not.

Sterling Parson. Star for short.

Privately, he called her Trouble.

At a few inches shy of six feet, her body toned, she walked with a self-possessed air that he recognized as more attitude than ability. She wore that swagger like a warning that all but shouted *Back off.*

Her long wavy brown hair was usually in a ponytail, occasionally in a braid and sometimes stuffed under a trucker's cap.

Despite the loose shirts she wore with straight-legged jeans and mean lace-up black boots in an effort to disguise her body, she'd be hard to miss. For sure no one in his bar had missed her.

The woman was unique in so many ways. Bold but somehow vulnerable. Composed, yet temperate. Beautiful...but only to a discerning eye, because she did all she could to blend in.

The big rig she drove had SP Trucking emblazoned on the side, yet she was far from the usual trucker they got as customers.

The day she'd first walked in, heads had swiveled, eyes had widened and interest had perked—but after Cade swept his gaze around the room, everyone had gotten the message.

The lady was off-limits.

Cade hadn't bothered to explain to anyone. He never did... except occasionally to family. Then only when pressed.

From the moment he'd first spotted Sterling, he'd sensed the emotional wounds she hid, knew she had secrets galore and understood she needed a place to rest.

She needed *him*.

Star didn't know that yet, but no problem. In his bar, in this shit neighborhood, he'd look out for her anyway—same as he did for anyone in need.

Moving to the window, he watched her leave. Her long stride carried her across the well-lit gravel lot, not in haste but with an excess of energy. He couldn't imagine her meandering. The woman knew one speed: full steam ahead.

After unlocking the door, she climbed into her rig with practiced ease. Head tipped back, she rested a moment before squaring her shoulders and firing the engine. She idled for a bit, maybe checking her gauges, then eased off the clutch and smoothly rolled out to the road. Cade watched until he couldn't see her taillights anymore.

Where she'd go, he didn't yet know—but he wanted to. He wanted to introduce himself, ask questions, maybe offer assistance.

Her preferences on that were obvious.

Except that tonight she'd watched him a little more.

Actually, she often noticed him, in a cautious, distrustful way. And she always came back.

Sometimes she'd sleep for an hour, sometimes longer. Tonight, she'd dozed for two hours before jerking awake in alarm.

A bad dream?

Or a bad memory?

If she kept to her usual pattern, she'd be back tomorrow night on her return trip. Maybe, just maybe, he'd find a chink in her armor. He glanced at the little table she always chose.

Tomorrow, he'd offer her something different.

AFTER TOO MUCH DRIVING, sitting through endless traffic in Colorado's summer heat and going without enough rest, Sterling returned to the bar. Aching from her eyebrows to her toes, it was a relief to pull in to the lot a littler earlier than usual.

She'd thought about finding another place to rest. Bars and truck stops riddled this side of the Rockies. Before discovering the Tipsy Wolverine, she'd often crashed in a different location each time, but here... For some reason she was mostly comfortable here. *Mostly.*

It was the bartender, she knew. He didn't say much, didn't thump his chest like an ape—because he didn't have to. His commanding presence let everyone know that he was the one in charge.

She knew it. In that bar, no one could hurt her because he wouldn't let them.

Sterling shook her head. It was a crazy conclusion, but she trusted her instincts. So far, they'd served her well.

Grabbing her discarded jacket, she climbed out of the truck. Higher in the mountains, the chill could seep into her bones, but here in the valley, it had to be in the midnineties. The temperature in Colorado was all about elevation. The higher you went, the colder it got. She'd learned that her button-up shirt would be fine in the valley, but if the road climbed—and it sometimes did—she needed warmer clothes. The air-conditioning in the bar often chilled her, too, especially when she napped.

Her long sloppy ponytail bounced and her heavy boots crunched on gravel when she strode across the lot. Some strange sensation sizzled inside her.

She refused to acknowledge it as anticipation.

The minute she walked through the door, she knew something was different. Two men, regulars that she recognized, sat at her customary table. That hadn't happened since her third visit months ago. The table was usually saved for her. Without pausing, she continued into the dim room, giving a casual glance around.

No, it wasn't extra crowded.

Yes, there were other tables available.

So why, then...

The bartender stepped in front of her, his nearly six and a

half feet of muscle drawing her to a sudden stop. "Could I have a word?"

Almost plowing into him sent her heart shooting into her throat. She was tall enough that few men made her feel small, but this one towered over her.

Damn it, she hadn't even noticed him approach before he was just...there, standing too close, crowding her with his size and strength. In a nanosecond, her body jolted into defense mode.

She hid her unease even as she considered her options of fight or flight.

And damn him, he *knew* it. She saw it in the way his gaze sharpened, how his mouth softened.

In sympathy?

Screw that. Sterling took a step back, ready to retreat. Not like fighting was an actual option.

Raising his hands, his expression impassive, he said, "At the bar would be fine, if you have just a minute. I'm still on the clock."

Her gaze skipped to her table, and seconds ago she'd anticipated resting her bones in that well-worn seat. Now some of her exhaustion had lifted.

"I can move them if you want me to," he offered quietly. "After I've explained."

She had no interest in conversing with him, being drawn to him in any way. Familiarity worried her, yet curiosity won out. To cover her caution, she offered a casual shrug and indicated he should lead the way.

No way did she want him at her back.

He gifted her with that brief smile again.

Such a nice mouth, she couldn't help noticing. Not that she cared. Nice or not, she refused involvement.

He turned and headed for the bar.

Drawing in a bracing breath, she followed. Nice back, too. And forearms. And his backside in those jeans...

Sterling frowned at herself and vowed none of it mattered.

No one else sat at the far end of the scarred, polished wood counter, and once she'd taken the last stool, he circled around.

"Coffee? Cola?"

"Coke is fine."

"I can throw you together a sandwich if you want."

In most cases, she refused food when offered to her, but here, from him, it seemed okay—especially with her stomach grumbling. "Sure, thanks."

He went through a half door that led to the kitchen behind the bar and returned a minute later with a ham-and-cheese sandwich and chips. After setting the food before her, he filled a glass with ice and poured her a Coke.

Sterling realized he must have coordinated this little meet and greet, because one of his workers took over filling orders without being asked.

Obviously he was up to something—but what?

Watching her a little too closely, he leaned a hip against the bar. "You don't miss much, do you?"

Her gaze shot to his. She had a mouthful and had to chew and swallow before she could answer. "Should I?"

"No, but few people are as aware as you are." He opened his own cola, drinking straight from the bottle. "My name is Cade McKenzie, by the way."

"I didn't ask."

"I know. But I thought if you knew more about me, you'd—"

"What?" Panic, maybe anger, sharpened her tone. "Loosen up? Like you more? Get friendly?"

"Stop distrusting me."

Had her wariness been so noticeable? Apparently. "I'm eating your sandwich. What is that if not trust?"

Her reasoning made him grin, showing straight white teeth, and good God, when he did that, he was too damn gorgeous. The amusement softened his granite edge, made him feel approachable.

And damn it, it sparked something deep inside her.

She concentrated on her sandwich.

"My brother owns a gym in town," he continued. "You've probably noticed him in here a few times."

Of course she had. The family resemblance was unmistakable. "He's younger, different-colored eyes."

Nodding at this additional sign of her awareness, he explained, "Different mothers, but we were raised together. I have a sister, too. She's the baby at twenty-six."

"Does she look like you, as well?" She hadn't seen any women at the bar that she'd have pegged as a relation.

"Similar features, only more feminine. Same-colored eyes as my brother, but her hair is lighter than ours."

It struck Sterling that she was chatting. Casually, easily. When had she last done that? The shock of it put her on edge. "I didn't ask for a family rundown."

"I know. Other than your usual table and an occasional drink, all you ask for is to be left alone."

"Yet here we are." Not that she could entirely blame him for that. She'd chosen to accept the food, the conversation. Nothing would come of it, though. Not more familiarity. Not friendship.

Definitely nothing beyond that.

He leveled that electric-blue stare on her. "I wanted to show you that I have roots here, that I'm not a threat in any way."

Refusing to lower her guard, she asked, "But *why*?" She didn't trust goodwill. A motive generally followed close behind.

"Because you're a good customer, a regular, and I get that you want your space—no problem with that—but I thought I could help."

Slowly, she ate another bite of the sandwich while considering him. The urge to walk away was strong.

Oddly enough, an equally compelling urge had her asking, "Help how?" Then she thought to add, "With *what*?"

He propped his elbows on the bar, leaning toward her as he eased into his topic. "So your table... I can keep it open for you if that's what you want. That isn't a problem. But since you usually catch a nap, I wanted to offer my office."

One of the chips caught in her throat, making her cough.

Thankfully, he didn't reach around to pat her on the back. He seemed to know touching her would be a very bad move.

Instead, he nudged her glass toward her.

It took three gulps before she could catch her breath. Then she gasped, "Your office?"

A big old *no* to that. Not in a million years.

"It locks from the inside, so you wouldn't have to worry about customers stumbling in on you."

Would she have to worry about him?

"I have a key," he said, using his uncanny mind-reading super-power. "But you could hold on to it while you're in there."

The offer so surprised her that she couldn't find the right words to refuse him. She settled on shaking her head. "No thanks." She preferred to be out in the open. Not that the public option always equaled safety—she'd learned that the hard way. But at least this space was familiar to her. She'd memorized it in detail and knew the exits, the number of tables to the door, that the big front win-dow was tempered glass and that Cade McKenzie kept a few weap-ons behind the bar—but generally wouldn't need them to restore order if it came to that.

That line of thinking took her attention to his hands. Big hands. Hands that would feel like sledgehammers if he made a fist.

No, he didn't need a weapon. He *was* a weapon.

Not deterred by her refusal, he continued explaining. "I only use the office before we open and after we close. Besides my desk and chair, there's a love seat, a few throw pillows. A private landline." His gaze searched hers. "You'd be more comfortable."

Suddenly, it struck Sterling as funny. Here they were, tiptoe-ing around the obvious: she *knew* he wasn't just a bartender. And somehow he *knew* she wasn't just a trucker.

Grinning, she sat back and studied him.

"That's nice," he said.

Taken off guard, she asked, "What?"

"Your smile."

Stymied by that, it took her a second to regroup. "Look, I haven't even given you my name."

"I'm aware."

"But you know it anyway, don't you?" She expected him to lie, and when he did, she'd have solid reason not to trust him. She'd pay for her food, walk out and drive away—never to return.

Doing his own thorough study, he let his gaze move over her face as if cataloging each feature...and liking what he saw. "I can't go into details, or explain, but yes, I know your name."

Her heart skipped a beat. He'd admitted it! What did that mean for their association? Part of her shivered with alarm, but another part, a part she'd like to deny, suffered the strangest sort of...relief.

If someone actually knew her, then she was no longer alone. She existed. She *mattered*.

Sterling shook her head. Maybe he wasn't as good as she assumed.

Caught between conflicting emotions, she narrowed her eyes. "Fine. Let's hear it."

Straightening, Cade did a quick check to ensure no one listened to them, then casually dropped his research bombshell. "Sterling Parson, but you used to go by Star. You're twenty-nine, got your commercial driver's license when you were barely twenty-two, worked for Brown Transportation for a while, then bought your own rig when you were twenty-six."

Her jaw literally dropped. Dear God, he knew so much. *Too* much. She'd been right to fear him—no, damn it. *Not* fear. Just good old caution, the same caution she used with everyone. The caution that kept her alive. He wasn't different, wasn't special, and she couldn't—

"My sister," he offered with grave seriousness, interrupting her private castigation. "She's a research whiz, and I was curious."

"About me?"

"About you," he concurred.

No apology, but an explanation? "You had no right," she whispered through stiff lips.

For a moment he looked away while using one long, blunt finger to trace a bead of condensation on his cola bottle. "You can call it second nature." He rolled a thick shoulder. "Or instinct." Tension ratcheted up when he looked into her eyes, making them both a little breathless. His voice sounded like a soft growl when he added, "I felt it was important to know."

Dazed, confused and, damn him, disappointed, Sterling shook her head. "Now I have to find a new place to go."

His focus never wavered from hers. "Whatever you're up to, Star, you'll be safer here. Give yourself a minute to think before you react, and you'll admit it."

"What?" she asked with a sneer. "You don't know what I'm doing? You don't know why? How...incomplete of you."

"I tried not to overstep too much."

That made her laugh, but not with any humor.

"You're drawing attention when I assume you'd rather not. No," he said when alarm stiffened her neck, "not from anyone dangerous. Actually, all the customers have been curious about you at one time or another. I don't think any of us have ever heard you laugh."

"You can't know who's dangerous and who isn't." More than most, she'd learned that it was sometimes impossible to tell.

Softly, he insisted, "Yes, I can. I know everyone who comes here. You can trust me on that."

She snorted. She wouldn't trust anyone ever again.

"Right now there are only locals, a few truckers and a few vacationers, but it's still better not to be noticed, right? In case anyone comes around asking questions?"

Regret froze her to the spot, leaving her a little sick to her stomach, full of angst. And yearning.

God, she had so much yearning.

This bar had begun to feel like…home? How absurd. It wasn't in any way special, and it wasn't even in a good part of town. It was just a place where she could relax, and she hated to lose it.

The location was ideal for her, being only thirty minutes from I-25 with plenty of places to hide in between, and closer still to other venues known for seedier practices.

She didn't want to give it up, but what choice did she have now?

Cade made a small sound of frustration, there and gone. "Your table is empty now," he pointed out.

Yes, she was aware of that. Standing, she pulled out some cash to toss on the counter, but Cade stopped her with a shake of his head.

"This one was on the house. Go get some rest—and think about my offer."

She really didn't feel like leaving yet. Now that she'd eaten, lethargy gripped her. Finally she nodded. "All right, I'll think about it."

"Thanks, Star. I appreciate it."

"As you pointed out, I *used* to go by that name. Now I'm more comfortable with Sterling."

"I don't think you're ever really comfortable, so let's not nitpick on the name yet."

Teasing again? The man had a dimple. How unfair! He was always so attractive, but now with satisfaction in his gaze and his sexy mouth curved? Devastating.

She didn't understand him. She didn't understand herself with him, either. Rather than let him see her confusion, she headed to the table, ignoring the curious glances from the regulars who knew it was unusual for her to chat up anyone.

Despite her new caution, the feeling of security remained. Within minutes of sitting down, she dozed off.

CADE KNEW THE second she nodded off. She sat facing the rest of the bar, her long legs stretched out to the chair opposite her, her arms folded over her chest. Uncaring what anyone thought, she slumped in the seat, more reclining than otherwise, let her head rest back against the wall and closed her eyes. Long lashes sent feathery shadows over her cheekbones.

He admired her nose, narrow with the slightest arch in the bridge; he considered it perfect for her face. Not too cute, not too big or small. Like her attitude, each feature of her face and body was unique.

Her breathing deepened and slowed, but she didn't snore. Didn't go completely lax, either. Hell, he doubted she ever did.

So much churning wariness probably kept her constantly on edge. He knew it affected him that way. He rarely slept soundly, but then, he didn't need much sleep.

With any luck, she'd doze right up until closing time at midnight. Since being a bartender wasn't really his vocation, he didn't keep usual hours for the bar. Most in the area were open until 2:00 a.m., but he shut down at midnight and didn't open again until 4:00 p.m. That gave him plenty of time for other pursuits, and when the two overlapped, he had reliable staff to cover for him at the bar.

They were only an hour from closing when two strangers entered. The frisson of awareness that settled in his gut told him they were about to have problems.

Instinctively, his gaze shifted to Star.

He found her sitting upright, alert, her eyes narrowed dangerously. Well, hell.

He'd never known a woman so acutely aware of her surroundings. In that, she matched him.

Didn't mean he wanted her getting elbow deep in danger, especially not when that danger just walked into his bar.

Subtly, he drifted his gaze between her and the men—hoping she'd ignore them, that she'd go back to sleep.

Should have known better.

While he watched in frustration, she pulled the tie from her hair and let it tumble down over one shoulder.

Fuck me sideways.

He'd always known the difference a woman's hair could make to her appearance. But on Star? This softer look had a near-physical impact on him. The woman had gorgeous hair. Longer than he'd realized, and a rich brown streaked with gold by the sun. He watched as she tunneled her fingers in close to her scalp and fluffed it.

He would have liked to do that for her. Hands curled loosely, he could almost feel that silky mass.

When her slender fingers flicked open three buttons on her shirt, he locked his jaw—not that she noticed. Keeping her focus on the newcomers, she parted the shirt until a fair amount of cleavage showed, then tied the shirttails at her waist.

It took her less than thirty seconds to go from plain and reserved to a total bombshell. The "hands off" signals were gone, and instead her demeanor screamed "up for grabs."

Why? What the hell was she planning?

When she stood, he cursed silently, reading her intent.

She didn't spare him a glance. No, she'd forgotten all about him, and that nettled, because she'd been his first thought when he saw the two men.

The second she stood, she caught their attention. Wearing a flirty smile, she sauntered toward them.

Cade seriously wanted to demolish them both simply for the way they looked at her.

When she reached the bigger of the two men, she asked, "Got a cigarette?"

The guy sized her up in an insultingly thorough way, then pulled the pack from his front T-shirt pocket, shook one loose and offered it to her.

Maintaining eye contact, she leaned down and slowly slipped a cigarette free.

Both men looked down her shirt.

The second guy asked, "Light?"

"I have my own outside, but thank you." She sashayed out the door, and it wasn't just the two new guys watching her. Every man in the place had his fascinated gaze glued to her ass.

Shit. Cade quickly, but casually, directed others to cover the bar. Pretending he needed a break, he went down the hall and into the private office he'd offered for her use. After relocking the door, he went to the single window in the room, opened it and hoisted himself up and out. It was an awkward fit for a man his size, but he'd practiced before, ensuring he had multiple exits if it ever became necessary.

He considered watching Star's back very necessary.

Circling around the bar on silent feet, he listened. Her boots crunched on the gravel, guiding him. She didn't go to her rig, but then, maybe she didn't want them to know which truck was hers.

Smart—except that they could ask anyone in the bar about her, and that would be one of the first things they learned.

Cade leaned around the corner, still hidden by shadows but able to see her. She hadn't lit the cigarette, but she kept it dangling between her lips.

What are you up to?

She glanced several times at the entrance, and when the doors finally opened, she made a show of frustration.

The one who'd offered a light smiled. "Couldn't find your lighter after all?"

She shook her head, sending that wealth of thick hair to move around her breasts. Wearing a sexy pout, she asked, "Did you bring one out with you?"

He produced the lighter, then teased her with, "Say please."

Taking the cigarette from her lips, she gave him a tight smile. "Really? Because there are twenty men inside who would be glad to give me a light—without stipulations."

"Seems to me you don't like them, or you'd have gone to them for the cigarette."

Her lips curled. "You think you know what I like?"

"I know you'd like more than a smoke."

At that, she laughed, a rich, husky sound that set Cade's teeth on edge. She played a dangerous game, and he hoped like hell she didn't push too hard.

"Maybe you're right." The finger she stroked along her cleavage drew the man's heated stare. "What's your name?"

"You can call me Smith."

She laughed. "Well, Smith, how much are you willing to give?"

Not for a second did Cade believe she meant to sell herself. No, she had a bigger game in mind, and it made him scared for her.

Cade knew Smith—*what a crock*—because he and his brother had kept tabs on the man for more than a month. They knew Smith was involved in plenty of shady deals, but he was just muscle, not brains. Someone else called the shots. Someone with more power.

Cade wanted them all.

With her impetuous rush to get involved, Star jeopardized his well-made plans. Never mind that she didn't know he had plans...

"Tell you what." The guy reached to a back pocket and pulled out his wallet.

Finally, she looked a little nervous, but still, she didn't back down. Honest to God, she raised her chin.

Luckily—because Cade didn't want to blow his cover—the guy offered a card instead of cash. "You want to make a big score, come by Misfits tomorrow night. I have a buddy in need of cheering up and you'd be just the ticket."

Restoring that cocky attitude, she glanced at the card, then shoved it into her own pocket. "What time?"

"Ah, so you don't mind the idea of being his...entertainment?"

She shrugged but asked, "Is he a total pig?"

"Most of the women don't complain."

Most of the women don't complain. Meaning some did...but it didn't matter? When Smith's friend finished with them, were they even able to complain?

Breathing slow and deep kept Cade from reacting. Somehow he'd ensure Star's safety, and eventually he'd bury Smith.

For a split second, she went blank—fear? anger?—before curling her mouth in another credible smile. "I take it you've given him other *gifts*?"

"He's partial to those with long legs and big tits."

With every beat of his heart, Cade wanted her away from the bastard, but he didn't intrude. Not yet.

Toying with a long curl, Star pretended the crude language and dark insinuation didn't bother her. "How much are we talking?"

Taken by surprise, Smith reached out, wrapping his fingers in her hair. "Enough, okay? Don't push me. Just be there at nine."

She didn't flinch, didn't show any pain and didn't back down. She actually moved closer to Smith. Too damn close. "Oh, I'll be there. And I'll expect you to make it worth my while."

He leaned forward, clearly intending to kiss her, and suddenly she freed herself—minus a few dozen strands of hair. "You pay first, sugar. I don't give out freebies." Before Smith could figure out what to do, she walked away.

To her credit, she went back into the bar and relative safety. But how safe would she be when she left?

Keeping an eye on the door she went through, Smith dug out his cell phone and pressed in a number. The light from the screen emphasized his twisted smile. "Hey," Smith said, when the call was answered. "Prep the back room, okay? I have a new one coming out tomorrow." He laughed. "Yeah, you'll like her. She fits your preferences to a tee." He listened, shook his head. "No, I'm sure she's not, but I'll follow her tonight just to be safe. One thing, and it's nonnegotiable." He waited, then said, "Once you're done with her, I'm next in line."

CHAPTER TWO

STERLING DIDN'T SEE Cade when she walked back in, and it left her
even more rattled. He made her feel safer, and right now, with her
skin crawling and her heart jumping, she needed that. Whether it
made sense or not, whether he wanted to protect her or not, she
wanted him near.

Ignoring all the interested stares, chin up, eyes straight ahead,
she went to her table. Belatedly, she remembered the stupid cigarette in her hand.

She never had gotten that light.

Just as well. She'd never smoked and would probably have
choked on the thing.

Suddenly Cade was there, brushing past her, making physical contact for a single heartbeat before he went back to the bar.

The touch shook her, and settled her. How the hell was that
possible?

Sterling watched him, but then caught herself and looked away.
Trying to appear casual, she pulled out her phone and pretended
to check messages, just to give herself something to do. Her hands
shook, but hopefully no one noticed. She worked up a smile just
in case.

The two men hung around, making no bones about watching
her. So...now what? If she'd thought ahead, she'd have realized
she needed an exit plan. But no, she'd seen them and, knowing

what they were, simply reacted. The desire to destroy them had encompassed her.

Uber. That's what she'd do. And her truck?

Damn.

Cade slid another drink in front of her. So low she barely heard him, he said, "My brother is picking you up. Dark gray newer-model Ram truck. I'll take care of your rig. Leave the keys on your chair when you're ready to go."

Sterling blinked at him, but he'd already turned away. Aware of the two goons keeping her in their sights, she caught herself. Smiling like she didn't have a care, she backed up her ruse of a fun-loving girl without caution and tossed back the drink.

Because of her life choices, choices that often put her in dive bars, she'd learned to hold her liquor. This time she didn't have to. Cade must have anticipated her cooperation because he'd watered down the shot.

Just how well did he know her?

And how the hell did he plan to take care of her truck?

So far he'd made a lot of assumptions, including that she'd accept a ride from his brother. She should refuse, but... Her gaze strayed to the scumbags watching her. Yeah, they'd be a problem.

How was Cade's plan any worse than taking a ride from a stranger in an Uber?

Keeping the frown off her face wasn't easy, not while being in such a pickle, but she'd thought fast on her feet before.

Okay, so he had a decent plan. Long as his brother didn't try anything funny, it could work.

Another glance at Cade and she saw him texting on his phone. When he finished, he murmured something to his employee—a medium-height, wiry fellow he referred to as Rob—and then went into the kitchen area.

Because she felt safe doing so, Sterling looked at Rob again. On her first visit she'd noticed his eyes. They were as black as Satan's, but somehow still kind. Or maybe, considering the overpowering presence of Cade, Rob's gaze only seemed kind in comparison.

When he announced the last call, she realized it was nearly midnight. Within the next few minutes, the bar began to clear.

Even the two goons headed out. Or pretended to. She didn't trust them not to hang around outside in the hopes of catching her alone.

Cade reappeared under the guise of picking up her empty shot glass. "My brother is out front. Go straight to his truck, even if Smith tries to talk to you."

In the same easy tone he'd used, she replied, "Who put you in charge? Just so we're clear, you're not my boss."

That gave him pause. Clearly he was used to issuing orders and having them followed!

"Star—"

She ignored the use of her old name—for now. In some ways, it was even nice to hear. Familiar from a lifetime ago, before her whole world had upended. "I've survived on my own since I was seventeen. I'm not an idiot, either. So I accept the help—but if your brother tries anything, I'll kill him."

Another hesitation, and then Cade nodded. "Fair enough."

He wouldn't argue in his brother's defense? What insanity was that? Or maybe he didn't consider her a serious threat, which meant he didn't know her that well after all.

Less than reassured, Sterling asked, "You're sure my truck will be safe?"

"Guaranteed. We shouldn't talk too long, though, so tell my brother when and where you want it, and we'll get it there."

Her brows went up. "Just like that?"

Instead of explaining how he'd accomplish it, he said, "You started this. Do you have a better option?"

Sadly, no, she didn't. Standing, she scooped up her jacket—leaving her keys on the seat as he'd requested—and then pushed in her chair. "I suppose I should thank you?"

His eyes narrowed. "Not necessary. But you might consider that trust we discussed earlier."

Before she could reply, he walked away.

It was with a lot of trepidation and heightened awareness that Sterling exited the bar. Bright security lights lit the front but left murky shadows in the surrounding area. Immediately she spotted his brother. He didn't leave the driver's seat, but he did lean over and push open the passenger door.

With every crunch of her boots on the gravel, she felt eyes on her. She didn't see the goons, but she didn't doubt they were there somewhere, watching her and speculating.

Pasting on a false smile, she waved to Cade's brother as if happy to see him. She wished she at least knew his name, but Cade hadn't seen fit to tell her.

From seeing him before in the bar, she already knew his brother was a good-looking guy—not quite as tall as Cade, but close, and his body was every bit as muscular, maybe even a little more ripped. She recalled that he owned a gym and figured he'd gotten that bod as a natural result of working with customers.

"Let's go," he said when Sterling got close, as if she'd been holding him up.

Fine. She didn't want to be a nuisance, but her recklessness was over for the night. She quickly checked the door, ensuring she wouldn't get locked in, before sliding onto the seat.

She barely had the door closed when he said, "Buckle up," and put the truck in gear.

Annoyance brought her teeth together. Did he have to be as bossy as his brother? "I was planning to, so save the orders for someone else."

That made him grin. "Touchy, huh? Cade warned me, so no worries. Where we headed?"

Cade had warned him? "I'm not *touchy*, it's just—"

"Yeah, yeah. I insulted your independence. Don't chew it to death." He glanced in the rearview mirror, then back to the road. "Your place? If so, I'm going to take the long way around to lose our tail. Cool?"

Startled, she asked, "We have a tail?"

"Yeah—don't look! Damn." He scowled in annoyance. "Cade said you could handle yourself, so don't act like a rookie, 'kay?"

How infuriating! Slumping back in her seat, she snapped, "I *can* handle myself—you just caught me by surprise, that's all."

He snorted. "Sounds like a lot of shit caught you by surprise tonight. Hang on." He took a sharp turn, then accelerated until she had no choice but to grab the door handle with one hand, the dash with the other.

These were not straight, flat roads.

Even though he'd explained why, it alarmed her that he was

speeding away from where she needed to go. "Look, you can drop me off at the mall—"

"Not a chance. Cade would have my head." His gaze ran over her, then returned to the road. "For whatever reason, he's decided to focus on you."

Now, that felt incredibly insulting! His "For whatever reason" made it clear he didn't see the draw.

But damn it, she was *not* going to be offended over it. She didn't want either of them to find her attractive. She really didn't.

Through her teeth, she said, "He can just un-focus."

"Yeah, right." With a snort, he replied, "Try telling him that, because he sure as hell never listens to me."

It seemed Cade had coerced his brother into this impromptu rescue, and he clearly didn't like it any more than she did. "Damn right, I'll tell him."

Judging by his grin, he found that amusing. "Yeah, you do that. Can't wait to hear how it goes. But tonight I'm dropping you at your front door—after I lose them."

She grew more irritated by the second. "If you think I'll tell you where I live—"

"You don't need to. Now shush a sec while I concentrate on driving."

Shush? *Shush!* The urge to blast him bubbled up, but she still didn't see anyone following them, and actually, a tingle of new alarm climbed her spine. What if he was just a good liar using a story to get her out of town?

She'd gut him, that's what.

Slowly, she reached for her ankle and the knife she kept strapped there, but no sooner did her fingers touch the hilt than headlights appeared behind them.

"Determined SOBs, aren't they?" He searched the road ahead of them, then the rearview mirror again. "If you want to get out of this, I'd suggest you not stab me."

Guilty heat flushed her face.

Especially when he added, "Not that I'd let you."

"You—"

In a long-suffering voice, he said, "The mall it is."

Now that she knew the threat was real, Sterling didn't much

like that idea. She'd be a sitting duck until she could find a ride. Sure, she was good at hiding, but it was past midnight, the air had cooled, and at this hour the mall was deserted. How hard would it be for the goons to find her—and then what?

Except that Cade's brother pulled in to a small, recently completed outlet mall instead of the larger mall she'd referred to. Turning off his headlights, he quietly rolled away from the security lights, circled around the back and stopped, facing the main road.

So he wasn't dropping her off after all, just lying low for a few. She could handle that.

"Where do you want your truck?" he asked casually, as if they weren't hiding from danger. He half turned to face her. "I disabled the interior lights, but I can't use my phone yet. We don't want to tip our hand, right? But as soon as it's clear, I'll let Cade know. No reason he should have to stay out any later than necessary."

His ease afforded her some of her own. Getting comfortable in the corner of the door and the seat, as far from him as possible, Sterling considered him. "Cade knows how to drive a rig?"

"Big brother knows how to do a great many things. Ask him to jump out of a plane? No problem. Run five miles without breaking a sweat? Piece of cake. Swim underwater—"

"Do I detect some hero worship?"

"Hell yeah. Big-time." He turned back to the road, listened a second, then nodded in satisfaction. "There they go."

A car sped past them at an impossible speed, given the winding mountain roads. Subtly, Sterling let out a relieved breath. "We can head out now."

"We'll give it another thirty seconds. We don't want them to notice us, but neither do we want them to double back and find us, right?" He smiled at her. "Timing is everything."

Cade's brother was a little too cocky for her taste. She started to tell him so, but then he put the truck in gear and gradually moved forward again until he was at the edge of the road. From either direction, all they could see were streetlamps, but no traffic.

"So," he said, once they were on their way again, this time headed toward where she lived. "You and Cade?"

Denial rushed forward and she shook her head. "No." There

wasn't a scenario of her with…anyone. Never had been and never would be.

"No?"

Did he have to sound so disbelieving? "I frequent his bar, that's it."

"Uh-huh. Cade overreacted because those were just Good Samaritans hoping to find you alone on a mountain road. Got it." He drove more leisurely now. "So where do you want your truck?"

This time the question didn't take her by surprise. "I have an office."

"Makes sense." He handed over his phone. "You can text Cade so I can keep my hands on the wheel."

He'd handed her his phone? For a few seconds there, she just stared at it with the same fascination she'd give a snake. But this could be her opportunity to learn more about Cade McKenzie. Past messages with his brother could tell her a lot.

Unfortunately, when she got around to looking at the phone, all she saw was one message: Pick her up out front.

She scrolled, but that was it. Nothing else. No other numbers in the phone, no other communication, at least none readily available. If she could dig around a little…

Glancing at Cade's brother disabused her of that notion. The jerk was grinning again.

Giving up, she texted, Take the rig to her office, and she put in the address. But her curiosity didn't wane, so she asked, "What is this exactly? Some supersecret cell phone communication?"

"Sure, let's call it that. It makes us sound cool, right?"

His good humor wore on her—then the phone dinged and she looked down to see a reply from Cade. Is she behaving?

Of all the… Without alerting Cade's brother, Sterling texted back, No. She kicked my ass n took over. Bitch is hard-core. Pretty sure she never needed our help.

To which Cade replied, Star? That you?

Damn it, her lips twitched. She curled a little more in her seat, the phone held close, and almost forgot about his insufferable brother humming beside her. Yeah, it's me. How'd you know?

Brother would never call u a bitch.

So the goofball driving had some redeeming qualities? Good to know.

She tried to figure out what to say next.

Cade beat her to it. You okay?

She wasn't but wouldn't admit it to anyone but herself. Yup, NP. That is, no problems other than his brother, but she saw no reason to go into that. It'd only make her sound petty. My truck?

Getting it there now. Be safe tonight.

Did he have to treat her like a teenager? She knew how to take care of herself, and seriously, she would have been fine on her own.

Somehow.

Narrowing her eyes, Sterling texted, You 2. She waited, hoping that might offend him, but he didn't reply back.

She refused to acknowledge the disappointment she felt. After a few more seconds, she handed the phone back to his brother. "Do you have a name?"

"Course I do. It's on my birth certificate, all legal-like."

Such a frustrating man! "Care to share it?"

"No can do. After tonight, I hope to never see you again. In fact, tonight shouldn't have happened. Cade knows better." His gaze slanted her way. "You sure you two aren't boning?"

Good God, he was so ridiculous; it almost softened her mood. Instead of smiling, she dryly replied, "Pretty sure I would have noticed if we were."

"Ha!" He had no problem grinning. "See, you're getting the hang of it now."

"Meaning?"

"All that turbulent animosity is a waste of good energy. You were over there crackling with hatred, on the edge of imploding, when snarky comebacks are easier, and more effective anyway."

"Effective?" Getting used to him and his odd insults, Sterling let her spine relax against the seat back and stretched out her legs. "When you're just laughing at me?"

"Not *at* you," he denied. "Jesus. *With* you. Lighten up, already."

"One thing—I wasn't *crackling with hatred*." What a stupid way to put it.

"Then what?"

"Confusion? You haven't exactly been forthcoming, and I'm not sure what's going on."

"I'm rescuing you, that's what—but only because Cade asked me to."

"And I can't know your name because it's top secret?"

"Exactly. Consider me an enigma." He bobbed his eyebrows. "You intrigue me, though, because Cade is a hard nut to crack."

"So he wouldn't normally have offered his help?" Did that mean he considered her special—or was she in more trouble than he could ignore? Not a good thought.

"He would have helped you without you ever knowing. That he made it personal is downright fascinating."

Yeah, she had to admit, she found it rather fascinating, too. "Will my truck truly be there when I check in the morning?"

"Yup. It'll probably be there in another twenty minutes, but I hope you'll pack away some of that prickly pride and go inside for the night. Lock everything up nice and tight and don't go anywhere alone for a while."

She'd already planned to stay in for the night, but she wouldn't share that with him. Enigmas didn't deserve full disclosure.

"Ah, you've clammed up again? I get it. I wouldn't like someone saving my ass, either."

She rolled her eyes. "You haven't saved my ass—"

"Beg to differ."

"But with every word out of your mouth, my curiosity expands. So tell me, what makes you think I'll still be in danger even after I'm home?"

"You kidding? For Cade to get involved, I'm sure it was life and death, right? Dude is usually so cool. And that means, despite my excellent driving, someone could figure out where you live."

Her place was secure, so she wasn't worried about that. "Cade is cool, but you're not?"

"I'm learning." He shrugged. "See, I used to be a hothead, but big brother has a way of tamping that shit down, ya know?"

He made it sound like he'd been a hothead in younger days, but then Cade showed up and gave him a guiding hand. Did that mean Cade hadn't always been around?

"Now, don't start speculating," he warned. "My lips are sealed."

"Is that a joke? Your lips haven't stop flapping since I got in your truck."

"Flapping? I have several lady friends who would object to that description. *Flapping*," he repeated with a snort.

Extreme exasperation had her huffing. "Might be a good idea for you to work on that sarcasm next?"

"Was I sarcastic?" He was on the verge of laughing as he turned down her street. "Guess your chipper personality just brings it out of me."

"You don't have to sound so cheerful about it."

He barely managed to bank his grin. "Look, my point is that anything you want to know about Cade you'll have to get from him, not that he'll tell you anything."

"Except that he's a bartender?"

"See, you've got it." He pulled in to her apartment complex. "Is this place protected?"

"It's safe enough." Two could play the closemouthed game. "Don't worry your pretty head about it."

Showing no reaction to the insult, he said, "Wasn't planning to." He forestalled her getting out of the truck by adding, "Here. Cade said to give you this." Opening the glove box, he pulled out a cell phone.

She didn't take it. "Have one, but thanks anyway."

"Yeah, sure, I figured that. But this one has his number already programmed in."

It could also have a tracker or something on it. She forced a snarky smile. "If I took that, I'd just ditch it."

Nonplussed, he stared at her, followed by a laugh. "You're something else—let's not speculate on what. Okay then, how about this." Pulling a small notepad and pen from the center console, he jotted down a number. "Now you have it, but it's just paper, right?" He held it up, flipping it back and forth. "Not a threat. Does that work?"

"Why not?" Quickly pocketing it, she slid out of the car. "Thanks for the ride."

"You sure you don't want me to walk you up?"

"Positive."

"Suit yourself, but I'm waiting right here until I see your kitchen light come on."

Sterling spun around to frown at him. How did he know the kitchen window was the only one facing this lot?

Still being a goof, he wiggled his fingers in the air and said, "Woo-ooo, we enigmas are so mysterious."

And damn it, there was no way she could hold in her chuckle.

Course, the humor ended the minute she entered the apartment building. She liked the place because it was spacious and open, without a lot of nooks or corners for anyone to lurk. Still, it was a nice feeling to know Cade's brother was there, waiting to ensure no one bothered her.

Keys already in her hand, she went up the carpeted stairs to the second floor and unlocked her door. Soon as she stepped inside, she pulled the knife from her boot and locked up again, not just the doorknob lock but also the dead bolt she'd installed. Crossing the living room, she checked inside the closet, then strode through the kitchen and dining area to the bathroom, where she peeked inside, even glancing into the bathroom cabinet and the glass-enclosed shower, then into the bedroom. This was the only room where someone could adequately hide, so she looked first under the bed—easy enough because she didn't use a bed skirt. The closet here was bigger with more clothes, so she took a few seconds to move them around before heading back to the dining room to check the patio door, which was thankfully still locked, the additional bar in place.

Stepping into the kitchen, she couldn't resist peering out the window to where she saw Cade's brother leaning against the front fender of his truck, arms folded, staring up at her window.

Damn it, she smiled…and stepped back to flip on the light. Seconds later he drove away.

Huh. Actual, bona fide protection courtesy of Cade and his crazy-ass brother. She couldn't trust it—no really, she couldn't.

Enigma? He had that right. There was far too much she didn't know about Cade, and that made his concern suspect.

But…it didn't feel suspect. It felt genuine.

Blast it all, it felt *good.*

CADE WAITED AS long as he could, then called his brother. Soon as Reyes answered, he asked, "She's settled?"

"Far as I can tell," Reyes said, and then, "What the hell have you gotten yourself into?"

"It's complicated."

"If you mean the lady, no, she's not. In fact, I thought she was pretty clear. She means to demolish someone and doesn't want our help."

True enough—with one problem. "She zeroed in on Thacker, who told her his name was Smith."

A long pause preceded Reyes's explosive *"No fucking way."*

"'Fraid so." It enraged Cade. "From what I could pick up, she's meeting him tomorrow."

"She's to be the entertainment?"

Base entertainment was the only use Thacker and his ilk had for women. "That's what it sounded like."

"You realize your girlfriend is going to fuck up a month's worth of work."

"Not my girlfriend," Cade corrected. "But yeah. Somehow we need to escalate things."

"Dad is going to blow a gasket."

"I'm aware." Cade resented that his father still tried to pull all the strings, as if they were mere puppets. "He'll get over it."

Laughing, Reyes accused, "You're not going to tell him, are you?"

"I'll tell him—a few hours before it all goes down."

With a low whistle, Reyes let him know what he thought of that plan. "And Madison? You plan to clue her in?"

Their sister, the home base of their surveillance, was absolutely necessary. "Yeah, I'll talk to her in the morning. Go get some rest. Tomorrow is going to be—"

"An unadulterated clusterfuck."

"You don't have to sound so cheerful about it."

Reyes laughed. "Funny—your girlfriend told me the same thing. Later, bro."

Girlfriend, Cade thought with a shake of his head. As if he had room in his life for anything that frivolous.

CHAPTER THREE

HELL OF A position to be in, on the outside looking in, but Cade knew he had no one but himself to blame. As predicted, his father went quietly ballistic, but there was nothing new in that, at least whenever he dealt with Cade.

Reyes, of course, treated the whole thing like a lark. And his no-nonsense sister was as pragmatic as ever. For her, this was business as usual.

None of that made it easier for him to accept that Star mingled with human traffickers while he waited in the most disreputable of their vehicles, an aging, rusted white van with darkly tinted windows.

He'd parked across the street from the property in a run-down business district. Part bar, part hookup, a 100-percent members-only establishment, Misfits was, as they'd learned through meticulous research, a place for acquiring women and girls—against their will.

If Cade had his way, he'd go in, rip apart every bastard involved, then demolish the building so nothing was left but the blood of the abusers…and maybe a little dust. Unfortunately, he'd gotten voted down on that solution. He understood why, but that didn't make it any easier to bear.

Using binoculars, he watched through the front window of the squat brick building as Star was shown in. Currently the atmosphere inside the bar was all about music and dancing, but two burly guards stood just outside the door.

Not to keep people from entering, but to ensure no one left without permission.

The original plan had been to keep tabs until they could nail the one in charge, but Star's involvement changed that.

For as long as he lived, Cade would remember the horror on the faces of the five women they'd already rescued from Misfits. Kept in the back of an airless truck, ages varying from seventeen to thirty-three, they'd been to hell and back before his sister had ferreted out the transfer and they'd arranged to intercept en route.

Because they worked with anonymity, he and Reyes had merely pulverized the drivers—instead of killing them—and then left them for local authorities to pick up after a hot tip.

They'd ensured the freedom of the traumatized women. His sister had followed updates about them and knew three of them had returned to family, one moved far away and another was in the women's shelter his father funded.

He had to believe they'd recover, but still they visited him in his nightmares.

If only he could find a way to shut down these fucking enterprises *before* they abused anyone. His father, who ran the operation, had no qualms about them using deadly force when absolutely necessary. Anyone who thought to enslave another deserved nothing less than death.

Cade believed that clear down to his soul. When he killed the heartless pricks, he did the world a favor.

Just then, he spotted Star dancing in the middle of several guys. Damn, the lady had nice moves.

Had Star noticed Reyes sitting at a booth? Not much got past her, but Reyes had subterfuge down to a fine art. Without Cade's military training, Reyes could fit in with the coarsest street toughs.

His brother was there as fast backup if it became necessary. With any luck, though, this was a trial of sorts, where they only wanted to see how far they could push Star, instead of imprisoning her tonight.

For once, Cade was glad he'd joined his father's family-based enterprise, though their reasons were different. Cade had resisted as long as he could, to the point that he'd enlisted with the army at eighteen in an effort to put distance between him and his only parent.

Unlike some of the new recruits, he'd taken to basic training, liking the structure enough that he went on to airborne school, and RIP—the Ranger Indoctrination Program—and finally, he'd served with the Seventy-Fifth Ranger Regiment. Military life suited him, and he would have made it his career, but after a lot of deployments carrying heavy weight, along with hard landings from jumping out of planes, his multiple leg issues had forced him into a medical discharge.

That didn't mean his no-fail mentality had changed, or that he didn't stay in top-notch shape. In a pinch, he could even sky jump from another plane.

He just couldn't do it on a regular basis.

Teaming up with the family in their effort to combat human trafficking was the only means he had to continue using his skill set.

Star danced past the front window again. She smiled, but he could already tell she was nervous. Dressed in a black breast-hugging T-shirt with an open gray button-up shirt over that, and skinny jeans that outlined her ass and legs, she looked like a wet dream—at a time when Cade wished she was a little less noticeable. His keen interest moved down her body from her sparkling eyes to her feet—and he grinned when he saw that she wore her shit-kicker boots. He'd bet those clunky things had steel toes, perfect for causing damage.

Sterling Parson had her own unique style, and he liked it. A lot. He liked her attitude. Her perseverance. Her bravery.

All good qualities, but did she also have what it took to weather the upcoming interview?

While he watched, she danced past a booth, stumbled and practically landed in Reyes's lap.

His brother looked surprised, but Star did not. She laughingly said something to him, patted his cheek a little harder than necessary, then danced away with a different guy.

Shit.

Seconds later his phone dinged with a text message. He hated to take his gaze off her, but he already knew it would be from Reyes.

Sure enough, the message read: She said to back off.

Like hell he would. Cade returned: Stay put.

Through the binoculars, he saw Reyes laugh and stow his phone again.

For another hour, things seemed to go okay. She was handed one drink after another, though he couldn't tell whether or not she actually drank any of them. She dodged grabby hands while keeping her grin in place.

When a guard led her off down a hallway, Cade tensed.

Showtime.

They knew the layout of the building, and Cade easily guessed that they were moving her to the back room, where they could privately intimidate her.

Reyes staggered like a drunk, following after them, but he'd be forced to veer off into the john. Closer, but not close enough to shield her.

It took a precious three minutes for Cade to drive around the back, staying far enough away to remain inconspicuous. Another goon guarded the back door, but luckily side-by-side windows gave him an adequate view inside of the room.

Two women were there with her now, one laughing uncontrollably while the other, with a few bruises, looked very shell-shocked. There were also three men: the two guys she'd met at his bar and another hulk of a guy who'd just walked in.

Up to that point Star had stuck to her role of a carefree, unsuspecting party girl, not overcome with giggles like the one girl, and not fatalistic like the other.

Whatever was said just then got her tight-lipped with some strong emotion that resembled part fear, part rage. Cade couldn't tell for sure.

In fact, the only thing he knew for certain was that he had to get her out of there. *Now.*

STERLING HADN'T BEEN prepared for the double whammy. First, she was introduced to a woman who'd been clearly abused. She appeared to be in her early twenties, either drunk or doped up, with an underlying fear that kept her breathless with panic.

That smack of reality was bad enough, really driving home

her precarious position, locked in with monsters and little hope for escape. It reminded her too much of another time when she'd been locked in a room.

She'd been young and helpless then.

This time, she wasn't.

Knowing the danger and hoping to spare someone else the things she'd suffered, she'd gone into this with eyes wide-open—though admittedly with no solid plan or exit strategy.

On the heels of that first surprise was the second shocker, the one that really did her in.

Mattox Symmes. Twelve years had passed since she'd had to see the cruel sneer on his wet lips. Twelve years since he'd looked at her with those dead brown eyes as if she weren't a flesh-and-blood person.

Twelve years that she'd used to grow stronger, braver, to bury the past and give purpose to her present. She'd never thought to see him again, though she'd often thought of killing him, *dreamed* of killing him.

Still built like a freezer with legs and arms, and just as brutish as she remembered. His shoulders stretched the seams of his dress shirt, his neck too thick for the collar. The receding silver hair made his forehead seem more prominent. His gut was more prominent, too.

And he still looked at her like merchandise. *But*...he didn't seem to recognize her!

Needing to know for sure, she held out a limp hand and summoned up a careless smile. "Hello, there. I'm Francis." She waited for him to correct her, to say he knew the name was a lie.

Instead, he took her hand and smiled. "Now, aren't you a nice present."

Oh. Dear. God. Mattox was the man she was supposed to cheer up?

No. *Hell* no. She couldn't do it.

Entertaining him was not on her agenda. Cutting his throat, yes. Cheering him up, not so much.

She knew she had to come up with a real plan—fast.

The effort to retrieve her hand only got her fingers crushed. He tugged her closer. "Have we met before?"

Her heart lodged in her throat, making her short laugh sound borderline hysterical. "Pretty sure we haven't. I think I would have remembered you."

"Hmm." He continued to study her, his dead eyes appraising. "How long have you been in the area?"

"My whole life." Another lie, since she'd moved here after escaping. When had *he* relocated? Or did he have contacts all over the country? A morbid thought.

Sterling told herself that she'd changed, not just emotionally, but physically, too. At seventeen she'd been skinny, with dyed purple hair, a ring in her lip and an excess of dramatic makeup.

Her rebellious stage, as her drug-addicted mother had called it when she was clearheaded enough to notice what her daughter looked like, which wasn't often.

"I think I would have remembered, as well," Mattox finally said, before towing her over to a chair so he could sit. The chair groaned under his weight. Sprawling out his tree-trunk thighs, he freed her fingers, yet she didn't dare move.

In the locked room, where could she go? The windows behind her were accessible, but too high for her to get through quickly, even if she managed to break one before getting grabbed. Smith and his crony stood there grinning by the door. The bruised girl silently wept while the other couldn't stop snickering over everything. It was almost more than Sterling could take.

Besides, if she tried to move away, he'd react as all predators did, by capturing, subduing. Devouring. He would enjoy her fear. It would probably provide the entertainment he wanted.

"Goddamn," Mattox suddenly complained. "We have one too many in here." He gestured at Smith.

Smith roughly grabbed the laughing woman and put her on the other side of the door, where a guard all but dragged her away. Only then did the woman start to protest.

Her humor wouldn't last. Not for a second did Sterling think they'd let the woman go, and eventually the drugs would wear off. Best chance of her survival? If Sterling managed to kill these three men and whoever else was involved.

As Smith again closed and locked the door, her tension coiled with familiar emotions. The sense of helplessness. The burning hatred.

"Now." Mattox sat back and laced his fingers over his gut. "You two can strip down. Make it quick, because I'm short on time."

The other girl openly sobbed as she hurriedly stripped off her sandals and pants, tripping herself twice and making the men laugh. Fucking pigs. Sterling contemplated kicking Mattox in the nuts—but that would only get her killed.

Did Cade's brother have a plan? Or was he just visiting the bar for his own hookup? He hadn't left when she'd told him to, so did he know this was a location for buying and selling women? He'd seemed sharp, and Cade was most definitely more than a mere bartender.

"Jesus, Adela. Quit that caterwauling," Smith ordered, giving her a shove that sent her into the wall.

Adela. It was the first time Sterling had heard her name. How long had she been here?

Long enough to be scared witless, obviously.

Somehow, someway, she'd get herself and the other girl out of this. Until a genius plan occurred to her, she'd just have to play along. If she could distract them, maybe they'd leave Adela alone.

"So," she said, shrugging the unbuttoned shirt off one shoulder and shimmying so her boobs bounced. "How about I do this slow, like a tease? Would you like that?" It might give her an opportunity to get the knife from her boot. If nothing else, she could straddle Mattox's lap and use her necklace blade to slit his throat.

She'd tucked the necklace inside her T-shirt, but even if he saw it, he wouldn't recognize it as a weapon. It looked like nothing more than a decorative metal medallion on a long chain, but by the push of a small button, the disk opened to reveal a curved, razor-sharp blade that when used correctly would be deadly.

She knew how to use it, and here, in this moment, she wouldn't bat an eye at ending Mattox.

The impatient bastard showed his teeth in an evil smile. "No, I don't think I want to wait. Take off both tops." He stared into her eyes, the smile vanishing. "Now."

Well, hell. She tried to tease, but a tremor had entered her voice when she said, "Anxious for the goods, huh? Fine by me, but when do I get my money? I was told I'd be paid for this little performance, and I prefer cash up front."

Smith snorted. "Let's wait and see if you're worth it." Softer, he complained, "Adela sure as fuck wasn't, were you, doll?" He reached for the girl, who screamed. Sterling turned, prepared to attack him despite the consequences—and suddenly a chunk of concrete crashed through one of the windows, sending glass everywhere. A second later, the lights went out.

Chaos erupted with Adela shrieking and the men cursing as they lumbered around, but Sterling seized the opportunity. In a practiced move, she swiped the knife from her boot and stabbed toward the chair where Mattox had been sitting.

Her knife sank deep...into chair padding. How the hell had such a big man moved so quickly? Putting herself behind that chair, Sterling listened to the sounds of a vicious fight ensuing, trying to place bodies.

She couldn't see dick and wasn't about to use the flashlight on her phone, knowing that'd only draw attention to her. Hearing Adela's whimpers, she felt her way along the wall until she reached the girl.

Someone hit the floor in front of them, and what sounded like another body crashed into the wall where she'd just been. Whoever did the demolishing did so silently, efficiently.

Oh, she heard the grunts and groans of the men going down, but from the big shadow doing the damage? Not a peep.

Her hand closed around Adela's arm. The door behind her opened to let two more men charge in. Out in the bar, she heard pandemonium break out with panicked shouts and a lot of scrambling bodies, probably in a rush for the exit.

"Come on," Sterling said, dragging Adela with her. It surprised her that the girl didn't fight her, didn't resist in any way, and she'd stopped sobbing. Maybe because escape seemed imminent.

Someone ran into them, almost knocking Sterling over, but she managed to keep her feet. She dragged Adela along until she felt the doorknob for the men's room that she'd noted when they'd led her down the hallway. Inside, the room was dark and foul, but Sterling didn't slow. On the opposite wall, the light of a streetlamp filtered through a grungy window.

"Let's get out of here, okay?" She didn't wait for Adela to answer.

The window was narrow, and it opened out instead of up, but she'd figure it out. She released Adela, then shoved the knife back into her boot to use both hands to force the rusted knob to turn. Knowing they could be found at any moment, her heart thundered and her palms sweat.

"I can't go," Adela whispered.

"What?" The window creaked ominously, like a special effect in a horror movie, opening inch by inch. "It'll be fine. You'll see. I can hoist you up first."

"No, I can't. They'll kill me."

Why did she have to get stubborn now? "They can't kill you when we're gone," Sterling reasoned. "I promise, I'll get you someplace safe."

"Your house?"

What? Since she wasn't about to reveal her own private location, she said, "No. I know another place—"

"I can't risk it." Adela drew a breath. "I should stay. We both should."

Terror did strange things to people, sometimes paralyzing them with the worry of repercussions. Sterling understood that, but she wasn't quite sure how to overcome it.

At least Adela wasn't sobbing anymore. Wasn't hysterical, either.

Someone shouted from the hallway. A flashlight shone from beneath the door.

"We have to go *now,*" Sterling whispered, reaching for the vague outline of Adela's body.

The girl backed away. "No. No, I can't."

"At least take this." Sterling fished a card from her pocket and thrust it toward Adela. "It's my number—in case you change your mind." The card had a phone number but nothing else. It wouldn't lead anyone to her, but it could be a link to freedom for a victim.

She'd handed out those cards a dozen times in recent years.

Adela took it, then opened the door and yelled, "I'm here!"

Hating herself for failing, mired in regret that she couldn't help Adela, Sterling turned and, with one boot on the edge of the sink, hoisted herself up and through the partially opened window. She scraped her spine along the edge of the casing, her hip and thigh, too, before kicking and wiggling to land hard on her side on the rough gravel drive. Something cut through her jeans. Her palm cracked on a solid surface, and one of her fingers bent unnaturally.

For a moment, in her crumpled position, her body couldn't assimilate the pain. Then feeling rushed in, and with it a welcoming wave of adrenaline.

Too bad she didn't know where Reyes had gone. She had to admit to herself she wouldn't mind some muscle right about now. Unfortunately, in the dark chaos, she couldn't attempt to find him. She was on her own, so she had to get to it.

Teeth locked, she lumbered to her feet and took off awkwardly, running as fast as she could down an alley, behind two abandoned buildings, through a parking lot and finally to the main thoroughfare. A stitch in her side kept her half doubled over—and then she noticed the blood.

Ignore that for now. Ignore the people gawking, too.

Focused only on escape, Sterling hobbled toward the lot where she'd parked her car several blocks away from Misfits. She hadn't wanted to risk being followed, but she hadn't planned on leaving battered, either. Despite the expanding pain, she walked a wide path around the car, ensuring no one paid her undue attention, before taking the key from her boot and unlocking the driver's door.

As always, she checked the back seat, saw it remained empty and dropped behind the wheel. She hit the door locks first and then, with shaking hands, started the black Fiesta she drove when she wasn't in her rig.

What had happened with Cade's brother? Was he still in the bar? Was he the one who'd caused the ruckus?

For only a second, she considered circling back to make sure he was okay, but when she raised her hand to the steering wheel and saw her unnaturally bent finger, another slice of pain jolted her. Right now, she couldn't help anyone.

She stepped on the gas and hoped that Cade was there, watching out for his brother.

She had his number at home, and once she recovered, she'd call him. She had so many unanswered questions…

But for now, she only wanted to put distance between her and

Misfits. A couple of miles out, she pulled in to a well-lit Walmart parking lot and slowly worked off her loose shirt to tie it around her bleeding thigh. God, with her mangled finger, getting it done really hurt, but even without tightening much, it'd stem some of the bleeding.

By the time she got home, she felt like one giant pulsing bruise. She still used extreme caution in going up to her place, every step a trial of determination.

As usual, the apartment building was quiet and she didn't run into anyone. Severely limping now, she forced herself to keep to her routine, checking the doors, beneath the bed and in the closets, before staggering into the bathroom.

Under the bright fluorescent lights, she freed the shirt from around her thigh and winced. A chunk of glass embedded in her skin left an inch-wide puncture. Seeing the mess she'd already made on the floor, she more or less collapsed into the bathtub.

With a harsh groan, she caught the edge of the protruding glass with blood-slick fingers and, gritting her teeth, slowly pulled it free. Swamped with self-pity, she tossed it toward the garbage can. More blood blossomed on her jeans.

Two slow, deep breaths helped, as did her lame pep talk. *You're okay. Everything will heal.*

For now, you're safe.

She needed to clean the wound or she'd be facing bigger problems, like infection or even blood poisoning. There was no one to do it for her, hadn't been anyone for too many years to count— if ever.

Stripping off her clothes caused more than a few guttural groans, as well as a light sheen of sweat. Her lace-up boots and tight jeans especially proved difficult. Stupid skinny jeans. She hadn't been skinny in a very long time, and it took a major incentive to get her to wear anything that uncomfortable.

Killing a human trafficker topped her list, but still...

It took every ounce of agonizing grit she possessed to get naked. Panting with the effort, her clothes in a heap on the other side of the tub, Sterling inspected the damage.

Black-and-blue swelling bruises marred her skin from her waist to her ankle. Christ, no wonder she hurt. If only Adela hadn't balked, if only she'd gotten that window open a little more. Failure left a bitter taste in her mouth.

She didn't want to move, but what choice did she have? It hurt like hell, but she could bend her leg, so she assumed it wasn't broken.

Slowly sitting upright, she turned on the shower and, once the water warmed, inched forward to sit under the spray, her forehead resting on her knees. At some point she must have zoned out. She didn't know how long she'd sat there, but the lack of hot water revived her. Teeth clenched, she carefully washed her thigh. When she reached to turn off the water, renewed pain seized her.

Her finger. With so many aches to choose from, she'd all but forgotten about the ring finger on her right hand. Looking at it now, she knew she'd dislocated it in her fall.

Switching to her left hand, keeping her right tucked close to her body, she shut off the shower and, leaning heavily on the wall, managed to get upright. Her thigh continued to ooze blood, so she dried it as best she could and applied several butterfly bandages, then wrapped it in gauze.

Rather than get her bed wet, she eased her injured hand through the sleeve of her big terry robe, wrapped it around her and gimped her way to the couch, where she curled up. Exhausted, she thankfully slept.

CHAPTER FOUR

CADE TRIED CALLING HER. He even tried tapping quietly on her door. It was two in the morning, far from a decent hour to call on someone, but he was surprised he'd lasted this long without getting hold of her.

He and Reyes had rounded up several women, as well as Smith and his cohort, but they'd lost sight of both Star and the young woman who'd been with her. That bastard Mattox had gotten away, too, and it tortured Cade thinking he might have Star. His sister was on it, and she'd locate Mattox eventually—when it might be too late.

No, he couldn't accept that, so here he was, checking Star's apartment and praying she was safely inside.

He knocked again, hard enough that a neighbor stuck her head out and cursed him.

Somewhere between eighty and ninety, eyeglasses askew, hair frazzled, cranky and nowhere near properly dressed, the woman snapped, "What the hell are you doing?"

Great. Not what he needed right now. "My apologies, ma'am."

"Just keep it down," she barked, then slammed her door loudly enough to wake up the rest of the building.

Cade gave serious thought to breaking into Star's apartment. If she wasn't in there, he'd start scouring the area to find her—

"Who is it?" Her weak voice came through the closed door.

Fresh alarm mingled with relief, because at least he'd found her...unless she wasn't alone?

His gaze shot up to the peek hole in the door. Stepping back so she could see him, he said, "It's Cade. Let me in."

Nothing happened.

He leaned closer to the door. "Swear to God, Star, I'm about two seconds from knocking down the—"

The lock clicked and the door opened.

One look at her and uncontrollable rage returned. That was something that never happened to him. He worked best in cold deliberation, detached, proficient...but this was Star, and somehow she'd always jacked his control.

Stepping in and quietly securing the door again, he asked, "Who did this to you?" She looked like she'd been through a war.

With a pronounced limp, her face taut with pain, she went back to the couch and gingerly lowered herself. Instead of answering his question, she asked one of her own. "Why are you here?"

Several lights were on in the apartment. "Are you alone?"

She sat back. "Yes." Her robe parted and he saw her right leg.

Locking his jaw, he came to kneel in front of her. "Ah, babe, how the hell did this happen?"

Trembling, she swallowed heavily and closed her eyes. "Babe?"

Seriously, an endearment was what she wanted to talk about now? "You can gut me later. Tell me what happened."

Though she didn't actually shrug, he heard it in her tone. "I landed hard when I went out the window in the guys' john. I'm okay, though."

No, she most definitely was not. The bruising started dark red at the top of her thigh and down the middle, but then spread outward to blue, green and black. Actually, he couldn't see how high it went because the robe didn't part any higher. He lightly touched his fingers to her skin, especially over the bandages that covered a blood-encrusted cut.

Lethargic, Sterling said, "It looks terrible, doesn't it?"

He'd seen similar bruising, just never on a woman. "My guess is a pulled hammy. I don't know how you managed to get home."

"Adrenaline, I think. *Not* getting home wasn't an option, right? But yeah, now it hurts like crazy."

He noticed she held her arm, too—which drew his gaze to her fingers. *Shit.* He winced for her, but first things first. Gesturing at her leg, he asked, "Mind if I take a look?"

Those velvety brown eyes of hers stared at him. "Actually, since I'm buck-ass under the robe, yeah, I mind."

He hadn't needed her confirmation on that. His body already knew it, and conflicting needs were bombarding him. He wanted to help her. Protect her. Touch her.

Look at her.

Stop being an asshole. He drew in a deep breath and tried to be businesslike. "You need to see a doctor."

"Nope. If that's why you came here, you can run along back to wherever you live."

"Star." He braced his hand on the couch. "You can't think I'd leave you like this."

Her eyes narrowed. "Why not? I'm not your *babe*, and I didn't ask you to—"

"Let me rephrase that." He hardened his own gaze. "I'm not leaving you like this."

They stared at each other, a battle of wills, until she relented with ill grace. Hell, she looked too spent to do otherwise.

"Fine," she groused. "Suit yourself. Not sure I could fend off anyone if you led them here, so if nothing else, you can be backup."

"I didn't, but in case *you* did, you're right. I make excellent backup." Now with a purpose, Cade stood. "We're going to handle this step by step, okay? First, have you taken anything?"

Eyes closed, body tight with pain, she asked, "Like...?"

"Pain meds? And you should have that leg elevated, under ice packs, or you won't be able to walk tomorrow."

She gave a short laugh. "Walk? I'm not sure I could crawl." She lifted her head, and her eyes barely opened. "I probably shouldn't admit this, but just showering took it out of me. All I want to do now is sleep."

His heart softened. "You can do that soon, okay? After I get you more comfortable. So you need something for pain."

"I have aspirin in my medicine cabinet."

"And a first aid kit, apparently." She hadn't done a terrible job, but he could do better. "I'll properly clean and dress that cut, too. You know how you did it?"

"Chunk of glass." Again she put her head back as if any effort at being alert was too much. "It's in or near the trash can in my bathroom."

To know what he was dealing with, Cade went to retrieve it. Discarded clothes littered the floor, including bloodied jeans and her boots. She'd left a knife and a necklace on the counter. No, not a necklace. Though he recognized it as a hidden weapon, it took him a second to figure it out. With the press of a small mechanism built into the medallion, a claw blade opened out.

Jesus, what had she planned? Just how deep was she into her vigilante crusade?

Worrying about that would have to wait until he'd seen to her injuries. He found the chunk of glass. It appeared to be part of a broken bottle, still covered in Sterling's blood. In fact, she'd gotten blood everywhere—the floor, the tub, the edge of the sink...

The first aid kit was left open on the counter. Since the rest of her apartment was tidy, he'd pick up the mess for her once he had her better settled.

Next he detoured into the kitchen to find a bottle of water. Her fridge was almost barren, her cabinets cluttered with packaged food but nothing healthy. Figuring out something for her to eat would take a trick.

When he returned with the kit, three store-brand pain tablets and the water, she appeared to be sleeping. "Star?" he asked quietly.

"Hmm?" She sounded lethargic.

"Can you take these?" He touched her lips, and that got her more alert, her dark eyes watchful. He badly wanted to kiss that soft mouth, but all he said was, "Open."

She did, and he dropped them in, then handed her the water.

After swallowing the pills, she took several more drinks until she'd downed half the bottle. "No one's ever taken care of me."

No one? *Ever?* "Then let me show you how it's done."

Contemplative, she frowned at him, then gave up. "Fine. I'm starving, too. I don't suppose you know how to cook?"

"Better than you, apparently." He knelt down again and gently peeled away the butterfly bandages that had helped, but not enough. With the condition of her leg, it had to hurt like crazy.

"I didn't sleep at all last night," she explained, a mixture of pain and running the words together. "I haven't eaten since early this morning, either. Add in tonight's...*excitement*, and yeah, I'm shot."

"Excitement. Right." Cade let that slide to silently concentrate on the job at hand. "I'm sorry," he said, dampening a cotton ball in antiseptic. "This is going to sting."

"I know." She clutched the couch cushion with her left hand. "Go ahead."

Her breath hissed out as he worked, so he tried to distract her. "Do you often go all day without eating?"

"Do I look like I'm starving?"

Definitely not. Sterling had a strong and shapely body that had caught his attention the moment he first saw her. Broad shoulders for a woman, hefty breasts and an ass he wanted to grasp with both hands. She didn't play up her assets in any way, and Cade thought she was sexy as hell because of it.

"So you skipped food out of nervousness?"

"I don't get nervous," she denied—then caught her breath as he cleaned a spot of debris from the edge of the cut.

"So why didn't you eat?"

"I was busy prepping." She scowled at him. "Are you about done?"

He'd take her annoyance over the sight of her pain any day. "Almost. You could really use a few stitches, but since the bleeding has almost stopped, we'll stick with bandages." The robe barely preserved her modesty, not that she seemed concerned. The woman was utterly unaffected by his nearness and her own nakedness— or else she hid it well.

Whichever, he appreciated how well she handled it. Any show of shyness now would have made it that much more difficult.

When he finished, he lightly covered her again with the edges of the robe. "Now." He sat beside her.

Making it clear she didn't like his nearness, she gave him another scowl.

"That finger is dislocated." She'd either need a trip to the ER after all...or he'd need to set it for her.

Looking away from her injured hand, she whispered, "I know."

Very gently, Cade took her hand, then trailed his fingertips over the swollen knuckle. "Does anything else on this arm hurt? Your wrist, elbow?" She was guarding it pretty good.

Lips pressed together, she shook her head.

"Are you sure?" He held her wrist firmly in one hand, the dislocated finger in the other. "Have you tried moving it?"

"Yes. I was reaching for the faucet when— *Ngahhh!*"

Before she could finish, he'd tugged the finger back into place and now gently held her hand in his, trying to soothe her. "Shh, I know. It's damn painful. Take some deep breaths."

"Go to hell!" she snapped, but she curled closer to him and moaned.

Cade had trouble swallowing. He'd set fingers before, his own included, but this was different. One arm around her, his other hand still holding hers, he kept her close. "I'm sorry, babe."

Her breath shuddered in. "Don't be." Still a little shaky, she said, "You fixed it for me."

"You should really see a doctor—"

She inhaled deeply, let it out slowly and eased away from him. "I'm sure it'll be fine."

The stubbornness started to grate on him. "Does anything else hurt?"

Her choking laugh sounded with pain. "What doesn't hurt? It was a stupid idea to go out that window."

Since he'd been there to get her out, Cade agreed. But she hadn't known that. "I think it showed a lot of initiative."

She huffed a breath. "It was better than staying, I guess."

Before he could think better of it, he had his hand on her tangled hair, smoothing it down. "Can you tell me what you were doing there?"

"You first."

He looked up in surprise. "So you knew it was me?"

"I thought you might be around somewhere."

Talking seemed to help her collect herself, so Cade settled back beside her. "I was keeping an eye on you." He could tell her that much. He wanted her to know...what? That he cared, yes. That whatever she was up to, he could handle it for her. "What did you hope to accomplish, Star?"

Hand trembling, she swiped a tear off her lashes as if it offended her. "I was offered money, remember? What's your excuse?"

She had to be the most maddening person he'd ever encountered. "I can't go into it."

"Yeah? Well, ditto for me. Guess we can both keep our little secrets, okay?"

Cade tried a different tack. "You said you're hungry. Let's get the rest of the injuries looked at and then I'll see what I can put together."

"You already covered it, and I can rustle up a bowl of cereal or something."

He doubted she could rustle herself to bed, but he refrained from saying so. "Nothing else hurts on your arm? Your shoulder, back?"

"My back's a little sore, but hey, I scraped my spine on the window casing, then damn near landed on my head and shoulders, so... Guess I'm lucky I didn't break my neck."

The thought of that leveled him, made his heart thump and his lungs constrict. "Let me take a look."

Eyes narrowing, she curled a little away from him. "Don't tell me you're a doctor?"

"No, but I have some field experience—"

"Aha. Military." Pouncing on that, she said with triumph, "I knew it."

"And since you refuse to get actual medical attention, at least let me see what I can do." Seconds ticked by while she considered it.

"Yeah, all right." She struggled to sit up.

Carefully, he helped lever her more upright.

"I need panties," she said. "And maybe a button-up shirt. Then you can do all the doctoring you want."

The timing was all wrong, yet he teased, "Promise?"

"Get cute and you can get out."

Pleased to see her attitude back in full force, Cade murmured, "Sorry," and helped her to her feet. "Can I help you dress?"

"You might have to. It took all I had just to get my robe on."

He hadn't expected her agreement, but he went along without a word, letting her lean on him as they made their way to her bedroom. Once there, she settled cautiously at the foot of the bed. "Panties are in the top middle drawer."

A new experience—helping a woman *into* her panties. Reyes would find it funny as fuck, but Cade was an eon away from humor.

He opened the drawer to a jumble of colors and fabrics all stuffed in together. Most were cotton, some with lacy trim, others nylon or ultra-sheer. Such a selection. He glanced over his shoulder. "You have a preference on full coverage or barely there?"

She smirked. "If by full coverage you mean granny panties, you won't find any there. But nothing too skimpy, and preferably cotton."

"Color matter?"

"Not to me."

Meaning it could matter to him? *Hmm...*

His hand looked too big sifting through her delicate underthings. Did her bras match her panties? Somehow he didn't think so, not unless it was a special occasion for her.

Did she consider sex a special occasion?

He'd like to find out. *Don't be an asshole.*

Deciding on hot pink with little yellow flowers, he turned and found her barely awake, her shoulders slumped, her head hanging. It wasn't a look he'd ever expected to see on Sterling Parson.

It bothered him. Too much. Somehow she'd already burrowed under his skin. When had that ever happened? Never.

Kneeling in front of her, he said, "Here," and helped to get the pretty panties over her feet and up to the knees she had pressed tightly together.

Standing, her uninjured hand braced on his shoulder, she said, "Not a word."

His face was level with her stomach, his hands bracketed outside her knees, her hand warm on his shoulder. Scenarios winged through his mind, heating his blood, tensing his muscles.

If she hadn't been hurt, he would have leaned forward, pressed his face against her, breathed in her heated scent...

One day soon, he'd be back in this position—once she'd fully recovered. *Not being an asshole, remember?*

Steeling himself, Cade looked up at her face.

Her gaze avoided his. "I mean it."

"I know." Watching her expression kept him from looking at her body, at the warm, silky flesh teasing his fingers and wrists as he tugged the panties up, under her robe, and smoothed them onto her hips.

It took a lot of iron control, but Cade stood. "Shirt?"

"No, I've decided to keep the robe, but you can look at my back if you want." Turning, she opened the belt and let the shoulders droop down.

More bruises, of course. He hadn't expected anything else, but at least these weren't as bad as her leg. Lifting her thick mass of hair with one hand, he touched, lightly prodded, but she barely flinched. "I think the worst of it is your leg and that finger."

"My finger feels better already, but yeah, my leg is crazy stiff."

He had a hot tub at his place, but inviting her there would cause more problems than he wanted to deal with. That is, if she'd even accept, which he doubted.

"How about we get you comfortable on the couch with an ice pack on your leg? I'll tape your fingers, then get food together."

"Wow, this whole 'being waited on' thing is nice. I had no idea what I've been missing."

The sarcasm made it easier for her, Cade knew, so he didn't reply as he helped her back to the living room.

MAYBE IF SHE'D had a different background, having Cade see so much of her under such crummy circumstances might have been more embarrassing. Truth? Her biggest issue wasn't nudity. It was being dependent on him.

That sucked rocks big-time, though she had to admit he made it easier than it could have been. He was so blasted matter-of-fact about it, like he did this sort of thing all the time.

Did he? No, somehow she knew he wasn't anyone's toady. Nice that, for right now, he'd be hers. Besides all the pampering, the view was pretty sweet. And stirring.

Yup, even though she felt like the walking dead, her hormones took notice of him. When he'd been on his knees? Downright fantasy inspiring.

Sterling wondered if he could really cook. Probably, given he did everything else with ease. Maybe someday she'd find out for sure, but right now she didn't have any basic ingredients for him to work with. Instead they dined on pizza rolls—fresh from freezer to microwave—with colas. It was the best she had since he'd discounted cold cereal and packaged cookies.

She felt better being clean, her finger straightened and taped to the one next to it, her thigh, resting on pillows to elevate it, numb from the ice he kept rotating, and food in her belly. Not good— good was nowhere on the horizon—but definitely less annihilated.

Less alone in the world.

Not that she'd start to depend on Cade. Hell no. The man was far too secretive about every single thing.

"So." She idly rubbed an area of her leg not covered by ice. "What happened at Misfits? Was that your brother's plan, to cause pandemonium? I saw him, you know, before I got taken to that back room."

"Actually, that was all my doing, with only a short warning to my brother." He leaned forward over her injured leg to readjust the ice, then explained, "The other night when you left my bar to draw out Smith—who is actually Thacker, by the way—I listened in, so I knew he'd propositioned you."

What? No way. "I didn't see you."

With a shrug, he explained, "Neither did he, because I went out the office window and hung in the shadows. I knew right away you'd be walking into a trap, so I set up a hasty plan."

"You could have told me."

"So you could tell me to butt out? Not a chance."

Yeah, she probably would have. Far too often, pride overrode common sense. "I knew his name wasn't Smith."

"I figured."

So at least he credited her with some sense. "Were you in Misfits, too?"

"Outside, watching through a window. I knew what that bastard was likely expecting, and whether you were agreeable or not, I wasn't about to let you go through with it."

"Let me?" she asked quietly, with a fair amount of menace.

"Figure of speech, but accurate. I had the ability to stop it, so I did. Are you really going to protest now? Would you have handled it better on your own?"

Handle it? Ha. She'd been stuck with no way out, and he'd basically saved her. Unable to meet his direct gaze, she looked down, feeling cornered.

Damn it, she wasn't good at gratitude, at even recognizing it when she felt it, but she knew that had to be the emotion sitting heavy on her chest. "So...*surly* is generally my default mood, ya know?"

Instead of being insulted, he gave a small laugh. "I've noticed."

Peeking up at him, seeing the actual smile on his mouth had a strange effect on Sterling. They sat close, alone together in her apartment, and she wasn't exactly immune to his personal brand of attention. "Anyway," she said, reining in her unruly thoughts, "yeah, I appreciate the help you gave."

Trying to see her face, Cade tipped his head. "No problem."

For him, it hadn't been. In the darkness of the bar, she hadn't been able to see the ass kicker versus the ones getting their asses kicked, but somehow she knew Cade was the first. She remembered the silence from him, how he hadn't even breathed heavily while taking apart everyone in the room—except her and...

Adela! Sterling jerked her head up. "The woman who was in that room with me? Do you know what happened to her? Is she okay?"

With a small, regretful shake of his head, Cade said, "No idea, sorry."

Deflated, she decided it was past time for some truths. "Okay, enough. You were there with your brother. I was there. We don't trust each other—I get that. But I seriously need to know what happened."

Cade gave her a silent scrutiny.

Desperation wavered in her voice. "Please?"

It took him too damn long to nod, and he still didn't give in completely. "I'll share a truth, then you share. Deal?"

Dirty pool! She had reason for needing to know, but what reason could he have for not wanting to tell her?

Unaffected by her scowl, he said, "Take it or leave it, Star."

Ha! He knew she wouldn't refuse. "Fine. But you tell me what happened to Adela first."

"I can't. I told you that. But," he said before she could interrupt, "we nabbed Thacker—that is, Smith—and his buddy Jay, the two bozos who showed up at my bar. My brother also found several women locked in different rooms."

Her heart dropped hard. She grabbed his wrist. "You got them out?"

His gaze went to her hand, making her acutely aware of what she'd done. His wrist was so thick her fingers couldn't encircle it. Hot, rock-solid and dusted with soft hair—now that he'd drawn her attention to it, her palm tingled...and that tingle seemed to travel up her arm and on to places better forgotten.

"Sorry." She hastily withdrew.

"You can touch me anytime you want."

Such a thrilling offer! "I don't—"

He cut off her protest. "Those women are safe now, but we couldn't locate you, the other woman or..." He paused.

"Mattox?"

Cade's brows shot up. "He actually introduced himself?"

She understood his surprise. Mattox tended to keep a low profile, leaving it to his lackeys to do his dirty work, except for when it came to procuring women. Then the slimy bastard insisted on taking part.

Even more telling, though, was the fact that Cade obviously knew Mattox, or knew of him. So, she'd nailed it: being a sexy bartender wasn't his main vocation. Plus she now knew he had military experience. What, exactly, were he and his brother up to?

She wasn't sure how to answer him without giving away her own secrets. After considering it, she said, "No introductions were necessary."

"You already knew Mattox?"

"Yup." Knew him, despised him, badly wanted to see him suffer. "You did, too, right?"

He bypassed that to ask, "How? You'd met him before?"

"No, you don't. One question at a time. So tell me. What exactly was your plan at Misfits?"

"Keep you safe, period," he replied without hesitation. "Your turn."

"Bull! You already knew the place and the players, so don't try to tell me—"

"I've been aware of Misfits and what they do for a while. But I was there last night because that's where you went. Otherwise, I would have continued to..." He fell silent.

"Surveil?" she offered helpfully. "Investigate?" Damn it, what exactly was his role in all this?

One steely shoulder lifted.

Not good enough. Throwing caution to the wind, she looked him over. "So this is what you do? You find and expose human-trafficking rings?"

Nothing, not even a blink.

"And then what?" Were they actually on the same mission? That'd be cool. More and more, she liked Cade. She *mostly* trusted him. It'd be great to have her own personal badass around when she needed him, and the man was certainly easy on the eyes. Win-win.

"It's my turn to ask questions." He rubbed her foot through the blanket.

Almost stopping her heart.

Yeah, a foot rub was definitely not in her repertoire of experiences. Had to admit, though, it felt downright heavenly.

"So tell me, Star—"

"Sterling."

He gave a brief nod of acknowledgment. "What were you hoping to accomplish with that stunt?"

She supposed someone had to make the first move, right? Might as well be her. If she gave a little, surely he'd do the same, and maybe they could clear out the secrets between them.

Normally, she'd never consider such a thing. The less people knew her and what drove her, the safer she felt. But of all the men in all the world, she actually *liked* Cade—especially now that she realized they had a common goal: to bust up sex trafficking, free the women captured and punish the ones responsible.

With that decision made, she pondered where to start. "I hadn't figured on Thacker showing up at the bar." It was her haven... probably not anymore. "He never had before, at least not that I know of?"

Since she posed it as a question, Cade confirmed it for her. "It was his first time in."

Sterling nodded. "I've been aware of him for a while."

"How?"

"Mmm... I've talked with a few women who knew him. Yeah, vague, I know, but that's all you're getting on that." Unless he shared a few nuggets, too. This had to be an even exchange. "I kept wondering how I was going to get to him—"

"Jesus." Raking a hand over his short hair, Cade sat back and frowned.

There went her foot rub. Bummer.

"Then I saw him at the bar. Poof, he was within my reach. I saw it as an opportunity I couldn't resist."

"An opportunity for *what*? To get mauled? Raped? Sold?"

Having her worst fears thrown at her brought back her scowl. "Sheesh, what a downer. Have a little faith, why don't you?"

"Star," he warned.

"Sterling," she automatically corrected. When she'd started her new, empowered life, she'd changed everything—locale, appearance and nickname. "I thought I'd get a feel for Misfits, see how they ran it, you know? Getting in without an invite isn't easy, so this was the only way."

"No, it wasn't."

Right. Evidently he'd already been in there. His brother, too. They saw Misfits for what it was. Not that either of them had bothered to tell her that, even though they knew she'd planned to go.

Seeing yet another opportunity, Sterling rethought her argument. Since Cade seemed determined to keep her safe, she could use that to her advantage. It wasn't like she wanted to tackle Mattox and his perverted pals on her own. That path led to failure, as she'd already discovered.

But with Cade's help? His brother's assistance?

She just might be able to get somewhere.

Smiling with her new intent, she stared into Cade's stunning blue eyes and suggested, "If you would share with me, we could coordinate." His entire expression hardened. If she hadn't already decided not to fear him, that look alone would have set off her alarm bells. Funny that she somehow knew Cade was different.

Now she had to convince him that she was different, too.

CHAPTER FIVE

GAUGING HIS REACTION, Sterling prompted, "You could do that, right? Get in, same as your brother?"

Voice dropping to a quiet but firm whisper, he warned, "This is not a game you should be playing."

"Says you. I feel differently." For the last few years, it was the only game she played, and she called it revenge, atonement, even satisfaction.

"You still haven't told me why."

Was that worry—for *her*—putting that particular dire expression on his face? Interesting. "Why doesn't matter. You see—"

"It matters a lot."

"Anyway," she said, stressing the word to make it clear she didn't appreciate his interruption. "If all had gone well, I might've ended a few monsters and freed a few women."

Incredulous, he stared at her as if she'd grown two heads. "Things did not go well."

A reminder she didn't need. Trying to sound cavalier, she returned, "No, but you saved the day."

Too quick for her to stop him, he flipped the ice packs and blanket aside. Indicating the deepening bruises on her leg, he said, "You call this saving the day?" Catching her wrist, he lifted her hand with the two fingers taped together. "Does this look like I'm some kind of hero?"

Whoa. That was a lot of anger, but oddly, it didn't concern her since he seemed to be angry on her behalf.

Given that Adela wasn't free and Mattox wasn't dead, Sterling considered her efforts a big old failure—and maybe, because she'd gotten injured, Cade felt the same.

Did he already feel responsible for her, just as she felt responsible for Adela? That possibility warmed her, but it also set off alarm bells. She'd been on her own too long to let anyone, especially a guy with secrets as big as her own, sidle in and take over.

Hopefully she hid her mixed reactions under sarcasm. "I'm here, alive, not mauled or raped or sold, so yeah. All in all, your diversion saved…well, at least me." She drew a breath. "That's something, right?"

Shoving to his feet, Cade paced the small area of her living room. Hers wasn't a tiny apartment, but with him prowling around it felt minuscule, as if his size and presence had shrunk the space. Looking at him was easy. All that fluid strength, tightly contained but ready when he needed it. She envied him that physical power.

He stopped to face her. "I do not want you hurt."

It fascinated Sterling, witnessing his protective instinct. Not something she was used to. "That makes two of us."

And actually, she didn't want him hurt, either, but she had a feeling he wouldn't appreciate her concern quite so much. "You said your brother got hold of Thacker and the other dude, and some women. What'd he do with them?"

He relented enough to explain, "The women were transported to a secure shelter. They'll get whatever help they need."

Nice. It's what she would have done, too. "And the scumbags?"

The look he sent her said it all.

Sterling whistled. "They're dead?"

He answered her question with one of his own. "Isn't that what you intended?"

"Yeah, but somehow I think you might have contacts that I don't."

"I have a lot of things you don't."

Was that supposed to be an insult? She laughed. "No kidding. Want me to name a few? How about big biceps and bigger fists? Muscled legs and granite shoulders. I'm tall, but you've got me on height, strength and ability." His irritation amused her. "My legs aren't short, but I know they're not as strong as yours. And while I'm not a weakling, I'm not on a par with you, either. Ability? I mean, I try. I have a lot of determination. But I'm self-taught, so I'm sure I don't have the same skill set you have."

"This is…" He turned away again, the set of his shoulders showing his tension as he paced. "I'm not sure how to handle you."

Handle her? She snorted. "You can't, so don't tax yourself. But can I make a suggestion? Try answering my questions and let's see if we find some common ground."

"We can't. Not on this."

Rolling her eyes, Sterling asked her questions anyway. "What shelter did you take them to? And how were you surveilling Misfits?"

He shook his head.

"All right, try these on for size." He had to tell her *something*, or their conversation was at an end. "How'd you know where I live? And where'd you learn to fight?"

Stubbornly silent, Cade rubbed his jaw, his gaze piercing as he stared at her. "It's almost morning. You should get some sleep."

Jerk. Extreme disappointment sharpened her anger. He didn't want to team up? Fine. She'd managed on her own so far. She didn't need him.

She didn't need anyone.

"Yeah, I am tired." She faked a widemouthed yawn. "Go on, run back to wherever you came from. Maybe I'll see you at the bar again sometime." She was just irked enough to add, "Or maybe not."

Cade went still, his nostrils flaring. Tone dark and deadly, he asked, "What's that supposed to mean?"

"It means I don't like you much anymore."

His eye twitched. "I didn't know liking had anything to do with it." Dangerously on edge, he stalked closer to her, braced one broad hand on the back of the couch, the other on the arm, and leaned down close. "You always stop at the bar after a haul."

Even showing signs of anger, his nearness fired her engines. Too bad she was out of commission. "So we're sticking with me as a trucker and you as a bartender? Fine by me." With mock innocence, she said, "I don't have deliveries for at least a week. Good thing, since I'm not sure I could manage it until my leg heals."

"Your leg is going to need more than a week, and if you're not a trucker—"

"Oh, but I am. Just like you're a bartender." Her sugary smile snapped him upright again.

"You know I am. You see me there often enough."

Sterling sighed. God, he was impossible. Also sexy and fit, and so blasted competent, how could she stay resistant? "You've seen me driving my rig. Done and done. All is as it seems."

Anger seemed to emanate off him in waves.

Oh, poor baby. Was she getting to him? More like driving him nuts, but whatever. "Did you like me better when I mostly ignored you? Well, too bad. You're the one who forced this...whatever it is. Odd friendship."

His gaze drilled into hers. "Sexual attraction."

Was he trying to shock her? Not happening. Since there was no point in ignoring him anymore, she grinned. "That, too."

His eyes narrowed. "Mutual respect."

Unwilling to give up too much ground, she looked away. "Possibly." She definitely respected his ability, but she didn't think he returned the favor.

"It's a beneficial relationship."

"How so?" Curious now, she took her own turn glaring daggers. "How do you benefit? Because I haven't agreed to anything."

"You will."

Anger stirred. "Are you talking sex?"

"I'm talking shared confidences."

"I'm the only one sharing!"

Acknowledging that with a nod, he straightened. "I need to clear a few things." He picked up her displaced ice packs and carried them back to the kitchen but continued to talk. "I don't have autonomy, so it's better if I don't act alone."

Now, that was a tidbit she could dig into. Her heart started pumping double time, and she carefully turned so her legs were off the side of the couch.

Hurt. Like. Hell.

But once he left, she'd have to get herself to the bathroom and bed, so she may as well start now. The longer she sat, the harder she knew it'd be.

She clenched her teeth and concentrated on bending her knee. Fire burned up her thigh. How was she supposed to stand or walk?

Needing a distraction and fast, she asked, "So you work with your brother?" Did he need to consult him before confiding in her?

She could hear him in the kitchen, emptying the ice packs in the sink, the clinking of ice cubes as he refilled them. The man was entirely too at ease in her apartment, but then, she imagined he took control everywhere he went.

He returned and, without answering her question, asked, "Could we make a few agreements? I'll let you know if I find Adela or Mattox, and you don't do anything else without letting me know."

Talk about a one-sided contract. "I don't answer to you."

He took in her strained expression, then moved forward to set the ice packs on the table. Slipping an arm around her, he helped her up. "Probably better if I don't tell anything more about them anyway."

"Wait, that's not what I meant." Leaning against him, with his arm around her back to support her and her hand clutching his shoulder, really drove home the differences in their sizes. Yes, she was tall, but he stood a head taller.

For too long they just looked at each other. When her gaze dropped to his mouth, he shook his head. "You're in no shape to start anything."

Of course he was right. If he let go, she'd probably fall on her face. A kiss, though... She could handle that.

He tipped up her chin. "Where are we going?"

Guess that settled that. "You're leaving." Pretty sure that was his plan, anyway. "And I'm making my way to the bedroom. Maybe the bathroom first, but..."

He waited. "But?"

"I need to know if Adela is found, if she's safe—"

"Then agree."

If she weren't so banged up, she'd...what? Her unique set of skills wouldn't get her anywhere with a guy like Cade, and she knew it. That was part of his draw, actually. A big part. Most guys just didn't appeal to her, especially when she knew she was stronger—emotionally, mentally and sometimes physically. She was definitely more ruthless than most.

But Cade wasn't the type of guy she could dismiss on any level. He proved that with his newest tactic. "Blackmail?"

"Negotiations," he countered, never fazed, never out of control.

What could she do but agree? There, it wasn't even in her hands. He'd removed all options for her, so she didn't have to feel guilty for the little thrill that came with her capitulation.

"All right, fine." To ensure he didn't know how she really felt, she added in a grumble, "Not like I'll be doing much for a week or two anyway."

Now that he'd gotten his way, Cade relaxed even more. It was subtle, the slight smoothing of his brows, the softening of his mouth, tension ebbing from his shoulders. He somehow felt closer, gentler...warmer.

"Bathroom first?" And then with concern, "Do you need any help?"

Not on her life. "You're pushing your luck, dude."

That earned her a small smile. "I don't count on luck anyway. I use good, sound calculation. But if you think you can handle it, I'll wait right out here. If you run into a problem, though, just let me know. I'm not squeamish."

She almost growled that she wasn't, either, but he might take that as an invitation. The day she couldn't pee on her own was the day she'd truly give up.

He left her leaning against the sink. She noticed that he'd tidied up for her. Her clothes were now in the hamper and the blood had been wiped up before it could stain. Nice. God only knew when she'd be able to get on her knees to scrub the floor.

The first aid kit was stowed under the sink, and her necklace hung over the knob of the medicine cabinet.

He'd opened it to expose the curved blade. Had he left it that way to show her he recognized it for a weapon—or because he hadn't known how to close it again? She'd bet on the first.

Cade McKenzie was a handy man to have around—in more ways than one.

While she was in there, she brushed her teeth. She gave her hair a cursory glance but didn't really care enough to mess with it. Stiff legged and limping, she opened the door and found Cade leaning against the wall, his arms folded over his chest.

He looked lost in thought, but he immediately stepped forward to put that steel band normally called an arm around her again. "Bed?"

"Yeah, but I need to lock up behind you first." She couldn't accomplish much tonight, so she might as well get some sleep. But she sort of hated to see their time together end, and she sucked at subtlety, so she asked, "When will I see you again?"

Standing there together, her more or less in his embrace, he asked, "What time do you get up?"

When she could walk? Usually by five. Now? She had no idea. "Maybe eight or so?"

"I'll have coffee ready."

He said that so casually she almost fell over. "You'll be here first thing in the morning?"

With the light of challenge in his eyes, he said, "Figured I'd stay over, actually."

"Stay over?" And she squeaked, *"Here?"*

APPARENTLY AN UNHEARD-OF OCCASION, if the expression on her face was any indication. That didn't surprise Cade. Everything she did screamed *loner*.

If he had his way, that would end.

"You might need me." Rather than give her too much time to think about it, Cade steered her toward the bedroom. "Don't worry about the doors. I'll lock up."

Holding his breath, he waited for her refusal, for her sharp stubbornness to kick in.

Instead she grumbled, "Fine. I suppose I wouldn't mind the help."

His eyes widened, but he kept his face averted so she wouldn't notice. On the heels of that shocker, renewed concern followed. Her quick acceptance meant she had to be in total misery. Tomorrow would be worse before things started to get better.

Getting her from the living room to the bathroom had been the longest walk for her, but her bedroom was only a few steps away now. "Let me turn down the bed."

From what he could see, she didn't use a bedspread, but she'd smoothed the bedding into place. Leaving her to hold on to the dresser, he pulled back the sheet and quilt, then plumped her pillow.

"So." Voice strained, she asked, "Where will you sleep? Pretty sure my couch isn't long enough to accommodate a guy your size."

He'd slept in worse cramped places but didn't say so. Turning to her, he took her arm and urged her to the bed. "Where I sleep is up to you. I can crash beside you without bumping your leg— or make do on the couch. Even the floor is fine."

On her back, her dark hair fanned out on the pillow and her hands clutching the quilt, she looked younger.

And a lot more wary.

"I've never slept with anyone before."

Cade felt the bottom drop out of his stomach. "You...?"

Annoyed now, she waved away his surprise. "I don't mean that. I've had sex. I've just never spent the night with anyone."

Way to stop his heart. "The night is almost over, so it wouldn't be more than a few hours anyway."

Looking to the side of the bed, maybe judging whether or not he'd fit, she said, "You're not clingy, are you?"

"If you're asking if I'd want to hold you, yeah, I would. But that's your decision." Trying to tease the worry from her expression, he promised, "I won't cuddle you in your sleep if you'd rather I didn't."

Disgruntled for only a second more, she scoffed. "All right, let's not chew it to death." Going all brisk, she levered carefully to her side—facing away from where he'd sleep. "Get the doors locked and do whatever you have to do. I can't keep my eyes open any longer."

An hour later, enveloped by darkness, Cade silently called her a fibber. She was faking sleep, but he wasn't fooled. Maybe being in here with her wasn't such a good idea if his nearness was going to keep her awake.

Kept him awake, too, but he knew his problem. Despite her injuries, despite her wariness, he wanted her. Didn't matter that it couldn't happen, didn't matter that he wouldn't let it happen even if she felt up for it—which she didn't.

At the very least, he wanted to curve his body around hers,

but she was so stiff beside him he thought she might startle if he reached for her.

Suddenly she made a small agonizing sound, breaking the spell.

Immediately he rolled toward her. "What's wrong? Leg hurting? I can get you more aspirin."

In reply, she snapped, "Just do it already."

His turn to go perfectly still. "It?"

"This cuddle stuff you mentioned. We're both awake, so you might as well—"

Not giving her a chance to change her mind, Cade carefully scooted closer until his body molded to hers, his legs fitting behind hers, his arm curving over the dip of her waist. Placing a soft kiss to the side of her neck, he asked, "Okay?"

Audibly breathing, she croaked, "Sure."

So warm, and surprisingly soft for such an attitude. He laced his fingers with hers over her stomach. "Relax."

Turning her head toward him, she asked incredulously, "Can you?"

"Eventually." He tugged her a little closer. "Close your eyes and take slow, deep breaths. If that doesn't work, I'm moving to the couch so you *can* sleep." When she said nothing, he directed again, "Breathe slow and easy."

Nodding, she sucked in a quick breath but did blow it out slowly, then repeated it...again and again, finding a smooth rhythm that lasted until her body went lax.

Cade knew the moment she nodded off, and then finally, he dozed off, too. Expecting her to stir off and on all night with discomfort, he was disconcerted to wake with sunshine filtering in through the window. Overall, they were in the same position they'd started in. Their fingers were no longer entwined, since she now had her uninjured hand tucked under her cheek, and his hand rested over her bruised thigh. Leaning up, he checked the clock on the nightstand.

Huh. He couldn't remember the last time he'd slept after nine, but it was damn near nine thirty.

On a soft groan, Sterling shifted—and went still. She jerked her head around, then winced in pain.

"Easy. Let me disengage first. Then I can help. You're probably going to be twice as stiff now." He tried not to jar the bed as he got up and pulled on his jeans, leaving them unsnapped. He didn't bother with his shirt or shoes yet. "Can you sit up?"

"No choice," she said, teeth clenched as she let him help her upright.

Her robe had come open, so he got an eyeful, one that'd stick with him for…oh, the rest of his life, probably. Injured or not, she had a killer body. He didn't mean to, but his attention snagged on soft white breasts, tipped with rosy nipples.

Morning wood settled in real fast.

Without saying a word, he pulled the lapels together and re-tied the belt.

"You go ahead and use the bathroom," she said. "I need a minute."

"You won't move?"

She snorted. "Might as well warn you now, I'm not at my best in the morning, so mosey on while I concentrate on becoming human."

Grinning, Cade smoothed her hair. "Be right back."

A half hour later, he managed to get his unruly gonads under control, and she managed to make it to the bathroom and then the couch. They ended up positioned the same way as last night, with ice packs on her elevated leg, but now with coffee in hand.

He waited until she'd almost finished her first cup and then said, "I'll need to head out soon, but I want to make sure you're settled first."

Over the rim of her mug, those dark velvet eyes zeroed in on his face, before drifting down his body.

Several times she'd done that, her attention starting in one place and ending up on his bare chest or his stomach. Each appreciative study left him a little warmer. At one point she'd even stared at the crotch of his jeans until he worried he'd get hard again.

With the memory of her bare breasts at the forefront of his mind, it wouldn't take much.

When he cleared his throat, her gaze lifted lazily back to his. "Hey, you don't want me looking, don't show so much."

The things she said—hell, even her reactions, all of it—were entirely unexpected. "No way am I the first shirtless man you've seen."

Brows going up, she saluted him with her coffee. "No, but most don't look like you, do they? You've got some serious hotness going on. Work out often?"

Every day, but he wouldn't boast about it. "I like to stay fit."

"Because you routinely tangle with bad guys?"

Cade knew she casually slipped that in hoping he'd automatically answer, maybe tell her more than he meant to. She was slick about it, but he wasn't that easy. "Habit. Lifestyle. Discipline."

"Yup, definitely military. And I guess that explains the tats?" She waited, but he only sipped his coffee. "You don't want to share yet? Bummer. I mean, we slept together, right? That should count for something."

"You think so? Then tell me—how often have you interfered with traffickers?"

"I'd rather know what the tattoos mean."

"I'll tell you—someday."

Turning away, she finished off her coffee and plunked the mug down on the table.

Disappointed, but not surprised, Cade strode back into her bedroom to pull on his shirt and grab his shoes and socks. He returned to the living room and took the chair adjacent to the couch to finish dressing.

She was still silent when he stood, provoking his impatience.

"I started," she whispered, "by picking up a girl on the highway."

Going still, Cade took in her expression, her carefully blanked mask that said so much, surely more than she meant to. Slowly, he reseated himself. "She was trafficked?"

Sterling nodded. "I knew the signs as soon as I saw her. Or suspected, anyway, but it didn't take me long to have it confirmed." Absently, she rubbed her leg. "It was cold, dark, and there she was, without a coat, her eyes…haunted. The second I pulled over, she got in and begged me to drive. She didn't care where as long as it was away. There were bruises on her arms, a few on her neck."

Getting up, Cade moved closer, sitting by her feet on the couch and curving a hand over her calf. "You got her somewhere safe?"

"She refused the police station. Airport was out without ID. Bus station was too shady, and the hospital would be too obvious, she said, because they'd know to find her there."

"They who?"

Sterling shook her head. "She didn't want to say." Her eyes met his. "But I talked her around."

Reading the vindication in her hard gaze unsettled him. "You went after them, didn't you?"

Bypassing that, she said, "There's a woman... I knew her years ago when I relocated. I trusted her." Sterling tucked back her hair with fidgeting fingers. "I got hold of her, and she helped me figure out what to do."

"Like what?"

"The thing is, knowing I made a difference, helping someone— it's empowering. Almost addictive." Flexing her toes, she winced, then shifted to get comfortable. "I couldn't give that up, so I've educated myself more."

Cade couldn't believe what he was hearing, but God help him, he knew this was her grand confession. It was truth, and somehow he had to bend his brain around it. "And so now you go trolling for victims?"

Insult sharpened her gaze. "There's no *trolling* involved. I'm on the most trafficked route in Colorado anyway, I'm in and out of truck stops, so yeah, I keep my eyes open, and when appropriate, I act."

A headache started at the base of his skull. "It's dangerous."

"Duh. But I can handle it."

He shot right back, "Like you did at Misfits?"

Pain forgotten, she sat forward and poked at his chest. "If you hadn't interfered, yeah, I'd have figured it out somehow. But you mucked it all up, didn't you? Now Adela is missing and Mattox is out there somewhere, so if anything, I'm in more danger now after your *assistance* than I'd be if I'd handled it on my own."

Cade nearly threw up his hands, but that wouldn't solve anything. He knew better than to let his temper take control. A man had to have a cool head to deal with most situations. Dealing with someone like Star? He'd let his anger fuck that royally.

Time to retrench, before she expected reciprocal confessions from him. Nothing had changed there. He still couldn't confide in her without implicating his family, and that was something he wouldn't do.

Getting up, he headed to the kitchen and rummaged through a few junk drawers before he found a pen and piece of paper. It gave him a second to collect himself and hopefully allowed her a minute to lose steam.

On his way back in, he preempted any angry outbursts by saying, "You're right. I'm sorry."

Mouth open—probably to blast him—Sterling paused, then clicked her teeth together. "I don't know if I accept your apology. It'll depend on what you tell me in return."

And there it was, the expectation of tit for tat. "We have a lot to discuss, but I really am running short on time, so how about giving me a list of groceries you want?"

She knew an evasion when she heard one. "Go. I don't need anything. My plan is to veg right here and watch TV."

"And what do you plan to do about food?"

That stymied her for a second. "Cereal is still in there."

"But your milk is bad."

Wrinkling her nose, she said, "Yeah, that happens a lot. Not your problem."

It bothered him that she'd seriously sit at home, hurt and without food, before she'd ask for help. Not that she had to ask, but it'd help if she didn't fight him every inch of the way. Now, of course, she had more reason than ever to be difficult.

"I do go after traffickers, with the end goal to take them out."

Eyes widening with an *aha* expression, she sat forward. "I *knew* it."

"We can compare notes soon, okay?" Maybe. Probably. Probably not.

"But right now I want to run to the store before I have to get home and then to work. If you tell me your preferences, I can get some meals figured out, stuff that you can just nuke or eat cold, like sandwiches. What do you think?"

"I think you're a real mother hen."

"My family would disagree with you, but I am realistic enough to know you aren't in any shape to go out, your cabinets are all but empty, and I doubt you'd open the door to fast-food delivery."

Without denying or confirming any of that, she narrowed her eyes. "Why does it matter to you?"

"Why do you fight me?"

Her mouth twitched to the side. "Maybe because you confuse me and I'm not sure of your motives."

Something he could sink his teeth into. Hopefully it wouldn't make her more resistant. "I like you. I'm sure you've figured out that I want you." He held up a hand. "Not that I'm trading favors—"

"I *know* that." Color, both embarrassment and irritation, warmed her face. "Give me some credit."

"Whether you and I ever get together, we're friends now, right? I'd help a stranger if I could, so of course I want to lend you a hand."

When she still didn't agree, he growled, "You like being disagreeable, don't you?"

Her mouth twitched the other way. "I don't want to be beholden."

"For food? You're telling me that once you're up and running again, you won't return the favor?"

Guarded, she asked, "Return it how?"

"Dinner? If you don't cook, we could go out."

"I cook." Touchy about it, she said, "I'm not helpless or dumb."

"Far from both," he agreed. "So we're on the same page here?"

"I'm not keen on going hungry, so feel free to play maid and chef."

God forbid she give an inch. Tamping down irritation, Cade asked, "Preferences?"

"I'll eat pretty much anything other than seafood, so get whatever's convenient. But I want the receipt so I can pay you back."

Knowing she'd insist, he nodded. "Fine."

She countered back with her own version of "Fine," loading the word with a lot of annoyance.

He picked up her keys so he'd be able to get back in and was almost to the door when she stopped him.

"One thing, Cade, and it's nonnegotiable."

Bracing himself, he waited.

"If you don't trust me with some details, you won't be welcome back, and I won't return to the bar. Maybe keep that in mind before you insist on doing my shopping."

Driven by her inflexible tone, Cade strode back to the couch, bent down and took her mouth in a quick, warm kiss—that really got to him. Her lips were soft, parted in surprise, allowing his tongue a brief foray. She tasted good and felt even better. He wanted to learn about that mouth. About all of her.

Before he got carried away, he stepped back but took in her bemused expression. She touched her lips, her gaze seeking his. First time he'd ever seen her speechless.

Next time she started haranguing him, he'd remember what worked. "I won't be long."

This time when he left, she didn't stop him.

CHAPTER SIX

THREE FLIPPIN' DAYS of laziness and Sterling was about to climb the walls. Sure, Cade continued to spend the night, getting in late after the bar closed and leaving late the next morning. But he still hadn't told her anything substantial. He answered her questions with questions of his own, to the point they were at a stalemate. The way he dodged getting to the meat of issues, she hadn't realized how little he'd shared until she started piecing it together.

Okay, so his buff bod distracted her. He slept in his boxers and didn't bother to dress until he was ready to go. What red-blooded woman wouldn't focus on that?

A couple of times now she'd wondered if he did it on purpose, just to keep her suitably dazed and on the edge of lust. If so, she didn't want him to stop.

She enjoyed it all too much.

The way he waited on her was sweet, too, but now she realized he'd sidestepped questions by cooking, tidying up the apartment, ensuring she had everything within easy reach before he left each day.

Finally, the bruising started to fade a bit and she could bear more weight on her injured leg. No, she wouldn't be doing any deep knee bends yet, and driving her rig was still out, but she was pretty sure she could handle her car—and her own shopping.

Which meant it was time for him to fess up, or she'd have to send him packing. It didn't make sense for her to share anything more with a man who so obviously didn't trust her.

She'd just finished putting a compression wrap on her thigh when Cade asked, "How often do you actually transport or deliver?"

"Often enough to be legit," she replied, standing to test her leg. "Seldom enough that I can use my truck for other purposes."

He stood close in case she needed his help but didn't yet touch her. "Like searching for women along trucking routes?"

"Bingo." Satisfied that she could manage on her own, she took a small trip around the apartment. Her leg remained stiff and achy, but she moved on her own steam. "Mostly I pick up freight overload from bigger trucking companies, which lets me be pretty footloose with my schedule. When I have other leads to follow, I can pass on the job offer, and I never have to book myself too far in advance."

Sounding impressed, he said, "That's genius."

"I know, right?" She stopped to rest, one hand on the divider wall that separated the kitchen from the living room. "Now it's your turn, so—"

Her phone rang.

Disgusted by the interruption, she warned, "Don't go anywhere," and returned to the coffee table, grabbed up her cell and glanced at the screen. "An unlisted number." She answered, "Hello?"

"Francis?"

Oh, hell. Knees going weak, she lowered herself to sit on the edge of the couch. Already guessing the answer, she asked, "Who's this?"

"Adela."

Her gaze shot to Cade's. As if he'd picked up on the sense of danger, he came to sit beside her.

"How are you, Adela?" Sterling used her name to let Cade know the identity of her caller. "I hope you got out okay?"

"I need help."

Not exactly a direct answer. "Okay. Where are you?"

"I'm afraid to tell you—but I thought maybe I could meet you somewhere safe? You...well, it seemed you wanted to help, right?

I'm sorry I wasn't as brave as you, but you can't imagine..." Her breath shuddered. "The things they've done to me, I couldn't risk it."

"I understand." Feeling Cade's gaze burning over her, Sterling tried to think. "What happened after I left?"

"I... I thought we'd stay at the bar, but they stuffed me in a car and drove to a different place."

"Where?"

"It doesn't matter. I got away, but now I don't know what to do. Please say you'll meet me."

Stalling for time, Sterling chewed her bottom lip.

"Francis?"

"It's okay. I'm here." Some anomalous emotion squeezed her lungs. Terror, likely. But also...uncertainty? Something here felt very, very wrong.

Cade shook his head at her.

The man dared to give her orders when he wouldn't tell her a damn thing? Screw that. She could make her own plans. "I hope you're somewhere secure, Adela, because I can't meet you for a few days."

"*Please!* I can't stay here. I'll get caught again, I just know it. They use horrible drugs and...and *violence*, and it scares me so badly—"

"Shh," Sterling whispered, hoping to calm her. "We'll get it figured out, I promise. You just need to stay safe a little longer."

After some heavy breathing, Adela asked, "Then you'll come for me?"

Heart clenching, Sterling vowed, "Of course I will, just not today. I hurt my...shoulder, when I went out the window." She couldn't say what prompted the lie, except that she'd learned extreme caution whenever dealing with traffickers or victims. "I'm sorry, but I can't drive yet. Another day or two and I should be better." Not giving Adela time to start crying again, Sterling asked, "How far do I need to go to meet you?"

After a lengthy hesitation, Adela blew out a shaky breath. "I'm off I-25. That's all I can say for now."

"But that covers a lot of ground."

"I'll be more specific when I know you're on your way."

With no other choice to take, Sterling nodded. "Okay, but give me a number so I can contact you tomorrow. We'll set something up for the next evening."

"No. I'll call you back." Agonized, Adela added, "I'm counting on you, Francis. Please, don't forget about me."

Hearing the finality in that small plea, Sterling said, "Wait—" but it was too late. She'd already ended the call.

The urge to throw the phone made it extra difficult for Sterling to gently place it on the coffee table, but that's what she did.

Then she ignored Cade as she concentrated on organizing her thoughts.

"YOU DID WELL."

Adela stayed silent. His moods could be unpredictable at the best of times, and this wasn't a good time. He detested having his plans upset, but she'd tried her best. It wasn't her fault the woman wouldn't cooperate.

"We'll give her a day to stew on it," he decided. "Then you'll call her in a panic to make the arrangements."

"A panic?" That suggestion didn't bode well.

Eyes full of malice pinned her to the spot. He smiled, reaching out with one hand to finger the shorter wisps of her hair over her temple.

She tried not to flinch, but she couldn't help it.

"When she sees you, she needs to know you're in trouble. She needs to be completely horrified by your condition." His meaty hand opened to cup her cheek. "Do you understand what I'm telling you?"

Unfortunately, she did. She shouldn't have been cold, but the chill of the inevitable seeped into her bones, making her shiver.

His thick hand slid down her neck and gripped tightly—seconds before his other hand made sharp contact with her jaw. Stars erupted and she would have collapsed, except that he held her by the neck.

STANDING, STERLING MADE her way to the patio doors and stared out at the mountains in the distance. It was a sight that used to soothe her. The vastness of the Rockies meant she could hide—but now it also meant she might disappear, and who would know?

Who would *care*?

This was the first time someone had contacted her directly. Usually when she helped a young woman, it was because she'd found her on the road or in the act of being traded. Truck stops were hotbeds of trafficking, which was the main reason she'd gotten her CDL.

Promising safety, she could usually talk a woman into getting into her truck. When conditions warranted it, when sleazeballs were keeping watch, she performed hasty kidnappings.

In her seven years as a truck driver, she hadn't made as much impact as she would have liked—but for the women she'd rescued, she'd made a big difference. They'd been given a second chance.

And in doing so, she'd given herself another chance, as well. A chance to add worth to her life. A chance to—

"How'd she get your number?"

The intrusion of Cade's voice disrupted her maudlin thoughts. A good thing, really. She couldn't afford too much introspection right now or she'd chicken out of what had to be done.

Glancing at him, she said, "I gave her a card the night we were at Misfits."

Fury and disbelief brought Cade slowly to his feet. "You did *what*?"

She curled her lip in disdain. Sure, she recognized his temper as concern, but the facts remained: *he didn't trust her.*

Whatever. She was done trusting him, too.

"Don't sweat it. All the card had on it was my number, nothing else, and I don't use GPS or public Wi-Fi on my phone. No one is going to track me down."

"I did."

Her brows climbed high. "Using my cell phone? No, I don't think so." Sterling turned back to the view, but she didn't really see it. Damn it, she had hopes of her and Cade teaming up, but he'd dashed them, and now she had to accept it wouldn't happen. "More likely you followed me home—or had someone else do it. Either way, it was a breach of privacy that I don't appreciate."

She hadn't heard his approach, so it took her off guard when

his hard hands settled on her shoulders. Her senses stirred, awareness spiking.

His reflection in the glass showed his resolve.

Against her back, she felt the heat of him.

Odd, but his nearness calmed her rioting thoughts. Since she
couldn't rely on him, that wasn't necessarily a good thing. To put
them back on track, she said, "I'll have to go after her."

Cade pulled her against his body, his arms folding over her
chest, enveloping her in his strength. "No, you won't. I can handle it for you."

"Oh, for sure, you look enough like me to fool her." Rolling her
eyes, she twisted around to face him. "She'll be looking for *me*,
an unassuming woman—"

Cade snorted.

"Not an imposing man. If she sees you, she'll bolt."

"You don't know that."

"I've handled it enough times that I can guarantee it. Men will
not be high on her trustworthy list."

"Is that the voice of experience?" Appearing far too solemn, he
cupped his hands around her neck, his thumbs keeping her chin
lifted. "It'd help if you told me how you got started with all this."

It saddened her far more than it should have, but Sterling shook
her head. "I don't think so. Interesting as this has been, it's going
nowhere. I got that message loud and clear." She pulled away from
him and hobbled toward the front door. "Time for you to go."

Cade didn't move. "I'm not going anywhere."

She spun back to face him and nearly lost her balance when her
bum leg gave way. "Yes, you are."

"You can so easily dismiss this?" He gestured between them.

"I don't even know what this is. You said you needed to talk to
others, to see what you could share. Well, you've had four days
and still nada. I'm done. I have things to do, and they don't include
dumping my past on you."

As she spoke, Cade seemed to get bigger, harder, maybe even
a little menacing. In comparison, his tone was soft—and somehow more lethal because of it. "I kept putting off talking to my
family because it's going to raise a lot of speculation. And I know
how they'll react."

Family, meaning not just his brother? Was his sis involved, too? "Secrecy all the way, huh?"

"It's what we've lived by for many years. You know it, too. The best way to keep private info private is not to share it with anyone."

Her heart sank. Had she really held out hope that her ultimatum would change things? Stupidly, yes.

He'd done the unthinkable, dangling the carrot of shared experiences…only to yank it away. "Leave."

Instead, he scrubbed a hand over his face. "I never knew my mother."

In the process of heading to the door, Sterling froze. Afraid that he'd say no more, she kept her back to him and stayed perfectly still.

"My father raised me from birth. I'm thirty-two now and not once has my mother ever tried to contact me."

When she got light-headed, Sterling realized she was holding her breath. She let it out softly, then sucked in fresh oxygen. "Maybe she didn't know how to find you."

"No, that wouldn't have been a problem."

She heard him moving and chanced a peek back.

He now sat on the couch, legs sprawled, hands braced on his thighs. "My father never married, but he did have a life partner." He shrugged. "She was like a stepmother to me. They loved each other, and when she was taken, it leveled him in a way I've never seen before. He was…crazed."

Cautiously, Sterling approached, her heart beating double time, and eased down beside him. "She was never found?"

"Oh, she was. Dad has the kind of money that can hire the best and hire the worst."

"I don't understand."

"They turned the state upside down. He observed it all, the interrogations—and the vengeance. Finally, he found her. It's bullshit, the way Hollywood paints human trafficking as some high-style wealthy man's sport. It can be, but that's not the norm. It's what exists in our own backyards."

Unable to resist, Sterling put her hand over his. "I know."

"She was found in a shitty little hotel room, drugged to the gills and…" He swallowed heavily.

Again, with emotion making her throat feel thick, Sterling whispered, "I know."

Turning his hand, Cade clasped her fingers. "One year to the day that she returned home, she swallowed a bottle of pills."

Seeing his pain made it fresh for Sterling. Tears burned her eyes, but a crying woman wouldn't help him.

A strong woman would. "I'm sorry."

"She'd left a note, a plea for Dad to do *something* so other women wouldn't have to go through that." His gaze locked on hers. "And that's all I can tell you for now. Don't ask me names or details, because I can't give them."

She was quick to nod. This was a moment, one she could cherish, one she could build on—and God, she wanted that. She wanted more than the emptiness her life had been.

It took her a second to decide on her next step, but it was instinct that brought her forward so she could sink against his big solid chest. Wrapping her arms around his waist, she squeezed him tight. "Thank you for telling me."

"Is it enough, Star?"

Damn it, she was starting to like the way he said her name.

He nuzzled against her hair. "Will you promise me you won't go after Adela alone?"

Feeling the weight lifted from her shoulders, she nodded. "Yes. I promise."

That got her crushed against him. "Let's go over what we know."

This. This was what she'd wanted. Someone to collaborate with, to help her with her plans. A sounding board that'd give her a new perspective.

Nodding, Sterling forced herself past the satisfaction of having a cohort to address the business at hand. "Adela said she was staying off I-25, which doesn't tell us much."

"Except that it's known as a trafficking route."

Sterling knew that well. "Along the front range, drivers can easily travel from city to city and into other states. Here's the thing." With one last squeeze, Sterling straightened. "I've picked up three women along that interstate, all of them about an hour south of Colorado Springs in the same general area."

"You think it could be related?"

"Makes sense, right? It's how I knew about Misfits and—Thacker. But only if it's a widely spread organization. One of the women was from a spa that later got busted."

"Thanks to a tip from you?"

Pleased that he'd give her credit, she blushed. "Yeah, sure. I mean, I couldn't just charge in there with guns blazing, right? So I anonymously clued in some people, luckily the right people, and it turned into a big sting."

"I actually remember that. Around eighteen months ago, right?"

So *he* kept track of such things? Interesting. "That's right. Eight men were arrested and the spa was shut down."

His phone dinged with a message. Impatient, he glanced at it and didn't look pleased. "The other women you mentioned?"

Of course, now she wondered who'd sent him a message, but he'd just started opening up and she didn't want to pressure him, so she let it go.

For now.

"One had been held in a prostitution ring that operated out of this nasty little hotel. They thought they had her too intimidated to run, but she'd only been waiting for an opportunity, and that happened during a severe rainstorm that knocked out power over a wide swath. Plus the downpour made it tougher for them to search for her."

"But you found her?"

"At a truck stop, hiding behind a building. Being female, she trusted me more than the male truck drivers."

He nodded. "And the third?"

"She'd only recently been abducted. She was able to get away by jumping out of a moving car while they were transporting her, so she was pretty banged up. It was cold and she didn't have the right clothes. I think it was desperation that brought her near the road. Good thing I found her before anyone else did."

His admiring gaze moved over her face. "You're pretty remarkable, you know that, right?"

Again his words warmed her. "Just doing my part."

"Above and beyond."

"Like you?"

"There are definite similarities, and I'd love to compare notes, but that was a summons from my father and it's never a good idea to keep him waiting." As he stood, he asked, "You'll be okay until I get back after work?"

Since he'd stocked the fridge with chicken salad and pickles and left croissants and chips on the counter, canned soup in the cabinets, he didn't need to worry about her going hungry. "I'm better every day. In case you didn't notice, I can get around on my own now."

"I noticed." Intense emotion darkened his eyes. "I'm looking forward to you being one hundred percent again."

She couldn't hold back the silly smile. "Yeah? Why's that?"

For an answer, he leaned in and took her mouth again, longer, hotter this time, his tongue teasing against hers, his breath warm on her cheek. He lingered—until his phone buzzed once more.

On a low growl, he moved away, but not far, just enough to separate their lips. His hand tunneled into her hair to curve around her skull. "Make no mistake. We've come to an agreement. You'll stay in today, and tomorrow we'll make plans together?"

"Tomorrow we can discuss plans," she clarified. "But I won't go out. I'm not quite ready for that anyway. I thought instead I'd do some additional research on the area where I found the other women."

"Good thinking. I'll see you tonight after I've closed up the bar." With one last, sizzling kiss, he left her apartment.

Sterling would like to know more about his father. His brother and sister, too. Hopefully tomorrow he'd share details.

Would she share, as well? She *did* trust him, she realized, so what would be the harm? Yet caution was her constant companion, so she'd consider all the angles before making up her mind.

Crazy, but she already anticipated his return—and more than that, the day when she'd be healed enough to make him live up to the promise behind those kisses.

DOGGED BY HIS father's assistant, who also served as a butler and chef, pretty much everything, Cade went through the opulent mountain home toward the back deck, where he knew he'd find his family. "I know the way, Bernard."

"Yes, sir," he acknowledged, while continuing to be Cade's shadow.

Cade glanced back at him. "I thought we agreed you'd quit with the *sir* nonsense."

"You requested," Bernard said in his grating monotone, "and I declined."

Knowing Bernard to be as stubborn as Star, Cade let it go as he continued on through the massive great room and out to the three-tier deck that offered an amazing view of the mountains, as well as his father's man-made lake. Sitting on fifty-two acres, surrounded by wilderness, guaranteed a level of privacy not found in the skiing towns.

Cade loved the house and the surrounding land—not so much these visits.

It was cooler up here, so his sister, immersed in reading something on her laptop, had a colorful shawl around her shoulders. Reyes sprawled in a chair, one leg over the arm, his expression pensive—until he spotted Cade.

"'Bout time you got here."

Curious over what that meant, Cade glanced at his father. Parrish McKenzie looked younger than his fifty-three years. Almost as tall as Cade, still fit thanks to the well-equipped gym on his lower level and a love of the outdoors, his father always made an imposing figure.

Sipping hot tea from a dainty cup and working a crossword puzzle, he looked nothing like a hard-core vigilante. Without looking up, he said, "You have some explaining to do."

At the same time, Bernard asked, "Something to drink, sir?"

"I'll take a beer."

"This early?" Bernard questioned, with disapproval.

"Not like I'll drink at the bar, so yeah. This early." Hell, it had to be noon. Not like he was having it for breakfast.

"Yeah," Reyes said, perking up at that suggestion. "Grab me one, too, will you, Bernard?"

His sister never stirred, but then, when she got immersed in research, she tuned out everything else.

The second Bernard left, Reyes sang, "Cade has a girlfriend."

Cutting his gaze to his brother, Cade warned, "Knock it off." He dropped into an empty chair at the table.

Reyes only grinned. "But that's why we're here. I just figured I'd throw it out there rather than keep you waiting."

Shit. It had been too much to ask that his father might not yet know about Star.

Finally Parrish put down his pencil and sent an enigmatic gaze at Cade. "This won't do, you know."

"Not up to you, so save the dictates." Cade accommodated his father whenever possible. This wasn't one of those times.

"If you want her," Parrish said baldly, "just have her and be done with it."

Reyes snorted.

Madison glanced up, brows lifted.

It struck Cade that he had to have the strangest family in God's creation. Keeping his expression bland, he asked Parrish, "Does she get a say in it?"

Hot color rushed into his father's face. As a champion of women, it was an insult that cut deep. "You know I wasn't suggesting—"

"So you just assumed she'd be on board if I'm interested? I appreciate the vote of confidence."

"Logical conclusion." Shifting his gaze to Reyes, Parrish asked, "What's so special about this woman?"

"No freaking idea."

Cade thought about tossing his brother over the railing. He could roll downhill until he hit the lake.

"Is she beautiful?" Expounding on that, Parrish said, "Describe her."

Uneasy now, Reyes glanced at Cade, then shrugged. "Tall, strong figure, average face. Nice hair. Definite lack of fashion sense."

Frowning in confusion, Parrish turned back to Cade for enlightenment.

It was almost laughable. Almost. "Looks aren't everything, Dad." And then to Reyes, "Though you have to admit there's something about her."

"She's sexy," Reyes agreed. "But that's not what Dad asked."

"It's the attitude." Cade didn't mean to offer up details, but the words came out anyway. "If you got to know her, you'd understand what I mean."

"Yeah, uh... I got a small taste of that attitude, enough to neuter me, so no thanks." To their dad, he said, "It'd take someone like Cade to go toe-to-toe with her. She's what you'd call *challenging*."

"Challenging how?"

"Let's just say she's not a 'polished nails and styled hair' kind of gal—more like 'I'll gut you and walk away smiling if you get in my way' type."

Appalled, Parrish asked Cade, "Is that something you want?"

Even Madison put aside her work to hear the answer to that.

Their reactions left him grinning. Was it so unheard of for him to be interested? All right, so he never let his personal life cross paths with his work—until now.

It wasn't like he set out to find a balls-to-the-walls woman. Nope. Had he been looking for someone to match his strength? Not likely, since he usually was attracted to ultrafeminine women. Actually, he hadn't been looking for anything.

Then Sterling Parson had walked into his bar one night and he hadn't been able to put her from his mind since then.

That was his business, though, no one else's, and he wouldn't sit here while they dissected her. "Maybe you all missed it, but I'm thirty-two, too old to explain myself, so leave it alone."

"But you need our help," Madison said, then fell silent as Bernard returned with beers, little sandwiches and some type of individual cakes on a round tray.

"Bernard!" she exclaimed, already snatching up two of the small cakes. "You know these are my favorites."

"Yes, I do. That's why I made them." He handed her a napkin, then refilled her tea before offering the contents of the tray to Cade and Reyes.

Glad for the reprieve, Cade took two sandwiches, popping one into his mouth right away. Good. Some kind of specialty bread, with a tangy sauce, sliced roast beef and fresh tomatoes. "Not bad, Bernard."

"You'll make me blush with that type of praise."

Laughing, Reyes grabbed a few sandwiches for himself. "We

all know you're invaluable, Bernard, so don't go fishing for compliments."

"Can't imagine what I was thinking." After setting the half-empty tray on the table, he turned to Parrish. "If you need anything else, let me know."

Parrish waved him off. "Go take a break. Maybe grab a swim. Put one of the pools to use."

"The indoor pool is heated just right," Reyes said, "but fair warning, the outside pool is cold enough to shrivel your..."

"Ahem." Bernard censured Reyes with a single withering look, then said to Parrish, "Thank you, but I need to start preparations for dinner." With a sniff, he added, "The meat must marinate. Perhaps I'll indulge a swim later this evening."

After the French doors closed behind him, Reyes burst out laughing. "I do love shocking him."

Parrish shook his head. "For twenty years I've been telling that man not to be so formal."

"He enjoys the pomp," Madison said. "Let him have his fun." Her eyes, the same bright hazel color as Reyes's, narrowed on Cade. "Now, as I was saying—"

"I don't want your help."

She smiled. "Sorry, but you're getting it anyway."

CHAPTER SEVEN

CADE TURNED HIS ire on Reyes. "Felt like you had to confess all, huh?"

Unfazed, Reyes shook his head. "Wrong tree you're barking up, there. I didn't say jackola." He gestured toward Madison. "Did you really think *she* wouldn't find out?"

No, it would have been more surprising if she hadn't. His baby sister didn't miss much. By accessing street cameras and security cameras on businesses, and with the help of good old-fashioned bugs, she had surveillance everywhere.

No problem when it came to work, but apparently she knew he hadn't been home the last few days, either.

Because he'd been staying with Star.

Cade shifted his attention to his sister.

Defiant, Madison elevated her chin. "Of course I told Dad. When you risk yourself, you risk the rest of us."

An insult he couldn't ignore. "You think I'd let harm come to you?"

She winced in apology. "No, not really. I didn't mean that."

"So you think what? That Star will hold me hostage until I tell her all about you?"

Parrish scowled at Cade. "Don't put your sister in an untenable position with divided loyalties. We work as a family. You know that." Admonishing, he added, "And she wouldn't have had to tell me if you'd done so instead."

"I planned to tell you soon."

"Why wait?"

Reyes started to speak up, likely with another joke.

He shut down when Cade turned on him. "I wouldn't if I was you."

Hands up, Reyes said, "Take it easy. Here on the balcony isn't the right place, but if you want a go at me, the gym is available downstairs."

Parrish slammed a fist to the table. "I didn't teach you to fight so you could maul each other."

For too many years, Parrish had been fanatical about his children learning both defensive and offensive moves. While he trained with one expert after another, always with the intent of one day getting the men who'd kidnapped his companion, he included his children so that they were trained, as well.

From the day his stepmother committed suicide, Cade was told his purpose in life was to seek justice for those who couldn't defend themselves. He, Reyes and Madison couldn't just be good—they had to be the best.

Once Reyes had stopped grieving his mother, he'd loved the discipline and had embraced the vigilante purpose with enthusiasm.

Madison, too, accepted her role as tech genius, falling into place from the age of nine.

Cade was different. He'd balked at having his purpose predestined by his overbearing father. Oh, he'd learned what he could. Training was a satisfying outlet for his sorrow at losing the only mother he knew, and having siblings he'd wanted to protect.

Fifteen at the time and already rebellious, he'd butted heads with his father at every opportunity—right up until he'd joined the military in defiance of his father's dictates.

"If you want to spar," Parrish said, "you'll do so when neither of you is angry."

Smirking, Reyes asked, "When is he *not* angry?"

Cade rolled his eyes. True, he used to stay at some level of rage day in and day out. But that was a decade ago, before the military had helped him tamp down the emotion under firm control. Reyes knew that, but Bernard wasn't the only one he liked to heckle.

"I'm not angry now," Cade said, "but I'd still be happy to kick your ass."

"Nah. I think I'll wait and take you by surprise." He grinned. "Ups my odds, ya know?"

Getting back to the matter at hand, Madison shared one of her gentlest smiles. "For what it's worth, I admire Sterling a great deal." She turned her laptop so Cade could see the screen...where she'd expanded her research to include a history of Star's life.

He didn't want to read it here, under his family's scrutiny, but he knew how proprietary Madison could be about her investigations. She preferred to keep everything in-house—literally—and under her own impenetrable security protocols.

If he wanted to learn about Star, he needed to read everything now. And there was the rub. "This feels like a huge invasion of her privacy."

Madison's smile quirked. "You don't think she'd read everything she could about you if she had access?"

Actually...he knew she would, if for no other reason than that she didn't fully trust him.

Aware of Parrish, Reyes and Madison all watching him, Cade pulled the laptop closer. At first he merely skimmed the details. Abducted at seventeen from her high school. Escaped at some point between then and her eighteenth birthday, because new photos of her emerged after that—driver's license, concealed carry permit (now, why wasn't he surprised that she'd carry a gun?), her CDL for driving. She'd used different names, lied about her age a few times and moved around a lot, all the way from Ohio to Colorado.

"Last page," Madison said. "Child protection services had been to her home multiple times before she was abducted. That probably explains why she didn't return for her mother's funeral, even though she was apparently free by then."

Various photos from different ages, some of them grainy, others clear, filled the file. Damn, she'd changed.

At one point she'd been more colorful, more dramatic, likely outgoing. Now she was usually so contained she was like a different person. Quiet, intense, focused on a single purpose...

No wonder she didn't want him to call her Star anymore. She'd reshaped her life, her appearance, her entire persona. She'd made herself into a different person altogether.

The reach of his sister's abilities never failed to amaze him. "How did you do all this?"

"Facial recognition software, mostly. It's easy once you have access to various databases. Biometrics map out features and match them up. I wasn't sure about a few of the photos, so I had to do some cross-referencing to be positive they were really her."

Parrish sat back, his hands laced over his stomach. "In case you didn't realize, she's a vigilante, same as us."

"But without our connections," Reyes said.

"Or our financial means," Madison added.

Were they championing her now? Cade didn't know what to think of that. Until Parrish wrapped it up for him.

"All of which means she could bring us down with her blunders." Parrish watched him closely. "You understand that?"

They all waited, while Cade's calm chipped away. He met his father's gaze. "You may as well save your breath, because I'll do whatever I can to keep her safe."

"I'd like to know how." Parrish picked up his tea. "It seems keeping her out of trouble is going to be a full-time job."

"Put our stuff away."

She would, but... "It's cold." Arms wrapped around herself, Adela listened to the hollowness of her footsteps on the warped wooden floorboards. Drafts circled her legs. Cobwebs hung in every corner. It smelled damp, as if moisture had seeped in.

The mountain cabin—more like a shack—offered only minimum comfort. A rickety cot, a small generator to run the coffee machine and the mini refrigerator, and a private cell tower so making a call wouldn't be a problem.

Nervousness sank into every pore of her body. Already the cabin looked dark. How bad would it be when the sun set behind the mountains?

She swallowed hard. "What if someone finds us here?"

"We'll claim we were lost and needed shelter." Mattox rolled a massive shoulder. "If that doesn't work, offer yourself up." He went to a dirty window to look out. "No matter what, don't leave the cabin tonight."

As if she would.

When she didn't answer, he turned to face her, his gaze piercing enough to make her tremble. "You heard me?"

"Yes." She looked around again, dreading the next few days. Hopefully Francis wouldn't make her wait long.

"You wouldn't make it to the road, not in the dark," he warned, "and you could run into a snake, a mountain lion or a black bear—"

"I won't step outside." God no, she wouldn't. The mention of snakes made other threats unnecessary.

She shouldn't ask. She knew better, but she heard herself say, "I don't see why we have to stay here."

His gaze went icy. "Don't you?" Stalking toward her, he growled, "You fucked up, Adela. That's why Misfits is temporarily shut down. That's why fucking Francis got away. That's why we're losing money as we speak, and that, my little idiot, is why we're stuck in this fucking cabin."

A spark of anger ignited, but she kept it under control. "I played my part. How was I to know someone would kill the lights or launch an attack, or that she'd be so quick at finding a way out?"

Disgusted, he said, "You didn't stop her, did you?"

"I called out!" God, she hated getting blamed—even if what he said was true. She should have found a way to stop Francis, but she'd drawn a blank at the woman's lack of fear and her daring, plus it had been so damn dark she couldn't see her hand in front of her face. "You'll get her back."

For the longest time he studied her, his expression unreadable. Then he touched the bruise on her face as if fascinated. "Yes, I will—although I'm starting to wonder if she's worth the trouble."

Her eyes widened. "You think she'll stop now? That she'll just go away?"

"No, but it might be better, easier, to put a bullet in her skull and be done with it."

Adela was sure he didn't mean that. "So you've given up on making her pay?"

"No. We'll stick with the set plan." With a shrug, he added, "It'll work—if you play your part."

Glad that he'd relented, Adela promised, "I will."

Mattox tipped her face one way, then the other. "You look very much like a battered woman."

Which was the point, the very reason he'd struck her like he did. She held his gaze.

As if she stumped him, Mattox shook his head, then looked around the cabin. "For this insult alone, I'll make her beg for death. You can count on that."

Now that he was back to normal, Adela went about fixing them a light meal. Silence settled in, other than the occasional creak of an evergreen swaying or the whistle of wind.

Soon she'd contact Francis again—and then hopefully this would all be over.

CADE'S BROODING SILENCE was starting to get on Sterling's nerves.

They sat at the small dinette table sharing the country breakfast they'd prepared together. He'd handled the bacon, eggs and toast. Mostly one-handed, she'd done the fried potatoes.

Impossible to remember the last time she'd cooked so much food for the start of her day. Her normal practice was to grab a protein bar and a cup of coffee. Because she didn't have it often, the food tasted extra delicious.

It felt good to be functioning again, to be off the couch and properly dressed. Okay, so she wore only a big T-shirt and yoga pants—her typical at-home clothes. She'd even gotten her hair into a ponytail, no small feat with her fingers still taped together.

An hour ago she'd awakened with his arm around her, his breath warm on her neck, excited by the possibilities of their new relationship.

Shortly after that he'd gone all silent and introspective. He hadn't even commented on her getting dressed, the jerk.

Tired of waiting for him to perk up, she demanded, "What's wrong?"

That got his gaze up from his plate. "Nothing."

So he'd make her drag it out of him? Fine. Not like she had anything more pressing this morning. "Couldn't sleep?"

"I slept fine. You?"

She ignored the question to ask another of her own. "Trouble at the bar last night?"

"No." Frowning, he set aside his fork. "Why?"

Well, that left only one other possibility. "Daddy get on your nerves? Or was it that annoying brother of yours? Don't tell me you got a cease and desist on sharing, because we already agreed."

His mouth quirked at her wording.

She did love his mouth, the shape of his lips, the crooked way he smiled...how he'd tasted. And that strong jaw, now covered in dark, sexy stubble.

Oh, and those electric-blue eyes—which were now trying to peer into her soul. "Uh-uh, no you don't." She pointed a crispy piece of bacon at him. "I see what you're doing, but you have some explaining to do first."

"As I recall, I did all the explaining last night—and today was to be your turn."

"Actually..." She thought about it, but if she told him a few select details, would he further reciprocate? She'd never been this curious about a guy, so the lure of learning more tempted her into agreement. "Okay."

"Okay?"

Ha. She'd caught him off guard. Always a good thing. Spreading out her arms, she said, "What do you want to know?"

Taking that question far too seriously, he pushed aside his empty plate and folded his arms on the table. "You're too passionate about helping others, so I assume you have personal reasons?"

Something in his tone... Why did this feel like a test? Did he already know the answers and he wanted to see if she'd be upfront? Irritation sharpened her tone. "Why can't I just be a Good Samaritan?"

"You can. You *are*. The way you tried to help Adela, how you're worried about her still, is commendable."

"Yeah, someone should pin a medal to my T-shirt. At least give me a gold star sticker, right?"

His shoulders flexed—and he ignored her sarcasm. "But it's more than that, isn't it?"

So. Much. More.

She'd never really had a chance to talk about that awful time.

Her mother...no, she hadn't been clearheaded enough to listen, and there'd been no guarantees she wouldn't blab to the wrong person.

With Cade sitting there waiting, his expression warm, open and caring, the timing felt right to get it off her chest.

Sterling stared at the remains of egg yolk on her plate. "So... I killed a dude."

She waited for a gasp, for questions, maybe even accusations.

Nothing. No reaction, definitely no outrage or shock.

When she worked up the nerve to look at his face, all she found was honest empathy etched there. It almost choked her up.

Screw that. Making her tone as dispassionate as she could, she quipped, "He had it coming, though, you know?"

"Then I'm glad he's gone." Reaching across the table, his hand palm up, he offered her something new.

Understanding.

Theirs needed to be a business relationship...preferably with benefits. Getting emotionally involved with him could pose a problem.

But even knowing that, she couldn't resist lacing the fingers of her left hand with his. Unlike any other man she'd known, Cade made her feel delicate in comparison to his strength.

With him, it wasn't an unpleasant feeling.

Brushing his thumb over her knuckles, he asked, "Will you tell me about it?"

Telling him would be better than getting all maudlin. "Yeah, sure. Not much to tell, really. I got snatched during my junior year, right after I left school. Two guys. They were flirting and I stupidly fell for it."

"Got too close to them?"

"Yup. I made it so damn easy." She blew out a breath. Self-recriminations got her nowhere. She'd lived through it, learned from it and would never again make that mistake. "I was in a van going...somewhere, before I could even figure out what had happened. For the rest of the day they transferred me around from one place to another, moving me farther from home each time. Then I killed the dick who paid to use me, and got away."

His hand tightened around hers, not painfully but in reaction to that stark recounting. "How did you kill him?"

"I'm not sure I want to talk about this." But when she tried to pull her hand away, he held on.

"I told you about my stepmother."

True, he had. "You didn't force the pills on her, though."

Both his hands held hers now. His nails were short and clean, his fingers long. Slightly calloused. Very warm.

Very masculine, and they made her think of things that involved his hands and long fingers—

"I'm not going to judge you, Star, and I swear to you, your secrets are safe with me."

Jostled from her inappropriately timed sexual thoughts, she used her bandaged fingers to trace along his knuckles, up to his thick wrist and then over the downy hair on his forearms. "You know, it's the oddest damn thing. I was aware of you all that time at the bar, and then we started talking and I felt like I could trust you."

"Because you, lady, have good instincts. Same as me."

Sterling eyed him. "You saying you trust me?"

"I wouldn't be here if I didn't."

Hell of a compliment there. He did that a lot, heaping little bits of praise on her and making her almost glow with it. Could she do this? Could she repay his understanding with a brief, glossed-over version of what had happened that night?

Sensing her uncertainty, he asked, "Have you ever told anyone?"

No, she hadn't. "Never seemed like a good idea."

"But now? With me?"

Would it make her feel better? She sort of figured it might. "All right, fine. I got put with several other girls. Some of them had already been..." She swallowed hard. "It was awful, Cade. Seeing them, knowing what they'd been through, made it all the more real. They hadn't gotten away, so how could I?" The guilt swamped her again, strong enough to choke a horse, because she *had* escaped.

And in doing so, she'd left others behind.

Cade said nothing, but he held her hand steady in his and somehow it felt protective. If only she'd had someone like him back when she'd needed him most.

All she'd had was an addict for a mother, and a society that barely knew she existed.

"Like I said, they shuffled us from one place to another, as if we were cattle. Or even…boxed goods, you know? Not people. Not humans with a heartbeat, or girls who felt fear and pain. They didn't acknowledge any of that. They didn't care." This detailed stuff was for the birds. It made her tremble like that long-ago girl who'd been so terrorized. "So anyway," she said, more brisk now, "we ended up at this big old house that was mostly bedrooms, with a small sitting room, one upstairs john and a tiny kitchen. Each bedroom had a lock on the outside of the door. They some-how advertised us and people put in orders, like…pizza. Except instead of thick crust, they wanted a heavier girl. Red hair, black, like pepperoni or sausage. Fresh…" She swallowed hard. "Or a little more seasoned."

Cade briefly closed his eyes. Yeah, if he thought it was hard to hear, he should have tried going through it— No. No, she wouldn't wish that hell on anyone. She'd gladly kill those who instigated or added to the misery, but she wouldn't make them suffer the same humiliations and abuse that she had.

"Guess I got ordered up. Gullible teen with purple hair and a pierced lip who cried a lot. Sounds delicious, right?"

"Don't." His voice turned to rough, broken gravel. "Please don't downplay what you suffered."

Suffered, an apt word. Looking away, Sterling nodded. He didn't need to know that downplaying it was the only way she kept it from taking over her life. "The guy was disgusting, old with a beer gut and jowls, and he literally savored every second of my shock. But he showed up half-drunk, and after that door was locked on the outside, he locked it on the inside, too. Just to intimidate me more, I think, but turned out that was his biggest mistake."

Cade's eyes turned steely. "With the door locked, no one else could get in?"

"I figured it would slow them down, at least—if they even heard the scuffle and bothered to investigate. They were used to hearing screams and cries and…rough stuff, so they played loud music in the hall."

Mouth tightening, he growled, "I wish they were all dead."

"You and me both." And if she had her way, eventually they would be. "So like I said, he had a bottle with him and I offered to pour him another drink. Just desperate to buy some time at first, but the idiot agreed, and when I got close to him, I smashed the bottle in his face." Bile seemed to clog her throat, cutting off her air.

Cade waited, gently stroking her palm...letting her know she wasn't alone.

It helped, enough for her to continue.

"It stunned him, but he was still upright, looking at me like he couldn't believe my audacity. That really set me off—that he'd be surprised because I fought back, that I wouldn't just meekly be raped—and since I had the broken neck of the bottle in my hand, I... I jammed it into his throat and twisted it deep."

Without hesitation, Cade said, "Good for you."

Trying a smile that felt a little sick, Sterling skipped past the massive amount of blood that had gone everywhere, the god-awful gurgling sounds the man had made. "That was the start of my great window caper. It was a hell of a drop, and I was afraid I'd break my legs, or maybe my neck, but I figured it was worth the risk."

"Jesus. You were on the second floor?"

"Yeah, but the ground broke my fall." This smile was a little more genuine. She'd gotten past the worst of it and Cade hadn't rained down judgments, so she guessed he was okay with it. Or at least he got it, that she'd done what she had to. "Knocked the wind out of me, and you should have seen the bruises I got then."

As if he couldn't quite believe it, Cade slowly shook his head. "That was exceptionally brave and resourceful."

She wrinkled her nose. "I should be honest and say I had second thoughts once I was hanging out the window, but my grip slipped and I didn't really have any choice. Luckily that room faced the back, not far from an alley. I had no idea where I was, but I knew where I didn't want to be."

"So you ran."

"Down alleys, through buildings, across backyards. I think I ran that entire day, weaving my way as far from them as I could get." She shrugged. "In fact, I pretty much ran for a whole year."

"You didn't go home?"

"Mom wasn't really into helping anyone but herself, and most times she couldn't even manage that."

"How did you survive?"

"Halfway houses, soup kitchens. A little thievery. There was a woman at one halfway house who worked with battered women. I've contacted her since, when I first helped another woman. She's the one who told me what to do."

"I'm glad you could trust her."

"Trust her? No. But I liked her, and she was good for info." It seemed one memory churned up another, until it felt like she was living it again. "This elderly guy busted me stealing some of his laundry." That particular memory lightened her mood. "Know what he did?"

"I'm guessing he didn't call the cops?"

"He gave me more clothes, including some that had belonged to his deceased wife. He fed me, too, and didn't complain when I insisted on staying outside so he couldn't trap me. He told me I was smart for being cautious, but that if I was going to hang around, I might as well earn some money."

Cade stiffened.

She quickly said, "He offered me a job working on his lawn."

Relaxing again, Cade asked, "Cutting grass and stuff?"

"And trimming bushes, edging the lawn, picking up old tree branches. He kept that place pristine."

Cade actually smiled. "I like him."

"One day after this big storm had made a mess of things, he came out and started helping me work. We didn't talk or anything, we were just there together, getting the job done. After a while he insisted I take a break, and we sat together on a bench drinking colas." At the time, it had seemed the most normal, most domestic thing she'd ever done. "Finally he asked where I went when I left his place. At that time, I used to crash in the park, or I'd catch a snooze in an all-night diner."

"Not safe."

"Eh, it feels fine when you don't have any other options. But then he showed me his garage. Said he had a sleeping bag and I could lock the doors so at least I could rest without worrying. He didn't ask me to sleep in his house, but I think it's because he knew I wouldn't." Remembering brought a sense of melancholy that left her eyes glazed with tears. "He was so brusque about everything, real no-nonsense attitude, but he showed me that as bad as those bastards were who'd tried to use me, there were equally good, kindhearted people in the world."

Lifting her uninjured hand to his mouth, Cade kissed her knuckles. "Was he a truck driver?"

"Retired, but he had been, so yeah, the trucking company was his idea once he knew what I wanted to do. I stayed with him for years. We cleaned out the garage, and he put an actual room in there for me, with my own toilet and tiny shower. I had a chair and a TV, a cot to sleep on." She realized how lame that sounded, but for her, it had been a real home.

"It sounds comfortable."

"I swear," she whispered, "he was like my grandpa."

"Did neighbors assume that relationship?"

"Not likely, with him being Black." She grinned. "But he didn't have any close neighbors anyway. Didn't have any family left, either, since he and his wife had never had kids."

"You loved him."

The tears spilled over, so all she could do was nod.

Cade reached out to gently brush her cheeks. "I'm so glad you found him."

It took her a minute to regain her composure. Normally she would have been more embarrassed for the pitiful show of emotion, but as he'd said, Cade was different. With a sniffle and a clearing of her throat, she whispered, "When I was twenty-two, he helped me get my CDL, even gave me a reference for Brown Transportation. I worked there until I was twenty-six."

"Why didn't you stay there?"

"Gus passed away in his sleep. I knew we'd gotten close, but it stunned me to find out he'd left me his house. Isn't that crazy?"

"Sounds like you were as important to him as he was to you."

"Not even close, but God love that man, he made me feel…valued." More tears fell, and this time she angrily swiped them away. "There was a note with the will. He kept it vague, I guess in case anyone else read it, but he said to sell the house and use the money, with what he had in his accounts, to do what I needed to do."

Cade still held her left hand, but now he gripped it as if he couldn't let go. "You didn't want to stay in his house? Find a regular job?"

"Me? No way. I'm not cut out for that, you know? Gus had provided a lifeline and I grabbed it. When he said he knew what I needed to do, he was right. I *need* to do this." That god-awful guilt shortened her breath and compressed her lungs, but she admitted her greatest sin. "When I escaped, I left other girls behind."

"You alone couldn't have helped them."

No, she wouldn't accept that, wouldn't take the easy out. She'd let her fear run her. All she could do now was own the truth. "I could have led police there. I did try calling it in once, but it was a week later before I thought of it, and I'm guessing after what happened, they'd moved on."

Cade sat quiet for far too long. He kissed her knuckles again, started to speak but didn't. Finally he said, "Hearing all this…it occurs to me that I might have been too pushy."

"No denying that." He'd pushed his way right into her life, but she enjoyed having him there. More than she'd ever thought possible. "Too late to take it back now."

As if magnetized, his gaze caught hers. "I'm guessing some things might be…difficult for you."

Not liking the way he verbally danced around it, she said, "A lot of stuff is difficult, so what? If you mean something specific, spit it out already."

"Sex."

"Oh." He was concerned that she was traumatized still? Well, yeah, in some ways she was—but that wasn't one of them. "You know me now, right?"

"I hope so. I'd like to know you even better, but yes, we're getting there."

"So do you *really* think I wouldn't have fixed that?"

Skeptical, and obviously a bit confused by her wording, he repeated, "*Fixed* it?"

"With what I do, I knew I had to overcome some things. Getting caught would be bad enough, but if the thought of regular sex with a non-psychopathic guy left me paralyzed, how would I deal with a freaking monster who treated women like trained dogs?"

Finally he released her hand. He looked steady enough, but she saw the fire in his eyes and the acceleration of his breathing. "And you fixed that…how?"

He looked so intense right now that she could guess how he'd looked when he broke into Misfits. "Cool your jets. It's nothing bad."

"Define *bad.*"

"I had sex," she said with a shrug. "Few different guys, few different occasions. Until it wasn't so scary anymore."

Sitting back hard, Cade studied her. "Did you like it?"

"I didn't hate it." Not the last few times. "That was the important part. Now I'm in the camp of take it or leave it."

Seconds ticked by. "Except with me."

The man did not lack confidence. "Yup. There you go again, standing out from the pack. I liked kissing you, so I'm guessing the rest will be fun."

Slowly, he pushed back his chair and stood.

Sterling held her breath, but when he reached for her, he only stroked her ponytail, down and over her shoulder, until his fingers cupped her chin. "When we get together, it'll be more than fun. I'm going to make damn sure you love every second."

Wow, now she could hardly wait.

CHAPTER EIGHT

CADE WAS PATIENT, always, but two additional days passed without a word from Adela. He knew the waiting wore on Star. He understood that. With a woman in need, every day—hell, every hour—could mean life or death.

Using the time to get closer to Star, he'd kissed her a few more times, each a little longer, a little hotter, easing into her life. She was so open about what she liked, and she clearly liked intimate contact. It astounded him that she hadn't been more sexually active, but it made sense, given what she'd been through.

He wanted to be the one to show her just how hot sex could be—with the right person. So far she was on board with that plan.

She was recovering quickly but still had a limp to her walk, and she couldn't yet make a fist with her injured finger. Until she was 100 percent, he wouldn't let it go beyond kissing. For now, it worked as extended foreplay, wearing her down, softening her attitude. Not that he wanted to change her.

It was the hard-core woman who'd drawn him.

But when they came together, he wanted her totally involved, as ready as he was, maybe even more anxious for the ultimate release he'd give her, though how that was possible when he wanted her nonstop, he didn't know.

For now, sleeping with her each night was enough. Torture, yes, but he wouldn't be giving it up anytime soon.

He knew eventually he'd have all of her.

And then what?

His life wasn't set up for a significant other. Any day now his father could send him off on a mission. Reyes might hear something at his gym that required follow-up. Madison might uncover a lead.

He hadn't yet told Star that the main reason he ran a bar, besides fitting into the neighborhood, was because conversations from seedy characters could be overheard. More than a few times he'd gotten information he needed because too many drinks lowered caution. He could subtly ask the right questions and get good information that he then followed up on.

There'd been a man who bragged about the internet arrangements that had gotten him a few hours of pleasure. Another who'd laughed about how cheaply he'd bought time with a girl.

Keeping his hands off them was difficult, but when it led to bigger stings, Cade could hold it together.

Same with Reyes and his gym. All different types came in to bulk up. Even if they didn't talk about personal involvement, word from the street was usually sound. Reyes would hear enough to know when a new crew moved into an abandoned house or if a different guy was suddenly offering services from the corner.

Parrish had planned it all well. He'd purchased the bar and gym at opposite ends of the same downtrodden area, instructed each of them on what they'd do—and then he'd fully expected to be obeyed.

That part of the equation still annoyed Cade, but he couldn't deny they were effective. Not just in Ridge Trail, Colorado, but all over the US, since many of the roads here were used to transport women, kids and sometimes men in and out of various states. A local lead often branched out to different headquarters. Not all traffickers were on a grand scale, but some were—and they all deserved to be eliminated.

"I need to get back to work soon." Star didn't look up to make that announcement. At the dining table, her laptop open, she said, "I've had a few requests for deliveries."

Cade understood, but he didn't like it. When he had to take off to follow a lead, would Star understand? He might not see her for a day or two, or more. Would she demand answers that he couldn't give?

Unwilling to borrow trouble, he joined her at the table. "Local drives?"

"One is for an overnight, but two others are local." Brows scrunched up, she studied the screen.

"Problem?"

"I keep thinking about Adela." She rubbed her temple wearily. "She was supposed to have called by now. If my stupid leg hadn't been hurt—"

"You still needed time to plan."

"I know. But it's been too long now. What if I'm gone on a job and she needs me?"

Knowing he had to be careful here, Cade tried for an offhand tone. "If you're away, you could call me with the details. I could follow up for you."

She slanted him a look. "We've been over that, right? You're a guy, so not trustworthy. She probably wouldn't let you get anywhere near her."

"She might if you told her that *you* trust me."

Slumping into her seat, she sighed. "I don't know. There are some things I prefer to do myself."

Right—like *most* things. That prickly attitude was a part of her personality, like her sarcasm and her inner strength. Altogether, they were…sometimes annoying, yes. But he also saw them as tools she'd used to survive, and for that he was profoundly grateful.

For now, she was safely ensconced at home, she slept with him every night, and each day a little more of her reserve melted away.

She had a strong will—but so did he. In the end, he'd convince her to see things his way.

When her phone buzzed, they both turned to look where she'd left it plugged in on the end table next to the couch.

"You rarely get calls," Cade noted.

"Rarely, as in never." She bolted out of the chair, limped hurriedly across the room and frowned at the screen. "Unlisted number again."

"Put it on speaker."

"Magic word?" she asked, but then did as he requested without making him say "please," answering on the fourth ring. "Hello?"

"Francis?"

Star gripped the phone tighter. "Adela? Hey. I thought you'd call before now. I'd about given up on you."

Voice choked, Adela said, "Please don't. Please don't give up on me."

Gently, Star said, "No, I won't."

"I'd have called sooner, but I couldn't."

Cade didn't move.

Star didn't appear to be breathing. "Why not?"

"I think he's found me, Francis." Softly weeping, she said, "I was in a cabin without cell service, and when I went into town, I saw him there. If I don't get away soon, I'm afraid he'll kill me."

Carefully sitting on the couch, Star said, "Tell me exactly where you are."

"I want to," she said in a small voice. "But you can't call the police. One of the cops is a regular. He'd lead Mattox right to me."

Eyes narrowing at that info, Star promised, "I won't tell the police, but I can't help you if I don't know where to find you."

"You'll come alone? You swear?"

Star's gaze met and held Cade's as she answered. "Yes, I swear."

Closing his eyes, Cade vowed that wouldn't happen. He wouldn't *let* it happen. If he had to dog her day and night to ensure she didn't try this on her own, that's what he'd do.

"All right." Adela sniffled. "I trust you."

"When should I come for you?" Star asked. "Right now?"

Like hell. Already Cade was reconfiguring his schedule, who he'd get to cover for him at the bar, how quickly he could arrange for Reyes to be backup.

He didn't doubt that his brother would do it. Come to that, Parrish would also extend all the protections he could. But that shit took time, and if she left right now—

"No!" Panic sharpened the single word. Then Adela immediately tried to explain. "Tonight. When it's dark. That way he…he won't be able to see us leaving."

"All right." Standing again, Star went into the kitchen and retrieved the pen and paper, then carried them back to hand to Cade. "Give me a number to reach you."

"No, it's too risky."

"I need *something*, Adela. At least an address or directions."

"Right." She breathed audibly, then asked, "You really won't say anything to anyone?"

Star rolled her eyes over the continued—frustrating—worry, but replied in a soothing tone, "I already gave you my word."

"You tried to save me that night. At Misfits."

"Yes, but I understand why you were too frightened to go then."

"He would have killed me," Adela claimed. "Right there on the spot. I didn't think you'd actually get away, but you did."

"We'll both get away this time, okay? Now quickly, tell me where to find you."

With only the briefest hesitation, Adela said, "There's a small town. Coalville. It's only five or six miles off I-25. As you enter the town, there's a stone church. Right after that, take the dirt road. It'll lead you up to the cabin where I'm staying. In case Mattox is watching the roads in that area, turn your headlights off."

It all sounded majorly fucked to Cade, even as he jotted it all down.

Star must've agreed, because she suggested, "Why don't you just meet me at the church? That'll be easier, right?"

"But if you don't show up, I'll be too exposed."

"I'll be there, and being close to the road will give us a better chance to escape." Not giving Adela a moment to change that plan, Star asked, "What time?"

"I guess…ten?"

"I'll be there. Adela? Try not to worry. I won't let you down."

"I can't thank you enough, really, but I should go." Nervously, she whispered, "I never know if Mattox has men watching the town looking for me. I'll go back to the cabin for now and wait."

"Until ten."

"Thank you, Francis. You're a lifesaver."

Deflated, Star returned the phone to the table, then just stood there.

It would be easier to have her cooperation, so Cade came up

behind her, drew her back against his body and kissed her temple. "I'm going to help."

As if he hadn't spoken, she said, "Good thing my leg is so much better. I have a lot to get done now."

"Like what?"

Looking at him as if he were nuts, she said, "Like I need to rent a car. No way am I letting anyone track me down by my ride. And of course I want to go scope out that area. It could be a trap. Could be Mattox forced her to make the call."

He found no fault with her deductive reasoning. "It does seem a little too pat."

"She did agree to switch locations, and hopefully the church is more in the town than the cabin would've been. But… I don't know. Something doesn't feel right."

Turning her, Cade cupped her face in his hands. "You have incredible instincts, honey, so trust them."

"Yeah, I do." She frowned. "Those instincts are telling me something isn't right." She looked up at him. "But I still have to go."

"I know." Only she didn't need to go alone. "Will you trust me?"

Head cocked in challenge, she asked, "Trust you how?"

"I have…resources."

Her mouth twisted. "That you can't discuss."

A reality he couldn't get around. "Let me have the area checked. We'll be discreet. I can get you the alternate car, too. No need to use a dealer."

"Huh." Sounding impressed, she said, "No kidding? Just like that?"

"Yeah, just like that."

For several seconds, Star considered it. "The thing is…" She moistened her lips while carefully selecting her words. "I do trust you, because I know you. These other obscure peeps you talk about—they're big unknowns, and I just don't go there. So how about *you* trust *me* to get this job done without your interference?"

He didn't like having his assistance labeled as interference, but he got where she was coming from. He wouldn't trust the unknown, either. Still, he couldn't let her do this alone.

Looking past her, he checked the clock on the wall. He had only a few hours left if he wanted to accomplish all that needed to be done—with or without her approval.

He needed to accelerate their relationship—but would she see that as underhanded? Find it difficult to forgive—or insanely satisfying? Hard to say, and unfortunately, it was the only thing he could think of. His time to slowly win her over had abruptly run out.

"Is your leg healed enough?"

"I won't be running any races yet, but yeah, it's fine. Hardly sore anymore."

Yet she still limped—and he couldn't let that matter. Not now. "Good to know," he whispered as he bent to her mouth, kissing her softly at first, just moving his lips over hers until she leaned into him—which he took as a sign of agreement.

One hand at the back of her head, the other sliding down to her backside, he aligned her body with his. Hell if he wasn't already hard, but he'd wanted her for so long that giving himself permission was like flipping a switch. He was now *on* and only hoped he could get her there, too.

With all she'd suffered in her past, he planned to take it slow, to make use of the entire two hours he had. He could scramble last-minute with plans, but he wouldn't rush this.

He wouldn't rush her.

Her lips opened to the touch of his tongue, and the kiss quickly became hot. He turned his head for a better fit. She did the same. Her fingertips curled against his chest. Her hips nudged his.

Open mouths, lots of tongue play, heavy breathing. Now petting, too... Christ, she'd escalated things fast, but then, she was like that, a lit fuse waiting to explode.

He'd take a sexual explosion over her temper any day.

Urging her head back, he trailed his lips to the velvet skin of her neck, her warm throat, that sensitive spot beneath her ear. Tilting to give him better access, she gave a soft groan.

"Wow, I like that."

Had no one ever...? No, he didn't want to think about her healing brand of sex, meant only to help her over an emotional hurdle, with no thought for pleasure.

He'd drown her in pleasure, and she'd never forget him.

The comfortable clothes she wore made touching her oh so easy. Liking the feel of her beneath the stretchy yoga pants, he opened his hand wide to enclose an entire cheek, then trailed his fingers down the cleft—then under, to touch her more intimately.

Gasping, she went to her tiptoes but didn't pull away.

Her tightened nipples, covered only by the soft cotton of her loose T-shirt, pressed against his chest. With a love bite, Cade encouraged another gasp...one that faded into a vibrating groan.

"Mmm," she whispered. "Do that again."

"Which part?"

"All of it?"

Even now, when he'd launched to the ragged edge, she made him smile. Star had substance, both emotionally and intellectually.

And in her curves. God yes, those curves.

She was as soft as a woman should be, but with core strength. She was bold enough to speak her mind, as she'd just done, and brave enough to travel to a remote area alone, without backup, to save a woman in need.

How the hell was he supposed to resist that enticing mix of attributes?

He couldn't.

With her active participation so obvious, he stroked her waist, then slipped his hand under her shirt and up to one heavy breast. He held back his own groan, but the warmth of her, the silkiness of her bare breast, made him forget his resolve.

"Cade?"

He came back to her mouth for another deep kiss. She tangled the fingers of her left hand into his hair, and with the right, she cupped his face. He felt the roughness of the bandage on her fingers and turned to gently kiss those, too. "Hmm?"

"Is this your way of coercing me?"

Stark reality crashed onto his head. Had his motives been that base? That cold? Not with the way he'd always wanted her. Hell, he'd been looking for an excuse to rush his own self-imposed timeline.

Since he hadn't heard anger or accusation in her tone, just curiosity, he straightened to look into her eyes.

She gave him a smug, knowing smile.

Nothing got by her. He wouldn't have lied anyway, but now he knew she wouldn't have fallen for it no matter his reasons.

Before he could say anything, she grinned and cuddled close again. "Understand, I'm not complaining." Her uninjured hand traveled to his ass. "And if you live up to your promise, I might even be swayed to take you along."

Now, why that outrageous comment fired his lust, he couldn't say, but he crushed his mouth down on hers again. Full participation, that's what he got from her.

No reserve. No remnants of bad memories.

Such a remarkable woman in every way.

"So much enthusiasm."

God, she pushed his buttons. And humbled him. "Thank you for understanding."

"That you're not a user? No problem."

Her faith meant more than she knew, prompting him to another kiss, this one full of tenderness. And yeah, lust.

No way to dodge the lust.

"Bedroom?" she suggested, when he came up for air.

Cade smoothed her hair and cupped her cheek. Unique in so many ways. "No argument from me."

Smiling in satisfaction, she took his hand and led him through the kitchen-dining area, past the bathroom and into her room with the still-rumpled bed.

His conscience decided he needed one more confirmation, so he started to say, "Are you sure—"

But she pulled the T-shirt up and off, and he forgot he had a conscience. Shoulders back, spine straight, chin elevated. Her breasts were a handful, yet somehow she'd always downplayed that asset with her wardrobe choices. Her rib cage tapered into a smaller waist, then flared out for her shapely hips. His gaze lingered on the slight curve of her belly, exposed by the low-fitting yoga pants. Every inch of her fascinated him and made him want more.

"You're staring."

Without lifting his gaze from her body, Cade shrugged. "How could I not? You're perfect."

"Ha. I'm still bruised some, you know. It's all these hideous shades of green and yellow now. Really nasty."

Insecurity, from Star? That, more than anything, helped him gain a measure of control even though she stood there half-naked, tempting every basic instinct known to man. "I've seen bruises before, and I saw part of yours today before you dressed."

Wrinkling her nose, she tugged the band out of her hair so that it fell free. "Then you know what I mean."

Reyes was right. She did have incredible hair. Having it loose and tousled around her naked breasts added to the sensuality of the moment. "They're just bruises, babe, and they don't keep me from wanting you."

"Good thing, I guess, since I want you, too." She nodded at him. "Shirt off."

All too happy to oblige, Cade reached back for a handful of material and stripped it over his head.

"You still haven't told me about these tats." She moved closer, first trailing her fingers through his chest hair, then tracing the edges of one tattoo, a waving American flag that twined from his right shoulder to his elbow. Eyes dark with interest, she teased that soft touch to the eagle on his right pec.

He had another on the back of his left shoulder of a soldier drifting from a battlefield into heaven. All in all, pretty self-explanatory. "How about after?"

"After we do the nasty?"

She wanted to make it less than it was—but he wouldn't let her. "Nothing nasty about it. Not between us." He gathered a thick hank of hair in his fist, resisting her breasts for the moment. It felt cool in comparison to her hot skin. "Okay?"

"Another promise. You've got a lot to live up to."

"I'll do my best." And with that he cupped a breast, kneaded gently, then bent to circle the nipple with his tongue.

"Okay." Shakily, she drew in a breath. "Let me just get my pants off."

"Soon." He drew her in, sucking softly—then not so softly—while she moved her hands all over him. "Easy. Don't hurt your fingers."

"Worry about what you're doing."

The order amused him, especially since he understood it. "All right." He shifted his attention to her other breast, but at the same time he worked his hand inside the loose waistband of her pants, his hand cupping over her heat.

"You're a tease," she complained, her head tipped back, eyes closed. "Men aren't supposed to tease."

"Me and you, Star. I told you, we're different." He kissed her slightly parted lips. "Quit trying to put us in a category."

Her heavy eyes opened. "Fine. But I've been waiting for this for too long, maybe even before I admitted I wanted you. So now is *not* the time for teasing."

God, he loved her forthright way of speaking. "You need to come?"

Her eyes flared, and a wash of color tinged her cheeks. "Well... I need *something*, okay? So stop playing around."

"All right." He went to his knees and reached for the waistband of her pants. "But one of these days you're going to like the way I play."

"One of these days—meaning you plan to stick around?"

Digging for future plans? What could he say? He wouldn't make promises until he knew he could keep them, so without answering, he tugged the pants and her panties down to her ankles. "Step out."

At first the only thing she did was breathe deeply.

He took his time looking at her body. And a hell of a body it was. Gorgeous legs, despite the bruising that drew his lips. He skimmed them over her skin as if he could heal the last remnants of her injury. The cut had closed nicely, but she'd have a small scar. He pressed a soft kiss to that, too.

The rest of her...so beautiful. He'd admired the length of her legs plenty of times, but seeing her like this, totally bared, ramped up the churning need. Sliding his hands to her hips, he leaned in—

"Wait." Sleek with muscle, her long thighs flexed as she balanced with a hand to his shoulder. Hastily, awkwardly, given the lingering stiffness of her injured leg, she kicked away her pants. Free of clothes, she straightened, nodded down at him and said, "Go ahead."

Cade actually laughed. Physical need consumed him, yet he'd never known anyone quite like her. In every way imaginable, she was incredibly special.

She was *his*.

She might not know that yet, but somehow he'd make it so, starting right now. "Anything you don't like—"

"Yeah, you'll hear about it." Again she threaded her fingers through his hair. "You curl my toes, Cade. I never knew that was a real thing."

He smiled again. "Let's see what else I can curl."

OH. MY. GOD. Over and over again, Sterling repeated that in her mind. She had Cade McKenzie, all six feet, five gorgeous inches of him, kneeling in front of her, touching her in incendiary ways while kissing her belly and thighs.

Now that she could play with it—and basically use it as an anchor—she found that his hair was thick and soft on top and in front, and she liked the way the shorter sides and back felt against her fingertips, like velvet almost.

Soon as he finished what he was doing—because she wasn't about to interrupt again—she planned to glut herself on his bod.

With his lips nibbling at her hip bone, he stroked over her sex. Yeah, she had to lock her knees for that—and then he pressed a finger into her, growling at finding her so wet. What did he expect? From the moment he started seducing her, she'd wanted to melt.

Didn't matter that he might have started this to get his way. It was as good a reason as any, right? Especially when it got her what she wanted most.

Him. Naked. With *her* naked. Full-body contact—and a big payoff in the way of pleasure.

Besides, he'd find she wasn't easily manipulated, awesome sex or not. If she invited Cade along, it'd be on her own terms, for her own reasons.

She had a feeling he'd meet her halfway, and until then, why not enjoy herself?

As he slowly fingered her, she not only heard but felt his groan. The pleasure built, coiling, heating... She wanted it bad. This, now, and more.

So much more.

She whispered that, *"More,"* aloud and got a second finger because of it. Much as she enjoyed watching the flex and roll of his broad shoulders, sensation compelled her eyes to close. Her head tipped back of its own accord, as if her neck offered no support.

Her knees were getting to the same point, especially when he used his other fingers to open her...and she felt his mouth.

Biting her lip to hold back the groan, she tightened. His tongue... yeah, that velvet tongue performed some magic, touching her just right, exactly *there*, over and over again, leisurely at first while he made sounds of enjoyment, then with more deliberate purpose.

She couldn't stay quiet any longer. Her nipples throbbed, needing him, but not enough to ask him to stop. The sweetest, almost painful ache curled in her lower belly. Despite the way she'd been pampering her leg, her thigh muscles tensed, a necessary adjustment to keep her upright so he could continue.

Shifting, he opened his hand on her behind and pressed her closer—then drew in her clit for a soft suckle and, good God, she cried out. Without restraint.

Who cared?

An incredibly powerful orgasm raged through her, leaving her one giant pulsing beat of sizzling sensation. Panting, a little sweaty, she realized she'd curled over him when he finally let up. Yup, that had pretty much wiped out her backbone. Maybe all her bones.

He shifted her so he could stand.

"Don't let go," she warned, unwilling to open her eyes. "I'll fall flat on my face."

Against her ear, he whispered, "Never," in a way that sounded like he meant more than this single moment. Her heart seized at the thought, but then in some crazy, gallant, straight-out-of-a-film move, he lifted her into his arms and placed her on the bed.

"Oh," she mumbled, stretching a little, snuggling into the bedding. "Well done. Very romantic."

Grinning, he opened his jeans. "You think so?"

"Yup." No way was she going to miss this. She managed to keep her eyes wide-open, didn't even blink. "Promises made, promises kept. I'm now a believer."

"And just think," he said, shoving down his jeans to stand there buck-ass and incredibly stunning, "we're not done, yet."

Wow, he was put together fine. Better than fine. It was as if someone had taken all things she considered masculine and expertly pieced them together. Dark chest hair, roped muscles over arms and legs, long bones and obvious power.

A big cock.

Sterling cleared her throat. "Looks like I won the lottery."

His smile went crooked. Pulling his wallet from his jeans, he dug out a condom. While she watched in fascination, he rolled it over a very rigid, pulsing erection.

Her mouth went dry. "What if I'd wanted to touch that?" When he glanced at her, she nodded at his crotch. Honestly, every inch of him fascinated her. She wanted to explore him—without a rubber in the way. In fact, she wouldn't mind stroking that firm butt, too, and those muscular, hair-dusted thighs, his flat abdomen with that sexy happy trail.

"It'd be over too quick," he said, stretching out atop her and pecking her mouth. "Next time, I promise, you can touch all you want."

"Hardly seems fair, considering."

Using his knee, he opened her legs and settled between her tingling thighs. "Complaining?"

On principle alone, she considered it, but he was already stroking her breasts, thumbing her nipples, and she felt that hard cock against her... "Nope. No complaints from me."

"Good." He sealed his mouth over hers—and thrust into her.

Holy cow. In sheer reaction, her hips lifted off the bed. He filled her up, the fit snug, the glide smooth, wet, pure pleasure, but it was so much more than that, too.

It was Cade's scent making her light-headed, the sleek feel of his taut skin under her hands, the provoking sound he made deep in his throat—a sound of pure, unadulterated lust.

Yes, she'd gotten used to sex.

Yes, there'd been times when she'd somewhat enjoyed it.

None of those times had anything in common with this.

She wrapped one leg around him, keeping him close, and lifted her other along his hip.

"Easy," Cade whispered against her throat. "I don't want to hurt you. Your leg—"

"Shut up, Cade." She grasped his butt in her uninjured hand

and urged him to move, at the same time *she* was moving, rocking against him, twisting…exciting herself on the hard length of him.

He laughed roughly and took over.

It was a hard ride, one she encouraged however she could. Keeping him locked to her, she bit his shoulder, licked the spot, then sucked on his hot skin as another climax rocked her.

Grinding into her, Cade put his face to her neck and growled out a long, harsh release.

Huh. Hearing other guys come hadn't moved her at all. But Cade? She wanted to cuddle him—and how nuts was that? You didn't cuddle a tiger, right? But she couldn't let him go, couldn't stop putting soft kisses along his shoulder, couldn't stop stroking his hot skin.

It was a good ten minutes before she moved, and even then, her limbs felt sluggish and uncooperative. Yes, her leg throbbed like a son of a bitch, but it was worth it.

"Good going," she whispered in a teasing grumble as she tried to adjust. "How am I supposed to deal with Adela or Mattox when my muscles have turned to noodles?"

An utter stillness settled over him, replaced seconds later by determination as he levered up, bracing his arms on either side of her shoulders. "You let me help."

He surrounded her with his size, his scent, his iron will. Didn't bother her at all. "Your muscles aren't limp?"

"I'll recover. Quickly." He pressed a firm kiss to her mouth. "This, what we just did, was a commitment."

What? No way. "Who says so?"

"I say so." Far too serious, his intense gaze drilled into her. "You're strong, Star. Strong enough to share the burden without worrying that I'll take over. I won't, you know."

She snorted at that. "You already are."

"No, babe. I want to share the plans, the setup and the risk. I'm guessing you don't know this yet, but it's easier that way."

"What's easier?"

His expression softened. "Everything." With extreme gentleness he smoothed back her hair. "Everything is easier when you're not alone."

"So…" Knowing she was out of her depth, Sterling tried to

think, but it wasn't possible, not right now with his body all over her body, his gaze catching her every thought. Full honesty, then. "This wasn't a one-off?"

His smile was so tender that it turned her soft, too. "Once isn't near enough for me. Don't tell me it was for you."

"I want more." More of him, more of this. Maybe the sharing he mentioned, too.

"Good." He released a pent-up breath. "Difficult as it'll be, we have to get out of bed, shower—"

"Together?"

"*Alone*, because I have calls to make."

She pretended to pout, but seriously, showering with him would have been nice.

"We need to coordinate plans. I need to prove to you that having me along will be a good thing. But if we shower together...?" He shook his head. "All my good intentions will go right out the window, because now that I've had you, I won't be able to keep from touching you." He cupped her breast. "Kissing you." He nuzzled her neck. Near her ear, he whispered, "Tasting you—again."

Sterling shivered. "You're promising a lot."

"Don't let it scare you." Laughing, he dodged her smack, caught her hand and pressed it down beside her head.

"I'm not *scared*."

"Wary, then." He pushed off the bed but took the time to look her over as he picked up his boxers and jeans. "Take a few minutes more if you want. I'll shower first."

She watched him walk away with a sense of...peace? That, or something equally serene, invaded her very soul. It was a new, unfamiliar feeling, one of many thanks to Cade.

He was right, of course. He did scare her, mostly because she hadn't relied on anyone in a very long time. Maybe because she liked Cade so much, because she really wanted to rely on him, it made it somehow worse. More alarming.

But she wasn't a wimp, so she got out of bed and went for her laptop. She had a lot of research to do. Maybe that'd get her mind off the naked hunk currently in her shower.

Doubtful, but she'd give it a try.

CHAPTER NINE

AFTER THE EXPLOSIVE SEX, Star finally agreed to let him take part in retrieving Adela. He would have assisted her anyway, but having her agreement simplified things.

He'd known they would be good together. After all, the chemistry was through the roof.

Yet the depth of what he'd felt, the extreme connection, had surprised him. He'd like nothing more than to spend an entire day in bed with her, exploring her incredible curves and enjoying her blunt, uninhibited way of responding.

Impossible when they had so much to do.

They'd already picked up the alternate vehicle from his family's private lot, a reinforced van with darkened windows that he and Reyes used when they expected gunplay. The black matte paint helped hide it in low light, plus it had incredible speed for a van.

He'd spent an hour trying to convince Star to let his family take part. Her protestations—that she didn't know his family, so how could he expect her to trust them?—made sense.

He understood and offered a compromise, suggesting, "Just my brother, then." Reyes made one hell of an ally. If there were ten men waiting to ambush Star, Cade could handle them. He had no doubts on his own ability. But a sniper bullet? Mattox was the type of cowardly abuser who might do anything, including lure her in for a fast death.

Making a woman suffer was more his speed, though, but Cade wouldn't take chances either way.

"You've already met him," he reminded Star. "He'll stay out of the way, but he'll be an extra set of eyes just in case something goes wrong."

"He's annoying," she announced, as if that settled it.

Laughing, Cade couldn't deny that she'd nailed Reyes. "It's true, my brother takes extreme pleasure in pushing people over the edge. But he's reliable, capable and loyal."

With ill grace, she growled, "Fine. So he's a sterling example of humanity."

"Let's don't go overboard." He knew and accepted his brother's faults—same as Reyes did for him.

With a frustrated growl, she said, "Involve him if you want." She gave him a hard glare. "But he's *your* responsibility."

Cade could just imagine Reyes's reaction if he heard that insult. Struggling not to smile, he said, "I appreciate the vote of confidence."

"Is that what it was? Felt more like me giving up because you wouldn't let it go."

That had been hours ago, and she was still bristling about it as they prepped to take off.

In the back of the van, Cade reached out to touch her cheek. "I have to do what's necessary to keep you safe."

Mouth firming, she slid the Glock she'd just checked into a holster at her hip and stared up at him. "Long as you know I feel the same about you."

That declaration deserved a kiss, but he kept it soft and quick to say, "I assume you've practiced shooting left-handed?" Her injured finger wasn't taped now, but it was still swollen and no doubt painful.

"You're asking me now?" Grinning, she indicated the small arsenal they'd amassed by combining their weapons. She reached for a Smith & Wesson .38 revolver to put in her ankle holster. "I plan for all contingencies, including an injured right hand, so yeah, I've had plenty of practice. I'm more accurate right-handed, but I can make do with my left, especially if it's a target as big as Mattox."

As she tugged the leg of her jeans over the gun, Cade asked deadpan, "Packing anything else?"

"My knife," she said, turning to shake her booty at him so he'd notice the sheathed knife at the small of her back. "But I'd only use it if I got caught up close."

No way would he let that happen. Cade drew a breath.

Seeing her so heavily armed had a dual effect on him. He believed she was proficient at protecting herself; her ease with all the weapons reassured him of that. At the same time, he wished he could insist she hang behind and let him handle things. He'd get Adela, and kill Mattox if possible, but he knew Star well enough to know she'd never go for that.

If he suggested she sit this out, she'd not only refuse, she'd revert to handling things on her own.

"Let me help," he said when she lifted the bulletproof vest he'd brought for her. It was the one thing she seemed unfamiliar with. He dropped it over her head, then adjusted the Velcro straps so it properly fit her.

While she pulled on her button-up shirt, which was a tight fit now, he put on his own vest, and then the tactical belt that held more ammo, nylon cuffs, a Taser, knife, strobing flashlight, flash bang and two Glocks.

Brows up, Star nodded at the flash bang. "A grenade? Really?"

"Nonlethal, but good at disorienting people—in the case of a mob. There's no telling how Mattox might set this up."

"*If* he set it up," Star said, then asked, "You don't believe Adela?"

He stashed the first aid kit into a panel of the van, along with other emergency items. "I don't think I do," Cade admitted, "but mostly because I don't think you do, either. Want to tell me why?"

She appeared to like his answer. "There's something about her, right? I've dealt with traumatized women before. I *was* a traumatized woman. But this just feels a little...off. Not enough that I won't help her, but yeah, I've got my guard up, big-time."

"Do you know what triggered that feeling?"

"She knows Mattox. I know him, too." Casual as you please, she tossed out, "He's the bastard who had me kidnapped all those years ago. The one who was in charge, who ordered me into that room with a drunken rapist, who employed the goons who stood guard."

Completely floored with that last-minute disclosure, Cade stared at her in disbelief. Pretending it was nothing, Star pulled the cargo door closed and locked it. Gaze averted, she started past him for the driver's seat, but he caught her arm.

At first, no words came to mind. She looked at him in mild inquiry, but he wasn't buying it. She knew she'd just dropped a bombshell on him, and now she waited to see what he'd do.

Sensing there was a lot riding on his reaction, he forcibly tamped down the extreme annoyance trying to take precedence. "You have a history with Mattox?"

"Yeah, but the big lummox didn't recognize me. Remember, I looked way different back then."

That she'd kept this from him left him seething. "Is there a reason you didn't tell me before now?"

"Couple of reasons, actually. One, I figured you'd freak out."

Cade took a step closer to her. "I do not *freak out*."

"No?" She pointedly looked over his rigid posture. "What do you call this?"

"Furious?" He caught her shoulder before she could spin away. "Damn it, Star. You know you should have told me."

"Because we had sex? Get real." She pointed a finger at his chest. "That's one reason why I didn't. You're acting all territorial and stuff."

"How do you figure that?" Hell, he felt that way, sure. But he'd kept from showing it.

Or had he?

No, he definitely had. If he'd had his way, she wouldn't be in the back of a bulletproof van strapping weapons all over her lean, sexy body, making plans to charge into danger.

"It's the way you look at me now," she explained, as if it surprised her that he didn't know.

He pulled his chin back. "How do I look at you?"

Mouth turning down, she quipped, "Like you think you have me all wrapped up."

Yeah, right. "I'm not deluded." She was a loose cannon. God, he wished he had a little control over her... No, he didn't.

Part of what he admired most about Star were her guts and fortitude. She might bend, but she would never break.

He found that confidence sexy as hell.

And deep down, a small part of him thought she might be strong enough to handle the life he'd chosen.

Most weren't.

Tell other women that he eliminated human traffickers at any cost? They'd bail real fast.

Only Star saw it as an opportunity to team up.

"Maybe not deluded, but if I'd told you earlier, you'd have wanted me to stay behind—which isn't happening, so don't even go there."

He let his own anger show. "Don't assume my thoughts."

"I don't have to. It's right there on your face."

"Regardless of what you think you see, I know this is important to you. And you're important to me."

Her belligerent expression faltered. "I am?"

New irritation surfaced. "How the hell can you be surprised over that?" He cut her off when she started to speak. "I care enough that I'd like to stand with you, but I wouldn't stand in your way."

"Wow. Okay." A small smile formed, then went crooked. "Do I owe you an apology?"

"Damn right. You withheld info that I need to share with Reyes."

That took care of her softened mood. "I don't see why."

Cade already had his phone out. "Your past relationship with Mattox ups the chance that this is all a ruse to get to you."

Scoffing, she said, "I told you, he didn't recognize me."

"You can't be sure of that."

She threw up her hands. "Aren't you the one who said I have good instincts?"

The text he sent Reyes was brief and to the point. "You're giving me second thoughts on that." Given her gasp, Cade assumed the insult hit home.

"Well, too bad." Suddenly she moved against him, hugging him as tight as she could while they wore bulletproof vests.

Definitely not the reaction he'd expected. Automatically, his arms went around her. Without thinking about it, he rested his face against the top of her head, breathed in the warm musk of her skin and hair, and relished the feel of her.

How had she become so important to him so quickly?

Voice lower now, a little confused and a little worried, she said, "I watched Mattox's face at Misfits. It leveled me, seeing him again after so long. I don't mind telling you I was struck with a sort of blindsided panic."

Cade wished he could have spared her that. It had to be rough, having her past just show up like that.

To reassure him, she pressed back to make eye contact. "There wasn't a speck of recognition. I swear, he had no idea who I am." Biting her lip, she added, "He didn't know that he'd ruined my life so long ago."

"Listen to me, babe, okay?" Here she stood, armed to the teeth, ready to take on the world—and her abuser. She'd suffered that recognition alone. She would have done this alone, too, if he hadn't found a way to talk her around. "You need to be ready to shoot. Shit goes sideways, don't think about it. Just protect yourself." Abusive assholes were expendable. She was not. "If anything at all sets off a warning, promise me you'll get out of there, okay?"

She nodded. "You betcha."

A returning text from Reyes dinged into the silence. Are you sure there won't be any other surprises?

No, he wasn't, but he replied: Just be ready for anything.

Reyes sent a thumbs-up emoji.

Putting the phone on vibrate and pocketing it, Cade said, "Time for us to go."

She nodded and got behind the wheel. He disabled the interior lights and then sat behind the passenger seat, where he'd have a view out the windshield and could also easily see Star. There was no more talking as she drove out to the meeting place.

Coalville was a minuscule town, a population of around one hundred, give or take any recent deaths or births, with most of the residents being elderly. The quick research they'd done claimed it was a ghost town—a story that started back in the early 1900s when a mine explosion caused over fifty deaths and effectively destroyed the growing mining industry.

"If anyone lives here," Star murmured, "they must be up in the hills somewhere." She drove slowly over railroad tracks onto broken pavement that turned to gravel...that led to a dirt road.

The van's headlights bounced over scrubby bushes and boulders along the narrow sides of the road. They passed a couple of shacks that appeared abandoned, two mobile homes nearly rusted through and a small store with most of the windows boarded up.

"Should I kill the lights?"

"No." That's what Adela wanted them to do, and he wasn't in an accommodating mood. At the end of the bumpy, uneven road, Cade spotted the church. "Nice and slow. Reyes is already in place. If he's spotted anything shady, he hasn't said so."

"Where exactly is he?"

"Up in the hills somewhere, well hidden but with a good view."

"Wouldn't he have been noticed getting there?"

"Nah, he's good."

The van bounced roughly over deep ruts. Brittle branches from pinyon pines and junipers scraped against the roof. There were no streetlights and the moon wasn't bright this night, so heavy shadows lurked right outside the headlight beams.

Grime-darkened windows and dirty clapboard indicated the church had lost its congregation. It was the last building before the road climbed up the mountain.

"I don't like it," Cade muttered.

"Shh," she said in return. Without looking at him, she stopped the van several yards away. After a moment, a woman stepped out on the front stoop. "That's her."

"Let her come to you," Cade insisted.

"She's not. She's probably worried that I might be Mattox." Drawing a deep breath, Star opened the door and stepped out.

Cade swallowed his curse and did the same, sliding silently out the cargo door and hunkering down low, in a better position to defend her if necessary.

In a hushed voice, Star called, "Adela?"

"Who is it?" Adela gripped the railing and peered toward the van. "Francis?"

Star stepped out farther, moving to the front of the van so the lights hit her. "Quickly. Let's go."

Taking one step toward her, Adela asked, "Are you alone?"

"Yes," Star lied. "C'mon."

And suddenly Adela had company.

STERLING WASN'T ALL that surprised when two men, dressed all in black, came out of the church around Adela, each of them armed, each of them aiming at her. Worse, she spotted movement in the scrub bushes to the right, and more to the left.

Surrounded? No, she wouldn't accept that.

They were all in the darkened shadows, but she stood in the light—an easy target. That got her feet moving.

Knowing she'd never get back in the van before they were on her, she ducked behind the open driver's door and glanced back for Cade.

The van was empty. How had he moved without her hearing it? He was like a damn wraith! A sound snapped her back around. In the three seconds she'd used to look for Cade, the dude had gotten far too close.

She smiled as she pointed her Glock. "Move and I'll put one in your forehead."

Laughing, he continued edging casually toward her. "You're lucky he wants you alive."

Screw that. She shot at his leg, but the bullet hit the dirt near his feet. Damn lousy left-handed aim—not that she'd wanted to kill him. Yet. And at least it made him dive off to the side for cover.

Since that had worked, she fired left and right, too. No one cried out, but she definitely heard some fast rustling.

Take cover, you goons. I won't go easy. She wouldn't go at all... not until she got what she'd come for. "Adela!"

"I'm so sorry," Adela wailed.

Sterling searched the darkness. Voices seemed to echo here, with the mountains around them, the night so still. Narrowing her eyes, she detected movement far ahead on the road.

It appeared someone—maybe Mattox?—was dragging Adela away.

How many men were there? So far she'd noticed four—if the men trying to close in around her were alone. There could be more. If they worked in pairs...insurmountable odds.

Mattox wasn't taking any chances, but then, he never did.

Was Adela in on it?

When a bullet zinged over her head, Sterling ducked—then looked back at the loud groan. A man was on the ground, clutching his leg and cursing a blue streak. Clearly he'd tried to sneak up behind her, but Cade's brother, wherever he was, must have spotted him.

Night-vision goggles? Seemed probable.

Just then, she saw Cade disable a different man with one vicious punch to the face. The man stiffened, then fell hard. Another launched at him, but in a very smooth move, he pivoted and elbowed the guy in the throat, sending him gagging and gasping to join his buddy on the dirt road. While he was down, Cade planted a boot in his face and the gagging stopped.

Huh.

She searched the immediate area but didn't see anyone else. "Is that it?"

His incredulous glare burned her. "There are now four bodies down around us, but a few of them might not stay that way, and I counted at least two more, so get in the van." With practiced ease, he disarmed the downed men. One of them groaned, but Cade ruthlessly punched him silent again.

"Wow." He had incredibly effective fists.

As he gathered up the weapons to dump in the cargo area, he repeated, "Get. In the. Van."

"Then what?" Before she took orders, she needed to know the plan. "More of them might be waiting on the road ahead." She should have already figured out a way to retreat, but instead she'd been focused on all the wrong things.

Like an unlikely alliance between Adela and Mattox.

And what Cade had said to her.

Could he really care that much? Given the way he'd protected her, he might.

She heard Adela scream again, but she couldn't see anything.

"Don't even think it," Cade ordered as he put nylon cuffs on the men. "You're staying here with me."

She knew that taking charge probably came naturally to him, and now wasn't the time to argue, especially since it was a good thing he'd come along.

If he hadn't, Mattox would already have her again, and her odds of getting away from him a second time wouldn't be favorable.

No, she wouldn't argue, but she did grumble, "I'm not an idiot."

She wouldn't chase after Adela into unknown circumstances, but what to do about her?

It was only a small sound that alerted her, a soft-soled shoe crunching on the loose dirt and gravel road.

Swinging around, she managed to get off one shot before a big bruiser knotted a hand in her hair and jerked her around the door toward him.

"I'm done fucking around with you," he growled.

She nutted him as hard as she could. Using her injured leg for balance, she lacked some of her usual power, but she still connected solidly.

Groaning, he loosened his hold, just not enough, and with the way he pinned down her arms, she was as likely to shoot her own foot as his if she dared to fire.

So instead she headbutted him. Her aim was off because she nailed him right in the nose. Blood sprayed.

"You little bitch—" he spit...just before a fist flew over her shoulder and knocked him out cold.

With his arms around her, she suddenly found herself crashing toward the ground.

Cade caught her, drawing her upright and pressing her back against the van. Face twisted with fury, he stomped the downed man, once, twice.

"He's out," Sterling whispered, awed by his violence. "Cade, he's out." She caught his arm. "Let's go while we can."

His jaw locked, but he did stop pulverizing the guy. Muscles pumped and expression deadly, he turned to her. "You're all right?"

She had that dude's blood on her face, but she nodded. "Fine."

"Stay put," he said, already moving away. "I'll be right back."

What the hell was that supposed to mean?

She got her answer a second later as the battle erupted behind her. Two men against Cade? Clearly not a problem for him.

How many more? A freaking army? She stayed alert, constantly looking around in case anyone else joined in, but she didn't see any others.

The man nearest her, the one Cade had stomped, stirred. Following Cade's cue, she kicked him in the face and put him out again.

She knew the dirt road continued on and then curved back to

meet the paved street that would lead to an interstate on-ramp. Far ahead she saw the sudden glow of red taillights.

Whoever had Adela was getting away.

What to do? She couldn't give chase, not now.

Cade rejoined her, and together they watched the taillights fade away.

The eerie silence left behind seemed almost threatening. Neither of them spoke until his phone beeped.

"Your brother?" she whispered.

He ignored the question, saying, "In the van and lock the door," while half lifting her to do just that.

She quickly secured the lock but then stepped into the back to help him inside. He was already there, slamming the door and locking it.

"Stay down." He read the text. "My brother is giving chase on the car that took off."

They heard the roar of a motorcycle and briefly saw the lights flash over the road, and then he was gone. "That was him?"

"Yeah." He sent off a message, then shoved the phone in his pocket. "Are you hurt?"

A few hairs missing, but… "Not a scratch, thanks to you."

"Your leg? Your finger—"

"I'm fine, Cade." Just trembling from an adrenaline dump. "I heard Adela scream. Do you think your brother will be able to catch up?"

"He'll be in touch soon. Get behind the wheel, okay? Let's get out of here."

Through the windshield, she saw the long expanse of darkness. "It's safe?"

"Yes, as long as we don't linger." Gingerly he removed his vest.

That's when she realized…he'd been shot! Her legs seemed to give out and she dropped into a seat. "Oh my God."

"I'm fine," he said absently, lightly touching a wound near his collarbone. "Just a ricochet."

"But…you're bleeding!" Regaining her feet, she started toward him.

He caught her hand and kept her from touching his chest. "I need you to drive, babe. Can you do that?"

Filled with new purpose, she nodded fast and rushed to the driver's seat, putting the van in gear. "Hospital?"

For three seconds, he considered it, then growled out a breath. "No. I need to go to my dad's place."

"But..." She glanced back at him. "You could be seriously hurt."

"Dad is a surgeon. Or was, anyway. He's still the best option." Cade joined her in the passenger seat, not really moving like a mortally wounded man. With the first aid kit in his hand, he gave her directions.

Panicked fear tried to take over. "That's at least forty minutes from here."

"I know." Using a cotton pad, he covered the injury. "It'll be okay." His mouth tightened. "The bullet didn't go deep."

She started forward in the darkness, her gun in her lap. Actually, he had his with him, too. He was far too alert, one hand holding that makeshift bandage in place, the other holding his weapon as he constantly scanned the area.

They got to the highway without any trouble. Still...

Longest. Drive. Of her *life*.

She kept glancing at Cade. "How you holding up?"

His mouth quirked. "Worried about me?"

"Well...yeah." Her tone plainly conveyed what she thought of that stupid question. "I didn't know... When did it happen?"

His expression went dark and deadly again. "Right before that bastard grabbed you."

Reaching over, she patted his tensed thigh. "Down, boy. I told you, he didn't hurt me."

"It'd be a different story if I hadn't been there with you."

Yeah, he couldn't resist making that point. "Maybe." Most definitely. She'd been far outnumbered, and outmaneuvered, too. "I'm not one hundred percent yet. Usually when I nut a guy, he's out. That dude had brass balls or something." She smirked. "I did smash his nose, though—I mean, before you completely rearranged his face. Pretty sure he's never going to look the same again."

Cade continually checked the mirrors. "It's not a joking matter." His glare burned over her. "I want another promise from you."

She almost groaned. She did give a quick roll of her eyes. "What now?"

"Whether Mattox recognized you or not, he's out to get you. That much is clear, yes?"

"He sent a small army, so yeah, not like I can deny it."

"Swear to me, until we have him locked away, or preferably dead, you won't try to deal with him or Adela on your own."

Her heart tripped, then settled into a fast, steady drumming. "You signing on for an extended period? Because there's no way to know how soon something like this could be wrapped up."

With no hesitation at all, he stated, "That's exactly what I'm doing. I don't care if it's a month, six months or a year." Tension poured off his big body, and he added in a hard, don't-argue voice, "We work together."

The warm glow started down deep in Sterling's jaded soul and fanned out until she couldn't keep the smile at bay. They were pretty crazy circumstances, and she was incredibly worried for Cade—despite his macho posturing—and still she couldn't repress a smile. "All right, you have my word." Urgency rushed back in on her. "Now no more talking. And don't you dare bleed to death!"

CHAPTER TEN

GETTING SHOT WAS never a good thing. Cade didn't say it to Star, but it was his distraction with her that caused the mishap. The bastard had just grabbed her, and the man he'd been binding had managed to pull away. He didn't get in a clean shot, not with the way Cade broke his arm for the attempt, but the gun had discharged, the bullet ricocheted off the ground...and he got nicked.

Luckily below his face, but unluckily right above his vest. It hadn't slowed him down, not with Star being manhandled, but it sure as hell hadn't felt good, either.

His dad and Reyes would be worried. Then once they knew he'd be okay, Reyes would find it hilarious, and his dad...would have a fit. Not that Parrish McKenzie had ordinary fits. No, he'd condemn and harass and overall be a pain in Cade's ass.

He should have killed that prick who'd dared to lay hands on Star. Knowing what they had intended, he'd wanted to kill them all. If Star hadn't been involved, he probably would have, but that type of cleanup, with a witness around, would have really sent his father through the roof.

He'd have enough explaining to do already.

Chewing her bottom lip, Star's gaze repeatedly darted to him. It was almost endearing, seeing her fret, because he hadn't figured her for the type. If anything, he'd thought she'd take the same tack as his dad and bitch him out for it.

She needed a distraction, so he said, "I didn't see Mattox."

"Neither did I, unless he's the one who dragged Adela away."

Every bump in the road sent an echo of pain through him. "Might have been." A text dinged on his phone. Getting the damn thing out of his pocket wasn't easy this time. Knowing it would be Reyes, he locked his teeth, twisted, and finally pulled it free of his back pocket. He glanced at the screen.

"What?" she asked. "Is that your brother?"

"Yeah. He's caught up with them. It was definitely Mattox who took Adela."

Hands tightening on the wheel, Star asked, "Is she okay?"

"He says she is and that he'll explain soon." Reyes wanted to know where they could meet up. Given his injury, Cade had no choice but to text back: Home base.

The return text came fast. You shitting me?

Of course, his brother wouldn't just accept that when he knew home was the last place Cade wanted to be. He had to explain, but he kept it simple. I'm fine, but caught a ricochet.

On my way.

Damn. A full house. He glanced at Star. "Would it be pushing my luck to make one more request?"

"What's wrong?" Her gaze swept over him before returning to the road. "You won't pass out, will you?"

Cade snorted. "No, I won't fucking pass out. I told you, it's not that bad."

"You're still bleeding," she accused, her voice going a little high with stress. "And here we are, taking the long way to help."

He wished he could take her hand, but his were now smeared with blood. "Stay with me."

"I'm not budging."

That quick answer didn't reassure him one bit. "I mean it. No matter what."

Her brows climbed high. "Just what the hell does that mean? What are you expecting to happen?"

No help for it. He had to be up-front, if for no other reason than to prepare her. "I'm expecting you'll want to run once you meet my family. But don't."

"Bunch of scary ogres, huh?"

He wasn't about to go into detail. "Let's just say they can be overwhelming."

Softer now, more sincere, she vowed, "A pack of wild dogs couldn't chase me off, okay? We're sort of like partners now. And partners stick together."

They were a hell of a sight more than that, whether she wanted to admit it or not. But for now, partners would do. "I'm going to hold you to that." He indicated the next exit. "Get off here."

When the road quickly narrowed and climbed the mountainside, she asked, "Where are you leading me?"

"I told you, my father's place. It's home base for what I—we—do. And FYI, he's not going to be pleased."

She frowned. "With me or you?"

"Both—but mostly me."

Her neck stiffened. "Then why are we going there?"

For an answer, Cade lifted the pad and saw that the bleeding had almost stopped. "He can handle this—quietly." Taking in her profile with her brows now set in an obstinate line, he said, "Hospitals report gunshots, and that would bring up too many questions that we don't want to answer." She started to speak, probably to say something grouchy, judging by her frown, but he said, "Veer to the right."

"This isn't much of a road."

"That's the point."

Craning her neck, she looked up through the windshield. "Are those security cameras?"

"Two of the twenty scattered around the property."

Star fell silent. Awe? Intimidation? Or wariness?

They ascended a few more miles, and there in the distance, lights glowed. Day or night, the mountain retreat made quite an impressive sight. Stone columns climbed high to support a curved roof over a sprawling deck, backlit by floor-to-ceiling windows that overlooked the mountains.

Eyes rounded, Star pulled up to the gated entry.

"You need to enter the code to get through the gate." He shared the series of numbers and letters with her, and the wide iron gates opened.

Star paused. She looked as though she wanted to turn around and leave.

"It'll be fine," Cade told her. "If anyone can handle my family, it's you." At least, he hoped that was true. Before her, he'd never considered putting it to the test.

Incredulous, she blinked at him, then frowned at whatever she saw on his face. "You're ready to keel over, when you promised you wouldn't!" Misgivings gone, or buried under her worry for him, she stepped on the gas.

There'd be no keeling. It'd take more than the paltry injury he had to make him do that. But if it propelled her past her nervousness, he didn't mind the misconception.

And in fact, he did feel wretched. Loss of blood, maybe.

Well, that and the fact that he was about to break a cardinal rule. He'd meant what he said, though. He didn't know another woman who could deal with what lay ahead. Star was the exception. Always. In everything.

With her, he believed it'd work out.

DRIVING PAST TALL aspens and magnificent boulders, Sterling pulled up to...a freaking lodge. "That's not a house."

"It is."

"No." She shook her head and pointed at a different home off to the side. "That smaller place over there, *that's* a house." The place in front of her...she'd never seen anything like it, not even in a magazine.

"That's my sister's private cottage. Drive right up to the front door there and help me inside before I lose more blood."

That silenced her. But God, she was caught in conflicting emotions. Cade took precedence, most definitely, but this, all this grandeur and wealth? Not her cup of tea.

She put the van in Park, turned it off and rushed around to his side. He'd gotten out on his own steam, thankfully, because Cade was a huge guy and she wasn't sure she could bear his weight on her own, especially not with a bum leg. At the door, she leaned on a buzzer. "Didn't they see us driving up? What good are security cameras if you don't—"

A tall man jerked the door open, already glaring in fury. "What in God's name...!"

The only way to brazen through a situation was to really brazen it through. "Out of the way, man," she barked. "He's been shot."

Immediately the man tucked his own shoulder under Cade's other arm. "I'll take care of him. You may leave."

Leaning heavily on them both, Cade stated, "If she leaves, I leave."

That caused a visual standoff between the two men—until Sterling slugged the stranger in the ear. "He. Is. *Bleeding.*"

Impotent fury darkened the man's face. He looked like he wanted to say or do something—to her—but instead he bellowed, "Bernard!"

The sound echoed around a grand sky-high foyer.

"She follows us," Cade warned.

The man said nothing, but he didn't try to stop her. Another man—she assumed poor Bernard—came to a halt before them.

"What in the world."

"Get the door," the man said, but before Bernard could do that, Cade's brother came to a screeching halt on his motorcycle and bounded in.

"Run every red light?" Cade asked.

"And drove ninety," his brother said, moving her out of the way so he could take Cade's other arm. "But I'm here, so don't complain."

Securing the door, Bernard said, "I'll get things prepped," and then he rushed off.

"Can you walk?" his brother asked Cade.

"I'm fine—but I'd like to see you try to carry me."

The older man snapped, "Don't you two start."

They all ignored *her.* If she'd wanted to leave, now would be her chance.

Of course she didn't. She'd promised Cade, and besides that, she wanted to see with her own two peepers that he was okay.

So she meekly followed along.

A pretty young woman came out of a room, took in the scene

before her and immediately set aside a laptop on a polished table to rush ahead of them. She now led the pack, while Sterling pulled up the rear.

They went across the great room, which really was great, before they veered off to the left and through the wide expanse of the kitchen, around a powder room, down a small flight of stairs, where the woman opened doors...into a lab?

Disbelief rounded Sterling's eyes and turned her in a circle as she took it all in. It looked like an honest-to-God operating room. Just what had she stepped into?

The men helped Cade to a white-sheeted bed that the handy Bernard had just finished making up with sheets from a metal cabinet.

Cade's brother neatly ripped open his shirt.

Blood was...everywhere, and Sterling felt her knees going weak. She reached out until her hand flattened on a wall, offering needed support.

Bernard set out a tray of stuff that looked too ominous for her peace of mind.

The older man, not Bernard, was busy scrubbing his hands and muttering, "You are the most stubborn, difficult—"

"Son. I know," Cade said, not really sounding like a man with a bullet in his chest. In fact, he was staring at Sterling, so she tried not to look so worried. "Reyes is the constant joker and Madison is the most obedient."

Reyes and Madison? Difficult *son*?

Her gaze slowly traveled to the sink where he washed. So that fire-breathing dragon was Cade's father? Yes, she saw the resemblance now, but...

Madison took offense at what he'd said. "Obedient? That's a lie."

Cade snorted. His brother did, too.

Madison folded her arms. "Don't take your temper out on me because you were foolish enough to get shot." Then to their father, who was now pulling on surgical gloves, Madison asked, "Is it serious, Dad?"

Sterling gaped at her. Serious? He'd caught a bullet! In his *chest*.

"No, it's not," Cade said, still not sounding all that wounded. "Damn bullet deflected off a rock and came back on me."

"You coulda shot your eye out," Reyes mused.

Madison reached out to swat him, but he ducked away.

They were all certifiably insane. From one to the other, Sterling stared—until she got snared again by Cade's gaze.

His father leaned over him, pressed...and announced, "It stopped at his collarbone, but luckily it doesn't appear to have broken anything."

Good news? At the moment, Sterling would take any she could get.

Utilizing scary surgical-type pincer thingies, his father poked and prodded while Cade gritted his teeth.

Madison stood stoic and Reyes was thankfully silent as he paced.

Bernard held a metal bowl...which clinked when the man dropped something into it. "Bullet's out. Let me make sure there's no other damage."

"X-ray?" Bernard asked.

Cade's father peered down at him. "Are you hurt anywhere else? And don't hold back."

Sounding disgusted, Cade said, "No."

"A few stitches, then." He turned to Sterling. "You're not sterile, so please remove yourself."

Of all the...! That sounded like a truly terrible insult. Reyes and Madison—were *they* sterile? Or Bernard?

But he must have meant them all because Reyes went to Madison and, with an arm around her shoulders, led her to the door. Bernard stepped away.

And that left only her.

"Bernard?" Cade called out, still looking at her.

"Yes?"

"Don't let her leave."

His father rolled his eyes, dismissed them all and began a thorough cleaning that, to Sterling, looked worse than what had come before it.

Feeling a little sick, she told Cade, "I'll be right outside the door."

"You'll wait in the kitchen," his father said without looking up.

"Since my son has quite a bit of explaining to do, you may as well get something to drink."

"Come along," Bernard said gently. "I'll get you settled."

She didn't want to. But damn. These people were daunting, far more so than Mattox with a gun.

THE SECOND THEY were alone, his father gave up even the slightest pretense of politeness. "What the hell were you thinking?"

"That I make my own decisions? That I want her with me? That you don't run my life?"

A deep growl crawled up his throat, but his hands were steady and competent as he numbed the area. "You could have been killed."

Without Star to focus on, Cade stared up at his father. "No more so than on any other job."

He paused. "We cover every possible scenario."

"Best we can, I know. I did the same tonight. That's why I convinced Reyes to tag along." He felt the tug of the first stitch going in, but no pain. "When you explode, don't include him. Against his better judgment, he did it for me."

Instead of doing some of that exploding that Cade expected, his father sighed. "Is the girl truly that important to you?"

Cade didn't doubt that his father had already surmised much of what had happened. Pesky details were only finer points of an overall view. "You already know the answer to that."

He finished stitching in silence. Once he was done, he treated the area with something and applied a light bandage. "You'll stay here tonight and tomorrow so I can keep an eye on this."

"Not without Star."

Moving away to wash his hands, his father remarked, "You shouldn't call her that. I've read your sister's report, you realize. Sterling Parson has good reason for having shed that name, and you endanger her by using it."

Cautiously, Cade sat up. His head swam a little, but he'd suffered worse injuries and he had a good grasp on what his body could and couldn't do. He took stock, flexed each arm and surmised that he'd walk out of the lab on his own. "I won't let any-thing happen to her."

With a sound of exasperation, Parrish turned back to him. His face was pinched. His eyes were narrowed. He looked pissed, but he said, "I suppose we should get to know her."

It was that concession more than anything else that allowed the residual aches and pains to swamp back in on Cade. Until he'd known if he had to fight his own family, which had been his presumption, he hadn't allowed himself to feel much of the dis-comfort.

The others would follow Parrish's lead, and he'd just offered an olive branch. Surprising, and very much appreciated.

Resigned, his father said, "I'll take you to your room so you can wash up and change clothes. Then we'll have a little talk with our guest."

Each of them had their own living quarters in the main house, for situations of this type. They were used when necessary, kept prepped otherwise.

Cade had his own house nearer to his bar, Reyes lived nearer to his gym and Madison had insisted on the separate cottage.

It was times like this that made having the quarters so conve-nient. He hated to admit to his own limitations, and he *could* make it back to Star's place if he needed to, but he didn't relish the idea of bouncing along the rough roads again.

Nodding, he carefully let his feet touch the floor. His head spun, but not too badly. "It was Mattox," he admitted. "And he had Star once before. He's the one who started her on this path of vengeance."

"You don't say? Hmm." Again with his arm around Cade, Par-rish started them forward.

His father was not known for an excess of sympathy, and he def-initely didn't indulge coddling. Cade had never wanted or needed either, and Reyes pretended he didn't care. But Madison? He and Reyes tried to make up for his father's lacks, but Cade wasn't sure if they'd succeeded or not. He understood Reyes, but his sister was often a mystery to him.

Right now, though, Cade was glad his father didn't fuss with him, trying to insist that he rest. Not yet. Not until he convinced Star that she needed to spend a few days with him.

Here, where it would be safer.

Where they could come up with a better plan—to end Mattox, once and for all.

STERLING HAD LEFT that home surgery center feeling pretty numb. Passing the powder room reminded her of the blood, and she detoured in there to wash her hands and face but couldn't do anything about her shirt. She still wore the bulletproof vest, but with Cade hurt, she hadn't even thought about it.

A knock at the door got her moving again. "Hold on." She smoothed back her hair, made a face at herself and stepped out.

Bernard smiled gently. "Come to the kitchen and rest. I'll get you something to drink while I prepare food."

She didn't need rest; she needed Cade.

No, she didn't *need* anything. Certainly not a guy. But she would stick around for a bit just to talk to him again.

It wasn't until she sat down at the kitchen table that Sterling realized how badly her leg thumped and her finger throbbed. Even her scalp hurt now, from where the goon had pulled her hair. And that damn vest nearly suffocated her. With Cade safe in the bosom of his lunatic family, all the discomforts settled in and made themselves known.

She wasn't sure what to think about these people yet. Cade's father was obviously wealthy. His sister tall, slim and beautiful. His brother still a raging pain in the butt.

But anyone could see that they loved one another.

Even the stuffy Bernard, who was trying so hard to look unconcerned as he prepared food, couldn't adequately hide how much he cared.

They were a family in every way that mattered. Blood related. Loyal to one another. Comfortable with heckling—and confident in assistance when needed.

And here she was, stuck in the middle of them, feeling like a mutt Cade had dragged home.

It didn't help that Reyes hadn't stopped staring at her with the same fascination he'd give a cockroach.

She tried to ignore him, she really did, but waiting to know how Cade had fared sent her temper spiraling and she couldn't grapple it back under control. Glaring at Reyes, she snapped, *"What?"*

Lifting his chin, Reyes said, "Just trying to figure it out."

Honestly confused by that answer, Sterling asked again, this time with less animus, "What?"

"You got my brother shot."

Hands fisting, Sterling bolted to her feet and leaned over the table. "I've had just about enough of you."

He eyed her up and down without concern, still showing only curiosity.

It unnerved her, damn it. "In case you failed to notice, Cade is a big boy and he makes his own damn decisions. Do you honestly think I could've stopped him from going along? For your information, I tried."

"And failed," Reyes said.

"But don't you see?" Madison said. "That's the lure."

They planned to verbally dissect her? Screw that.

Sterling pivoted to Madison. At least this sibling was calm and apparently not that interested in provoking her. "What's that supposed to mean?"

It was Reyes who answered, "All that." He gestured at her rigid posture. "Apparently Cade likes them fiery."

Madison gave him a quelling look, saving Sterling the trouble. "I think Cade likes her because she's as strong as he is."

One side of Reyes's mouth quirked in a way that was so familiar to Cade's smile that Sterling's heart clenched.

Then he ruined it by saying, "Since she's standing while he's on a table bleeding, maybe she's even stronger?"

"You're an asshole," Sterling accused, choking out the words around the lump in her throat. She strode away before she did something truly appalling. Like cry.

Silence throbbed behind her, until Reyes ordered, "You can't leave. You heard what big brother said."

Like she would without first seeing that Cade was okay? She wouldn't, but she replied, "Don't plan to, but I don't have to stay in the same room with a jackass!"

She'd take a turn around this mausoleum and hopefully get herself in check before returning to the kitchen.

But first...she headed out the front door and to the van.

Madison came trotting behind her, then just fell into step with her. Pretending she wasn't there, Sterling opened the door of the van, yanked off her shirts, then ripped open the fastenings on the vest and tossed the heavy thing inside.

Madison said not a single word while Sterling stripped down to her bra. In fact, she got comfortable against the side of the van, watching as Sterling pulled back on her T-shirt. Madison held out her button-up shirt, her expression enigmatic.

Shrugging it on, Sterling slammed the van door and walked away without thanking her. She went back inside the open front door of the house, aware of Madison trailing her.

The silence dragged out until Sterling wanted to scream, but she clamped her lips together and managed to keep quiet. Where to go? She couldn't imagine traipsing through the house without an invite. Besides, it was so damn immense she might get lost. From the great room she spotted doors that led to a deck and darted that way.

Naturally, Madison followed.

Outside, gulping in the damp evening air, Sterling leaned on the railing. Being here like this, in the quiet night, the majestic mountains barely discernible in the moonlight, she felt incredibly small. Insignificant.

Then Madison shoulder-bumped her. "This is better than leaving, right? You had me concerned for a minute there. I wasn't keen on tackling you."

Tackling her? Though her eyes narrowed, Sterling kept her gaze trained ahead, doing her utmost not to react.

"By the way, you shouldn't let Reyes rile you. He does it on purpose, you know, but if he doesn't get a reaction, he loses interest."

Damn it, that deserved a response, and she heard herself say, "What if I reacted with a fist to his face?"

Madison went still—then burst out laughing. "Oh, I'd love to see that. But you should be forewarned, we're all excellent at fighting. Dad made sure we studied a wide variety of disciplines. The only one I know who can best Reyes is Cade. My guess is that if you tried to punch him, you'd probably end up in some ridiculously undignified hold that would only infuriate you more, and then Cade would be angry with him and he'd pulverize Reyes, and then Dad would be upset. Me, too, I guess. I love my brothers, even though they're far too alpha and bossy. It's always distressing when they go at each other."

Very slowly, Sterling turned her head to stare in amazement at this particularly chatty sibling. "Maybe I should shoot him instead?"

"Well, as to that..." Grinning, Madison caught her hair in a fist to keep it from blowing in her face. "We're all pretty good at anticipating that sort of thing, too. Which makes it really curious that Cade allowed himself to be shot. Did you see how it happened?"

Sterling snapped her mouth shut and looked away. If Cade wanted to explain to his sister, then he could. Right now, she wanted to concentrate on ignoring the girl so she'd go away.

Turning to lean her back on the rail, Madison wrapped her arms around herself. "It's chilly out here."

"Feels good." Damn it, she hadn't meant to reply.

"Cade will be fine, you know. He's probably busy trying to order Dad around, and that never goes well. Neither of them seems to realize it, but they're just too much alike to always get along. Dad isn't a dummy, though. He'll see the situation for what it is and then it'll be fine."

Sterling wondered if her eyes had crossed yet. Had she really thought this sibling wasn't provoking? Unable to ignore everything Madison had just said, she gave up. "What, exactly, is that supposed to mean?"

"Dad knows when to cut his losses. He won't like it, but Cade brought you home, so he's obviously going to get his way."

"He didn't *bring me home*." Did Madison consider her a stray mutt, too? "He needed me to drive him here because he had a bullet in his chest."

"Oh, please. Cade could have driven—or even removed the bullet himself. He defines *tough guy*, you know."

Yeah, she did kind of know it.

Madison leaned closer, as if in confidence. "Personally, I think he saw it as a good excuse to push his own agenda."

"His agenda?"

Madison nudged her again. "You."

Bernard tapped at the doors, then stuck his head out. "I have food prepared, if you'd like to return to the kitchen now."

Before Sterling could decide what she wanted to do, Madison linked her arm through hers and pulled her along. "Thank you, Bernard. I'm suddenly famished."

Indulging her own whisper, Sterling asked, "Is he a butler?"

"Bernard? Oh, he's pretty much everything." Then louder, Madison added, "You take excellent care of us, don't you, Bernard?"

"I try."

And...that told Sterling nothing.

The only upside was finding Cade in the kitchen when she got there. His hair was wet and finger-combed back, he wore a clean dark T-shirt and fresh jeans, socks but no shoes, and in no way did he look like an injured man.

His gaze searched hers as she strode in, then moved to his sister with silent question.

Madison released her, saying, "We were just enjoying the view."

"Can't see much at night," Reyes pointed out.

Sterling shot back, "A black void is still more pleasant than you."

His mouth twitched. Then he said to Cade, "I like her."

Throwing up her hands, Sterling decided to stop wasting her time on that particular annoying brother so she could concentrate on Cade. Stopping before him, she took in the visible edges of a square white bandage at the base of his throat.

Maybe that's why her voice emerged all soft and feminine when she asked, "Are you okay?"

Enfolding her in his arms, Cade drew her close and asked, "Were you worrying about me? I told you I was fine."

Carefully, Sterling rested her cheek against his shoulder. Knowing for a fact that he was okay, seeing him hale and hearty, left her legs weak with relief. "I've never had to worry about anyone before."

"Baloney," he replied. "You worry about everyone."

Interrupting their moment, Reyes said, "You can stop worrying about Adela. That conniver is not a victim. In fact, from what I saw, she might be helping to run the show."

CHAPTER ELEVEN

CADE WANTED TO hear all about Adela and his brother's impressions, but a few other things took priority. Giving Star one last hug, he urged her to a chair.

Bernard had "thrown together" one of his incredible pasta dishes, and Cade wanted her to eat before she got more distracted.

Taking the seat next to her, he asked, "What do you want to drink?"

She stared at the angel-hair pasta smothered in a cream sauce that Bernard had pulled from his private stash for just such an occasion.

Bernard said, "I suggest sauvignon blanc—"

"Got a cola?" she asked instead, interrupting him. "Anything from a can is fine."

Smiling, Cade glanced at his family, daring them to say anything derogatory. "I'll have the same."

"I, as well," Madison said.

God bless his sister. Cade gave her a grateful smile.

Parrish said, "Pour me a glass, please," and took his seat at the head of the table.

Grinning, Reyes looked from one to the other. "Damn, this is fun. Guess as long as we're going with variety, I'll take a beer."

Appalled, Bernard stared at him. "With my pasta?"

"Yeah, but you're not the one driving me to drink, so don't sweat it."

Cade gave him a warning look, but Star smiled sweetly.

Once everyone was served, Bernard fixed his own plate and sat to Parrish's right. It was unusual for him to do so, but being unaware of the family dynamics, Star didn't seem to think anything of it.

No doubt about it, Bernard was curious about Star, and with good reason. Cade had never brought a woman home before. There were rules against such things, and he'd just crashed through them all.

Taking a bite of the pasta, Star gave a low groan that had each man staring at her. "Oh, Bernard." Another groan. "This is amazing."

Bernard actually flushed. "Thank you."

Pointing her fork at Reyes, she said, "So spill it. What do you know about Adela?"

That sounded so much like an order that Reyes took his time replying, and not with an answer but another question. "You're not surprised that she might be in cahoots with Mattox?"

"Nope, but I'd like details."

"We already suspected her," Cade explained.

"But naturally you rushed ahead anyway." Parrish made no bones about his disapproval.

"Hey, that was my fault." While twirling more pasta around her fork, Star said, "She contacted me, so I felt I had to be certain. Even tonight, it wasn't one hundred percent clear if she was a victim or helping to set a trap. And it *was* a trap, big-time. Dudes swarmed out of everywhere. I lost count. Six, maybe seven."

"Eight total," Reyes said, and Cade could see he was starting to relax. How could he not with Star being so casual?

"Night-vision goggles?" she asked. "Awesome. I need some of those."

"They come in handy," Reyes agreed. "I take it you couldn't see much?"

"Not in that darkness. Anything away from the headlight beam was more shadow than anything else."

"Yet you seemed to know when someone was moving in."

She shrugged. "Just sensed the movement, you know? Or heard a small sound."

"So astute," Madison enthused. "Dad, isn't she amazing?"

"Don't answer that," Star dared to order Parrish, then said to Madison, "I'm as far from amazing as a person can get, so don't fool yourself. I completely dicked up tonight. If it weren't for Cade—and actually, you, too, Reyes—I'd have been toast."

"You'd have been in Mattox's capture," Parrish stated with blunt insistence.

"Yup." She gave an exaggerated shudder. "Not a place I want to be, so gratitude all around, guys. Thanks for saving my bacon. And, Cade, seriously, I am so damn sorry you got hurt."

Everyone fell silent again. Cade knew she wasn't what any of them had expected.

She was better. More refreshing.

Pride, that's what he felt. Star handled his family with more ease than he'd expected, mostly by just being her usual candid self.

Reyes raised a brow at Cade. "She must have been hangry before. She's much more agreeable now that she's fed her face."

"Food is always good," Star agreed with a wink at Bernard. "Especially when it's this delicious."

Heat crawled up Bernard's neck. "Again, thank you."

"And you," she said, playfully growling at Reyes. "You do like to push those buttons, don't you? I considered punching you in your face, but your sister warned me against it." She smirked. "Considered just shooting you, too, but Cade might not like that. For some reason I can't figure out, he seems fond of you."

Reyes burst out laughing, earning a look of censure from Parrish, which he pretended not to see. "You want to spar sometime, lady, just let me know. You're welcome to my gym any day."

"I might take you up on that." Plate empty, Star pushed it back. "But I'll wait until my leg and finger have completely healed. Now, enough of the pleasantries. Tell me what you saw with Adela before she decides to call me again. I need to know how to handle things."

Slumping comfortably into his seat, Reyes held his beer loosely in one hand. "Adela and some other guy got out at an empty lot. Mattox was there. I assumed they were going to meet up with anyone else who'd been able to crawl away."

"I left them bound," Cade said. "Unless someone releases them, they'll be there awhile."

Parrish looked up from his plate. "You didn't kill them?"

Deadpan, Cade said, "You tend to frown over random murders that you haven't sanctioned. And at that point, I didn't know I'd be bringing Star back here."

"He was trying to tiptoe around the rules," Reyes offered. "Not all in, but not out, either."

Eyes wide, Star looked from father to son and back again. "Wish someone had told me the options. I wouldn't have had a problem sending a few of them to hell."

Realizing that he'd said so much, Parrish scowled. "This conversation didn't happen."

Star pretended to lock her lips and toss away a key.

Her antics had Reyes chuckling again. "No worries about anyone left behind. Mattox used the phone, so I assume he sent a lackey or two back for his men. If someone else finds them, it's not a worry. They won't say anything about us being there because that'd just expose their own agenda." He turned his attention to Star. "Your little victim gave Mattox hell."

"Seriously?" Star leaned forward, her arms crossed on the table. "You couldn't have misunderstood?"

"I know a female temper when I see it," he assured her. "Adela jabbed him in the chest, her mouth going the whole time. Mattox argued back, but she didn't look afraid. Mostly it looked like a lovers' quarrel."

"Euewww." Revulsion twisted Star's mouth. "Knowing what a disgusting ape Mattox is, I don't want to imagine that. It's too gross, but I suppose anything is possible. She did seem determined to hang back at Misfits, even though I could have gotten her out of there. And after that, when she claimed to want help escaping, she insisted that I come alone. You'd think she'd welcome an army, right? More rescuers would up her chances of getting away."

"If you knew all that," Parrish said, "then why did you go?"

"Because Mattox could have been forcing her." She shrugged. "You know he controls women, and most would do whatever he said to avoid the consequences."

"True enough." Reyes turned to Cade. "I followed them to another house. We can fetch her easily enough if that's what you want to do."

"Just like that?" Star asked.

"When we formulate an actual plan together, we're more successful than not," Reyes said.

Cade stroked her arm. "One of us could grab her while the other gives cover."

"And I can figure out the best time for it," Madison offered. "If Adela isn't under lock and key, it could be even easier. I'll sort that out."

"Not saying it'd be a piece of cake," Cade clarified, "but we can do it."

"With proper surveillance followed by careful planning," Parrish insisted. "Not this…" He flagged a hand at her. "Running off half-cocked business, like what happened tonight."

"Got it, but I don't think we should do that," Star said, thinking out loud. "With the extra info Reyes got, this could be a good opportunity to get all the players. Adela still thinks I consider her a victim, so it should be easy enough to set her up."

Overruling that idea, Cade shook his head. "Once we have her, we can question her."

"And she may or may not confide in us, right?" Star argued. "But if we use me as bait—"

Every muscle on his body clenched. "No."

Reyes, Parrish, Madison and Bernard all went still at his uncompromising tone.

Undaunted, Star continued as if he hadn't refused. "I can pretend to let her capture me, with you guys all keeping track."

The hairs on Cade's nape stood on end. *"No."*

"You were all just boasting about your skill. Well, just think, we could uncover Mattox's whole operation."

Shoving back his chair, Cade rose to his feet to tower over her. "I said no."

Parrish sent him a look of disapproval for the outburst. "It's actually a sound plan."

"The hell it is," Cade shot back. "You know what could happen to her."

Slowly, Star stood to face him. "I'm aware of the risks. I'm also aware of the rewards."

"We'll come up with a different plan," Cade said with finality.

Trying to break the tension, Madison smiled. "And this time, we'll all work on it together."

STERLING LOOKED AROUND the suite of rooms with dread. Even this, Cade's private section of the mansion, was nicer than anything she'd ever known. Way more upscale than her cheap apartment— an apartment she actually liked and, until now, had thought was pretty spiffy. She should have headed home after dinner instead of letting them all bulldoze her into staying over.

Madison had acted like it was a done deal.

Reyes had told her not to be dumb.

Parrish had insisted, with a stiff smile, that she was welcome.

Even Bernard had promised an amazing breakfast in the morning.

But Cade was the deciding factor, saying it was her decision— and if she left, he'd go with her.

Tough as he might be, getting jostled along mountain roads wouldn't be good for him. How could she put him through that with her stubbornness? So here she was, looking around in amazement at his sitting room, kitchenette and bedroom.

The ceilings were high, tall windows everywhere, and it all looked like a designer's dream, like something she'd see in a magazine of the rich and famous.

"Bathroom is right through here," Cade prompted, opening a door to an opulently decorated retreat.

Smooth stone covered the floor and the walls of the shower, a vessel sink topped a carved but masculine cabinet, and a lit mirror and heated towel shelves polished off the decor.

"Wow."

He came to her, looping his arms around her waist. "Why don't you shower? I'll give those bloody clothes to Bernard to wash."

Appalled with that idea, she pushed him back. "Not happening."

"Bernard wouldn't mind."

"I mind." She looked around again. "I'll wash my shirt in the sink and hang it in the shower to dry."

A quiet knock on the entry door had them both looking that way. Madison stuck her head in and searched the couch and kitchenette before spotting them in the bedroom, then smiled. "Oh, good, I was afraid I might be...interrupting."

"And you opened the door anyway?" Cade teased. He released Sterling from his embrace but kept his arm around her waist as he led her into the sitting room. "We were just discussing Star's clothes."

"Then I have perfect timing." Madison held out a stack of shirts, a pair of loose cotton pants, a blow-dryer, a round brush and a bottle of lotion. "I noticed when she got rid of the vest that she could use a change of clothes."

Looking down at her shirt, Sterling groaned. "I'd forgotten about that jerk bleeding all over me or I'd have...figured out something before dinner." No idea what she could have done, but she scowled up at Cade anyway. "You let me sit at that table with your family looking like this. Why didn't you remind me?"

"Because no one cared."

"But...at dinner?" She wasn't stupid. She knew his family understood decorum better than she did, but even she knew you didn't share a meal with polite company while wearing some cretin's nose blood on your shirt. Her cheeks actually went hot with embarrassment.

Cade ran a hand over her head. "Bloody shirt or not, I wanted you to eat, relax and get to know everyone."

"And that's what we did," Madison said happily. "So mission accomplished."

Yeah, she'd tried. For the most part, she'd managed to get along, too. That is, until Cade blew up about her excellent plan—a plan she hadn't yet given up on. It would work; she believed that.

And the important thing was to stop Mattox once and for all.

"The shirts are stretchy," Madison was saying, "so they should fit okay. We're both tall, but I'm skinnier than you, so I grabbed cotton drawstring pants instead of jeans."

There was nothing skinny about Madison McKenzie. Cade's sister had a tall, willowy body with gentle curves that Sterling thought was far more appealing than her own sturdy figure.

"I figured you could sleep in one of Cade's shirts." Grinning at him, Madison added, "Didn't think you would mind."

"Thanks, hon." Cade drew his sister in for a one-armed hug, then took the stack from her.

"Yeah," Sterling said, a little overwhelmed with the generosity. "Appreciate it."

"We'll talk more at breakfast, okay? Bernard usually has everything ready by eight, but since we're up so late, I asked him to make it nine. Will that work for you?"

Sterling looked at Cade. His house, his schedule.

He nodded. "That's fine. We'll see you then." He followed Madison to the door.

Sterling saw them whispering but couldn't hear what was said. Probably something she wouldn't like anyway. This time when Cade closed the door, he locked it, then came past her in the bedroom to ensure the French doors leading to a patio were also locked. With that done, he set his sister's offerings in the bathroom.

"No more interruptions." Opening a dresser drawer, he pulled out a snowy white T-shirt and handed it to her. "Want some boxers, too? Or how about you go without?" He gathered her close, one large hand caressing her behind. "I won't mind."

Concerned for his injury, Sterling gently rested a hand to his shoulder. "Let me shower first, okay? You don't want to hug this mess."

He treated her to that crooked smile and, leaning in, kissed her without drawing her close. "Use whatever you need in the bathroom. Toothbrush, lotion, shampoo and conditioner. Make yourself at home, okay? I'll fold down the bed."

Standing there, Sterling looked past him at the king-size bed, then stupidly whispered, "We're sleeping together? In your dad's house, I mean?"

He actually laughed. "No one will know."

"Bull."

"Okay, so they'll all assume. We're adults, babe." His grin faded into a tender smile. "And I want to hold you."

She wanted that, too. "But you were shot. What if I bump you?"

"I'll keep you too close for that." He kissed her again, this time lingering until her toes curled in her boots.

It took her a second to regain her wits. Then she breathed, "All right." It had been an exhausting and disappointing day, and she was still worried about Cade. Snuggling close, reassuring herself that he was fine, sounded too nice to resist. "Be forewarned, though, if Reyes says anything tomorrow, I can't be held responsible for what I do."

"Whatever you do, I'll help." He steered her into the bathroom, leaving after a smack on her behind. "Let me know if you can't find something you need." He closed the door before she could come up with more objections.

Of course she knew her reservations were absurd. As he'd said, they were adults.

But she'd never before stayed over with a guy in his father's house. Cade had probably sneaked in a lot of girls, but their formative years were vastly different. Overall, there'd been no fathers for her to deal with, not even her own. A grandfatherly figure, yes, but that was different, since she'd lived in the garage and never, not once, had she considered inviting a guy to share that precious space with her.

She pampered herself for a bit, but not as much as she'd have liked with only Cade's masculine products at hand. At least the lotion Madison had brought smelled more feminine. She slathered it on, occasionally lifting her wrist to sniff it again. Lavender, maybe. Or something more exotic. Whatever the scent, she liked it.

Her hair was thick, and by the time she'd dried it, nearly an hour had passed.

Sterling glanced at herself in the mirror. If she weren't so tall, Cade's T-shirt would have covered more of her. Instead, it barely reached below her backside. Of course, that made her think of the affectionate smack he'd left there, and his comment...

He's injured, she reminded herself. *No sex, not tonight. Maybe not for a while.* Still, as she opened the door and stepped out, her nipples pulled tight.

Already stretched out in the bed, his big, gorgeous body bare except for snug boxers, his shoulders propped against the headboard, he looked relaxed, maybe even asleep.

Until his eyes opened.

"Sorry I took so long." She stood there, framed in the light from the bathroom.

His slumberous gaze traveled over her. "Feel better?"

"I didn't feel bad." Not really. Tired, frazzled, achy...but not bad. Feeling like a feast he wanted to devour, she tugged at the hem of the shirt.

A morbid thought occurred to her—how awful it would be if... *when*...they went their separate ways. No other man would be like Cade. And no other man could make her feel the way he did.

Standing here now, in this moment, seeing the naked desire on his face, it was easy to think they could carve out a real relationship, yet all she had to do was look around to be reminded that they came from very different worlds.

Because of the circumstances, his father and brother were tolerating her, and Madison was kind. If he hadn't gotten shot, he would never have brought her here. This was a one-off, because Cade's family loved him.

"What are you thinking?" He left the bed to stalk toward her. "I think you just wrote a book in your head, didn't you? Will you tell me about it?"

Not being a dummy, Sterling determined to enjoy it all while it lasted. She wouldn't waste a single second by moping about an uncertain future. Heck, there was a chance Mattox would kill her, so what did the future matter?

When Cade got close, she touched the bruising she could see around his bandage. "I was thinking that, even wounded, you are seriously sexy." Tilting into him, she lightly brushed her lips over the heated skin of his chest. His chest hair tickled, and he smelled indescribably good. "I hate that you got hurt because of me." He frowned, and she quickly corrected, "I mean, I hate that you got hurt, period. It's just extra sucky that it happened while you were helping me."

Taking her hand, he lifted it to cover the bandage. "I know better than to get distracted. That's not on you, okay? I was where I wanted to be."

"Because I was there. If I hadn't involved you—"

"Then I wouldn't have you here now." He stroked an open hand down her spine and over her rump to cup a bare cheek. Grinning, he bent to nuzzle her neck and whispered, "With your sweet ass available."

Sterling laughed. It was that sort of thing, the playful compliments and sexual teasing, that she enjoyed so much. "I'm putting my sweet ass in the bed. The bathroom is all yours."

"Give me five minutes. And don't you dare fall asleep."

The second the door closed behind him, Sterling hurried to the bed and got under the covers.

In only three minutes, Cade emerged. He'd showered earlier but hadn't shaved. She liked him like this, his hair a little messy, not as precisely groomed, the beard shadow adding a rugged edge to his appeal.

It wasn't until he reached his side of the bed that she noticed the condoms on the nightstand. Her eyes flared, but he didn't notice as he clicked off the light and slid in beside her. In one smooth move he drew her against him and his mouth covered hers, stalling any protests she might have made over her concern for his injury.

Those large, rough hands slowly roamed everywhere, along her back, her shoulders, her thighs, yet they returned again and again to her behind. If she could have caught her breath, she might have laughed. He really did like her backside, when she'd never thought much about it.

He wasn't taking any chances on her using his wound as a reason to turn him down. How could he want her so much? It had to be magic, because no one else ever had.

Finally getting her mouth free, she whispered, "Slow down."

"Say yes, and then I will." He kissed a searing path along her throat to her ear.

He teased with his tongue, making her squirm. "Yes," she agreed. "With one condition."

"No conditions in bed, babe."

"I insist." Gently pushing him to his back, she crawled over him and sat on his abdomen. Her leg protested, but not enough to change her mind.

Staring up at her in the darkness, he held her waist and bent his knees so his thighs supported her back. "Lose the T-shirt."

It seemed second nature for Cade to give orders, but here in bed, she liked it. After whisking off her top, she said, "Now."

"Now," he agreed, shifting his hands to her breasts, lightly tugging at her nipples and obliterating her thoughts in the process. "Did I tell you how much I love these?"

She was starting to think he loved everything about her body. Dropping her head back, she let him have his way.

"So damn sweet."

He toyed with her nipples so long that she knew she was wet and beyond ready. "Cade..."

Leaning up while urging her down, he strongly sucked one nipple into the wet heat of his mouth.

Holy smokes. His tongue rasped over her, and she felt it in other places, especially between her legs. "That's enough." If he didn't ease up, she'd come before he ever got inside her.

He closed his teeth gently around her—and tugged insistently. Her breath shuddered in and released as a broken groan. She didn't mean to, but she rocked against his hard abs.

Humming his approval, he switched to the other breast.

"Whoa," she gasped, struggling for air.

"No."

Oh, what he did with mouth, lips, tongue and teeth... But he'd been shot, and she couldn't let this get out of control. *"Yes."*

With a last leisurely lick, he rested back on the bed. Her harsh breathing filled the air. His hands continued to stroke all over her.

Trying to regain control—as if she'd ever had it—Sterling braced her hands over his pecs, but that was a mistake. His skin burned, his muscles all knotted tight. He was closer to the ragged edge than he wanted to admit, and that turned her on even more.

"You're rushing it," she accused softly.

"You liked it."

"Yeah, course." She wasn't dead yet! One more cleansing breath helped to calm her racing heartbeat. "But seriously, Cade, you're hurt, regardless of how you want to minimize it." Getting words out wasn't easy, not with her nipples wet and aching. "To make this work—"

His fingers contracted on her hips. "It was working just fine."

"You need to let me take care of you."

He was silent a moment, just thinking. "Take care of me how?"

"You'll be still, and I'll do all the moving."

He snorted, and yeah, she got that. During sex, it was pretty damn hard to not move. "I mean it, Cade."

Lowering his arms to his sides, he said, "Go for it."

"I need you to relax."

"I'm relaxed."

She tsked. He felt like steel under her thighs. "Will you promise to tell me if I hurt you?"

"Hell no."

Such a *guy*. "Then I'll just have to be extra careful." Stretching out over him, she lightly teased her lips over his, dodging him when he tried to deepen the kiss. "Behave."

He choked on a laugh.

She trailed her tongue along his bristly jaw...to his ear. Closing her lips around his earlobe, she waited to see if he'd react the same as she had.

He did. Arms closing around her, he gave a vibrating groan and even turned his head a little for her.

Sterling ran her fingertips over the shorter hair at his temples, around to the back of his head to hold him still as she opened her mouth on his throat, grazed him with her teeth and sucked to give him a love bite.

His long fingers tangled in her hair, fisting gently.

Careful to keep pressure off his bandaged area, she rocked against him, deliberately teasing the hard cock straining beneath the material of his boxers.

A little roughly, he steered her mouth to his and took over the kiss. She didn't mind that...but then, she couldn't think straight. In fact, she wanted him too much to think.

Right *now*.

Maybe it was the chaos of the day, the resulting fear from him being hurt, but she felt totally out of control—a novel thing for her. She'd never had a craving like this, but she craved Cade.

The kiss went on and on while she touched him everywhere, moved against him, drove them both to the brink.

Pulling her mouth away, she sat up and away from him, then began wrestling off his boxers. He lifted his hips to help...and there he was. Long, hard, throbbing.

Sterling didn't think about it, didn't plan it; she just gave in to her desires.

Taking him in her fist, she kissed his erection, tentatively at first, just brushing her lips over his velvety length. The heated, musky scent of him encouraged her. His choppy breathing did, too.

Wanting more of him, she licked—from the base up to the head—and felt him go rigid. She liked that enough that she growled low and drew him in for a soft, wet suck.

CHAPTER TWELVE

CADE HAD TO grip the sheets to keep from taking over. He couldn't stop his hips from lifting. Or quiet the groan that rumbled from his chest. Her tongue…damn, her tongue kept lapping over the sensitive head of his cock, and he thought he might explode.

Star wasn't skilled, but she was damn sure enthusiastic, and that seemed to be all that mattered.

Her hot little mouth slid down his length, back up again, over and over while her hand squeezed and her wet tongue tasted him—no, he wouldn't last.

"Condom," he nearly gasped, reaching to the nightstand as he said it. "Babe, put the condom on me."

With a small, hungry sound, she took him deep again.

"Star… God." He squeezed his eyes shut and thought of everything under the sun except what she made him feel. That lasted five minutes, maybe, and then he knew he had to end the torture.

Tangling a hand in her hair, he gently tugged. "Let up, babe, or it's over for me."

Slowly, as if she hated to stop, she released him. Breathing deeply, eyelids heavy, she licked her lips. "I liked that."

His eyes had adjusted and he could see her well enough to know she was every bit as stoked as he was. "I more than liked it." He decided to do the condom himself. Keeping his gaze locked with hers, he used his teeth to open the packet, then rolled it on. Even touching himself pushed his control.

"Stay on your back," she whispered, already climbing over him. "I like being able to see so much of you."

So her eyes had adjusted, as well? "No complaints from me." He held her waist as she positioned herself, rubbing her wet heat against him—before sliding down, taking all of him, in one steady move.

Christ, she was wet. And so hot. They both groaned.

Everything became fast and furious at that point.

Star had strong legs and she rode him hard, moving how she wanted, needed. With her hands braced on his biceps, he couldn't touch her as much as he'd like, but her breasts were right there, bouncing with each hard thrust, each roll of her hips. Her fingertips dug into him, and she tipped her head back on a low, throaty cry.

Lifting into her, Cade kept up the rhythm until she slumped forward, replete enough that she forgot about his wound and collapsed against him. Hell, he barely felt it with so much sensation pulsing in his erection.

Holding her hips tight to his, he easily rolled her to her back and hammered out his own mind-blowing release. Damn, she pleased him. Wrung him out, too.

In no hurry to move, he relaxed over her.

Long minutes passed like that, him resting on her warm, giving body, her sprawled legs around him.

Her choppy breathing had evened out, her thundering heartbeat slowed, and she lazily toyed with the hair at the back of his neck.

Soft and warm, she complained, "You ruined my plans."

Smiling, Cade lifted up to see her. And yeah, he felt it in his chest, around the bruised wound. But hell, it had totally been worth it. "How's that?"

"I didn't want you to exert yourself." She kissed his shoulder. "How are you? Okay?"

"Actually, I feel terrific." Tired, but also oddly satisfied. He turned to his back to take the pressure off his collarbone but gathered her close to his side.

To his surprise, she got out of the bed. "Hey." Catching her hand, he asked, "Where are you going?"

"I want to take care of you. Don't budge." She pulled free, warning, "I mean it," before disappearing into the bathroom.

The sounds of running water reached him. Then she stepped from the bathroom, beautifully naked, not in the least shy. Because she left on the bathroom light, he saw that she held a tissue box and a damp cloth.

As she reached the bed, she said, "I'm getting rid of the condom and washing you."

What? Cade started to sit up, but she already had hold of his now flaccid dick. Leave it to Star to do something totally different. With every other woman, he'd had the honor of cleanup. Choking on an odd mix of embarrassment and tenderness, he said, "You don't need to—"

"Shush." She dropped the spent rubber into a tissue and then smoothed the damp rag over him. He twitched.

So maybe he wasn't so spent after all. How could he be when she concentrated on him like that?

Grinning, she glanced up at his face. "This is all so interesting."

"This, meaning my junk?"

"Yeah." Leaning forward, she pressed another kiss to him, then said, "Be right back," and strode off again, all sassy and without a care.

Of course, Cade watched her. She had *such* a fine ass.

He didn't know how he'd gotten so lucky, but he knew she was worth fighting for, whether that meant fighting his family, fighting traffickers or fighting the lady herself.

EVERYONE LOOKED UP the second they stepped into the breakfast room. Surprised, Cade realized they'd kept them waiting. From the stove, where Bernard had been keeping the dishes warm, he began serving.

Star had assumed they'd eat in the kitchen again, but Cade explained that wasn't the norm, just something that seemed to happen during unusual occurrences.

The breakfast room was large and airy with windows that faced the mountains and the man-made lake below. There was no end of incredible views in his father's home.

Sipping from his coffee, Reyes glanced up, caught Star yawning and lifted a taunting brow. "Cade didn't let you sleep, huh?"

"Don't start," Cade ordered, unsure how she'd react. This morning she dragged a little, and yes, she kept yawning, but then, they'd had a trying day yesterday, and a satisfying night...that hadn't allowed for much sleep.

Today, he felt the activity in his collarbone but he wouldn't complain. No way did he want Star having any regrets, not when it was his own fault for waking her once in the middle of the night by nibbling on her shoulder. He hadn't been able to resist, but then, she'd come awake with her own intentions, completely on board in a nanosecond.

"What?" Reyes asked with mock innocence. "She looks... exhausted."

Taking a seat across from Reyes, Star picked up the silver knife at her place setting and studied it quietly. When she glanced at Reyes, Cade had to stifle a grin. He knew exactly what she was thinking.

Even sluggish, Star didn't disappoint, saying to his brother, "On top of all your other skills, are you good at dodging knives?"

Smile banked, Reyes sat back. "Depends. You planning to use it up close or throw it?"

"I'm thinking...throw it."

Reyes's amusement grew. "It's not really a throwing knife."

And, Cade recalled, Star had said she kept her knife for close contact.

"True," she agreed, placing the knife beside her plate—and reaching to the small of her back, where she kept a real blade strapped in a clip-on holster. She lifted it for Reyes to see and asked sweetly, "What about this one?"

Bursting out a big laugh, Reyes said, "Should I be ducking?"

"Not right now." She returned the lethal weapon to the sheath. "If I decide you deserve it, I'll wait until you least expect it."

Grinning ear to ear, Reyes flagged his napkin in the air. "Then maybe I should call a truce. What do you think?"

"If you stop needling me...maybe."

Bernard handed her a glass of orange juice. "A hearty breakfast will improve dispositions all around."

Star inhaled the scents of breakfast meats, scrambled eggs, muffins and potatoes. "It certainly smells good enough to cause miracles."

Laughing, Madison loaded her plate. "This is fun, isn't it?"

That earned her a quelling frown from Parrish. "We have plans to make."

"I know, but usually we're all deadpan other than Reyes and Cade sniping at each other." She turned her smile on Star. "You're shaking things up, and I, for one, love it."

Bernard set fresh-cut fruit on the table. "I, as well."

Everyone looked at Reyes, but with one hand he just waved his napkin again while forking two sausage links with the other.

The ease with which Star dealt with his more bothersome sibling amazed Cade. Reyes didn't warm up to many people. Most never really knew him. He excelled at showing only what he wanted others to see, but with Star, he'd relaxed and opened up.

That may or may not be a good thing, considering Reyes's brand of humor could wear thin quickly, but so far Star didn't seem bothered.

Putting a hand to her back between her shoulder blades, Cade stroked her. He loved touching her, and he enjoyed the way she got up on his brother, how she didn't let Parrish intimidate her.

The urge to kiss her again nearly had him skipping breakfast, except that she was obviously hungry.

Parrish gave him a frown, making it clear he didn't condone the familiarity. Too bad. With Star near, keeping his hands to himself wasn't possible. Smiling, he let his father know what he could do with his judgment.

While helping himself to a slice of cantaloupe, Parrish said, "I assume Adela called you from an unlisted number."

"You assume correctly," Star said. "She's been very cagey about any details. It took some coaxing—or she wanted me to think I had to coax her—just to get a location on where to meet."

"She doesn't live in Coalville," Madison said. "I already checked. My guess would be that she's in another area altogether, that she chose Coalville because, one, it'd be easy to set a trap. Two, not many witnesses, since the town is so tiny. And three, it gave quick access to I-25, meaning she could make a hasty exit once she had you under wraps."

"Any idea why she wants you?" Reyes asked.

"I don't know her." Star shrugged while dishing up a bite of fresh pineapple. "I assume it's Mattox who wants me, and he's either forcing her to help, or she's a willing accomplice."

That careless attitude rubbed Cade the wrong way. "It occurs to me that you're in more danger now."

Brows lifting, Star asked, "How do you figure that?"

"They probably don't know where you live, but they do know that you frequent the bar. It'd be easy enough to ask around there and find out about your truck. You travel that way often. Some of the roads are long, lonely stretches."

"Perfect to shanghai me? You could be right." Star sipped her juice. "But you're in the same shape, right?"

Cade conceded the point. "If anyone at that church recognized me, then yes, they'll trace me back to the bar."

"And you travel back and forth, too," Madison pointed out.

Yes, and Cade hoped they'd come after him instead of Star. He could handle himself, but if they overwhelmed her...

No, he wouldn't consider the possibility of her being taken again. He'd kill them all before he let that happen.

Parrish held silent, watching, listening, allowing them to work it out. It was his way—not that he hesitated to interject whenever he chose to, but he considered discussion a learning opportunity. That he didn't object over Star's participation in what would normally be a family matter meant that he trusted Star, at least in part.

"Your trucking business is an issue," Reyes said. "It's too hard to monitor you if you go far."

Cade waited for her reaction to being monitored, but she skipped right past that.

"Thing is, it gives me legitimacy for what I do. No one questions a truck at a truck stop, right? And I have a reason to repeatedly hit the east-west expressway where long-haul trucks pass through."

Chiming in, Madison said, "That's why that area is ideal for human trafficking."

Glancing around the table, Star asked, "So you guys set up a bar and a gym for legit businesses, huh? Makes sense. I imagine both of you hear all the nitty-gritty, right?"

Reyes didn't answer, so Cade said, "That's the idea."

"You've rescued a lot of women?"

"Quite a few, yes." Parrish fidgeted with his napkin, then crumpled it in his fist. He asked Cade, "You completely trust her?"

Shocked, Cade knew exactly what his father was ready to do. It was unheard of, yet they'd all seen how concerned she'd been for him. And Reyes had probably explained to Parrish just how hard Star had fought against those men trying to take her. Anyone could tell she had the right edge, a sharp intuition and a core strength that couldn't be faked.

Aware of Star looking at him, wanting clarification for what was happening, he nodded. "Yes, I do."

Bernard quickly pulled up a chair, expectant anticipation in his eyes as he took in each person at the table.

"Whoa," Star said, growing wary as tension thickened the air. "You're not planning to put me through a blood rite or anything, are you?"

Clasping her thigh beneath the table, Cade said, "I believe my dad is ready to tell you more about the task force he funds."

"A task force? No kidding?" Fascinated, Star folded her arms on the table. "That sounds pretty awesome."

"It is," Madison enthused. "It's at the heart of everything we do."

"But we keep our involvement quiet," Parrish explained. "It's always best to avoid obvious links to your private life."

"Probably easier to do if you have a lot of dough, right?"

"Yes," he allowed. "Wealth has its advantages."

"Benevolence being one of them?"

Parrish gave a slight nod.

Since no one else was jumping in to explain, Cade did the honors. "The task force is possible because of Dad's funds. It ensures victims get counseling, plus legal representation when needed."

Bernard took over. It wasn't often he got to brag on Parrish. "They also get financial assistance to start over, and guidance so that all legal avenues are used to convict the ones responsible."

"We make sure we have it all zipped up," Reyes said. "Dates, names, addresses, witnesses—the whole shebang."

"Wow." Impressed, Star asked, "I take it that's for the perps who don't die in the process?"

Bernard put his nose in the air. "There are, necessarily, a few who do."

She grinned at the way he said that with proper gravity. "You won't see me crying about it. I'd wipe them all out if I could."

"But you're just one woman," Reyes pointed out. "Unless you join us."

Eyes flaring, Star blinked at Reyes. Her gaze shifted to Parrish and Bernard, then to Madison, before she slowly pivoted to face Cade. "Is that a joke?"

"No." Cade squeezed her knee. "It'd be safer for you, and you'd have more effect."

As if they couldn't hear her, she leaned closer. "But I work alone."

"You work with me."

"Just that once!"

Cade considered her attitude, but he couldn't convince her here with his family all riveted. "I think maybe we need to talk privately. Are you done eating?"

"What? Oh, yeah." Standing, she picked up her plate and started for the kitchen.

"I'll do that." Bernard rushed around the table.

She kept going. So did Bernard.

Madison fretted. "She needs a minute, doesn't she?"

"She's been alone a very long time," Cade explained. He'd sway her, but he didn't delude himself that it'd be easy. Star was one of the most independent people he'd ever met, and with good reason, she didn't trust easily. Yes, she'd taken to him fast enough, once he'd introduced the idea, but he was one person, not a family unit.

And his family... Cade glanced at each of them. His father had initiated this, but he still didn't speak up. Cade pushed back his chair. "I'll convince her."

"I hope so." Rubbing his mouth, Reyes stated the obvious. "It's going to be a problem if she wants to walk away at this point."

"She won't." Cade picked up his own plate and went after her.

He stalled when he didn't find her in the kitchen, but Bernard said, "She went out the side door to the deck," as he took the plate from Cade. "I had to wrestle the dishes from her. She's a very determined young lady, and she was most insistent that she 'pull her own weight,' even though I explained that this is part of *my* job." He made a rude sound. "But she's wonderful and I like her—as long as she understands the parameters of my domain."

Sounded about right. "I'll talk to her," he promised again and almost laughed. He had a growing list of things that required his skill at convincing. Usually not a daunting task, but with Star? She could be very bullheaded.

She wasn't in back, which would have put her in line with the windows where his family dined. Instead she'd taken up a corner of the wraparound deck, facing the side yard with tree-covered hills.

The second he stepped out behind her, she said, "Don't start," without turning to face him.

"Come on."

That got her attention. She glanced back with suspicion. "Where are we going?"

"I thought we'd take the trail down to the lake. One day we can fish there, if you'd like. Or take out kayaks. It's a private lake, so pretty damn peaceful."

Bracing her back on the railing, she smiled at him. "That sounds nice."

"Today, we'll just walk." And talk. He held out his hand.

She didn't take it right away. "Are we going to have a fight? You want to get me alone so your family won't hear me yelling?"

So damn astute. He snagged her hand and pulled her forward into his arms. "I want you alone so you can speak freely."

She snuggled close. "Wasn't I already doing that?"

He couldn't help but laugh. "Do you need to be a hard-ass to the bitter end?" Pressing a kiss to the top of her head, he suggested, "Meet me halfway here, okay?"

"You're right," she said, surprising him. "Sorry."

Disbelief had him levering her back. "Do you ever say the expected?"

Her mouth opened, then snapped closed as she gave it thought. "I have no idea what the expected might be, so I don't know if I do or not. Other than brief exchanges with clients who want to hire me to carry a load, or when shopping or requesting food, I don't really have conversations with anyone."

"What about the women you've helped?"

Uncertainty darkened her eyes. "More like a question-and-answer deal. Like if they had a specific place to go, if they wanted cops involved or not, or if they needed a trip to the ER. Stuff like that."

He imagined she was a lot more compassionate than she made it sound, but he got her point. "Come on. We'll go this way." With her smaller hand held securely in his, Cade tugged her to the spiral stairs that led down to the lawn. From there they circled around for the worn footpath to the lake.

"It's a long walk?" she asked.

Depended on the perspective. "It'll take us ten or fifteen minutes to get down there, but with a lot of nature to see along the way."

"I wasn't complaining, just curious." Tipping her head back, she peered up at the bright blue sky. "It smells different here."

"Fresh," he agreed. "All the trees and earth and the scents from the mountain…"

Smiling, she bumped him with her hip. "You love it here, don't you?"

"The land, yeah. Who wouldn't? There's something about being surrounded by the mountains, all the peace and quiet, immersed in nature. The scrub oak brush is something to see in the fall." Would he be able to show her? He hoped so, and that brought him around to the reason for their walk. "It was a huge concession for Dad to include you."

"I figured." Distracted by a boulder, she said, "Look at the size of that rock," and proceeded to climb atop it.

As agile as a mountain goat, she clambered up to the highest spot about six feet off the ground, then spread her arms wide. Cade moved around to the side of the boulder so he could catch her if she fell.

"I declare myself king of the mountain."

God, he loved seeing her like this. Playful. Relaxed. Mostly unguarded. "You might have to take that up with Bernard, since he claims he holds that title."

Laughter bubbled out. "No way! Stuffy Bernard does? Are you pulling my leg?"

"He loves it here, says it calls to his soul."

"I can believe it." She inhaled deeply. "It's awesome, for sure." Putting her head back and closing her eyes, she breathed deeply, but then abruptly looked down at him again. "What's up with Bernard? Does he live here? He's like a butler, right?"

"He and Dad have been best friends a long time, back before Reyes and Madison were born. As Dad's wealth grew, Bernard came along, working various jobs, though Dad swears he wasn't helping Bernard, that Bernard made his life easier because he could trust him. He moved in after Marian died—"

"Marian was his love? Mom to Reyes and Madison?"

Cade nodded. "Dad was a mess, and he was so consumed with grief, Bernard picked up the slack where he could. He loves to cook, though, and he's an organizational whiz, so that's mostly what he does."

"Huh. So he's part of the family?"

"Very much so." Tired of the distanced chatting, Cade held out his arms. "Jump."

"Ha! Not on your life." She looked around for an easy way down.

Cade knew she'd find that getting down was the hard part. "Chicken."

Her gaze clashed with his. "Take that back or I might just launch at you, and we both know I'm not a lightweight."

Cade mimicked her "Ha!" and left his arms up for her. No, she wasn't a delicate woman, but compared to him, she was still very female, smaller boned, curvy where he was straight, soft where he was hard. She needed to stop underestimating his strength. "Trust me."

Her brows pinched together. "Have you forgotten you were injured?"

No, but he wished she would. "I'm fine." If he said it often enough, maybe she'd finally believe him.

Softer, with worry, she explained, "I don't want to hurt you."

"I promise you won't." He waited and knew the second she

planned to prove him wrong. Using her strong legs to propel her
forward, she did indeed launch at him.

He was grinning before she landed against his chest and was
grinning still as he swung her around, going with the momentum
until they stopped, body to body, her feet off the ground. Yes, that
impact jarred him, but the pain was minimal and the reward made
it worthwhile when she fit him so perfectly.

Not just physically, but in so many other ways, too.

Against her lips, he whispered, "Told you so."

Her laughter made it tough to kiss her, but he persisted until she
slumped against him, her arms tight around his neck, her mouth
open, her tongue greeting his.

It would be so easy to get carried away, but he didn't think she
wanted to get naked on the mountainside. Plus, yeah, he wouldn't
put it past his brother to break out the binoculars.

When Cade moved to kiss her throat, she whispered, "You are
a certified stud."

"Don't forget it."

She laughed a little too hard over that, so he set her down and
again got them walking toward the lake. It was ten minutes of
peaceful quiet before they reached the edge of the water.

They had a dozen things to discuss, but Star's awe kept him
quiet. Her eyes went soft and wide as she took in the reflection of
junipers and fluffy clouds on the placid surface of the lake.

This early in the day, you could see to the rocky bottom. Rough
boulders bordered one whole side of the large lake, with thick ev-
ergreens behind that. It was only this section that offered easy
access to the water. Cleared per his father's instructions, a pebble-
covered shoreline made it easy to fish.

Random wildflowers grew from between rocks, drawing hum-
mingbirds that flitted here and there. Overhead, red-tailed hawks
soared.

Silently, Star went to the water's edge and reached down to trail
her fingers over the glassy surface, sending ripples to feather out.
"Do you ever swim?"

"The water is always freezing."

She glanced back. "Is that a yes or no?"

"I have, yes. So has Reyes."

"But Madison has more sense?"

He grinned. "A nice way to put it."

"Women don't feel the need to prove things the way guys do."

"Oh, really?" He climbed up to sit on a flat sun-warmed rock, his arms resting over one bent leg as he stared out at the lake. "So that wasn't you who felt it necessary to challenge my brother?"

Joining him, she accepted the hand he offered to help her up. "Totally different," she said as she got settled. "Your brother needs to be knocked down a peg or two."

"I do that on a regular basis."

Leaning against him, she said, "I can't challenge your dad."

"No?" Cade had been wondering how to bring it up, but he should have known Star would beat him to it. She wasn't one to shy away—from a subject, danger or anything else. "Why not?"

Her shoulder lifted. "He's your dad. I don't know what to do with dads, but I do know I won't like being under his thumb. He's a dictator, isn't he?" Wrinkling her nose, she specified, "Super bossy, I bet. And if I go along with this whole...alliance, he'll expect me to toe the line. But that's not me."

As Reyes had said, there wasn't much choice at this point. That was Cade's doing. He'd brought her here, forcing the issue and putting his father in an untenable position.

But he didn't regret it.

After drawing her between his legs so he could wrap his arms around her, Cade propped his chin on top of her head. He relished the light breeze that blew over his face, and the way she rested her hands over his forearms. "You think I toe the line, babe?"

A sudden stillness settled over her. "Did I insult you?"

A little late for her to worry about that now, but he didn't want her to change, not when he already admired so much about her. "I butt heads with my dad plenty often enough."

"So how do you deal with him?"

"By listening when what he says makes sense." Which, much as it annoyed Cade, was most of the time. "When I disagree, I say so."

"Does he ever listen to you?"

Only when Cade wouldn't relent, but he didn't want to scare her off. "How about we put it this way—if you work with us, what's the worst that could happen?"

"I could lose my cool and…"

"What?"

"I don't know. I might make an ass of myself."

That candid confession had him barking a laugh, which had her turning on him. He kissed her before she could blast him.

"So what?" She looked like such a thundercloud that he kissed her again. "You're allowed to be human, honey. I am. Reyes and Madison are. My dad…well, he's more distant, very driven, but he's not bad. You *can* deal with him." One more kiss, this time teasing. "You know the best things that could happen? You'd be safer—and I'd know you were safer, so I wouldn't worry about you. You'd be able to help a lot more women."

"In more meaningful ways."

"Not what I said. I'm sure for any woman you've helped, it made a life-altering difference."

She stared out over the lake. "You think I can do this?"

Insecurity? From Sterling Parson? He hugged her. "I have faith in you."

Her scowl hadn't lightened up, but she grudgingly said, "Okay— on a trial basis."

That wouldn't do, but for now he'd accept it. If nothing else, it'd give him time to talk her around.

And then what?

He didn't know for sure, but she fit so well into his life, he wasn't ready to let her go. Not today, not next week.

Not for the foreseeable future.

CHAPTER THIRTEEN

CADE WOULD HAVE been happier if he could have convinced Star to stay at his father's house, but he'd known that wouldn't happen, not without him there, and he had to go to work.

At least he'd talked her into coming to the bar with him instead of going to the apartment alone. Nothing unusual in her being at the bar. During deliveries, she'd often stopped in and stayed for hours. He doubted anyone would pay any attention.

She'd had to turn down two jobs for now, but for how long would she do that? If Adela didn't call back, then what?

He'd go after her, that's what. One way or another, this had to end. It was the only way to be fair to Star.

Tonight they'd go back to his father's—he'd used the excuse of Parrish checking his wound in the morning—but after that? Star made her own decisions, and she wasn't big on concessions. But then, she was also smart and she'd understand the need for extra security until Mattox was locked up or dead.

"I should check on my truck tomorrow. I never leave it to sit this long."

"We can do that, no problem." Cade pulled in to the parking lot of the Tipsy Wolverine. His tendency was to park around the back and go in through that door, so when they left, it was likely no one would notice that they were together.

"Now that we're a thing..." She let that hang out there for a bit before continuing, maybe waiting for him to object.

Of course he didn't. Putting his SUV in Park, he asked, "What?"

Relief brought a brief smile to her mouth. "How did you come up with the name of this place?"

"Don't put that on me." He turned off the car. "The name was already on it when Dad bought the place. I came out of the military and got dropped into the Tipsy Wolverine practically in the same week." Pretty sure his dad had wanted to lock him down while he had the opportunity. "The name was already known, and I don't really care, so I never bothered to change it."

"What a disappointing answer." She opened her seat belt. "I was all set for a good story."

Laughing, Cade got out and started around to her side of the SUV. She didn't often let him open her door for her, but the instinct was there anyway.

Luckily he had amazing peripheral vision. He caught the rush of movement and automatically reacted, turning and kicking out at the same time.

He caught the tallest guy in the knee, watched it buckle awkwardly, but didn't have time to follow up as two more men charged him.

Dodging a short pipe aimed at his head, he buried a heavy fist into that fool's gut, followed by a head-snapping pop to the chin.

Something broke over Cade's back, almost taking him down as he staggered forward, but he caught himself and spun with another kick. He missed the man's face and only hit his shoulder. It was still effective enough to knock the guy on his ass, only he didn't stay down.

With only a quick glimpse, Cade realized all three men were young, probably no older than midtwenties. Had Mattox run out of muscle, or did he consider these boys expendable?

Willing Star to lock the car doors, he concentrated on ending the attack quickly.

They were definitely injured, but other than the one with a busted knee, they weren't yet out of the fight.

Handling that swiftly, Cade grabbed one by the throat, lifted and slammed him hard to the ground. Stunned, the breath knocked out of him, he didn't fight as Cade flipped him over to pin him down with a knee pressed between his shoulder blades. The rough gravel would cut into his face.

No more than he deserved.

The third fellow thought that'd be a good time to press his advantage, but Cade was using only one knee on the guy he held down, leaving both arms and a foot free.

"You're a dead man," the third guy said, then dived at him.

Cade flipped him, too—did they not learn? In a finishing blow, Cade punched him in the nuts.

An inhuman sound squeaked out of his gaping mouth, and pain curled him tight.

"Someone better start answering questions fast," Cade said. He got to his feet, pulled up the guy he'd been holding down and slammed his face into the wall of the bar. He crumpled backward without a sound.

Gaze locked on the goon with the badly mangled knee, Cade smiled. "Looks like you're it." Knowing the man he'd just nutted wouldn't function again anytime soon, he started forward.

The guy tried to crawl back but couldn't get more than a few inches before Cade hauled him up with a fist in his hair. "I'm going to ask questions, and you're going to give me answers. Got it?"

Face contorted in pain, he gasped, "Yeah, man, let up."

"Name."

"My name?" he asked, confused.

Tightening his hold, Cade lightly kicked his knee, earning a groan. "I'm only asking each question once."

"Right, yeah. I'm Paulie Wells."

"And the other two?"

"Brothers."

The one with crushed gonads growled, "Shut up, Paulie."

"You want another?" Cade asked him.

Wincing at the threat, he curled tighter to protect his jewels.

"That's…that's Ward Manton. You knocked out his bro, Kelly."

Cade dug a hand into Paulie's pocket and found a wallet but no cell phone. He checked for ID, saw Paulie had told the truth, then searched him for weapons before letting him fall into a whimpering heap.

He turned to Ward. "You like wielding pipes, my man?" Cade strode over to where it had fallen and picked it up, hefting it in his hand.

Ward amused him by looking both defiant and terrorized. "Just business, dude. Nothin' personal, I swear."

"Whose business is it?"

Shifty eyes darted around. "We, ah, we were just robbin' you, that's all. It's cool."

Cade spun the pipe in his hand, then rested it against Ward's temple. "That's your one and only lie. Tell me another and you won't be able to talk for a very long time." He paused to tell Paulie, "If you don't sit your ass down, I'll break the other knee."

Paulie promptly stopped looking for an avenue of escape and instead put both hands to his head, his expression lost.

Back to Ward, Cade tapped the pipe none too gently to his temple. "Do we understand each other?"

He heard *"Euewww"* and glanced back to see Star standing behind the open car door watching. Damn it, he would have preferred she stay hidden.

But of course, she did the opposite and stepped out. "If you're going to splatter what little brains he has, will you warn me first? I'd rather look away."

"Better yet," Cade said calmly, "why don't you get back in the car and—"

"Nope." She sauntered forward. "I'm not missing all the fun. In fact, I'll check this one while you do your brain splattering."

Ward eyed her warily, his gaze going from his still-unconscious brother to Star, then to Cade.

Kneeling down by Kelly, Star efficiently went through his pockets, tossing out a wallet, then a knife, brass knuckles and nylon hand ties. "Looks like they had a party planned." With the small collection in front of her, a look of icy rage on her face, Star said, "Maybe I want to watch you cave in his skull after all."

Kelly groaned, and without a blink, Star brought her elbow hard to his temple, knocking him out again. To Ward, she said, "You better start talking fast or neither of you will have any brains left."

Cade wasn't happy with her interference—the less low-life

thugs knew about her, the better. Couldn't tell her that right now, though, not with their audience.

Glaring down at Ward, he whispered with tight control, "Were the brass knuckles for her or me?"

Properly terrified, Ward stammered, "For…for you, dude. You're big. We weren't gonna hurt her none. Mattox wants her in one piece."

"That answer is the only thing saving your ass." Cade shoved him over to his face. "Give me the cuffs."

Star lifted a brow at the order, then shrugged and carried everything to him. While he bound Ward's hands, she slipped on the brass knuckles. "I like these." Her feral gaze dropped to Ward. "Let's see how well they work."

Cade had to jump up to keep her from breaking Ward's jaw. Quietly wrestling her into submission, he said, "Not now. I have more questions for them."

"He was going to use these on *you*," she practically yelled in his face, the brass-enhanced fist almost touching his chin.

"Was never going to happen. They're children. You can see that."

"What I see is that they're a bunch of cowardly goons." She kicked past Cade's restraint, landing that steel-toed boot to Ward's shin.

Howling, Ward tried to scuttle away from her.

Fighting amusement as well as frustration, Cade urged her back more. "Hey," he whispered, "you're giving away too much. No need for them to know you care."

Nostrils flaring and expression red with antagonism, she said, "Well, I *do*."

Cade couldn't help it. He laughed. Leave it to Star to growl that declaration at him with murder in her eyes during a violent altercation. "Good to know."

She blinked, then shoved away from him. "You have a warped sense of humor."

"Maybe." He put his mouth to her ear so the downed goons wouldn't hear. "Now get it together, *Francis*."

It took her a second. Then she gave a stiff nod. Just as low, she said, "I want credit for letting you handle things."

His eyes flared.

Unconcerned, she pointed out, "I didn't jump to your defense right off since I saw you had it handled. You can thank me."

"Thank you."

She nodded and moved on. "No phones?"

"Let me check Ward. I have a feeling he's the head of this comic trio." Sure enough, once he'd roughly gone through Ward's pockets, he found an old burner phone, a slip of paper with the bar's name scrawled on it and a nearly empty wallet.

There were only three numbers saved in the phone, none with contact info. He toed Ward with his boot. "Who's going to answer if I call these numbers?"

"Those two," Ward said, giving a slight nod toward his brother and Paulie. He didn't have much range of motion with his face in the gravel.

"And the third?"

Ward's face tightened.

"Need some incentive?" Cade asked. "I suppose I could turn her loose on you. Let her bloody up your face a bit, but I should warn you, she's damn strong and has a solid punch—"

"Mattox," he snapped. "It goes to Mattox." Then in a whine, "Dude, he's going to kill us."

"Mattox is the least of your worries right now." Cade wanted to ask about Adela, but the bar would open soon and customers would start showing up. He still had to clean up this mess. Besides, the clowns on the ground around him didn't look like the type to have any real info.

"What are we going to do with them?" Before he could answer, Star said, "FYI, I called for backup. Should be here any minute."

Renewed anger rushed through Cade. He said one word. "Who?" If she'd called the cops, that'd be a huge problem.

Cocking her head, she listened, then looked out at the road. "That's probably him now. Yup, it is."

Reyes pulled up and without a word joined them, his gaze going over each man. "From Mattox?"

"Yeah." Relieved that Star hadn't brought authorities in on things, Cade still said, "I could have handled it."

"Women," Reyes commiserated, just to rile her. "Guess she was worried about you."

And of course it worked. Star gave him a killing glare. "I still have my knife."

Hands in his back pockets, Reyes pursed his mouth, then shifted his gaze to Cade. "Gunning for her?"

"It's what they said."

Star jammed her fist at Reyes, showing off the brass knuckles. "They were going to use these on him."

His mouth twitched. "Pisses you off, huh? Well, no worries, doll. I'll handle them."

Her eyes narrowed. "By *handle them*, you better mean beating them to a bloody pulp!"

"If that's what it takes," Reyes promised, taking a pack of nylon cuffs from his pocket.

Snorting, Star said, "You're a little overprepared, aren't you?"

Shrugging, Reyes said, "You were all hysterical—"

"I was not!"

"So I thought there might be a mob or something." He grinned at her blustering indignation. "Now, why don't you wait in the bar? I'll handle this."

"Ugh." Face flushed, she snatched ties from him and stomped over to Kelly to deftly bind his hands behind his back. It roused him, but Star was already working on his ankles, pushing up his jeans, dragging down his socks so the nylon was tight against his skin. He wasn't going anywhere.

"Ward?" Kelly struggled, twisting his head to try to see his brother. "What's going on?"

"We're done," Ward groaned. "Done."

"So much drama." Reyes was quick, and a little brutal, in how he bound Ward. Then he quickly gagged all three of them. Hoisting Ward over his shoulder, Reyes carried him to his truck and dumped him in the bed none too gently.

It took a little time to get them secured to grommets and concealed with a tonneau cover. It was a tight fit in the short bed, but bound and gagged as they were, no one would discover them.

Appearing a little worried, Star asked, "Where are you taking them?"

"Someplace private, where I can do a proper interrogation."

She bit her lip. "Will you kill them?"

Reyes slowly grinned. "Now you're worried about that? Just minutes ago you wanted them annihilated."

"Forget it." She started to stomp away.

Reyes caught her arm—then shocked her by pulling her into a hug. "Rest easy, hon. Once I've found out what I can, I'll hand them over to someone else."

"Who?"

Arms folded, Cade leaned back against the truck and explained, "We have contacts who'll make sure they're off the street and that they're legally punished for their part in Mattox's plans." Interesting that Star allowed Reyes to hold her. Was it possible she didn't dislike his brother as much as she pretended? If they got along, it'd make things easier.

For Star.

"They won't die, though," Reyes assured her.

Shoulders relaxing, she glanced at Cade. "You said it yourself, they're boys. If anyone's going to die, I'd rather it be Mattox."

With another hug, Reyes said softly, "I'm glad you're not quite as bloodthirsty as you pretend." Not giving her a chance to blow up on him, he released her and headed around to the driver's side.

Cade put a hand to Star's back and together they followed. Lower, so the men wouldn't hear, he said to Reyes, "I took a cheap phone off one of them. I'll give you time to get well away from here before I call the three numbers."

"If you call now," Star mused, piecing it together, "they might realize their plan backfired. They could set a trap to attack—"

"Me on the road," Reyes finished. "I'd almost like them to try." He looked back at the truck bed. "That is, if I didn't have cargo."

Nodding, Cade explained what he'd learned from Ward. "I think he's telling the truth about those numbers, that one will lead to Mattox, but I'll let you know."

Reyes nodded at Star's hand. "Plan to keep that little decoration?"

She curled her fingers around the thick brass knuckles. "Yup."

Shaking his head in a laughing way, Reyes got in the truck and drove off.

"Come on." Cade drew Star around to the bar door. He wanted her safe inside before he got more distracted with details. "We'll give it fifteen minutes so Reyes is off the worst of the winding roads. Then we'll call."

"We?" she repeated, as he relocked the door behind him. Strolling to a barstool, she took a seat, her long legs stretched out, one elbow resting on the counter.

She looked sexy as hell sitting there. Part of it was that she took the attack in stride. Star was unlike most people; she didn't fall apart under pressure, and in fact seemed to gain an edge.

Except when she'd lost it a little over those brass knuckles. He didn't want her worried about him, but he also enjoyed the show of concern.

Sidetracked for a moment, he asked, "What did you say to Reyes when you called him?"

Rolling her eyes, she gave a soft laugh. "He's a damn doofus— and a giant liar. I was *not* hysterical. Can you even imagine?"

No, he couldn't.

"I gave him the facts—maybe I gave them a little quickly, you know? I told him we'd pulled up to the bar and three guys tried to jump you."

"Just like that, huh?"

"Mostly like that. But yeah, I didn't know if there was a fourth or fifth around somewhere, or if Mattox was hiding nearby with a gun. So I told your brother to get his butt over there in case the tide turned." She rolled a shoulder. "Didn't take me long to realize you had it under control—which is kind of astounding, I have to say. Wimpy guys or not, it was three to one, with a pipe and a chunk of wood, but in no time, you had it all well in hand."

So it was a chunk of wood they'd broken over his back? He hadn't been sure. In the long run, it hadn't mattered. "Appreciate the vote of confidence." He went behind the bar to start prepping. Workers would show up shortly. They wouldn't have long alone.

"It's earned." She turned on the stool to keep him in her sights. "So the number we're going to call?"

"I assumed you'd want to be a part of it."

"Part of it? You do realize I'm the one who should call, right? I mean, in case Adela answers. She'd hang up on you, but there's a chance she'll talk to me. And if she does, she might give something away. I might even be able to goad her into losing her pretense of being a victim. It's worth a shot."

Actually... "You're right." After he finished the bar prep, he checked the time, poured them each a cola over ice and set the cell phone on the counter between them. "On speaker."

"You betcha." Almost rubbing her hands together, she opened the screen, went to the first number and pressed to dial it.

"IF ANY EMPLOYEES show up early, we can step into the office."

"Got it." With Cade leaning close, Sterling listened as the phone rang and rang... No answer.

"One down," she said, aware that her palms were a little sweaty. "Probably went to his brother or Paulie, as Ward said."

Cade lifted her chin. "You have great instinct, babe. I've told you that enough times. If anyone answers, just go with your gut. You've got this."

His confidence helped shore up her own. Yes, she could do this. If it was Adela, she'd play her part depending on what the other woman said or did.

Drawing a breath, Sterling moved on to the next number. Each ring caused her tension to notch up.

Again, no answer. Crazy that this was making her so nervous. They were away from the danger for now, and even better, she had the dynamic McKenzie family as backup. Whatever rolled out, it'd be fine.

But she knew, of course. Her frazzled nerves were based directly on one particular McKenzie. A specimen of the first order, impossibly strong, remarkably fast, unshakable and... He hadn't denied that they were "a thing." That made the risk about more than just her, because now it was about *them*.

That made it so much worse.

She'd already discovered firsthand that seeing him hurt sent her into a tailspin.

"Two strikes," Cade said, and he brushed his thumb over her cheek. "Third has to be a charm."

Sterling nodded and pressed the last button.

Immediately following the first ring, a deep voice growled, "Tell me you have her."

Ah. Mattox. Amazingly enough, her nervousness left and she settled in with a smile. This she could handle—as Cade predicted, her instincts kicked in with a vengeance.

"Hello, Mattox."

Silence, then a snarled, "You fucking bitch."

Sterling actually laughed. "What? You figured I'd be stuffed in a trunk by now or something?" That thought struck her, and she glanced up at Cade to mouth, "Car?" How had those three hoodlums arrived at the bar? In the middle of the chaos, she hadn't even considered that.

Cade shook his head and whispered, "Later."

Unaware of her sudden distraction, Mattox said, "I thought I'd have my hands on you any minute. It would have been such a pleasure—for me."

"So those boys you sent after me were planning to meet you somewhere?" She sat up a little straighter, all teasing gone from her tone. "Tell me where and I'll come to you right now, you miserable pig."

"I don't think so," he said with a laugh. "I'll get you soon enough."

"Really? How do you think to do that? You must be running out of lackeys by now. How many have I already brought down?"

Mattox snorted. "I doubt you've done any real damage, sweetheart. More likely your hulking bodyguard—but he won't be around forever."

The thought of him getting hold of Cade sent a wash of ice through her veins. Cade wouldn't appreciate her fear, and Mattox would try to use it against her, so she purred, "Oh, please. Please, underestimate me. It'll make gutting you so much more satisfying."

Cade shook his head. Apparently he didn't want her goading Mattox quite that much, but hey, too late to pull back now.

"So where's Adela?" Sterling asked. "Is she standing right there, listening to our conversation?"

"Is that what this is?" Mattox replied. "A conversation? I thought it was me telling you how fucking bad you're going to suffer before I cut your throat and watch you bleed out. You want to hear details?"

Aware of Cade's hands curling into fists, she said, "Not particularly."

Of course, that didn't stop Mattox. "I have plenty of men left—and they'll each get a turn with you. Might have to make them draw straws to see who goes last, because by the end there won't be much of you left."

Though her stomach turned, Sterling laughed. "That's a lot of bold talk for a dead man." She hesitated, but the timing felt right, so she added, "Especially since you tried handing me out once already, and all you got for your troubles was a corpse."

Like the ticking of a bomb, the tension stretched taut—until it detonated. *"You fucking whore!"* Mattox roared. "You're the one who got away!"

"Ding-ding-ding!" All pretense of calm shredded away as she got to her feet and smirked down at the phone. "I recognized you right off, big disgusting ape that you are. But you had no idea, did you?"

He snarled something low, but then snapped, "That was years ago, when I was still starting out. After all this time, the meat starts to look the same."

God, she wished she could kill him right now.

Cade took her hand and held it. Strong, steady, sexy Cade. He was counting on her, and she wouldn't let him down.

When she didn't reply, Mattox asked, "Do you have any idea of the trouble you caused me?"

Ah, it bothered him that he hadn't made her lose her temper. Good. Sterling smiled. "The upside is that when you're dead, your troubles will be over."

"You think you're smart?"

"Smart enough to get to you when you least expect it. There's not a hole deep enough for you to crawl in, not enough men to watch your back, to keep you safe. You better sleep with one eye open, because the second they both close, I'll end you."

He hung up and Sterling wanted to pitch the phone. Instead she peeked at Cade and asked, "Did I go overboard?"

Eyes like the center of a flame and jaw clenched tight, he drew her forward to lean over the bar. "I will never let him touch you."

Wow. She hadn't even realized his temper had risen. He'd seemed so cool during the call. He tried to act cool now, too, but yeah, she saw all that fierce rage in his eyes. "Er...thanks?"

Not amused, he put his mouth to hers. And proceeded to devour her. Holy smokes, possessiveness had really gotten his engine revving.

To soothe him, Sterling stroked the side of his face.

He let up but kept her close, his forehead to hers. "Sorry."

"No worries. Kind of turned me on."

He looked into her eyes—and laughed. "There can't be another woman like you in the entire universe."

And just like that, he lightened her mood. Unfortunately, a knock at the back door interrupted them, and shortly they were joined by employees, and then customers, too.

They had a lot of plans to make. Mattox would be coming for her—or rather, he'd send more men after her. Odds were, he'd try to take out Cade first. Obviously Mattox knew Cade, maybe even recognized him from the church.

She bit her lip, thinking about that. It was time to follow through on that trap, and if it required using her as bait, Cade would just have to get over it.

Talking him around wouldn't be easy, but she figured Parrish, Reyes and Madison would agree. They'd vote on it or something, she'd win, and finally she'd get the chance for her revenge. Now that Mattox had crossed her path again, she had to end him or die trying.

Once that was done, what would happen with her and Cade? She didn't know. For now she'd have to take their relationship one day at a time.

She glanced over at Cade as he served two pretty women sitting at the bar. The women flirted, their expressions showing awe, but then, Cade was such a big dude he had that effect on a lot of people.

He smiled at them, but it was his patented polite smile, not the kind he gave to her—the kind full of secrets and shared lust and so much more.

Over the next few hours, in between customers, Cade used the phone. Each time he held her gaze while quietly talking.

Strangers came in, putting her on guard, but no one that acted suspicious. They drank, talked and left.

She was starting to think it'd be a quiet night, and she even considered dozing like old times.

And then the call from Adela came in.

CHAPTER FOURTEEN

"FRANCIS?"

She blinked, for once unsure what to say. "Yeah... Adela?"

"Oh, God, I was so afraid you'd be dead." Voice shaking, Adela whispered, "I knew he was trying to get you, and I'm so sorry. I couldn't figure out how to warn you."

Sterling caught Cade's eye to let him know what was happening, but he was stuck in a crowd. It'd take him a few seconds to get away, so she moved out of the main room of the bar and into the hallway where she could better hear.

"Are you still there?" Adela asked frantically.

"Yeah. So..." What to say? "I'm surprised to hear from you."

"I'm sorry, Francis, but listen to me. He's hiring men. A *lot* of men. He said he knows where to find you."

Sterling really didn't trust the woman. Not that she ever had completely, but now? She accepted Reyes's take on things, yet the thinnest doubt remained. Having been in captivity once herself, Sterling understood better than some how you said and did things that normally you would never consider.

Doing those things had allowed her to escape.

They'd allowed her to survive.

Was Adela trying to escape—or trying to entrap her? Sterling didn't want to believe that another woman would be so cruel, but too many things didn't add up. "How do you know all that?"

"I don't have much time. He'll be back in a minute, but I was able to listen through the door. He's...*enraged.* Francis, God, the things he's planning to do to you..." She started to cry.

Damn it, that sounded real enough.

"It's all my fault," Adela sobbed. "I shouldn't have involved you."

Twisting her mouth, Sterling considered things. It'd probably be best if she didn't question Adela's motives, so instead she asked, "How does he plan to get me?"

"He said he knows where you live. Or will know. I'm not sure. He plans to follow you, I think. Oh, Francis, you have to be careful. You should just go away—" Suddenly Adela screamed.

It sounded like the phone crashed to the floor. Sterling heard a man's voice. *"Stupid bitch."* Loud thumps. Slaps.

Worse.

With her heart caught in her throat, Sterling heard Mattox snarl, "When the hell will you learn?"

Frozen in horror, Sterling listened to Adela's hysterical, babbling voice, pleading, crying out... She winced at a louder crash, and then—deafening silence.

Her heart hammered in her chest.

There was rustling, and then, "Is that you, Francis?"

Sterling didn't reply. Anger roiled inside her, helping to settle the fear and upset.

"She's bleeding," he said, his tone taunting. "If she dies now, it's your fault."

The call ended.

Blindly, Sterling stared at the floor, trying to assimilate what she'd heard and what she knew.

"Hey." Joining her, Cade slipped both hands around her neck. "What's happened?"

"I don't know." She shook her head. "Something. Or maybe nothing." She gazed into his stunning blue eyes. "Either Mattox just beat Adela badly, or they're working together and want me to... I don't know. Act hastily? Or just feel bad, maybe."

"If you're mired in guilt, you can't think clearly." He drew her into his arms. "Whatever happened, none of it is in your control."

"But what if Adela is innocent? What if she really was trying to escape?"

"Reyes didn't think so."

She pushed him back. "Reyes could be wrong!"

"Could be, but probably isn't."

For once his calm, in-charge tone annoyed her. She was ready to lose it, and Cade was unaffected. "I still want to know for sure."

"I have some news that might help." He kissed her forehead, then took her hand and led her to the office. Once inside, he closed the door and leaned back on it, his arms folded over his chest. "The three stooges gave up a few locations before Reyes handed them off."

"Locations for Mattox?" Finally, some good news! "Why are we still standing here? We should check them out."

"Reyes is doing that right now."

"He's one man! He can't be in three places at once."

"No, but my sister can. Remotely, that is. She's able to tell which buildings are occupied, which ones have activity."

Sterling didn't ask how. So far as she could tell, Madison had scary tech ability that'd be well over her head. "And?"

"An old house seems more likely than the other two. Mattox hasn't survived this long by being careless, so odds are he'll be relocating real fast. If Reyes gets lucky, he might be able to follow him, find out where he holes up."

That sounded beyond perilous. "What if he gets caught?"

"Worried about Reyes now, too?"

"You aren't?"

Taking mercy on her emotions, Cade admitted, "A little. He'll check back in soon."

How long was *soon*? Pacing, Sterling absently took in the room. Neat, of course. A solid but plain desk, comfortable chair—and the short sofa he'd offered her for napping. "We need to find out how the men got here today. There weren't any cars in the lot. Did they park somewhere close by?"

"Actually, they told Reyes they were dropped off so we wouldn't see a car and be alerted. They were to use my own SUV to bring you in."

Her mouth went dry. "You mean us, don't you? Bring *us* in?"

He looked away. "They don't want me, honey. I'd only be in the way."

No. Charging up to him, Sterling went on tiptoe to say, "Don't you dare act indifferent about someone trying to kill you."

For the longest time Cade just stared at her. "You understand the situation. You don't need me to tell you anything."

No and no again! Fear pushed her away from him. She needed distance to think, a way to lessen the awfulness of that possibility.

Cade caught her before she got far, pulling her into his arms and holding her when she tried to get away. "Why is it you can handle it if someone threatens you, but this is a problem?"

Her laugh sounded almost hysterical. "You, dead? No, I can't handle that at all."

His expression softened. "Did I look in danger of dying?"

No, he hadn't. He'd dealt with those men as easily as he would have children. *But they won't all be that way.* "You're not invincible, you know."

She felt his smile against her temple. "I know. But I am highly trained for all situations, so the odds will always be in my favor."

Right up until they weren't. God, she felt sick.

"We need to stop and think now, okay?" He led her to the couch and sat down with her. "While I have Rob covering for me out front, tell me everything Adela said. We'll sort it out."

Because she wasn't sure what else to do, Sterling started at the beginning of the call and gave every grisly detail until she finished with what Mattox had said.

The calm retelling aided her, giving her a new perspective. "They might have wanted to panic me."

"If Adela is working with him."

She nodded and met his gaze. "I have to know for sure."

"We all do, okay? None of us takes chances with the lives of innocent people. That's first and foremost."

Yes, she'd realized that right off. Cade and his family were the good guys—and they were far better organized than she could ever hope to be on her own.

Calming even more, Sterling asked, "So do you have a plan?"

"I do, and it involves luring them in. Letting them think they have the upper hand, when in fact we're the ones in control."

"Awesome." It sounded like they were thinking along the same lines. "It's like I said, right? Use me as bait, but I'll be safe because you guys will be on it."

His expression went blank. Then a second later he scowled. "Close, but I'll be the bait instead of you."

"What? *No.*" If he'd thought it through, he'd already know why that wouldn't work. "They want to *capture* me, but you they want *dead.*"

"They'll take me alive, hoping it'll help them get to you."

"You can't know that!"

He kissed her fast before she lost her cool all over again. "I have to get back out to the bar, but I promise you, Star. We'll go over every detail, and we'll all be in agreement before anything is put in motion. Does that work for you?"

What could she say? It worked for her only because she'd never agree to anything that dumb. But damn it, she had joined their little group, and what if she got outvoted, instead of the other way around?

Hand to her churning stomach, she gave a grudging nod, but deep in her heart, she had a very big problem.

She'd already fallen in love with Cade McKenzie—and nothing dicked up clear thought like an overblown emotional attachment. Well, hell.

KNOCKED TO THE FLOOR, her jaw aching, her lip split, Adela scooted to sit against the wall. Thacker entered the room quietly, keeping a wide berth around Mattox, and handed her a cloth filled with ice.

Busy watching Mattox, she didn't thank Thacker. He looked nervously at Mattox, then sidled out of the room again, closing the door softly behind him. The cell phone, probably busted, lay on the floor between them.

Mattox was out of control in a big way. She hadn't lied about that. The floor shook beneath his stomping stride.

He'd made two turns around the room, knocking furniture out of his way, before he paused in front of her. "You okay?"

"Yes." Quickly, not trusting his feet, she stood but stayed against the wall.

"That shouldn't have happened."

"It was her fault, not yours." She tried to smile, but the swelling in her cheek made it difficult, and with him glowering at her… "She infuriates you. I understand."

Taking her wrist, Mattox lowered her hand to see her face. Whatever he saw tightened his mouth in disgust. "She's going to pay. For everything."

He said it like a promise, so she replied, "I… I know."

"We have to relocate, the sooner the better. Be ready in five minutes."

Adela watched him storm out. He had a mercurial temper, but his rages didn't last long, thank God. She'd probably be dead already if they did.

When she knew he was far enough away, she picked up the phone. The screen was cracked, but it seemed to work still. Not that she had anyone else to call.

"Sorry, sugar. My plans got changed." Sitting in yet another car, one of ten that Parrish had purchased for different occasions, Reyes stared through the windshield at the front of the old house. Patience might be his weak link. He detested downtime. If he had his druthers, he'd just plow into the house, find Mattox and beat the prick to death.

Unfortunately, no one wanted him to do that, least of all his father. The plan was to bring down the whole shebang, not just one man, but damn. Stakeouts were boring as shit.

"Reyes," she complained. "I already had dinner planned."

Seeing movement behind the front window, Reyes narrowed his eyes and said in distraction, "Sorry, Annette. I'd be there if I could."

"You could come over when you get done with…whatever you're doing."

"Family stuff." He lifted the binoculars and looked at those windows more closely. Yup, that was definitely shadows shifting. "I'll have to eat on the fly."

"So we won't do dinner first." Her voice went low and throaty. "I'll still be here all night."

"You're tempting me, doll." Unfortunately, he couldn't afford a distraction. "It could be late."

"So wake me when you get here." She added in a singsong voice, "I'll be naked."

A quick visual flitted through his mind. Annette's curly blond hair and sexy smiles, big boobs and shapely legs... "Sold." Yes, he was that easy when it came to sex. "If I can wrap it up before midnight, I'll be there. But if I'm a no-show, it won't be lack of interest for that intriguing offer, okay?"

"I'll make it worth your while."

The front door opened, and Reyes rushed to say, "I do enjoy how you tease. Gotta roll now, but keep the motor revving for me." He disconnected the call before Annette could say anything else.

Four people came out of the house. First was Thacker, the slimy worm, and he didn't even try for subtlety as he searched the area, a gun already in his hand.

Behind him was Mattox...*dragging* Adela along with a bruising grip on her wrist.

Well, hell. The binoculars gave him a very clear view of Adela's battered face. Someone had socked the lady, and none too gently. Head down, short brown hair tangled and shoulders slumped, she followed meekly to a clichéd black sedan, where Mattox shoved her into the back seat.

Frowning, Reyes wondered what had changed. Did he need to reevaluate the situation?

He rubbed his chin, sorting through it all as he'd been taught.

No, he wouldn't make up his mind, not yet. Not until he had more to go on.

With that thought, he tailed the car from a safe distance, checking constantly to ensure he hadn't picked up a tail himself. That's what he and Cade would have done. Switched it up. Let someone think they were following along, while they were actually being followed.

A short time later, he called Cade. Soon as his brother answered, Reyes said, "Best as I can tell, they're heading back to that cabin in the woods, near Coalville."

"Ballsy," Cade said, "since we're already aware of that area."

"Yeah, but it was a good hideout, and situated where it's easy to spot anyone coming or going. If it came to that, they could hide in the mountains, or in one of the old coal mines, plus I can't follow them there. They'd be onto me in no time."

"For now you're safe?"

"Yeah, just rode past. I'll circle around a few times, just so they don't catch on to me. Then I'll hang out an hour or so to make sure they're not moving again."

"I want you to be extra careful," Cade said. He explained about the call Sterling had gotten. "Mattox is unhinged, and I have no idea what's going on with him and Adela."

"Yeah, as to that… Someone knocked her around. The scene was total opposite of the other day. Fucker dragged her out of there and she looked cowed."

"Shit."

"Yeah, hard to read them, but I retract my earlier conclusions, at least until I can see more—which might be difficult with them hiding away. Doubt there's any electronic eyes there for Madison to pick up. Hell, might not be Wi-Fi, either."

Cade didn't answer, but Reyes knew the silence meant he was thinking. Cade was like that. Quietly methodical in all he did, whether it was plotting or kicking ass. Impressive stuff. He'd always admired his big brother, but no, he wasn't much like him.

Cade could handle a stakeout all day and never lose his edge. Sometimes it was eerie. He didn't know what the military had done to his brother—but then, Cade had always been somewhat remote. Deep. A loner.

Sad part was, he dealt with women the same way—or at least he had until Sterling charged in. He grinned, just thinking about it.

She was one hell of a surprise.

Not that his brother avoided female company. Hell no. But a relationship? That was the shocker. Anyone who knew Cade could see he'd staked a claim. The amusing part was that Sterling seemed every bit as possessive.

"Star is worried," Cade said, interrupting Reyes's thoughts. "Mostly because she's not sure of things, either. I trust her impressions on this, so I think it's more complicated than we first considered."

"I agree she's sharp." Reyes took an exit to circle back and make another loop. "I just got an idea. If Madison could come up with an eye of some sort, I could sneak in later tonight and hook it up. Maybe at the main entrance to the town. It's one dusty road, right? Should be easy enough to do, and then we'd at least get a heads-up if Mattox leaves there. If Madison has anything super high-tech, we might even be able to tell if he leaves alone or with Adela."

"Good idea, the sooner the better. You want me to get hold of her to ask?"

"Just so you can relay to me? No, I'm already bored to tears. I'll make the call."

Without comment on his complaint, Cade said, "Then keep me posted. And I mean, posted as in every hour or less. Star isn't used to worrying, but she's worried about you."

His brows shot up. "No shit?" The grin came slowly. "Now, ain't that sweet?"

"Check in," Cade ordered again, "and let me know what Madison has to say."

"You got it." As he drove past, he did see Thacker just departing, but Reyes was close enough to see he was alone. So he'd dumped Mattox and Adela somewhere inside the town or up in the mountain? Without transportation? Or was Thacker just running an errand?

He called his sister and explained the situation, adding with concern, "There's not a lot of light in this section—"

"I know just the thing," Madison said, and it sounded like she was on the go.

"I'm guessing we'll probably need three of them."

"Perfect," she enthused. "I've got it covered."

"It needs to be something I can install superfast."

"Won't take me more than a few minutes to get them each going."

"What— *Whoa*." No way in hell did he want Madison getting physically involved. "You won't be installing them."

"Course I will. You can keep watch. I think you're forty-five minutes from me, but I'll leave within five. I'll call you when I'm close so we can meet up. No reason we can't sneak in there together."

Talking tech always excited Madison, but Reyes wasn't at all keen on her being in the same vicinity as Mattox. "We'll meet and you can talk me through how to do it."

"Byeeee," she said, and the call ended.

"Son of a…" Reyes cut short his discontent, knowing it wouldn't do him any good. If he could figure out exactly where the three cameras should go, he and Madison could get out of there quickly. Thinking of what they needed to know, and what would be least dangerous for his kid sister, he chose a post next to the railroad tracks—it would catch anyone attempting to arrive or exit that way. The second could go on a telephone pole but would require him standing on his car to get it high enough so it wouldn't be noticeable. That'd exclude Madison.

Under the overhang of the shabby church would be the perfect spot for the third camera because it would also catch anyone coming down the mountain on the narrower trail. But did he dare let Madison do that? Could he stop her?

Probably not.

He wouldn't let anything happen to her, though. They'd use extra care, which meant it'd take a little longer, but he'd deal with it, and Annette would just have to deal, too.

Once he had that worked out in his mind, he drove south to the next exit, found a gas station a mile down on the right and called his sister.

"I'm on my way," she assured him. "Where do we meet?"

He gave her directions, then tried insisting again, "I'll put up the cameras."

"Reyes." Exasperated, she stretched out his name. "I have to be there anyway to ensure they're properly connected and that I can access them. The three I have are motion activated, but that could still mean an animal, a bird or even a tree branch moved by the wind would kick them on. I'll be able to remotely clear recordings, which will be on my server and impenetrable from outside, so that we don't have a cluttered feed."

Making a winding motion with his finger, Reyes said, "That's all over my head. I'm talking about actually getting them mounted—"

"I want them done a certain way. You can ensure no one sees me."

"You realize you sound as stubborn as Cade."

"Thank you." With laughter in her tone, she said, "Love you, brother. See you shortly." Again, she disconnected him.

Sisters, he grumbled to himself. Yes, he knew he was sexist—most especially when it came to a baby sister he loved. Did he know she was capable? Yup, he did. Was he confident she could do it with or without his help? No doubts.

But that didn't mean he wanted his sis in the line of fire. Not if he could help it.

Couldn't stop her, though. Madison was sweet, but she didn't put up with any macho crap. So he slumped in his seat, drummed his fingers on the steering wheel and waited.

She arrived sooner than he'd expected, which was good, since he'd already been away from the site too long. Typical of Madison, she immediately took charge, but at least she allowed him to drive. They rode to the site together, all the while with her chatting about the cameras and what they could do.

For the most part, Reyes tuned her out, uninterested in the technical details that fascinated her when he'd rather work out the logistics of getting her safely in and out of the area.

He just knew Cade was going to have his head, being he was ten times more protective than Reyes.

Fortunately for him, he was able to park down the tracks away from the small main road, close enough that they could sneak into Coalville on foot, unnoticed. Since she insisted on installing each one, he had to hoist Madison onto his shoulders to get two of the cameras in place, but she was incredibly efficient, as well as silent, in getting that completed. After only a few brief adjustments, she wrapped it up.

As he lowered her back to the ground, she whispered, "Now I just need to connect them to my device so I can transfer it all back home and voilà—I'll have eyes here."

"You're so clever," Reyes murmured absently, while constantly scanning their darkened surroundings. So quiet, not even a rodent stirred.

Sort of electrified the small hairs on the back of his neck.

If he didn't have Madison with him, he'd creep around a little, see if he could figure out exactly where Mattox had hunkered down, maybe discover if Adela was okay.

But not with her along for the adventure. "Let's go." Reyes nudged her forward, considerate of her slower pace while she picked her way over the rocks and rubble.

When they reached the car, they both did a quick check around it, ensuring they hadn't been discovered. Madison flipped on her phone light just long enough to see that no one had hidden in the back seat. Then they went dark again.

Reyes drove slowly without headlights until they merged onto the interstate. He flipped them on and released a tight breath at the same time. "I'll take you to your car." And he'd follow her home, just to be extra safe.

Annette would keep, or not. He wouldn't leave his sister's safety to chance.

He checked in with Cade a few times, and yeah, big brother was all PO'd over Madison being involved at the site. Reyes listened, and since he didn't disagree, what could he say? "It wasn't *my* idea."

Cade still chewed his ass, but in that controlled way that sounded more like a disappointed father—as if he needed two of those. "Next time, I'll call you and you can try your hand at talking her around."

Cade exhaled sharply, but said, "Be safe tonight."

Rolling his eyes, Reyes said, "Yeah, same to you."

It was two long, grueling hours later before he got to Annette's front door. She'd left the outside lights on for him, making him smile. Since he had a key, he let himself in without a sound.

Unlike him, Annette was far too trusting.

Not in a million years would he give a key to anyone other than family.

Inside, he flipped on the foyer lamp. The house was quiet, and he didn't sense any threats—something he always checked—so he slipped off his shoes and started down the hall.

Her bedroom door was open, and with the light from the foyer barely filtering in, he saw her slender form in the bed, stretched out on her stomach...and naked as she'd promised.

Already getting hard, Reyes caught the edge of the sheet and slowly pulled it to the foot of the bed. Annette shifted to her side, curling her luscious bod to keep warm.

Yeah, he'd help her with that.

Without taking his gaze off her body, he removed his wallet and placed it on the nightstand. Quietly, he set his gun beside it. Then his knife. Annette knew not to touch his weapons, but he always put himself between her and them anyway.

He peeled off his shirt and tossed it to a chair, then opened his jeans and tugged down the zipper.

Annette opened her eyes, purring sleepily, "Reyes?"

"You expecting anyone else?" If so, he wouldn't stay.

Going to her back, she whispered, "Come here."

"Yes, ma'am." He finished stripping and climbed in beside her.

Out of the three women he currently visited, Annette was the most affectionate. Cathy, an exec in the business world, wanted her booty calls scheduled in advance, and he had to be prompt. Unlike Annette, Cathy wouldn't tell him to come by whenever.

Lili loved to call him when the mood struck her. If he was available, fine; if not, she moved on to the next guy.

Annette would do the same, but she always swore he was the best. And after sex, she wanted to laze around together. She wasn't clingy—none of them were, or he wouldn't visit them—but she did enjoy an extra closeness.

Tonight, he wouldn't mind that, either.

Her hand snaked down his chest and went straight to his dick. "Mmm, already ready for me?"

"I was ready the second I stepped in the door."

Laughing softly, she kissed his chest, his ribs…and slowly worked her way down.

Annette had an *amazing* mouth, meaning his night would definitely be more rewarding than his day had been.

CHAPTER FIFTEEN

STERLING WAS EXCITED about seeing Reyes's gym this morning. It was yet another facet of the whole McKenzie operation, and she wanted to learn as much as she could.

It might give her a leg up in dealing with Parrish, because she was pretty sure their relationship would take some adjustment.

Relationship. With Cade. With his siblings and father. With the awesome Bernard. She wanted to hug it all to her chest and cherish it for however long it lasted.

She was always cautious when she went out, but Cade took it to a whole new level. Getting jumped last night hadn't helped. He'd been extra attentive in delicious ways, but she knew he'd also strained his injury. His father hadn't been pleased this morning when he insisted on checking things, but he wasn't really the doting sort, either. More like a sour general.

Getting from the bar to her apartment so she could get some things last night, and then back to his father's house, had taken twice as long as it should have just so Cade could backtrack twice, his way of guaranteeing no one followed them. By the time they'd actually gotten to bed, she'd been exhausted.

Not *too* exhausted, not when Cade had stripped down and curved around her, all hot and hard and keenly interested. She'd taken quick advantage of that and the incredible pleasure he offered.

But she felt the lack of sleep catching up with her today.

Good thing they were doing something fun.

A massive front window showed the interior of the gym where Reyes stood on a mat instructing two men. He wore only shorts and wrestling shoes, and she had to admit he was a good-looking guy.

"What's he teaching them?"

Cade shrugged. "I'm guessing basic defense."

Through the window, she watched as the guys went into a stance. Reyes continued to instruct, right up until both men charged him.

Her brows climbed up in delight as Reyes lowered a shoulder and tossed the heavier of the two men. Just as quickly, he tripped the other. While Cade's brother still stood there instructing, the other two men sucked wind from their backs.

Sterling laughed.

"Amusing, right?" Cade put an arm around her and steered her to the door. "We can watch for a while, or you're welcome to try out the equipment."

More interested in seeing than doing, Sterling shook her head. "I'm not dressed for it."

"There's not a dress code, babe." As he often did, he stroked along her spine down to the small of her back over the soft cotton T-shirt she wore, then down to the seat of her faded jeans, where he lightly copped a feel of her backside. "Other than your boots, you're fine. You'd just need to remove them before you stepped on a mat."

One of these days she'd get used to all the familiar touching, but it was going to take a while. Trying not to show how deeply he affected her, Sterling asked, "You know all this stuff, too?"

"I do."

She leaned into him. "Then I'd rather you teach me."

His slow smile did crazy things to her. "It'll be my pleasure."

It was nice to know that his brain stayed centered on sex as often as hers did.

A sign on the door read "Walk-ins welcome, but we can't guarantee all equipment will be open."

Once she stepped inside, she knew why: the place was packed.

The interior was more spacious than she'd realized. Every inch utilized in one way or another by sweat-damp people ranging in age from late teens to early sixties, male and female alike.

In the back section, heavy bags hung from reinforced beams and, beyond that, speed bags. It appeared to be mostly younger males using those. Stationary bikes lined one wall, occupied by women and elders. Various racks of weights and bars, with a few benches, took up the opposite. One of the men doing bench presses had grotesquely huge arms...especially in comparison to his thin legs.

Cade whispered, "No balance. Reyes has tried to tell him, but he focuses on that one exercise and won't do anything else."

Sterling snorted, then glanced around at the women. A few of them seemed mostly concerned with looking stylish, standing around in their cute clothes and chatting. Others were clearly there to work out, their hair in ponytails or clips, sweat dampening T-shirts or sports bras.

One gal in baggy sweatpants, an oversize T-shirt, shoulder-length blond hair held back with a wide band and earbuds in her ears, popped her neck as she walked to a heavy bag. She wore fingerless gloves and shin guards.

She looked absurd in her getup but didn't seem to care—and that impressed Sterling.

"I'm going to talk to Reyes a few minutes," Cade said. "Want to join us?"

"I'd rather look around." Whatever they discussed, Cade would tell her later. Why risk letting Reyes provoke her temper when she didn't need to?

With a long look, Cade said, "Stay where I can see you." He touched her cheek. "Everyone in here is probably fine, but Reyes can't know each person, and I'm not willing to take chances right now."

"You don't think you'd notice someone dragging me out the front door?"

His fingers spread, threading into her hair and cupping her head. "There are two back doors, one out of a break room and another at the end of the hall near the bathrooms."

Ah, yeah. If she went to the bathroom, and someone was waiting… "I'll stay within range if you will, too," she promised, then sauntered off.

Something about that other lady drew her. As Cade had noted, she had good instincts. Something inside her screamed that the woman had trouble on her heels and could use a friendly face.

Often Sterling felt that way with the women she helped. She was good at reading them, at knowing what to say and when, whether to push or just wait.

Odd, but she hadn't quite felt that connection with Adela, or at least not consistently.

Finding one heavy bag unoccupied, she gave it a tentative push. The woman stood next to her, giving the bag hell—and ignoring Sterling. She seemed intent on abusing her legs. Even though she wore shin guards, Sterling winced.

With the earbuds in, she couldn't really give a friendly "Hey" to break the ice, so she moseyed on. But her gaze repeatedly went back to glimpse the woman working. She was so intense, so focused that Sterling couldn't help but be impressed.

And worried.

Fifteen minutes later, while she idly examined a weird contraption that looked too complicated for her to figure out, Cade and Reyes joined her.

So much for avoiding the annoying brother.

And with him stripped down so much, ignoring his presence wouldn't be easy.

As if he'd read her thoughts, he said in a singsong voice, "Hi, Sterling."

With a roll of her eyes and a sigh, she turned to him. "What's up, troublemaker?"

Reyes grinned. "Let's head to the break room. I could use a cold drink."

"First…" Damn, Sterling really hated to involve him, but if he knew the woman, maybe he could put her worries to rest. "So, don't stare, but the lady back there, kicking the stuffing out of the heavy bag?"

Curious, both men glanced that way.

"You guys suck, you know that?" Hands on her hips, Sterling scowled at them. "I said don't stare, but you both did."

"There's staring, and then there's *staring*," Cade said. "Besides, you didn't specify it was anything like that."

She rolled her eyes.

With his gaze still on the woman, Reyes asked, "What about her?"

Already frowning, Cade gave her a longer look, too. "Something's off."

Sterling nodded. "Fear is working her hard."

After a lengthy perusal, Reyes cursed softly. "You're right."

It reassured Sterling that she wasn't imagining things. "Do you know her?"

Reyes shrugged. "She's been coming in for about a month but keeps to herself."

"So no?"

His mouth flattened. "No."

"Huh." She'd expected Reyes to have some snappy comeback, but instead he looked displeased. With her? No, with himself. Digging a little, she said, "Haven't hit on her, huh?"

That got his eyes narrowed. "This is my gym. Think what you want of me, but I take my pleasure elsewhere."

His sincerity made Sterling feel a little bad for deliberately provoking him—but *only* a little. "Scruples. Bravo." Aware of Cade grinning and Reyes growling, she turned to keep the woman in sight. "She's not here to stay in shape, or to bulk up or trim down. She wants to know how to hurt people."

Cade slanted a look at Reyes. "Told you she was astute."

"I never denied it." Propping his hands on his hips, Reyes asked, "If she wants to learn offensive moves, why didn't she ask for instruction?"

"Maybe because you look like that?" Sterling nodded at his body, and when she did so, she couldn't help eyeballing his sweaty, naked torso. Not out of interest, but because he really was a specimen.

She noticed him the same way she might a really nice pair of stilettos. She appreciated the style, but you'd never catch her wearing a pair.

Rocking back on his heels, Reyes asked, "What the hell is that supposed to mean?"

"You're intimidating." Much like Cade, Reyes had muscles everywhere. Not overblown, but very defined. His eyes were hazel, like Madison's, instead of electric blue like Cade's, but they were still nice.

He was almost as tall as Cade, too, but he wore his dark hair a little longer, and his attitude was a lot less restrained.

"I've never intimidated you," Reyes pointed out.

She grinned. "I'm not the average woman."

"True enough." Laughing, Cade drew her into his side. "You're above average."

Reyes groaned. "It's almost nauseating the way you two fawn all over each other."

"Oh?" Feeling devilish, Sterling asked, "So I know how to bug you, while getting awesome benefits at the same time? Sweet." Even as she spoke, she cuddled closer to Cade and walked her fingers up his chest.

"Hey, I run a reputable business, you know," Reyes mock-complained. "Take that foreplay elsewhere."

Cade reached for him, but he ducked away, then asked, "So you think my size has put her off?"

Sterling wasn't sure if he threw that out there because of real interest or just to get her off molesting Cade. But whatever, she'd save the good stuff for when she had Cade alone.

"You are big," she admitted.

He and Cade both grinned, and she knew exactly what they were thinking.

Willing herself not to blush, she spoke before Reyes could. "But it's not just because you're tall and fit. You're...sexual?" Considering that, Sterling shook her head. "Yeah, not a great word, but you know what I mean."

Both brothers now stared at her, prompting her to roll her eyes again. "A woman who's unsure of men wouldn't want to approach someone as cocky as you."

More disgruntled by the minute, Reyes said, "I'll have you know, plenty of women like me just fine the way I am."

"I bet they do." She snickered. "The thing is, the same reason why those other women like you is probably why that one prefers to watch a video or something on her phone. At least, I think that's what she's doing. See how she keeps looking at the screen and repositioning her stance?"

Cade nodded. "Trying to mimic the moves...but not really doing them correctly. It's tough to figure out without in-person instruction."

While Reyes was distracted watching the woman, Sterling sent her elbow into his stomach. "You need to offer."

"Ow, damn." Scowling, he rubbed his side. "Maybe, but not now. She's heading out."

Without being obvious about it, they watched the woman walk to a duffel bag she'd left in the corner near a wooden bench. She dug out a bottle of water and took a long drink. After storing it away again, she located a small blue towel, which she used to dry the sweat from her face and arms. Then she removed her earbuds and unplugged them from her phone, stripped off the protective gear and stuffed everything into the bag, located keys in the front pocket, and started for the door.

Judging by the frowns the brothers wore, they didn't like having to wait any more than Sterling did, but Reyes was right—stopping her would seem too presumptuous, especially when she already seemed...well, not exactly skittish, but more like reserved. "You're sure she'll be back?"

"She's been here every day for a month," Reyes said. "So unless you scared her off with all that staring—" This time he dodged her elbow. Laughing, he predicted, "She'll be back. And yes, I'll see if I can figure out a way to offer."

"Thanks." Looking up at Cade, she asked, "You two finished your talk?"

With a nod, Cade took her hand. "You want a tour around the place, or would you rather head out?"

"A tour." She added to Reyes, "I'm impressed, by the way. Nice place you run here."

Grabbing his chest, Reyes pretended to stagger, but the second Sterling turned away, he mussed her hair and took the lead. Anxious to show her around? It seemed so. Little by little, she was starting to like Cade's brother—or at least she was learning to tolerate him.

Reyes strode ahead of them, and yup, the back view of him was impressive, too. Nowhere near as nice as Cade's, but she glanced around and saw many of the women looking their way. Sterling they didn't even see, because Cade and Reyes held all their attention.

And here she was, right in the middle of them.

Overall, not a bad place to be.

THE NEXT MORNING, wearing snug shorts, a clingy tank top and battered sneakers, Star looked entirely different—and downright edible. Cade watched as she twisted her long hair up onto her head. He couldn't take his eyes off her. No matter what she did, or how she dressed, he found her irresistible.

But like this? Her body clearly outlined under the close-fitting clothes, those long, toned legs on display... He wasn't a saint. Far from it. And right now, he'd rather take her back to his room, where they could both get naked.

The more he had her, the more he wanted her.

It was like an addiction—Cade's first, since he avoided vices. This vice, though, sating himself on Star's unique brand of sex appeal, he didn't mind at all.

The plan was to spar here in the privacy of his father's private gym so he could assess her ability, fine-tune what she already knew and teach her a few new tricks.

Most important, she had to be able to defend herself. If anything should happen to him, which was unlikely but still possible given his vocation, he needed to know Star would be okay.

"Quit primping," he finally said, knowing it would rile her. "If someone attacks, you won't have time to put up your hair."

She snorted and strode out to the middle of the mat. "You might have to pay for that."

Banking a grin, Cade joined her, then easily ducked the swing she threw and followed it by tripping her to her back.

Instead of being annoyed, she stared up at him with a smile and a droll "That was slick."

Little by little, he got used to her attitude. She got angry when someone tried to take over, him included, but she was always up to learn something new and didn't mind being instructed.

Or tripped to her back.

Cade held out a hand. "Your turn to try it." He showed her the moves, when to pull, how to use her feet in combination with her hands and body, and by the third try, she nailed it.

"Good job," he praised as he rolled back to his feet. "Especially since I'm a lot bigger."

Her mouth twisted to the side. "You *let* me do that."

"To see if you could, yes. While I'm coaching, that's the best way. We'll get to the hard-core stuff soon, I promise. One step at a time. Okay?"

"If you say so." She got into her stance. "Ready when you are."

For the next hour they practiced hard, and by the end, Star was a lot smoother. No matter how many times she hit the mat, she didn't get frustrated or angry.

She brushed herself off, asked pertinent questions and tried again.

She had so much moxie it made him want her even more. How was that possible?

Groaning, she rolled to her back. "I think I finally understand it. Thanks for not losing your patience."

Amazing. How many women—or men, for that matter—would thank him for repeatedly tossing them to their backs? Star was unique because her motives were unique, and they aligned with his in a way he hadn't expected to find. Definitely not with a woman he desired.

She wanted to be highly trained to successfully attack, defend and rescue those in need, even against the most insurmountable odds. Her mettle impressed him, as did her dogged attitude.

"Hello," she teased. "Yoo-hoo, Cade. You still with me? You're just staring."

Shaking his head, he squatted down beside her and got back to the business at hand. "That's one move," he explained. "We'll work every day until you have a cache of ingrained responses. The idea is for it to be automatic. What one person does triggers what you do, preferably without you having to think about it."

"That's what you do, huh? The other night at the bar, it amazed me how easy you made it look."

Drawn by the way her sweat-dampened shirt stuck to her

breasts, how the waistband of her shorts rode low to reveal a strip of her flat, damp stomach, he felt himself stirring.

"Bad example, because they weren't much challenge at all. With trained men, it'd be a little tougher."

Her lips quirked. Still breathless, she pushed a hank of hair off her temple and asked, "Tougher, but not impossible?"

Cade couldn't claim an ounce of modesty, not when it came to his ability. "I'm good."

Her voice dropped as she purred, "At many things."

That did it. He started to reach for her, but she utilized the move he'd taught her and lunged for him instead.

Laughing, he countered it by catching her to him, then rolling her to her back to come down over her, pelvis to pelvis, his hands holding her breasts but his elbows catching some of his weight.

Eyes gone heavy, she asked, "Is this a legit move?"

"Damn right," he said, devouring her mouth with a kiss that made him forget about further lessons. Star always tasted so good, and now her exertion had intensified her scent. As he breathed her in, it added to the sudden onslaught of lust.

When he moved to kiss her throat, she whispered, "Then I'm glad it's you teaching me instead of your brother."

Reyes? Jealousy slammed into Cade, and he reared back to scowl at her—only to see her barely repressed grin. He should tell her that joking like that wasn't allowed. He opened his mouth—

Taking swift advantage of his distraction, she bucked him to the side and straddled his hips.

Laughing in triumph, she said, "That was a joke, for crying out loud."

"I'm not sure it's funny."

She only laughed harder. "All's fair in love and war."

Thoughtful, Cade caught her waist to keep her still and asked, "Which are we?"

Her expression shut down at the question. "Um…"

Yeah, maybe he shouldn't have asked that. Star was still skittish about any references to their relationship. He knew he had to go slow, to give her plenty of room.

Every day that got a little harder.

For now, he slowly grinned, then flipped her again and said, "You're too easy."

"Jerk." She smacked his shoulder, then blanched and carefully pulled aside the neckline of his shirt. "I keep forgetting you're wounded. Maybe because you don't act like you are."

"I forget myself. It doesn't hurt anymore." When he was this close to Star, his physical need blunted everything else.

He started to kiss her again, but she protested. "No. I'm gross with sweat. Let's go shower first."

Clearly she was getting used to being in his father's house. One of these days he'd have to tell her that he had a place of his own. He hadn't yet because he didn't want her to insist on leaving.

If Star weren't with him, he'd be home alone right now, but Mattox's last threats had been extreme and they didn't yet know what was going on with Adela. He hadn't said it to Star, but they'd take care of that soon. Another reason to stay here. Being in his father's fortress during a sting was not only the safest place to be, but it also provided the quickest way to get info.

While they were still sprawled together on the floor, the door opened and Reyes and Madison stepped in.

Seeing them entwined, Reyes quipped, "Not sure that form of defense will be effective."

Maybe he needed to teach his brother a new lesson, Cade thought as he moved away from Star. She sat up but didn't yet say anything.

"Got any gas left in the tank?" Reyes asked her.

She rolled her shoulder. "Could be. Why?"

"I want to give it a go."

"Nope."

"Chicken?" Reyes asked.

Slowly, Star looked up. "If you persist, I'll agree. But I strongly advise you wear a cup, because I'll go after your vulnerable spots full force."

Scowling, Reyes tucked his hips back, his hands protectively folded over his junk. "That's not how you spar."

"That's how *I* spar—with you." Her smile looked evil. "I have wicked knees." She clenched a hand. "And my fist isn't too bad, either."

"Damn." Reyes turned his accusing gaze on Cade. "What the hell are you teaching her?"

Already grinning, Cade held up his hands. "I'd say the animosity was taught by *you*."

"Men and their precious jewels," Madison complained. She kicked off her shoes and stalked closer. "Come on. I'll go a round or two with you, and the boys can observe."

Star's smile slipped. "I don't think—"

"I'm trained," Madison promised. "But I'd prefer not to get my lady parts wounded, so how about we make this a teaching moment? Cade and Reyes can then offer suggestions. They are good at this sort of thing, you know."

Brows up, Star looked at him for confirmation. Cade nodded. "Madison knows what she's doing, and she is good, so why not?" He gave Reyes a shove that nearly took him off his feet. "Even my brother occasionally has valuable input."

Under her breath, Star grumbled, "It's the audience I object to," but she got to her feet and quickly tucked loose hairs into her topknot. With a glare at Reyes, she said, "No color commentary, got that? Just pertinent facts."

"Yes, ma'am." Then he said to Madison, "Go easy on her."

Star drew a big breath, got in a stance—and barely stopped Madison when she shot in on her.

Standing next to Reyes, Cade watched Star deflect one move after another. To his brother, he said, "She's actually better than I realized now that she's with someone closer to her own size."

"She's fast," Reyes agreed. Then with a sideways glance at Cade, he added, "But how often will she get attacked by someone smaller?"

True enough. Madison was shorter than Star, though both were tall, but she was probably thirty pounds lighter. Where Star was sturdy, Madison was delicate.

His sister compensated for that with speed and agility, and a refined skill in technique. He could see that both women had forgotten about the men watching while they enjoyed the combat.

Star, especially, looked invigorated. She even laughed a few times, either when she missed Madison, or when she caught a hit or kick.

Reyes stepped closer, calling out to their sister, "Wrong leg. Left...*now* the right."

"Block it," Cade countered to Star. "That's it. You have to immediately move."

"When she reaches for you, grab... Yeah, that's it."

Star had tried grabbing Madison's wrist, but Madison knew that move and how to counter it. She locked her own hand over Star's and pivoted, and Star ended up with her arm twisted behind her, forced to her knees.

Cade briefly stepped in to show Star how to avoid that trick. He encouraged them to go through the same scenario three more times before he was satisfied that Star had it down.

Once she'd nailed it, he had them reverse so that Star knew how to use the move to subdue an attacker.

"She's a quick learner," Reyes said.

Without taking his eyes off the women, Cade nodded. "A natural survivor. Always has been."

"Didn't have a choice?" Reyes asked without his usual caustic humor.

"No, she didn't." Distracted, Cade said, "You're being defensive, Star, instead of offensive. Don't try to escape until you have control."

This time Reyes demonstrated, and with him in teacher mode, Star didn't seem to mind.

Life would be easier if those two got along. Ignoring him wouldn't do her much good, would in fact only encourage Reyes to ramp up the taunts. So far, Star had managed by giving as good as she got, and Cade had a feeling she'd earned Reyes's respect because of it.

More kicks were thrown, punches blocked.

"How about another lesson?" Cade asked. "That is, if you're both up for it?"

"Sure," Star immediately said, rolling her head to work out a kink in her neck, shaking her hands to loosen them up again. "I'm game."

"Fine by me," Madison agreed.

"This one might work better if Reyes takes part." He beckoned his brother to the mat.

Reyes stepped in with a grin, rubbing his hands together. "Which one is my victim?"

For that comment, Madison kicked his feet out from under him. Since Reyes wasn't expecting the attack, he went down, but he shot right back up with a laugh, pointing at his sister and saying, "Sneaky. And you already know payback is hell."

While he shared that silly threat with Madison, Star got an impish look in her dark eyes—and copied his sister's move so that Reyes went down again. This time he sprawled out with a chuckling groan. "They're ganging up on me, Cade! Get control of this lesson already."

"You're a good sport," Star said, her wide smile proof that she was having fun.

As if requesting help, Reyes raised a hand to her, but she backed away shaking her head.

"We're not both fools," she laughed.

Loving the way Star fit right in, Cade drew her close for a quick kiss, then explained what he wanted them to do. "Reyes is going to behave himself for this demonstration, isn't that right, brother?"

"Me? Maybe you failed to notice that I'm the one on my back?" Saying that, he rolled to his feet and gave both women a *try me* look. They snickered but didn't engage.

"Reyes is going to invade your space."

"You got it," Reyes said, knowing the lesson and stepping in close to Star—at least until she leaped back. "Hey, I can't show you if you don't let me get hold of you."

Rife with suspicion, Star asked Cade, "Why can't you demonstrate?"

"You're too comfortable with me." He thought of the expression on her face after she'd joked that all's fair in love and war. And without thinking, he'd replied, *Which are we?*

She'd looked ready to bolt, and it bothered him, because Star didn't run from anyone or anything. Love? Yeah, he was there, but clearly she wasn't.

Not yet, anyway.

He'd sway her eventually by building on their shared inclinations and showing her how great they'd be together.

With that goal in mind, he gestured for Reyes to continue.

This time, Star went stiff, but she allowed him to put his arm around her and crush her close into his side—just like a creep would do.

"Now," Cade said, walking her through the process of freeing herself. It took a few tries, especially since Reyes wasn't making it easy for her. Then she nailed it, getting a firm grip on his brother's wrist, ducking under his arm and, in the process, twisting his hand up behind him. Immediately, she put her foot to Reyes's ass and shoved him forward, giving her the opportunity to flee...if she'd been in real danger.

Madison applauded.

Reyes did, too, actually, but Cade tried to keep it on point by saying, "If you try that move, be ready to race away as fast as you can, but keep in mind that it'd only work if you're in a congested area where you can quickly find help."

"Or if your attacker is severely out of shape," Madison added. "It's a disgusting reality that *just* fleeing isn't usually the best option."

"So let's give me a weapon," Reyes suggested, "and you can show her how to take it from me."

Intrigued by that, Star held up a hand while breathing hard. "Give me five. Then we can try that."

That's how they ended up working an hour more, with all of them involved in one way or another. Twice she'd successfully taken the dummy knife from Reyes. The concept was the same with a gun, and eventually they'd practice that, too.

But for now, before Star completely collapsed, Cade called a halt. He and Reyes were fine, but then, they took physical training to an extreme. The women, however, looked completely spent.

Hands on her knees, sucking in air, Star said, "That was invigorating."

"Right?" Madison agreed, gulping her own breaths. "I got more of a workout with you than I ever do with my brothers."

"You two are more evenly matched," Cade said. "That's a good thing, but also problematic."

Reyes stepped forward to offer them each water. "You did great, Sterling. You have a natural ability, but Cade's right. Next time we need to wear protective gear so we can really push it. You were both holding back. Cade and I sometimes do the same for simple sparring, but the best way to learn is to go full force."

"Sweet," Star said, accepting the water and chugging it down. "What kind of gear?"

"Headgear and face protector, for starters," Cade offered. "It'll ensure against broken noses or cracked jaws while you practice face strikes. Mouthpiece to protect teeth. Some pads would help, too." His family always took self-defense seriously.

"Sounds good." Star finally straightened, still breathing hard, yet smiling. "The better prepared I am, the more I like it."

Madison grinned, too. "My sentiments exactly." She tossed a towel to Star. "Give it a few days, and then we can work on marksmanship, as well."

And speaking of that… Cade took Star's hand. "You can shower in a minute, but first I want to show you one more thing."

As they crossed the length of the lower level, all the way to the other side, Reyes and Madison followed along. It made Cade wonder if Parrish knew they were congregated downstairs. No doubt he did, because not much slipped past his dad, but he wouldn't take part in giving Star the tour of their armory. Later, perhaps over lunch, Parrish would weigh in with his thoughts—and no doubt judgments.

Didn't matter. Star would be working with Reyes and Madison, and that's what he'd wanted.

Things with Mattox would come to a head very soon. Madison kept a log of movement. They wouldn't stay hidden long, and they all needed to be prepared.

CHAPTER SIXTEEN

NEVER IN A million years would Sterling have guessed that she'd one day be in a freaking mansion practicing lethal skills with three totally badass people. Talk about unbelievable things to happen... This one would top her list.

Reyes had actually been fun, and Cade was such an amazing teacher. Everything he did fascinated her even more.

Plus, she loved it that Madison was *so* incredibly proficient—which meant that, one day, Sterling could be that good, too. It gave her a rush, made her blood sing and had her eyeballing Cade hungrily, wondering when she might be able to get him alone.

How working herself into a sweaty mess and turning her limbs to noodles could make her hungry for sex, she didn't know, but then again, there'd been a lot of close contact with that big hunk she currently got to call her own. What red-blooded woman wouldn't react to all those warm, straining muscles, the incredible scent of his heated skin, his sexy take-charge attitude and bone-deep confidence? Cade was the whole, delicious package, and she wanted to gobble him up.

Reyes and Madison were still following along, and Sterling knew she needed a shower, but she figured if he wanted to show her one more thing, she may as well indulge him. He'd certainly indulged her long enough, teaching her so many valuable moves.

He led them all to a back room that appeared to be mostly

empty, with a few crates and storage boxes stacked around. There was no drywall on the walls, only exposed studs.

Sterling wondered if there was something in one of the boxes that Cade wanted to show her—until he pressed a concealed lever on the floor and a section of wall swung open, exposing another room behind the insulation.

Eyes flaring wide, she slowly stepped inside to take it all in. Holy smokes. The hidden room was smallish, maybe eight by eight, and it was utilitarian in design—linoleum floor, concrete walls... and an astounding display of weaponry. "You have an arsenal."

"We're prepared," Cade countered.

"For your own private war?" She didn't say it as a criticism, more in awe. Strolling along the back wall, Sterling took in rifles, revolvers, handguns of every make and model. Grenades, smoke bombs, flash bombs. Long knives and switchblades. Tasers and batons. She also noted helmets, body armor, camo and utility belts. "This is remarkable." On another wall, ammo filled multiple shelves, surely enough to last them for a good long while.

Madison and Reyes stood aside, silent and watchful, apparently leaving this introduction to Cade.

That worked for her. In fact, she'd like it even better if they gave her some privacy with Cade, but she knew that wasn't going to happen. They might quibble with one another, but the siblings were close. Probably came from protecting one another.

"I'm fascinated," she said, to put them all at ease. "Impressed, too, and I'd love to try every one of them." She ended her circuit of the room in front of Cade. "Got some specific reason for showing me this?"

He put his hands on her shoulders. "We don't leave things to chance, so if Mattox doesn't make a move very soon, we'll go after Adela. I want to know that you can protect yourself—when I'm not available to do it."

Aw. That was sweet. Surprisingly, it didn't insult her. Facts were facts, and although she'd already known it, today's practice reinforced that Cade was far better trained for combat. Being military, that made sense. But of course, he'd taken it well beyond that. She'd never met another person so wholly equipped to handle danger of any sort.

He and his siblings were trained pros, and she was not.

Sterling accepted that she had a lot to learn. One day she'd love to be on a par with them. Until then, she liked that Cade would look out for her—if it became necessary. Knowing he wouldn't let her be hurt made her feel better about being bait to lure in Mattox. Sure, Cade still thought he'd do the honors, but she'd talk him around somehow.

Her plan made more sense.

She smiled. "Thank you." *For so many things.* Getting close, she hugged him tight. "*Now* do you think we can get that shower? I'm ready to melt in my own sweat."

Reyes laughed, and a definite note of relief resonated in the sound.

Had they expected her to be shocked—in a bad way?

She wasn't. If anything, she loved that they were so well prepared to care for others. It was what she'd always wanted to do, had tried to do, but obviously they did it better.

"That's my cue to head out," Reyes announced. "I'm already running late for the gym."

"And I need my own quick shower before I get back to monitoring things," Madison added. "Bernard will only cover for me so long before he loses interest."

Once they were alone, Cade closed up the room and led the way to his suite.

Taking his hand, Sterling pulled him into the bathroom and clasped the hem of his clinging T-shirt, tugging it up and over those scrumptious abs, broad chest and rock-hard shoulders. She paused at the sight of his injury. It didn't seem to bother him, but the skin around the stitches was now more discolored. "I hope you didn't overdo it."

Without replying, Cade finished tugging off his shirt, then returned the favor by removing hers and her sports bra, as well.

Breasts bared, Sterling trailed a finger over one of his tattoos. She wanted to trace the design with her tongue, and thinking about it sent a curl of desire through her. "I've been worrying about Adela. I'm glad we won't wait to save her."

"If she needs saving."

Yeah, there weren't any certainties yet. "Reyes said she was hurt. That's enough for me."

"I know." He opened his hand on her cheek. "As long as you don't try anything on your own, we can push it whenever you want."

Nice, so he'd leave it up to her instead of Parrish? That was an unsettling idea. After all, they had a smooth-running outfit. She ran more on emotion.

But thinking logically, she got the idea of throwing a wider net. That method would ultimately save more women...but could she sacrifice Adela for a possibility that may not pay off? "How do you feel about it all?"

Without hesitation, Cade said, "I don't like it when things don't add up. Something is going on between them, I just don't know what."

And that made it riskier. If she had to worry only about herself...

"What?" he asked, his thumb brushing the corner of her mouth.

Guessing how he'd react to her thoughts, she smiled. "Every time I see you, I'm struck by how lucky I am."

That got him refocused real fast. "You think I'm any different?" In rapid order, he removed the rest of her clothes, even kneeling down to tug off her sneakers. "Every part of you, Star, this—" he ran his hands up her bare legs, around to her backside to draw her in for a kiss to her stomach "—but also the way you smile, your core strength, your occasional insecurity and your bold attitude—"

"Hey," she protested shakily. "I'm not insecure." *Liar.* She knew she sometimes was, and apparently he knew it, too. But he didn't disagree. Strong and bold, those were attributes she didn't mind.

"The way you argue," he added, with a nibble to her hip bone. "God, how you smell, how you feel—I love all of it, everything about you, inside and out."

Her lips parted. *Love.* Earlier, when he'd teased about love and war, she'd at first gone blank...and then accepted it as a joke, nothing more. But this? The way he looked at her now?

Honest to God, Sterling didn't know what to do, what to say. She knew how *she* felt, but him? She didn't have a clue. "You confuse me."

Smiling, Cade rose back to his feet. So tall. So damn strong. So freaking impressive in every way.

As he finished stripping, he said, "I don't know why you'd be confused. You're sexy, smart, quick-witted, strong, compassionate—"

Embarrassed heat flushed her face. "That's enough."

"Not even close." Taking her shoulders, Cade turned her away from him so he could free her hair. His fingers were gentle as he loosened the band and slid it free. "You're a remarkable person in so many ways. Do you honestly think I can be around you without wanting you?"

Wanting, sure. She wanted him nonstop, too. But he'd mentioned *love* again. Frowning, she turned to face him. "Instead of standing around talking, how about we make use of that warm shower? Together."

Cade pressed a soft kiss to her mouth. "Love the way you think."

Her eyes widened. Did he use that damn word on purpose now?

With a lazy smile, he turned on the water and got out two towels. A little numb, Sterling stepped under the spray to soak her face and hair. She needed to stop gawking over the things he said. She also needed to know if he meant anything substantial by it, but she was too cowardly to ask.

Getting in behind her, Cade took the shampoo bottle from her. "Let me."

Why not? If she was going to stand there feeling stupid, she may as well let him take over.

And take over he did. In diabolical ways.

Massaging the shampoo through her hair was somehow very erotic, especially when she felt his powerful body behind her. Cade made her feel small—and very feminine. It was unique for her, and her hormones loved it.

After she'd rinsed her hair, he picked up the soap and, keeping her back to his chest, proceeded to clean her.

All over.

Slick fingers worked her nipples until she couldn't breathe. Her breasts felt heavy, so sensitive that she trembled all over. "Cade..."

"Shh." He kissed the side of her throat. "I love touching you."

She groaned at his insistent use of *love*, but she couldn't muster up a real protest. Trying to distract him, she moved her backside against his erection, but being the man he was, he lightly sank his teeth into her shoulder.

Delicious sensation prickled all over her body, every nerve ending electrified. Good God, she felt close to coming, and all he did was play with her breasts. "Let's go to bed," she pleaded. *Pleaded.* It was both appalling and exciting that he'd reduced her to that needy voice.

"Not yet." He licked the spot where he'd given her a love bite, and those broad, slightly rough hands coasted down, over her stomach, her thighs, between them...

Pressing back against him, Sterling tipped her head to his strong shoulder.

"That's it, babe. Don't fight me."

Fight him? What a joke. He was bigger, stronger and currently far more in control.

"Feel how slick you are?"

Very aware of her body's response, she gave another small groan. He pressed a finger into her, worked her carefully, then pulled out only to add a second finger.

She clenched around him. It felt so good—but she wanted more than his fingers. Reaching back, she clamped a hand onto his thigh to ground herself. With her other hand, she covered his and pressed his fingers deeper, then moved sinuously against him.

She was close, so close, if he'd only—

Cade pulled away, then repositioned her. "Lean against the wall. That's it. Now open your legs."

Eyelashes spiked with the shower spray, Sterling looked at him through a haze of lust—and did as ordered.

Lowering to his knees, Cade touched her again. Her breasts, down to her belly, lower, exploring, and pressing his fingers in again. Nuzzling against her, he found her clit and licked.

"Oh, God." Sterling locked her knees, her eyes squeezed shut, her head back...

He drew her in, sucking, teasing rhythmically with his tongue while keeping those long fingers thrust deep—on and on it went until an incredible climax crashed through her. Like, literally *crashed*, stealing the strength from her limbs, wringing a harsh cry from her throat, putting tears in her eyes even.

Luckily the shower would hide that, but wow. She tunneled her fingers into his close-cropped hair and rode out the pleasure until she felt herself slipping down the wall.

Cade caught her hips and stood in a rush. His mouth on hers, his tongue delving, that solid erection pulsing against her belly.

She reached for it, but he caught her hand, lifted it to his mouth for a tender kiss and said, "Not this time, babe. I'm too close to acting stupid."

Gulping breaths, Sterling managed to get her eyes open. A tiny bit, but enough to see that the blue of his eyes had turned incendiary. Curious, she whispered, "Stupid...how?"

"Forgoing protection."

"Oh." He turned away before she admitted that she wouldn't mind. Actually, the idea of feeling him and only him sparked a new stirring deep inside her.

In extreme haste Cade washed and rinsed, then turned off the water, grabbed the towels and pressed one against Sterling's chest.

"I would do the honors, but I need you too damn much. Get dry, or close to it, and let's go to the bedroom where I can grab a rubber."

Her mouth twitched with a secret little smile of happiness. She'd never seen Cade so frazzled.

She'd never been wanted that much.

Her heart expanded, making her chest feel tight with emotion. Lazily, while watching him, she dried off, then flipped her hair forward and wrapped it in the towel.

She was still bent forward when Cade hoisted her over his shoulder, making her laugh.

"I like the way you lust for me," she admitted. "Especially since I lust for you so much."

"Good to know." He put her on the foot of the bed so that her legs hung off the end, then strode to the nightstand to grab a condom and quickly rolled it on. "Turn over."

Since she was already on her back, she blinked. "Do what?"

Without waiting for her to understand, he flipped her to her stomach and kneed her legs apart.

Curious, she lifted up on her arms to look back but went flat again as he gripped her hips and drove into her.

He filled her completely and was already thrusting, lifting her up to meet him each time he sank deep. His thighs met the back of hers, his firm abdomen slapping against her softer backside. Another climax started to build, and she knotted her fingers in the bedding.

"Star," Cade growled low, the sound almost tortured. "Can't wait." Reaching around and under her, he found her clit again, did no more than lightly pinch, holding her like that as he continued the hard rhythm, and far too quickly they were both coming.

It was so deep this way, his thrusts more powerful, and she loved it. Every second of it.

Because she loved him.

This time the knowledge didn't frighten her. Heck, she was now too exhausted to be frightened. Her thoughts were blessedly free of any angst. Even long-buried fears seemed to have evaporated, leaving her utterly replete.

Resting over her, still in her, Cade murmured, "Every time."

"Hmm?"

"Every time…is somehow better."

In total agreement with that, she sighed. "Mmm."

She felt his smile on her shoulder, then the tender kiss he pressed there before he pulled away.

Sterling wasn't sure she could move, not even for an earthquake, but Cade took care of it, cleaning her with his towel, then scooping her up and placing her in the bed, even tucking her in. He kissed her forehead and whispered, "Be right back."

It was the last thing she heard…until he woke her sometime later.

AFTER ARRIVING AT the gym an hour ago, Reyes had repeatedly lost his concentration.

It was her fault. That cute little mystery woman.

Even while listening in on a trio of knuckleheads talking about some underhanded business—one that could pertain to his family's pursuits—Reyes couldn't keep his eyes off her.

She appeared to be close to his age of thirty—maybe a little younger. Honey-blond hair swung loose to her shoulders, dipping and swaying each time she landed a kick or threw a punch.

Improperly.

He chewed his upper lip. She did okay, and she put plenty of effort into it, but her stance was off. To get the best impact with her strikes, and to avoid getting thrown off balance, she needed to lead off with the other leg. She also let her hands drop each time...

Why the hell was he still dwelling on her?

He heard one of the guys say, "Seriously, man, easy cash. Just gotta be ready to pull the trigger."

Ears perking up, Reyes listened more closely.

"I traded my hardware a month ago," another complained.

"Damn, G, they'll give ya the firepower to protect the deal."

"What kind of deal?"

"The fuck does that matter?"

Reyes silently sighed. *G?* As in *gangster*? What a misnomer for the strung-out, scrawny fool sporting very amateurish tattoos all up and down his skinny arms.

"I don't know, man. I got that bum beef already. Don't wanna be messin' around."

"There'll be four of us," the recruiter continued. "Meetin' out at some farm. I was gonna catch a ride with you."

While listening, Reyes studied the woman.

What curves she lacked up top, she made up for with a really stellar ass.

Suddenly her attention snagged on him with a nasty glare.

Oops. Busted.

Busted looking at her *butt*. Definitely not cool.

Even all narrowed with annoyance, her blue eyes were nice— a soft color, thickly lashed.

Dismissing him, she turned away, which made his gaze return to that premium part of her anatomy. She didn't get back to work, though; instead she stood there with her hands on her hips, her shoulders set in annoyance.

He hadn't meant to interrupt her workout...but he also hated to miss anything else the knuckleheads said.

He heard "Aspen Creek," but the rest was indistinct, and now they were heading out, spines bowed, feet shuffling.

One of them glanced toward him. Reyes met his gaze. "Can I help you?"

"You seen Mort?"

Having no idea who Mort might be, Reyes lied, "He usually shows up later in the day."

"Tell him I was lookin' for him, yeah?"

"And you are...?" For certain, they hadn't come to his gym to work out, but then again, it's why he had the place, so cretins like that could pass along info.

"Hoop."

Novel name. "You got it, Hoop. You want to leave a number?"

"He has it."

Reyes looked back at Will, who manned the desk. "You see Mort come in, tell him to call Hoop." Then he walked away from Will's confusion, because Will had no idea who Mort was, either.

Satisfied, the two-bit thugs left.

Reyes waited until they were out of sight before he went to Will. "If you see anyone named Mort, let me know."

Will had learned not to ask questions, so he just nodded. He was a good worker, always showed up, and because Reyes paid him extra, he knew to keep his mouth shut and his eyes open.

The mystery woman regained his attention.

Guessing that she wouldn't linger much longer, Reyes moved toward her through the crowd. Occasionally he answered a quick question for a patron, all the while keeping his gaze on her.

He was pretty sure she felt his attention, but she didn't look at him again, not until he reached her.

Lips tight—very plump lips, he couldn't help noticing—she pulled out her earbuds and draped the cord around her neck.

Damn it, he never hesitated to speak his mind with women, but with her being so unapproachable, he floundered.

With a resigned sigh, she looked up at him and asked politely, "What?"

"I'm Reyes McKenzie, owner of the gym—"

"I know who you are."

She did, huh? But he noticed she didn't introduce herself. He rubbed his neck, shifted his feet like a friggin' schoolboy and waited.

This time she rolled her eyes before saying, "Kennedy Brooks. I've signed up for a year, but if there's a problem with my membership—"

"There's no problem." Surprised him, though. Most didn't choose the yearly option. In this part of town, people sometimes didn't know from one week to the next if they'd have money or time. Most of his clientele was fluid, which was how his father had planned it. Lots of people coming and going made it easier to catch information from the street.

He'd tell Will to let him know from now on whenever they sold a big membership.

"Kennedy." Somehow the name fit her. She probably stood five feet five, making her damn near a foot shorter than him. "You need any help?"

She shook her head. "No, thank you."

He should have walked away, but he didn't. With Sterling's certainty in his mind, Reyes said, "If you want to defend yourself—"

"Just getting in shape."

Complete BS. She'd said it too quickly, and she didn't meet his gaze. "I don't think so."

She'd just been ready to punch again but paused at his reply. Slowly, she turned to face him. Crossing her arms and cocking out a hip, she looked him over with mere curiosity.

No interest. Nope. Just like…she wondered why he was still bothering her.

Reyes sighed.

She half smiled. "Why do you say that?"

"I've been watching you," he explained, hoping that'd lead into more.

"I noticed you watching," she replied, with no invitation to extend the conversation.

Well, too bad for her.

"I was watching because I see the difference between getting in shape and learning how to fend off attackers."

"Huh." Very sexy lips curled. "Well, that confirms something for me."

For whatever reason, he found himself stepping a little closer to her. "What's that?"

Her chin lifted. "You're not a mere instructor."

Her insight nearly blew him over, but he quickly recovered. "I already told you, I own the gym."

"So?" She rolled a shoulder. "You're more than a mere gym owner, too."

He opened his mouth, then closed it. Her lips were *really* distracting, especially when curved in a superior smile.

"You think you're the only observant one here? No, Mr. McKenzie, I notice things, too."

"Reyes." Mr. McKenzie was his father, for Christ's sake.

"Like you listening in to those young toughs. I noticed that, as well. Did you hear anything insightful?"

Well, hell, this lady was dangerous. "I give my attention to everyone who comes in."

"Yes, there's attention, and then there's listening in on a conversation to ferret out info." She gave his own words back to him. "I see the difference. So, Mr. McKenzie, how about you mind your business and I'll mind mine, and we'll get along just fine."

Well... He really had no idea how to react to that, so he merely saluted, said, "Carry on," and stalked away. He wasn't running, but it did feel like a strategic retreat.

This time he felt her gaze drilling into his back.

Later, he'd give Sterling hell. For now, though... Kennedy intrigued him even more. He couldn't get her off his mind—and the fact that she didn't pack up and leave immediately, that she stuck around, glancing at him every so often, felt almost like a dare.

Or an invitation? Not likely.

He wouldn't act on it anyway, not yet. He didn't want to be a creeper who bothered the clients. But he wondered if she reconsidered her stance, maybe she'd approach him next time.

It was a nice little fantasy, one that included him getting his hands on that plump backside... Shaking his head, he retrieved his cell phone and sent Cade a message about what he'd heard. Four guys probably didn't mean anything, but a farm in Aspen Creek might. Never hurt to share the tidbits he heard.

He'd just finished when Will called out to him. "Hey, Reyes, you have a call."

As he headed to the desk, he decided it was time to get his mind off a certain prickly-but-somehow-sexy woman. He wasn't a glutton for punishment like his brother.

Yet even as he made that vow, his attention wandered back to her. He needed things with Adela and Mattox to blow; that'd give him something else to focus on.

While speaking with the head of a youth group about sponsoring a field trip, he deliberately turned his back on Kennedy. When he heard the front door open, he jerked around and saw her walking through it, her gym bag in hand.

Even while keeping up with the phone conversation, Reyes tracked her movements through the big front window. She scanned the parked cars, up and down the street, her gaze watchful. Made sense for the neighborhood, but he sensed it was more with her, like an ingrained wariness.

Most people took safety for granted; clearly Kennedy did not.

Reyes saw the moment her attention snagged on something out of range of the front window. Frowning, she tossed her bag into a little red compact, relocked the car and headed slowly, cautiously along the sidewalk and out of view.

What the hell?

Too curious to ignore it, he wrapped up the call so quickly he bordered on rudeness, ending with, "Sorry, something's come up, but sure, I'd be glad to sponsor. Just give the details to Will. Thanks." He handed the phone to Will, then hurried out the door just in time to see Kennedy walk between the two buildings.

All kinds of shady shit happened in the alleys. Never mind that it was the middle of the day, or that he wore only shorts.

Reyes went after her, his stride long and fast—until he spotted her kneeling next to some garbage cans. Behind a broken-down cardboard box was...a very mangy cat.

"Careful," he said softly, already moving forward to join her.

"Shh," she replied without looking up, as if she'd already known it was him. "He's scared."

Reyes could imagine. The cat, who had probably once been white but was now too messy to tell for sure, had very strange eyes, one pale gray, the other mustard yellow, and a little...googly. Mud and filth streaked his face, and part of his tail was missing.

He hunkered back, eyeing Reyes.

"Do you think we can catch him?"

Staring at her, Reyes asked stupidly, "Catch him?"

"He's hungry," she cooed.

Cooed.

For him, she'd been all snippy and smug, but for a mangy cat—And then he heard a softer, squeakier little sound. Ah, hell. Resigned, he let out a groan.

"Shh," Kennedy said again.

Her bossiness made him grin. "That's not a tomcat."

She didn't look at him, only asked, "No?"

"You don't hear it?"

"What?"

"Kittens." The tiny meows came again—very nearby, in fact.

Her eyes went wide, her mouth forming a soft O. Then she breathed, *"Kittens."*

Yeah, he knew exactly what that expression meant. Either way, he'd have helped the cat, but kittens changed the manner he would have used.

When she started to stand, he said, "No. Don't start looking for them yet. They're close by, but we might spook the mama if we disturb them before we've won her over."

Trusting him, at least on that, Kennedy nodded. "Right."

Reyes considered the situation. "If she's nursing, she needs to eat."

"I was trying to figure out how I'd sneak in a cat, but a cat with kittens?" Kennedy turned to him. "Where I'm staying, pets aren't allowed. What are we going to do?"

We? Minutes ago she'd told him to buzz off, but now they were working together? Okay, he'd take it. "If I can corral her, I can put her and the babies in my office for now." Responsibility for the cats would give them a neutral link, one that might bridge the divide so she'd tell him what she was up to, and whose ass he needed to kick for her.

"Would you really?" Excited now, she smiled at him, a genuine smile that made him want to lick her mouth.

Down, he ordered himself. "Keep an eye on her while I go find a box. I packed food for later today—we might be able to use it to lure her in." *We.* He used that word, reinforcing it for her.

And she didn't object.

But that was a little too easy, so he wanted it confirmed. As he stood, he asked, "You *will* be back to help me figure this out, right?"

"You know I come to the gym nearly every day. Of course I'll be back." Just then, the cat crept out enough to butt her head into Kennedy's extended hand. "Aw."

The lady looked very different when she was being all gentle and sweet. She looked a little too appealing, in fact.

Maybe seeing all that overblown chemistry between Sterling and Cade was starting to wear on him. Not that he wanted anything that substantial...but it did have him looking at Kennedy differently.

Before he said or did something stupid, he went inside to get what he needed. He returned with a nice-sized cardboard box, a plush towel in the bottom of it and half of his chicken salad croissant.

Kennedy had the cat nearly in her lap at that point. "After this, I'll pay for her food and whatever else she needs."

No way would he commit to that. "Let's just see how far we get today, okay?" He held out the sandwich.

Kennedy gave him an incredulous look over his bait. "Croissant? You?"

What did she think, that he sustained himself on Cheez Whiz and beer? "It's delicious—but I didn't make it."

Her brows leveled out. "Ah, girlfriend?" Then on the heels of that, with a darkening frown, she asked, "Wife?"

That particular acerbic tone caused a laugh that startled the cat.

While she won the scraggly thing over again, Reyes said around a big grin, "No girlfriend, definitely not a *wife*."

Her jaw flexed over the way he stressed the word, but she said nothing. It took only seconds to locate the kittens in a torn bag of trash. Reyes carefully transferred them into the box. There were only three, thank God. He double-checked, looking everywhere. The mama, still on Kennedy's lap, went alert and immediately started fretting...until she found the food.

Making a sound somewhere between a purr and a growl, she devoured it but still kept her eyes on Reyes. She ate the entire sandwich, croissant roll and all, which made him realize just how hungry the poor thing had been.

When she finished, she went into the box with her kittens, circled once, then lay on her side to lick her paw while the kittens nursed.

Yeah, that melted even his own heart a little.

Standing close to his side, Kennedy whispered, "She was starving."

He glanced down at her, then had to look away again. He'd never seen a woman with quite that particular mix of tenderness and sympathy.

"She'll be fine now," he assured her, slowly closing the box so she couldn't leap out the minute he moved her. He was about to suggest that Kennedy walk with him, one hand on the cardboard flaps, until he got the animals inside, but his phone beeped, and when he checked the message, he saw it was go time.

CHAPTER SEVENTEEN

WATCHING STAR STIR awake from her nap was a distinct pleasure, one that Cade wanted to enjoy every day for the rest of his life.

She still had a towel, now lopsided, on her head, and a hickey on her shoulder. He lightly brushed his fingertips over the mark.

The core of his basic nature was to protect his own, and she *was* his now, whether she'd accepted that as fact or not. Eventually she would. He'd see to it. "Hey, sleepyhead."

On a sinuous stretch, she murmured...and settled again.

Knowing he'd caused her exhaustion with sexual excess left him aching with renewed lust—and love. The urge was to cradle her close, coddle her, spar with her, train her, make love to her and then start all over again. Conversations, meals, showers, danger, sex... Sharing with her made everything better.

It struck him that he needed a lifetime of that, a lifetime with her.

The emotional overload left him combustible, agitated and needing her again. He curved his hand around her shoulder, absorbing the satiny feel of her skin, the warmth.

Her lashes barely lifted. "Cade?"

Smiling at her, he said, "You taste so good I'd prefer to have *you* for lunch. But since everyone will wait on us..."

Eyes popping open wide, she stared at him in blank surprise. "Lunch?"

Damn, she was a sweetheart with that comical confusion on her face. "Bernard has outdone himself, and he's waiting for your praise."

"Bernard," she repeated, before coming up to one elbow and groaning. "It's time for lunch already?"

"You've been asleep awhile."

She reached up to keep the towel on her head. "But I *never* nap."

Leaning in, Cade whispered, "Guess the awesome sex tuckered you out. I gave you two big Os, if you recall."

The fog left her gaze and she grinned. "Of course I recall. Sex with you makes up my favorite memories."

Severely disliking how she worded that, he clarified, "Reality."

"What?"

"Us, together. That's reality, not a memory."

She softened, her lips curving. "You do like to say confusing things, but if everyone is waiting, I need to make myself presentable instead of trying to figure you out."

She made to get out of the bed, but with a kiss, Cade took her down to the mattress again, his chest against the soft cushion of her breasts, one leg thrown over hers to keep her still. He searched her gaze, determined to gain an admission. "Tell me you understand, babe. Say that you like our relationship."

"You kidding?" She ran her fingers along his jaw, around his ear to his nape. "Course I do. I'm not dumb."

That answer didn't really satisfy, either, but then, short of her telling him how much she cared, no answer would. Cade gave her a firm kiss. "Dad checked my stitches, bitched because I'd pulled one, and redressed it. If he says anything in front of you, ignore him."

Blanching, she whispered, "Your dad knows what we were doing?"

Cade almost choked on his humor. Because teasing her was so much fun, he used the same hushed tone she'd had. "Yes." Scorching heat rushed into her face, leaving her cheeks blotchy. The grin broke through. "He knows we were *sparring*."

Relief took away her starch. "Not nice, you butthead. You knew what I was thinking."

"I couldn't resist. Seems to happen a lot where you're concerned." With a last firm kiss to her mouth, he rolled out of the bed, then hauled her up. "Bernard has hot roast beef sandwiches with caramelized onions on crusty bread—that's the description he insisted I share, along with the warning that you'll want to enjoy it while it's hot, so hustle up. Lunch is in fifteen minutes."

"Ack." Beautifully naked, she darted around him, already whipping away the towel. "You should have told me all that five minutes ago!"

Sitting on the side of the bed, Cade listened to the blow-dryer and smiled with bone-deep satisfaction. Had he done this much smiling before Star? He didn't think so. For most of his life he'd been driven. Driven to buck his father's dictates, then to succeed in the army, and now to right wrongs for women and children exploited by traffickers.

Singular focus kept him on track, or at least it did before Star. Now he enjoyed thinking of her, seeing her, touching her. He'd always do the best he could, but responsibilities had moved aside to make room for pleasure.

To make room for Star.

When the noise quit, he found himself saying, "I have a decent place of my own."

The door jerked open and Star stood there, still naked but now with her hair loose the way he liked it. She stared at him a moment, then stalked forward to get clothes. "A place other than this apartment?"

He'd never really thought of these rooms as his apartment, but then, he knew he had a small home to call his own. Star didn't. "I bought it after I was medically discharged from the army while serving as a Ranger."

Pausing with her panties halfway up her legs, Star's gaze clashed with his. After a second, she pulled them up and came to sit by him. Breasts bared, eyes watchful.

Cade said nothing, leaving it to her to ask any questions she had.

"You were a Ranger?"

"Once a Ranger, always a Ranger, so I'm a Ranger still, medically retired."

Uncertainty trembled in her fingers as she tucked back her hair. "Medically retired, why?"

It felt good to share with her, to finally, completely open up. He laced his fingers with hers, moving her hand to his thigh. When with her, he couldn't touch her enough. "After a lot of deployments and hard landings when jumping from planes, I had multiple leg issues."

"You jumped from planes?" Surprise was immediately followed by concern. "You're hurt?"

"I'm in prime physical shape for the average man."

The concern shifted to amused interest. "Heck yeah, you are."

"But for a Ranger?" Keeping his attention off her breasts wasn't easy. "Not so much."

That statement left her disgruntled. "Who says so?"

His mouth twitched. "Don't act like you're sorry I'm here."

"What? No, course not." She stood again and reached for her bra. "So tell me about your house—and how come we're not there instead of here?"

He'd known that would be her response. "Like I said, it's small. Two bedrooms, one I use for storage. Family room, eat-in kitchen, bathroom. A single-car garage. There's a nice big basement, though, so I have my workout gear down there. Nothing like Dad's downstairs setup, just bare concrete walls and floor, exposed pipes and all that."

She pulled up straight-leg jeans, tugging a little to get them over her perfect ass, and then pulled on a loose shirt. "And we're here because?"

"It's the safest place to be right now."

Brows pinching in thought, she sat beside him again to get on her socks and those shit-kicker boots of hers. "If I wasn't with you, would you feel the same?"

"You are with me." He trailed his fingers through her hair. "And you matter to me, Star. A lot."

Some turbulent emotion brought her gaze snapping to his. He saw her slender throat work, watched her lick her lips. Shooting for cockiness, she said, "Ditto."

He wasn't buying it. Her attitude was mostly uncertainty, not disinterest. What would she do if he said that he loved her? With everyone waiting, he decided not to put it to the test.

Bent at the waist to tie her boots, she said with nonchalance, "You're the only one who calls me that now."

"Star? It suits you."

"I thought Star had disappeared years ago."

Very softly, he said, "I found her again."

Denials hung in the air, but she didn't give them voice. Instead she stood and held out a hand. "Come on. I'm starved."

Knowing this was difficult for her, Cade let her lead him out. "Before I got to know you, I called you something else."

"Yeah? You called me Sterling?"

"No." They started up the steps.

"Then what?"

"Trouble." Catching her at the top of the stairwell, he pinned her to the wall. "Massive trouble—especially to my libido."

Her laugh sounded almost like a giggle, and damn, that pleased him. "Your libido is fine."

"It's in hyperdrive around you."

Dodging his mouth, she said, "Lunch is waiting."

"Then give me a kiss to carry me through the next hour or two."

Challenge sparked in her dark eyes and she focused on his mouth. Small but capable hands slid around his neck. "All right."

Damn. She leaned forward—and singed him.

He shouldn't have started this when he knew the others were waiting, but he wasn't about to end it, either. She nibbled on his bottom lip, licked the upper, sealed her lips to his and dueled with his tongue.

He had his hips pinned to hers, grinding against her, when he heard the door open.

Star freed her mouth and immediately used his shoulder as a shield. Cade concentrated on breathing.

Behind them, stunned silence reigned, and then Bernard stated, "Lunch will not keep, so I hope this will." He slammed the door again.

Shoulders shaking, Star held on to him.

"I have a boner."

The snickers turned into full-blown howls.

It was nice, hearing her laugh so freely. He wanted to hear it more often. "It's not that funny."

She tried to catch her breath, took one look at him and fell into another fit.

To get even, Cade moved his open palm over her breast, whispering against her ear, "Your nipples are also telling a tale."

That earned him a groan and a tight squeeze. "If I wasn't so hungry, I'd say to hell with lunch, but after all that exercise this morning, I think I need to eat."

"We have the rest of our lives," he said and tugged her through the doorway before she could stop sputtering.

Getting past her reserve was a challenge, but also strangely satisfying. And fun.

Especially since she liked the physical side of their relationship as much as he did. The rest? He didn't know yet, but he refused to believe he was the only one falling hard.

"BERNARD, YOU OUTDID YOURSELF." Sitting back, one hand to her full stomach, Sterling sighed. Much as she wanted to see Cade's home, she would definitely miss Bernard's cooking.

For the moment, she refused to dwell on why Cade hadn't yet shown her his place. There'd been opportunity, before the danger ramped up, so why hadn't he? Did he want to keep his personal life separate?

Even to her skeptical mind, that didn't make much sense, not with the careless way he threw around the *L* word. And what was that comment in the stairwell? *The rest of our lives.*

Like maybe he expected them to spend that life together?

Hoping for too much could lead to the biggest disappointment she'd ever known—and God knew, she'd known plenty. But she couldn't help herself. Her heart had already launched on a gleeful path of "what if?"

Was it possible?

If he had something to say, why didn't he just come out and say it already? All those verbal clues that she didn't know how to decipher were making her a little nuts.

"Oh, hey," Madison said, sitting forward to stare at her laptop. "We have movement."

Cade's sister had alternated between eating, joining in the casual conversation and scanning her screen. No one had commented on the laptop set on the table before her.

"What is it?" Out of his seat, Cade went behind Madison's chair, one hand braced on the back of it, to see for himself.

The expression on his face warned Sterling, apprehension instantly filling her.

Why? She wanted to get Mattox, so she needed to know the truth about Adela. It's what they'd been working for, what she wanted.

But she'd just been contemplating her future and now reality came crashing down around her.

"It's go time." Already with his cell out, Cade keyed in a message.

"Getting hold of Reyes?" Parrish asked.

"He'd messaged me earlier about some guys hanging out, talking about a job tonight. No idea if they're connected, but it's possible."

"My instincts are telling me this is it." Madison glanced up. "Tell Reyes to make arrangements to leave the gym."

Getting her gumption back—sort of—Sterling asked, "He has someone to cover for him?"

"Every eventuality has been prearranged," Parrish explained.

Of course it had. Clearing the sudden lump of nervousness from her throat, Sterling asked, "Do you see Mattox? Is Adela with him?"

Already shaking her head, Madison used her mouse to take a few screenshots. "It's a ten-foot box truck and I'm willing to bet there are women inside. Here comes a car."

"Reyes said he'll be ready in five, just waiting for directions." Returning his phone to his pocket, Cade went back to looking at the screen with his sister. "That's Mattox getting out of the back seat. I can't see if Adela is in there."

Sterling sat still, listening as they coordinated around her. She felt like a useless lump, but she was out of her element and didn't want to slow anyone down.

"He's opening the back of the truck—I wish one of the cameras showed that view!"

Cade rested a hand on his sister's shoulder. "The three cameras are helping, hon. Will you be able to follow them?"

"Probably, or at least enough to get a fix on where they're going. Tell Reyes to get over to I-25 near there. He needs to be closer to pick up the tail once we know."

Almost at the same time, Sterling's phone rang. Startled, she gave an inelegant jump.

All eyes turned to her.

The lump in her throat expanded, but she managed a cavalier smile that carried over to a neutral tone. "Hello?"

"Francis?"

That panicked voice had her sitting forward. Was Adela not with Mattox?

Quickly, she put the phone on speaker and said, "Adela. I haven't heard from you in a—"

"You have to help. *Please*. He has new women, Francis. They'll be in the same shape as me, but if you can figure out a way to stop him... I didn't know who else to call!"

Knowing how the others would react, but wanting to gauge Adela's reaction, Sterling suggested, "The police?"

Parrish shook his head at her. Alarm raised Madison's brows.

Cade just held up a placating hand, indicating they should wait and let her do her thing.

So what was her thing? Somehow, while falling in love with Cade, she'd forgotten.

"Not a good idea. I told you, he's bought off some of the cops."

So Sterling hadn't tripped her up on that. Did Mattox have a few cops in his pocket? It'd be worth finding out. "How do you know?" It wasn't unheard of for a cop to be complicit, but it was rare, and she figured Cade and his family would have forewarned her if the problem was around here.

"I don't have much time! He could be back to the cabin any minute."

"What cabin?" Sterling asked, playing along—just in case. "Where?"

"It's a shack in the mountain, near Coalville."

Brows shot up everywhere. Adela admitted it? She was either truly desperate or riding out with Mattox right now.

"But that doesn't matter," Adela rushed on. "He has eight new girls. I overheard him talking about north on I-25, something about meeting at an abandoned farm near Aspen Creek."

Cade's entire demeanor changed. It was amazing to witness as he started texting Reyes again.

Gently, with understanding and sympathy, Sterling asked, "If you don't want cops, how do you expect me to handle it?"

All she heard was heavy breathing. "I thought... I thought you had that big guy with you. Mattox has been furious that he was able to fight off all the men he sent after him. He even said some of his guys are still missing."

Huh. Adela had managed to hear a lot. "He's one man, Adela. And I assume Mattox won't be alone."

"No. He doesn't go anywhere without personal protection, plus I think he hired on a few more."

Sterling waited.

"I'm sorry. You seemed so resourceful..." Adela caught her breath. "Guess I was wrong, so maybe you could go ahead and try the police? Just, please, don't tell anyone I tipped you off. He'd kill me if he ever found out."

"I can come get you from the cabin—"

"No, he's leaving people here to watch me. It'd be too dangerous. Besides, I don't matter right now. I just don't want those other women..." She drew a shaky breath. "I want them to have a chance, okay? But I have to go now. If I don't hide this phone, he'll know." The call died.

Just like her nerve. Just like her backbone.

Sterling looked up at Cade. Dear God, she wasn't sure what to do.

"I've got this," Cade said, his voice firm. "Did I tell you that Rangers are critical thinkers? We are, so let me handle things."

Relieved that this time she didn't have to sort it out alone, Sterling swallowed back her misgivings and came to her feet. "Okay. Right." She'd made her voice firm. She wasn't a wimp and she wouldn't start acting like one. "So what do we do first?"

Parrish's discerning gaze missed nothing. He turned to Cade. "You're good to go?"

"Glad things are finally in motion," he said. "The men Reyes overheard at the gym also mentioned Aspen Creek."

Madison frowned. "What else?"

"Four men, and Mattox is ensuring they're all strapped."

"You've devastated his organization," Parrish mused as he pushed back his chair and began to pace. "First getting Misfits shut down, then going through his men. He's afraid to operate until you're out of the picture. This is his Hail Mary, a last desperate attempt to try to regain his footing."

Desperate? Sterling wondered if Parrish was delusional. "Four men," she emphasized. "All armed."

Cade shook his head. "Bozos, Reyes said. Nothing to worry about."

Incredulity tensed her body. "You can't know that."

Perturbed by her tone, Parrish zeroed in on Cade. "Do we need to wait, to investigate more?"

"Forget the number of men. There may be eight women. Eight innocents."

"If she wasn't lying," Madison pointed out.

Resolute, Cade said, "I'm not willing to chance it."

Parrish's eyes narrowed, but he nodded.

Not good enough, not for Sterling. "If they're armed..."

"I'll disarm them."

Of all the idiotic— She couldn't believe he was that arrogant.

Cade held out a hand to her. "Come on. We'll need to leave quickly so we can rendezvous with Reyes on the way."

Knowing she had to find her own arrogance and fast, Sterling nodded.

"Bernard, would you please keep an eye on things here while I help them get ready?"

"I'll be diligent," Bernard announced while taking her seat. "If anyone moves, I'll alert you."

"Thank you." Madison jogged around and ahead of Cade.

Getting ready, Sterling found, meant donning body armor, strapping on guns, and stowing a sniper rifle and plenty of ammo. Much better stuff than the knife necklace she'd worn to Misfits. God, that felt like a lifetime ago.

When she'd been all alone in the world.

Shaking off those maudlin thoughts, Sterling put her knife in her boot, the brass knuckles in her rear pocket. With Madison's assistance, it was such seamless prep that within minutes she was seated in the passenger side of Cade's SUV while he had a few quiet words with his father. Madison had returned to the kitchen as command central.

Through the window, Sterling watched as Parrish put a fatherly hand on Cade's shoulder. Seeing that touched her heart. Cade's father was nearly as tall as him, still very fit, and for once she detected concern in his gaze. This, she realized, was how Cade would look as he aged. Distinguished, impressive and in control.

Maybe Cade had inherited his attitude from Parrish, too. With their cool command, the two of them were very different from Madison's joyful persona and Reyes's maddening personality.

The more she looked at Cade, the harder her heart pounded.

This could be it. She could die—worse, *Cade could get hurt*— and all her newfound happiness would mean absolutely nothing.

This caring stuff was awful. How simple her life used to be when she had no one, when even *she* didn't matter that much. Now she was crazy in love and worried sick because of it.

It changed everything.

Cade slid into the driver's seat and started the SUV.

Looking back at Parrish, she found him still standing there, his hands clasped behind his back, watching as they drove away.

Sterling lifted her hand in a wave. He returned the gesture. Parrish might be a dictator, but he obviously loved his kids.

How stressful must it be for him, having his sons in the field?

Facing forward again, she glanced at Cade. His hands rested on the steering wheel, his posture relaxed. It all felt surreal.

"Everything okay, honey?"

"Yes." *No.* She wasn't sure anything would ever again be okay.

"You're staring."

"Because you are devastating to my senses." *And I need to absorb more of you while I can.*

Smiling, Cade handed her his phone. "Here, Madison will send updates, in case they get too far ahead of us."

Her palms felt sweaty when she accepted the cell. Why? She'd done stuff like this before... Okay, *that* was a big lie. She'd never done *anything* this complex.

But she'd wanted to, right?

Apparently sensing her turmoil, Cade put a hand on her knee. "We'll pick up Reyes shortly."

Knowing Cade's brother was also effective in this crazy stuff, that he'd be good backup for Cade, made her feel a tiny bit better.

Again, anticipating her reaction, Cade drew a bottle of water from the door and handed it to her. "Hydrate."

Hydrate, she mocked silently, even as she took a quick drink. His "business as usual" attitude was really starting to irk. "What about you? Don't you need to drink some?"

"If I do, I have another bottle."

So calm, so matter-of-fact.

Get it together, Sterling ordered herself. Cade was smart enough to know if he couldn't handle the situation. She should take comfort in his confidence, not get annoyed by it.

Scenery passed in a blur, much like her thoughts. Madison texted once to say that she'd confirmed two men in the truck, and one in the front seat of the car chauffeuring Mattox.

Sterling read the message to Cade and sent back his simple acknowledgment, but her mind scrambled on the math. Four men hired, three accompanying Mattox, and Mattox himself... That was *eight* men.

Against the three of them.

And they still didn't know if Adela was along for the ride, complicit in everything, or cowering, possibly injured, back in an isolated cabin.

Not long after that, they turned down a narrow road off the highway and picked up Reyes. He'd parked his truck behind some trees and strode out with the same insouciance as Cade.

She was ready to chew her nails, and they acted like it was nothing.

Cade got out and walked around to meet his brother at the back of the SUV.

Twisting in her seat, Sterling watched as Reyes suited up, starting with a back holster that held two handguns. Unlike Cade, Reyes adjusted his bulletproof vest right over his T-shirt.

Too antsy to sit still, Sterling got out to join them.

Reyes glanced up with a smile. "Hey, girl. How's it hanging?"

"Hey."

Far too perceptive, Reyes did a double take, but wisely chose not to comment on the visible tension in her frame.

Instead, he picked up the semiauto precision rifle. "It's going to rain."

Cade shrugged. "Every afternoon, this time of year. You won't melt."

"I'd rather not calculate wind, though."

When Sterling frowned, Cade explained, "Reyes will cover us from farther away."

That was news to her. "He won't be with us?"

"I'll ensure no one sneaks up behind you."

Well...that was reassuring. "You're a crack shot, huh?"

Tugging on a lock of her hair, Reyes said, "Even with wind and rain." He closed the back of the car. "Let's go. I'll drive."

So that Cade could ride shotgun, Sterling took the back seat. Heavy clouds moved in and around the sun, one minute making it gloomy, the next leaving the day bright. She knew they were right. Rain was inevitable, and it fit her mood.

If they all got through this day unscathed, she'd reevaluate how she lived her life. Cade mattered. His family mattered.

And by God, that meant she mattered, too.

CHAPTER EIGHTEEN

THEY CAME INTO the farm from the side, skirting around scraggly woods, making their way over a neglected field. Given that dried stalks remained scattered about, she guessed someone had once grown corn.

Age and neglect had ravaged the farmhouse, the windows all broken, the roof half gone. Farther back, and to the right, an old weathered barn remained standing.

If not for the box truck and black sedan parked behind it, Sterling would have thought they had the wrong place. But no, the evidence was there. Had they come in through the front, they wouldn't have seen either vehicle parked in back.

Both men were quietly focused as they took in a big gnarled tree near a fence line, a massive boulder and an old trestle bridge over a creek.

"There," Reyes decided, nodding at the bridge. "I'll have a better line of sight from there."

Cade nodded. "I'll circle around and come in on that side of the barn. I'll be able to see what I'm up against and you'll be able to cover me."

"Should I pick a few off right away?"

"That would just announce us and might not be necessary anyway. Wait and see how it goes."

Sterling frowned at them as they went over plans. There were eight men out there, waiting, anxious to kill Cade and probably Reyes, too.

Anxious to get hold of her.

In no way did she feel equipped for this—but how could she say that when they were so freakishly calm?

Reyes lowered the binoculars. "I only counted five inside the barn. Think they're planning to stash the women there?"

"How secure could it be? Wouldn't take much to have the whole structure falling down around them."

"What if it's a trap?" When both men turned to her, Sterling curled her fingers until she felt her nails digging into her palms. "What if one of them has a sniper rifle of his own? He could pick us off as we close in."

"Not likely," Reyes said. "I'm not sure these buffoons can manage that much planning. The punks at the gym definitely don't have any talents beyond finding their way into trouble."

"Mattox is not a punk," she insisted. "He's a bloodthirsty, heartless bastard who would take pleasure in killing all of us."

Slowly, Reyes lowered the binoculars. Seconds passed before he spoke, and again he chose to overlook her trepidation. "A few of them have gone to the back of the truck. They don't appear to be aware of us."

"Mattox?" Sterling leaned forward, staring hard, but without binoculars of her own, she couldn't make out any people. "Did you see him?"

"Neither of them look thick enough. Besides, I can't imagine Mattox doing the grunt work."

"We've stripped him of his resources." Cade took another look. "He's here. I sense it."

Sterling whispered, "Me, too." Somehow she knew Mattox was there…and she knew everything about this was wrong.

Cade glanced back at her in sharpened awareness. Dissecting her. Analyzing her. Coming to conclusions.

How could eyes so cool be so scorching?

In defensive belligerence, she asked, "What?"

"Now isn't the time to hold back. If you have suspicions—"

"It feels *wrong*," she blurted. "All of it. In my gut, I know we're being set up." Sitting back, she waited for their derision. She waited for their doubt.

The brothers shared a look.

Reyes surprised her by saying, "Gut feelings have kept me alive more than once."

Cade nodded. "So this might not be the cakewalk I anticipated."

Now that she had their attention, Sterling started to relax.

Until Cade caught her hand. "I don't want to piss you off, babe, but I have a favor to ask."

Reyes hummed a little, drummed his fingertips on the steering wheel and went back to surveying the barn.

With a terrible foreboding, Sterling lifted her chin.

"I think you're right. I think it's a setup of some sort—but it's nothing I can't handle."

Tension burrowed into her every muscle. "You've gotten through things like this before?"

"Many times."

Clearly he wasn't retrenching—and she wasn't willing to hold him up. "Okay, so let's go. The waiting is worse than the doing."

Cade didn't budge. His hold on her hand tightened. "Since it likely is a trap, we need someone at the wheel, ready to go, in case we have to bounce in a hurry."

Of course she knew where this was going. "You mean me?"

"You're good. I'd never say otherwise." His low voice seemed to brush over her skin like a reassuring caress. "Put to the test, I know you'd handle any situation. No doubts at all, I swear. But the truth is—"

"You and Reyes are better at this." A blatant truth.

"We're bigger. Stronger." His thumb rubbed over her clenched knuckles. "And yes, better trained for this."

It galled, knowing that Cade was giving her an out.

He must have known that, too, because he tacked on, "It's either you or Reyes—"

Reyes snorted but continued studying the barn. "Still only see five. No women."

Sterling knew she should have been gracious, should have accepted the excuse with gratitude, but instead she said, "I'm agreeing under duress."

His shoulders relaxed, telling her that her decision had mattered to him.

Before Cade, the concept of the future had no real meaning. Now she wanted to see what happened between them. She wanted to know what tomorrow, the next month, an entire year would bring. "You need to understand, Cade. I'm going to be very worried for you. *Very.*" It horrified her that her voice wavered with emotion. "Damn it, you've stolen my edge!"

"I'll go get in position." Taking the rifle from the floor near Cade's feet, Reyes left the SUV, then kept low as he cut across the field. He'd have to wade out into the creek to climb the trestle, but she didn't have a doubt he could do it.

With terrible timing, Sterling realized she liked Reyes now. Heck, in such a short time, the entire McKenzie family had become dear to her.

When Cade got out and circled around, she stepped out to meet him, oblivious to the light rain that immediately dampened her clothes and hair. Without missing a beat, he pressed her to the side of the SUV. His rough hand cradled her cheek. "The timing is fucked, but I need you to know something."

"Wha—"

"I love you."

Her heart shot into her throat and stuck there, feeling as big as a grapefruit. Unfair! *Now* he decided to make it all crystal clear, with her rowdy emotions flying out of control?

At her stunned silence, his mouth quirked. "I *love* you, Star."

It took a second, but she found herself smiling, as well. "Cade—"

"There's no way in hell I won't come back to you." He punctuated that with the briefest of kisses to her slightly parted lips but then wasted no more time talking. "Get behind the wheel, keep the doors locked and stay alert."

He took it one step further, practically putting her in the seat himself, locking the door and quietly closing it.

He hadn't given her a chance to tell him how she felt, and now she desperately wanted to. Did he not trust what she'd say? Was he uncertain of her?

A laughable idea. She was a complete nobody, without special talent, no family, nothing to recommend her, and he was...

He was everything to her.

Cade loves me. She hugged his confession to her heart, and in that moment, she believed it would be all right.

Had he known her misgivings? Course he had. Cade missed nothing. He'd deliberately saved her by saying they needed a driver. That hadn't been discussed in their prior plans, so she knew he'd come up with it on the fly.

Somehow, he truly knew her, well enough to understand her even when she had trouble understanding herself. Without the excuse he'd given her, she *would* have gone along. And she likely would have been up to the task.

She knew it. Cade knew it, too. And that's what mattered.

He'd been considerate...because he loved her.

More focused because of that, she stared ahead, already losing sight of Cade, still unable to spot Reyes. She picked up Cade's discarded binoculars. If it became necessary, she'd lend a hand.

Otherwise, she'd be right here—waiting.

SPOTTING REYES ON the bridge, positioned behind a beam, Cade stole low through the high weeds and cornstalks until he was on the other side of the barn, then crept forward. Once he got close enough, he could hear men talking. Not Mattox, not yet, but he sensed the bastard was near.

"Think they'll show?" someone asked. "Should have been here by now, right?"

"Have a look around. Take someone with you."

Cade flattened his back to the rough, weather-bleached boards and waited. The men murmured low, mostly complaints about the rain. Then one said, "You check around back. I'll go this way."

Perfect. He could take them on two at a time, but individually would be quieter, ensuring he didn't alert the others.

The first started around the corner. Slouched, one hand shoved in his pocket, the other hand holding a revolver at his side, he spotted Cade a second too late.

Snagging the much smaller man into a tight choke hold that both kept him silent and immobilized him, Cade torqued up the pressure until the man's skinny legs gave out and he slumped. Lowering him to the ground, Cade quickly wrapped his mouth with duct tape, then secured his hands and feet with nylon cuffs.

He stuck the guy's weapon into his waistband and in less than thirty seconds was at the back of the barn—where he caught the startled surprise of the second guy as he stepped into view. Hair in a ponytail and missing two front teeth made the sight pretty comical.

When the thug opened his mouth to scream, Cade slammed his fist into his face, putting him down, dazed, but not yet out.

Easy enough. Straddling him, Cade gripped his throat tight. "Make a sound, and you're dead."

Blinking fast in panic, the idiot went still. Cade released him but only to land another hard punch, and this time it put him to sleep. He trussed up that guy much like the first.

Reyes had spotted five, so he had three to go.

A twig snapped, and Cade looked back to see two more men standing there, and if their wild-eyed expressions meant anything, they were scared spitless. They each held guns but hadn't yet aimed them.

Even more reckless, they were within reach.

Slowly, Cade smiled—then spun, leg out, taking them off their feet. They crashed into each other.

Either Mattox was getting really desperate by using wannabe street toughs with no training, or he didn't care if they all died.

Not that Cade committed random murder, but still, he took them apart pretty easily, even while preparing for another threat to show. He bound their hands and feet, and when he heard the shot, he knew it was Reyes.

On the other side of the barn, someone howled in pain. The last man? Or maybe Mattox.

Back on his feet, Cade peered into the barn, saw it was empty and felt fury expand. Where the fuck was Mattox?

He had a few prisoners who might be able to tell him.

Turning back, he met the gaze of one of the punks.

Face bloodied and eyes wild, he watched as Cade strode toward him.

Trying to scuttle back, the panicked guy asked, "Who the fuck are you?"

Cade kicked him in the ribs. With his hands bound, he couldn't block the strike at all. "Where's Mattox?"

"Goddammit!" he yelled, trying to curl in on himself. "Fucking asshole!"

The outpouring of profanity didn't faze Cade. He aimed his Glock. "You have two seconds. One, t—"

"He's in the farmhouse!"

"Shut up, Mort," the other man growled. "Mattox'll cut your fuckin' throat."

"And this one will shoot me, man! Either way, I'm dead."

In the house... "Why?"

"Don't want his biz told, that's why."

Idiot. Ignoring Mort, Cade stepped on the other one's nuts, hard enough to make him scream. *"Why* is he in the house?" With the house barely standing, the barn would have been a better choice.

Urgency beat in Cade's brain. He needed to see Star, needed to touch her. Needed to know—

Mort stammered, "Some sort of setup, dude. We don't get details. Now let up 'fore you kill him."

Blinding rage coalesced. *Star.* It all became a blur at that point. He quickly gagged Mort and the other idiot. Then in a flat-out run, he headed for the house.

THE GUNSHOT SCARED STERLING, making it impossible for her to stay in the car. Heart rapping, she got out with the binoculars and stared, but everything must have been happening on the other side of the barn.

Had Reyes fired, or had one of Mattox's men?

Caught in indecision, she chewed her lip—and suddenly Adela slammed up to the fender of the SUV. Swinging around to face her, the gun already in her hand, Sterling gaped in shock.

Adela's mouth was swollen, crusted over with dried blood, and one of her eyes was blackened. A purpling bruise spread out on her jaw. "What in the world—"

"Francis..." Now half draped over the hood of the car, her

legs unable to hold her, Adela groped her way around. "Please. Help me."

Empathy took over, sharpened by rage, and Sterling snapped to attention. "What happened?" After holstering the gun, she hurried over to put an arm around Adela. "Mattox did this to you?"

"Yes." Slumping against her, Adela held on for dear life. Her clothes were torn, a dirty T-shirt ripped from the hem halfway up her midriff. Jeans ragged and dirty. Hair tangled.

Struggling with the deadweight, Sterling tried to steer her to the side of the SUV so she could open the door and get her inside. "Easy. Take a few breaths." She reached for the handle...

Adela laughed as she pushed her back, taking her off guard. She had Sterling's gun in her hand.

Things clicked into place easy enough. "Huh. So I was right. You're part of the setup."

"Don't lie!" Adela raged. "You had no idea."

Curling her lip, Sterling said, "I suspected you all along."

Stymied, Adela's mouth firmed, her eyes narrowed and she looked ready for murder.

Sterling immediately considered how to react, what she'd do, when she'd do it. It'd be dicey, but she wouldn't go down without a fight.

Then Adela surprised her by smiling. "Did you know I arranged it all? Ah, I see that you didn't."

All? No, she wouldn't buy that. "Mattox doesn't take orders from a woman."

"Of course not. He's all man. He's all *mine*." As if gloating, Adela said, "I suggested how to get you, and he liked the idea. It's worked before."

Worked before? What the ever-loving hell.

"I don't want to kill you out here. Mattox would be disappointed, so turn around and walk."

At the moment all Sterling felt was stark anger and firm resolve. Cade was near, but she'd handle this without distracting him. He already had his hands full.

"Move!"

Smirking, Sterling asked, "And if I don't?"

Adela limped closer. "Mattox will shoot your boyfriend right in the face." Glee twisted her abused features. "He has him, you know."

Cade told her to trust him, so that's what she'd do. Keeping her expression impassive wasn't easy, but Sterling gave it her best shot. "You've already proven yourself to be a liar, so why should I believe you? If anything, Mattox is already dead."

"No!" Closer still, Adela's breath rasped harshly. "Mattox has him, and if you don't come along, I'll shoot you in the leg and drag you there."

If Adela got near enough, Sterling felt certain she could disarm her. But no, she stopped with too much distance still between them.

To goad her, Sterling snorted. "You can barely keep yourself upright."

"Fine. I'll shoot you in both legs and tell Mattox where to find you."

On the off chance Cade had been outmaneuvered, Sterling wanted to be near him to help, so going along suited her. "Fine. To the barn, then."

"No, not the barn." Adela stayed behind her. "The house."

The house? "You're kidding, right? There is no house."

"Two inner rooms are intact." Breathing heavily, probably in pain, Adela snapped, "Hurry up. It's going to rain again."

Sure enough, lightning flickered in the distance, and the sky grew dark and menacing.

Outlined by the coming storm, the house looked like a specter of bad things to come.

It seemed a good idea to keep Adela talking. "Was taking a beating part of your grand plan? You look like you've been through hell and back."

"That's *your* fault! He can be more tempered, except when you've enraged him. You forced us into hiding, forced him to lose business." Adela laughed brokenly. "Now he's going to make you pay."

"Looks like you already did."

"Mattox can be very gentle. Once he's finished with you, he'll be gentle again."

It twisted Sterling's stomach to witness such madness. "You forgive his abuse that easily?"

With a shrug in her tone, Adela said, "It was necessary to reel you in. No, I didn't like it, but there's a lot of necessary things I don't like—especially the way Mattox obsesses about you." She made a giggling sound. "He'll be so thrilled to see you again."

"Somehow I don't think *thrilled* is the right word."

"Oh, but it is. He doesn't like hurting me, but you? He's going to take great pleasure in hearing you cry."

Sterling steeled her resolve. If she let it, fear would weaken her. She couldn't think about Mattox, about what he might do to her if things went wrong. She'd never again be a victim.

She wouldn't.

Adela prodded her hard in the spine, probably leaving bruises behind, before scuttling out of reach again. Perverse bitch. But even as Sterling thought it, she felt pity. It seemed pretty clear that Adela wasn't well. Whatever she'd gone through in her life had left her damaged enough to see Mattox as a hero.

She glanced back, but already Adela had put enough space between them to be out of reach. She might be insane, but she wasn't taking any chances on Sterling getting her hands on her.

"See the light in the house?" Adela gloated. "They're in there. Who knows? Your man might already be dead…or dying. So hurry it up if you want a chance to say goodbye."

Yes, she did hurry, going so fast that Adela had difficulty keeping up with her. Whatever motivation Mattox had for beating Adela, he'd overdone it, leaving her weakened and hurt.

Sterling went up the broken front steps, alert to any opportunity to turn the tables. So far there'd been none.

Missing boards in the porch forced her to pick her way cautiously before she stepped over the threshold. Rainwater puddled on the floor beneath an entirely collapsed section of roof.

Up ahead, in one contained room, Mattox stood, gun in hand, massive shoulder propped on a mold-covered wall, face twisted with cruel satisfaction. "Well, well, well. You actually did it, Adela."

"I told you I would." She shoved Sterling forward, almost making her fall.

Senses keenly attuned to the danger, Sterling noticed the eerie silence.

Mattox didn't have Cade.

Relieved, she breathed easy again. Cade was still out there with Reyes, and that meant she had a chance. They all did.

"Ah, I see the hope in your eyes," Mattox crooned. "It's lovely, truly it is."

"I told her there were women in the truck," Adela said with a sneer. "She doesn't yet know that you actually brought more men."

"Four more," Mattox explained. "They're already out there scouring the farm for your hulking friend."

Sterling leveled an unimpressed stare on Mattox. "You sent more sacrifices to be slaughtered?"

"I sent them fully armed."

"And you think that'll help them?" She scoffed. "So far no one you sent has even been a challenge."

Mattox didn't seem bothered by that. "It's true, I've been forced to use the dregs of society. They're not exactly reliable backup, but there's strength in numbers, so I'm confident they'll be dragging in his body any minute."

Sterling allowed a slow, smug smile. "Amazing. You really don't realize that you've sent them all to their deaths, do you?"

The relaxed posture left Mattox and he shoved upright. "Bullshit."

"They were in the barn, right? Well, they're useless now. Hear that silence? Think hard and you'll know what that means. Better still, you'll know that you're next." The words no sooner left her mouth than blinding pain exploded in her skull and she dropped to her knees. Jesus. Fighting off a rush of nausea, Sterling watched stars dance before her eyes.

Tsking, Mattox said, "Don't say things that set her off. Adela is unpredictable in her dedication to me." He smiled at the other woman, his expression bordering on tender. "What if you'd accidentally killed her?"

Heaving, Adela snarled, "She had it coming."

"Sick fucks." Sterling had the forethought to withdraw the knife from her boot before struggling awkwardly to her feet. Keeping it hidden was a challenge, but she pretended to stumble into the wall so she could slip it into the back of her waistband. To distract them both, she said to Adela, "You'll pay for that."

Enraged, Adela started to lunge forward.

Sterling braced for impact. At the moment, with her temples pounding, she wouldn't mind breaking Adela's neck.

Unfortunately, Mattox interfered, snatching Adela away none too gently, then cupping her bruised cheek in his meaty mitt. "I don't have a quick death in mind for her. You don't want to rob me of my pleasure, do you?"

Faced with so much hatred, it wasn't easy to keep a cool facade, but Sterling gave it her best shot.

It didn't help that Adela snuggled against his wide frame with complete adoration. "I'll behave."

Worse, Mattox coasted fat fingers over her swollen cheek and bloodied mouth, frowning a little, then pressing a tender kiss to her forehead. "I know you will."

"Gawd," Sterling groused. "If you two don't knock it off, I'm going to puke up my guts."

He glared at her for that remark but said to Adela, "Give me your gun so you aren't tempted to shoot her too soon."

Uncertain, Adela offered it up, then flinched when he roughly snatched it away. He shoved it into his pocket, meaning he now had two guns.

Wincing inside, Sterling again took in Adela's battered face. Mattox definitely had to die—but could Adela be saved? Didn't seem likely.

To be sure, Sterling asked, "So you don't have new women held captive?"

"Oh, he does," Adela bragged, regaining her attitude. "They'll replenish some of the profits *you* cost him."

Nope. Not a chance in hell of saving her. At that point, knowing other women were terrorized because of her, Sterling no longer cared.

Instead of speaking to Adela, she asked Mattox, "If they're not here, then where?"

"You think I'd tell you?" He evaluated her new posture against the wall but didn't seem to notice anything amiss. "No, I'll keep that information to myself, but I will tell you that they'll be transported soon." He eyed her distress with interest. "That bothers you? Well, it's partially your fault. I need cash, and they'll each earn a fair price. No daily rentals, as I had planned for you way back then. These women will be pets... Perhaps you'd like to be one, as well? Maybe even my own personal pet."

"Seriously, dude, I'm going to puke."

Mattox grinned. "When I'm done with you, you won't have such a smart mouth."

Adela scowled. "I thought we were going to kill her?"

Licking his thick lips, Mattox murmured, "Yes—*after* I've gotten my fill."

Trepidation kept her guts churning, but Sterling eyed him up and down with disdain. "You won't live long enough to make those threats a reality."

Fury brought Mattox forward. Stopping a few feet from her, he demanded, "Call out to him."

"Him?" Sterling asked, pretending confusion.

"If she plays dumb again," Adela shouted, "shoot her in the leg!"

Mattox raised his brows at her ruthless suggestion.

Stalling for time, Sterling asked, "What do you want me to say?"

"Yell his name." Mattox grinned with satisfaction. "That should do it."

Drawing a slow, deep breath, Sterling called out, "Cade?"

No answer—not that she'd expected one. Cade wasn't stupid. She had no doubt that he already had a grasp of the situation and all the players. He had a plan, and he would come for her. She only prayed he didn't get hurt in the process.

"I think I need to make you scream." Adela started to move forward.

Again, Mattox pulled her back, this time with keen impatience. "Call him again, and you better make it good."

Trying to determine which way Cade would enter, Sterling quickly scanned the open areas of the half-demolished house. Mattox had his back protected by a wall, so Cade couldn't come in behind him. That probably meant he'd enter through the side of the house where much of the structure was missing, or the front doorway that Sterling had used.

Either way, they'd see him coming, and that would make him an easy target for Mattox.

Just then, three rapid shots rang out. They echoed over the barren fields, making it impossible to pinpoint a direction.

In her heart, Sterling knew it was Cade, doing what he did best—kicking ass.

Adela blanched. Equally rattled, Mattox swung his heavy Glock around and took aim at her chest. "Call him! Make sure he knows I have you."

If Mattox thought that would save him, he'd find out otherwise.

"Call him, call him," Adela sang, her eyes going vague with excitement. *"Call him."*

By the second, she became more unhinged.

Sterling filled her lungs. "Cade!" To appease Mattox, she added, "I'm in here, Cade."

Eyes glittering, Adela held her breath.

The silence dragged out while Mattox's flinty gaze bounced back and forth between the two entrances—and suddenly Cade dropped through the hole in the ceiling, landing on his feet right before them.

A sort of blindsided panic held them both enthralled, but not Cade. Incandescent rage seemed to emanate from him. He appeared bigger, as invincible as he claimed. Turning fast, he violently kicked the gun away from Mattox, likely breaking his forearm in the process. While Mattox flailed, Cade grabbed him by the throat, lifted him from the floor and slammed him into a crumbling wall. His boulder-sized fist connected with Mattox's crotch. Then a forearm to his face cut off the scream of pain. Last, a punch to his throat.

Mattox was done for, a heavy deadweight hanging limp from Cade's grip.

It all happened so fast that Sterling stood there staring, riveted by the fluid ease of his attack.

Adela's shrill, earsplitting scream of rage jolted her back into action. She watched Adela scrabble for the gun.

She's going to shoot Cade?

Like hell! Throwing everything she had into a tackle, Sterling took them both down hard. She was bigger than Adela, surely stronger...and yet she wasn't fast enough.

The gun discharged with a deafening explosion.

Fighting a rush of suffocating fear, Sterling managed to glance up. But no, Cade hadn't slowed at all. His heavy fist repeatedly hammered Mattox's face.

"No!" Insanity made Adela stronger. Despite Sterling's efforts, she forced the gun around again, snarling like an animal, consumed with hatred.

Sterling tried, but she couldn't wrest the gun from her. *No, no, no.*

She would not let Cade be shot.

Savage protective instincts surged up...and her lessons kicked in. She reacted, fast, harsh. Brutal.

Just as Cade had taught her.

Her elbow slammed into Adela's already injured nose, crunching it and sending out a thick spray of blood. It dazed her long enough for Sterling to grab her knife and, without pause, drive the blade deep, once, twice, a third time.

Just as quickly, Sterling withdrew, moving back in horror.

Mouth going slack, eyes wide and sightless with shock, the gun slipped from Adela's hand. Blood pulsed and oozed from the wounds in her midriff.

Trembling with the aftereffects, Sterling saw her try to speak, then slump flat to the floor. Lifeless.

They weren't yet safe. Tamping down the horror of what she'd just done, she snatched up the gun and got back to her feet in time to see Cade release Mattox.

The floor shook as his body landed.

A big blackened hole gaped in his side. Adela had killed him. Somehow that seemed fitting.

The queasiness returned in a rush, but before Sterling could assimilate all the sights and scents of death, Cade had her, crushing her close, his face in her hair.

God, he felt good. Warm, safe...*alive.*

"Are you hurt?" He thrust her back, his gaze searching over her, his hands examining her arms, her waist, down to her hips.

Sterling rested a trembling hand against his steeled shoulder. "I'm okay."

"You don't look it."

Maybe because her head was splitting now that the adrenaline waned. She made a lame gesture toward Adela's body. "She cracked me in the back of the head with the gun."

Immediately, Cade turned her. "Aw, babe, let me see."

"It's all right." It annoyed her that she'd gotten caught like that while he stood there without a scratch other than his knuckles.

Tenderly, Cade sifted his fingers through her hair, lightly prodding her skull. "Damn. You have a massive goose egg." He turned her again to look into her eyes.

"I'm fine, Cade. I promise." Shock settled in, making her shiver and shake. "You?"

For an answer, he pressed his mouth to hers. The kiss wasn't sexual but reassuring. Soft, lingering, comforting.

From behind them, Reyes asked, "Some new form of resuscitation? Because I *know* you're not making out when we have shit to do."

Cade ended the kiss but didn't step away. He gathered her to his chest and said to his brother, "Madison called it in?"

"Ambulance and cops will be here any minute." Looking past Sterling to the bodies, he asked, "Dead?"

Sterling didn't have an answer to that.

Stepping around them, bypassing Mattox, Reyes went to one knee and pressed his fingers to Adela's throat. "Light pulse. She might make it."

In a truly gallant move, Cade lifted Sterling into his arms and turned to leave the destruction behind. Once outside, he moved a good distance from the house—and didn't put her down.

"Do you think Adela will—"

"Either way," he said, "that's not on you."

Understanding that and accepting it were two different things. "I couldn't let her shoot you."

Jaw flexing, arms tightening, Cade struggled with himself, all while his vivid blue eyes held hers captive. "Just so you know," he rasped in a growl, "I'm never letting you out of my sight."

Liking the sound of that, Sterling rested her head against his shoulder and whispered, "Good."

CHAPTER NINETEEN

As soon as they'd gotten home, his dad checked Star, going over all the signs of a concussion. She did have a slight headache but otherwise seemed fine. Introspective, but not lethargic. Quiet, but responsive to questions asked. No blurry vision, and hungry enough to eat a few cookies.

Though she grumbled about it, Cade stayed with her while she showered and changed clothes. There were many things he wanted to say, but he could wait. He had her with him, she was safe and that's what mattered.

When she'd finished dressing warmly, they moved outside to the deck, where the cool mountain air revived her. She hadn't complained when he'd sat down and pulled her onto his lap. In fact, she'd been so silent it worried him.

With her attention on the mountain view, Star said, "It's a good thing that Mattox is gone."

"A very good thing."

"Even though she didn't mean to, I'm glad that it was Adela who killed him."

They knew that an ambulance had taken Adela away, but no one really thought she'd make it. Previous injuries from the sick games she'd played with Mattox had already worn her down.

Cade didn't know how many beatings she'd taken, but Adela participated in hurting women and she'd wanted to hurt Star, too. She'd done her best to lure them into a trap.

If she died, he wouldn't lose sleep over it.

"Have you heard from Reyes yet?"

His brother had gone after the captive women, using the details Cade had gotten from one of the men hired to kill him. "He checked in."

"And?" Twisting around, Star faced him. "Were they there? Those men hadn't lied?"

Their loyalty to Mattox ended as soon as Cade had started wiping them out. "Once Reyes found the women, he allowed the task force to take over." Not everyone realized that his father founded the task force, and that they were, ultimately, answerable to him—which meant they could keep tabs on the women to know, without a doubt, that they were helped.

That, more than anything, was important to his father. To him, Reyes and Madison, too.

And now, obviously, to Star, as well.

She searched his gaze, and as understanding dawned, she again relaxed against him. "We need to know where Mattox got them."

"Working on it." In fact, that was the next step, and his sister was already chasing down leads. The thugs hadn't known much about the operation, but Mattox's driver, and the bastards who'd brought the truck, proved to be better informed—once they'd been persuaded to talk.

Luckily his father had great contacts in both law enforcement and politics. Within a few hours, Parrish had learned that the police had rounded up all the fucks involved. There were a few unavoidable fatalities beyond Mattox—and maybe Adela—but with any luck, there'd be nothing to trace the incident back to them. Not that they couldn't handle it, but it offered unnecessary complications.

If anyone did sniff in that direction, Parrish would handle it.

Star's small hand opened over his chest. "I want to be a part of that, okay?"

She could be a part of everything, as far as he was concerned. "That's a given, babe." But he added, "You can be involved as much, or as little, as you like."

"Good. They all need to be destroyed."

"Agreed." Cade knew she was working things out in her mind.

Yes, she'd done some awesome work on her own, but the violence today was at a new level.

For him, it was routine. For her...not so much.

"Everything that happened today..."

Her voice trailed off, so Cade didn't push it. He just held her, his hand coasting up and down her arm, over her hip and back.

"When I was taken all those years ago, I was nothing but a victim."

A victim who had used her wits and bravery to escape. Sadly, not every person in her position had a chance to do the same. "No, babe, you were a survivor."

She turned her face to kiss his throat. "I got away, but I was still...still a casualty. Helping other women helped *me*, too, because I felt useful, like I was making a difference."

"I understand."

"Today, leading up to things, I got so nervous I couldn't think straight. It was terrible."

Again Cade said nothing. He'd picked up on her growing anxiety and had tried to spare her. In that, he'd failed.

She drew in an audible breath, rubbed at her eyes and shivered again. "I learned that I can handle it, you know? I did okay today."

"You did amazing. I keep telling you, you have incredible instincts and you're a fighter. But it's more than that. You're a natural defender."

She kissed his throat again. "Why do you say that?"

A fresh wave of fury ran through his veins. Knowing Mattox had been *that close* to her, knowing that Adela had hoped to witness her murder, kept him teetering on the edge of rage. He wanted to secure her safety, he wanted her to let him care for her the way he wanted to—the way she deserved.

He wanted to spend his life with her. To share everything. Especially commitment.

He wanted marriage.

Tilting up her chin, Cade looked into her eyes, hoping she'd see everything he felt. "You protected me today."

A wry smile twisted her mouth. "Well, I tried, but I'm not sure it was necessary."

"If Adela's aim had been better?"

Wincing, she said, "Well, she did get off a shot."

"Just one, because you acted fast, ensuring she didn't get another. You were there, and I trust you, so I was able to focus solely on Mattox." But he'd lost his control, and that never happened. "Because of what he did to you in the past, because he dared to come after you again, I wanted to kill him with my bare hands. If Adela hadn't shot him, I would have beat him to death."

She swallowed heavily. "You almost did. I was…impressed. You moved like a very agile wrecking ball."

Cade wanted to give her time, but it wasn't easy, not when she looked at him with her heart in her eyes.

He wanted it all. Did she?

Just then, Parrish opened the door and stuck his head out. "You two might want to come see this."

They each looked up, but Parrish was smiling, so Cade wasn't concerned. "In a bit."

"You'll be sorry if you miss it."

"Well, now I'm intrigued." Scooting that sweet rump over his lap, Star got to her feet. Looking a little desperate for a change of topic, she took his hand and tugged. "Come on. I need a distraction."

Cade didn't, but he let her pull him to his feet, then held her back until his father went inside ahead of them. She might not have a concussion, thank God, but Cade could see that her head hurt. It was there in her pinched expression, the shadows under her eyes.

"Before we go in, I want you to know that I'm incredibly proud of you."

Her bottom lip trembled before she caught it in her teeth.

Not exactly the romantic declaration he wanted to make, but definitely something she needed to know.

"I don't think anyone's ever said that to me before."

No, probably not. Her life hadn't been an easy one. She'd conquered more hardships than any person should have to, and was still beautiful inside and out, strong and independent, caring and sexy. "What you did, how you handled yourself, was nothing short of remarkable."

Leaning into him, her forehead against his chest, she shivered. "I was afraid if I showed my fear, they'd just feed off it. That's what happened when Mattox first had me. They all loved fear, like it was a big joke." Her hands fisted in his shirt and she confessed, "But I was afraid, Cade. So afraid."

"God, me, too."

That got her gaze up to his real fast. "You?"

"Don't you dare be surprised by that." Tears filled her eyes, shredding his heart. "Please don't cry."

"I'm not," she denied, sniffling.

He brushed her cheeks, catching the tears on his fingertips before cupping her face. "I've never in my life been that afraid. If I'd lost you..." He couldn't finish that thought. Putting his arms around her, he gathered her close. "I *can't* lose you."

Swiping her eyes on his shirt, she swallowed, nodded. "I don't want to lose you, either."

Cade started to remark on that, but they heard the laughter from the great room and it drew Star's attention. She gave a tremulous smile. "Are they having a party?" Curiosity took her to the door, and since he wasn't about to leave her side, Cade followed along.

In the great room, they found the usually stuffy Bernard on the floor, long legs crossed, with a very grungy cat rubbing against his chest.

Star stalled. Cade stared.

"Yes, precious," Bernard crooned in a ridiculous voice while stroking the cat's back. "You're a beauty, aren't you, darling? Such a sweet little mama."

"Little?" Cade eyed the long, gangly cat currently getting white fur all over Bernard's dark slacks.

"Mama?" Star asked at the same time.

"Kittens." Sitting opposite Bernard, Madison gazed down into a cardboard box. "Three of them."

Star made a beeline for the box, dropped to her knees, and seconds later a beautiful smile bloomed on her face. Emotion bubbling over, she lifted a tiny ball of fur to her cheek.

God, he loved her. So goddamn much it was killing him. He thought of how she'd stood strong, how despite her fear she hadn't buckled. And now seeing this, that soft, tender side of her...

She smiled toward him. "Cade, isn't it adorable?"

Still holding her gaze, he whispered, "Very."

Arms folded, Parrish stood by the fireplace, watching it all with a slightly dazed expression. Reyes was there beside him, his stance aggressive.

Amused by that, Cade joined them. "Where did—"

"It's my cat," Reyes stated, his muscles bunching and his chin jutting.

Holding up his hands, Cade fought a grin. "Okay. No problem. So you got a cat. Makes perfect sense. Can't imagine a better time for it."

The blatant nonsense stole Reyes's angry edge, and with a roll of his eyes, he said, "It's not like I planned it. She was in the alley next to the gym. Starving, trying to care for those three little fur balls. What could I do?"

"You had to take her in," Cade agreed, clapping his brother on the shoulder. "I'd have done the same."

"That's all understandable," Parrish said. "You wouldn't be my sons if you could turn a blind eye to any suffering. The shocker is Bernard." Smiling in disbelief at his old friend, he said, "Just look at him. Have you ever seen anything like it?"

Now on his back, unconcerned with his usually impeccable clothes or his gawking audience, Bernard laughed as the cat walked over his chest to butt into his chin.

Cade shook his head. No, most definitely he hadn't. "I didn't know he liked animals."

"Neither did I," Parrish admitted. "I knew he was a loyal friend, that he loves you all like his own, that cooking is his passion and that he's a ladies' man—"

"He *what*?" Reyes asked.

Yeah, that was news to Cade, too. From what he'd observed, Bernard cared about many things—his appearance, his job...all of them. But sex? "Where the hell does he find the time?"

"Where there's a will, there's a way" was all Parrish said. "But in all the time he's worked for us, he's never mentioned having a soft spot for animals."

Reyes stared in disgust as the older man sat up again, hugging the cat to his cheek, much as Star had hugged the kitten. The difference was that the cat hung from his arms, her crooked, mismatched eyes half-closed in bliss, her broken tail twined around Bernard's forearm.

"I didn't bring her home as a gift to him. I just…" Reyes ran a hand over his head. "I couldn't leave her alone at the gym, right? I mean, that was my intention at first. But I got the call to get moving, so I didn't have time to set her up as nicely as I meant to. After I wrapped up things today, I kept thinking about her, and it bothered me."

"Understandable," Cade said, while fighting a grin at his brother's discomfort.

"I stopped by the gym on my return. She was in the box with the kittens, but it was a tight fit. She needs a real bed, cat food, too, and—"

"A litter box," Star added as she joined them. She'd put the kitten back in the box, but that sweet little smile remained on her face. "You're keeping the cat?"

Reyes stared at Bernard. "Hell, I don't know if he'll give her back." Slanting his gaze at Star, he said, "And that's going to be a problem, because Kennedy will want to know where the cat went."

"Kennedy?" Parrish asked.

"Sterling pointed her out to me at the gym." Then to Cade, Reyes added, "The hedgehog teaching herself defense techniques?"

"You talked with her?" Star asked.

"I offered her help, but she wasn't receptive. In fact, she was downright insulting about it." Gaining steam, Reyes glared at Star again. "She'd already figured out that I'm more than a gym owner. Said if I didn't want her snooping in my life, I shouldn't butt into hers."

"Huh." Star fought a grin. "So she's not only cute, and maybe in danger, she's also shrewd. I like her already."

Aggrieved, Reyes rolled his eyes.

Madison stepped up. "Want me to look into her background? What's her last name?"

Succinct, Reyes said, "No."

"Why not?" Star asked. "You guys didn't hesitate to check up on me."

"Cade was interested in you." Denying it a little too strongly, Reyes said, "Totally different story with Kennedy."

"Uh-huh." Madison nudged Star, making it clear she wasn't buying Reyes's declarations. "I want her last name—just in case."

"*Anyway,*" Reyes said with irritation, "she's the one who found the cat. I just followed her when she started down the alley."

Brows up, Star said, "You followed her?"

On the spot, Reyes flung a hand toward Bernard, then rounded on their father. "What am I supposed to do now? She expects to see the cat at the gym."

Parrish always had an answer. "Tell her you took it home to better care for it. It doesn't sound like she wants to get close to you, so that'll keep her from demanding a visit. But if she does want to see the cat again, invite her to join you on a trip to the vet."

Approving that plan, Cade stepped in with his own advice. "The cat and kittens will all need to be checked. You should get that scheduled right away."

When the kittens started mewling, the cat looked up, abandoned Bernard and hurried back to the box.

Covered in white fur, grinning ear to ear, Bernard strode over. "She'll need several things, but for now I can put together some food and better bedding. Tomorrow, I'll go to the store."

Madison gave him a hug. "I never knew you were such a big softy, Bernard."

That put his nose in the air. "I'm not."

Reaching out, Parrish plucked a clump of fur from his shirt. "You do an incredible impression."

Bernard shrugged. "I adore cats."

"Since when?" Cade asked.

"I was raised on a farm. My parents grew corn and soy, and we always had cats around." One thin hand smoothed his silver hair back into place, and in his usual lofty tone, he announced, "I've missed them."

Everyone stared at him.

Clearing his throat, Reyes took a step forward. "Look, the cat is my responsibility—"

Eyes narrowed and mean, Bernard took a step, too. "She's staying here." The challenge was clear—a first for Bernard.

Taken off guard, Reyes retreated, hands up in surrender. "Fine. No problem. I appreciate the help."

"Oh my," Star breathed.

Cade glanced at her, then followed her gaze to where the mother cat sat by Bernard's feet, a kitten in her mouth.

Bernard went comically mushy all over again. "You're bringing me your babies?" he asked in a high, silly voice. "Oh, you precious, precious thing." He sank down and accepted the little bundle. "I'm overwhelmed."

They all shared another look. Star couldn't hold back her grin, and it got to Cade. After the melancholy following the sting, she was happy again.

Relieved, aware of several strong urges, he pulled her to his side.

Madison leaned against Reyes, patting him in sympathy. After all, he'd gotten, and lost, a pet in record time. "I have some leads we can follow based on where the women were grabbed."

Jumping on that, Reyes asked, "All from the same area?"

"Very close. I've configured a map and I have a few ideas."

"It's getting late." Stressing that it was time to take a break and regroup, Parrish gave a pointed look at Star, which luckily she missed.

Knowing the toll it took to do their specific jobs, Parrish was keen on physical and emotional health.

Star, being new to it all, would especially be affected, so Cade gave his father a nod of appreciation for understanding and not pushing her.

"We can plan our next move tomorrow—" Looking down at Bernard, Parrish shook his head. "I was going to say over breakfast, but now I'm not sure."

"There will be breakfast." Bernard cuddled all three kittens in his arms, and he looked deliriously happy. "Just don't expect anything fancy."

Cade wasn't about to miss that perfect segue. "Star and I are heading downstairs. We'll see you all in the morning."

She was still trying to say her goodbyes when Cade led her from the room and to the stairs.

"Why are we rushing?"

"Because the way I need to kiss you, I figured you'd prefer we were alone."

Warmth entered her dark eyes and humor lifted the corners of her mouth. "Too impatient to wait?"

"Something like that."

She took the lead, passing him by, making him laugh out loud, until they reached his rooms. After securing the door, she started undressing—on her way to the bedroom.

"Wait up."

"Found your patience, huh?" Her T-shirt hit him in the chest and she kept going, her hands busy on her jeans. "Well, I don't want to wait."

With his longer stride, Cade caught her before she got her jeans down any farther than her knees.

Lord help him, how she looked bent over, her perfect ass on display, was enough to test his strongest convictions. But she'd been hurt, and whether or not she'd admit to the ache in her head, he wouldn't forget it.

Pulling her upright, he slid an arm under her hips, scooped her into his arms and went to the barrel chair adjacent to the dresser. Sitting with her again in his lap, he took her mouth.

He meant to be gentle, but she already had her slender fingers clasping his jaw, keeping him close while she consumed him. Her warm tongue stroked, her sharp little teeth nibbled and, yeah, he lost it.

"I want you," she groaned, shifting around so she could grab his shirt, peeling it up and over his head. Her scorching gaze traveled over his chest, and she leaned forward to lick a tattoo.

He wasn't made of steel. "Your head—"

"Is fine." Breathing hard, she leaned back to see him again. "It's my heart you need to worry about right now."

"Aw, babe." This time he kept the kiss short and sweet. "I will always protect your heart, I swear."

Emotion softened the lust, made her lips tremble. "My heart needs to feel you, around me, in me. Give me that. Please."

She'd easily outmaneuvered him, and Cade knew when to relent. Kissing her more deeply, he stood and carried her to the bed.

IT FELT GOOD to have Cade hold her so easily, proof of his strength and his affection. Even better was how he carefully lowered her to the mattress, then stripped away her jeans and panties.

That compelling steel-blue gaze moved over her. "You'll tell me if your head—"

"Yes." She patted the bed beside her. "I'll tell you."

He stripped out of his own clothes, robbing her of breath with his remarkable body. Now, being turned on, his abs were tight above an impressive erection. Always, his body hair fascinated her, how it spread out over his chest, how that happy trail led down to his cock. Every single part of him, from his military haircut to his patrician features, his granite body down to his feet... She loved it all. So very, very much.

Not unaffected by her rapt attention, Cade snagged a condom, opened the packet and rolled it on.

The second he stretched out over her, her hands went exploring, relishing the warmth of his taut flesh, the flex of firm muscle, his indescribable scent that both incited and soothed her. A little overcome, Sterling hugged him tight with her nose in his neck, breathing him in.

Cade said nothing—not with words, anyway. He used his hands and lips, the stroke of his tongue and the press of his body to tell her how much she meant to him.

Now, after everything, she believed him. This was real. Solid. A commitment she could count on. Security she'd never known she wanted but relished so very much.

He kissed her, teasing at first, just brushing over her lips, tracing with his tongue—until her breath caught and she arched up against him.

Angling his head, he let his tongue sink deep. Hot, wet. Possessive.

Sterling's fingertips gripped his shoulders, and that seemed to fire his blood even more.

"You're mine," he rasped, reaching down between their bodies to find her sex, to slide his fingers over her warm wetness... to press in, fill her, make her cry out with escalating sensations.

Marveling, Cade breathed, "Damn, you're close already."

In agreement, she pulled him into another tongue-thrusting, molten kiss while tightening around his fingers, rolling her hips against him, needing and taking.

He pulled away, but only to readjust, and then it was his cock pressing into her. Braced on his forearms, his hands holding her head and his mouth eating at hers, he rode her hard.

And she loved it.

Their combined sounds of pleasure filled the room. Desperation grew. Pleasure coiled tighter and tighter.

The second the high, vibrating moan escaped her, Cade put his head back, jaw clenched in concentration, until she began to ease in the aftermath of her orgasm. Tucking his face to her neck, he growled out his own release.

For only a few moments, he gave her his weight. With limbs tangled, all aches and pains forgotten, misgivings shelved, Sterling felt entirely at peace.

When she sighed, he struggled up to his elbows again. "Hey. You okay?"

"Mmm. I think you've found a cure for headaches. I'm blessedly numb."

The smile showed in his eyes, if not on his mouth. "Is that so?"

"Don't look so pleased. You already knew you excelled at *everything.*"

Something else joined the humor in his eyes. Affection.

Love.

"Look who's talking." Rolling to his side while keeping her tucked close, Cade heaved a big breath. "We both need some sleep."

She did, but she didn't want to sleep yet.

As usual, he seemed to know her thoughts. While stroking her back, her hip, he asked, "Something on your mind?"

Never had she thought to be in this place—a place of satisfaction and contentment. Admitting to the fears that had always plagued her seemed incredibly easy, at least with Cade.

"Star?" He lifted his head. "What's wrong?"

"I've always assumed a normal life wasn't possible for me, and I was right."

"Hey." With the edge of his fist, he nudged up her face.

She pressed a finger to his lips and spoke around the choking emotion. "I was right, but this, with you, isn't normal."

The tension in his shoulders eased a little. "It's exceptional."

"Very much so. You've given me what I didn't think I could

ever find. A place to fit in." The damn tears spilled over, but this was Cade, so she didn't mind. "I never used to cry."

"Not on the outside," he agreed, and his hand settled under her breast. "But here, in your heart, I think you were very sad."

How could he know her so well? Easy—he loved her. Well, it was time she opened up, so she smiled and said, "I appreciate how you trust me, how you recognize what I can do...and what I can't."

His mouth touched hers. "You can do anything, babe."

Love swelled her heart until there were no hollow corners left in her soul. "No, I can't. And now I don't mind that. We complement each other, you and I. I feel safe with you when I'd forgotten what safe felt like."

His eyes went a little glassy, too. "I will always protect you."

"I know. Just as I'll protect you."

He smiled and said softly, "I know."

With her newfound freedom and confidence, Sterling said, "You love me."

"More than I knew was possible."

That seemed like enough. "I want to live with you," she stated.

"I want to marry you," he countered. "Naturally we'll live together."

Marriage. It had always sounded like the standard norm, a normal she'd never have.

Now it sounded like *them.*

Sterling hugged him, letting his scent surround her, his strength cradle her, and knew she'd found the most incredibly perfect man—for her. "I love you, too. So damn much."

"Will you marry me?"

"Yes, please." Giddy happiness consumed her. "As long as we don't live here—not permanently, anyway."

Cade grinned. "I think it's time I showed you my house."

"Tomorrow," she whispered, already comfortable against him. "You might not have noticed, but I had a trying day."

EPILOGUE

EVERYONE WAS IN the breakfast room when they finally made it upstairs. Cade was surprised they'd waited on them, or so he assumed, until Bernard came in looking harried.

He carried a large tray of dishes...with his hair uncombed and his shirt untucked.

Cade shared a look with Star, who appeared equally boggled, then glanced at the others. Madison hid a smile. Parrish looked harassed.

"He's already been out," Reyes complained with a glare at Bernard. "Buying things for *my* cat."

Going rigid, Bernard paused by the table. "Her name is Chimera."

Left eye twitching, Reyes said in a soft, lethal tone, "You named my cat?"

Nose up, arrogance in full force, Bernard glared at him. "Better than calling that beautiful creature *Cat*."

"Beautiful?" Reyes leaned forward, his elbows on the table. "She has mismatched eyes and looks like she was run over by a mower."

"Her eyes are *stunning*, and now that I've bathed and brushed her, her fur is gorgeous, as well."

Astonishment dropped Reyes's mouth open. "You—"

At the head of the table, Parrish cleared his throat. "Enough on the…"

Bernard stabbed him with a look.

Parrish quickly amended, "Chimera. Food would be nice, preferably before it gets cold. Or did you only plan to stand there and let us smell it?"

The tray clattered to the table. In rapid order, Bernard set out scrambled eggs, muffins, fresh fruit and a plate of sausages.

Before he could leave, Star said, "Thank you, Bernard. I don't know how I got by so long without your cooking. You're a master."

Smug, Bernard sent Reyes a look. "Thank you. It's nice to be appreciated."

That earned a round of protests from everyone, but Bernard wasn't moved. For a moment there, Cade thought he'd flip them all off as he exited the room in his lofty way.

They dealt with a lot of crazy shit, but Bernard in that particular mood? Strangest of them all.

The stillness lasted all of three seconds before everyone started laughing. Madison pushed back her chair. "I'll go soothe the beast." She nudged her brother. "And you—stop needling him."

Reyes grinned. "No can do. The more I complain, the more determined he is to care for that… Chimera."

Cade snorted. "Good save. He did seem adamant about her having a name."

Even Parrish chuckled. "I've never seen him so rattled. He went out bright and early, buying everything from food and dishes, to catnip and toys, to bedding and brushes. He rushed back, afraid Chimera would miss him."

Star laughed. "She probably did."

"Didn't sound like it, given the racket she made while he bathed her. He had to change clothes, but then Madison came in, and shortly after that, Reyes showed up, so Bernard didn't have a chance to properly spiff up. You know he's fanatical about having food ready."

Plate already filled, Reyes settled in to eat. "I had no idea what I'd do with the cat, but Bernard has offered the perfect solution."

"There are still three kittens," Cade pointed out.

"And I have two siblings. Problem solved."

As if someone had just handed her a million dollars, Star squealed. "I get a kitten?"

"When they're old enough to be weaned—though I imagine Bernard will demand visitation rights."

Cade was smiling when Star turned a worried frown on him. "I'd love a kitten, but it's your house we're talking about, so I'll understand—"

"It'll be our house."

That got everyone quiet again. Reyes even paused in midchew with his mouth full.

Madison returned with Bernard in tow. He still looked frazzled, but he'd at least smoothed his hair. Or maybe Madison had done that for him.

Now that they were all present, Cade decided to make an announcement, before Reyes stirred Bernard up again. "I asked Star to marry me."

All eyes turned to her. Wearing a cheek-splitting grin, Reyes said, "I'm guessing you said yes, or he wouldn't be looking so pleased."

"Of course I said yes. I'm not a dope."

In seconds, Madison was right back out of her seat, circling the table to grab Star in a hug. Appearing pleased, Bernard lifted his orange juice in a toast. "Welcome to the family."

Even Parrish smiled, saying to Cade, "Finding the right woman for you is the greatest gift you'll ever receive. I'm happy for you."

That sobered them all. It was a stark reminder that Parrish had found his love—and lost her to violence. That loss had determined how he'd raised his children, and how they lived their lives.

Seeking justice.

Because of that, he'd met Star.

Such a lifestyle shouldn't have been conducive to a prolonged relationship, much less love or marriage, yet if it wasn't for his sharpened insights, he might not have noticed Star right off.

Knowing he owed Parrish a debt of gratitude, Cade looked at him, an older version of himself, and said simply, "Thank you, Dad."

Star leaned into his side, smiling, happy. "Yeah, thanks. For a bunch of stuff, but mostly for raising such an awesome son."

Being an ass, Reyes asked, "Do you mean me or Cade?"

Bernard threw a napkin at him, and Parrish protested the disruption. Ignoring them all, Madison opened her laptop while eating.

Star turned to Cade, grinning. "Don't tell them I said this, but your family is truly awesome."

As Cade looked at each of them, old resentments faded away. He'd been coerced to this life, but because of that he had Star. They were still nuts, but they were his. He hugged Star tight. "I agree."

* * * * *

Stronger Than You Know

To Kimmy Potts,

You graciously answered my request on my Facebook page for more information on Colorado, and I truly appreciate it. Not only that, you also answered all of my pesky follow-up questions! I know the Smoky Mountains, but the Rockies…not so much. You were a huge help, Kimmy, and I'm glad I didn't need to fly to Colorado for further research. (Not that I'd planned to, but still…) Thank you x 10!

I have to say, I have the absolute BEST readers in the entire world.

Big hugs,

Tori Foster

*Please note, any location errors that got through are my own!

CHAPTER ONE

EVEN BEFORE KENNEDY BROOKS'S Uber driver turned the corner to where she lived, her skin prickled with alarm. It was well past midnight, a fact that couldn't be helped.

She should have been home at dinnertime.

One delay after another had obliterated her schedule to the point she had to rebook her flight. After hours spent sitting in the airport, exhaustion pulled at her. She wanted nothing more than to collapse in her bed, with her own sturdy locks in place.

When the scent of smoke infiltrated the closed windows of the car, her heart beat harder. She had a terrible feeling that there'd be no rest for her tonight. Maybe not even in the foreseeable future.

"What do you suppose happened?" her driver asked, pointing to the strobe of red lights that pierced the dark night.

"Fire," she breathed. And not just any fire, but in the apartment building where she lived.

Firetrucks, police and EMTs were everywhere. Neighbors she recognized clung together, many wrapped in blankets to ward off the cool Colorado evening air. Crowds of curious onlookers also lined the street, having left their own buildings to gawk.

Lifting a shaking hand to cover her mouth, Kennedy took in the enormous blaze that engulfed the entire building—including the floor where she would have been sleeping.

The driver couldn't get close, and she didn't want him to. "Stop here."

He glanced at her in the rearview mirror. "Hey, you okay? Is that your building?"

"Yes." She swallowed heavily. *What to do, what to do?*

Because she'd learned caution the hard way, Kennedy pulled additional money from her wallet. "Wait here, please."

The young man eyed the cash, glanced back at the fire and finally took the bills. "For how long?"

"I just need to make a call." She hesitated again. "I'm going to stand directly in front of your car, in the beam of the headlights." She needed privacy for the call, but she didn't want to be alone in the dark. "Leave them on, okay?"

"Sure."

Knowing she couldn't delay any longer, Kennedy hooked her purse strap over her shoulder and neck to keep it secure, dug out her phone and stepped from the car. It was an uncommonly cool September night, yet she felt flushed with heat, as if she could feel those flames touching her skin.

There was only one person she knew who might be able to deal with the present situation.

It was fortunate she had his number programmed into her phone, because her trembling hands refused to cooperate.

As the phone rang, she kept constant vigilance on her surroundings. She could almost swear someone watched her, yet when she glanced back at the driver, she couldn't see him for the glare of the lights in her eyes.

"Hello?"

Reyes McKenzie's sleep-deep voice caused her to jump, and not for the first time. He was six feet four inches of hewn strength, thick bones and confident attitude. A man with a big, sculpted body, thanks to the gym he owned—and his voice reflected that, bringing an instant visual to mind.

Pretty sure he had other interests, as well, which would explain the edge of danger that always emanated from him.

Just what she needed right now.

Clutching the phone, hoping he'd be receptive, she whispered, "Hey. It's Kennedy."

Sharpened awareness obliterated his groggy tone. "What's wrong?"

Yes, Reyes was definitely the right person for her to call. Never mind that he had a wealth of secrets—for some inexplicable reason she trusted him. Mostly, anyway.

Tonight she had little choice in the matter. "Reyes, I need you."

She could hear him moving as he said, "I can be out the door in two minutes. Fill me in."

God bless the man, he didn't hesitate to come to her rescue. Before anything more happened, Kennedy gave him her address—something she hadn't wanted to share before now. Life had a way of upending plans, and hers had just been sucked into a treacherous whirlwind. "I'm not actually in the apartment building, though. I'm at the corner, behind a line of emergency vehicles, with an Uber driver. I don't know how long he'll let me hang out, though."

"Are you hurt?"

That no-nonsense question held a note of urgency.

"No." *Not yet.* "Could I explain everything once you're here? I'm afraid it's not safe." She felt horribly exposed.

"Forget the Uber driver, okay?" The sound of a door closing, then jogging steps, came through the line. "Get close to a firefighter. Or an EMT. *Stay there.* It'll only take me fifteen minutes if I really push it."

Nodding, Kennedy looked up the street. The officials all seemed so far away, and there was a lot of dark space between here and there. "I... I don't think I can."

"Shit." A truck door slammed. "I'm on my way, babe, okay? Get back in the car with the Uber guy and drive around in congested areas. Don't go anyplace deserted, and don't sit in one spot. Tell me you understand, Kennedy."

"I understand."

"Circle back in fifteen. I'll be waiting."

Yes, that sounded like a more viable plan. "Thank you, Reyes."

"Keep your eyes open." He disconnected, likely to concentrate on driving, and suddenly she felt very alone again. Reaching into her purse, Kennedy found the stun gun and palmed it. She'd practiced with the damn thing but had never actually used it on anyone.

She didn't want to use it tonight, either, but she felt better for having it.

All around her, smoke thickened the air and tension seemed to escalate. She opened the back door and slid into the car, saying to the driver, "Could you drive, please?"

Exasperated, he twisted back to see her. "Listen, I have to pick up another guy from the airport. I can't just—"

"I'll make it worth your while, I promise."

He eyed her anew, his gaze dipping over her body. "What's that supposed to mean?"

Oh, for the love of... Kennedy knew she was a mess. She'd pulled her hair into a haphazard ponytail, her makeup was smudged, and her clothes were sloppy-comfortable, suitable for a long flight. There was absolutely nothing appealing about her at the moment. "It's not an invitation, so forget that. Just lock the doors and drive for fifteen minutes. Stay in busy areas—no dark, empty streets—and then you can bring me back here. I'll give you another forty bucks."

Considering it, he continued to study her.

A movement beyond him drew her startled attention. There, from the long shadows, two men crept toward them. "Lock the doors and freaking drive!" she screamed.

Disconcerted, he, too, looked around, and the second he noticed the men, they broke into a jog.

Coming straight for them.

"Jesus!" Jerking the car into Reverse, he backed away with haste, almost hitting a telephone pole. Spinning around, he punched the gas and the small economy car lurched forward down the empty street. Again his gaze went to the rearview mirror. "Who the fuck was that?"

Looking over her shoulder, seeing the men fade away, Kennedy sucked in a much-needed breath. "I don't know," she whispered. *But I know they haven't given up.*

REYES DROVE LIKE a lunatic. His Harley would have been quicker, but he couldn't quite picture Kennedy strapped around him with the wind in her hair. Plus, he had no way of knowing if she'd be dressed for the cool night. Grim, he pulled up to the cross street in front of her apartment building. The road was closed off to through traffic, and the firefighters were still hard at work. Crowds had been pushed far back, held at bay by police officers.

Glancing around, he didn't see Kennedy.

But he did spot two shifty-looking dicks keeping watch on everything. Dressed all in black, with black knit hats pulled low, they watched the streets instead of the fire.

Narrowing his eyes, Reyes did a quick survey of the area and didn't see anyone else. The majority of people appeared to be enrapt with the fire—unlike these two.

Getting out his phone, he pulled up his recent call list and touched Kennedy's name. She answered before the first ring had finished.

"Reyes?" she asked with shaky urgency.

"Where are you, hon?"

"I couldn't come back. Two men are watching for me."

"Yeah, I see them. Did they bother you?"

"They charged after the Uber car, but my driver got us away. I... I don't know what they want."

"I'll find out. Give me two minutes, then circle by. I should be ready by then." Belatedly he thought to add, "I'm in my truck." Because Kennedy came to the gym he owned, and because they'd partnered in the rescue of a big alley cat, she was familiar with his ride.

"What?" With breathless panic, she screeched, "What do you mean you'll find out? You can't possibly—"

"Sure I can." For a while now, he and Kennedy had been dancing around the fact that they both had secrets. When faced with danger, she'd called him, so obviously she understood the extent of his ability.

Tonight seemed like a good night for her to learn a little more about him. "Did you hear me, Kennedy? What did I say?"

"Two minutes," she repeated blankly. "Reyes, don't you dare—"

Seeing that the guys had noticed him, Reyes smiled and disconnected. Leaving the truck, he started toward them, his attitude amicable. "What happened, do you know?"

The men looked at each other. The taller of the two said, "Looks like an apartment fire."

"Yeah, I can see that." He was only ten feet away now. "Who started it?"

They shared another glance, and Stretch spoke again. "Who says anyone did? Might've been faulty wiring."

"Nah." He continued to close the distance, his stride long and cocky—with good reason. "Pretty sure you yahoos had something to do with it." He grinned. "Amiright?"

Stretch reached inside his jacket, and Reyes kicked out, sending him sprawling backward. He landed hard, the wind knocked out of him.

His shorter friend took an aggressive stance.

Bad move. With a short, swift kick of his booted foot, Reyes took out the guy's braced knee. He screamed in pain as his leg buckled the wrong way.

Quickly Reyes patted him down, removing both a knife and Glock. Still squatting, he shifted his attention to Stretch just as the guy got back to his feet.

Maybe hoping to mimic Reyes's moves, Stretch tried to plant his foot in his face.

Reyes ducked to the side, grabbed his ankle and yanked him off balance again.

Down he went for the second time. Unfortunately, he cracked his head and, without so much as a moan, passed out.

"Well, hell." Turning back to the shorter dude, Reyes prodded him. "Who are you and what did you want with the girl?"

Dazed with pain, his face contorted, the guy gasped, "What girl?"

"Dude, you are seriously whack. Want me to bust the other knee? I can, you know." Using the muzzle of the Glock, Reyes tapped his crotch. "Or maybe you want me to smash these instead?"

Rolling to his side, he cried, *"No."*

Heaving a sigh, Reyes stood. "What a wuss. C'mon, man. Give me something. It's not like I really *want* to hurt you, you know." *Not much, anyway.* But when he thought of these two planning to harm Kennedy...yeah. Red-hot rage. "I'll give you to the count of three. One. Two."

"All right! We were hired to grab her. That's all I know."

"Bullshit. There's always more. Like where were you going to take her? Who wants her? And why?"

"I don't know, man! We were paid half, and once we grabbed her, someone would call with an address. After we dropped her off, we'd get the other half."

"Yeah? Planned to do this whole thing blind, huh?" Reyes heard Stretch groan and knew he was coming around. Probably a good thing.

"I mean...trust only goes so far."

What a joke. Who the hell was dumb enough to trust these two? "Maybe your buddy has more info on him. If I find out you're lying, you won't like what I do."

"Bolen woulda found out same as me, when we got the call."

Sounded legit, but Reyes wasn't taking any chances. Going over to Bolen, he quickly searched him, removing another gun and also taking his wallet. Inside he found a stack of hundreds, but nothing useful. When Bolen tried to sit up, Reyes pistol-whipped him. He collapsed again.

Glancing back at the other guy, who made a failed attempt to get up, he asked, "What's your name?"

"Herman."

"Ah, dude, you said that so fast I'm not sure I believe you." When Reyes reached for him, the guy flinched away. "Man, you are seriously not cut out for this line of work." He shoved him to his side and pulled his wallet from his back pocket. It, too, was padded with bills. "You guys got a nice paycheck for kidnapping, didn't you?"

"I need an ambulance."

"Yeah, probably. Pretty sure I fucked up your kneecap. You might never walk the same." He searched through the wallet, curling his lip at a condom, a few interesting business cards for local joints, a coupon and a receipt. "Tell you what. Once I'm gone, you can try to crawl down there by the fire you set. EMTs are still caring for the people you hurt. Course that might raise questions you don't want to answer, right? One thing could lead to another, then you and your busted leg might end up rotting in prison." Reyes pulled out his driver's license. "Huh. Herman Coop. Well, Herman, now I know how to find you. And trust me, if you ever bother the girl again, I will. You won't like the outcome of that."

"God," Herman groaned, sweat soaking his face from pain.

"When good old Bolen comes around, you tell him I'm watching him, too, yeah?"

"Who the fuck are you?"

Headlights bounced around nearby, and he sensed it was Kennedy returning. With an edge of menace, he intoned, "Your worst nightmare." Seeing Herman's face, Reyes barely bit back his laugh.

He did enjoy spooking the knuckleheads.

Coming to his feet, he considered alerting the nearby cops, but he didn't know how that might implicate Kennedy. Hell, he didn't know her secrets or how serious they might be.

Should have listened to his family and researched her. In fact, he'd be willing to bet his computer-tech sister hadn't listened when he'd told her to step down.

Research was what she did, after all.

Then he and his brother followed up in whatever way was necessary.

For now, though, all he knew for sure was that there was more to Kennedy Brooks than she let on.

He nudged the thug with the edge of his boot. "On your stomach, lace your fingers behind your head, and don't move or I'll send your balls into your throat."

It took a lot of effort for Herman to painfully maneuver around, but the balls threat often worked wonders. Choking on his every agonized breath, Herman got into position.

"Stay like that," Reyes warned again as he began moving away, one of the guns held at the ready in his right hand, the remaining weapon and wallets balanced in his left. He glanced behind him and saw Kennedy stepping out of the car, her eyes huge in the shadows. The driver lurched to the trunk, practically tossed out a rolling suitcase and allowed her to snatch a laptop case out of his hands. While she tried to get her luggage upright, the driver sped away.

Leaving her standing there alone.

Giving up on the goons, Reyes jogged to her. "Come on."

Staring at the load he carried, she whispered, "What did you do?"

"Gathered intel, that's all. Move it." He got her to his truck, dumped the confiscated items onto the floor and practically tossed her inside. "Buckle up, babe." He took her laptop case from her and shoved it to the floor as well.

After putting her enormous suitcase into the back of his truck, he gave one last look at the fallen men and a quick glance at the still-raging fire. The night had turned into a clusterfuck of the first order. But, hey, Kennedy had called him, not anyone else.

Overall, he'd claim it as a win.

TREMBLING FROM HER eyebrows to her toes, Kennedy wrapped her arms around herself as Reyes drove away, putting the fire farther and farther behind her. Physically, anyway. Emotionally? She knew what could have happened, what might have been intended, and it left her painfully aware of her own vulnerability.

Hadn't one tragedy in her life been enough? "Reyes?"

"Hmm?" As if he hadn't just annihilated two men and stowed multiple weapons near her feet, he flashed her a smile meant to reassure. "You okay?"

The interior lights created a bluish glow over his dark hair and limned his wide, muscular shoulders. No man should look as good as he did.

From the first moment she saw him, she'd made note of his physique. Every moment since then had been an exercise of resistance.

Kennedy peered down at the floor. Two big guns, a wicked-looking switchblade and a couple of wallets shared space with her laptop case, leaving her feet little room.

Those men had planned to use those weapons on her. She felt sure of it.

After adjusting the heater, Reyes patted her leg. "I've got you, honey. You're safe."

Odd, but she did feel safe. The road ahead was long and dark, and she had no idea where they were going, but Reyes wouldn't let anyone hurt her. She believed that.

"Babe? You're worrying me."

It shouldn't have surprised her, but it seemed her call had further changed the dynamic of their relationship. They already had a loose friendship, formed during the joint rescue of Chimera the alley cat, so they were beyond being merely gym member and gym owner.

They'd never dated. She'd deflected his efforts to get to know her better. Instinctively, she knew Reyes was more than a simple man running his own business. Others might take him at face value, but she'd experienced things others hadn't, and it had changed her forever.

With his secrets, as well as the lethal ability he usually tried to downplay, Reyes reeked of danger.

Plus, avoiding involvement with any man suited her just fine.

Now, that didn't seem possible.

She might be bordering on shock, but she hadn't missed the things he'd called her, like *babe* and *honey*. If he'd ever used endearments before, she didn't recall it.

Usually she wouldn't like it. Tonight? She wanted more than just his affection. She wanted his protection. She wanted his comfort.

She wanted him to promise her it would be okay.

Her eyes burned as she stared at him. She could pretend it was from the smoke, though she knew better. "I don't have anywhere to go." The enormity of the situation was sinking in, bringing a tinge of panic with it. "Almost everything I owned was in that apartment." Another thought occurred to her, and she gasped. "My car! My car was parked in the lot behind the building…"

"Shh." Reaching over, he clasped her knee, his thumb rubbing against the side of her thigh through her leggings. "I'll handle it, okay? For now, just tell me what happened."

Quickly she tried to tally her cash. She had credit cards—would it be safe to use them? "I don't know where to go."

His hold on her knee firmed. "With me. You go with me, Kennedy. We'll work it out."

Swallowing heavily, utterly relieved that she wouldn't be alone, she nodded. "I guess I'll get to see Chimera, so that'd be—what?" The way he grimaced made her fear something had happened to the cat, too. When they'd rescued her from the alley, she'd been half-starved and nursing three kittens. Reyes had taken the animals home with him, but so far she'd been joining him on the vet visits and splitting those bills.

"Chimera isn't with me right now."

Unreasonable anger swelled. "You got rid of my cat?"

"No! Damn, do you always have to think the worst of me?" He

released her leg and squeezed the wheel with both hard-knuckled hands. "She's with my dad right now. Or actually, my dad's man."

"Your dad's man?" Kennedy blinked. "What exactly does that mean?"

He shook his head. "Tell you what. Let's come back to that later, okay? For now, just know that Chimera is well loved and cared for." He tipped his head to the pile of stuff he'd dumped on the floor. "Check out those wallets, see if you know either of those bozos. Keep their licenses out so I can give their names to my brother."

"Your brother? The guy who's even taller than you?" She'd seen him once at the gym, along with a woman who looked equally beautiful and badass, as if she could chew rusty nails while seducing someone.

The relationship to the brother had been plain. Both men shared superb physiques, incredible height and gorgeous faces. Reyes's eyes were a warm hazel, but his brother's had been bright blue. At six foot four, Reyes was tall, but his brother had a few inches on him. Of course she'd noticed the brother—it would have been hard not to—but unlike the other women at the gym that day, Kennedy hadn't gawked.

"Babe, if you keep questioning everything I say, we're never going to get this show on the road."

Get the show on the road? Her life was in a shambles and he cavalierly—

"I got this, okay?" He glanced at her, then returned his gaze to the dark road. "Cooperation would be nice, but you have my word, I'm not going to let anything happen to you."

And there it was, that cockiness she knew would make her feel better. "Okay. Thank you."

His grin created an over-the-top dimple in his cheek. A man like Reyes McKenzie didn't need the added charm of dimples, for God's sake.

"Licenses?" he prompted with an endless store of patience.

"Right." Having a purpose galvanized her. Her fumbling hands accidentally dumped one wallet, and she didn't care. Quickly she located both IDs, studying the faces, hopeful of making sense of what had happened. "No." Deflated, she dropped back in the seat. Damn, she really had to get a grip. "I've never seen them before."

"No big deal." He glanced at her again. "How'd you get out of the apartment?"

"I wasn't there. I was on my way home from the airport after a weekend in Texas."

With no expression at all, he asked, "Doing what?"

She really didn't feel like summing up her entire life for him, but she supposed it was necessary. "I'm a professional speaker, specifically for schools and colleges." Every muscle in her body tensed. She watched his profile, counted five beats of her heart, then made herself whisper, "I cover the dangers of human trafficking."

Slowly he nodded, as if that answered a question he hadn't yet asked. "You have that knowledge from experience?"

Five more heartbeats, each strong and steady. It was a practice she'd learned to remind herself that as long as her heart beat, she was alive.

And as long as she was alive, she had hope.

Tonight she had more than hope.

She had Reyes McKenzie.

"Should I gather from your silence that you don't want to talk about it?"

Giving up her scrutiny of his face, she stared out the passenger window. "I talk about it all the time. Professional speaker, remember?"

Accepting that, he asked, "How old were you?"

So matter-of-fact, as if she hadn't just imparted life-altering news. Most people were taken aback at the mention of something as heinous as trafficking. They balked and usually changed the subject.

None of which would help a person taken into captivity.

What victims needed, especially young people, was information. Ways to avoid being taken, and what to do if they were.

No one had ever reacted as Reyes just had. So what was his real vocation? Definitely, he did a lot more than just running a gym.

"I feel like everything I say causes you this painful introspection. I'm sorry for that, okay? But the best way for us to tackle this is to first understand it."

Kennedy knew he was right. She filled her lungs with a bracing breath. "I'd just turned twenty-one. Fresh out of college. A know-it-all." In truth, she hadn't known a damn thing, not about the real world. "I tell kids what to watch for, how important it is to have situational awareness, and what it means to risk going out alone."

"Did you get taken from Texas? Or here in Colorado?"

"Florida," she answered. Going into speaker mode, she insulated herself from harsh memories. "I was jogging on the beach, enjoying my solitude, thinking about my future..." She remembered it all in sharp-edged detail. "The next thing I knew, men had me, one with his hand so tight over my mouth I thought I would suffocate. I lost a sneaker in the sand. My shirt ripped."

Again he cupped her knee, the simple connection offering needed comfort.

"I got stuffed into a van and taken to a house with a few other women, some of them drugged unconscious." Tension gathered along her neck and upper spine. "That was punishment if you tried to get away. I saw two women held down while another woman injected them."

"The woman who injected them—she worked with the traffickers?"

"Yes." And that was something Kennedy still struggled with. How could one woman do that to another? She'd made a point of being the opposite. She helped not only women, but also children and some men.

"It's an ugly business. Anyone who's not a monster can't make sense of it."

Very true. "After a few weeks, I got away only because another one of the captives sacrificed herself. Literally." Kennedy rubbed her forehead, thinking of Sharlene and how she'd tried to mother everyone, even the women who were the same age as her. "There was one guy known for cruelty. He wasn't satisfied with rape. He..." Her throat closed. These were details she didn't share during her talks, not because they weren't important, but because they were far too personal.

Reyes lifted his hand from her knee, turning it palm up, waiting. When she put her hand in his, he enfolded it in his strength. Somehow, he seemed to know what to do to help.

Amazing.

"Her name was Sharlene. She was thirty years old and the most beautiful soul I've ever met. More than once she convinced a man that he wanted her instead of one of the other girls. She'd tell us to be really quiet, to avoid eye contact, and then she'd draw attention to herself." Kennedy stared at him. "She was used so poorly, and she did it anyway—to spare the rest of us."

"She did that the day you got away?"

"Yes." Kennedy tightened her hold on his hand. "The bastard decided he wanted Sharlene and me both, so I had to go along. So many times, when it was just us girls in the room, Sharlene would coach us on what to do, what to say, opportunities to look for."

"She gave you an opportunity," Reyes said quietly, as if he already knew.

"She did, and it saved me." The shallow breaths she'd been taking left her lungs starved, prompting her to suck in a deep, desperate inhale. "I knew that if there was a window near, I should go out it. If there was an unlocked door, I should try. If a car was moving slowly enough, I should take my chances on jumping out." That night had been dark just like this one, but instead of cool, crisp air, the skies had hung heavy with heated humidity. "We were on a busy street and the customer, who was driving, braked to avoid another car that switched lanes. I didn't know Sharlene was going to do it. I was pretty much just sitting there shaking. But all of a sudden she kicked the back of his seat hard, sending his face into the steering wheel. She kept kicking, too. I saw blood go everywhere. Then one car crashed into another, and the handler who rented us out was in the passenger seat and he reached back for her." Kennedy tightened her hold on Reyes. "He had a gun, and he was threatening to kill her, but all she did was yell for me to go." Kennedy swallowed hard, then whispered, "So I did."

After lifting her clenched fingers to his lips for the brush of a kiss, Reyes asked, "You jumped out of the car?"

"And into insane traffic. Tires screeched and horns blared. More cars crashed. People stopped. One man came running over to help me, another couple was already on the phone to call the police. I looked back, and the guy who'd been driving was dead." Heavy remorse, forever present, settled on her shoulders. Not for the cruel bastard who'd thought he could rent women to rape. But for a friend she'd lost too soon. "Sharlene also died in the wreck."

"The prick riding shotgun?"

"He made a run for it. I don't know what happened to him, but the police were amazing. Even with me babbling and sobbing, they understood. They did this incredible coordination between departments, all while caring for me. By the time the sun came up, they'd rescued the other women at the house and had arrested the creeps who'd caused so much harm." Tears burned her eyes, and building emotion thickened her throat. "Sharlene didn't just save me, she saved them, too, and lost her life in the process." Blinking away the tears, Kennedy sniffled. "She'll always be my inspiration for bravery, selflessness and morality. To me, she'll always be my hero."

"What was the handler's name?"

She shook her head. "They were careful not to use names around us. I'd recognize him if I saw him, but that wasn't enough for the police to find him."

Sharlene had died, and that miserable excuse for a man had gotten away.

He was still out there somewhere, and that fact, more than any other, haunted her every day.

CHAPTER TWO

KNOWING KENNEDY LISTENED, that she was sharp enough to draw a lot of conclusions from his conversation with Cade, Reyes finalized his plans. After hearing her heartbreaking experience, he'd had to do something.

Something other than pulling over and holding her tight.

Other than going back to kill the two thugs he'd left disabled.

And telling her his entire backstory was a giant no-go. His family would have a fit.

So he called big brother.

Cade, a retired army ranger and one of the calmest, most take-charge people he knew, excelled at focusing on the critical data.

Plus, when he was honest with himself, Reyes could admit that Cade had an overall positive influence on his life. Yeah, Reyes had once been a hothead. From his midteens, he'd solved all his frustrations with fighting or fucking. And God, he'd had a lot of frustrations—many that he hid beneath caustic humor. After Cade medically retired from the military, he'd stomped the worst of Reyes's rebellious nature into the dirt. Cade wasn't unduly harsh. He definitely wasn't a bully. But, over and over, in the most impressive ways, he'd refined Reyes's ability through firm control.

To this day, his brother was the only person he knew who could still best him. Didn't stop Reyes from challenging Cade. Often.

A man had to have some fun.

Now with Cade on the phone, and on the job, Reyes felt proactive rather than reactive to Kennedy's problem.

Cade would not only take care of her car, he'd get the names of the guys he'd disarmed to their sister, who would find out everything there was to know about them. Madison's research skills often left him awed. Before she was done, she'd know more about the two yahoos than they knew about themselves.

She'd been raised to do exactly that, and a whole lot more.

Like the rest of the family, his sister was tall and, when need be, dangerous in her own right.

In contrast to the McKenzies, Kennedy was downright tiny at around five feet five inches. She was also fierce in her attitude and independence.

At the gym, he'd watched her work hard to master a skill set that remained out of her reach. Unlike most who came to the gym, Kennedy didn't exercise to bulk up or shed weight, or even for reasons of fitness. Over and over again, day after day, she practiced offensive moves. Kicks and strikes meant to disable. From the first, Reyes had wondered what motivated her.

Now he knew, and, Christ, he hated it.

"I'll put out some feelers, see if there's any talk on the street," Cade said. "I'll check that her car isn't bugged, then store it at my place. Soon as Madison has some news, I'll let you know. Anything else?"

"No, that's it for now."

"Why am I not buying it? Why am I getting the impression you're a little more invested than usual?"

Because you're incredibly astute. Reyes shook his head. "That's the pot calling the kettle black." After all, Cade had rushed into matrimony the last time he'd found himself assisting a woman. And not just any woman, but one that brought her own store of trouble to the table. Reyes grinned, thinking about his sister-in-law. "Not all of us fall head over ass during a mission."

"Is that what this is?" Cade asked. "A mission?"

"Notice you're not denying the head-over-ass part."

Cade ignored that. "You and I are not the same. I don't go off half-cocked, even when I'm falling hard. You, on the other hand, tend to stay in a perpetual state of boiling over."

True enough. "I got it covered. Let me know what you find out, and tell Madison not to worry."

"We'll both worry if we want to." Getting serious, Cade added, "Call if you need me. For anything."

"Will do." Reyes disconnected, then glanced at Kennedy.

"Let me guess. Your brother was warning you against any machinations on my part?" She chafed her arms. "So far your family seems far too suspicious."

"Here's the thing," he said, refusing to let her rile him. "I never take women to my house."

She snorted at that. "Yeah, right."

"Didn't say I don't get around. I do."

"Bragging? Lovely."

"It isn't bragging," he insisted, a frown forming despite his efforts to stay even-tempered. Truth was, he never lacked for female company. "Just trying to explain why my brother was…"

"Alarmed?"

"Cade? Ha. No, he doesn't get alarmed." He never missed a damned thing, either. "Big brother could be in the middle of a three-alarm fire, during a tornado, with a murderer on his heels, and he wouldn't blink."

Wide-eyed, Kennedy said, "Wow."

Yeah, he'd just spewed way more than he meant to. "Point is," he stressed, making a concerted effort to get back on course, "I take my pleasure elsewhere, not at my home."

"Is that some sort of scruple or what? No, wait," she said, her gaze discerning. "Whatever it is you *really* do, you have to keep it private. Can't manage that if you have bed partners traipsing in and out."

"Know what?" He couldn't help smirking. "That sounded so old-fashioned it should be tarnished." When she started to grumble, he spoke over her. "I'm breaking a hard rule for you, so a little appreciation would be nice."

Grudgingly she said, "Thank you."

"Just know that I'm not taking you there for any reason other than safety." He shot her a quick glance. Having her dark past confirmed, he had to consider how unsettled she might be alone in his company—especially since she didn't buy his front as a gym owner. "I won't come on to you or anything."

She slanted him a look. "I wasn't worried."

"No?" Hell, now he didn't know if he should be insulted or not.

"I've gotten good at sizing up people. Not saying I automatically trust my instincts. I still use a lot of caution. But it should be obvious I trust you overall, otherwise I wouldn't have called you tonight."

That could have been a simple lack of options. "Do you have family?"

She hesitated far too long before shrugging. "Mom and Dad. They don't live close, though, so I couldn't call them."

Wow. If what she'd described had happened to *his* kid, he'd never again let her out of his sight. "No one you're dating? No close friends?"

She shook her head. "For the longest time I stayed on the move. Ridge Trail is the first place I've settled down since—" she flapped a hand "—everything happened."

His heart gave a hard thump in sympathy. He knew only too well how it felt to be chased by your past. "My place is secure. We'll lock down while Cade and Madison do their thing. Early tomorrow, they'll check back with what they've found, and we'll go from there."

She gave him another look of wonder. "So...that just opened up about a million more questions."

"I know, right?" Even as a part of the inner circle, the reach and ability of his family sometimes astounded him. "The important thing is that you'll be safe tonight, you can get some rest, and tomorrow we can figure out our next step. How's that sound?"

"Like I'm out of my depth."

"Yeah, you are. But I got it covered. No more questions tonight. I'm good at prioritizing, and number one is food and then sleep. Unless you're not hungry?" Some people couldn't eat when they got nervous. "If not, we can go straight to sleep."

"I'm not sure I could sleep yet, so I'll opt for food."

"You got it. Anything in particular you want? At home I can throw together a sandwich, or I have cereal. Cookies. Canned soup. Oatmeal."

"A sandwich would be great."

"Good, then we don't need to stop." He'd rather get her settled in, to know for a fact she was out of harm's way. If she'd wanted a burger or something, he'd have worked it out, but this was easier.

He was nothing if not adaptable.

This, though? Yeah, hadn't seen it coming. Knowing Kennedy had secrets, and having those secrets burn down an apartment building and come after her with guns—two very different things.

His phone rang and, knowing it'd be family, he answered.

True to form, Madison relayed information without a greeting. "No one died in the fire. Sounds like a few people were taken to the hospital for smoke inhalation, and a whole lot of people lost everything, but Dad said he'll help with that."

Good old Dad. Parrish McKenzie never hesitated to toss around the cash. "That was quick."

"Did you expect me to be slow?"

"Nope. Just didn't know Cade had gotten hold of you already. Figured he might wait until morning."

"Don't be absurd." Madison's voice softened. "How is your lady friend?"

Lady friend? Talk about old-fashioned… "Kennedy isn't like us," he said, and figured that covered it all.

"If there's anything I can do, for her personally, I mean, let me know."

Driving one-handed, he shrugged. "She has luggage with her, so I'm guessing her immediate needs are covered."

"Luggage? She'd been on a trip?"

Feeling Kennedy's hard stare, he said, "Texas."

"I need details."

Of course she did. Madison always wanted more details. It was a trait of her talent. "Because?"

"Duh. It could be related." Suddenly she demanded, "Put her on the phone."

"Hell, no." The last thing he wanted was for his sister to chat up Kennedy, making his rescue into something it wasn't.

"I'll locate her number and call her if you don't, then you'll have to explain that one."

A frown gathered. "How the hell would you do that?"

"Easy peasy." As if ticking off the high points, Madison said, "She's registered at the gym. She likely gave her cell number there. It'd be a piece of cake to access that data—"

Growling low, Reyes said, "Fine." He knew his sister didn't make idle threats. She might be beautiful, with a deceptively delicate quality about her, but like the rest of the family, she had mad skills, plus a backbone of steel and the determination of an ox.

Lowering the phone, he said to Kennedy, "My sister wants to talk to you."

Without a word, her expression enigmatic, Kennedy held out her small hand.

Damn, these two could be difficult.

Well, they couldn't have *everything* their way. As the driver of this rescue mission, he had some rights. Defiantly hitting the speaker button with his thumb, he handed it over to Kennedy.

Proving she knew how irked he was, Kennedy smiled and held the phone loosely against her knee. "Hello?"

"First," Madison said. "You're okay?"

"Yes, I think so. Still shaking horribly, but I guess that's to be expected."

"Of course. Your voice sounds strong, though. A good thing, especially when forced into my brother's company." Sotto voce, Madison added, "He's an adorable pain in the ass."

"I've noticed."

Reyes felt his eyebrows climb. Kennedy considered him *adorable*? Screw that.

The pain-in-the-ass part he couldn't really deny.

Her tone brisk, Madison said, "I take it you've been through things like this before?"

"Unfortunately—but I'm not going into that right now."

Madison had just learned something he didn't know. "What and when?" he demanded, and was thoroughly ignored.

"Understandable," Madison said. "Though eventually I'll know it all."

Eyes narrowing, Kennedy asked, "What is it you do?"

"Reyes didn't tell you? I'm the tech guru. When he or our brother need research, I pull it together."

"Research for…?"

"I'm sure Reyes will explain in his own sweet time," Madison said smoothly. "Now, short and succinct, tell me where you've been, if there were any mishaps or you noticed anything out of the ordinary."

Without hesitation, Kennedy said, "I flew into Texas on Thursday morning early. I went first to the prearranged hotel so I could unpack, get food, rest a few minutes. A couple of hours later I was picked up by a hired driver."

Madison jumped in. "Anything off about the driver?"

"No. He took me straight to the meeting place. I caught a cab back to the hotel later."

"He didn't talk to you? Didn't watch you unduly?"

"Not that I noticed," Kennedy said. "I was busy going over my notes. For me, each talk is slightly different depending on where I give it, if it's for high school or college age audiences. I speak on human trafficking, and each location has its own unique cautions."

Madison never missed a beat. "You share what you've learned?"

"I try. The least I can do is tell young people what to look for, what to avoid. What to do if they're taken."

Reyes could practically see his sister sorting through that information, but Kennedy pushed past any further questions Madison might have asked.

"I had speaking engagements Thursday, Friday and Saturday nights, then again on Sunday afternoon. I'd taken my luggage with me to the last location, a high school, so I could leave directly from there for the airport. Again, a hired driver picked me up."

"Nothing unusual?" Madison asked again.

"No."

"Do you remember the name of the company?"

Kennedy shared it without pause, proving she noted details. "It wasn't until I got to the airport that everything went haywire. My flight was delayed by three hours so I went for a bite to eat. Right as I was finishing up, a kid accidentally dumped a cola on me. After I assured the frazzled parents that it was fine, I went to the restroom to change."

Reyes gave a small smile. Of course Kennedy would reassure the parents. He hadn't known her that long, and still he'd recognized right off that she had a big heart. Otherwise, she wouldn't have set out to save Chimera. The alley cat hadn't been cute, but she had been hungry, and Kennedy had immediately decided to care for her.

Yes, Kennedy could be prickly, but he figured that had something to do with her past, and her understandable wariness.

"The line was long," Kennedy continued, "since a flight had just let out, so it took me forever to get into the restroom. I had to take wet paper towels into the stall with me, but it was impossible to wash properly. In fact, I'm still sticky."

"You can shower at Reyes's place."

Kennedy flashed him a lingering look. "Yes, that would be nice."

Real nice. Annnnd...now he had that image stuck in his brain. At the gym, he'd seen Kennedy working out in snug shorts and loose T-shirts, so he knew a little something about her body. She was short, toned, not overly endowed up top but she had a lush, well-rounded bottom that constantly snagged his attention.

Lately, too many of his fantasies centered on that perfect ass. Didn't matter if he'd just indulged in a sexual marathon with another woman, before the night was over, his brain focused back on Kennedy.

"Anyway," she said, unaware of his musings, "by the time I finished, I'd missed the next flight, too. At that point, I was ready to cry, I was so exhausted. Luckily, the flight attendants managed to get me on a connecting flight the next hour, but it turned into a long, frustrating night."

"And then you got home to find your apartment building burned down." Full of sympathy, Madison asked, "Anything sketchy about the Uber driver?"

"No. Poor guy was scared to death. I felt bad for him." Kennedy heaved a sigh. "I knew the minute I saw the commotion something was terribly wrong."

"Something personal?" Madison asked.

"Yes." Looking out the windshield, Kennedy hesitated. "I felt the danger. I *knew* someone was after me, and it made me ill to realize people could have died in that fire." She swallowed heavily. "Because of me."

"You're too smart to blame yourself for that," Madison assured her. "I agree it's unnerving to realize someone is so determined. I'm glad you trusted your instincts."

"Instincts are a powerful thing. I never ignore them." She bit her lip. "Not anymore."

Huh. So even if she didn't always trust her instincts, she didn't ignore them. Reyes considered that smart—because he was the same.

"I'm going to let you go now," Madison said gently. "When you get a minute, sometime in the morning, use Reyes's account to email me all the details of your trip. The names of the schools, addresses and any descriptions you can recall about the drivers. Anything, no matter how insignificant it might seem."

"Thank you. I feel better knowing I'm not alone in this."

Reyes scowled. What was he? Invisible? *He* was the one who'd rescued her. He would *personally* see that she was kept safe.

Here, in this moment, he didn't even care how long it might take.

When Kennedy's cool hand rested on his biceps, everything inside him snapped to awareness. Weird. His body had stopped reacting like that long ago. During personal introspection, he admitted that he was a sexual glutton. Apparently, all the variety had blunted the excitement of heated sex.

Yet here he was, all reactionary and overheated.

Couldn't deny it, he liked Kennedy's touch. He wanted more of it. In more interesting places.

But first… "Say goodbye, Madison, so Kennedy and I can talk."

Kennedy's smile teased. "Again, thank you, Madison. I'll get the info to you right away. In fact, I have my schedule in my laptop case. I always print it for quick reference. It has most of the details you want."

"She can take a pic with my phone," Reyes said. "I'll text it to you."

"Perfect. I know your phone isn't compromised, but I'm not sure about hers. Maybe keep her off it?"

"Ha!" said Kennedy. "I don't need Reyes to keep me off it, as long as I know it's not permanent."

"I'll sort it out quickly," Madison promised. "Be safe, you two. And if you need anything, don't hesitate to let me know."

Kennedy handed him the phone. Instead of disconnecting, he

took it off speaker and put it to his ear. "I need someone to cover for me tomorrow."

"Cade's taking care of it. He knows your employees."

"Great. I'll be in touch."

"Go easy, brother. She's strong, but some of that strength is a front."

Naturally, his sister knew this part of their call was private; otherwise, she never would have said such a thing. The three of them had worked together for so long it was easy to anticipate each and every move. "Got it. Thanks, hon."

She blew him a kiss and the call ended.

Holding out her hand to reclaim the phone, Kennedy said, "Interesting family you have."

He acknowledged that with a smile. She'd only witnessed the tip of the iceberg. Long ago his dad had made a decision that affected them all and determined their fates. Cade had rebelled and joined the military instead, but he and Madison, overall, had dutifully fallen in line with the plan.

Digging through her briefcase, Kennedy located several papers. Using Reyes's phone, and the number Madison had just called from, she sent images of each paper to his sister.

"That's quite the itinerary," he murmured.

"Which is why I keep it all typed out for easy reference." Once she'd put his phone in the console between them and stored her papers again, she got cozy in the corner and simply watched the dark scenery pass by.

Twenty minutes later, he pulled down the long winding drive to his secluded cabin. Sitting straighter in her seat, Kennedy looked around. "So…you're off the beaten path."

Did that worry her? Was she afraid to be isolated with him? Going for nonchalance, he said, "Easier to stay safe that way."

Her piercing gaze landed on him. "But we aren't that far from your gym. However did you manage it?"

Damn. He'd taken the long way around to his house with the sole purpose of throwing her off. Hadn't worked. "You know Ridge Trail. Go half an hour in any direction and you're lost in the mountains."

"We're not lost. *I'm* not lost." Looking at the towering trees that lined the drive, she mused, "I knew you were taking the long way, but I didn't realize we'd end up here."

"Here?"

"In a place like this." Hands on the dash, she leaned forward. "Oh, a rustic cabin."

In the distance, yellow lights showed through the tinted windows and outside each corner of the house. It looked warm and welcoming. "Rustic on the outside, comfortable on the inside." With every security amenity a dude like him could need.

While Kennedy darted her gaze everywhere, he pulled into the garage and parked beside his Harley. With a press of the garage door remote, a steel reinforced door slid back into place and locked with a comforting clang.

"Wow." She eyed him again. "I feel like I was just imprisoned."

"Believe me, you learn to like that sound." It meant no one could intrude and he could sleep in peace. "Each lower-level window has galvanized steel webbing that is locked in place at night."

"As it is now?"

"Yes." He sat still in the truck, his wrists resting loosely on the steering wheel, half turned toward her. He was unwilling to rush her. The last thing he wanted was for her to be skittish with him. "There are escape routes out the roof in the upper master, and under the rolling island that divides the kitchen and the dining room. It's small. Really small, I guess." He shifted, a little uncomfortable now that he thought about it. He could afford a bigger place, but what would be the point? He had to clean it, since he didn't allow anyone else into his sanctum. Well...except that now he was allowing Kennedy. "Only about fifteen hundred square feet, though it's enough for me."

With a soft sigh, she settled back in the seat and smiled at him. "It's sweet of you to give me time to adjust, but honestly, I'm beat. I'd rather see your house, take a shower, eat and then crash—if it's okay with you."

Her smile gave him one of his own. "You're not nervous?"

The rude snort she issued should have insulted him; instead, he laughed. "Got it. You don't see me as any kind of threat. Glad to hear it." Getting out of the truck, he headed around the hood to open her door, but she'd already done that and stepped out.

Over her shoulder, she slung her purse strap, then the strap for her laptop case. Both looked heavy enough to bring her low, but her posture warned him against offering to take them. Instead, he hefted her suitcase out of the bed of his truck.

Kennedy wrinkled her nose at the weapons and wallets. "I'll leave those to you."

"No problem. Here." Hastily, he stepped past her and did a quick finger press on the interior door that opened into the house. All the locks were biometric and opened only to his touch, though he could also operate them from his cell phone.

Stepping into the laundry room, he set down her luggage and offered his hand.

Kennedy ignored him as she looked through the room and into the hall. To the left was a half bath, and straight ahead was a guest bedroom and bath.

"This way." He led her up the hall and around the corner to the great room, which combined the living room, kitchen and dining area all in one big open space.

"Wow," she said again, her head tipped back to take in the high ceilings, the spiral staircase that led up to the master and the abundance of windows. "This is amazing."

Shifting again, Reyes did his own quick scrutiny. Pretty much everything was wood or rock, including the heated slate floors on the ground level. Upstairs he had wood floors with colorful rugs. "You like it?"

"It's beautiful. Somehow I never pictured you in a place like this."

"No?" Where had she pictured him? Sleeping in his gym?

"Everything is so detailed. And *clean*. My gosh, there's not a speck of dust anywhere. Not even a smudge on all these incredible windows." She turned a slow circle. "I love the spiral staircase. May I go up?" Already she'd slipped the straps from her shoulders and let the bags down to the floor.

"Sure." He trailed after her, wishing he'd had time to make his bed. He remembered tossing the quilt as soon as he'd gotten her call.

She went through the bedroom and into the master bath, staring at the dark gray slate that climbed the wall of the wide shower, the natural wood slab sink, the dark oval tub and brass fittings.

"OMG," Kennedy whispered. "This is stunning."

Tension gathered at the base of his neck. Why did he feel so dumb? "I, um, eliminated the third bedroom to make the master bath and bedroom bigger."

"Whoever put this together is a genius."

His mouth firmed. "I did."

Eyes flaring, she stared at him, then settled into a smile. "A man of many talents. You just keep amazing me." With that bizarre compliment she pivoted and headed back to the bedroom.

Reyes hurried to catch up with her.

She slowed as she entered the room. "These floors aren't heated?"

"Nah. I like it cool when I sleep."

"Me, too." Trailing her fingertips over the surface of his dresser, she strolled around the room, taking in the headboard that spanned one entire wall to accommodate the extrawide mattress. It had built-in end tables, bronze wall sconces and a niche for a few books. "You read?" she asked.

Okay, that went too far. Crossing his arms, he leaned against the wall and gave her an insolent stare. "Yeah, learned when I was four or five. I can write, too. Spell, do math, all sorts of complex shit."

Her mouth curled into a grin. "I meant do you read for pleasure?" She pulled a book to see the title. "Woodworking?"

The muscles of his shoulders drew tighter. "I made the sink in the bathroom."

"Astounding." Shaking her head, she slid the book back into place and pulled another. "Horror?"

"Why not?"

Moving on to yet another, she said, "Ah. A biography of famous and not-so-famous killers."

It always helped to understand the twisted psyche. "So?"

Done perusing his books, she lifted the quilt from the floor, shook it out and replaced it on the bed. "This is beautiful. Homemade?"

"Not by me." Damn it, if he didn't get her out of the bedroom soon, he'd do something stupid. "Local quilters. When I saw that one hanging outside, I asked if it could be doubled. Took a few months, and cost a small fortune, but I like it."

"So do I." Going to the window, she stared out. "No drapes?"

For an answer, he walked to the nightstand and picked up the remote. With a touch, the windows gradually lightened to make the interior visible from the outside. Always cautious, he immediately darkened them again. "Nifty, right?"

Keeping her back to him, she whispered, "So you're not only a physical specimen and incredibly handsome, you're a craftsman, a designer and, apparently, wealthy. No wonder I never bought the whole gym-owner bit."

"I *am* a gym owner." Physical specimen? Handsome. Those compliments drew him closer. "How else do you explain the physical fitness?"

"Some of it has to be genetics." Knowing he was nearer, she half turned her head. "Is your dad as physically perfect as you and your brother?"

"Now, how do I answer that?" Carefully, slowly, he settled his hands on her shoulders. Little by little, he thought he might be starting to understand her mood. "If I say yes, I'll be admitting that I'm perfect, and we don't want that."

She rubbed her face on a tired laugh. "You're perfectly exasperating." Surprising him, she leaned back into his body. "Reyes?"

"Hmm?"

"Your bedroom is up here, and the guest bedroom is down there, but I don't want to be that far away from you."

"No problem. As you might have noticed, the bed is huge."

"Ridiculously so." She turned to face him, staring up at him with a wealth of emotion in her eyes. "I promise to stay on my side of the bed."

"Yeah, no problem." He leaned closer to tease. "But if you wander over in the night, I promise not to mind." Straightening again, he took her hand and drew her along behind him. "Come on. You can shower in the guest bedroom while I make those sandwiches. If you don't mind, I can take a look at your phone, too."

"It's off," she promised. "Isn't that good enough?"

"For now, yeah." Turning it on just to see if anyone had contacted her wouldn't be a bad idea, though. Never knew when someone might make it easy by being too cocky. He didn't expect that—most shit like this went the hard route. Still... One look at the exhaustion on her face and he decided to let it go. "Where do you want your things? Upstairs for the night with us, or down here in the guest bedroom?"

Indecision had her gaze flicking to the suitcase, her laptop case and her purse. "The suitcase will be fine down here. The others can go up."

"You've got it." He carried the overstuffed bag into the guest room and set it on top of the bed. "Should be a few towels under the sink. You need anything else? Soap, toothbrush?"

"Thank you, but I have it all with me."

He rubbed his hands together, hesitant to leave her. She looked small and worn-out, and she had to be running on last reserves. "All right, then. I'll have sandwiches ready in ten minutes, but take your time."

For a few seconds more, she continued to stare up at him. "What would I have done tonight without you?"

Smoothing down her mussed honey-blond hair, he admitted, "I have a feeling you'd have figured it out."

"I'm glad I didn't have to."

Damn, much more of that and she wouldn't get her shower because he'd be kissing her. "Me, too." With one last brush of his thumb over her warm cheek, he walked out of the room, pulling the door closed behind him.

CHAPTER THREE

DRESSED IN LOOSE pajama pants and a baggy T-shirt, her hair caught up in a ponytail, Kennedy walked across the heated floors, listening for Reyes. When she didn't hear him right away, fear wormed in.

Incidents like what had happened tonight never failed to transport her back to that time and place when she'd been at the mercy of people who'd had none. Standing in the quiet house, out in the middle of nowhere, feeling very much alone, she became that frightened woman again.

Reflexively, she put her hand to her heart, counting the beats. One, two, three... Alive. She was still alive.

"Hey."

Her gaze shot up, and she found Reyes standing there between the kitchen and the living room. He was now barefoot, shirtless, and his jeans hung low. He also watched her closely, as if waiting for any unsettling reactions.

She had a reaction, all right. Fear immediately diverted to sizzling awareness.

Forcing a smile, she said, "I didn't hear you."

"I was texting with my brother. He has your car."

"Already?"

Reyes shrugged and turned back into the kitchen, leaving her to follow. "By the way, my sister-in-law, who until recently drove a semi, thinks your little red compact is cute."

Stomach rumbling, she went in to sit at the table. "It *is* very cute." Two place settings were arranged, each plate holding a sandwich cut in half, chips and a few pickles. "God, I'm starved," she said as she sat.

"Dig in." He opened the fridge. "What do you want to drink?"

"A cola would be great, but then I'd never sleep, so...water?"

"Sure." He withdrew two frosty bottles and brought them to the table, cracking open the caps on each before setting them down. "I did a sort of cold cut combination. Hope that works for you. Turkey, ham and salami."

She lifted a slice of wheat bread and saw lettuce, tomato and onion. "Mmm. Lots of veggies, too."

"With cheese and mayo." He smiled at her.

She took a big bite and hummed in bliss. Once she'd swallowed, she said, "It feels like I haven't eaten for days, but I always overeat when I'm anxious."

"Anxious?"

"Nervous." She flapped a hand. "Uncertain."

He paused. "With me?" Before she could answer, he asked, "Should I grab a shirt? I should grab a shirt, shouldn't I?" He started to leave the room.

"No, goofus. This is your house and you should be comfortable." Yes, he kept her hyperaware, but she wouldn't tell him so. He was cocky enough already.

"It doesn't bother you?"

He bothered her plenty, in interesting ways. "Burned-down apartment building? Armed men? It's that stuff that put me on edge." Seeing his expression, she grinned. Had he thought she was anxious about crawling into bed with him?

She was, just a little, but it wasn't in her nature to admit to weaknesses. Not when she could help it.

"Glad to hear it." He went back to devouring his sandwich.

She didn't. "You make me grateful, Reyes. Seriously. If not for you, I'd probably be in some expensive hotel right now, scared to sleep and fretting about what to do next."

It took him a second, and finally he accepted her explanation.

"You told my sister other stuff had happened. You want to tell me about that while we eat?"

She'd rather not. Not tonight. Then again, the sooner things were resolved, the sooner she'd feel safe again. She picked up her sandwich. "Could it wait until tomorrow?"

"Depends on how critical it is, and if it has anything to do with what just happened."

Always so pragmatic. "The thing is, if I start talking about all that again, the hot shower I just took will be useless. I'll be all tensed up and then I won't be able to sleep. If we wait until the morning, when I'm fresh and the sun is out, it won't feel so overwhelming."

He studied her as if looking for the lie. "You promise there's nothing I need to know tonight?"

"I honestly don't think so. It will wait." As he'd said, she was safe here.

"All right then," he decided, as if he was the one in charge.

Whereas his autocratic attitude used to rub her the wrong way, now it seemed somewhat reassuring. Still, she pretended affront. "Gee, thanks."

"Am I coming on too strong? At this point in my life, it's habit. Nothing I can do about it." He held out his arms. "You get what you get."

"You being an alpha and all that."

"Well, I am, yeah. But also, I know about this stuff, right?"

Stuff being heinous people lacking a heart and conscience?

Apparently, he didn't need confirmation. "One thing I've learned is that the more info you have, the better you can deal with threats. If that makes me alpha, hey, I've been called worse."

She laughed. "You're nuts, Reyes, but you really do make me feel better."

Smiling with her, he let his gaze travel over her face in what felt like minute detail.

Flustered, she grabbed up a pickle and popped it into her mouth.

Finally he murmured, "I like you like this."

In so many ways she was out of her comfort zone, a common occurrence with Reyes McKenzie. "How's that?"

"Less…antagonistic? Smiling and laughing a little."

Ah. Yeah, she'd been cautious about getting to know him, at least until they'd found the cat outside his gym. "I'm imposing on you," she said. "It would hardly seem fair to be disgruntled about it."

"Is that what you call your attitude at the gym? Disgruntled?"

Her face warmed. Okay, so she hadn't been the friendliest person around. She hadn't been outright rude, either—or had she? "It was different after we found the cat, don't you think?" It had been for her. "I started to trust you a little then."

"Only a little?" He tsked. "When you ran into trouble you called me, so I have to believe you have ultimate trust."

"At least in your skill set."

"And my integrity?"

"Talk about old-fashioned." His serious expression didn't change, so she shrugged. "Sure. I assumed you'd be able to help, and I trusted that you would." He'd reacted faster than she'd expected, and with a lot more violence. Not that she'd complain.

Clearly he had a network of sorts set up with his siblings, yet she didn't know why. That, as much as his overall carefree outlook on life, kept her guarded.

"Surprised you, didn't I?" He gestured. "With how quickly I got things done, I mean. Bet you weren't expecting that."

"No, I wasn't." Idly she nibbled on her chips, wondering what he was thinking. "Reyes?"

He glanced up. "Hmm?"

"I don't want you to feel responsible for me. Tomorrow morning, I'll work this out, whatever it is. You're not stuck with me or anything like that."

"No worries. I have big shoulders. I don't mind taking on a little responsibility."

He couldn't mean that, not when he'd set up his life as a bachelor. If she believed him, he'd never even brought another woman into his beautiful home. She cleared her throat. "Thank you, but *I* mind."

Eyeing her, he said, "I thought you wanted to wait until morning to sort things out."

"I do."

"There you go."

Exasperated, she gave up. "Fine."

Unlike most people, he didn't chime in to have the last word. He just smiled.

For the next few minutes, they finished eating in comfortable silence. She went to brush her teeth while he put things away. She felt like a slug, but if it had been up to her, she'd have left everything on the table until the morning.

This time when she stepped out of the room, he was waiting for her. "I brushed my teeth, too," he said. "Took my shower earlier before you called. So...you ready to head up?"

Hello, anxiety. She, Kennedy Brooks, was about to sleep with a certifiable hunk. Granted, it wouldn't be a sexual thing. That didn't stop her from imagining it all in a fast-rolling reel of images.

It felt incredibly momentous to nod, to allow him to take her hand, to be led up the spiral stairs and to his room.

"Did you lock up downstairs?"

"Happens automatically, and sensors tell me if anything unlocks." Releasing her, he turned back the quilt. "You're safe here, Kennedy. Swear."

Why did her mouth go dry? She nodded.

"Which side of the bed do you want?"

"Which side do you usually use?"

"The middle?"

"Oh."

He grinned. "Mind if I sleep in my boxers? It's a requirement, you know. All bachelors who live alone either sleep in the raw or in their shorts. I'm offering shorts as a concession to our sleepover. I promise it doesn't make you any more susceptible." He held up his hands. "I respect boundaries, no matter what I'm wearing." He flashed his dimple at her again. "Or not wearing."

Kennedy stared at him, awed that he'd spewed so much nonsense in a single breath. True, sleep pants wouldn't have hindered him in any way. It was just the idea of him wearing the additional barrier to his oh-so-awesome body. Unfortunately, she'd already been rattled by the idea of sleeping in the same bed with him. Rattled, yet very determined not to be alone with her unruly worries.

Now she'd have to deal with him being mostly bare?

He stood there waiting, a look of amused expectation in his

eyes, and it was in that moment she realized that he hoped she would protest. Not only that, he assumed she would.

That man was never serious, not even in a life-and-death situation like they'd experienced only hours ago. Well, she wouldn't give him the satisfaction.

"No biggie," she said, her tone all breezy and unconcerned, while anticipation hitched her heartbeat into a gallop. "I don't want you to be uncomfortable."

"Awesome."

Now she waited...but he didn't remove his jeans. Darn. She'd been braced for the impact of seeing him mostly bare and, given his grin, he knew it.

He surprised her by suggesting, "Since you're being so agreeable, how about we snuggle? That'll be a hell of a lot easier than trying to keep to my own side of the bed." Before she could mentally digest that, he asked, "You like snuggling, right?"

No way would she admit that her life had been devoid of anything even close to snuggling. Get that close to a man? No thanks. Reyes though... "I'm not sure it would be smart to—"

"I've had a shock today," he said with ludicrous gravity. "Don't know about you, but I could use some human contact. Strictly platonic. No hanky-panky." He put his nose in the air. "I'm not that easy, so don't get any ideas."

Crazy Reyes. "How many platonic relationships have you had with women?"

"A few." This time he really did look somber. "Here's the thing, Kennedy. I would never do anything to further stress a woman who was already distressed."

"And you've dealt with distressed women before?"

His voice gentled. "Pretty sure you already know the answer to that."

"I do." She didn't want either of them to get too serious, not right when they were going to bed. Not when she hoped to get some actual sleep. "Snuggling it is. I can keep my hands to myself, no problem. You're tempting, but you're not irresistible."

"You wound me." He gestured at the bed. "Climb in."

Climb was an accurate term, given the expanse of that oversize bed. She chose the side farthest from the door with the idea that if anyone did get into his house, he'd be better equipped to stop them.

Settling on her back against the downy soft pillows, she pulled the quilt up to her chin.

He gave her one long look, then switched off the light. She heard rustling and knew he was stripping down to his shorts. Inhaling deeply through her nose, Kennedy tried to relax.

When the bed dipped, she tensed all over.

"You're like a cobra, ready to strike. Is it safe for me to get comfortable?"

Nodding, she choked out, "Yes."

With great care and a deliberate lack of haste, he scooted closer, put an arm around her waist and drew her into full contact with his body.

Hot. Hard. And, great, he smelled enticing, too.

"Turn to your side." As he said it, he guided her, so that she faced away from him. One thick arm slipped under her head, the other pulled her closer still. "Now sleep."

That had to be a joke! Seconds ticked by, then minutes. His heat sank into her. Her breathing aligned with his, slow and deep. He didn't move, didn't let his hands wander, and gradually she started to relax.

Lethargy crept in.

Sleep beckoned.

Yet she knew he was still awake. She knew he'd stay awake until she dozed off. When more time passed and he hadn't done more than hold her safe and secure, she realized what he'd done. And why.

"Reyes?"

His voice sounded deep and dark behind her. "Yeah?"

"You knew I needed this, didn't you?" Even though she hadn't known it. "That's why you suggested it."

"I don't need a reason to want to cuddle with a hot babe, but yeah, I figured we both could use it."

Kennedy seriously doubted he had any such need, which made the gesture even nicer. And *hot babe*? As if. She knew she made a decent appearance, but *hot* was not a word applied to her.

"I've probably said it a dozen times today, but thank you."

He pressed a soft kiss to her temple. "Sleep."

Relaxing into him, she did just that.

REYES WOKE BEFORE she did, but then, he always woke early. Didn't matter what time he went to bed, or how much sleep he got. The sunrise triggered an inner alarm clock. Sometime during the night, Kennedy had turned to face him, and now one flannel-covered thigh was draped over his junk.

Course he had morning wood.

Luckily she slept through him gently rearranging her. Slipping from the bed, he yawned, stretched and scratched his chest. All the while his gaze remained on her.

It was a unique but not altogether unpleasant feeling to have a woman in his house. In his bed.

In this light, her golden hair looked darker, all the different shades hidden beneath murky shadow. Overall, her honey-blond hair had streaks of lighter blond, brown and even a few hints of red. All natural, he assumed, because she didn't strike him as a woman who spent much time in a salon. He'd yet to see her hair styled in any way. Sleek ponytails, the occasional braid and sloppy topknots were more her speed.

His gaze tracked down her small, sweet body.

The gentle slopes of her breasts barely showed beneath the big shirt. Her arms, one resting limply over her middle, the other turned up by her head, looked delicate and softly rounded in the most feminine way.

Despite all the work she did at the gym, it didn't show. There were no obvious muscles, definitely no bulk. He could say she was toned, without excess weight. Except when it came to her ass.

Plenty of plump curves there.

Not only was Kennedy short, she was very fine boned. Delicate hands, fingers slightly curled, were half the size of his.

Drawing a breath, his attention moved to her parted lips. That mouth was at the top of the list of things he'd noticed about her, with her attitude being first, and her stellar ass being second. Her mouth was usually set in a stern line, at least when talking to him. While trying to improve her speed at striking and kicking, she sometimes pursed her lips. When worried, she chewed her bottom lip.

She displayed a lot of emotions with her mouth, and it never failed to intrigue him.

Hell, *she* intrigued him, in ways no one else ever had.

Why she affected him so strongly, he couldn't say. It had happened the day he met her, when she'd bombarded him with her suspicious nature.

His thoughts traveled back as he recalled it, an occasion he'd locked into his memory bank because it had been so unique.

Prompted by his sister-in-law, who had insisted that Kennedy looked like a woman needing help, Reyes had approached her with the thought of offering his services.

For far too long, she'd simply ignored his presence. When he hadn't budged, she'd had no choice but to acknowledge him.

She hadn't been polite about it.

The way she'd snapped, *What?* amused him now.

At the time, it hadn't been quite so entertaining. *I'm Reyes McKenzie, owner of the gym—*

I know who you are.

She hadn't given her own name, so he'd stood there, waiting.

Until she rolled her eyes. *Kennedy Brooks. I've signed up for a year, but if there's a problem with my membership—*

There's no problem. The only problem he'd noticed was that she didn't know what she was doing. *You need any help?*

No, thank you.

Some invisible force kept him from walking away. *If you want to defend yourself—*

Just getting in shape.

That obvious lie had brought out his most forthright manner. *I don't think so.*

Instead of being impressed with his insight, she'd seemed merely curious. *Why do you say that?*

I've been watching you, he'd admitted, just to see what she'd say.

I noticed you watching, she'd countered, showing her own plain-spoken ways.

Reyes had forged on. *I was watching because I see the dif-*

ference between getting in shape and learning how to fend off attackers.

Well, that confirms something for me.

For whatever reason, he'd found himself drawn to her. *Yeah? What's that?*

You're not a mere instructor.

Obviously she had her own store of acute insight. *I already told you, I own the gym.*

You're more than a mere gym owner, too.

That straight shot had leveled him, leaving him at a loss.

You think you're the only observant one here? No, Mr. McKenzie, I also notice things.

If on that day someone had told him that Kennedy Brooks would end up in his bed, and that she'd be there not for sex but for protection... Yeah, he might've believed it. He'd known right off that she was into something, that she had deep secrets.

And that he wouldn't leave her to fend off danger on her own.

Astounding. Not that he'd save someone in need—that was his stock-in-trade. But that he'd feel compelled to make it personal? Only with Kennedy.

Studying her, Reyes smiled.

For a while now, he'd been taking note of Kennedy's every move. What time she came into the gym, how long she stayed, what she did there and how she acted as she went out. Without being too obvious to the casual observer, she was attentive to her surroundings. She had an air of alert wariness.

His sister-in-law was right, of course. Kennedy Brooks had a whole lot of *something* going on. He needed to figure out what.

Silently he headed into the bathroom, easing the door mostly closed behind him. To keep from disturbing her, he left off the light and didn't let the door click shut.

He was standing there at the toilet, lost in thought, when suddenly the light came on, blinding him. Over his shoulder, he looked back to see a sleep-rumpled Kennedy staring at him in mute, open-mouthed surprise.

"Hey."

When she tried to speak, nothing came out.

Funny stuff. To fill in the silence, he said, "Had to drain the pipes, you know." She still didn't move, and he couldn't, considering he was in the middle of things. "Don't usually do this with an audience, but if you have some kink I don't know about—"

Sharply pivoting, she almost ran into the wall, staggered around and through the doorway and, all in all, fled the scene.

Smirking, Reyes finished up, then washed his hands, did a quick brush of his teeth and splashed his face. He wasn't about to waste time shaving yet.

Expecting to find her in the bedroom, he stepped out, but the rising sun proved the room was now empty. He cocked an ear and detected sounds in the downstairs bathroom.

What an interesting morning. He'd awakened with sleepy women before, but not in this house, and none who weren't comfortable with the whole scene.

Without dressing, he snatched up his cell phone from the nightstand and started down the stairs in time to hear water running. She was likely doing her own quick cleanup before facing him. Not that she needed to. The whole bed-head look and wrinkled sleep clothes worked on her.

Hell, if he let it happen, he could be half-hard already.

Determined not to spook her, he called out, "Coffee in the kitchen in ten." He didn't get a reply.

In less than one minute, he had the coffee prep done, and the smell of freshly ground beans filled the air. He set out two mugs, sugar and powdered creamer, in case she wanted either, then he took a seat at the table and switched his phone from sleep mode.

It pinged immediately, indicating one or both of his siblings had also awakened early. He saw he'd missed a call from Cade, and hit Redial.

His brother answered with, "Both are dead."

Reyes's brows shot up. To make sure he hadn't misunderstood, he asked, "The dudes I mangled?"

"Bullets to their brains. Good thing they were shot in the forehead and not the back of the head, because the ammo used blew out with an explosion."

Imagining that, he grimaced. "Meaning a shot to the back of the melon would have destroyed their faces, leaving them unrecognizable."

"Exactly." Grimly Cade said, "You need to find out who Kennedy knows that might commit execution-style murder."

"Don't tell me you feel bad for those bastards."

Cade didn't bother replying to that idiot gibe. They were both capable of offing traffickers when necessary, and neither of them would feel an ounce of remorse when it meant women would be spared their abuse. "If they weren't dead when I got there, I might have been able to interrogate them—"

Aka coerce them by whatever means into spilling their guts.

"—or at the very least I could have tracked them. Now there's nothing but cold bodies."

"Cops see you there?"

"Stop trying to provoke me."

Reyes grinned. No, Cade wouldn't be spotted. He was far too slick for that. "So now it's up to Madison to do her thing."

"She was up and at it when I got to Dad's half an hour ago. I'm not sure she went to bed last night."

"Yeah, I know how she is when she starts researching. One thing leads to another."

"And another and another, and she refuses to stop until the trail goes cold."

"If it goes cold." With Madison, that seldom happened. She could uncover stuff the FBI couldn't find. Leads that started in one direction often fanned out in new ways that kept her intrigued.

"Talk to Kennedy," Cade said. "Then let me know what you find out."

"On it." Speak of the devil, Kennedy dragged herself into the room just then. "Later," he said to Cade, disconnecting the call and coming to his feet to pull out a chair for her. The girl looked like a very appealing zombie. That sweet bottom dropped into the seat as if pulled by forceful magnets. She managed to get one hand up in time to catch her head, and then she sat there, boneless, her eyes barely open.

For some ridiculous reason, Reyes felt charmed. "Not a morning person?"

Without answering, her eyes sank shut.

He chuckled and headed for the coffee carafe. It was still sputtering when he pulled it free and filled two mugs. After setting both on the table, he asked, "How do you take it?"

Again without replying, she lifted the mug to her mouth, sipped, sipped, sipped, sighed, and said, "Cream and sugar."

On the verge of laughing, Reyes dumped in a spoonful of sugar, waited while she watched on with heavy eyes, and then dumped in another.

She murmured, "Thank you."

"I have powered creamer or milk."

"Milk, please."

Happy to wait on her, especially since it gave him insight into her preferences, he fetched the milk and dropped in a splash. Lifting one finger, she touched the bottom of the carton, urging him to pour more until the mug was full again.

Before he could use the spoon, she stirred it with her finger, then popped that finger into her mouth with an appreciative "mmm" that made him tighten all over.

Sinking back into his chair, his gaze glued to those lips, he said, "So you know, that's crazy suggestive."

As if she hadn't heard him, she brought the mug to her mouth and gulped. "Oh, *that*." Another long drink, leaving the mug half-empty. "Yeah, that'll help." Sleepy eyes finally focused on him.

He felt it with the same intensity as that sucking lick to her finger. He tried to joke, but the words came out low and gravelly. "You, lady, pack a wallop."

Her lip curled in disdain. "You must be really easy."

"Actually, I'm not." If anything, he was damned selective with his female company. First rule, the woman couldn't have designs on happy-ever-after. Not with him.

Where did that leave Kennedy? Where did he want it to leave her?

"I'm not convinced," she said. Stroking her fingers through her tangled hair, leaving the off-center part totally crooked. She indulged a giant yawn. "I know what I look like. Had to face myself in the mirror."

"After you eyeballed me." Folding his arms on the table, he watched her, then slowly smiled. "There it is. That rosy blush."

"See this?" She tipped her mug at him. "Only half a cup gone.

I'll need the rest of this and two more before I verbally spar with you, so take pity on me and stop right now."

The strangest damn thing happened. Affection crowded in, taking the lead over sexual interest. Huh. The anomalous sensation left him confused, but not for long.

This was similar to what he felt with his sister-in-law, only it was different, too, because he didn't want in Sterling's pants.

Kennedy was a whole different story.

CHAPTER FOUR

REACHING OUT, Reyes smoothed the hair she'd mussed, liking the softness of it, the warmth. Freed from all restraints, it skimmed just past her shoulders. "All right."

Gulping the rest of her mug, she said, "None of that, either. My sluggish system doesn't know what to make of it."

Tenderness joined the affection. "Here, let me get you a refill."

"My hero."

As he fixed his mug, he asked, "Didn't sleep well?" He couldn't recall her waking, but then, he'd slept soundly himself.

"I don't remember a thing." She sighed heavily. "Odd, right? You'd think something so unfamiliar…"

The words trailed off. Did she mean sleeping with him was unfamiliar? Or sleeping with anyone? To find out, he asked, "Unfamiliar?"

She shook her head. "Doesn't matter how I slept. I always struggle in the morning. For sure, finding a guy at the john jolted my heart, and I'm not sure I've recovered yet."

"Next time," he promised, sliding back into his seat, "I'll go downstairs so you can have the connected bath."

She was just about to sip again, but at his words, she slowly lowered the mug. Wide blue eyes stared at him agog.

"What?"

She blinked twice. "Next time?"

A slipup. He had no idea what would happen next. "Figure of speech."

For two seconds more, she continued to stare at him, then gave an accepting nod and went back to consuming her coffee.

"Breakfast? I can do bacon and eggs, or pancakes."

"I'm not a big breakfast person." She idly turned the mug. "Please don't misunderstand. I get that this was an intrusion on your private space, and it's awkward for me as well, so I'm not hinting."

Damn. Unsure what to say, Reyes just waited.

"What am I going to do today? I mean, will it be safe for me to use my credit cards? I can set up a long-stay hotel, and public transportation will be fine for a while, at least until I can get my car and get things sorted with insurance. But is it okay for me to do that?" She chewed her bottom lip. "Again, not to impose on you, but everything still feels very unsafe to me."

Tackling her points in the same manner she had, he replied, "I know you're not hinting. The number one thing, though, is that you're not alone in this." He wouldn't let her out of his sight if he didn't know it was safe. Cade would find out what he could, and then, he assumed, he'd get her set up somewhere other than the run-of-the-mill hotel scene. "I agree, it's probably not safe. I didn't have a chance to tell you this yet—" and he wasn't sure until this moment that he wanted to tell her "—but the guys who came after you last night are dead."

The coffee mug nearly slipped from her hand. She quickly set it down. "Dead? You hurt them that badly?"

"No. After we left, someone shot them." He touched his forehead. "And whoever it was wanted to make sure they wouldn't recoup."

"Oh, my God."

The ringing of his doorbell further startled Kennedy, who nearly jumped out of her seat.

"Shh. It's okay." He nodded at the security screen mounted on the wall beside a cabinet. "It's just my nosy sister."

She turned and stared. "I thought that was a TV."

"Nope." Pushing back his chair with a resigned sense of his

future being forever altered, he said, "Finish up your coffee. I'll be right back."

At first she appeared ready to protest, then she glanced down at her clothes, wrinkled her nose and shrugged. "I'm not ready to move, so no arguments from me."

The second he opened his door, Madison breezed in, her laptop in hand. "What took you so long? Don't try telling me you were in bed because I know Cade already spoke with you. And being you're in your drawers, I assume you haven't showered yet."

"Haven't done much of anything yet." But, yeah, with his sis underfoot, he definitely needed some jeans. "Kennedy is in the kitchen." Which wasn't so far away that she couldn't hear their every word. "Don't spook her while I get dressed."

"I don't spook that easily," Kennedy called back.

That prompted Madison to smile. "I like her."

"You don't even know her."

She hefted her laptop. "Wanna bet?" Without expounding on that, she hurried toward the kitchen, leaving Reyes undecided on which way to go.

Should he run interference between the two women to ensure Madison didn't overstep? Or would it make sense to face the situation in more than snug boxers?

The idea of clothes won out, so he rushed up the steps, taking them two at a time. If he left them alone too long they'd probably start plotting against him.

Grabbing up his discarded jeans from yesterday, he yanked them on, and then did the same with his badly rumpled T-shirt. While zipping and snapping the jeans, he headed back down in time to hear Madison ask, "Who's Jodi Bentley?"

A lengthy pause gave him time to reenter the kitchen before Kennedy finally said, "Just a woman I know."

Having helped herself to coffee, Madison surveyed Kennedy while sipping. "Hmm. I'd say it's more than a mere acquaintance."

Still slumped in her seat, Kennedy shrugged. "We share a similar background, that's all."

"Both of you were trafficked?"

The bald way his sis tossed that out there made Reyes want to muzzle her.

Kennedy, however, merely gave her a long look. "Is this a show of your research skill?"

Pinching the air, Madison said, "A tiny example. There's more." Opening her laptop and quickly typing, she spun it around to show a shadowy figure next to a car.

Breathing a little deeper, Kennedy lost her relaxed posture. "That's Jodi."

"Yup." Touching the screen in the far right corner, Madison said, "And there's your fire."

"Jodi was there?" As if clearing away her shock, Kennedy scowled. "How and where did you get that photo?"

"There's a security camera at the all-night diner on the corner. It picked up the image."

"They gave you their footage?"

"Ah, no." Madison checked a nail. "Not exactly."

Reyes rubbed a hand over his face. Ignoring his sister, he sat down and took Kennedy's hands. "Remember, I told you that Madison is the researcher? Well, she's better than good."

"You didn't say she hacked private businesses."

Not at all bothered, Madison stated, "I hack anyone—when I think there's a good reason."

"You," Reyes said, shooting her a look, "need to pull back a little."

"No." Adamant, Kennedy freed her hands and squared her shoulders. "I want to hear it all. I need to know what I'm up against."

"Well, as to that," Madison said, "you, alone, aren't up against anything." Munificent, she spread out her arms. "You now have some of the best backup you'll ever find, short of calling out the military."

So many emotions stole over Kennedy's features. Shock, resistance, horror... And hope.

Clearing her throat and making a wild grab for composure, she asked, "Why would you want to help me?"

"I don't mean just me, since my siblings will most certainly be involved." Madison elbowed Reyes. "Now would be a good time for you to say you're in."

He held up his hands. "I'm in—but I had already told Kennedy that."

"As to why I'd help, it's because you're eyeball deep in a huge conspiracy, and I can't quite sort it all out. Jodi had something to do with it, but maybe not everything."

"Jodi is a very nice person," Kennedy insisted. "She's also a victim, and sometimes misguided."

"Yes, I have it all in my notes. Is she capable of killing two men? I believe so." She waited for Kennedy to confirm it, and when she didn't, Madison continued, "Do I think it was her? Not necessarily." Rapidly switching the photos, she pulled up another that showed a dark, ancient sedan. "I tracked your friend by the plates on her car. No such luck on this one, but notice the person returning to the car? Dressed all in black. Hand inside his jacket— as if returning a weapon to a holster."

No way could Reyes miss the relief on Kennedy's face. "So you don't think Jodi shot them?"

Madison's smile showed her triumph. "Obviously, you *know* she's capable, which puts to rest the issue of whether or not she could. But did she?" Madison shrugged. "It's also possible she was working with this other person." Again she watched Kennedy.

With no reaction at all, Kennedy waited.

"Or not. We'll have to sort it all out."

Chugging the rest of her coffee, Kennedy stood. "I need to shower, dress and figure out where I'm going, so if you two will excuse me." She didn't wait for a reply, just skirted around the table and headed into the guest room, closing the door with a firm click of the lock.

"Huh." Madison sat back. "Will she scurry out a window?"

Hell, he didn't know if that was her intent. "Not without setting off an alarm." His sister had done exactly what he'd feared. She'd come on too fast, too strong. Sometimes Madison forgot that not everyone lived in a cutthroat world of murder, mayhem and retribution.

Reyes rubbed his eyes, then dragged his hand down his face. "How bad is it?"

"Scale of one to ten? I'd say an eight or nine."

"Damn."

"Yeah. She's in deep doo-doo." Madison did a few more page scrolls. "Many of these places she went were innocuous enough. I was even able to find a few of her recorded speeches." She glanced up. "I sent those to you, as well as a digital copy of her book."

"Her book?"

"A memoir of having been trafficked. Tragic stuff, but she's sold really well."

"What do you title something like that?"

"*No One Is Safe: The Sad Truth of Human Trafficking.* There's a whole chapter on monsters among us. Very insightful stuff. I could almost feel her terror in some of those chapters, but she's also very plainspoken on how she's dealt with it."

His stomach cramped. Yes, he should probably read it to get a better understanding of what Kennedy had gone through. Not that he didn't already know the worst of it. He'd saved enough women and kids, as well as some men, to understand the harsh impact trafficking had on a person.

For that person to be Kennedy? Whole different thing.

"She's a terrific speaker," Madison said. "Very down-to-earth with workable info. She doesn't look like a celebrity, doesn't dress like one, either." Madison brought up an image of Kennedy on-stage in jeans, with a nice blouse and blazer. "Because she seems like one of them, young people listen to her. They can relate. On this last trip, she got a lot of questions. Twice, after a lecture, she agreed to meet privately with students."

He'd listen to at least one of the speeches as soon as he could. "Anyone sketchy?"

"I don't think so, at least not obviously so. She also went to dinner with one of the professors at the college." Madison glanced at him. "A man." She went back to her laptop.

Everything masculine in Reyes went on alert. "What man?"

"Like I said, a professor. He seemed okay, but obviously I'll look into him more."

"Yeah, you do that." And in the meantime, he'd find out...what? Kennedy wasn't his. He didn't even want her to be his.

Ignoring his turmoil, Madison continued, "This friend of hers, Jodi Bentley, is more than a little misguided. It appears she's playing vigilante."

Since Reyes and his siblings did the same, he wouldn't condemn her out of hand for that. "Details?"

"She drove one guy off the road. I think she'd planned to kill him, but a cop was nearby and arrived before she could. Turned out the guy had outstanding warrants for kidnapping and suspected murder. Jodi claimed he'd been chasing her, and since it fit, no one questioned it."

"Sounds to me like she did the world a favor." And, yeah, it worried him.

"Another guy went home with her from a bar, and he was never seen again. Friends of his at the bar said she'd come on to him hot and heavy. She claims they went to a park to boink, he got too rough and she walked home. That time she had a black eye, so again, there weren't a lot of questions asked."

"But you're suspicious."

"I've got six or seven more stories like those, but the real kicker?" Again she spun the laptop around for Reyes to see. "This isn't the first fire she's been near."

"Holy shit." Eyes glued to the screen, Reyes took in the grainy image of a young, scrawny woman standing on the sidewalk among other spectators, watching a home go up in flames.

Madison tapped a finger over the woman. "She'd been renting the house down the street for only a month. Right after the fire, she moved."

Tension crawled into his neck, along with a rush of determination to his blood. "You think she'd want to hurt Kennedy?"

"Not really, but something isn't adding up. Is she capable of killing? Yes. Is she familiar with fires? Evidence makes it seem so. Did the poor woman have a horrific background? Most definitely. Let's just say it bears more investigation."

"What about the other guy you saw on the scene? The one who appeared to be tucking away a weapon?"

"Without plates, he's a little more difficult to track."

"Only a little?" Even though Reyes had witnessed his sister's tech magic, there were still times when she left him awed.

With a shrug, she closed her laptop. "I'll be going through other camera feeds to see if I can pick up anything else, but it's doubtful. I've already looked at the most obvious ones without luck."

"Let me know—"

"ASAP if I find anything. Naturally." Then she tipped her head. "So, you and Kennedy."

"No." Reyes pointed at her. "Do *not* do that."

Her secret little smile set off alarm bells in his head. "I hope you like her, because she'll need to stay with you for a while."

His molars clenched. "I'll find her a secure place."

"No place is secure enough if she's alone."

"Bullshit. I can tuck her into a protected facility and have her stay put." Even as he said the words, he knew he was full of it. He didn't want her on her own, alone and afraid.

Even more than that, though, he didn't want his family manipulating him. Sure, Madison might have altruistic motives, but that didn't mean she knew what was best for him.

Arms folded, Madison narrowed her eyes. "Oh? For how long, because this won't get wrapped up anytime soon. You want her 'staying put' for a month? Two?"

He shot back, "You want her to live with me *that* long?"

Clearly disappointed in him, she shook her head. "This might be a good time to remind you that she lost nearly everything. She has a suitcase of stuff, and nothing else. Any photos, artwork, all her clothes—anything and everything personal, gone."

Shit. Turning his back on his sister, Reyes walked to the kitchen patio doors to look out. Aspens in fall shades of butter yellow, golden amber and crimson red dotted the landscape, mixed with russet scrub oak brush and backlit by a sky made vivid blue by the morning sunrise. This home was his retreat, his and his alone. It was where he worked out his frustrations, sparing the rest of the world—and his family—his occasional foul mood.

"You want me to turn my life upside down for Kennedy." Madison didn't just want it, she expected it.

"If you have a better idea, go for it. Just know that, left on her own, she doesn't stand a chance."

Pressing his forehead to the cool glass, Reyes held silent. He knew what he had to do. Hell, what he *wanted* to do. Once his sister hit the road, he'd get the ball rolling.

That didn't mean he had to embrace the damn implosion of his carefully constructed life.

When a door closed a little too loudly, he turned fast, but realized right away it wasn't an entry door, but the bedroom door.

Which had already been closed. Unless... Kennedy had come out and they hadn't heard her.

But, of course, she would have heard them.

He and Madison stared at each other.

"Oops," his sister said. "Guess the girl has stealth."

"Time for you to go." Otherwise, Kennedy really might try crawling out the window.

Already standing and gathering her purse, Madison said, "No problem. By the way, it's safe enough for her to use her phone, but she shouldn't send any texts or emails detailing her location. Whoever is on her, they're not tech savvy enough, or connected enough, to do much digital tracking, but we can't rule out a hacker. However, she should avoid all areas familiar to her because I have a feeling Jodi, or her goons, might be watching for her to pop back up. It could be dangerous."

"Unless she's with me."

Satisfaction curved Madison's mouth. "Unless she's with you." She came over to kiss Reyes on the cheek. "Good luck."

Knowing he'd need it, he said, "Thanks," and walked her out. After watching her drive away, he knew he couldn't put it off any longer.

It was time to explain things to Kennedy, whether she wanted to hear him out or not.

"WHERE THE FUCK IS SHE?" Delbert O'Neil demanded as he paced, occasionally taking a deep draw on his cigarette. Kennedy should have been in her bed. She should now be nothing but cinders. Instead, she was unaccounted for, and that meant she was still a threat to him.

Thanks to her he'd lost everything, including his life savings. Wasn't it enough that he'd had to start over, that for weeks while hiding out he'd gone with little to eat?

By God, it should have been enough.

Yet every time she opened her damn mouth at a high school or college campus, she risked exposing him again.

"We'll find her," Golly said, despite all evidence to the contrary. "If it hadn't been for that damned ape who came after her, we'd have her right now."

Del liked the sound of that even more than her dying in her sleep. He'd get some payback on the bitch...and *then* she could die. He rubbed the snake tattoo on his neck and wondered why it felt like a tightening noose.

Twice, Kennedy had done this to him.

"Relax," Golly ordered, his twisted smile full of anticipation. "I have a few street informants watching for her to pop up. She can't lie low forever. Even if she tries that, eventually she'll have another speaking gig and we'll be able to grab her then. That, or else Jodi will lead us to her. She's as good as yours." He prodded his tongue through a hole where two teeth should be, repulsing Del. "And the other one will be mine."

DRIVEN BY PRIDE—STUPID, foolish pride—Kennedy continued stuffing her few belongings back into the suitcase.

She had to leave. Of course she did.

Reyes had made it clear that he didn't want her here. She had no right to further disrupt his life. Not only that, but his sister made her uneasy. Madison was tall, slim, incredibly beautiful—just like her blasted brothers—and she was every bit as cocky, too. Maybe not with physical ability, but the woman understood her skill. A skill she had used without apology to invade Kennedy's life.

Did the whole damn family have to be overachievers? Were they all lethal, even Madison?

She'd met Cade a few times at the gym, and it took no more than a single glance to know he owned any situation he was in. The man was even taller than Reyes, so he had to be six-five. His sweeping gaze missed nothing, and calm confidence could be his middle name.

Whereas Reyes was brash, Cade was quietly in control.

And Madison was cheerfully certain.

Who *were* they anyway?

The tap at the door made her stiffen. There'd been several times in her life when she'd been horribly lost. Very alone. Frantic and uncertain what to do.

This was quickly turning into another one.

Girding herself, she walked to the door and opened it with what she considered admirable nonchalance. "I'm almost done."

His frowning gaze went over her and then to the bed, where her suitcase lay open. "Almost done with what?"

"Getting ready to leave." The nervousness sounded in her tone, though not overly. "Would you like to drive me somewhere, or should I call...someone?" She had no idea who she could call.

A muscle ticked in his jaw. Stepping in, he filled the spare bedroom with his size, his presence, the sheer magnetism of him. "Let's talk."

"I don't think so, Reyes. Truly, I appreciate all you've done. You've gone above and beyond, and it's time I quit cowering and instead acted like an adult."

Folding his arms, he leaned against the door frame. "Pretty sure you always act the adult. I've never seen otherwise. At least, not until shit went sideways, and you're not equipped to deal with it, honey."

"Yes, I know." *He* was equipped, but also unwilling. "I'll work it out."

Not moving, he asked, "How?"

Why did he have to press her? Going back to her suitcase, she jammed in the overflowing clothes and started to zip it shut. "I'll hire someone."

"No."

"No?" Temper spiking, she turned on him. "What do you mean, no? It's not up to you."

"Sure it is." He pushed away from the door frame.

Oh, hell. Kennedy backed up, which effectively froze him in his tracks, at least for a few seconds.

Quickly recovering, he strode forward. "I would never hurt you, so don't do that."

"Then quit crowding me." A dumb thing to say, since he was still a few feet away.

"This," he bit out, leaning into her space until their noses almost touched, "is crowding you."

His hazel eyes glittered gold, fascinating her. She put one hand flat to his chest and said succinctly, "Back off."

To her surprise, he did, jerking around and running a hand over his hair. "You're not going anywhere, all right? That's just dumb."

"You arrogant dick."

He turned again, this time presenting a slow grin. "What did you call me?"

"You heard me well enough." Where had she left her laptop? Her phone? "I know this is all a joke to you, and I'm aware I come off as less than savvy in dealing with the scum of the earth, but I've survived the horrors of trafficking, and I'll figure this out, too. The almighty Reyes McKenzie can tell me goodbye with a clear conscience."

Back to being the arrogant dick, he stared at her. "That's even dumber than talking about leaving."

For the love of... Taking a stance, she asked, "Which part?"

"All of it, but especially the part where I think you're not savvy. Saying something dumb and being dumb are two very different things. Trust me, I have no illusions about your intelligence."

Well, that was something at least. "Good. So you know I can deal with—"

"Nope."

His attitude infuriated her, and she stayed chill only by an act of sheer willpower. She even got her stiff lips to smile. "Again, it's not up to you."

"We agree you're smart, right? So," he continued before she could say a single word, "a smart woman wouldn't budge from where it's safe."

"Maybe not, but a proud woman wouldn't stay where she's not wanted." She lifted her chin. Let him deal with *that*. "I clearly heard you say you could stick me somewhere safe. Let's go with that." She unfolded her arms to hold them out in concession. "I promise I will stay put. You won't even have to twist my arm."

Reyes worked his jaw. "Here's the thing. You don't really know what I want, since I didn't know until just this second. All that bullshit earlier with my sister was just me blustering." He moved in again, this time taking her shoulders.

Why did he have to be so big? Damn near a foot taller than her. And *solid*. Good God, the man was like chiseled stone, only warm.

"I want you here, Kennedy. In fact, the only problem is that I want you a little too much."

Her eyes flared. "What's that supposed to mean?"

"I'm a dude. You're a woman. I'm sure you'll figure it out."

She shook her head. "A big fat *no* on that."

"Yeah, I already ruled it out, too, you being dependent on me and all."

"I am *not…*" No, she wouldn't lie. At the moment, she was dependent…somewhat, damn it.

"It wouldn't be ethical. And then, of course, there's your background." He eyed her. "You still struggle with that? I'm guessing you do. Who wouldn't, right? But you have to know the last thing I'd want to do is make you uncomfortable, or put you on the spot. And never, not under any circumstances, would I pressure you."

"You're pressuring me now."

"To stay." His hands kneaded her shoulders. "I meant sexually. To keep you safe, I'll definitely pressure you if I need to." He bent his knees a little to look more directly into her eyes.

Damn him, he was potent. In fact, she found herself leaning into him a bit.

"I'll do whatever it takes then. I want you to know that, okay? Sometimes that might mean me giving orders."

"I don't think so."

"And sometimes you'll have to follow those orders."

"Like hell."

"But I'll always have a good reason, and hey, if necessary, I'll apologize once we're safe again." He tried one of his charming smiles on her. It was more effective than not. "Deal?"

Unable to help herself, Kennedy slumped forward until her forehead came into contact with his firm chest. *Holy smokes, he smelled good.* "I had just resigned myself to leaving."

Carefully his arms closed around her. "I know. Have I convinced you to stay?"

Still inhaling his delicious scent, she asked, "So now you're giving me a choice?"

"I'm not into kidnapping, so maybe."

The "maybe" made her laugh. He was so outrageous. She lifted a hand to rest against his shoulder. "I'm scared and, as you said,

I'm smart enough to know I'm out of my depth. So, yes, I'd like to stay." For now. "I haven't yet locked down any new engagements, so my schedule is open."

"You were taking time off? A vacation?"

"Actually, I was only going to work on my next book. I can set up in here so I'm out of your way, okay? You won't even know I'm here."

He snorted. "Trust me, I'll know." His palm moved up and down her spine, both soothing her and making her far too aware of him as a man. "You're writing another book?"

"With all the digging your sister did, you surely know that already."

He tried to lever her back so he could see her face, but when she resisted, he hugged her instead. "Yeah, I knew you'd published one book. Didn't know you were starting another."

"The results of trafficking go on and on." She still wasn't over it. She didn't think she'd ever be over it. "For anyone recovering, it might be helpful to know the resources that are available, the things I've done to help me feel more in control of my life, and to know that difficulty sleeping isn't uncommon."

He pressed his mouth to her temple. "You slept all right last night."

Because she'd been with him. Likely the difference was in not being alone, but telling him that might obligate him to keep her close each night, and she wouldn't intrude on him more than she had to. "Usually I hear every little sound, and once I do, I can't just assume it's the house settling or the wind stirring branches. I can't assume it's anything less than an intruder."

"Even though it never is?"

She went still. Knowing she had to tell him soon didn't mean she was ready to do it now. Of course, an astute guy like Reyes didn't miss much.

This time his hold on her shoulders was too firm, and she couldn't stop him from pressing her back the length of those long arms. His probing stare dissected her. Grim, he demanded, "When?"

CHAPTER FIVE

GOING OVER THE details made her nerves jangle, adding a quiver to her voice that she hated. "A month ago, I heard someone on the balcony off my apartment." That struck her with new awareness, and she gave a humorless laugh. "Or rather, what used to be my balcony. I got up to look, as I always do." Unable to hold his gaze, she stared down at his chest and whispered, "There was a man there. He'd just climbed over the railing."

"Damn." Gathering her against him once more, Reyes gently rocked her. "He didn't get in?"

Kennedy shook her head. Retelling this was so much easier while Reyes held her. "I had my gun in my hand—"

Back she went again so he could do another long stare. "You have a gun?"

She gave him a "duh" look. "That night all I had was a small .38 with a laser pointer, but now I also have a Glock." She blew out a breath. "Stupidly, I'd left my phone on the bedside table. All I could do was stand there staring at him, the gun aimed, the red dot on his chest until he smiled at me and vaulted back over the rail."

Again he hugged her. "You called the cops?"

"Yes. They came right away, took a description and looked around. In the end, they wrote it off as a likely burglar and promised to drive by often for the rest of the night, but I couldn't stay there. I went to a hotel, and the next morning I bought additional security stuff for all around the apartment. Alarms for everything. Bars for the balcony door and windows." She cleared her throat. "I also bought a screamer—one of those little handheld things where you press a button and it makes a loud, piercing noise? Plus, I got a stun gun."

His mouth firmed in disapproval, but what did she care? She'd needed protection, and she couldn't rely on anyone else.

"The cops didn't know your history or they'd have—"

"What? Protected me from the boogeyman? We both know it isn't that easy."

He smoothed a hand over her hair. "Yeah, we do." Glancing at her suitcase, he asked, "You have the weapons on you?"

"Yes." She never went anywhere without them, not even when she traveled. It was why she always checked her bags.

Moving to the suitcase, she opened it again, lifted aside a sweater and a pair of jeans, and removed the heavy firearm case that held her guns. Gingerly she set them out.

Not so gingerly, Reyes lifted them with an expert touch, looking them over. "Plenty of ammo?"

"Yes." She lifted away the egg crate foam to show the bullets beneath.

"Where's the stun gun?"

"In my purse now. I got it out of my luggage once I left the airport, before I got my ride." Exiting the room, she went up the spiral staircase on light feet to reach his bedroom. Her heart beat a little faster, now for entirely different reasons.

Reyes came in behind her. He must have returned her weapons to the case, because he was empty-handed. It didn't surprise her that he hadn't made a single sound on his approach. The man moved with stealth even when there was no reason. It seemed to be an intrinsic part of his psyche.

Being in a bedroom with him again caused her to babble. "Here it is." She put her hand in the grip to show him how she'd use it. Much like brass knuckles, it allowed her a firm grip. "I like the way this one is made. Instead of having to poke someone with a long stick, I just squeeze the handle and it works, plus it has a really bright flashlight. See the spikes? Those can be removed, but why would I?"

"Never know when you might need to gouge someone."

The deadpan way he said that put her on edge.

Carefully, he closed his hand over hers and relieved her of the weapon. "Tell me what else is going on, okay?"

She probably should, but first she needed out of the bedroom. Hurrying past him, she trotted back down the stairs and...wasn't sure where to go. Her gaze bounced around, taking in her options. The kitchen, then.

Her butt had just settled in a chair when Reyes appeared in the doorway. "So." Lifting one brow, he asked, "Are we done racing around the house?"

Feeling like a fool, Kennedy nodded.

He gestured at the chair opposite. "If I grab a seat, you won't bolt out of the room?"

"No." At least, she hoped she wouldn't.

With his hands raised to look less threatening—the ass—he came forward and eased into a chair. "I didn't mean to spook you."

Kennedy snorted. "You didn't." The memories did. The harsh reality of the threat did. The insidious fear did. Best to get it all said. "A few weeks after the prowler on my balcony, there was another incident in the grocery parking lot. Middle of the day, other people around." Her mouth went dry, remembering the brazenness of the attack. "I was loading my groceries into the back seat and a guy asked for my cart. I said sure, took the last bag, and while my hands were full he started shoving me into the back seat. Another guy was already getting behind the wheel. My car is keyless and the fob was in my purse over my shoulder, so he started the engine with no problem."

Something violent glittered in Reyes's hazel eyes. "Clearly you got away."

"I tried to scream." Her throat grew tight, so tight she couldn't seem to get enough air. "But he put his hand over my mouth and I thought he would crush my jaw. I dropped the bag I was holding. A can of peas fell onto my lap."

Quietly, calmly, Reyes listened, his gaze locked with hers as if to offer silent support.

"I used that can to bash in his face."

"Yes!" When she startled at his exclamation, he moderated his tone. "Good for you, honey."

For some reason, his praise made her feel better. "Blood went everywhere. It looked like I'd fractured his eye socket. His nose was crushed." She swallowed heavily. "I hit him again."

Slowly Reyes smiled. "Good girl."

At any other time, that patronizing phrase might have offended her. Now? It just felt nice to know he approved of her actions.

She took pleasure in saying, "*He* screamed, loudly enough to draw plenty of attention. I quickly joined him, and soon people were swarming around us. A black car screeched up next to mine, the two of them jumped in, and then they were gone. The whole thing probably lasted less than three minutes, but God, Reyes, it felt like a lifetime. I knew what would happen, what they would do, and that made it worse."

"I'm so damn proud of you," he said with gruff sincerity. Slowly, he slid his hand, palm up, across the table. Offering her his touch. A connection.

How could she resist? Clearly she couldn't, so she placed her much smaller hand in his and was immediately engulfed in his comforting strength.

"You know how hard it is to keep your head when being attacked, but you did it, Kennedy. You fought hard, and sometimes that can make all the difference."

Nodding, she squeezed his hand. "Or no difference at all."

The truth of that hung between them.

Watching her, he lifted her hand to his mouth and kissed her knuckles. "All those workout sessions at my gym are starting to make sense."

No reason to fudge the truth any longer; Reyes now knew it all. "I know I'm small, and not all that strong, but there are ways to slow a man down, right? That's what I was trying to learn. I can't best a man, but if I can thwart him, then I'd at least have a chance to get away."

He seemed to come to some decision. "No more talk about leaving here, okay? Not until we have this all wrapped up."

"That could take a long time." Or it might never happen.

"Nah. Like Madison said, you have a team at your back now.

So let's come to some agreements." He turned as businesslike as
Reyes could. "One, you'll stay here, and no more talk of leaving.
Done and done. Two, I'll get your car for you, but you have to give
me your word you won't take off."

She didn't want to go anywhere alone until she knew it was
safe, so she shrugged. "No problem." The thought of ever again
being held in captivity paralyzed her with fear.

"Three, we'll spend the next few days replacing things you lost,
starting in about an hour. I'll be your escort-slash-bodyguard-slash-
whatever, and you'll be patient with me. Agreed?"

Her mouth twitched. "You're not so hard to be around, now
that I know you better."

Disbelief narrowed his eyes. "Yeah, okay. Believe that if you
want."

Just by being himself, he'd lifted her mood. "Which part?"

"That you know me."

Ah, so he didn't deny being difficult. "You're still an enigma?"

"A deadly wraith in the night, capable of almost anything."
He grinned.

"Almost anything, huh?"

The grin morphed into a tender smile. "I'm not capable of hurting you, Kennedy. I need you to know that."

Just as quietly, she whispered, "I do."

Satisfied by that, he said, "Four, when I have to be at the gym,
you'll go with me. I can instruct you so you'll know some lethal
shit, and when Cade is around, he can give you some pointers, too."

A workable solution, except that... "I can't keep up that pace
for eight hours."

"I know. I have an office there with a private bathroom, comfy
chair, secure browser and a small fridge. It'll be yours to use until
I wrap up my day."

She honestly didn't know what to say, so she settled for, "Thank
you."

"No thanks necessary. I do what I do, when and how I want to
do it." He released her to stretch, which, yes, made her stare. He
said, "I need to shower and shave and all that. Start a list of anything you might need. We'll knock off what we can today. First,

though, we'll stop somewhere for breakfast. You might not be a fan, but I always put fuel in the tank before I tackle the day."

"All right." Thinking out loud, she said, "I have a pen and paper in my laptop case. I'll get started on that right now."

"Hey." He touched her arm. "You can use your laptop, and even your phone if you want. But don't contact Jodi. Let's see if she reaches out to you."

"She *is* a friend, you know."

"If you say so, but she was there at the fire, so why hasn't she reached out, if for no other reason than to make sure you're okay?"

"I don't know, but I'm sure there's an explanation." She really needed to make it clear about poor Jodi.

Reyes didn't give her a chance. "We'll discuss it tonight, maybe on a conference call with Cade and Madison so we can put our collective heads together. How's that sound?"

She wasn't at all keen about the idea. Yes, she trusted Reyes, but there was so much she didn't know about him, and it seemed that every new thing she learned only created more questions.

As he started out of the room, she realized he wasn't waiting for a reply anyway. "Make yourself at home. I'll be right back."

Then he was gone, and she was left thinking about Reyes. About all he was doing for her.

And about him naked in a shower.

Things were going to get horribly awkward, and she couldn't even blame Reyes. It was her own fault—for finding him so fascinating.

CADE CALLED WHILE they were still on the road, and since he wanted to talk about Jodi, Reyes put the phone on speaker. "I told Kennedy we'd go over this tonight."

"It needs to be now," Cade said. "Jodi was scoping out the gym this morning."

The hell she was! When Reyes glanced at Kennedy, he saw the same surprise on her face that he felt. "Was she watching for Kennedy?"

"That's the safe assumption. Maybe she's hoping to touch base with her."

Kennedy was already shaking her head. "I never told Jodi about the gym. If she knows, it's because..."

Reyes didn't need her to finish that thought. "She's been keeping tabs on you? I'm liking this chick less and less."

Madison interrupted, saying, "Be nice, Reyes. She's Kennedy's friend, and she was once a victim."

Very quietly, Kennedy whispered, "Being a victim isn't something that stays in your past."

Reyes gave her a sharp look. "Meaning?"

Kennedy gave a slight lift of her shoulders. "You recover, you regain your strength—but you also learn, which means you don't forget, you rarely let down your guard, and trust doesn't come easy."

"My wife would very much disagree with you," Cade said.

Kennedy's eyes widened. "Your wife was—"

"Yes." He paused. "And she's the strongest person I know."

"I'm sorry, but strength doesn't obliterate the aftereffects. We push on," Kennedy explained. "We survive, and we put a pretty face on things, but for the rest of our lives we know exactly what can happen. Most people never give the risks a thought. They go through each day with the easy assumption that they're fine, that they'll always be fine, with no grasp of how quickly their safe, normal existences can be destroyed." She drew a breath. "But I know. Those who have survived it know. And we don't let ourselves forget."

The sobering words brought down a repressive silence to hang thick and heavy in the air. Reyes reached over to clasp her knee. She covered his hand with her own.

Connected, he thought. He and Kennedy connected in ways he never had with any other woman. Damn, that was so unusual, it sort of shook him.

"You're right," Cade murmured. "It changes a person."

Reyes asked, "Is that what happened with Jodi?"

"Yes." Kennedy stroked over his hand, tracing along the hard ridges of his knuckles, then down to the sensitive skin between. The provoking touch didn't feel deliberate, but rather a necessary distraction to her own thoughts. "I met her four years ago, when she was only twenty. I'd had one of my first speaking engagements at a college, and afterward, as I was leaving, I sensed her following me. She was this sullen figure, half-hidden under an oversize hoodie. I knew something was horribly wrong. It was there when her eyes met mine, and how she looked at me."

"How was that?" Reyes asked.

"With desperation."

He appreciated that his brother and sister stayed quiet so Kennedy could forget they were listening in. Not that she would. She was too sharp for that, and far too aware of her surroundings. Their silence offered only the illusion of privacy.

"I rarely take risks with other people, regardless if they're men or women, young or more mature."

"You shouldn't." Reyes found her touch incredibly distracting. "Evil has no gender or age."

"I know." Her explorations trailed along his thumb. "But something about Jodi was different. More vulnerable. She needed me, so I invited her to lunch. She doesn't trust most people, either, and still she came with me, and we ended up talking for two hours. I got the distinct impression that she'd mostly given up on life."

"If that's so, why was she at the college?"

"My guess is that she was looking for something, anything, to give her purpose so she wouldn't dwell as often on what she'd gone through." Giving up her intent study of his hand, Kennedy shifted away and crossed her arms. "That's why I took up speaking, you know. It makes me feel like I'm helping."

"Is that also why you write?"

"It's cathartic," she said. "Spelling it all out helps me understand it, and gives me a sense of control. Jodi hadn't found a direction yet. She was still floundering in her fear and hatred. Once we became friends, I think it helped her."

"You're not sure?" Reyes asked.

"Jodi disappears for long stretches. Sometimes a month will go by before I hear from her. Then I'll get texts for three days in a row. I just never know with her."

"So," Cade said, "we can't be certain why she was checking out the gym."

"She was stealthy about it," Madison said. "Hanging out across the street, trying not to be obvious."

Kennedy stared at Reyes. "There have been times when Jodi thought I was in trouble, and she acted without discussing it with me."

"Example?" Cade prompted.

"One time after I'd spoken with this gigantic group, a guy asked me out. He was loud and obnoxious about it, saying he'd help me through all my troubles, like I was a joke." Her mouth firmed. "Overall, I ignored him. Things like that happen sometimes. A lot of people get uncomfortable with my story. Guys try to laugh it off. Girls make snide comments about it, as if I'd brought it on myself."

"Immature, clueless brats," Madison commented, though not with any heat.

Kennedy agreed. "They're young and dumb, and thankfully, reality hasn't yet knocked them down. What they say doesn't matter much to me."

Much? In that moment, Reyes wanted to protect her from everyone and everything, even mouthy college knuckleheads.

"Jodi takes the insults to me more personally. Apparently, she was there that day, and she waited until she found the boy—"

"Man," Cade corrected. "If he's college age, he's a man and should behave like one."

Kennedy's amused smile slipped into place. "I get the feeling that being a man might mean something different to you and Reyes."

Reyes couldn't deny that. His father had treated him like a man before he'd ever become a teenager. From a young age he'd been taught that stupidity wouldn't be tolerated and cruelty was an unforgivable sin, most especially where women were concerned.

"Anyway," Kennedy said, exasperated with them all now that his siblings were speaking up. "Later that night, she caught him alone and hit him in the back of the head. He ended up with a concussion and twelve stitches."

Damn. Reyes didn't blame Jodi for wanting to defend her friend, but that was a pretty harsh way to go about it.

"You know it was her?" Madison asked.

"I didn't, not at first. The police contacted me after some of the other students told them the guy had been hassling me. I was at the hotel restaurant having dinner, so they knew I hadn't done it. At the time I didn't have a clue what might have actually happened. Later, though, when I thought about it, I got a... I don't know. A hunch? I contacted Jodi the next morning and found out she'd been in the audience when she told me how much she'd enjoyed my talk."

Reyes frowned. "Does she live near the college where you were speaking?"

"Honestly, I'm not sure where she lives. She seems to travel a lot."

Maybe, Reyes thought, she traveled to follow Kennedy. Creepy. "You asked her flat out about the guy?"

"Yes. She didn't confirm it, but neither did she deny it. Basically she repeated back to me one of the things I often say in my lectures—that no one has the right to treat you as if you don't matter."

None of them said anything for far too long.

Finally Madison spoke up, directing her comment to Reyes. "I've put a few safeguards in place. When she comes near the gym again—and she will—we'll know it right away."

"I suggest the direct approach," Cade said.

Kennedy stiffened. "What does that mean?"

"I'll go up to her and find out what she's doing." Reyes lifted a shoulder. "No biggie."

"Absolutely not!" Turning to half face him, Kennedy insisted, "I'll call her and—"

"No," Reyes said.

At almost the same time, Cade and Madison echoed him.

"If she's involved in the fire," Madison explained, "our way is better."

"And if she isn't, no harm done," Cade said.

Kennedy gave him a dark frown. "You and I will discuss this later."

"My brother is smart, Kennedy. You can't strong-arm him just by getting him alone."

Reyes grinned at Cade's observation. Would Kennedy try to badger him into doing things her way? Probably.

Less blunt than Cade, Madison said, "We really do know what we're doing. Trust us, okay?"

Kennedy's eyes narrowed. "Actually, I have no idea what you're doing. Now might be a good time to tell me."

Of course, no one spoke up. Grunting, Reyes muttered, "Thank you for nothing" to his brother and sister. "I'll handle it, okay?"

"Sounds like a plan," Madison said. "Enjoy your day."

"Don't go overboard," Cade warned. "And keep me posted."

With the call ended, Reyes put his mind to choosing a place for breakfast. He scanned the streets, looking for somewhere that wasn't too busy.

"Well?" Impatience crackled in that single word Kennedy threw at him.

How come everything she said or did made him want to grin? For such a small woman, she sure packed a lot of attitude. Even in such an untenable position—with thugs after her, a sketchy friend and the loss of her possessions.

"How about I give you the broad strokes?" Hopefully, that would appease her. No way could he share the nitty-gritty. Other than immediate family and, of course, Bernard, his father's assistant, chef, butler—and now cat kidnapper—no one knew the details of their operation. Yes, Cade had confided in Sterling, but only because he'd fallen in love with her.

Even thinking it made Reyes curl his lip.

He and Cade were alike in many ways, but they also had a lot of differences. For one thing, Reyes had no intention of getting married. Not now, maybe not ever.

"If you're thinking of lies to tell me, don't bother."

Her derision tickled him even more. He was grateful to see that all the turmoil hadn't dented her dominant persona. "Nah, I wasn't. Just ruminating on my life, I guess." He glanced at her, saw she looked more confused than ever, and laughed. "So here's the big picture. My family works to rescue trafficked victims, sometimes with the law, sometimes not." *Often* not, but yeah, he probably shouldn't go into that yet. "It's like a task force, covering a lot of ground. Rescue, counsel, financial assistance, all that."

Cutting right to the chase, Kennedy asked, "Have you killed anyone?"

Damn, way to throw a guy off guard. "I'm not sure that's part of the broad strokes."

"I'd like to know."

"Yes?" He rushed to add, "Only assholes who really deserved it."

The funniest thing happened. Instead of being outraged, Kennedy gave him a firm nod, and whispered, "Good."

Whew. What a relief to know she wasn't horrified.

Then she said, "Of course, you'll understand that Jodi feels the same way." She gave him a placid smile. "She feels everyone she's hurt also deserved it."

Everyone she'd hurt? Well, hell. The day just totally soured.

EVEN AS KENNEDY wondered what Jodi might have gotten into, she felt the need to defend her. Dread warred with loyalty. If Reyes knew it all, would he feel honor bound to see Jodi locked away? She'd never be able to bear that.

With the hope of making Reyes really understand, she formulated her thoughts. Luckily, Reyes didn't press her. Not yet anyway. He waited until they were seated on the terrace of a trendy local restaurant outside Ridge Trail before ramping up the questions.

"Let's hear it, but keep your voice low."

Looking around, Kennedy wondered who he thought might hear. It was a cool morning and few people were lured by the mountain views. Those who had ventured outside were at the other end of the terrace.

"Isn't it amazing how quickly people grow accustomed to things? It's absolutely beautiful out here, yet the crowd is inside." She shook her head.

"Have you gotten used to the scenery?"

"No. I'm still in awe whenever I look at the mountains."

"Me, too." He waited while a young man brought them water, offered coffee and left behind menus. "You shouldn't drink so much caffeine."

"I lost everything last night. No bitching about my coffee."

He grinned. Without perusing the menu, he asked, "Know what you want to eat?"

She'd never been here before, but obviously he had. As she skimmed the selection, the pricing staggered her. "Um…you remember that I'm currently penniless, right?"

His expression softened. "We'll get that sorted out later, okay? For now, it's my treat."

Glancing at the French toast, she winced. On top of his offer to replace her necessities, the meal seemed extravagant. "Not to be crass, but covering my expenses—for now—won't strain your finances?"

"Nah. It's all good."

Giving up on the concern, she laid aside the menu. Fine. He'd chosen the place, and he seemed familiar with it, so why should she grovel over breakfast? "Yes, I know what I want."

"Perfect. I'm starved." He lifted a hand and within seconds the young man was back.

Kennedy ordered the French toast, fresh berries and bacon.

Reyes requested the same, and added scrambled eggs and home fries.

How he stayed so ripped while consuming so much food, she couldn't imagine. Of course, he ran a gym and was physical all day long, which probably explained it.

"Now, before our food gets here, spill the beans. What nefarious stuff has Jodi gotten into? Don't fudge the truth or leave out anything. I need to know what I'm up against."

Yes, to be fair, he needed to know everything. After a fortifying sip of her coffee, she cleared her throat. "First, let me explain something about Jodi, okay? Unlike the place where I was held—" and basically rented out "—Jodi was outright bought and owned by a man who was, from what she's said, pure evil."

"Any man who participates in trafficking is evil." He held up a hand. "Still, I get your meaning."

"There were times he closed Jodi in a small room in the basement. It was his idea of punishment if she wasn't performing up to his standards. Once, he left her there for two days. No food or water. By the time he let her out, she said her spirit was broken. She only wanted to eat, bathe—and to never go back to that room." Fingers of red-hot rage clenched around her windpipe, forcing her voice to a ragged whisper. "No matter what she did, though, he found reasons to lock her away again and again. She never knew if she'd be punished for an hour, a day, or if he'd leave her there to die. Jodi said that was the worst torture of all. Not knowing."

As he often did, Reyes reached out to her. His strong fingers closed oh-so-gently around her forearm, then trailed down until he could hold her hand in his own.

It astounded her that his touch helped so much. For a second there, she'd gotten lost in the details of what Jodi had suffered.

Putting her left hand to her chest, she counted her heartbeats. The combined facts that she was alive and that Reyes planned to keep her that way helped her to find her composure.

"You do that often," he said softly.

She'd been staring blindly at the table. At his observation, her gaze snapped up to his.

When he nodded at her left hand, she realized his meaning.

Never before, not even to Jodi, had Kennedy explained the small gesture that signified so much. It was private to her, central to her struggle with a past that still haunted her today.

"Containing your heart?" he asked, his tone still amazingly gentle.

With his hand offering safety, his hazel eyes showing so much understanding, the words just came out. "I'm feeling my heart beat."

His thumb moved over her fingers, but he didn't say anything.

"It's dumb," she said, feeling a little self-conscious.

"No, it's not. Anything that reminds you you're alive is a good thing."

Oh, wow. He actually got it. An emotional tsunami hit her. She couldn't speak, so she nodded, and Reyes didn't press her. He continued to watch her, almost like he'd never seen a woman before—or maybe like she fascinated him in some way.

A bizarre way? She hoped not.

Just then, their food arrived, relieving her of the awkward moment. He took care of thanking the server, commenting that it smelled good, asking for more coffee and, in the process, giving her a much-needed moment to clear her head.

When they were alone again, she said, "Thank you."

He chided her with a half smile. "No more of that, remember?"

"I can't help it." He was just that wonderful. Far more than she knew a man could be, especially a big buff alpha like him. "You can't know how much I appreciate…everything." Most especially the way he grasped her innermost thoughts.

"Does that make it better?" he asked, shaking out her napkin and leaning over to put it in her lap, overall pretending that she wasn't frozen still. "Talking about it, I mean."

"I don't know." The speaker in her came forth, and while she cut into her French toast, she began to ramble. "I've never really talked about my personal experiences. What I share in my speeches is a general impression that applies to a lot of people, in a lot of situations. The specifics of what happened to me… I've put some of them in my book. Writing things and saying them aloud are very different."

"Maybe you need to talk about them more." He forked up a bite of egg. "With me."

Yes, with him, she probably could. From the start, Reyes had been different. Cocky, yes, but with the ability to back it up. Assured, but in a very nice, take-charge way.

Concerned, and that was what had worried her most. She'd worked hard to regain her life, and Reyes saw right through the facade to the hyperaware, ever-vigilant, still very afraid girl who knew that, alone, she didn't stand a chance against the cruelty of the world.

CHAPTER SIX

THE IDEA OF sharing her innermost thoughts, her basest fears and most humiliating moments left her shaken, so she deflected. "I thought you wanted to know about Jodi."

"That, too." As usual, Reyes let her off the hook. "Go ahead and eat. We're not in a rush. I have the whole day free."

No problem there. She was finally hungry, and the breakfast really was delicious. In between bites, she shared some of Jodi's characteristics. Like her brusque insistence of going it alone. Her staunch defense of any woman injured by a man. The very meager way she lived.

"How long was she with the bastard?"

"A few months. She's never said exactly, but I know it was long enough that she'd given up hope. Unlike my situation, she was alone. At least I had Sharlene and the other women. We made a unique sort of family, weird as that sounds."

"Not weird at all. Even in terrible circumstances, there's comfort in numbers."

See, how could she not be impressed with his insight? "Jodi was alone, mistreated, desperate, and I hope you don't blame her for—"

"If she killed the fucker, I'll cheer her on."

"She did." Once the blurted words left her mouth, Kennedy went still, anxiously waiting to see how Reyes would react. He surprised her by *not* reacting.

Around eating, he asked, "How'd she do it?"

This was Jodi's secret, and Kennedy had never shared it before. "You can't tell anyone."

"Okay." He nodded at her food. "You need to eat, hon."

No, she wasn't buying it. "Just like that? You won't say anything to Cade or Madison?"

"No reason. They already suspect she's crossed a few lines, and if Madison wants to know details, she'll figure it out." He rolled one shoulder. "Just know that you never have to question my word. If I can't keep something secret, I'll say so. If I say I will, then I will."

Had she offended him? She didn't think so. It felt more like he wanted to reassure her. Again. "I wasn't questioning you, not really."

"Good. So how'd she do it? I'm guessing he didn't leave any weapons around."

"No. He'd had weapons, some that he'd used to threaten Jodi, but they were always locked away where she couldn't get them."

Right up until the tide had turned.

Her heart beat a little faster. Nervousness did that to her. Reyes might treat this little convo as no big deal, but to Jodi, it would be the biggest betrayal imaginable. Unfortunately, Kennedy wasn't sure what else to do. "The room he put her in was small and dark. The door locked on the outside. She said it was bare concrete, with damp walls. Always cold." Imagining it made her shiver. "All she had was a bucket for a toilet, and a wooden pallet to keep her off the floor. No blanket, no water or food. No way to stay warm." Feeling more of the chill Jodi must have suffered, Kennedy lifted her coffee cup in both hands, cradling it close.

Reyes's eyes narrowed. "I hope he didn't have an easy death."

She glanced around the restaurant. No one was near. No one paid them any attention other than a few women giving Reyes sly glances. Not that she could blame them. He owned the space by his presence alone, not to mention his size and that too-handsome face.

Dropping her voice to a barely there whisper, Kennedy continued the gruesome tale. "Jodi managed to break up the pallet by busting it against the wall. Then she dragged the edges against the rough concrete wall to sharpen them."

"Clever."

She'd always thought so. "Jodi could have starved before he returned, but she used her misery to build her rage. She was waiting next to the door when he finally came in."

"And?" he prompted.

Again, images formed in her mind, turning her stomach with the ugliness of it all. "She stabbed him with a jagged piece of wood. She said it wasn't a fatal blow, but the wood broke off in his side, and she had several pieces that she'd gotten ready. She...slashed and stabbed until he went down and didn't get up."

"Grisly," he said, not at all disturbed. "She got out of there, then?"

Kennedy shook her head. "She locked him in the room first, then yelled through the door that she'd call an ambulance for him if he gave her the combination to his safe. Jodi said he could barely talk, that he was hurting bad, bleeding everywhere. She'd... Apparently she'd cut across his face, laying open his cheek and injuring his eye. She said he was begging for help, afraid he'd go blind."

"Fuuuuck," Reyes said, sounding impressed. "Guess she got a little payback."

"He was desperate, and he gave her what she wanted. She found cash and weapons in the safe, and also her purse, which still had her ID and stuff. She grabbed some of his clothes so she could change once she was well away. Then she found the keys to his car, and..." Kennedy shook her head. "She left."

"No ambulance, huh?"

Still, Reyes didn't seem disturbed. "She never told anyone, and she never went back. Unless someone found him, he died in that room."

"A fitting end for him."

"There were times when Jodi wanted to check the house, to make sure he was dead and gone. I always managed to talk her out of it."

"Good." He went back to eating. "It's risky to revisit a site."

"Know something about that, do you?"

Scoffing, Reyes didn't take the bait. He just nudged her plate at her. "There've been times since then that Jodi went after people?"

Kennedy really hated to share this part, even knowing she had to. "I don't have names, or even many details, but she told me about a guy who'd been abusing his wife. She sabotaged his car somehow and he ended up going over a bridge. He survived, but hurt his back, and Jodi was satisfied that he wouldn't walk again, so he couldn't hurt his wife."

Reyes offered no judgment.

Rubbing her forehead, Kennedy said, "She also took credit for a few pimps who were found dead, as well as a guy who'd paid one of the pimps for time with a seventeen-year-old girl."

"Is that it?" he asked without inflection.

Kennedy shook her head. "She went after a drug dealer who was preying on kids. He's dead, too. OD."

Softly Reyes said, "Jodi's gotten around."

"If the stories are all true, yes she has. I've done everything I could to convince her to stop. I've urged her to start building a better life for herself."

"She doesn't yet know how."

"No, she doesn't. And the longer she plays vigilante, the more concerned I am that she won't stop—until someone stops her."

"A worry for you, I'm sure." He again nudged her plate. "If that's it, will you please eat before your food gets any colder? We have a lot of shopping ahead of us."

She had a feeling Reyes wanted time to think. He was certainly quiet for a while after that.

Once they'd finished up their food, Kennedy accepted a refill on her coffee.

"Seriously, hon, you consume way too much caffeine," he commented.

"You can have your vices and I'll have mine."

"My vices are more fun."

Assuming his were all sexually related, she shook her head. "Jodi said she'd never admitted what she'd done to anyone other than me. With the first guy, I don't blame her."

"Of course not."

Kennedy knew if she'd been braver, stronger, she'd have done the same thing. Instead, she'd allowed herself to be intimidated until Sharlene gave her life to free her.

No, she didn't blame Jodi. Too often, she blamed herself.

And the rest of it? The other people Jodi claimed to have hurt or killed? Honestly, she just didn't know.

A WEEK WENT by in an incredible rush. Having a woman in his house was, at times, more pleasant than he could have imagined, and other times beyond frustrating. Like the way Kennedy slept in the guest room now.

Reyes hated it.

He'd *liked* holding her, but the very next night, she'd quietly made her preferences known and had slept apart from him ever since.

His subtle suggestions that she might be more comfortable with him, that his bed was big enough, the mattress more comfortable, had only brought out her infuriating manners.

She'd politely say, "The guest room is very comfortable, but thank you," and he didn't know how to press the issue without also pressing her.

That, he wouldn't do.

Why did she have to get all stubborn now and deny them both?

Other than their sleeping arrangements, everything else was easier than he'd expected. He, Reyes McKenzie, a man who'd put careful boundaries around his privacy, now relished having a woman in his space.

And not just any woman, but a woman he couldn't touch.

Never in his life had he thought he'd be in a situation like this—and liking it.

She'd damn near shopped him to death those first few days, saying it was his own fault since he wouldn't let her out of his sight. True enough, she'd offered to let him sit in the mall restaurant while she gathered everything she needed, but he, being a glutton for punishment and feeling over-the-top protective of her, had stuck as close as her shadow.

He'd also covered those expenses, and it seemed like Kennedy would never get over it. Hadn't anyone ever helped her? Didn't matter how many times he assured her he could afford it, she got touchy about paying him back once she could access her funds.

He was independent, too, so he got it. But in some strange, chauvinistic way, he'd savored the act of providing for her.

So he had some caveman genes? Go figure.

In the end, all her careful selections, based on price and comfort, worked out. She now had warmer clothes for the chillier fall weather, plus hiking boots for their evening walks, which had become routine.

Kennedy shared his fascination with the mountains. She could walk forever, discovering creeks, exploring shallow caves and memorizing birds. Sometimes they followed easy paths, and other times they labored over rough terrain. He loved it all, and sharing with Kennedy made it somehow special.

His cabinets now held her favorite snacks, which were mostly things he didn't eat, but he enjoyed watching her enjoy them.

How twisted was that? Here he was, a grown-ass man, sexual in the extreme, but the way Kennedy licked her lips while eating a cookie made him hot.

He really needed to get laid, and soon.

But he wouldn't leave her alone to see to that, so...celibacy ruled his immediate future. Which wasn't to say he didn't appreciate his time with her.

"I need a shower," she said, as she climbed into his truck.

"You can use the showers at the gym, you know." They spent each morning and afternoon there together. Already Kennedy had gotten better at a few basic moves, though she wasn't a natural like his sister-in-law, Sterling. Overall, Kennedy didn't have the same killer instinct or a rabid desire to hone deadly skills. For her, it was more about survival. She didn't want to maim, as Jodi had done. Or stay and fight, as Sterling would insist on doing.

Kennedy wanted enough advantage to flee.

"I'm not big on group showers." She wrinkled her nose. "There are always other people there." She gave him a look. "Do you realize the women walk around naked like it's no big deal? They dry their hair, chat with their friends and apply makeup, all while entirely nude."

No, he hadn't known that. Interesting. "You're shy, huh?" Or was it that the trauma of her past made her more private about her body?

Yeah, that would make sense. Frowning, he got behind the

wheel, all the while checking the area to ensure no one, including Jodi, was looming around.

"I've always been reserved when it came to my body."

"There's no reason," he said with total honesty.

Half smiling, she ducked her face. "I used the sink in your bathroom to clean up, and I changed clothes, but it's not the same as a nice long shower."

No, he supposed it wasn't. And damn it, he didn't want to think about Kennedy lingering under a warm spray.

In more ways than he could count, she was the total opposite of his brother's wife. Put in a similar situation, Sterling would have owned the showers and anyone in them. In part, her alpha attitude made her perfect for Cade.

But Reyes wouldn't like having a chick around who was every bit as ruthless as him.

"I mean it, you know. You have a nice body."

Her eyes flared. "You've never seen my body."

"I've seen you in snug shorts." He rolled a shoulder. "You have a really nice ass."

Kennedy almost choked. "That's..." She shook her head. "Um, thanks."

Her modesty was kind of cute, now that he knew it was just part of her nature and not something wrought from abuse. "Did I embarrass you? Sorry. I don't know a lot of shy women."

"I'm not really shy. Not about most things."

"Just your ass?"

Laughing, she slugged him in the shoulder. "I got a lot of work done today. Your office is comfortable."

Often while at the gym, after a few hours of instruction from him, Kennedy would retreat to his office to write her book. He'd read most of the one already published, and that made it even more difficult for him to be apart from her.

He was most at ease when he had eyes on the woman.

"Glad to hear it."

Once they were on the main road to his house, Kennedy retrieved her phone from her purse and checked her messages. That was a pattern for her. While doing drills, or writing, she kept the phone in her bag so it wouldn't distract her.

Now, as she flipped through texts, he immediately sensed that something was wrong.

The urge to pull over, to give her his undivided attention, warred with the need to secure her in his home. He wasn't Cade, all even-tempered and shit. Hell, he was the opposite of Cade. "What is it?"

"You're not going to like it."

Probably not. Anything that put that worried expression onto Kennedy's face automatically irked him. "Tell me anyway."

She nodded, looked at the phone again, and said, "I just got a text from Jodi."

Well, that wasn't horrible. At least he hoped it wasn't. "Took her long enough. What does she have to say?"

Kennedy chewed her bottom lip. "She, um, is warning me that you're dangerous."

"She's right." He gave her another quick glance. "But remember, I'm not dangerous to you."

"She said you wreak destruction wherever you go."

He snorted. *How the hell would Jodi know?* "A little dramatic, but whatever."

"None of that bothers me, Reyes. I'm glad you can be ruthless."

"So what's the problem?"

"Jodi wants to meet me tonight."

"No."

"She said I can stay with her—"

"No fucking way."

Frowning, Kennedy said, "You realize that your vocabulary deteriorates whenever you get annoyed or when you're taken by surprise."

"I'm not taken by surprise." He scowled, letting her know what he thought of that notion. "But I don't want you going anywhere. Your friend might be unbalanced."

Kennedy didn't deny that.

What would he do if she decided to bail on him? It wasn't yet safe. Hell, they still hadn't discovered anything pertinent, and until they did, he couldn't resolve jack shit, which meant she was still in danger. "You remember she was at the fire, right?"

"It's not like I'd forget."

That was something, at least. He gave the situation quick thought, trying to gauge what his family would say about it, then he shrugged. They weren't here, and he had to make a decision. Once they got home, Kennedy would barricade herself in the guest room again and he'd lose his chance to persuade her to his way of thinking. "Now might be a good time to ask her why she was there, to see her reaction."

Kennedy considered that for a moment. "If I do, she's going to ask me how I know."

"Or she'll deny it."

"No, I don't think she'd lie to me. As far as I know, she never has."

"So you'll tell her the truth that a security camera off another business picked up her image. You don't need to mention Madison, though."

"I'm not sure I'm good with half-truths."

"Sorry, honey, but it's necessary. Until we know how Jodi is involved, you can't trust her."

She stared at the phone, her troubled thoughts showing in her frown. "All right. Should I call or text?"

"Call. And put her on speaker."

Her chest expanded on a deep breath. "God, this feels like such a betrayal."

"I'm sorry." He meant it. "Your safety comes first, okay?"

Nodding, she let her thumb hover over the screen...and finally pressed the phone icon.

It rang only once before a frantic voice answered. "Kennedy, thank God. Tell me you're all right."

"Yes, I'm fine."

"People deliberately burned down your apartment building."

She shot Reyes a look as if to say, *See? She's transparent.* "I know. I'd just gotten home from a trip. It spooked me."

"That's why you're with the big guy?"

"I met him at the gym where I work out." She cradled the phone closer. "Jodi, what were you doing at my building that night?"

"Trying to watch out for you. Jesus, Kennedy, I didn't know you were still out of town and when I saw the whole thing burning, I panicked. I thought you were inside."

"But how did you know to be there?" she pressed.

"So here's the thing. You can't tell that hulk, okay? I don't trust him. He's incredibly shifty."

"He's not, actually," Kennedy replied. "He's one of the good guys, Jodi."

"There are no good guys. They're all creeps, as you should know by now!"

Reyes reached over to touch Kennedy's knee, letting her know he wasn't insulted, that in fact he got Jodi's anger.

She nodded, then said gently, "You trust me, Jodi. So trust me to know a monster from a protector. Reyes won't hurt me, I promise."

"Maybe not physically," Jodi sneered. "Some just use women as conveniences. He's that type of man, Kennedy. Do you know he's banging several women already? While he's with you?"

Kennedy's brows shot up. "While I've been with him, he hasn't gone anywhere, and what he does in his free time is his own business. We're not together that way."

For some reason, it irked Reyes to hear Kennedy say that. It was true, but still...

Sharp with disbelief, Jodi hissed, "You don't care that he's using them?"

It bothered Reyes that the woman's voice had risen. She teetered on the brink of rage, and it wouldn't take much to push her over the edge.

"You don't know him, Jodi, but I do. If he's sexually involved with anyone, it's consensual. I don't think he'd lie to them, either. Odds are they're as satisfied with an open-ended agreement as he is."

He noticed that Kennedy avoided his gaze.

New concerns intruded. There were only three women he'd seen lately, and if Jodi knew about them, then it meant she'd been spying on him for a while.

Which likely meant she'd been spying on Kennedy, too, and had seen her with him at the gym.

Kennedy must have figured the same thing, because she said, "Listen to me, Jodi. I need you to explain a few things, all right? First, *why* were you at my apartment?"

All the heat evaporated from her voice. "You're like family to me. The only family I have. I've watched over you for a while."

Pressing back into her seat, Kennedy paled. "By hanging outside my apartment? By following me?"

"Sometimes, yeah. You remember that jerk that was hassling you, right? I want to make sure no one else bothers you. You're not like me. You don't fight."

Briefly closing her eyes, Kennedy nodded. "That's true. I've tried to get better, and I'm more in shape. I'm just not much of a fighter."

Now wait a minute! Reyes hated the hint of shame he heard in her voice. Of course she was a damn fighter. Anyone could see that.

"I knew you'd been out of town," Jodi continued. "I try to keep up with your schedule."

Kennedy's gaze met his.

Disturbed, Reyes turned down the drive to his house. The fine hairs on the back of his neck stood on end, and he used extra caution surveying the area.

"All right," Kennedy said, trying to soothe her. "You were there and you saw something?"

"I thought you were already back. You were supposed to be back."

"I had delays." Kennedy rubbed at her forehead.

"I'm glad, because if you hadn't, you'd..." The words trailed off, then renewed with a vengeance. "I saw those assholes dicking around your apartment! I *knew* they were up to something, and I was right."

"When I saw the fire," Kennedy said, "I called Reyes. He picked me up. You didn't see that?"

"No, I left once everyone was out of the building. That's when I figured you weren't in there."

If she'd already left, then who killed the two men?

Kennedy asked her exactly that, being more direct than Reyes expected. "Those two men were found with bullets in their heads."

"I know," Jodi said. "Good riddance."

Kennedy stiffened. "Did you...?"

"No, but I would have." Her voice lowered with grave determination. "The world is better off without their kind. I didn't have a chance to get to them, so I'm glad someone else did."

"But *who*?"

"I figured it was your boyfriend."

"He is not my boyfriend, Jodi. I already explained this to you."

"Okay, okay. Don't get your panties in a bunch. I'm just saying. He seems like he's capable, right? Who's to say he didn't off them?"

"I say he didn't. Remember, he was with me."

"Yeah, okay. So someone else did us a favor."

By the second, Kennedy got more frazzled. "You've been following Reyes, too?"

"Sometimes. I mean, I'm not going to trust him with my girl, am I?" Her attempt at levity fell flat. "He's a creep."

Dark with suspicion, Kennedy asked, "Do you know the women he's been with?"

"No. Want me to check into them more?"

"No! Absolutely not."

Reyes squeezed her knee, then pressed the garage door opener so he could pull inside. Immediately, he shut it again.

Already he felt better, knowing Kennedy wasn't exposed to her lunatic friend. He hadn't seen anyone following them, but there was a chance Jodi was good enough to be somewhere on the property and not get spotted.

After a steadying breath, Kennedy reclaimed her calm. "I don't want you to do anything else, Jodi, okay? I mean it. I'm an adult and I can take care of myself."

"Yeah, right," she said with caustic sarcasm.

In contrast, Kennedy softly chided, "That's not kind, Jodi."

Seconds ticked by, then Jodi said, "Sorry. I just don't want to see you hurt again."

"Then don't assume the worst about Reyes, don't spy on his girlfriends and, please, trust in my instincts and intelligence."

"I guess this means you're going to stay with him."

"Do you know where he lives?" Kennedy whispered, her spine going rigid. "Have you followed him home?"

"No, but I've seen him at the gym, and I've seen him visit women." She paused. "He's cagey, you know? Not easy to tail." Jodi huffed out a breath. "When can I see you?"

Reyes shook his head, not wanting her to commit.

She accepted that without question. "I don't know. Right now

I'm working on my book and trying to get my life reorganized after the fire and everything."

"Plus, it's not really safe for you to be out alone."

"No, it's not."

"Okay, so stay with the hulk. But promise me, if he does anything he shouldn't, if he hurts you in any way, you'll let me know. I swear to you, I'll end him."

Jesus, the girl was unhinged. Reyes met Kennedy's horrified gaze. Again he shook his head. He wasn't worried, so Kennedy shouldn't worry, either.

Keeping her gaze locked with his, Kennedy stated, "If you attempt to hurt him in any way, I won't forgive you, Jodi. Do you understand?"

"No sweat. I've got my hands full with another jerk anyway."

"Wait. *What?*"

"I'll be in touch, okay? And remember. You need me, all you gotta do is call."

Kennedy sat forward. "Jodi, don't—"

The call ended with all the subtlety of a thunderclap. Kennedy redialed immediately, but this time Jodi didn't answer.

"It's okay," Reyes said, hating that the girl had upset her. "Take a breath, babe."

Gulping in air, Kennedy visibly struggled with everything she'd just heard. Reyes gave her plenty of time, until the automatic overhead light flicked off, filling the garage with shadows.

Galvanized, he opened the truck door and got out. The look on Kennedy's face bothered him. She had enough worries without adding Jodi to the list.

With a long, purposeful stride, he circled the hood. For once, Kennedy was still sitting there. Not waiting for him to do the gentlemanly thing, but rather in a fog of dread.

He unhooked her seat belt. "Come on, hon, it's going to be okay." He took her purse and gym bag, and when he closed his fingers around her arm, she finally reacted.

Looking at him, Kennedy whispered, "She's irrational."

"Sounds like." He eased her out of the truck, more cognizant than ever of her small frame. With his arm around her waist, he led her inside. "It's not your problem."

"She's my friend."

"She's obsessed with you." Someone had to state the obvious. "That's not healthy."

"You heard her." Kennedy halted in the mudroom to kick off her sneakers, then she took the gym bag from him, and her purse. "She doesn't have anyone else."

Reyes smoothed her hair, left unruly from her activity at the gym. Her blue eyes were big and soft, her lips trembling.

And he wanted her like he'd never wanted another woman.

"We'll figure it out, okay? First things first, though. We need to let Madison know Jodi has been following me, that she knows about..." Shit. He rubbed the back of his neck.

"Your women?" Kennedy asked, her tone just a tad too detached to sound authentic. "Yes, you should let Madison know about that." She pivoted away. "I need that shower, now more than ever."

He let her go, mostly because he wasn't sure what to say.

She'd staunchly defended him to Jodi, stating unequivocally that he wouldn't misuse women. Hell, she'd even defended Annette, Cathy and Lili, correctly assuming that they were strong women who made their own decisions.

He'd never lied to a woman to get her into bed.

He never would.

If anyone wanted more than just sex, he walked away.

Yet here he was with Kennedy, who wanted nothing at all except his protection.

At the moment, that didn't seem to matter. She *knew* him, better than any other woman. In some ways, better than his family.

On top of that, there was a lot to unravel with everything Jodi had admitted.

Keeping Kennedy safe remained his top priority. Getting closer to her felt vital.

As he went through the house, he thought about everything he had to juggle, including his own confusion, but for the moment, he felt uncommonly...content.

It was because of Kennedy, and damn, he wasn't sure what to do about it. He was still a die-hard bachelor. Cade had made the whole relationship thing work, but as he often reminded himself, he wasn't Cade. A woman didn't fit into his life, the life groomed for him by his father.

But then, he didn't think Kennedy wanted to be a part of his life. So why was he tormenting himself about it?

Because he wanted her. Bad.

And that, he could have...if only she wanted it, too.

CHAPTER SEVEN

"YOU SURE YOU know what you're doing?" Del asked. He was damned tired of hanging around this run-down excuse for a cabin with nothing to do but smoke and think. He wanted to get back on the street, get his connections going and start acquiring girls he could rent out. Until then, he was bleeding what little cash he'd saved.

"You need to learn patience," Golly said, probably for the hundredth time. "With patience comes great rewards."

Hearing that nonsense, Del was fairly certain he and Golly had little in common. To him, selling women was a business. Not so for his cohort in this miserable scheme. Golly was obsessed with a scrawny girl and had some sick, twisted plans for when he captured her.

He was also completely repulsive. Throughout his life, Del had met some real disgusting characters, but none were as unbalanced as this one. It was bad enough that many of his teeth had rotted out, that his bald head was perpetually sweaty and that his shirts seldom covered his gut. Did he have to continually smile as if his brain had malfunctioned?

Sick prick.

Making a decision, Del stubbed out his cigarette and stood glaring at the man. "I'll wait a little longer, then I need to move on." Yes, he wanted Kennedy. He wanted to make her sorry for having crossed him. Mostly he wanted to remove her as a threat. The rest of the world had forgotten about him, but Kennedy?

She would never forget; he was fairly certain of that. It had taken him a while, but he'd finally located her here in Colorado. He was *that* close to ending her for good, but he had to move with caution, which was why he'd agreed to team up with the sick fuck now rocking in a wooden chair and humming.

What bothered him even more than the unnatural manner of the guy? That face. Del would bet the man had always been butt ugly, but an unhealthy fixation gave him the appearance of a demon from hell.

And that goddamned smile made it all the worse.

Yeah, if they didn't find Kennedy soon, Del would cut his losses and move on. He lit another cigarette.

No bitch was worth this much trouble.

THAT NIGHT, after debating with herself for far too long, Kennedy reluctantly returned to the living room instead of staying in the guest room, as was her norm. She'd tried to stick to her plan of giving Reyes as much space as she could so her time spent at his home wouldn't feel so invasive.

Already he'd reordered his life to accommodate her. She'd never known anyone like him. Who did that for a mere acquaintance?

Obviously, a man of Reyes's caliber.

He might act irreverent at times, and there was no denying he had a high opinion of his ability, plus his blatant sexuality was as much a part of him as his height and good looks.

And he was so much more than that. Smart, caring, gentle, practical, efficient.

Proud.

Gorgeous.

She'd brought so much trouble to his door, and it was all amplified by Jodi's volatility. Asking for anything more was unforgivably selfish, and yet here she was.

She found Reyes half sprawled over the couch, his head in the corner of the armrest, one muscled leg stretched along the cushions, the other braced on the floor. He had a laptop balanced on his hard abdomen and was focused on something he read.

Of course he noticed her silent approach. He missed nothing. Glancing up, his expression went wary. "Hey."

After dinner, she'd insisted on doing cleanup, where she'd lingered as long as she could, too unsettled to want to be alone. Finally, around eight thirty, she'd gone to the guest room. That was over an hour ago. Clearly, given her current habits, he hadn't expected to see her again until the morning. But for every second she'd spent pacing the room, her agitation had grown. She'd been unable to calm her rioting emotions.

And she'd been unable to stop thinking about Reyes.

It wasn't that she didn't trust Jodi, because overall she did. She didn't think Jodi would ever hurt her. As Reyes had said, Jodi was clearly obsessed with her.

But what if she hurt Reyes? He'd deny even the possibility, though people couldn't dodge bullets. Did Jodi own a high-powered rifle?

She honestly didn't know.

Another worry worm that had crawled into her brain was the idea that Jodi didn't understand boundaries, and she was so single-minded about protecting Kennedy that she didn't seem to distinguish right from wrong.

Would Jodi do something completely over-the-top that, in effect, could end up hurting her? Yes.

Now here she was, afraid for Reyes, riddled with guilt, worried for Jodi—and for the women Reyes visited.

Closing his laptop and setting it aside, Reyes sat up. "Everything okay?"

Now that she stood before him, she felt far more awkward than she'd anticipated.

She shook her head. No, she wasn't okay.

He was on his feet instantly, his hands clasping her shoulders, drawing her close. "Jodi has you rattled?"

"Yes." God, it felt good to let him hold her. *Too* good. It would be dangerous to depend on him that much, so she pressed back, robbing herself of his physical comfort. "I've been thinking."

He waited, and when she couldn't seem to vocalize the rest, he prompted her with, "Okay."

That made her smile. Silly Reyes. Always trying to comfort her. Always succeeding. "Can we sit?"

"Sure, yeah." He cleared a spot, then eased down with her, still keeping her close.

Such a big, badass guy, who always took care with her. Knowing she'd confused him—heck, she had herself confused, too—Kennedy leaned into his side.

So warm and strong. Resting one hand on his chest, she settled against the curve of his shoulder. "Let me get this said, okay?"

"All right."

"If you want to visit a woman, you should."

Arrested, he went perfectly still. But not for long. "Damn it, Kennedy—"

"Let me finish," she urged.

Frowning down at her, his mouth flattened, he gave one firm, annoyed nod.

"I know you think you need to stay here with me, but it's enough that you let *me* stay. Even if you're not here, it's safe, right? I promise I won't step outside. You shouldn't be locked down just because I am."

"My turn, yet?"

"No." God, this was difficult. "If you're staying in tonight—"

"You know I am."

Yup, that was relief turning her bones to noodles. Had she really thought he might race out the door just because she gave him permission?

Maybe she should do more than that.

Maybe she should encourage him to go...have his needs met.

God, that idea galled her, but she was determined to be fair to him. "I already knew you didn't spend your nights at home. Jodi confirmed it, therefore there's no reason for you to be discreet about it. You have a right to live your life."

"Damn right I do." He levered her up and across his lap as easily as he would have moved a throw pillow. She landed on his hard thighs with startling awareness. "No one tells me what to do or not do. Cade tries sometimes. Dad often gives it his best shot. Even Bernard has put in the effort a time or two."

She was on Reyes's lap. Everything he'd just said breezed in one ear and out the other.

The position was unlike anything she'd known. When was the last time anyone had held her?

So long ago that she couldn't remember.

"Are you listening to me?"

Not really. For some reason, he was running down the list of his family members as if they had some bearing on the situation. For the life of her, she didn't know why.

Kennedy sat stiffly, trying to give him the attention he demanded. But...

This was not at all what she'd expected when she ventured from the guest room.

His big hand came up to cradle the side of her face. "Pay attention, okay?"

She nodded. "Yes, okay."

Showing his doubt, he slipped his thumb under her chin and tilted her face up more. "If I wanted to go out, I'd go out."

"You can't *want* to stay cooped up here with me."

"Why not? You're good company." The thumb under her chin began a slow caress. "At least you are when you're not hiding in the other room."

Hiding. That summed it up nicely. "This is all so different. I'm used to being alone. I don't know what to do."

"With me?"

The way he asked that, it sounded sexual. Funny, but it caused a flutter in her stomach that didn't come close to resembling panic or even discomfort. "I don't date, Reyes. I don't sit around having casual conversations with men. I never sit on a guy's lap."

"So?"

Right. What exactly was her point? "I do my speaking, I engage with the audience, I answer questions, and then I go home to work on my book."

"Alone."

"It's what I prefer." Or rather, what she used to prefer. The fact that she was here now, *sitting on Reyes's lap*, proved that being alone didn't appeal as much at the moment.

His gaze searched hers. "Are you saying you'd rather I go out? That you want time away from me?"

"No!" Good God, running him out of his own home was the very last thing she wanted. Unsure what to do with her hands, she folded them together in her lap. He might be casual about their current position, but she wasn't. "Actually, I was going to ask you something."

"Shoot."

It would be better to just get it out there rather than keep agonizing over it. In a rush of words, she asked, "Since you're staying in, could I sleep with you again?"

The house got so quiet Kennedy could hear the steady thumping of her heart.

He cleared his throat. "You're ready for bed now?"

It was barely ten, but... "Yes?"

"No problem." In rapid order, he set her on her feet, moved his laptop to a table and began turning off lights.

Watching him, Kennedy said, "I guess after speaking with Jodi, I'm a little more nervous than I thought."

"That chick could spook anyone." He stood beneath the only remaining light near the stairs.

"I don't think I'd be able to sleep on my own. My brain would just keep churning over problems. But that first night here, with you, I slept well."

He held out a hand. "I know what you're saying, and what you're not. Don't worry that I'll take it the wrong way, okay?"

She took two steps toward him before pausing again. "I know it doesn't make sense for me to tell you to go out, then ask you to sleep with me."

"Makes perfect sense because I'm not going out, so we might as well share the bed."

He was the most confounding man ever, the way he just rolled with a situation, no questions asked. Surely, nothing like this had happened to him before.

Could he really know her that well?

She couldn't resist taking his hand. God knew he offered it often enough.

They started up the steps, with him measuring his stride to match her own.

Part of her shopping expedition had included warm pajamas. She wore the snug-fitting thermal bottoms with a looser matching top. After her shower, she'd left her hair free to ward off the headache trying to claim her. Her teeth were brushed, she'd applied lotion to her skin, and now...now she really wanted her thoughts to settle instead of jumping in a dozen different directions, each one more unsettling than the last.

At the bedroom door, he said, "I need to brush my teeth. Go ahead and get under the covers." He stepped into the bathroom and closed the door.

She knew he'd showered at the gym, and she assumed he wore his jeans out of deference to her. He'd adopted that habit ever since she'd moved into the guest room.

Maybe he thought she'd opted for a different room because his casual near-nudity made her feel threatened.

In truth, she enjoyed looking at him. Sure, she might be forever affected by her experience, but that didn't make her blind. In many ways, Reyes was like a work of art. A living sculpture of long bones, pronounced muscles and delectable body hair.

The door opened and he stepped back into the room to find her still standing there.

Smile going crooked, he chided, "You haven't moved."

"I got lost in thought."

"Yeah? About Jodi?"

Shaking her head, she asked, "Why are you wearing jeans all the time?"

Coming to a halt, he looked down at his jeans as if he'd forgotten he had them on, then he scratched his jaw. "I figured it was the polite thing to do."

She gave an exasperated sigh. "Because you think it makes me uncomfortable?"

"I thought it might, and didn't want to take the chance."

Heading to the bed, she said, "Well, it doesn't. But even if it did, I don't want you adjusting things for me. Your comfort should come first. That's what I'd prefer, okay?"

"So if I just go naked around the house, you're okay with that?"

She had the covers lifted in her hand, one knee on the mattress about to climb in, but at his statement she almost fell in face-first. "Naked?" Straightening back to her feet, she dropped her hands to her hips and eyed him with suspicion. "You're just messing with me. No way do you prance around here naked."

"Prance, no."

Her mind conjured an image... "Be serious, Reyes."

He laughed at her sharp tone. "Sorry. Gotta take my pleasures where I can." Sporting a big grin, he shucked off his jeans but left on his boxers, turned off the light and got into bed.

Leaving her standing there feeling foolish. "So you don't walk around here without clothes?"

"Not often."

This time she rudely huffed, sure that he was only baiting her to get a reaction. She slid between the cool sheets, and immediately Reyes tugged her close, curving his body around hers.

His minty breath teased her cheek. "Get comfortable in whatever way works for you, as long as it's near me, and then we can get some sleep."

"I want you comfortable, too," she whispered.

"So you know, I'm a hell of a lot more comfortable like this than with us sleeping in separate rooms."

She turned her head enough to face him, but her eyes hadn't yet adjusted. She had the sense of him being very near, yet she couldn't make out his features. "You said you've never brought a woman here."

"Haven't." His hand smoothed over her hair, then tucked it back behind her ear with a tenderness she felt in her heart. "There's a difference in being home alone and knowing a woman sleeps just downstairs."

His temperature seemed to have risen, sending his heated scent to envelope her. "This is nice," she murmured.

"Very." He pressed a kiss to the top of her head. "Now sleep."

Held against his body, listening to his deepening breaths, Kennedy felt his hold loosen as he fell asleep.

There couldn't be another man like Reyes anywhere.

Without thinking about it, she whispered, "It's a good thing you don't want me, or we wouldn't be able to do this."

His arm immediately snuggled her closer, and his husky voice, low and rough, sounded very near to her ear. "I've wanted you from the first time I saw you. Make no mistake about that."

Her eyes popped open wide.

"Since we enjoy sharing the bed, from now on you sleep with me. Only sleep. And if you ever want more, just let me know." Putting a final kiss to her ear, he breathed, "Now sleep. If we talk about this much longer, I'm gonna get hard and that'll bother you and we'll never get any rest."

He wanted her. Enough that he could get an erection from talking? Kennedy had no idea what to say. She stared into the darkness, her eyes rounded, her heart galloping…and the strangest sort of thrill curling around her heart.

Huh. Reyes McKenzie had done the impossible.

He'd sparked her interest. Now she needed to figure out what to do about it.

THE WEEKEND ROLLED AROUND, and Reyes walked through the house whistling. Who knew he could be so happy with sexual frustration? Being celibate with Kennedy made all the difference. For several days now she'd slept with him each night.

Each day, she tried to figure out when and how she could leave. He understood that. Their investigation had come to a grinding halt with no new clues and no new leads to follow. She wanted to get on with her life.

Each day he became more determined to keep her around a little longer.

How long, he didn't know. Sooner or later, she'd need her own place, yet every time he thought of it he got a bad feeling. Something wasn't right. Whoever had come after her was just lying low. Eventually they'd crawl out of the shadows again, and when they did, he wanted to be with Kennedy so he could ensure her safety.

Sitting at the kitchen table, sipping yet another cup of coffee, Kennedy looked lost in thought.

He'd learned to make an entire pot instead of only a few cups. Sometimes it seemed she sustained herself on worry and caffeine, along with the determination to help others avoid her fate.

"It's Saturday," he said, aware of her gaze lifting to his body.

As she'd requested, he'd gone back to wearing only his boxers in the morning, at least until he dressed for the day. More than a few times, he'd caught her looking him over.

He wasn't quite sure what her intense scrutiny meant. With another woman, yeah, he could assume. But this was Kennedy, and she had a troubled past.

"I know." She smiled at him. "The pancakes were amazing. Give me a few more minutes and I'll clean up."

"You've done all the cleanup, lately. It's my turn."

"I clean because you always cook." As if that bugged her, she said, "I know how to cook, too, you know."

As he carried plates to the dishwasher, he said, "No biggie. You can do dinner whenever you want."

"That's not what you said the last five times I asked."

He shrugged. "I didn't want you to feel obligated. But sure, if it means that much to you, I don't mind. Just not tonight. It's Saturday, so I figured we'd go out."

She perked up at that. "Out? Out where?"

He heard the excitement in her voice and felt like a dope. Of course she wanted to get out. Other than their one breakfast at a restaurant, the entirety of her social life had been going to the gym and back. Her life was literally on hold, the danger still out there with no way for them to address it.

"Dinner and a movie?" he suggested.

Standing, she carried her now-empty cup to him. "I'd rather visit this Bernard person so I could see Chimera. You keep telling me you still have the cat, but in all this time, I haven't seen her. *And*," she stressed, when he started to speak, "you refuse to take me to see her."

"Because it's complicated."

Adorably cute in her pajamas, she growled, "Either you have the cat or you don't."

"Fine." He gave up. "You want to see Chimera? I'll talk to Bernard today and see when we can visit."

Narrowing her eyes, she looked at him askance. "You make it sound like some grand concession."

Yeah, because he'd wanted to take her out, not drag her to his father's house, where she'd be dissected and where his relationship with her would be up for discussion. He could already hear his dad lecturing him.

Who needed that shit?

"Look," he said, ready to launch into something, probably something obnoxious, that was interrupted by the doorbell.

Before Kennedy could get all panicky, he cursed. "My sister. And damn it, it looks like she has Sterling with her." More or less stomping out of the kitchen, he went to the door and shouted through the intercom, "I'm not dressed. Give me five."

"I won't look," Sterling said, then she snickered.

Aware of a blur behind him, Reyes watched Kennedy dart toward the guest room. "No hiding," he called after her.

"Just getting dressed," she assured him, seconds before she disappeared from sight.

Fuck it. He opened the door to let in his sister and sister-in-law. "Coffee's in the kitchen. Kennedy is changing out of her pj's. I'll be right back."

Sterling boldly stared at him, then snorted. "Those boxers are no different than the shorts you wear for working out."

Madison, not in the least interested in what her brother wore, headed to the couch with her laptop. "I'm here to see Kennedy anyway."

That brought him away from the stairs and back into the living room area. "Why?"

"The cops did a massive, coordinated statewide search of missing youths. Found a lot of them, too, and in the process, they also arrested several suspected traffickers. I want Kennedy to check out the photos to see if anyone looks familiar."

That sounded interesting. "Got it." He rushed upstairs to take a speed shower, clean his teeth and shave. He dressed in a long-sleeved pullover and worn jeans. Carrying his shoes and socks, he headed back down.

Kennedy was already neatly dressed in a flannel shirt, skinny jeans and thick socks. She'd pulled her hair into a high ponytail and put on a touch of makeup.

Cute. She wanted to impress his family.

She was going about it the wrong way, but he wouldn't tell her so.

Sterling now had a cola, and Madison had a bottle of water. Curled in a chair, Kennedy asked numerous questions, which Sterling fielded like a pro, telling her only so much without admitting to anything private.

They were mostly questions on fighting styles, and Kennedy seemed duly impressed with their answers.

Reaching to the small of her back, Sterling pulled a wicked blade from a sheath. "Check out my new knife."

Gingerly Kennedy accepted it, handling it like a live grenade.

Madison's laptop was open, but so far no one was looking at it. Reyes lifted it, going through the photos with a practiced eye. He didn't see anyone familiar to him, but then, that was the problem with the ever-growing trade.

When the women started talking about fashion or, in Sterling's case, the lack thereof, Reyes decided this might be a good time for him to dodge out. He could talk to his dad, let him know that he might have to bring Kennedy by, and he could warn Bernard not to be so damned possessive of the cat.

Yes, the cat *was* Bernard's now. Reyes had relinquished ownership when Bernard turned to comical mush over the critter. Pretty sure if he'd pressed the issue, Bernard would have challenged him.

Then his dad would be pissed, and probably Madison, too, because they all considered Bernard one of the family.

Shaking his head, Reyes said, "If you ladies are going to hang out here awhile, I think I'll head over to Dad's to check on... things."

Madison shooed him away. "I'll give you three hours while Kennedy and I get better acquainted."

Better acquainted? What the hell did that have to do with searching through arrest photos? He didn't like the sound of it and was about to protest when Sterling got to her feet in a rush.

"No way." She pointed at Reyes. "You're going to the house to spar with Cade and I want to take part."

Why couldn't his sister-in-law just go along like Madison had? She never let anything slide, and she never missed an opportunity to sharpen her edge.

Reyes tried a smile that felt like a snarl. "I thought you were going to visit."

"Ha!" Sterling narrowed her eyes on him. It was an effective look for her, both mocking and, for some, intimidating. "You know I don't get into the whole girl-talk thing."

Madison glanced up with indignation. "I hardly think researching traffickers fits that description."

"You're talking clothes, not creeps."

"They're going to search through arrest photos," Reyes reminded, trying to divert her.

Sterling huffed. "And that'll take how long? Once they're done, we both know the chitchat is going to veer to female stuff."

"News flash, Sterling. You're female."

She rolled her eyes. "Barely."

Of all the... "My brother would disagree with that assessment."

"Your brother is incredibly unique." She shrugged it off. "So far, he's the only one I know who makes it worthwhile to be female."

Kennedy's fascinated gaze took it all in. "Why don't you like being female?"

Just to irritate Sterling, Reyes answered before she could. "Being smaller and weaker grates on her. She'd rather kick ass than fix her hair."

"Hey." Madison glared at him. "Some of us enjoy doing both."

"Yeah, I get it," Reyes said, with enough inflection to insinuate that Sterling did not. "You happen to be both lethal and feminine. Apparently, most can't figure out that balance."

Slowly smiling, Sterling said, "Oh, now I'm really going to enjoy sparring. Plan to bleed."

He groaned. When Sterling got in that particular mood, she could be a total bear. He wouldn't actually bleed, but he would be wearing a few new bruises before they wrapped it up. "I didn't agree to spar with you."

"You will."

He narrowed his eyes. "So maybe I'll give as good as I get."

"You can try."

Damn it, they both knew he could flatten her—if he wanted. The problem was that she *was* his brother's wife. Cade loved her more than life, and if his scuffling got too rough, Cade would take it out on him. "I'm *sparring* with you," Reyes stated, emphasis on *sparring*. "Save that painful shit for your husband."

"Chicken."

Ignoring Sterling, he made an impulse decision and bent to press a kiss to Kennedy's forehead. "Call if you need me, otherwise I'll be back before Madison is ready to go."

It took her a few seconds to recover from the affectionate peck. She blinked several times, then lifted her chin. "I'm getting curious about all this sparring stuff. I think watching would be fun."

"Another day," he said easily, and moved on before she could challenge that dismissal. He leveled a severe look on his sister. "Don't overdo it."

After giving him another airy wave, Madison situated the laptop on the coffee table and gestured Kennedy over to sit beside her so they could look at the images together.

Sterling turned to Kennedy with a quick apology. "Sorry to visit and run—"

"I understand," Kennedy assured her.

Still, Sterling explained, "Sparring with the guys is special. I always learn something new."

"I'm in no way offended," Kennedy promised. "Go have fun."

Fun. Frustrated, Reyes walked out of the room with Sterling dogging his heels. He literally *felt* her behind him as he went down the hall and out into the garage. If he thought he could leave her behind, he would.

But one thing he'd learned about Sterling—dealing with her was never easy. In her current challenging mood?

It'd be downright impossible.

CHAPTER EIGHT

"I CAME OVER WITH MADISON," Sterling said. "Since I hadn't planned to leave—until you offered better entertainment—you'll have to give me a lift back."

Great. More isolated time with her. *If only he'd kept his mouth shut.* Reyes plastered on an insincere smile. If she knew she'd irked him, she'd only dig in more. "No problem."

His lack of enthusiasm made Sterling laugh out loud. "You are so transparent, you big fraud." When he started around to open her door, she made a sound of derision and hauled herself up into the truck.

Stopping to stare at her, Reyes propped his fists on his hips. "What if I'd planned to take my bike?" He hadn't had the Harley out recently. The day was cool, but the sun was bright.

Already jumping back out of the truck, Sterling said, "Awesome. Let's do it."

Figured she'd like that idea. Cade would kick his ass for real if he had Sterling strapped around him on the drive to his father's place. For such a calm, in-control guy, his brother was ridiculously territorial with his wife. "No, I don't think so."

"Spoilsport." Again she jumped easily into the truck. As he pulled out of the driveway, she added, "Reyes has a girlfriend," in a low and annoying singsong voice.

The truth was, he loved his sister-in-law, most especially because she had brought Cade back into the family. His big brother had avoided that duty by joining the army rangers. When he medically retired with a bad knee from too many jumps out of moving planes, he'd reluctantly returned to the family...yet an emotional distance had remained.

From the start, Cade had bucked their father's iron will. He wanted to choose his own destiny, not fall in line with his father's plans.

When he met Sterling, though, he got a whole new perspective on what family meant, mostly because she didn't have one and therefore appreciated his.

They'd all pulled together to get her bacon out of the fire. Of course, that hadn't stopped Reyes from teasing her mercilessly. He'd at first considered her a pushy broad who'd played at being a badass. Hadn't taken him long to realize she wasn't playing.

The lady had endless stamina, a backbone of steel, a streak of bravery a mile wide and endless determination to learn. He liked her. More than that, he respected her.

Maybe he should tell her that to end their not-so-subtle war.

Nah. Pretty sure she enjoyed it as much as he did. Or at least, as much as he did when he wasn't worried for Kennedy.

"Not denying it, huh?"

Reyes took his sunglasses from the visor and slipped them on. "What's that? Did you say something?"

Sterling grinned. She was a tall, bold woman with strong features, a sturdy, rockin' body, and a lack of fashion sense. When she smiled? Downright beautiful.

"You like her. Admit it."

"I like her." He more than liked her. Not that he'd do anything about it.

"Wow." Clearly Sterling hadn't expected that reply. "So how does she feel about you?"

It occurred to him that his sister-in-law might make a good sounding board. She'd been through a devastating experience similar to what Kennedy had endured. The big difference was that Sterling appeared to bounce back. Like a boxer, she refused to show weakness in any way. Long before she'd met Cade, she'd had some understandable hang-ups concerning sex—but she'd forged onward, involving herself in sexual situations until she no longer froze, for the sole purpose of ensuring she wouldn't cower when threatened. Her whole focus had been on helping others, and she knew she couldn't do that if the threat of sex left her emotionally paralyzed.

Because of her resolve, she'd learned to "get through it" without anyone realizing how she disliked the whole physical thing.

Now with Cade… The two of them could barely keep their hands off each other. Sterling had gone from tolerating sex to wallowing in the pleasure of it.

Which meant his brother did a fair amount of smiling these days.

"Trust me," Sterling said, "if it takes that much thought trying to figure it out, she's not into you. Women aren't that subtle."

Never a dull moment with his prickly sister-in-law. She had a razor-sharp wit that he couldn't help admiring. "I could use some advice."

Slapping a hand over her heart, Sterling pretended to swoon back against the door.

"Knock it off. I'm serious."

As if she didn't believe her ears, she said, "You want *my* advice?"

Damn, couldn't she ever let up? "Never mind. It was a bad idea."

"No way, now I want to hear this. Behold, a serious woman. Tell me what's troubling you. I'm all ears."

The humor caught him off guard, making him snicker. "I don't know how Cade tolerates your sarcasm."

"He doesn't earn it, that's how." Shifting to better face him, she grew serious. "Come on, give. All ribbing aside, you're my brother now and I care about you. I'll help if I can."

Yeah, that was the sister-in-law he loved. She could charge into danger with the best of them, and she also had a heart of gold. "You know what Kennedy went through."

"Yeah. Hope the dick who did that to her is buried deep."

One guy was. The other? He didn't know. "She's…guarded still."

Plainspoken as always, Sterling asked, "You mean about sex? With you?"

Reyes frowned. "You're jumping the gun."

"So you don't mean sex?"

Why in the world had he thought she'd be subtle about the topic? "Damn it, will you let me talk?"

She pretended to zip her lips.

After shooting her a quelling glance, she remained silent and waiting, and Reyes released a deep breath. "Sex between us hasn't come up. I'm not an idiot where women are concerned. I pick up on stuff. Kennedy's not into it, not just with me, but I think with anyone. I think she's..." Not damaged. Never that. "I don't think she's given sex a thought since she got away."

"Can I speak now?"

Why not? "Have at it."

"Kennedy obviously doesn't know what she's missing. In her mind, sex is still all about humiliation, lack of choices and pain— basically the total opposite of fun. Given what she's been through, she's probably not looking to change that."

"You did."

"Yeah, well, you know I can't stand being cowed by anyone or anything. To me, sex was a handicap to overcome."

"And you managed that." Could Kennedy?

"Yeah, I did. Sex was no longer an agony, but it was a far shot from enjoyable." She bobbed her eyebrows. "Whole different story with your oh-so-amazing brother."

"I figured." It felt both strange and natural to have this discussion with Sterling. "The last thing I want to do is spook Kennedy, you know? I want her to feel safe with me."

"She does. Guaranteed."

"Yeah? You really think so?"

"She's smart, right? She would have moved on already if she didn't trust you."

At least that was something.

"Here's what I'd do," Sterling said. "Build on that trust. Like the way you kissed her goodbye today? Totally took her by surprise, but she didn't mind. It just wasn't something in her wheelhouse. I doubt she's let any guy get close enough for an affectionate peck. Do that a few more times."

Not a problem. "And?"

"Trust opens the door to other things. Right now, she's got her guard up, even with you. I mean, a smart woman doesn't want to take the chance on being hurt twice. So while she doesn't think you'd do anything heinous to harm her, she's still protecting herself. When she lets down those walls, she'll notice things."

"Like?"

"Like your very fine physique and sexy attitude. Actually, she's probably already been clued in on that, she's just not sure what to do about it."

Reyes felt heat burn up the back of his neck. A compliment from Sterling was a damned uncomfortable thing.

Either she didn't notice his unease, or she flat out didn't care. "You know how to seduce, right? I mean, you are Cade's brother, so I assume—"

Affronted, he growled, "Knowing how and thinking I should are two different things."

In a soothing tone, Sterling explained, "I'm not saying to come on hot and heavy. That'd be all wrong. Just help her ease into things. I know if she gives you a back-off signal, you'll respect that."

"Yes."

"So there you go. When she realizes she likes the contact, that a kiss isn't an ugly, unwanted thing, that it makes her want more, then you can deliver. Little by little, though, okay?" She landed a friendly punch to his shoulder. "I know this family has some superior genes coursing through the bloodline, but a guy is a guy is a guy. Don't think she's all enthused when she might not be. Wait until she makes it clear it's what she wants."

"I wouldn't pressure her." For some reason, it was important to him for Sterling to understand that.

"I know that, Reyes." Briefly she touched his forearm, as if to emphasize the sincerity of her words, then she retreated again. "I guess that's why you want to spar? Have some pent-up frustrations to work out?"

Something like that. "Just keeping my edge."

"If you say so."

Which translated to: *You are so full of it.*

He liked Sterling, he really did. If nothing else, she always kept it real.

NOW THAT THEY WERE ALONE, Madison launched right into work. "Over the past month, our local Human Trafficking task force teamed up with the state and did a huge sting. They not only rounded up a bunch of missing kids, they got multiple traffickers."

Freezing in horror, Kennedy breathed, "The kids are okay?"

"They are now, yeah. Many of them were runaways and such, and they're getting help. Some were being groomed to be prostitutes, but for most, it hadn't happened yet."

Thank God.

Madison scooted closer. "Not every situation is like yours."

"I know that, but they're all awful."

"I agree. But what I meant is that sometimes the kids are coaxed into it, not forced. They have someone taking care of them when no one else has—and sometimes just because they think they're misunderstood and they're rebelling against their parents. Being out with a 'protector' who ensures they have food and pretty clothes, it's seductive. Then the sexual favors start, and pretty soon, once they're used to that—"

"The trafficker asks for more." Kennedy hated them all. Each and every one of the monsters who preyed on the vulnerable, either through emotional control or physical abuse.

"Yes." She touched Kennedy's hand. "But they're rescued now, and the ones responsible will be prosecuted. What I need you to do is look through these images and see if you recognize anyone."

Kennedy took the laptop from her and settled back on the couch. Photos of men, and a few women, both facing forward and in profile, filled the screen. "How did you get these?" They looked like official police photos.

Madison smiled but didn't answer. "Click on each image to enlarge it." With a pat to Kennedy's hand, she stood. "I could use a cup of coffee and maybe a few cookies. You?"

"Sounds good. You want me to make it?" She now felt fairly comfortable in Reyes's home. A dangerous thing, that. A part of her knew she should be expending every ounce of free time trying to figure out how to leave; instead, every day she became more settled.

"No, you look through those. I'll be right back."

An hour later, with a looming headache and eyestrain, Kennedy admitted defeat. "I'm sorry, but I don't recognize any of them." Which only meant there were too many horrible people in the world.

"That's okay. It was worth a shot."

Another hour passed while they talked and strategized. Kennedy liked Madison. The woman was far too pretty with her fawn-colored hair and wide hazel eyes that matched Reyes's. She had to be six feet tall, slender but toned, and though she had a fragile femininity about her, Kennedy believed she could do serious damage.

Never would she underestimate any of the McKenzies.

When the doorbell rang, Kennedy nearly leaped off her seat.

"Oops." Madison glanced up at the nearest monitor. "I was enjoying our visit so much, I didn't even notice someone approaching."

Far less cavalier, Kennedy's heart lodged in her throat, making her rasp when she asked, "Who do you think it is?"

"Oh, look. He's staring right into the security camera. Isn't that clever of him?"

Kennedy gaped at her.

"It's hidden, you know, but he spotted it." Finally realizing that Kennedy was frozen beside her, Madison smiled. "No worries. It's just Detective Albertson. What a surprise."

"You know him?" Kennedy started to relax.

"We've never met. He's been keeping tabs on my family, so I've been keeping tabs on him."

As she headed for the door, Kennedy panicked. "Wait! Should you open that?"

Gently, and with understanding, Madison said, "It'll be okay, I promise. I won't let anyone hurt you."

She wouldn't let... Good grief. Was everyone in the McKenzie family so cocksure of themselves? Of course, she believed Madison was capable, but the man was big, muscular, and he just might have his own set of skills.

Launching from her seat, Kennedy quickly backed up to the kitchen entry, which also put her in line with the hall. If she had to make a run for it, she'd go to the guest room she used, lock the door and dig out her weapons. In fact, maybe she should do that now.

Too late.

Madison swung open the door to reveal a… Wow. Seeing him for real instead of through the camera, the guy looked like a male model. Not as tall as Reyes and Cade, but then who was? He was still six-two, with broad shoulders beneath an expensive suit.

Sandy-brown hair, with gold streaks that made it a few shades lighter than Madison's, and dark-as-sin eyes, made him a devastatingly handsome man.

Madison smiled. "Hello, Detective Albertson. How nice to see you."

The detective had been staring at Madison in a surprised yet absorbed way—until her words registered. Then he straightened, on alert. "We haven't met."

"No," Madison confirmed. "We haven't."

He looked past her into the house, locked on to Kennedy for a heart-stopping moment, then gave his attention back to Madison. "Miss Madison McKenzie."

Madison actually seemed pleased that he'd said her name. "That's Ms., if you don't mind."

He acknowledged that with a nod. "I wanted to speak to your brother."

"Which one?"

"The one who lives here?"

She laughed. Kennedy couldn't credit it.

And, damn it, she was still tempted to run.

"Unfortunately, Detective, he's away at the moment. Would you like to come in?"

Kennedy almost choked. She didn't want a stranger in the house!

Sensing her unease, Madison glanced back. "It's okay. Detective Albertson is a very good, honest cop. Isn't that right, Detective?"

Confused by the familiar way she addressed him, he ran a hand over his mouth. "You've been studying up on me."

"Tit for tat, you know."

Flirting? Was Madison actually *flirting* with the man? They were all certifiable…but also proficient, damn it. She trusted that Madison knew what she was doing. Sort of.

Maybe.

Still undecided, Albertson hesitated, then finally nodded and stepped in. "Thank you."

"Coffee?" Madison asked as she headed to the couch and casually closed her laptop.

Not missing a thing, the detective's suspicious gaze zeroed in on the device. "Sure, thanks."

Madison looked to Kennedy. "Would you mind?"

"Oh." Shaking herself, Kennedy said, "Sure," and hurried away. She needed a minute to herself, and this would help. As she poured the coffee, she tried to think.

Reyes would be furious, she didn't doubt that. Would he be mad at her, or just his sister?

Didn't matter. Reyes was the one she trusted—his sister, she barely knew. So she used her phone to quickly send a text to Reyes.

your sis just let in Detective Albertson. They R talking & it seems ok but thought you should know

Immediately she got a reply: On my way. She was about to put the phone in her pocket when another text came in: Stay behind Madison.

Obviously, he believed his sister could protect her. For the moment, that was good enough for her.

"So." MADISON COULDN'T help admiring the handsome detective. His sandy-brown hair was a bit too long, curling at the ends in what might have created a boyish look if it wasn't for his strong jaw and sinfully dark eyes. Such a stunning contrast, that lighter hair with the dark chocolate gaze. With brothers like hers, most men seemed far too ordinary in comparison.

Not so with Crosby. Having never experienced lust at first sight, she sighed.

The good detective shot her a suspicious look, to which she smiled...and yes, that only made him more wary.

It wasn't only his looks worth noting. Since he'd been checking into them, he had to know that her brothers were very dangerous people. So was she. Yet here he stood, in Reyes's house, gazing at *her* with cautious interest—something most men didn't dare to do.

That dark stare did funny things to her insides. She'd have to get used to the detective in small doses. "If you're here for a reason, I suggest we get to it."

Now he smiled. "Suddenly in a rush?"

"Well, since Kennedy surely texted Reyes, and since he'll race over here just to throw you out—and I do mean *throw*—yes, it might be wise to find out the reason for your visit."

That took care of his smile. Annoyance gathered his brows together. They were a few shades darker than his hair and added even more interesting dimensions to his face.

"You're threatening me with your brother?" he growled.

"Oh, no, I'm happy to finally meet you in person. Remember, I offered you coffee." Louder, so that Kennedy would hear, she said, "Although I'm starting to wonder if that meant making a new pot, since it's taking so long."

Wearing a hot blush, Kennedy finally slunk back. She set the cup on a coaster on the coffee table, then backed a safe distance away.

Clearly she didn't trust Albertson, which sort of amused Madison. "Crosby—may I call you Crosby?" She didn't wait for him to answer before continuing to Kennedy. "Crosby is fine, I promise. You can trust my judgment. That said, I don't mind that you contacted Reyes, I promise. No reason to blush."

Now Kennedy frowned, too. "I think you're trying to embarrass me."

"Not at all. I just want us all to be honest." She turned back to Crosby. "Now, why are you here?"

He rubbed a big-knuckled hand over his mouth. "We've arrested a lot of shady men lately—"

"I'm aware."

"Yeah, well, maybe you don't know that there was one particular man I want, but he wasn't in the mix. I thought you might know something about that."

Madison almost clapped her hands. "We're collaborating? Oh, how fun! Do you have an image?"

"I do. So you know, it's inside my jacket pocket."

"Not going for a gun, huh?"

"No, I'm not, so don't overreact."

That he understood her capability flattered her. Few men would even acknowledge her talents, much less respect them.

Slowly he withdrew a small, crinkled photo and handed it over.

"Hmm." Madison studied the black-and-white of a balding guy in slight profile, which showed a scraggly ponytail hanging down his neck. He had a very weak chin, an ugly smile and a few missing teeth. "I'm sorry, but he doesn't look familiar."

Kennedy gave up her suspicion of Crosby in favor of seeing the photo for herself. Silently, she stared at it. "Are you able to give a name to go with the image?"

Madison watched Kennedy more closely. She saw...maybe not actual recognition, but definitely a flash of something.

As if delivering a curse, Crosby muttered, "Rob Golly."

Kennedy's head jerked up. She stared in horror at Crosby, which brought him closer to her in a rush.

"You know him, don't you?"

"No," she said, stepping closer to Madison. "No, I don't."

Madison touched her arm. "But you've heard of him?" Was his a name she'd learned during her time being trafficked?

Or...was the bastard somehow tied to Jodi?

Starting to tremble, Kennedy asked, "Why are you looking for him?"

Crosby noted Kennedy's unease and he solicitously indicated the chair.

Gripping the photo enough to add new wrinkles to it, Kennedy sank onto the cushion.

Madison chose a spot on the couch and patted the seat beside her.

Ignoring that, Crosby sat at the other end, as far from her as he could get, and retrieved the coffee. He sipped, no doubt using that time to formulate how much he wanted to share.

"You can tell me, you know," Madison assured him. "I'm completely trustworthy."

He shot her an incredulous look. "You're completely...something. *Trustworthy* isn't the word I'd use."

Smart man. "Okay, give. Who is Rob Golly and why do you want him?"

Keeping his gaze on Kennedy, Crosby said, "I've been tracking him for a while. Over two years, actually. He's a known abuser of women, the worst sort of scum you can imagine."

"Oh, I don't know," Madison murmured. "I have a very developed imagination."

Kennedy gaped at her in horrified disbelief. "You're treating this like a joke."

Oh, my. Kennedy definitely knew something about the man. "I'm sincerely sorry," she said, keeping her tone soft. "I never meant to make light of it."

Kennedy firmed her lips and nodded.

Glancing at Crosby, Madison felt sure that he, too, saw how tightly strung Kennedy had gotten over the man. "Go on."

He gave a small nod. "Golly moves around a lot, renting old houses where he'd keep women as prisoners. I finally tracked down his last house."

Kennedy literally held her breath.

Until Crosby added, "But he wasn't there."

Covering her mouth with one hand, Kennedy frowned. "What do you mean, he wasn't there? You had the wrong house?"

"Right house, but Golly was nowhere to be found."

"How do you know it was the right house?" Madison asked.

"All the signs were there. A room in the basement meant to be a cell. A door with too damn many locks on it." His right hand curled into a fist, and he rasped, "Blood on the floor."

"That sounds horrid," Madison whispered, no longer in a flirting mood.

"The worst nightmare a person could imagine." Crosby sat forward, all his attention on Kennedy. "I had the right place, I know it. But Golly was gone, and so was his last victim."

Kennedy said nothing, but her eyes went glassy with unshed tears.

Falling back on her training, Madison asked, "Did you check the yard? Sounds like old Golly might have a few bodies buried around the property."

"Nothing at that house, but at another we found remains."

Madison didn't know how much longer Kennedy could hang on. She looked ready to implode, with fear, anger. Any minute now, Reyes would come crashing in and all hell would break loose.

She would wait for him outside to warn him to behave, except that would mean leaving Kennedy alone with Crosby, and Reyes would be furious if she did that. If she took Kennedy with her, that would leave Crosby alone in Reyes's house. Another sin in her brother's eyes.

What to do?

"Tell me, Detective, when did you join the trafficking task force, and why were you tracking Golly in particular?" In her experience, most men enjoyed bragging. Not her brothers, not to strangers anyway, but for most other men it appeared to be a basic masculine trait.

Crosby surprised her silly by saying, "I'm not on a task force. My interest is personal, and you won't distract me with your questions." His smile looked the opposite of friendly, more like an issue of clear challenge. "I'd rather hear about you, your brothers and the head of it all, your father."

CHAPTER NINE

REYES KEPT HIS foot pressed hard on the gas pedal, weaving in and out of traffic. With every minute that passed, every mile he covered, his blood burned hotter.

How fucking *dare* his sister let a stranger into his house? She knew better.

After he'd finished sparring with Cade, they'd both gone to their respective suites within their father's immense mountain mansion to shower and change before meeting upstairs for drinks with Parrish. His father was keenly curious about Kennedy, and more than a little concerned about Reyes's involvement with her.

He'd denied any involvement, of course.

Neither Cade nor Parrish had bought his denials. The McKenzies were razor-sharp and cut through BS like a hot knife through butter.

Reyes had geared up for the inquisition, especially when he informed Bernard that he'd be bringing Kennedy over to visit Chimera the cat. Then her text had come in, and his only thought had been getting to her.

Cade had made the spur-of-the-moment decision to follow him home, just in case there was real trouble, while Parrish had told Reyes to trust Madison.

Right. Logic told him that the cop likely wasn't a stranger to his sister, but at the moment he didn't care.

Finally he turned into the long drive to his home, going so fast that the truck tires kicked up dirt and gravel. He screeched to a halt outside the garage, next to the silver sedan.

Fuming, he jogged up the walk—and the front door opened.

Kennedy said, "I'm sorry I overreacted," and then launched at him, her arms going tight around his neck.

Just as quickly, he moved her safely behind him and lifted his Glock.

Madison appeared next in the doorway. "I'd really prefer you not shoot the detective. Overall, he's been very helpful."

"Get out of the way, Madison."

She crossed her arms. "No, I don't think so. You're running on emotion and you know that's not wise."

Yeah, he did know it, but feeling Kennedy tremble behind him, he didn't give a shit.

Then she stepped around in front of him again, whispering, "Please don't do anything dumb. I'm fine, but I desperately need to talk to you, and I can't do that until Crosby and Madison are gone."

Crosby? Now why the hell did that fry his ass? "You know the fucker's first name?"

"Reyes," Madison sighed, making the sound long and aggrieved. "Get a grip, will you?"

Behind him, Cade pulled up. The door of his SUV slammed with foreboding.

Madison threw up her hands. "I know Kennedy texted you. I know she was worried." She came closer, stepping onto the walk, too. "But, Reyes, I promise there's no reason."

He was just about convinced when a man came out the door. "Honest to God, I've never before had two women trying to protect me."

"Trying?" Madison repeated. "If it weren't for me, you'd be eating dirt right now."

"Maybe I'm not the slouch you think I am."

Jesus, Joseph and Mary. He'd stepped into bedlam. Lowering the gun to his side, Reyes asked, "Do I need to kill him or not?"

Together, Madison and Kennedy said, *"Not."*

"Fine." He turned and shoved the gun into Kennedy's hand.

Horrified, she accepted it with the same enthusiasm she might give a cockroach.

To Cade, Reyes said, "Back off."

Cade held up his hands. "No problem. I, at least, trust our sister."

"Thank you," Madison stated primly.

In two long strides, Reyes reached the handsome bastard standing just outside his front door. Smiling in evil anticipation, he threw a punch too fast for the other man to duck and clocked him right in the jaw.

Staggering back, cursing, Crosby caught himself and took an aggressive stance. "That's not necessary, McKenzie."

"It is if you don't want me to rip you apart." He grabbed Crosby's arm and propelled him off the front porch to the yard.

This time Crosby went down from the sheer momentum of the attack, but he didn't stay down.

Bounding back to his feet, he surprised Reyes by snapping to Madison, "Stay out of it."

"I don't take orders from you," she informed him without heat, and stepped into Reyes's path.

Frustrated, Reyes looked to Cade. "A little help?"

Cade cocked a brow. "You want her pissed at me, too?"

Curses burned the back of his throat. "I won't kill him," he promised Madison.

"He's being helpful, you idiot. Why don't you just cool down and listen?"

"Because he dared to come to *my* house." Reyes advanced on his sister. "And *you* dared to let him in."

Suddenly, somehow, Crosby was in front of Madison. It so astonished Reyes that he came to an abrupt halt. "What the fuck?" He looked past Crosby to Madison, then almost laughed at her expression of chagrin. Grinning at the interloper, Reyes asked, "You're trying to protect my sister?" If Crosby admitted it, Madison would probably flatten him herself. "From *me*?"

"I'm the one you're pissed at," Crosby stated. "Focus on me. Not her."

Cade snorted a laugh.

Kennedy stood there wide-eyed.

"How sweet," Madison said, immediately hooking her arm

through Crosby's and more or less stealing his attention. "Since I know your intent is in the right place, I won't take offense." She grinned triumphantly at Reyes. "There, you see? He's an honorable cop, which is something I already knew, and which I wanted to explain to you, but you wouldn't listen."

Reyes eyed them all—then held out a hand to Kennedy.

Carrying his gun gingerly, proof that she wasn't all that comfortable with firearms, she immediately hurried to his side. Voice low, she urged again, "Let it go, please. We need to talk."

Nodding, he took the gun and slid it into his back holster, then said to the others, "Go home." Holding Kennedy's hand, he turned and walked into the house. She kept trying to look back, but he didn't let her.

Cade, intuitive brother that he was, got to the door before Reyes could secure it. "Not on your life," he said, pushing his way over the threshold. Giving Madison a look, Cade said, "Inside. Now."

For Cade, she did as she was told.

Unfortunately, she brought Crosby with her.

Kennedy kept both of her arms locked around one of his—like she thought she could restrain him?—and said, "If you'll all excuse us a moment?" She began hauling him toward the guest room.

Over his shoulder, Reyes glared at Cade. "Stay put."

"I'm not about to budge," he promised. And, in fact, he stationed himself between Crosby and Madison.

"Damn, he's smooth," Reyes complained right before he closed the door behind him.

Kennedy immediately began explaining. "The detective brought a photo with him. Reyes, I think it's the man who had Jodi."

Wow. Not at all what he'd been expecting. Quickly reevaluating the situation, he asked, "What makes you think so?"

"Back when I first met her, Jodi described Rob Golly to me. He's one of those balding men with a ponytail. Missing teeth. A weak chin. The photo matched all that."

Sadly, that description matched a lot of dudes. "That doesn't mean—"

She shook her head. "His name is unique enough to stick, right? And then there's Crosby's description of the house where Jodi was taken." She turned away, her arms hugged around her middle. "He

said he's been tracking Golly for a while. The things he shared..."
She shuddered. "Horrible, horrible monster. Jodi's held it together
only because she believed she'd killed him. If he somehow survived, if he's still alive, it'll destroy her."

"Or," Reyes said, his thoughts scrambling ahead, "she already
knows he didn't die, and that's why she's worried for you. Whoever knows her might be exposed to his vengeance. Worse, anyone she cares about could be used against her."

Kennedy blinked at him. "I'm not worried about me."

He gave her a level look. "No reason you should be since I won't
let anyone hurt you." He'd kill Golly and all his cronies before he'd
let them lay a finger on Kennedy.

She started pacing. "I need to copy that photo so I can ask Jodi
if it's him."

"Done. I'll take care of it."

Staring at him, her jaw loosened. "It can't be that easy. I got the
feeling that Crosby suspects your whole family. He even made a
veiled accusation about your father."

Ice skated down Reyes's spine. His voice lowered to a rough
growl. "What did he say?"

"Just something vague really, but it was how he said it."

"Tell me."

She licked her lips, thinking. "Madison was trying to engage
him in small talk. I think she was flirting."

"Doesn't sound like my sister." What the hell could Madison
be up to? "She pays no attention to men."

"Well, she's been paying a lot of interested attention to Crosby."

Probably Madison's way of softening the guy up, taking him
off guard, getting him to say too much. "How did that lead to my
father?"

"Madison wanted him to tell her more about himself, about the
task force or something like that. He said he wasn't on a task force,
that his interest in Golly was personal. Instead of going into it, he
wanted to hear more about her, you and Cade and your father, too.
Something about your father being the head of it all."

Son of a bitch. "I should have killed him," he snarled. Still
might.

Exasperated, Kennedy demanded, "Do you, or do you not, trust your sister?"

"Do." *But she'd been flirting?*

"And you don't indiscriminately kill men for asking questions, especially police officers."

No, but he could start. When she glared at him, he confirmed, "No, I don't."

"Madison isn't worried about him. When she saw him on the security cam, she recognized him. She opened the door and let him in without a qualm. I just... I don't know him, and I didn't think you'd want him here." She shrugged helplessly. "So I texted you."

"Hey." Reyes drew her against his chest. God, it felt good to hold her. On the drive back, he'd been running on a potent combo of instinct and adrenaline, anger and worry, unable to consider the possibilities of an intruder. "You did the right thing, babe. Anytime something feels off, even a little, I want you to let me know."

She dropped her forehead against him. "I've been here nearly a month, Reyes. This can't go on indefinitely."

His first impulse was to ask, *Why not?* He bit back that automatic response real fast. Why not? There were a million reasons, number one being that he didn't want a significant other. He liked his life of kicking ass when necessary, indulging in sex without emotional constraints, and fulfilling his father's edicts efficiently while never allowing the grisly details of the enterprise to overtake him.

"Shush." Holding Kennedy's shoulders, he stepped back and bent his knees to look into her pretty blue eyes. "You can't talk about leaving when we finally have something to go on. First thing we'll do is reach out to Jodi. I'll get that image from the cop, then we'll meet with her somewhere safe where I can control things."

"Jodi will never agree to meet with you."

"So we'll keep that part from her. Cade can be backup." Madison would, of course, provide necessary surveillance and digital security. "It'll be safe." Come hell or high water, he wouldn't let her be hurt. *Not ever again.*

Undecided, Kennedy visibly shored up her courage. "All right. But first you need that image. I won't upset Jodi without something concrete to show her."

Reyes cupped a hand to her cheek. "I don't want you to worry."

"Even you, Reyes McKenzie, don't get everything you want."

He grinned at her retreating back as she left the room. No, he wouldn't get everything. Pretty sure he might get Kennedy, though, at least long enough for them both to have a really good time.

Today, right now, that felt like enough.

DEL DIDN'T LIKE hiring others to do the dirty work, not when it was usually his favorite part. Imagining Kennedy's expression when he got his hands on her... It was all he'd had to think about lately, so yeah, he'd like to be there, up-front and real fucking personal.

Instead, he was stuck waiting with Mr. Butt-ugly, who kept grinning without saying anything.

Fucker got weirder by the day.

"Look, there's no reason to keep paying punks to handle things I could handle myself."

"Is that so?" Golly asked, still rocking, still smiling. "You're familiar with murder?"

"I don't want to *murder* Kennedy." Not right off, not after all this trouble. For a day or two he wanted her alive and kicking— then he'd gladly snuff her.

"You think *he'd* just let you take her?" Shaking his head, Golly said, "Don't be stupid. That one won't die easily. It'll take having more than one shooter on him, and even if they fail, I have two others in a truck, ready to ambush them on the road."

"Jesus, how many people are we paying?"

"Enough to get the job done."

Del *really* didn't like him. Worse, he sort of feared him—and that feeling grew more unsettling every day that he was stuck in Golly's company, witnessing his unhinged behavior.

There was no way of knowing when the prick might snap and kill everyone in sight.

The rocking abruptly stopped. "If it wasn't for me, you wouldn't even be close to getting your hands on that woman. *I'm* the one who knew to follow Jodi. I'm the one who discovered she was friends with Kennedy. The only reason you're involved at all is because

I want Jodi to see what happened to her so-called friend. I want her to know what you're going to do to that bitch."

For about the hundredth time, Del regretted ever meeting the whack job, and he really wished he hadn't agreed to partner up with him.

It was pure happenstance that they'd discovered their connection. Del had lingered late one night at a truck stop to shop the wares. He'd picked out a sweet little honey who'd looked strung out and willing to chance a ride with any stranger. Yet once he'd gotten her in the car, Golly had come out of nowhere and joined them.

The plan, he knew, had been to kill him, then rob him.

Instead, Del had done some fast talking, explaining that he didn't give a shit what happened with the chick. He had run his own business once, so he got it.

One thing had led to another, they'd ended up sharing a meal while bragging on their ruthlessness... At the time, Golly had managed to act sane enough. A dupe, for sure.

Now here he was, becoming more embroiled by the day with a certifiable maniac. There was no guarantee that Jodi would meet up with Kennedy tonight, but so far, following her was their only chance.

Kennedy, the conniving bitch, had all but disappeared off the face of the earth. Once her apartment had burned to the ground: poof. No more Kennedy.

"Why do you want Jodi so bad?" Del asked, watching the man through a veil of smoke while he sucked on his cigarette. "She ain't much to look at. You could grab another broad easy enough."

He rocked faster. "She took from me. Stole things she can never give back. For that, she'll pay."

Shit. He was back to sounding off the rails. Del moved away to look out the window, hoping that tonight would be the night.

"I'm going to make her pay," Golly promised from behind him. The rocking chair began to squeak. He was so agitated, he even laughed. "She'll pay, and pay, and pay until I'm satisfied she's paid enough. It's as easy as that."

Misgivings growing, Del asked, "What the hell did she take that was so important?"

And once Golly explained, yeah, he understood.

Now he almost felt sorry for the scrawny girl—but he still felt sorrier for himself. Del needed away from Golly and soon, before he too became a target.

KENNEDY SAT STIFFLY beside Reyes as he pulled into the remote area at eight o'clock. The rough ground was bumpy and his truck headlights sent deep shadows stretching from tall fir trees and pinyon junipers.

It felt eerie and dangerous. And, damn it, Reyes was too silent. She wasn't ready.

From the moment he'd started making his plans, everything had moved at lightning speed.

He'd talked a bit with Crosby, enough to get his measure, or so Reyes had said. Madison and Cade had taken part.

Never in her life had she felt more like an outsider. It was obvious that the siblings worked as a team, that they had an uncommon knowledge of things that went beyond even what Crosby had learned as a detective.

She'd tried to ask Reyes about it, but he'd gotten all hush-hush, doling out only a select few details that didn't really answer any of her questions.

Now here she was, ready to meet with Jodi if her friend showed.

Like Kennedy, Jodi had been uncertain of the whole thing.

With Reyes listening in, she'd called Jodi. Twice. No answer either time. It wasn't until the middle of last night that Jodi had finally called back, waking her from a sound sleep.

She'd been groggy and confused, but not Reyes. He'd pressed her away from his body, where she'd been snugly held, and quickly prepped her on what to say and not say.

He'd stayed silent beside her while she answered the call, but having him there had made it easier.

She'd told Jodi that she had to see her, and to her surprise, Jodi hadn't argued.

Instead, as if she'd been expecting the request, Jodi had arranged for the meeting at this remote location in the mountains. At one time it had been camping grounds, but the owner hadn't maintained the property, so other than a rut-filled road leading to what had once been a clearing, there was nothing around.

And the sun had set some time ago.

"Take a breath, babe. Everything is fine. Cade came in on foot and he's the best backup around. We have eyes on the truck so Madison can not only track us, she can see anyone else who might get near us. Remember, I won't let anything happen to you."

See, all *that*? Who the hell talked about eyes on a truck, meaning some high-tech surveillance stuff, and solid backup, meaning his brother was armed and ready to shoot if necessary?

Clenching her hands together, Kennedy asked, "Who are you people?"

"Shh. I'm gonna kill the lights now, okay? Then we'll go the rest of the way on foot."

And when they got near to the center of the clearing, Reyes would hang back.

She'd be alone, exposed.

No. He said he'd protect her and she believed him. God, she wished she was stronger, as clever as Madison or as fearless as Sterling. But she wasn't. She was just Kennedy Brooks, traumatized girl unable to move out of the past, trying to be a confident woman and failing far too often.

Reyes stopped the truck in a copse of tall trees. Everything went dark.

"Hey." He pried one of her hands loose, carrying it over to his mouth, where he pressed a warm kiss to her knuckles. "You've got this, babe. And I've got you. I swear, I won't let anything happen to you."

She nodded, knew he couldn't see her in the dark, and whispered, "I know. I'm just..." So cold and empty. "I'm fine."

"Yeah, you are. Extra fine." This time, he leaned in and his mouth brushed over her cheek, her jaw, down to the corner of her lips.

Holy smokes. That chased away the ice in her veins. "What are you doing?"

"Warming you up. Did it work?"

"Actually...yes." She exhaled a long breath. Funny, she did feel steadier. Who knew a kiss could accomplish that much? "Thank you."

"You and your gratitude." He flashed her a grin that did more to reassure her than all the words in the world. "Stay put until I come around. You have your flashlight?"

"Yes." She lifted the heavy utility light off the floor of the truck.

"Warm enough?"

No, but that had more to do with her nerves than the October temperatures in the mountains. She'd dressed appropriately, even had a stocking hat for her ears. "I'm—" She started to say *fine* again, but after his silly flattery with the word, she adjusted to, "Ready."

Without another word, Reyes got out and somehow, without making a single sound, came to her side of the truck and opened the door.

Wow, the man was a wraith. More and more, she wanted to know the backstory of what he and his family did.

Accepting his hand, she climbed from the truck. She, of course, made far too much noise as her hiking boots crunched over fallen leaves, twigs and rocks. Without the flashlight, she couldn't see, but apparently Reyes had no problem. He led, she followed, and with every step she tried to calm her rioting pulse.

They walked for maybe five minutes before he pulled her to a halt. Keeping his mouth close to her ear, he breathed, "I'm waiting right here behind this outcrop of rock. Go about ten steps and then turn on the flashlight. You'll see the fallen tree. That's where Jodi wants you to wait."

She remembered. Jodi had been adamant that she come alone. Reyes had flatly refused, promising to wait at the base of the road.

Obviously, a lie.

Supposedly, Cade was already in place, and Madison felt confident that Jodi would approach from a different direction. Reyes had agreed with her assessment.

It all seemed far too clandestine for her peace of mind.

Cautiously stepping away from Reyes, Kennedy counted her steps, tripped once, felt a juniper branch scratch her cheek and finally was able to turn on the flashlight.

She spotted the fallen tree right off. She also heard night sounds she hadn't noticed while standing so close to Reyes. Wind, animals, insects. The urge to look back, to prove he was still there, tested her resolve, but he'd schooled her on what not to do, and that was a biggie. He didn't want her giving him away.

What if a bear showed up? Or even a big spider?

The snap of twigs lodged her heart in her throat, and then Jodi stepped out from behind a tree.

Her friend kept her distance, her mistrust palpable. "Where's your boyfriend?"

The caustic question unfroze something inside Kennedy. This was Jodi, and that tone of voice was so familiar that it worked wonders for relieving her fears. "He's nearby if I need him," she admitted, and she could almost hear Reyes groaning his disappointment that she hadn't stuck to the plan. "Jodi, how are you?" Despite her worries, a genuine smile slipped up on her. "It's good to see you."

Lifting her chin, Jodi asked, "Do you mean that?"

"Yes, I do." Taking a few more steps, Kennedy bounced the flashlight around the area. "This is a weird place for a meeting. It feels creepy."

"To me, it feels safe."

"Safe from what?"

"Anyone. Everyone."

The reminder of Jodi's fear broke Kennedy's heart. Whereas she had, overall, moved on with her life, Jodi hadn't—and probably never would.

"Have you lost weight?" Jodi was a short woman, always on the thin side, yet with enough attitude for an Amazon. Tonight she looked positively frail. Even bundled up beneath a sweatshirt, Kennedy could see that she was at least ten pounds lighter. Her black leggings hung loose around her knees and bunched above her boots. The sweatshirt slouched off shoulders that were far too narrow.

Chin notching up even more, Jodi shook back her messy brown hair and sneered, "Someone's been following me, so yeah, I've skipped a few meals."

Oh, God. "Why didn't you tell me?" Taking two more steps toward her, Kennedy reached out. "You know I would help you however I can."

"Yeah? Glad to hear it." Jodi came closer.

Kennedy expected an embrace even though Jodi wasn't usually the hugging type.

Instead, Jodi took her by surprise by snaking an arm around her neck, snatching her back against a tree. Her shoulder thumped against the trunk and the flashlight nearly fell from her hand.

It took a second for the gesture to register, for Kennedy to realize that Jodi had her in a bruising choke hold. "What are you doing?" Not only was Jodi's arm clamped so tight under her chin that Kennedy could barely draw breath, but now Jodi had a gun in her hand, and she aimed it in the direction of where Reyes waited.

"I know you're out there," Jodi said, her voice hard and filled with anger. "Come out."

Kennedy frantically tried to twist away, which only prompted Jodi to tighten her hold. Obviously, this was a familiar move to her friend, and she had it fairly well perfected.

Kennedy was a few inches taller than Jodi, and probably had twenty pounds on her, yet she couldn't get free. Not without trying to hurt Jodi, and she didn't want to do that. Not yet anyway...

This was ridiculous! She thought about tossing the flashlight so she'd have both hands to work with, but that might make it difficult for Reyes to see her.

Reyes stepped out with his own gun at the ready. "Loosen up," he ordered. "You're hurting her."

Ignoring that, Jodi asked, "Why are you here?"

Unconcerned with his own safety, Reyes strode closer. "Try to hurt her," he warned, "and I'll put a bullet through your brain."

"I don't want to hurt *her*," Jodi shouted, sounding genuinely appalled by the accusation.

"Terrific. Then we should be able to get along because I don't want to hurt you."

"Says the big man with a weapon," she sneered.

"To protect Kennedy," he promised evenly. "And Jodi, if necessary, I'd protect you, too."

"Liar," she screamed.

"You don't have to take my word for it." Reyes stopped, his gaze unflinching. "Do you think Kennedy would lie to you?"

Her arm tightened in reaction. "Now that you've corrupted her, who knows?"

"Jodi." Little stars started to dance before Kennedy's eyes. "Can't...breathe."

"Oh, God." Immediately, Jodi released her, then had to help support her as she started to slump.

The flashlight fell from her hand with a thud. In the next second, Reyes was there, first taking Jodi's gun from her and then putting his strong arm around Kennedy's waist. "I've got you, babe. It's okay."

"Reyes." Finally able to gulp in enough air, she wheezed, "She's my friend."

"I know. Here, sit down." He lowered her to the fallen log and crouched in front of her. "Okay now?"

Her throat ached, but otherwise she felt okay. Her gaze sought out Jodi. The beam of the fallen flashlight skimmed over the ground, stopping at the toes of Jodi's boots and barely illuminating her face. One hand pressed to her mouth, the other to her middle. She looked devastated. Wounded, guilty, horrified...

"I'm okay, Jodi." Seeing the terror in her friend's eyes, Kennedy pleaded, "Please don't run. I really do need to talk to you."

Jodi was undecided, her muscles shifting, her eyes darting around.

Reyes looked up and beyond her, and then gave a soft curse. Almost at the same time, his phone buzzed.

"Stay low," he said to Kennedy, pulled out his phone to glance at the screen, then palmed his gun again. "Jodi, listen to me. We've got company."

"No." Frantically, she searched the area.

"My brother spotted three people coming up from the same direction you used."

"Brother?" she snarled, and then in the next breath, "I wasn't followed! I couldn't have been."

Keeping his voice calm and even, he said, "We need to get to my truck. Now."

A shot sounded, then sounded again and again in a terrible echo that split the quiet of the night. Immediately, footfalls thumped over the ground, shaking bushes and disturbing brambles.

"Assuming you can shoot, you need your gun," Reyes said. "Now get your ass over here, but stay low."

Oddly enough, Jodi did just that.

She stationed herself in front of Kennedy.

Well, that was embarrassing. "What should I do?" Kennedy asked. She desperately needed to feel useful.

Without answering, Reyes pressed them both down and used his own body as a shield. Silence descended, and somehow that was almost worse. There were two more shots, each coming from a different direction.

"They've fanned out," Reyes murmured, but he didn't look or sound worried.

Bully for him. She was worried enough for everyone. For Cade. For Jodi.

And especially for Reyes.

When his phone buzzed again, he withdrew it, used his thumb to unlock the screen and handed it to Kennedy.

Surprised, she quickly read the message aloud. "Retreating. Go now."

Just like that, he surged to his feet, swiped up the flashlight and said, "Hustle, babe, while we have the chance." He urged Kennedy forward with a hand around her upper arm.

"Jodi," she said, resisting just enough to grab for her friend.

Jodi ducked away. "My car—"

"For the love of sanity..." Reyes released Kennedy to snatch hold of Jodi's sweatshirt and then propelled them both along. "There's something you have to see, Jodi, so stop fighting. I'm not a threat to you."

Kennedy quickly took Jodi's other arm. "I swear it's true."

Subsiding, Jodi picked up the pace. "That was your brother who texted?"

"Yeah. He'll follow us out of here." Reyes drew the flashlight over and around his four-door Ram truck, likely ensuring no one was near it, and then he killed the light.

"Where's your brother's car?"

"Where no one will see it." He opened the rear door of the cab and hoisted Kennedy up into the narrow back seat with more haste than care, dropping the flashlight into her lap. "Figured you two would want to sit close so you can share that image on your phone."

"What image?" Jodi hauled herself in and scooted closer to Kennedy, which put her away from Reyes.

"No lights yet, okay?" Competence personified, Reyes got behind the wheel and started the truck in what felt like a single motion. The doors locked. "I'll tell you when."

"Okay, Reyes." Yes, Kennedy was rattled, but he was so calm and efficient about the whole process, she wasn't nearly as scared as she'd thought she'd be.

"I'm proud of you," he said suddenly. Leaving off the headlights, he turned a wide circle and easily made his way back to the uneven road.

"Me?" Kennedy asked. "Whatever for?"

"You kept it together," he said, while being vigilant to their surroundings. "You kept your priorities straight. You even understood your friend when I didn't. If it hadn't been for that, I might have..." The truck bumped along. "I didn't like seeing her restrain you."

Both women were silent, until Jodi whispered, "I'm sorry about that. I didn't mean to hurt her. I just... It was a reaction. To a threat, I mean."

"She knew that, I guess." Reyes blew out a breath. "I didn't."

"You don't trust me?" Jodi guessed.

"'Bout as much as you trust me, I'd say. Difference is that I trust Kennedy, and if she says you're okay, I believe her."

Knowing how confusing this had to be for Jodi, Kennedy patted her forearm. "Where are we going, Reyes?" To Jodi, information was power. She'd feel better with more details.

"Convenience mart or something. A place where there's plenty of light. Then you and Jodi can...talk."

"Without you giving me the evil eye?" Jodi asked.

"You'll get the eye," he said, "and everything that comes with it, because no matter who you are, no matter how much she trusts you, you've got trouble on your tail and I'm not letting it anywhere near Kennedy."

Jodi gave her the most comically bemused expression. "Who the hell *is* he?"

A good question. There were many layers to Reyes McKenzie, and Kennedy wanted to uncover each one. "He's a good man," she said simply, because that much she knew one hundred percent.

Jodi snorted. "Yeah, like Bigfoot and unicorns, huh?" She crossed her arms and slumped into the corner of the cab. "I think I'll wait and judge for myself."

Reyes left the dirt road and flipped on his headlights right before he turned onto pavement and accelerated, leaving the spooky campgrounds and danger behind.

Or so Kennedy thought.

CHAPTER TEN

KENNEDY WAS ABOUT to ask Reyes if she could now use the light from her phone when he gave a low curse.

Glancing in the rearview mirror, he asked, "You two buckled up?"

Kennedy watched Jodi quickly hook her seat belt, then she answered, "Yes. Why?"

"Hang on." He swerved sharply to the right.

Kennedy knocked into Jodi, with only the seat belt keeping her upright. The blinding glare of high beam headlights flashed into the back window of the truck, causing her heart to jump into her throat.

Reyes jerked the truck into the left lane and hit the brakes. Another truck went barreling past them and then immediately screeched into the middle of the road, stopping sideways.

He punched the gas and shot past them again, going half off the road and narrowly missing the front fender.

Kennedy felt like her teeth had been jarred loose. Knowing Reyes had his hands full, she kept as silent as possible so she wouldn't distract him, her body tense from her toes to her eyebrows.

"Are...are they after me?" Jodi asked.

"Or me," Reyes said. "Maybe Kennedy. Who the fuck knows? No worries, though, I've got this."

Again Jodi gave her an incredulous look, one that asked, *Is he insane?*

Kennedy shrugged.

Reyes drove faster and faster, but on this stretch of road, there was no other traffic, no exits—and no one to help.

"There's Cade," he said.

She looked back and realized another vehicle was now behind them.

"Do me a favor, babe? Duck down."

Confused, Kennedy asked, "Duck...?"

"Down," he barked.

When Jodi bent forward in the seat, Kennedy copied her.

A second later, gunshots rang out, followed by the screaming of tires and finally an awful crash.

Reyes pulled to the side of the road. Before Kennedy could get her wits about her, he said, "Lock up behind me," and then he...

He left the truck!

"Reyes!" Scrambling for the door, Kennedy opened it enough to shout, "What in the world are you doing?"

"Taking care of business." He pushed the door shut again. "Lock it."

With his eyes ablaze and his expression hard, Kennedy obediently hit the lock.

He gave one firm nod and turned away.

Good heavens. She'd never seen him like that. Peeking over the back seat, she watched him, utterly fascinated and scared to death for him.

In a long, purposeful stride, he approached their pursuers, staying just outside the direct beam of the other truck. It was twisted, the front end smashed against the rise of the mountain. Kennedy didn't see any movement.

Unhooking her seat belt, Jodi twisted about on her knees and watched, too. "Is that his brother coming up the other side?"

Until Jodi said it, Kennedy hadn't noticed Cade—strange, since he was so incredibly large. "Yes."

"They're unusual."

An understatement.

Jodi nudged her. "I think they can be just as dangerous as the goons who were chasing us."

"Most definitely." So far, Reyes was the most lethal person she'd ever known, and, given her background, that was saying something.

Together they saw Reyes and Cade look into the truck, then around it. Reyes pried open the damaged front door and leaned inside. The headlights went out and the grinding from the engine died.

When Reyes straightened again, he and Cade shared a short conversation. Apparently the danger was over?

Not that she'd believe it—until Reyes told her so.

"You wanted to show me something?" Jodi glanced around, wary as always, squinting into shadows and searching the long, empty stretch of road. "That's why we're here, right?"

Shoot. After all that, Kennedy almost didn't want to. "It's going to upset you, but I want you to know, I'm here with you every step of the way."

Stoic, Jodi straightened her shoulders. "What will the big guy have to say about that?"

Being honest, she said, "There's a lot I don't know about Reyes."

"Yeah, well, I thought I knew him, but clearly I only skimmed the tip of the iceberg."

Her cocky attitude didn't fool Kennedy. Jodi was afraid, the type of bone-deep fear felt by a woman who'd once been in hell. It'd be better for her if Kennedy cut to the chase instead of letting her dread build.

Pulling her cell phone from her pocket, Kennedy adjusted the settings. Earlier, she'd silenced it and turned down the brightness, and now she adjusted it back. "A detective came to see us. He's been hunting someone, and he thought Reyes might know something about him. Unfortunately, he didn't—but I think I may have recognized him."

"Him?" Expression changing, Jodi demanded, "Is it the man who had you? The one who got away?"

"No." Somehow, she thought that man was small-time when compared to Rob Golly.

And yet, both men were almost insignificant when compared to

Reyes. They were pure evil, but Reyes was bigger, braver, smarter, stronger. Also kinder, more caring, funnier.

He was all things good, which made him a perfect counterbalance to their cruelty.

She pulled up the photo on her phone. Thanks to Madison, it was a clearer, neater image than the one Crosby had carried. Glancing back at Reyes again, Kennedy saw that he stared toward her, keeping her in sight, ever vigilant, while speaking on his phone. Maybe talking to his sister? That'd make sense, given that Madison would be able to tell them a lot about this stretch of road.

Unable to put it off any longer, she took Jodi's hand in her own, locking their fingers together, and then turned the phone so she could see it.

A low sound, like that a wounded animal would make, slipped past Jodi's parted lips.

Heart breaking, Kennedy knew she had her answer.

"He's *dead*," Jodi rasped.

Maybe. "Shh. Let me explain, okay?" Jodi continued to stare at the photo. "The detective said he went to the house—I think the one where Golly kept you."

Jodi shook her head. "His body—"

"There was no body."

"I *killed* him," she growled, the words barely audible.

"Honey…are you sure?"

"Yes!" She tried to snap her hand away, but Kennedy held on.

If she released Jodi, her friend would probably leap from the truck and disappear. It's what Jodi did. She ran when threatened, and only reappeared when she thought Kennedy might need her.

Using that to her advantage, Kennedy whispered, "I need you here, Jodi. Whatever is going on, we can sort it out together."

"You don't need me!" She hitched her chin toward the window. "You have *them*, now."

Startled, Kennedy glanced back and found Cade and Reyes watching them, equal expressions of concern on their faces.

Ignoring them for the moment, Kennedy scooted closer to Jodi and lowered her voice. "They're men and they haven't been through what we have. We back each other up, remember? You're stronger than me, Jodi. I can help sort this out, but I need to be able to reach you when necessary. I need to know you're safe."

Settling her shoulders back against the seat, Jodi whispered, "You're strong, too, otherwise you wouldn't be crushing my fingers."

"Oh, my God, I'm sorry." Quickly she freed Jodi, and, as she'd assumed, Jodi was out of the truck in a heartbeat.

Kennedy heard Cade say, "Don't make me chase you. It's getting damned cold out here and cops could show up any minute."

"Or more thugs," Reyes added.

Kennedy slid across the seat to get out on Jodi's side. By God, if Jodi took off, she'd chase her down herself.

Trying to be as casual as everyone else, Kennedy got close to Jodi, then asked over the truck bed, "The driver of the truck?"

"Dead," Reyes said, already walking around to her. "We've made a plan."

"My plan," Jodi said, "is to get my car and get out of here."

Cade casually approached around the other side, but Kennedy wasn't fooled. There was a coiled readiness about both brothers, and she didn't think it was on her behalf. Shoot, they both knew she wasn't about to charge away from safety.

But Jodi? Yep, Jodi looked ready to take on the world. Alone.

"I know where your car is," Cade said. "The plan is for me to take you to it—"

"No."

As if Jodi hadn't interrupted, Cade continued with, "—so I can make sure no one else is lurking around. Then I'll follow you to a main highway. At that point, you can do as you please."

"But Jodi?" Reyes gave her a long look. "You need some backup. If Golly is out there, he might be the one who set the fire to Kennedy's apartment building."

"To get to me," she rasped, her hands clenched into fists at her sides, her expression grim.

"It's possible. I can't go into everything now. We're not safe standing here, so how about you keep us informed of where you'll be at all times?"

"I don't know." She pushed her hair from her face. "I'll think about it."

"Think while I drive you back to your car," Cade suggested.

Kennedy was impressed that Cade sounded so reasonable, so nonthreatening when anyone could see he was a walking weapon.

Just like Reyes.

When Jodi looked at her with indecision, Kennedy stepped forward. "Please? I won't be able to bear it if anything happens to you. You're like family."

"Family," Jodi repeated, as if weighing the word.

"Sisters," Kennedy stressed.

Jodi's mouth quirked. "I'd be the black sheep of the family, you know. The weirdo that everyone dreaded seeing."

"Not true." Kennedy moved closer, saying again, "Please, Jodi."

It took her far too long before Jodi found a flippant way to give in. "Yeah, sure. Why not? These two can't be more dangerous than Golly, or whoever is pretending to be him."

Oh, Kennedy hadn't even considered that. Someone pretending to be Golly? Was it possible?

"We need to roll." Reyes took her hand and tugged her to the front seat.

"Come on," Cade said to Jodi, gesturing toward his SUV. "Time to end this miserable night. The problems will still be there in the morning."

Kennedy looked over her shoulder.

Jodi walked backward to keep her in sight.

Near her ear, Reyes said, "She'll be okay, honey. I promise."

Wondering how he could guarantee such a thing, Kennedy nodded. "We'll talk in the morning," she called to Jodi.

"Sure thing." And with that, Jodi turned and fell into step beside Cade.

MISERABLE, INCOMPETENT FUCKS. Del glared as Golly disconnected his call and carefully set the phone on the table.

"What do you mean, they were both there but got away?"

At first, laughter was the only answer.

At the end of his rope, Del snapped, "Answer me, damn it!"

"He's better than we thought."

We? So far, Del hadn't been allowed much input at all. "Yeah? How's that?"

"We thought we had a setup, but it was the other way around. Somehow, that bodyguard of hers anticipated us being there."

"I wasn't anywhere except in this stupid dump!"

"It's a lovely cabin, not a dump, and you complain too much."

Del would have killed another man for that offhand insult, but this man? No, the way he watched Del made his skin crawl. "So what happened?"

"Shots were fired. My men were pinned down. The drivers I set to ambush them should have had it in hand, but that didn't work out, either, apparently."

Taking a chance, Del suggested, "So maybe I should plan the next—"

"No!" Slamming his hands down on the table, Golly rose to his feet and stared hard at Del, his protruding gut nearly busting the seams of his shirt. "She won't get away again."

"Jodi? Yeah, that's fine for you. But I need to stop Kennedy before she gets the cops on my ass again."

"I'll get them both," he promised, relaxing again, his twisted smile back in place. "Kennedy will be my gift to you."

Fuck that. Del didn't want to owe this man anything. It was past time he started making his own plans—separate from the lunatic. "Yeah, sure." Del decided it'd be easiest to just placate him. "Sounds good. Thanks." First chance he got, probably early tomorrow morning, he'd take off on his own. Once he did, he'd never again make a bargain with the devil—especially a devil who was bat-shit crazy.

ONCE THEY WERE ALONE, Reyes made haste getting them away from the area. He constantly checked the rearview mirror, regardless of how far they drove. Used to be, that would have made her nervous. Now she understood that it was just his way of using extra caution.

They were almost to his house when his cell rang. Driving one-handed, he held the phone to his ear and said, "All done? Great. Yeah, we'll be home in five. Tell Madison thanks for me, too." For a few seconds Reyes listened, then glanced at her and shrugged. "Sure, we can do that. All right, I'll see you both then."

"What?" she immediately asked.

"Cade tailed Jodi home. Jodi doesn't know that, though, so don't tell her. She thought he dropped back once they got to a more congested area."

"But he didn't?"

"No, he didn't. He circled back and followed her to a dive motel on the outskirts of town, to make sure no one else bothered her. We're nothing if not thorough. The motel, by the way, is near an I-70 on-ramp, not more than thirty minutes from Cade's bar, The Tipsy Wolverine."

Kennedy blinked at the name. *The Tipsy Wolverine?* "You're making that up."

"Nope." For only the briefest moment, he hesitated, then seemed to give a mental shrug. "I have a gym, Cade has a bar, we hear shit at both—that's part of how we operate."

A nugget of info? Desperately needing a new focus, Kennedy jumped on that. "Operate?"

"Patience, doll. For now, I need to tell you something else, but I need your word you won't say anything to Jodi."

If she didn't trust Reyes so much, his serious tone might really bother her. "All right."

"Cade tagged Jodi's car before he came after us. We'll have GPS on her wherever she goes. Usually that's something I'd keep to myself, but I'm telling you so you won't worry too much. She might get spooked and run, but we'll be able to find her."

Her heart, her emotions, softened. "To make sure she's safe?"

"Yeah."

Could he be more wonderful? "Thank you."

"You're not pissed?"

How could he think that? "I'm incredibly grateful that you're helping her."

"Whether she wants my help or not?"

Yes, Jodi had given that impression. And on the surface, she might even believe that she'd rather go it alone. But deep down?

Deep down, she desperately needed help. For a multitude of reasons, Kennedy was fairly certain that Reyes would understand. "She's so wounded," Kennedy explained. "So suspicious of everyone, I'm not sure she'd ever ask for help no matter how badly she needed it. It'd take a lot to earn her trust."

"You managed it."

"Only because we share a similar background."

He seemed pained by that reminder. "We're going to rendezvous with Cade and Madison at my dad's place tomorrow."

"Your dad?" she choked.

"Don't let him scare you, okay? No matter how much he scowls."

"Why would he scowl at me?" Even the possibility made her irate. She'd been through hell lately. She wouldn't let anyone, not even Reyes's father, treat her badly.

"Dad's just gruff, that's all. But hey, you'll finally get to see Chimera again, and you'll get to meet Bernard. I think you'll like him, mostly because he worships that cat."

"So I'll like Bernard but not your father?"

"Bernard, when he's not stealing cats, is a pretty likable guy."

Her mouth twitched. "He stole our cat?"

Reyes rolled his eyes. "That was humor. Sort of. None of us knew Bernard liked animals until I brought Chimera home and he went bonkers over her. When you meet him, you'll know how funny this is, but he was doing the whole baby-talk thing to her. Crazy. And those kittens? It was love at first sight. He did more or less steal the cat, but it made him so happy, I didn't really mind. I just act like I do to give Bernard a hard time, you know?"

No, she didn't know. It seemed that irritating people, especially family, was one of Reyes's favorite pastimes.

The whole idea of meeting his father and Bernard concerned her. It wouldn't be for the typical reasons a guy brought a woman home to meet the rest of his family. Not in her situation. It was more likely a safety issue, since that was his number one reason for keeping her around.

Alarming for sure. She'd already accepted that her life was on the line, but for them all to be involved... Maybe it was even worse than she'd thought.

To give herself some time, Kennedy turned to stare out the window, barely noticing the passing scenery, until Reyes pulled into the garage. It had been such an eventful day. Her stomach was still uneasy and every nerve seemed to be twitching.

Her world was again a scary place, but she wasn't facing it alone. And neither was Jodi.

That gave her more comfort than she could explain, and it was all because of Reyes.

Such a remarkable man he was.

Continually glancing at her, he turned off the truck and came around to her side, gently assisting her out of the truck as if he thought she might fall apart at any minute.

She *was* a little emotional, mostly with gratitude.

Everything he'd done for her made her want to hold him tight—so he'd hold her tight in return. While he and Cade, and even Jodi, had handled the threats fearlessly, she'd been a jittery mess.

They stepped into the house together, and, God, it felt good to be home. Maybe not her home, not long-term, but for now it felt more like home than anything had since her kidnapping.

"Jodi's right, you know." Reyes led her to the living room. "You're stronger than you think."

She gave a small laugh. "I was so nervous, I nearly crushed her fingers."

"That's not what I'm talking about." He tipped up her chin. "That shit tonight could have rattled anyone. Another woman might have been hysterical. But you, babe, you followed instructions without arguing, you didn't cry or fall apart and, not only that, you helped take care of Jodi." He threaded his fingers into her hair. "She thinks she's a badass, but that girl is shook. Being on her own would be a terrible thing, and you, with your big heart and logic, reached her when I'm not sure anyone else could have."

"Reyes." Giving in to her need, she put her arms tightly around him and borrowed some of his strength. Being this near to him, feeling his heat and breathing his scent, went a long way toward leveling her nerves, yet she continued to tremble.

Reyes didn't judge her, though. Nope, he saw the best in her. And damn it, she was starting to fall in love with him because of it.

"You're amazing," she whispered, and then confessed, "I don't know what I'd do without you right now."

REYES HAD NEVER had a woman cling to him like that, not without the addition of sex, but even then, it was different. Hungry or playful.

Not appreciative.

Kennedy's desperate hold, the tripping of her heartbeat and the feathering of her breath against his neck did something to him. Something unfamiliar. He tucked her closer, reassuring her. "You're all right."

"Because of you." She burrowed into him. "I know you don't want to hear it, but thank you."

"Shush. It's all right." Without meaning to, he pressed his mouth to the tender skin of her temple.

Her face turned toward him, and suddenly they were nose to nose, sharing breath and staring into each other's eyes.

A sexual moment for him, but he seriously doubted she viewed it the same way.

When he started to move away, she held him tighter. "I'm not upset."

"No?" She had every right to be. Someone was after her, Jodi or both of them. If the two fucks in the truck hadn't died, he could have questioned them. As it was, he'd removed their wallets and passed them to Cade. Hopefully, Madison would have plenty to share with him tomorrow.

"I was," Kennedy admitted. "The gunshots—"

"Cade had that in hand, and if one of the idiots got by him, I'd have taken care of it."

"So self-assured," she teased.

"I'm prepared," he said seriously. "Well trained."

And...he cared about her.

"Yes, it's been easy to see that you can handle yourself. But, Reyes, they tried to drive us off the road."

"And how did that turn out?" With two dead bodies, that's how.

She shook her head. "You amaze me. You stayed so blasted calm through all of it."

Taking her hand, he led her to the couch. He didn't pull her onto his lap this time, not when he was feeling so oddly territorial. Instead, he put his arm around her shoulders and drew her comfortably into his side. "Since you'll meet Dad tomorrow, I figure I better explain a few things."

"What things?"

"Long ago..." Hell, he sounded like the start of a *Star Wars* movie. "When I was thirteen, actually, my mother was taken, trafficked—and that changed Dad."

Horrified, she bit her lips. "God, I'm so sorry."

"He found her. Dad would have charged through hell for her, and a few times I think he did."

Kennedy rested a hand on his chest. "Is she okay now?"

He shook his head. "A year later, she committed suicide." He didn't want to dwell on that memory for too long. "I know what that type of abuse does to a person. I saw it in my mom—and I saw it in my dad. It changed him. He and Mom both came from money, then they made more of their own. Not bragging about finances or anything, just saying Dad had the funds and the motivation to turn his focus almost solely to taking down traffickers." He rested his chin against her silky hair, breathing in the scent of her while forcing all emotion from his tone. "That focus included grooming us—Cade, me and Madison—into weapons. We started learning every fighting technique there is, usually from the best trainers in the world. Hand-to-hand combat, grappling, boxing, mixed martial arts. We're versed in it all."

"Madison, too?"

"Yep. Though Dad groomed her for computer work, he wanted each of us to have a well-rounded education."

"Was there room for affection?" she asked softly.

"I guess. It was a difficult time, you know? Cade rebelled." Smiling, Reyes said, "He doesn't do well with orders, which is funny, since he joined the military to escape Dad's regimen. There, he excelled. With Dad? They're so much alike, they always butted heads."

"And now?"

"Sterling changed things. I think she blunted a bunch of Cade's anger and resistance."

"It sounds like you like her, but I got the impression you two don't get along."

"She's my sister-in-law and I love her, but yeah, I enjoy twitting her."

"You," Kennedy said, poking him in the stomach, "enjoy twitting everyone."

"Maybe." This whole discussion was easier than he'd expected, because Kennedy was so easy to be around. "Cade trained, the same as we all did. His pride demanded he be the best."

"How old was he?"

"Fifteen." Now that he'd started talking, Reyes wanted to share other things, too, things he'd never discussed with anyone, not even his siblings. "Cade is a half brother. Maybe that has something to do with how he's always been."

"Different mothers?"

"Yeah. When he was born, his mom gave him to Dad and moved on, and that was that. He's never met her. But to Madison and me, he's our big brother and nothing will ever change that."

"Of course. You were all raised together?"

He nodded. "My mom was basically his mom, too, until we lost her. We were all devastated, you know? And then Dad made his decision and we didn't really have time to grieve. On top of learning to fight, we're experts with weapons, from every improvised implement you'd find on the street to military grade."

"And that tricky driving you did?"

"Dad's covered every scenario," he confirmed. "Before you start thinking he's too mercenary, he also started a task force to help ensure victims are legally represented, that they get any counseling they need, and enough financial aid to start over."

"Wow. Your dad sounds pretty phenomenal."

"He is." He could also be overbearing, dictatorial and downright cold at times. Except that... Sterling had changed him some, too. Maybe it was getting Cade back as his son that made the difference. Reyes admitted, "I used to be a real hell-raiser."

"No?" she said with facetious surprise.

Reyes gave her a squeeze. "Dad didn't seem to care as long as I channeled my anger and energy into what he considered the right direction, which basically meant defending someone. But Cade? That dude is military through and through, and he's all about personal control. He put the stomp on my bad attitude real quick."

Rearing up, Kennedy frowned at him. "What does that mean?"

Her automatic defense made him grin. "It means anytime I got too froggy, Cade showed me that his quiet control trumped my rage every time. He always made it into a lesson. Like he'd block one of my punches, give me a smack, and explain why he'd managed it so easily."

Her scowl darkened. "I don't think I like the idea of him putting hands on you."

"Ah, hon, Cade and I have been sparring since we were early teens. This was no different. And I did learn. Funny thing, too, was that Dad would watch on with a satisfied smile, as if it made him proud to see Cade school me." He shook his head with a short laugh. "It's the truth, I'm a better man because of Cade. Better fighter, better strategist, probably a better son and brother."

"Did he teach you to shoot, too?"

"Actually, that's the one place where I'm better than him. I'm a top-notch marksman. Cade is good, better than many, but I have the edge there."

"Your family sounds absolutely fascinating."

He enjoyed this more than was wise. Having Kennedy curled up against him, her hand idly resting over his abs, her frowns and her smiles, her trust, felt like an amazing gift.

"What about your family?"

She ducked her face again. "There's just my mom and dad. They're both terrific."

"You haven't told them everything that's going on now?"

"They'd just worry." Her fingertips toyed with the buttons of his flannel shirt, stopping near his navel—and making him nuts. "They're quiet people, very involved in their church, and they were hurt so badly when I was taken."

Eyes narrowing, Reyes lifted her face. "Don't tell me they blamed you."

"No, of course not. Mom and Dad both cried for days when I returned. They'd aged so much, all from grief." She lowered her eyes. "They love me and I love them, but I couldn't stay in Florida. Not anymore. It was hard for them to grasp that type of evil. Mom would look at me and then suddenly crumble again. It was heartbreaking, for both of us. Dad couldn't bear seeing my mother so upset, and he felt like he'd somehow failed me."

"So you moved on?"

"Not the way you're saying it. I stayed long enough to convince them I was fine, then I moved away with a lot of happy fanfare, letting them think I was on an adventure for life." She sighed. "We talk often, and I try to get home at least once a year to see them, but I will never again deliberately worry them."

"Hey." He couldn't stop himself from pressing a kiss in between her brows, where a fretful frown lingered. "You were a victim, and parents are supposed to worry for their kids. That's not on you. It's on the bastards who took you."

Her gaze relaxed...then dipped down to his mouth. Yeah, much more of that and instincts would take over. He'd be kissing her hot and hungry before he had time to talk himself down.

He sat forward and, in a voice as casual as he could make it, he said, "It's getting late." He stood and pulled her to her feet. "I can be ready for bed in twenty minutes. How about you?"

She searched his face, her expression confused, a little embarrassed, but she managed a smile that didn't reach her eyes. "I need thirty minutes, so don't rush."

Reyes watched her head to the guest room, and he knew—oh, yeah, he knew—it was going to be a very long night sleeping beside her.

CHAPTER ELEVEN

WELL, HE HADN'T BEEN WRONG. An hour had passed and still he stared up at the ceiling, full of conflicts and hunger, both horny and swamped with tenderness.

Seeing that look on Kennedy's face when he'd abruptly moved away... He'd done that to her.

What should he have done instead?

He thought back to Sterling's advice, about how he should ease into things. He'd agreed to give it a try, and then instead he'd blown it.

There wasn't much he feared in life, but he detested the idea of pushing Kennedy, maybe making her uncomfortable with his lust.

"Reyes?"

Her voice was husky with sleep, and she shifted a little, turning to face him. "Hmm."

"Why are you still awake?"

Because I want you so damn much, and you're here, all sweet and soft beside me, and I can smell the scent of your shampoo and lotion, and the warmer, muskier scent of your skin, and it's making me nuts.

Of course, he didn't say any of that. "Just thinking."

"About?"

And...there went his brain again, pondering all the things he wanted to do with her. He turned on his side and levered up to his forearm. "Why aren't you sleeping? I thought you were out."

"Close, but I keep thinking about earlier."

"At the campsite? That's over, babe. You're here with me, safe."

Smiling, she touched his cheek, then his bare shoulder. "I meant on the couch, when I made you uncomfortable."

What the hell? "You didn't."

"It's just...the way you looked at me, well, I thought you were going to kiss me."

He'd been thinking of a hell of a lot more than mere kissing, but all he said was, "I would never take advantage of you."

"I know." Her fingers drifted across his chest. "But did I totally misread that? It's been forever since I paid attention to a guy, and now I'm worried I got my signals crossed. If so, that'd be really embarrassing." After all that, she drew a breath, and asked, "So were you thinking about it?"

Damn. He couldn't lie to her, not when she sounded so vulnerable. With a mental shrug, he admitted, "Yeah, I was thinking about kissing you—and more. Can't seem to help it around you. Just remember, you don't have to worry that I'll—"

"What if I wanted you to?" she interrupted. "Because I do. And it's the strangest feeling, wanting something I haven't even thought about for so long."

Reyes swallowed heavily. *What exactly did she want from him?*

"If you'd rather not, I understand."

"That's not the problem." God, he wished the room were lighter so he could really see her, not just the shadows and outlines of her features from the moonlight filtering through the darkened windows. "Why don't you tell me why you'd want me to?" Once the words left his mouth, they sounded lame.

Never in his life had he asked a woman to explain desire.

She scooted closer, opening her hand over his left pectoral muscle. "Until recently, the thought of getting that close to a man was repugnant."

"Things have changed, though?"

"With you, yes." Stroking over him, she seemed to relish the texture of his chest hair. She explored him—and it was sexy as hell. "Now I think about it all the time. Not just kissing you, but more."

Way to level him. "Kennedy—"

"I promise it won't mean anything," she rushed out. "I know it could be awkward if I got ideas, since I'm staying with you. Still... I just thought maybe you wouldn't mind." Her breasts pressed against his upper arm. "It doesn't have to be more than a kiss—"

He touched his mouth to hers, as light and easy as he could, but damn, a roaring sounded in his ears.

This was Kennedy.

This was red-hot hunger.

Go slow. Be easy.

Don't scare her.

Gently he framed her face in his hands and shifted her to her back. "I want you to tell me if at any point—"

She lifted up enough to seal her mouth to his, and he forgot what he was going to say.

In fact, he forgot his own name. As her mouth moved under his, he forgot that she'd been a victim, that he was her protector...

That this was only supposed to be a kiss.

Her arms snaked around his neck, and her lips parted to the touch of his tongue.

Half atop her now, Reyes slanted his head for a better fit and ate at her mouth with all the need burning up inside him.

With a soft groan, she shifted one of her legs alongside his hip, creating a cradle with her body. He liked that enough to trail a hand down her side until he could cup one full, soft cheek, lifting her more firmly against him.

His brain couldn't seem to wrap around the reality of what was happening. He'd wanted Kennedy forever, and here he was, one big hand stroking over the generous curves of her ass, his tongue in her mouth, their groans mingling.

This was *Kennedy.*

Being so fucking hot.

She wasn't at all like a woman caught up in past abuse. She wasn't timid or reserved. She gave and she took, and it was the most natural thing in the world.

Even when he had a fleeting moment of sanity, she quickly pushed him beyond it again. He left her mouth to kiss her throat and made a desperate attempt at control. "Babe—"

"Don't stop. Please don't." Her fingers tunneled into his hair and tightened. "Please."

"I won't unless you tell me to."

"Perfect," she purred, and steered his mouth back to hers.

Holy hell, she apparently wanted him every bit as much as he wanted her. Definitely not something he'd expected, but damn, it set him on fire.

Suddenly he had to touch and kiss every part of her. He wanted light enough to see, and he wanted nakedness to finally sate his imagination.

He wanted everything Kennedy Brooks could give, and then some.

Holding her face in his hands, he slowed her down. "I'm onboard one hundred percent, but I want your word that if anything bothers you, if you want me to ease up, or stop altogether, or—"

She smashed her fingers to his lips. "Do you have a condom?"

"Yup." He didn't mean to be abrupt, but the more agreeable she was, the hotter he got.

"Get it, then no more talking." She gave that quick thought, reconsidering apparently, because she added, "Unless you want to tell me something to do, something that you like."

He'd never survive this. Shifting her small, cool hand to his cheek, he whispered, "I like *you*, Kennedy." And that was more than enough.

Her expression softened. "I like you, too, Reyes." She brushed a tender kiss to his mouth. "Thank you for giving me this."

His eyes flared. She was thanking him for agreeing to have sex? "You are the most..." What? Sweetest? Funniest? Craziest woman he'd ever known? All of the above. "You're welcome," he said, then quickly slid to the side and turned on a lamp. He was already hard as granite and breathing too fast, but who cared?

Kennedy liked him.

He knew the truth—he more than liked her. His brain shied away from dwelling on that disquieting thought. At the closet, he got down a box of condoms, turned—and completely froze.

Her back to him, Kennedy pushed down her pajama pants, giving him a stellar view of the ass of his dreams.

His mouth went dry.

Straightening again, she tossed the bottoms toward the top already on the floor, and turned toward him wearing only minuscule rose-colored panties.

A wet dream, that's what she was.

When he continued to stare, she shifted.

"I'm not very endowed in the boob department."

"Babe, seriously, you're perfect." Proud shoulders led down to small, high breasts, her rosy nipples already pebbled tight. A narrow waist flared into generous hips and full thighs, down to shapely calves.

Visually, he devoured her.

Holding the box of condoms loosely in his hand, he strode over to her. "I've thought about you naked from that first day we met."

Her lips lifted into a cheeky smile. "I didn't think about you naked until we rescued Chimera."

Ah, that alley cat had proved most instrumental in his relationship with Kennedy. And, damn it, it was a relationship. That of friends, and soon lovers.

By far the closest relationship he'd ever had with a woman who wasn't related.

Reaching past her, he set the box on the bookcase headboard. He touched her hair, sifting the silky blond strands through his fingers and then settling them behind her shoulder. Leaning down, he kissed her throat, filling himself with the warm scent of her, absorbing her softness and accepting that she was his.

On a breathy sigh, she tipped her face up and away to give him more room. He cupped both her breasts, loving how they fit into his palms. Against her throat, he suggested, "Let's lose the panties, too."

She nodded but otherwise didn't move, so he did the honors, trailing his hands over her body, tracking all those sweet curves and the silkiness of her skin, down to her waist, her hips, then around to her bottom—and inside her panties.

Stepping against him, she opened her mouth on his chest, her hot little tongue tasting his skin, her sharp teeth scraping gently over him.

While stroking her, he eased her panties down. His arms were long enough, and she was short enough, that it was an easy thing to get them over her hips, and from there, they dropped on their own.

He was a visual man, and he absolutely loved women's bodies, so he held her back enough to look her over again.

"It's not going to change," she whispered with the first hint of nervousness. "This is it."

His gaze locked on hers. "Just so we're clear, you're the sexiest fucking thing I've ever seen, and I'm going to want to look at you a lot."

"Oh." Her chin angled up. "I'd like to look at you, too, so drop the boxers."

Ah, there was the confident, no-nonsense woman he knew. "Yes, ma'am." He took two steps back and quickly shucked off his shorts. Holding out his arms, he said, "I'm not shy. Look your fill, just make it fast because I'm dying to get you under me."

With her eyes on his dick, she murmured, "What if I want you under me?"

Was that nervousness, or just pure challenge? Was she saying it'd be easier for her in the dominant position?

He couldn't tell, so he said, "Whatever you want is fine by me." More serious now, he gathered her close for a devastating kiss. Yes, *this*. Skin to skin, heat combining… It couldn't be more perfect.

By silent agreement, they moved to the bed, both of them touching, stroking, exploring. Reyes drew her right nipple into his mouth, flicking with his tongue, then leisurely sucking, and she went a little wild. Her fingertips bit into his shoulders and her hips rose in a frantic rhythm against his.

Nice. He could have spent hours just doing this, but she wasn't patient enough for that. Her legs were shifting, her feet sliding over the sheets restlessly. Relieved that she wasn't having any bad memories, at least not so far, he lowered a hand to her sex.

That got her still real quick, mostly in bated anticipation. Smiling against her nipple, he stroked over her, parted her and teased her soft, damp lips with one finger.

Her body arched in response.

Her hand covered his and she pressed, urging him to move more quickly than he'd planned.

She was already wet enough that his finger pressed deep, even as her muscles squeezed around him.

Watching her, turned on even more by her need, he murmured, "It's like that, huh?"

"Shut up, Reyes," she groaned, already sounding near release.

Her long abstinence had left her incredibly tight, and apparently hungry. Taking her mouth again, he kissed her with every bit of finesse he possessed while rocking his palm against her mound in coordination with his thrusting finger. He was hard enough to be lethal, but he wanted to experience her pleasure first, to know he'd accomplished that much before he let himself go. He wasn't a bastard—her release mattered a lot to him—and so he concentrated on her, on each small reaction, the catch of her breath and every vibrating moan.

The problem was that as she got closer to the edge, so did he. Knowing he wouldn't last much longer, he brought his thumb up to her clitoris, and that almost did it for her. She gave a harsh groan and clenched around him, her heels digging into the mattress.

Beautiful. Urging her on with whispered words, he found a rhythm that pushed her ever closer. He added a second finger, stretching her carefully, spreading her slick moisture, then pressing his fingers as deeply as he could while continuing to tease her clit with the rough pad of his thumb.

She grew tighter and tighter, more restless, her breaths fast and shallow. He loved it, every freaking second of it. After a few minutes more, she came with a low, intense groan that absolutely did him in.

The second Kennedy went limp, he literally lurched over to grab a condom, rolled it on in haste, and parted her legs to settle over her.

"Yes?" he asked, needing her confirmation, needing to know she was still with him.

"Yes," she whispered, getting her eyes open and giving him a dreamy smile. "Definitely—"

He pressed into her in one long, smooth thrust.

"Yes." Gripping his shoulders, Kennedy caught her breath.

Yeah, maybe he should have gone a little slower. He was larger than a lot of guys, something other women had enjoyed. But this was Kennedy, and other women didn't matter anymore. It was what she felt, how she responded, that mattered to him.

"You okay?" She held him in a snug, wet vise, making speech near impossible. "Tell me you're okay, babe."

"Fine," she breathed, tightening around him even more, followed by a shifting of her hips.

"Ah, hell." Balanced on his forearms, he tipped his head back and drove into her with urgent need. Worry hovered around the periphery of his consciousness, because no matter the naturalness of her response, she had a dark past that could dredge up memories at any second.

But lust, tinged with something softer, stronger, drove him on despite that. As long as she didn't call a halt, he *had* to have her.

It helped that she moaned, that she hitched her legs around his hips and lifted into his every heavy thrust.

When he felt her tightening yet again, he wanted to shout with pure male satisfaction. Stiffening, her head back and her body arching, she cried out with another, stronger release.

That was it. Reyes couldn't wait a second more, so he let himself go.

Gone. Lost.

Probably a little in love.

And even that revelation didn't unsettle him. As he sank down against her, utterly replete, his world seemed at peace.

All because he had Kennedy in it.

ONCE DURING THE NIGHT, Reyes awoke to find her propped on an elbow, staring down at him.

"Hey," he said, still half asleep. "You okay?"

"Perfectly fine." She drifted a hand over his chest.

"Then why are you awake?"

"We forgot to turn out the light. The rain woke me and I remembered you were right here, that I could look my fill, and sleep didn't seem as interesting."

He lifted his head from the pillow and glanced at the window to see steady trickles of rain tracking over the panes. "What time is it?"

"I don't know." She leaned down to kiss him. "Go back to sleep."

The lecherous look on her face amused him. "So you can ogle me?"

"Sure."

He grinned. "I have a better idea." Pulling her up and over him, he kissed her and wanted to go on kissing her. "We'll sleep after, okay?"

Instead of answering, she took his mouth again.

Yeah, he could get used to this, all right.

THE NEXT TIME REYES WOKE, it was to see Kennedy's naked rump sneaking from the bed. Damn, but that was an eye-opener for sure. Tiptoeing, she slipped into his bathroom. Seconds later he heard the toilet flush, then the water running, and he glanced at the clock. Seven o'clock.

With a family meeting on the agenda, it was time to rise and shine. Indulging an elaborate stretch, he came fully awake.

A deep contentment had invaded his bones. Hell, he was smiling. Who woke with a smile?

Obviously, any guy lucky enough to have phenomenal sex with Kennedy.

Creeping over to the door, he peeked in and saw her cleaning her teeth with a toothpaste-covered finger.

Still naked.

Lord love the girl, she looked fine at his sink.

"You're welcome to use my toothbrush."

She blanched, jerked around to face him—finger still in her mouth—and glared. Turning back to the sink, she rinsed and spit before saying, "You were supposed to stay in bed."

"Why?" Eyeing her body, he propped a shoulder on the door frame. "You didn't."

Color suddenly tinged her cheeks. "I was trying to wake up enough to truly appreciate you." She indicated the toothpaste. "And I didn't want to have morning breath."

Reyes grinned... *Truly appreciate you.* Kennedy was absolutely the most unique woman he'd ever met. "Sorry to have spoiled your fun, but we can head back to bed if you want."

Her brows lifted over blurry eyes, her expression that of someone offered a gift. "Really?"

His grin widened. She truly amused him in the mornings with
her sluggishness. "We have a little time before we need to head
over to Dad's. We can sneak in a quickie if you want, but we can't
linger. I'm sure Bernard is putting together a big breakfast."

"So early?"

He shrugged. "We'd be cutting it close, but I can manage if you
can." It was his experience that women generally took longer getting ready than men did.

"Blast." Looking very disappointed, Kennedy said, "If you want
me verbally functional, I need coffee before I meet anyone. Lots
and lots of coffee." She huffed a sigh, then strode up to him and
stood, defiantly staring into his eyes. "Look, I know I started this
with wanting just a kiss, but we shot past that last night, right?"

"Er...right." Where was she going with this? Hopefully, she
didn't have regrets now.

Then again, she'd just been cleaning her teeth with a finger and
planning on keeping him in bed, so...

"Good, we're agreed." She opened her hand over his chest,
lightly petting him, testing the strength of his pec muscle, using
her thumb to brush over his left nipple.

"Kennedy—" Much more of that and she wouldn't get a single
sip of coffee.

Smiling up at him, she whispered, "Last night was a surprise.
You're a surprise." She pursed her mouth thoughtfully. "Actually,
I was the biggest surprise."

His heart softened. "Because you enjoyed yourself?"

"Far, far more than I knew was even possible," she confirmed.
"And now that I've had a taste, I'm not done."

Catching on, he asked, "You want more, is that it?" Definitely
not a problem for him.

"I really do. But actually, waiting until tonight might be a good
idea." She scrunched her nose. "I'm more alert in the evening, and
honestly... I'm a little sore."

Had he been too enthusiastic? "A shower would probably help."

"After coffee. But for now, can I count on a repeat?"

That quickie was sounding better and better. "Guaranteed."

A beautiful smile bloomed on her face. "Perfect." She stretched up on tiptoe to peck his lips, then headed for her top and bottoms. "Let's do coffee before I perish. It took all my resolve to accomplish cleaning my teeth without it. The rest might have been wishful thinking."

Reyes stood there grinning inside and out. He'd had sex, varied and often, but knowing he'd pleased Kennedy, that he'd overcome the ugly memories of her past, was a gift he'd always cherish.

Funny that, good as the sex had been, he still couldn't compete with caffeine. Should have known there wouldn't be a typical "morning after" with Kennedy.

She was different, so it figured this would be different, too.

With her, it was also better.

YES, REYES HAD SAID, in an offhand way, that his dad was loaded. She still hadn't expected *this*.

Good God, it appeared the man owned a mountain, or at least a good chunk of it, so that he had complete privacy.

And his house… Her eyes were round enough to drop out of her head as Reyes drove up higher and higher along the private road. When she spotted the smaller house to the right, she let out a breath of relief. Maybe his father lived there, and the other building was an upscale lodge or something.

But no, he went right past the very nice, moderately sized home.

"Who lives there?" Kennedy asked, thinking the smaller home felt cozier.

"That's Madison's place, though she, as well as Cade and I, have private suites in Dad's house just in case there's ever an emergency. His security is the best."

Kennedy stared at him, agog by that notion since Reyes had his place completely locked down. "Better than yours?"

Snorting, he said, "No comparison. Everything at Dad's is state-of-the-art shit, like the government would use, you know? Most of it isn't even available to the public. He has some crazy-cool stuff."

And Reyes's weird darkening windows weren't crazy cool? "If you say so."

He gave her a quick, knowing look. "Don't be nervous, honey."

"Oh, right. You tell me your father is an ogre and that he'll likely try to intimidate me, you say he has equipment not available to the rest of us mere mortals, and I can see he's insanely wealthy—but I shouldn't worry about any of that."

"No," he said gently, "you shouldn't. Dad is just…my dad, you know? Sure, the situation is a little different, but you'll hold your own, I don't doubt it."

"Cade and Madison will be there?"

"Sterling, too."

That was something, at least. Safety in numbers and all that. Being among his family would serve as a buffer against her new, somewhat raw awareness of Reyes as a sexual man. Left alone with him, she'd probably keep him in the bed all day.

He'd probably like the sex, but would he start to feel smothered? Already she'd practically insisted that he keep on sleeping with her, when that had never been his intent. He'd been very upfront about avoiding commitments.

Shame that her heart hadn't listened.

But even that, the sweet ache that filled her chest every time she looked at his impossibly handsome face, could probably be written off as lust. For so long she'd believed the scum who'd kidnapped her had stolen her sexuality in the process. In her mind, intercourse was something to be suffered, not enjoyed.

Yet with Reyes, the pleasure had been so intense she didn't know how to describe it.

"You have a certain look about you," Reyes mused aloud. "Want to share your thoughts?"

"Sex," she blurted, seeing no reason not to share. "It was all so hot and powerful and—"

"Wet," he agreed, his voice low and deep.

It felt like her stomach tumbled over in a very pleasant way. She fanned her face, feeling flushed. "Topic switch, okay? I don't want to be flustered when I meet your dad."

His satisfied smile nearly did her in, but he obliged her by asking, "What do you think of the house?"

"It's big enough to be a lodge that could hold a few hundred people." Not only did it sit partially in the mountain, but colorful aspens were everywhere, as well as giant boulders. Who needed landscaping when Mother Nature did such a remarkable job?

"You should see it at night, with all the exterior lights shining like amber along the stone columns. It's pretty. And the sunsets here are spectacular."

The sunsets at Reyes's house were beautiful, too. When she left there—because eventually she would—she'd miss it so much. The fresh air, the sounds of nature all around, sunrises and sunsets, the privacy. To her, Reyes had the perfect setup, and it was much nicer than this massive structure.

She didn't care if that wasn't fair. Yes, the house was beautiful, stunningly so, but herein lived Reyes's father, and she already disliked the man based on Reyes's descriptions.

He pulled right up near the front door instead of using one of the many parking spaces. After he turned off his truck, he asked, "Ready?"

Not even. Forcing her mouth into a smile, she nodded.

As usual, Reyes walked around to her side and played the gentleman while she continued to take in the grandeur of the place.

A circular deck on the second floor created a covered porch at the front double doors. Wings extended in both directions, sort of hugging the mountain, with the entirety of the house enclosed by a smooth stone wall. The same stone was used in the giant pillars that supported the second-floor deck.

She was still craning her head around, taking it all in, when the front doors opened.

Sterling stood there grinning at her, while a tall, elegant man fussed behind her. "My job," he stated in lofty tones, reaching past Sterling to wrest the doorknob from her hands so he could sweep the double doors wide. "Reyes," he said, and then he smiled at Kennedy. "And you must be Ms. Brooks."

She almost said, *Guilty*, but caught herself in time. "Hello. You have a beautiful home."

"Thank you. Though it's actually Parrish's, I claim it as well."

Ah, so this wasn't Reyes's father. He had to be midsixties, tall, thin, with silver hair and a reserved expression—except for his eyes. Those eyes were full of mischief. "You're Bernard?"

He surprised her by saying, "None other. And so we're clear right off, Chimera is mine."

Grousing, Reyes took her hand and tugged her over the threshold. "Let up, Bernard. She hasn't even been here a minute."

Bernard looked obstinate about it, so Kennedy turned to Sterling. "It's good to see you again."

Watching them, her gaze bouncing back and forth between Reyes and Kennedy, Sterling grinned. "Nice work, dude." She offered Reyes a high five.

Shaking his head in stern warning, Reyes took Sterling's wrist and lowered her arm to her side. "Behave."

"Never. At least not with you." She grinned at Kennedy. "I still owe him a whole lot of hassling, so you'll have to bear with me while I get it out of my system."

"Hassling?" she asked, confused by the whole exchange that had just happened.

"When I first came here, baby brother ribbed me endlessly, making me feel like a worn-out boot."

"I did not," Reyes complained, but he looked abashed as he said it.

"Come on." Sterling latched on to Kennedy's arm. "Bernard needs a few more minutes to finish up one of the most amazing breakfasts you'll ever have."

"Thank you," the stately Bernard said. Kennedy saw a definite twinkle in his eyes.

Sterling quickly propelled her through an immense room and toward a hall. "Where are we going?"

"I'll show you around. The place is big enough that, without a guide, you'll get lost." Over her shoulder, Sterling said to Reyes, "Go find your sibs. They have things to tell you. Kennedy and I will be along shortly."

Reyes didn't look happy about it, but neither did he reclaim her. No, he just let Sterling abscond with her.

Luckily, Sterling was with her, because it was true—Kennedy would most certainly get lost on her own.

CHAPTER TWELVE

"WE'LL BE EATING on the deck," Sterling said, "but no one is out there yet so we'll have a minute to chat."

Going through tall French doors, Sterling led her to a covered deck unlike any she'd ever seen. It seemed to go on forever and gave incredible views of snow-topped mountains, rocky terrain and a calm, beautiful lake.

"Wow." She could sit out here for hours, Kennedy thought. Tension seemed to seep away.

"Pretty, right?" Sterling indicated a table and chairs already set with china and a tablecloth. "It's getting chillier every day, so we won't get to sit out here too much longer. Figured we should take advantage of the sunny morning."

"You made the decision?"

Sterling laughed. "Bernard likes me, so he always gives me a choice." She leaned in a little closer. "I brag on his skills in the kitchen. Works wonders on softening him up."

That made Kennedy smile. "You like it here?" Because she felt really small, and almost…insignificant.

Turning to lean on the railing, Sterling said, "It's a little overwhelming, I know."

"Very." Moving to the railing, too, Kennedy stared out at the scenery and concentrated on conquering her nervousness.

"So…" Sterling nudged her. "You and Reyes did the nasty, huh?

And judging by the way you two were ogling each other, I'd say you even liked it."

Was she really that transparent? Did she want to confide in Sterling? She glanced up—because seriously, Sterling was a tall one—and saw her friendly but knowing smile.

She liked Sterling. The woman was like an open book, tossing out her thoughts without censoring, so that you didn't have to guess what she really thought about things. It appeared Sterling liked her, and she could use another friend, so... With a mental shrug, Kennedy said, "Yes, and yes."

"Awesome." Again Sterling offered a high five, and unlike Reyes, Kennedy accepted, reaching up to smack her palm to Sterling's.

"Before everyone joins us, I'll give you a fast rundown on the family, beyond what you already know, I mean. That way, you'll be better prepared."

"I'd appreciate that."

"First, Parrish tries to be snooty, but he's not so bad. Just stare him down. He respects that."

Kennedy could easily imagine Sterling employing that tactic. Her? Not so much. "Reyes told me a few things about him."

Snorting, Sterling said, "The brothers are a little biased when it comes to their dad. He's heavy-handed, and they're not the type of guys to take kindly to that. Cade was more open in his rebellion, to the point he skipped out and joined the military. Reyes hung around and just became an annoying ass."

The insult pricked Kennedy's temper. "He's not."

"Not to you, maybe."

Okay, yeah, she'd witnessed herself how Reyes baited not only Sterling, but Cade also. "Well, from what I've seen, you bring some of that on yourself."

"Oh, for sure." Sterling grinned. "Part of the fun of being in this family is getting Reyes riled."

Unable to resist, Kennedy conceded with a smile.

"Now, Bernard, well, he's the sweetest, but he's also a tad pompous. He takes the whole butler-slash-assistant-slash-chef thing way too seriously, complete with his nose in the air and pretentious manners. Only time I've seen him rattled was when he and Reyes were battling over the cat." Sterling chuckled. "Reyes never had a chance. Bernard was so cute, cuddling the mama cat, loving on her kittens. It was something to see."

The more Kennedy learned of Bernard, the more she understood why Reyes had let him have his way. "We were actually supposed to share responsibility for the cat."

"Yeah, well, that's one instance where I can't blame Reyes. When you get to know Bernard—heck, when you see him with Chimera—you'll know what I mean. Now, the kittens, they got divvied up. One for me, one for Madison, and one for Reyes."

"There's no kitten at Reyes's house."

"I know." She smirked. "Bernard is holding out on him, claiming Chimera will be lonely if she doesn't have at least one playmate. With how busy Reyes is, he hasn't pushed it."

Probably a sound arrangement. Kennedy was honest enough with herself to admit she couldn't care for a cat now anyway. She didn't even have a home.

The despondent sigh escaped her before she could stop it.

Sterling bumped her again. "I know stuff is rough right now, but Madison's unearthed some phenomenal info. Things *are* moving along." She slanted a look at Kennedy. "You're not in a hurry to leave Reyes anyway, are you?"

In a hurry, no. Still, he had a right to the life of his choosing. "I've imposed on him for so long already." If they could get the danger sorted, then she could regain her independence and if, at that point, Reyes was interested, he could let her know without the sense of obligation guiding him.

"Eh, these guys love playing the big macho protectors. Reyes is probably getting off on it."

"Ahem."

Going rigid, Sterling winced.

Kennedy looked back to see Cade grinning, Reyes frowning, Bernard utterly unperturbed, and a very handsome older man rolling his eyes.

Parrish, she assumed.

Regaining her aplomb, Sterling turned and said, "Deny it, Reyes. I dare you."

"And ruin your fantasies about me?" Far too intently, he approached Kennedy. "Hungry? Bernard says he's outdone himself."

"I said no such thing," Bernard replied as he took steaming dishes from a rolling cart and set them on the large round table. "It goes without saying that I always do my best. Today is no different."

Parrish caught her gaze and somehow held her captive. She couldn't blink, couldn't look away…

Sterling came to her rescue. "Dude, stop trying to intimidate her. She's been through enough."

At that, Parrish glanced at Sterling. "Already defending her? Why am I not surprised?"

"Because you know I'm awesome like that?" She winked and dropped into a chair.

Cade touched Sterling's hair as if endlessly enthralled by her, then he took the seat beside her.

Reyes pulled out a chair for Kennedy, and once she sat, he started to do the same, but Parrish beat him to it. Somehow he got around the table without her noticing, then he crowded in, boldly claiming the chair beside Kennedy. She now had Sterling on her right, and Parrish on her left.

Narrowing his eyes, Reyes grumbled but moved on, choosing to sit directly across from her.

"Where's Madison?" Kennedy asked, trying to act unaffected by the musical chairs.

"My daughter gets lost in her research."

With the food now on the table, Bernard said, "I'll let her know breakfast is served."

Once he'd gone inside, Reyes chuckled. "Boy, he's really turning it on today, isn't he?"

Cade said, "He's out to impress." Shooting his father a look, he added, "Unlike some people."

"I don't need to impress," Parrish stated. Turning slightly in his chair, he held out his hand to Kennedy. "Since my son doesn't see fit to introduce us, I suppose I'll handle it myself. Parrish McKenzie. And you're Kennedy Brooks."

Like she didn't know who she was? "That's right." She accepted his handshake, not at all surprised that his hand was as big as Reyes's. She got the impression that this older McKenzie was every bit as capable as his sons, just a little more seasoned. "You and Cade share a similar look."

"It's true." With a final, gentle squeeze, he released her hand and slid his napkin from a bronze napkin ring. "Madison and Reyes have their mother's coloring."

"But still your height," Kennedy noted. "Or was she tall as well?"

"She was..." Parrish hesitated as he looked inward. A smile touched his mouth. "Average height, I suppose, but she often appeared taller because she had such presence."

"Then I suppose they inherited that from her as well."

He gave her an odd look.

It occurred to Kennedy that she'd just made it sound like the senior McKenzie didn't have that same presence. Trying to recover, she tacked on, "And from you as well, of course."

"You're quick-witted, Ms. Brooks."

"Kennedy," she insisted.

"Do I make you nervous?"

"Yes?"

"You aren't certain?"

"I'm still taking your measure," she admitted. "I can't decide if it's being here, your attempts to intimidate, or the fact that Sterling hinted there'd be news today that has me a little on edge."

"Probably all of the above," Sterling said. "Just remember that I told you Parrish was harmless."

At that, Parrish made a rude sound. "You're the only one who thinks so."

Leaning forward to see around Kennedy, Sterling said, "Give it up already, or I'll have to switch seats with Kennedy and your son won't like that. Then he'll be butting heads with you again, and we'll never be able to enjoy Bernard's wonderful meal."

"It's fine," Kennedy said, shooting a desperate look at Reyes.

He shrugged, then lifted a lid off a covered plate. "You have a few choices here, Kennedy. Apple pancakes for starters, either with maple bacon or sausage links—"

"Or both," Sterling said, taking up the platter of meats to serve herself.

"—fresh fruit, a couple types of eggs, croissants—"

As he spoke, Reyes uncovered the feast, setting the lids on the cart behind him. Kennedy could barely take it all in. The amount of food presented was extravagant and, in her mind, wasteful.

When Reyes wrapped it up, he glanced at her and smiled. "I guess Sterling has the right idea. I'll get you some of everything."

"Small portions," she said quickly, watching as he loaded her plate. Her stomach was currently jumpy enough that she didn't want to chance things by overeating.

Parrish stood to fill her glass with orange juice, and then her coffee cup with a rich, steaming brew. "Cream and sugar?" he asked.

"Please."

Reyes passed her plate to her, now heaping with treats. She breathed deeply of all the combined scents, and decided she was hungry after all. "Oh, this is nirvana." Just as she forked up a bite, Madison came hustling through the doors. "Sorry I'm late, but I just made the most astounding discovery."

"Does it have anything to do with a certain cop?" Reyes asked. "'Cause I have it on good authority you were flirting with him."

Madison shot a glance at Kennedy. "Maybe a little." To her brother, she said, "So what? Detective Albertson fascinates me."

That earned a severe frown from Parrish. "It goes without saying that you shouldn't—"

"Yes, I know your preferences, Dad." Pushing her plate away, she opened the laptop and turned it toward Kennedy.

The bite in her mouth turned to sawdust. Kennedy tried to swallow and couldn't. She gulped down coffee, burning her mouth in the process, and then just stared.

She hadn't been prepared. Hadn't even suspected what Madison would show her.

There, enlarged on the screen, was the very man who'd fled the wrecked car on the day she'd finally been rescued.

Memories flooded back in on her, chilling her to the bone, then flushing her with heat. *Only a photo*, she reminded herself. *He's not here. He can't touch you.*

Reyes wouldn't let him.

She couldn't look away from his hated face. In a voice that didn't sound like her own, she whispered, "That's him."

A second later, Reyes snapped the laptop shut and circled around the table to put his hands on her shoulders. "Jesus, Madison. A little warning would have been nice."

Disconcerted, Madison rushed out an apology. "I'm so sorry. I was just excited with my find."

Kennedy managed a nod. "It's okay." It really was. She *wanted* to be kept informed. She just… The casual way they dealt with everything surprised her. "I appreciate all the trouble you're going to for me."

Sterling squeezed Kennedy's hand, and it felt like she understood. *Really* understood.

Possibly because she'd been through the same thing.

"I knew you were on his trail," Sterling said, "and that you'd narrowed down his location. But now you've found him?"

"I believe so." Madison nearly buzzed in her seat. "I'm sorry to throw more at you, Kennedy."

"I needed to know." With Reyes at her back, she felt better equipped to deal with the shock. "It's just… I had hoped he was dead."

"For sure, that'd be better," Sterling agreed.

"Eventually," Parrish said with quiet assurance.

Once she recovered from Parrish's comment—*had he just promised her that her abductor would die?*—she reclaimed her backbone. Everyone was watching her. Somehow, in the midst of this amazing meal, she'd hogged all the attention…by being pathetic.

"Where is he?" she asked Madison, trying for a note of interest instead of dread.

Now that she'd dropped her bombshell, Madison began filling her plate. "He's in Cedarville."

"Hmm," Sterling mused. "Close enough for us to come up with a plan."

"Probably chose that location for being near where I-70 and I-25 interconnect," Cade said.

"Giving him plenty of escape routes," Reyes added.

They were all so knowledgeable about human trafficking that Kennedy felt like a dunce. She'd suffered it, she'd learned what she could, but she didn't have their ease in discussing it, their quick assessment of the current situation.

"Given that he's not that far from Jodi, I'll set up surveillance around that entire area," Madison said. "I'll also get into any computers he has, see if I can find an agenda or financials or anything helpful."

"How?" Kennedy asked, both fascinated and boggled.

Madison lifted her brows. "How will I set up surveillance, you mean?" With a shrug, she said, "I'm good. I think I told you that already. I'll access any cameras in the area to see who's coming and going. They're staying at a Roadway Motel, in one of the separate cabins. Cheesy little dump, but surely they have some sort of security cameras, usually at the front and back doors, and sometimes in the lobby. Once I see what vehicle he's using, one of the boys can tag it for me. Then I'll be able to see them whenever they're on the road."

"GPS," Kennedy said, remembering that they'd done the same with Jodi's car.

"Exactly."

Bernard reappeared in the doorway, his critical gaze taking in her still-full plate. "Ms. Brooks, you aren't enjoying your breakfast?"

It felt very much as if she'd just been chastised. "I'm sorry. Madison was discussing business and I got distracted."

"Madison is always discussing business, and if you don't wish to go hungry you need to learn to eat while she does so."

Damn, now even the butler was giving her a hard time. She scowled.

Unfazed by that, Bernard added, "Once you've finished eating, I'd be happy to let you visit with Chimera and her adorable kittens."

As far as incentives went, that was a good one.

"Thank you, Bernard. I'll get busy eating right now."

He tipped his head in a nod of acceptance and went back inside again.

Kennedy glanced at Sterling. "He doesn't eat with the others?"

"Sometimes. It all depends on Bernard's mood." She gave a crooked grin. "They treat him like family, even when he really ramps up the airs, as he's doing for your sake."

He wanted to impress her? Kennedy couldn't think of the last time that had happened. Then again, it was better than being rudely scrutinized by Parrish.

The conversation turned casual while everyone paid homage to the magnificent breakfast. When she'd finished, Bernard appeared again with fresh coffee. He refilled everyone's cups, removed the empty dishes to the cart and again excused himself.

Kennedy had just sat back in her chair, the fragrant coffee held between her hands, when Madison again opened her laptop.

"Now that Bernard is appeased, I have one more detail to share."

"Course you do," Reyes said, already frowning. "Think you can use a little more tact this time?"

"Not really, because it's a bombshell." She turned to Kennedy. "Prepare yourself."

Good Lord, what now?

With a huff, Reyes came around to her seat. Standing beside her, he said, "Let's hear it."

"Delbert O'Neil isn't alone at the motel."

Kennedy did her best not to react to that, but dread poured through her. "That's the name of the man who escaped the car that day?"

"None other."

Sterling sat forward. "I heard you say '*they* were at the motel' earlier, but I assumed you meant him and a cohort. Don't tell me he has women in that room." Before Madison could reply, Sterling pushed back her chair. "Damn it, Madison, why didn't you say so right off?"

Cade stopped her with a hand lightly clasping her shoulder.

"Not women." Cade watched his sister carefully. "Not for a second would Madison let that slide."

Madison gently confirmed to Sterling, "No, I wouldn't."

"Damn." Sterling dropped back in her seat. "Sorry."

"No apology necessary, I promise." To the table at large, she explained, "Delbert isn't alone…because he has Rob Golly with him."

Kennedy's jaw loosened. Her brain scrambled to make sense of that. *Jodi's abductor and her abductor had teamed up together?* She reached back for Reyes's hand and immediately felt his fingers close around hers. "How is that possible?"

"It seems obvious to me," Parrish said, his expression a mask of cold rage, his tone softly lethal. "One of them knows that you and Jodi are friends, and he's looking for assistance to—"

"Don't say it," Sterling whispered.

But Kennedy already knew. Those evil men wanted revenge, against her, against Jodi. They wanted it enough that they were collaborating. Though her throat felt tight, her voice sounded strong when she said, "I understand." She stared back at Reyes. This was his expertise, after all. "What should I do now?"

Reyes gently tugged her from her seat and into his arms, where he held her close. "Easy enough." He stroked a hand up and down her spine. "You let us deal with it."

"Deal with it how?"

He shrugged. "Like Dad said, we kill them both."

FINALLY, HE'D GOTTEN AWAY. Del wiped his brow, wondering when, or if, he'd be the next target. Psychopaths didn't take kindly to having their plans disrupted.

The second Golly had left the cabin to get coffee from the diner next door, Del had pulled on his pants, grabbed a few of his belongings and dodged out to the parking lot where he got behind the wheel of his junker car.

After weeks in that deranged fucker's company, Del could practically taste the freedom. Cigarette butt clenched in his teeth, he inserted the key and turned it. Thankfully, the car started.

He realized his hands were shaking and his heart beat double time. Was this how the women felt when they were captured? Oddly enough, that realization excited him.

Usually he feared no one. When threatened, he reacted with deadly force. But the dude who'd been sharing the shack with him had too many people on his payroll, too many contacts who would know to look at Del first. He was part of a bigger machine, and if he crossed Golly...? Del knew he'd rather have cops after him than that vicious bastard.

At least the cops wouldn't torture him as payback, then dump his broken body off a cliff.

What Del wanted now was to grab Kennedy, maybe enjoy her

for a day, then he'd shut her up for good—and get as far from Colorado as he could manage.

First things first, he'd call on Jodi. One way or another, she'd tell him what he needed to know about Kennedy, and then all his plans would fall into place.

AFTER REYES AND KENNEDY left the deck for a stroll down to the lake, Cade glanced at his father. "What do you think?"

The senior McKenzie flattened his mouth. "Reyes isn't you. This could be nothing. Passing interest, maybe."

Sterling snorted. "Come on, Parrish. You're too sharp to believe that BS." She sipped her coffee. "I think he's in love and just hasn't realized it yet."

"Love?" Parrish dismissed that with a scowl. "That's a massive leap from mere interest."

Over the cup, Sterling narrowed her eyes at Parrish. "See, I expected *you* to have learned from past mistakes."

"Meaning what, exactly?"

Cade loved watching his wife put his stodgy, overbearing father in his place. She managed it in her frank, no-nonsense way, and even Parrish wasn't immune.

"Play nice, already," Sterling suggested. "Quit trying to alienate her, because you might just alienate Reyes, too. If she's going to be around, and I'm betting she will, what purpose does it serve to piss her off?"

Parrish gave Sterling a deadpan look. "Did I *piss you off*, Sterling, when we first met?"

"You and Reyes both," she confirmed, then she smiled back at Cade. "Good thing he was worth it, or I'd have disappeared that first day."

God, Cade loved her. From the start, Sterling, or Star as he called her, had proved to be the strongest woman he knew—with the biggest heart. She was unique, outspoken, capable, bold, and every so often, only with him, she also showed her vulnerability.

In every way, she was it for him.

Initially Cade had avoided commitment, thinking what he and his family did would be difficult for an outsider to digest.

Star had surprised him. She'd not only accepted it, she'd been excited to take part.

The woman who'd wanted to face the world alone, on her own terms, had seamlessly joined his family.

He glanced at his sister. "No talking to Detective Albertson."

She didn't bother to look up when she replied, "I'll speak to whomever I want. You're my brother, not my boss."

Cade switched his gaze to his father, waiting for his reaction.

"Madison," his father said silkily. "I expect you to keep your head."

"As opposed to how my brothers behave?" She shot Cade a tight smile and then held up a hand to forestall any protests from the men. "Your sexism has already been exposed, so spare me."

Sterling gave a small clap of approval.

"Has it occurred to either of you that Crosby might have information we don't?"

"We are *not* going to involve the law in this," Parrish stated.

Madison ignored that to say, "You raised me to balance what I give with what I take. Reyes and Cade aren't the only ones who can ferret out details by talking to others."

Cade sat back with a sigh. "You're literally looking for reasons to see him again."

"It's a shame that I must justify those reasons, while you and Reyes just go about doing as you please."

Grinning, Star elbowed Cade and murmured, "She's got you there."

Folding her hands on the table, Madison smiled at each of them. "Let me put it this way. I am in charge of research, and I expect the freedom to work in whatever way I see fit. I also expect the same level of trust given to my brothers." Her chin lifted. "Now, is there anything else you want to say on the subject?"

Star snickered.

Cade rolled his eyes.

After sipping his coffee, Parrish cleared his throat. And, wonder of wonders, he moved past the topic of Crosby Albertson to ask, "Have you found anything on Kennedy that we need to know about?"

"Anything that would make her unsuitable for Reyes?" Madison shook her head. "No. She has a full life that doesn't include fighting traffickers so, unlike Sterling, I can't see her teaming up with us."

"The way Reyes hovers over her," Parrish said, "I doubt he'd allow it anyway."

That earned a glare from Star. "*Allow* it? Get out of the Stone Age, will you? Kennedy is her own person and she can do whatever she wants. She doesn't need Reyes's permission, or your approval."

"Christ," Parrish muttered, "they've joined forces."

Cade sat back and crossed his arms. Overall, he agreed with his wife—but it was fact, not opinion, that Kennedy wasn't cut out for their line of work.

"As I was saying," Parrish continued, "Reyes isn't Cade. I can't see him accepting someone with your..." He paused at Star's dark look. "That is, he doesn't have the same constitution to work beside a woman he loves."

"Good save," Cade said with a grin. "Actually, I agree. Good thing Kennedy doesn't appear to want to join the business. Which brings me back to my question. What do you think? And don't try to sell me on that passing interest line, either. Just the fact that he moved her in—"

"And brought her here," Madison added while scrolling on her laptop.

"—says she's completely different to him."

"That might be true, but it becomes more and more difficult to keep our secrets contained when my children insist on bringing outsiders into things."

Madison laughed. "You already knew they weren't choirboys, Dad."

"And you?" Star challenged. "You've as much as admitted that you're going to coordinate with Crosby."

"He's been following Rob Golly for a while," Madison said without much attention. Still scanning pages on her laptop, she added, "Now that I know where Golly is, it doesn't seem fair to keep that from Crosby."

"You'll move cautiously," Parrish decreed, "and you'll keep the rest of us informed every step of the way."

"Of course." Madison smiled. "We are a team, after all." She closed her laptop and stood. "But since I have all the research data, the rest of you will just have to trust me when I say that Crosby isn't a threat to us."

As she made a grand exit, Parrish stared after her.

Cade and Star shared a look.

Apparently, Cade thought, he'd started a movement when he fell for his wife. Now he only hoped his brother and sister would end up as happy as he was.

REYES SAT ON a boulder and pulled Kennedy between his thighs, wrapping his arms around her to keep her warm. Here, by the lake, a brisk breeze sent a shiver up her spine.

He kissed the side of her neck. "Want to go back to the house?"

"No, not yet." She settled against him, her hands curling over his forearms, which he'd crossed over her breasts. "It's beautiful here."

"Yeah." He'd always liked the lake. In the warmest part of summer, he and Cade had often swum in the water that seemed to be forever icy, fed by the mountain streams. "You did well with Dad."

She turned her head so he'd see her smile. "He's a tyrant, but I think overall he's just concerned about you."

Reyes knew exactly what ailed his dad: fear of another son getting caught up in a romance. Sterling had already shaken things up. His dad probably feared losing control of the entire enterprise if Reyes got serious with Kennedy.

Thinking that, he pressed a kiss to her temple. Serious? Damn right he was serious. Serious about keeping her safe. Serious about wanting her to be happy.

Serious about…making love to her again.

Definitely serious about that.

"What will happen next?" she asked.

He wasn't entirely sure, since he'd taken her from the table before plans could be made. "Likely Madison will want a few days to figure out if the bastards have a pattern of any kind. When they're in the motel, when they're on the road, where they go and for how long. Stuff like that. Once we know, we can figure out where to grab them."

"What if…" She rested her head back against his shoulder and, after a few seconds, started again. "What if they take other women before then?"

"We'd go in sooner." Even now, Kennedy was worried about strangers instead of herself. It occurred to him that her entire career was meant to protect others, to prepare them, educate them, so they wouldn't suffer the same fate she had. "One thing to know, babe. We never turn a blind eye to abuse. If shit happens that alters our plans, we adjust accordingly."

She sat up and turned to face him, her expression drawn in worry. "Have you ever been hurt?"

"Few times." He carried her fingers to his upper chest, near his shoulder. "Did you happen to notice the scar I have here?"

"Yes."

"Knife wound," he said. "I demolished the fucker who did that, by the way." He moved her fingers to his thigh. "The scar I have here? Graze of a bullet. Prick was trying to unman me but missed." He showed his teeth in a savage smile. "I didn't."

Her gaze searched his, and suddenly she was against him, her arms snug around his neck. "You could have been killed and I never would have met you."

Then she might have died, too, because who else could she have called on the night of the fire? No one. He crushed her closer. "I didn't, you didn't, and we're going to keep it that way."

"Sometimes," she whispered, "I'm so afraid."

He didn't want that. A healthy respect for consequences, yeah, that was good. But actual fear? She'd had enough of that in her life already. "Can you tell me anything else about O'Neil?" He'd kill the man who'd once taken her, who apparently hunted her now, and he wouldn't have a single moment of remorse. "Anything at all would be good."

Her arms loosened as she eased out of his embrace. "He was a chain-smoker." Absently she smoothed a hand along the side of his neck. "He was meaner when he drank—and he drank all the time."

Fucker. Reyes would take pleasure in ending him.

"You saw what he looks like. Faded blond hair, under six feet, I think, but I couldn't say for sure."

Because she'd been so young, and so traumatized, every man

had likely felt huge. Who paid attention to little details when survival was top of the list? "Any tattoos?" he prompted. "Jewelry?"

She touched her throat, down by her clavicle. "A snake tattoo."

"What kind of clothes did he wear?"

"I don't know." Pressing her fingertips to her temples, she frowned. "Jeans usually, I think. T-shirts." Sounding shamed, she said, "I tried not to look at him."

"You're doing great, babe." Pulling her hands down, he pressed small, soft kisses to each of her knuckles. "Anything else?"

She shook her head. "I'm sorry."

"That's plenty for now." An especially cold wind blew over the lake, and Reyes decided it was time to get back to business. "Know what I want to do?"

Her eyes were big and blue, her honey-colored hair moving with the wind. "Plan?"

"Yeah, that first." He stood and tugged her to her feet. "Then I'd like to take you home and strip you naked, and spend the day in bed."

Slowly the darkness left her expression, and her mouth curled into a smile. "I like that idea."

He realized he was being a selfish ass, so he offered her an out. "Unless you'd rather take in a movie first? Or if you have any shopping to do?"

Wearing an impish smile, she pretended to think about it. "Let me see. A movie, or you naked? Such a difficult decision."

Teasing right back, Reyes reached for her breast. "Or maybe we should just make use of this boulder? I don't think my family would spy on us, then we could head to a movie when we leave here."

She surprised him by laughing. "Don't tempt me." Holding his hand for balance, she carefully made her way down the boulder, then laced her fingers through his once they had their feet on the ground again. "Let's go get this planning over with. I can call Jodi on the way home." She flashed him a smile. "And *then…*"

"I'll show you how nice a day spent in bed can be."

Together.

He thought it, but didn't say it.

He had a lot of things to work out, including his attitude on going it alone. Kennedy might not realize it, but she'd altered his thinking on things.

Hell, she'd altered his entire existence. His habits. His convictions.

Maybe even...his heart.

CHAPTER THIRTEEN

KENNEDY AND BERNARD played with the cat and kittens while Reyes, Cade, Madison and their dad sat around a massive desk in the library making plans. She'd been confused at finding all the kittens there, until Reyes explained that his siblings always brought them along when they came to his dad's house. It was a compromise that pleased everyone, most especially Bernard.

It was decided that he and Kennedy needed to meet with Jodi again, to clue her in on the players and the risks. Kennedy wanted to make sure that Jodi knew she wasn't alone, that she had substantial backup so she wouldn't do anything reckless.

Made sense to Reyes, although that also added the risk that his father's enterprise might be exposed. Extra care, everyone agreed, was necessary.

Cade and Sterling would shadow them to Jodi's place, just to make sure they weren't ambushed. There was a good chance the goons might already know where Jodi was staying.

After all, they knew Jodi and Kennedy were friends. They'd torched Kennedy's apartment. They'd tracked them to the campsite.

So far, they'd been pretty damned determined.

Given the go-ahead, Reyes would happily move on them now. Unfortunately, his dad and Cade disagreed with that plan. Madison insisted they needed more info first, just in case other women were already targeted or even imprisoned.

It wouldn't do to kill the creeps without first knowing all the details.

Sterling, forever over-the-top, said, "We could use me for bait again."

Reyes and Madison were already shaking their heads.

Cade stated firmly, "Fuck that."

And Parrish gave her a long-suffering look. "By now, you should have realized there are better plans than putting yourself at risk. Haven't you learned anything from us?"

Grumbling, Sterling sank back in her seat. "My way is more expedient."

"Your way," Cade growled, "will never happen again."

She shot Parrish a glare. "I blame you for him being so bossy."

He dipped his head in acceptance. "I'll gladly take the credit."

While they bickered, Reyes became distracted by Kennedy's laugh. He turned to see her snuggling Chimera and one kitten, while Bernard held the other two.

The kittens were bigger now, but still undeniably cute. And he had to admit, with all the lavish attention Bernard gave Chimera, she was now a beauty.

Her all-white coat had gone from shabby to thick, and as soft as rabbit fur. Her googly, mismatched eyes—one pale blue, one yellow-green—often stared at Bernard with undiluted love and trust.

Bernard had been good for the cat. It was still a shock, realizing that stuffy Bernard had grown up on a farm and absolutely loved animals. He was too damned aloof, but with Chimera, he was a giant softie.

Of course Reyes wouldn't take the cat away. Hopefully, Kennedy understood.

In the middle of his dad and Cade going over reconnaissance for the motel, Reyes asked, "How do you feel about having the cats here?"

The two men looked up, confused. Sterling smiled and Madison kept her attention on her laptop.

"What?" his father asked, thrown by the off-topic question.

"Chimera and her three kittens. They don't bother you?"

"Bernard takes care of everything," Parrish said dismissively.

"There has to be cat hair, though, right?"

"Bernard cleans after them," Parrish reminded him, as if that explained it all.

Reyes started to mention the cat box, then changed his mind. Both his father and brother were looking at him as if he'd just announced a flight to Mars.

"Told you," Sterling said. "Totally smitten."

Now they all stared at her.

"What in the world does cat hair have to do with that?" Parrish asked.

Sterling nodded at Reyes. "He's thinking of home, hearth and pets, that's what. If not with Kennedy, then who?"

"Butt out," Reyes told Sterling, then to distract everyone, he asked, "Any news on Jodi?"

"So far she hasn't budged," Madison said. "She ordered pizza, though, and that can be risky, too."

Reyes hadn't heard Kennedy approach until she stood right beside him. "If ordering food is dangerous, how is she supposed to survive?"

Without thinking about it, Reyes tugged her into his lap. *She* thought about it, obviously, given her very rigid posture. The rest of the family did, too, as evidenced by their alert stares.

For crying out loud, couldn't a guy—

The buzzing of his phone saved him, or so he thought until he answered the call and Annette's feminine, flirty voice said, "I haven't heard from you in forever and I have a desperate *need* to see you." The emphasis on *need* plainly meant sex.

Shit. Here he was, his entire family watching him, Kennedy on his lap, and one of his regulars on his phone. Or rather, Annette had been a regular, until Kennedy had moved in with him.

"Hey," he said, stalling while he tried to think.

Sterling, who was always perceptive, cocked a brow and grinned at him. "It's a woman," she decided aloud.

Knowing he wore a deer-in-the-headlights expression, Reyes wasn't surprised when Cade said, "Probably."

He really wanted to blast them both, but he had Kennedy slowly twisting around to frown at him and Annette impatiently waiting.

He cleared his throat. "Just a sec, doll."

Even Madison looked up at that point, disapproval plain in the set of her mouth.

Right. Bad choice of endearments, but damn it, it was what he always called Annette. Habit and all that.

Before he could explain anything to Kennedy, she gave him a tight smile and jolted off his lap. "I'll give you some privacy."

Reyes watched her stride out of the room. Where she'd go, he didn't know. The house was big enough that she might lose her way if she wandered too far.

But then Sterling muttered, "Asshole," in his general direction and went after Kennedy.

Well, hell.

Annette said, "Catch you at a bad time?"

"Actually, yes." Avoiding Cade's gaze and ignoring his father and sister, Reyes stood and, undecided where to go, headed out of the library and around to the foyer. That didn't seem private enough, so he stepped outside and pulled the door shut behind him. "So."

"C'mon, Reyes," Annette urged. "I'll make it worth your while."

Out of the three women he generally saw for casual hookups, Annette was the most affectionate, yet none of them were demanding. Of course, he usually saw each of them a few times a month.

After he'd gotten Kennedy settled in his place...well, he hadn't given other women a single thought. That realization made him frown.

Annette, Cathy and Lili didn't want anything other than convenient sex, which was why they worked out so well for him.

Until Kennedy.

Damn. He'd changed without even realizing it!

Disgruntled by that realization, Reyes said, "Sorry, but tonight is out."

"When, then?" Her voice grew a little more strident. "Or is it just that you've lost interest in me? If that's the case, hey, tell me now and you won't hear from me again."

See, this was why he avoided relationships. This crap was awkward. He started to go the route of "it's not you, it's me," but Annette was sharp and she'd see right through that.

Maybe honesty was the way to go. Why not? "Actually, I've met someone and she's occupying all my time right now."

Silence. Long, heavy silence.

Followed by...laughter?

"What the hell, Annette?" Pacing, Reyes walked along the considerable length of the covered front porch, barely aware of dropping temps or the increasing wind.

"Oh, my God," she said around continued hilarity. "I almost peed myself."

"It's not that funny."

She went silent again, then snorted. "Don't tell me you're serious?"

Slowly Reyes blew out a breath. Snapping at Annette made him feel like a jerk. In a less annoyed tone, he admitted, "Trust me, I'm as surprised as you are."

"More like blindsided, but... Congrats?"

"It's not all that," he muttered. Or was it?

"All right. Then when it ends, give me a call. Pretty sure I'll still be free." With another chuckle, she ended the call.

When it *ends*?

Why did everyone keep bringing that up? Kennedy was always trying to figure out when it'd be safe for her to move on. Now Annette, too?

Eventually it'd have to happen, right? He hadn't changed *that* much, and for sure his vocation would stay the same. Kennedy wasn't Sterling. Even if he wanted something more with her, something...permanent? He couldn't see her accepting the family enterprise.

She had an idea of things now, but he doubted she understood the scope of it all, or the fact that hunting scumbags and freeing victims was the focus rather than a side job. Everything else centered on it.

Besides, she'd made it clear already that she wasn't looking for anything permanent, either.

He thought of her expression when Annette had called. He'd label it a mix of hurt and disappointment. Her gaze had looked distant, her smile forced.

Could that be jealousy? Or just discomfort over the situation?

He was so lost in thought he didn't hear the front door open and close until his father said, "Staying out here won't solve anything."

Reyes turned, caught his father's enigmatic expression and shrugged. "Just finished my call." He shoved the phone back in his pocket. First thing, he'd get hold of the other women and make sure they knew he was out of commission for the foreseeable future. He didn't want to go through that awkwardness again.

Parrish leaned against a stone pillar. "Anything important?"

"Nah." Glancing at the door, he said, "Sorry for the interruption."

"You're distracted. That's dangerous."

"I'm not," he denied. Hell, even if he was, Reyes knew his training would take over when necessary. Like muscle memory for a fighter, his reactions had become instinctive. He was damned good at what he did, and beyond that, he would do whatever it took, however he needed to do it, to protect Kennedy.

Damn it, his thoughts had just circled back to her again.

Parrish didn't press him. "Cade will leave soon to check out the motel."

He didn't want to, but Reyes said, "I could go with him."

"Sterling is going. It won't be too dangerous since they're only going to scope out the egresses, the security cameras and the outlying area, and see if there are any guys on watch."

"Makes sense." His dad was reluctant to admit it, mostly because he worried for her, but Sterling knew what she was about. The lady had ingenuity galore, was a little too brave, and her instincts were pretty spot-on; however, she wasn't always as cautious as she could be.

"You," Parrish said with emphasis, "need to talk to Kennedy. Whatever your personal situation might be, work it out. Now that we're involved, we'll be seeing this through to the end. But she's still an outsider and if she gets resentful and talks, it puts us all at risk."

"She wouldn't."

Parrish studied him intently. "You're sure of that?"

"Hundred percent." It was a weird thing to realize how much he trusted Kennedy. "I doubt it's necessary, but I'll emphasize to her the need to keep things private." *After* he soothed her temper—and after they spent a few hours in bed.

That is, if she was still on board for that. It was never a good idea to make assumptions with women.

Never a good idea to keep one waiting, either, especially when her imagination might be in overdrive. "Where is Kennedy anyway?"

"Off with Sterling still."

Yeah, that didn't reassure him. He wanted to charge off to find her, but his dad was still giving him the stink eye, so he waited, doing his best to act like a man without a care.

Parrish walked to the end of the porch, his gaze off in the distance. "We'll get snow soon."

"You think?" He gave the darkening skies a critical glance.

"They're predicting a few inches, but if it turns into more, it could hamper us."

For some reason, Reyes found himself scowling. "Something on your mind, Dad?"

His father, still a big man with a strong physique, relaxed a shoulder against the stone pillar. "Your mother would have been proud of you, Reyes."

What. The. Fuck. Reyes looked around, but no, there was no one else to hear, so he rubbed the back of his neck and stepped closer. "You think?"

"She loved each of you equally." He glanced back. "Cade included."

"I know, Dad."

Cade might be a half brother, but no one in their family had ever made the distinction. He was a McKenzie, plain and simple.

Turning his gaze to the horizon, Parrish said, "Even before Cade went away, you were a wild one. Always too daring, always too quick to challenge."

More uncomfortable by the second, Reyes wasn't sure what to say. But he sensed his father needed to talk, so by God, he'd man up and listen. "I was a shithead."

A crease in Parrish's cheek told Reyes he was smiling. "That you were. All cocky bravado and such a know-it-all. So different from your reserved brother and your studious sister."

"Mom used to accuse me of giving her gray hairs."

Parrish laughed. It was a rare sound these days. "I miss her every single day."

"I know." Standing at Parrish's back, Reyes put a hand on his shoulder.

A full minute passed in companionable silence while the wind worsened and the temperature slowly dropped.

"My point," Parrish finally said, "is that I want you to know the difference a good woman can make to your life."

Because his father was often cagey, Reyes wasn't sure how to take that statement. Was he recommending Kennedy as the good woman, or cautioning Reyes that he should wait for more? "Tie the ends together for me, will you, Dad? I don't yet know if I want to be pissed or not."

Grinning, Parrish faced him. "When in doubt, you tend to go for pissed."

"Might happen now, too, so a little clarity would be nice."

"All right. I'm your father. I know you, understand you, and I sometimes see things in you that you don't see in yourself."

"Example?"

"You're different with Kennedy. You care more than you realize."

"And?"

Buffeting his shoulder, his dad said, "Relax. I'm not maligning the girl. Just the opposite, actually. I want you to know that there's more to life than vengeance, more than righting wrongs for strangers, more even than loyalty to your immediate family."

Whoa. When his dad decided to do a heart-to-heart, he went all in. Loyalty to family was a big one for him, which made it a big one for Reyes, too. "With you so far."

Parrish clasped his hands behind his back and again gazed at the tranquil surroundings. "Quiet nights in the evening with someone special—you can never discount the importance of that. Having that person to talk to when things happen..." His words stopped.

Reyes could have sworn he was struggling, and he couldn't bear it. "I get what you're saying, Dad. You had that with Mom."

"I had everything with her. In a very different way, Cade has that now with Sterling." His mouth firmed. "I want that for you."

Since that made him uncomfortable, Reyes asked, "And Madison?"

Groaning, Parrish shook his head. "Call me sexist, but no, I'm not ready to let go of my little girl yet."

"Little." He snorted, more to lighten the mood than anything else.

"Don't tell Sterling I said that. She'll eviscerate me—verbally if not physically."

True enough. He smiled at his dad, feeling an extra sense of companionship. "She's something, isn't she?"

"Beyond anything I ever expected," Parrish agreed. "And she's perfect for your brother."

"I know, right?" It still boggled his mind that his military-straight, control-freak brother had fallen headlong in love with a woman like Sterling. Boggled him, and made him happy as hell.

"Now for you." Parrish gave him a level look. "Kennedy is smart, accomplished, and she quickly adapts. I looked over Madison's notes on her, and it's astounding how she's moved on with her life, how she's always thinking of others."

"I noticed that, too. It's like she's fashioned her own existence to try to save others, not in the guns-blazing way we use, but by arming them with knowledge."

"It's admirable," Parrish said. "I respect her, and I like her. I especially like how she watches you. If she says things are casual, don't buy it. She's emotionally invested, and I think she's been through enough without adding heartbreak to the mix. If you aren't serious about her, let her go and we'll figure out some other way to keep her safe."

"No." Reyes tried not to glare, especially since he caught his dad's meaning. Parrish didn't want to see Kennedy hurt.

Reyes didn't, either. The idea that *he* might hurt her was excruciating. Still, he couldn't let her go.

Not now, not tomorrow or next week. Not ever?

Parrish again clasped his shoulder. "Figure out what it is you want, while keeping in mind what I've said. It isn't often that a woman can upend your world, and if she does, it probably means she's the one. Let the right one go, and you'll be regretting it for the rest of your life." Parrish headed for the door. "Now come inside. I'm freezing my balls off."

Cracking a loud laugh, Reyes followed his dad. Yeah, he had a lot to think about. But first he had to find Kennedy.

Dodging the rest of the family, he searched the house until he finally heard female voices coming from the kitchen. Peeking in, he saw Sterling and Kennedy sitting together at the table, and thank God, Bernard was nowhere around.

Reyes had started to intrude when he heard Kennedy say, "He has a right to his own life. If I'm not mad, you shouldn't be mad."

Sterling snorted. "There's no way you're sleeping with him and not at least a little irked that he's hearing from other women."

Right? She should be irked, shouldn't she?

Kennedy shook her head. "He's been with me nonstop, playing babysitter and protector and everything else, so I know he hasn't slept with anyone since I crashed into his life—though I did encourage him to."

Flopping back in her seat, Sterling said, "Shut the door! You can't mean that?"

"Granted, I was glad he didn't take me up on that offer. Pretty sure my imagination would have gone into hyperdrive if I'd known he was out sleeping around." Kennedy let out a huff. "But if he wants to talk to other women, if he chooses to arrange something, it's not for me to interfere. Our...association is casual at best. Once the danger's over, I'll move on and—"

"You can't be that blind."

"Not blind, no. But I'm a realist. All this?" Kennedy gestured as if to encompass the entire house with everything and everyone in it. "I'm not cut out for that life and Reyes knows it."

"Know what I think?" Sitting forward, Sterling folded her arms on the table. "I think you're usually pretty brave, but now you're being a chickenshit."

Kennedy sputtered.

Taking that as the perfect segue, Reyes strode in. "Feels a little different when you're the target of all her vitriol, huh?"

As she stood, Sterling smirked at him. "Since you're now here,

instead of off chatting with some other woman, I'll leave you to it."
She lightly elbowed him on her way out, murmuring, "Good luck."

"Thanks." Reyes took her vacated chair. Kennedy wasn't quite
looking at him, and color tinged her cheeks. "Sterling tends to cut
to the heart of the matter, doesn't she?"

"Maybe she doesn't know as much as she thinks she does."

He grinned at that. "Ah, so you're not being a chicken? You
really are okay with me making a few booty calls? Because you
know that's all it was with Annette, right? I didn't see her in any
serious way."

"Just when you had an itch?" she asked, mocking him.

It seemed easiest to just come clean, so he said, "I slept with
her, and with Cathy and Lili and, when the opportunity presented
itself, a few other women as well. We had an arrangement. They
didn't want anything other than sex, and neither did I."

"Yet she called you."

"Because I haven't…had an itch recently." He dipped in before
Kennedy could guess his intent, and put a firm smooch on her lips.
"These days, I'm only interested in sleeping with one woman."

She fried his ass by saying, "I guess there's something to be
said for convenience."

Sitting back, Reyes scowled. "Now you're just trying to piss
me off."

"No, I'm being serious." Leaving her seat, she went to the window to gaze out. "If I'm honest—"

"Yeah, let's try that." He stared at her proud shoulders and saw
her stiffen.

"Being honest," she began again, "it'd be less awkward for me
if I know you aren't with anyone else. But Reyes, I meant what I
said. You're doing enough for me as it is, and if you prefer to—"

"Just so we're clear," he interrupted in a voice gone low and
dangerous, "I'll be fucking furious if you think to sleep around
somewhere else."

She spun to face him, her brows up in surprise, not in the least
alarmed at his tone. In fact, she smiled. "That'd hardly be possible
when I have to stay glued to you for safety reasons." The smile
twitched. "I can't see you trailing along for that errand."

He narrowed his eyes.

"And I wouldn't presume to invite someone else into your house, so—"

Son of a bitch. He shot out of his seat and advanced on her. "I don't want anyone else, so for me it's a moot point. For *you*, if you're thinking of—"

Laughing, she pressed against him, her arms sliding around his neck, her body flush to his. "I'm glad."

"Glad?" He didn't understand her at all.

"Glad that you don't want anyone else." The smile softened. "Sterling is right. I was being chickenshit." Then she laughed again. "How could you think for even a second that I'd want another man with you around?"

"I'll admit I was stymied by the notion." While she snickered, he wrapped his arms around her waist and kept her *right there*, as close to him as possible—where she belonged. "I can't promise to have all the answers, babe, but I know this isn't convenience for me. I don't want it to end just because the danger does. I want a chance to see where it takes us."

The humor faded away, replaced by something nearing satisfaction. "That sounds serious."

"Feels serious, too." He nuzzled her temple, pressed a kiss to her brow, then another to the bridge of her nose, and finally planted one on her sexy mouth, long and hungry and probably inappropriate for his father's kitchen.

But hey, it wasn't every day that he spilled his guts out.

When he let up, Kennedy put her forehead to his chest. Around faster, deeper breaths, she whispered, "Count me in as long as you promise to let me know if you change your mind."

"Done."

"And FYI, when it's safe, I definitely need to get my own place." When he started to protest, she spoke over him. "It's the only way we'll both know for sure."

"I already know I don't want us in separate places." Now that he'd had her with him, he couldn't imagine any other scenario.

Sleeping alone? No, thank you.

Quiet dinners without their conversations? He'd pass.

Missing her pre-coffee zombie impression? Mornings wouldn't be the same.

"Uh-huh," she said. "That's why you spent so long talking to your caller?"

Ah, there was a definite edge to her words, and damned if he didn't like it. It meant she wasn't as blasé about sending him off to other women as she pretended.

Turning her own phrase back on her, he said, "FYI, I wasn't talking to Annette that whole time. In fact, my conversation with her was short and sweet, consisting of me saying I was off the market, and her laughing her ass off at me."

Kennedy frowned. "Why, exactly, did she laugh?"

"Because the idea of me being in a relationship is hilarious as fuck, I'm guessing." He kissed her again for good measure. "And there you have it. You're so special, so sexy and unique, you have me doing things out of character."

Her expression went through several changes, caught somewhere between displeasure and hope. Finally she sighed. "I don't understand you."

"Makes two of us." He grinned. "But I'm coming to grips with it, so I hope you do, too. By the way, I took so long because Dad cornered me on the front porch. He gave me a real heart-to-heart, the gist of which was that I shouldn't screw this up or I'd be regretting it the rest of my life. So here I am, trying to figure things out and, truth, Kennedy, I'm not getting a whole hell of a lot of help from you."

Her eyes widened. "I don't want your family to pressure you."

Laughing, he stepped back and snagged her hand, drawing her out of the kitchen. "That's what you took from all that, huh? For sure, you'll keep me on my toes." The humor swelled within him. They had a looming situation of life-and-death proportions, and still she made him laugh. There couldn't be another woman like Kennedy anywhere. "C'mon. Let's go home."

"And get naked and do all those amazing things again?"

"Now you're talking."

"I just need a few minutes to say goodbye, and to give Chimera and her babies one last hug."

Kennedy might not realize it yet, but she already fit in with his family. She didn't need to be a computer geek like Madison, or a fighter like him, Cade and Sterling. She fit because of who she was, not what she could do.

His family liked her. He more than liked her.

Was she the one for him? It was sure starting to feel that way.

CHAPTER FOURTEEN

THE SNOW WAS already falling by the time they left. Big, fat flakes that quickly gathered everywhere, covering every surface in white. Kennedy thought it was beautiful, adding a fairy-tale feel to the terrain.

Shivering, she huddled in the passenger seat, wishing she'd brought a coat.

"Not warming up, yet?" Reyes turned up the heater.

"Getting there." He wasn't shivering, but he was probably too busy watching the road to bother with the cold.

When his cell phone rang, Kennedy jumped, then immediately scowled, wondering if it was Annette calling back, or maybe one of the other women he'd mentioned.

He surprised her by answering hands-free, so that the caller was on speaker.

"What's up?" he asked. "Make it quick, because the roads are shit."

"Sorry to bother you," Madison said. "Jodi just left the motel. Cade and Sterling are ready to go, but you'd still reach her before they do."

"What in the world," Kennedy said. "Why would she go out?"

"I don't think she's someone content to be cooped up," Madison answered. "She probably wants to face the threat, not hide from it."

"If she's alone," Reyes said, adding enough ominous overtones to make Kennedy worry that the men had gotten to her already.

"Do you think she's been taken?" She wasn't sure Jodi would survive a second time.

"Doubtful," Madison said. "I haven't seen any movement with the men, but I still don't like it. We found her easily enough, so they could have as well."

Reyes quickly pulled over to the side of the road. "I'm on it."

Kennedy had no idea what was going on.

"Keep me posted," Madison said, and disconnected.

Reyes got out and growled over his shoulder, "Follow me."

Twisting, Kennedy saw him walk to the rear door, open it, then flip up the seat.

She got out and hustled to the back of the truck. The sound of her boots crunching in the snow seemed absurdly loud.

Reyes removed a rifle from the storage space and set it aside.

Her eyes flared. "Expecting trouble?"

"Always." He retrieved a Glock and a bulletproof vest. Turning, he handed her the vest. "Put that on."

Her heart started pounding double time. "You really think—"

"Don't know, and I won't take chances with you." He tilted his head to indicate he wanted her back in the truck. Not knowing what else to do, and already shivering, she carried the heavy vest back to her seat. After he slid into the driver's side and closed the door, he stored the rifle on the floor near her feet.

"This is nuts," she muttered aloud while struggling into the vest.

"Here, let me help you." He reached for the Velcro strips and tightened them around her. "Look at it this way. The vest will help keep you warm." He stole a kiss then put the truck back in gear.

She made an abrupt decision. "I'm going to call Jodi."

"Not a bad idea. If she's in a listening mood, tell her to pull over someplace safe and wait for us."

Nodding, Kennedy quickly pulled up Jodi's number. At first it rang and rang without answer, until she was starting to panic. "Come on, Jodi," she urged. "Answer, damn it."

"'Lo."

Releasing a tense breath, Kennedy got herself together and affected a casual tone. "Hey, what's up?"

"Heading out for a bite to eat. Why?"

"Oh? Could you…" She glanced at Reyes, who had his attention on the road and the accumulating snow. Without coming right out and saying so, he showed that he trusted her to handle this the right way. "Do you think you could put off your meal for just a bit? I'm on my way to see you."

"Why?" Jodi asked with suspicion. "You okay?"

"Yes, fine."

"After that mess we were in, you didn't seem fine. You seemed shook." She paused, then asked, "Where's your hulk? Don't tell me he's turned on you already?"

Kennedy almost gave into an eye roll. "He's right here with me, Jodi. Now can you pull over?"

"Not that I won't enjoy seeing you, but you should be holed up somewhere, staying safe."

Exasperated, Kennedy countered, "As should you. At least I'm not alone, but you are, and really, Jodi, I thought you'd stay put until you heard from me."

"Sorry, but I was getting antsy. I felt like a sitting duck, ya know?"

Yes, she understood that well enough. Between the fire at her apartment and Reyes taking her in, she had felt the same. "Please, pull over."

"I already took the on-ramp, but I can get off at the next exit. That's where I was headed anyway. There's a little diner that truckers use. Might take me another five minutes or so." Jodi named the exit and the diner. "How's that sound?"

Reyes held up a hand, flashing five fingers first, then two.

"I'll be there in under ten minutes. Go directly inside and wait, okay?"

"Sure, Mom," Jodi quipped. "Later."

"From what I saw of her car," Reyes said, "it's not exactly roadworthy in this weather." The wipers cleared the windshield of a continuous stream of snowflakes and ice. "I have a bad feeling, babe."

Well, hell. His bad feeling immediately became her bad feeling, too. "What's that supposed to mean?"

"Instincts kicking in."

Kennedy spotted the exit up ahead. "That didn't take any time at all."

"I know, but I didn't want to give her an exact time frame."

Because he thought Jodi might use the information to plot against them? She shook her head. "Still not trusting her?"

Reyes snorted.

Thanks to the snowstorm, the stretch of road was quiet with only a few cars present. "This is like a whiteout." It wasn't uncommon for Colorado, where the weather could be mild, then turn to a blizzard, especially at this time of year.

"At least it's not a bomb cyclone," Reyes murmured. "And luckily it's mostly melting on the road. Guess the pavement is still warm from the earlier sunshine."

Up ahead, alone in the lot, Jodi sat in her car with her cell phone in hand.

"Why hasn't she gone in yet?"

Reyes shook his head and then pulled in with some distance between them. "Stay put while I check it out."

"She won't want to see you."

"She doesn't get everything she wants. Now will you stay in the truck?"

Kennedy nodded. "Do you need the rifle?"

"Got the Glock," he said, stuffing it in the waistband at the back of his jeans and pulling his flannel shirt over it. "Sit tight. I'll be right back." Without another word, Reyes got out and closed the truck door.

Jodi saw him approaching. Her eyes widened as she twisted to look out the driver's window, staring toward Kennedy. Her mouth opened in a warning that Kennedy couldn't hear.

Reyes stiffened, started to turn to her, and suddenly a car came careening toward him, forcing him to jump back. He landed half over the back fender of Jodi's car, then got badly jarred when the other car crashed into hers. He ended up thrown to the other side.

Horrified, Kennedy screamed his name. *What to do?* Reyes had told her to stay put, but now she couldn't even see him. What if he was horribly hurt? What if he was knocked out, making it easy for them to kill him?

In a single heartbeat she noted there were four men, three

swarming out of the car and one still revving the engine as he slowly pulled away from Jodi's car.

Jodi was no longer in the front seat.

Mind made up, Kennedy removed her seat belt and grabbed the rifle. She had no idea how to use it, but they wouldn't know that. Maybe she could bluff long enough for Reyes to... She didn't know. Get his bearings? Recover?

Not die.

Just please, God, don't let him die.

She opened the door to step out—and hard hands grabbed her from behind.

DELBERT COULDN'T BELIEVE it when he got to Jodi's motel and found her driving away. He followed her to the mostly empty lot of a dive diner, staying back so she wouldn't spot him, and lo and behold, Kennedy was there. He couldn't have planned it more perfectly.

Seeing her made him want her even more. With success almost at hand, he felt the urgency burning through his blood.

Just as he pulled into the back of the lot, grateful for the thick snowfall that helped conceal him, an attack happened with a car trying to run over the big guy, no doubt to remove him so they could get to Jodi.

Didn't take a genius to know his cohort had set up the whole thing—without even telling Del about it! What a double-crossing bastard. Now Del was glad he'd bailed without a word. Let the prick have Jodi.

Del only wanted Kennedy.

Taking advantage of the chaos, he pulled up behind the truck and crept forward on foot. Thinking to use the butt of his gun to shatter the passenger window, he was stunned nearly stupid when Kennedy actually stepped out. So she wasn't a cowering girl anymore?

Better and better. He'd enjoy seeing her fight her fate.

Any second now that big bruiser could be on them, and Del would lose his chance.

While she was focused on the scene before her, he locked a tight arm around her throat, ensuring she couldn't make any noise, and jammed the barrel of his semiautomatic to her temple. "Drop the rifle or I'll kill you right now."

Her entire body shuddered, but she held on to the weapon.

The bitch had gotten a lot gutsier.

"Or," he breathed against her cheek, tightening his arm even more, "I'll tell the others to kill your boyfriend. What do you think?" She, of course, didn't know that he now worked alone, that he was as surprised as her to see men on the scene.

As she struggled for air, she dropped the rifle with a clatter.

Del looked up to see her bodyguard wasn't out of commission after all. No, he was rapidly annihilating everyone.

"Fuck." Spinning Kennedy around, Del smacked her hard in the head with his gun. Her eyes rolled back and she slumped hard into the door, shattering the window after all—and no doubt drawing attention to them.

She was a small woman, but her deadweight wasn't easy for him to lift, not with his gun still in hand.

Awkwardly dragging her, he stuffed her through the driver's door and climbed in beside her. In that single suspended moment of time, a golden-eyed gaze locked on his. Del saw his own death in those cold eyes. The big bruiser started toward him in a flat-out run.

With escape as his main goal, Del screeched out of the lot as fast as he could. He couldn't help the shudder of dread that raced down his spine. He'd seen a lot of shit in his days, but he'd never seen rage like that.

And it had been directed at him.

Glancing in the rearview mirror, he didn't yet see the big guy's truck following, so maybe he had a chance. Where to go, though? Not back to the motel where Crazy lived. That bastard would probably torture Kennedy just for amusement. By the time he finished, there wouldn't be enough of her left for Del to enjoy.

When she suddenly groaned, he glanced her way. Already a colorful knot swelled on her temple. She still looked dazed. "Be glad it's just me, girlie. If I hadn't left that crazy fuck when I did, you'd be dealing with real trouble right now." He snickered. "I mean, I'm trouble. But that other dude? Even I didn't want to deal with him anymore. I cut our association just today—and as luck would have it, I found you."

She shifted, and it occurred to him, perhaps a moment too late, that her feet were against him. Half-watching the icy road, he tried to adjust her, but then...

Drawing up her knees, she kicked like a mule, one foot catching him in the shoulder, the other in his jaw. The old car swerved on threadbare tires, sliding sideways on the slick roadway. The gun fell to the floor near his feet as he tried to keep from crashing.

Kennedy launched at him.

What the hell?

Like a pissed-off wildcat, she clawed at his face, scoring his cheek and jaw. Damn it, it hurt. Sure, he'd wanted a little fight in her, but not this berserker shit! *"Bitch,"* he roared. "You'll kill us both!" One-handed, he tried to fend her off, but she was throwing punches left and right, and somehow she managed to get him right in the junk.

Ah, *hell.*

Breath left him in a gravelly moan, and his hands went slack on the wheel. She took advantage, striking him again and again.

That did it. The car hit an icy spot and whipped sideways, slammed hard into a guardrail and then tumbled half over into a ravine.

He'd finally gotten Kennedy, only to die in the process.

AT THE LAST POSSIBLE SECOND, Kennedy realized they would wreck and that it would be bad. She grabbed for the seat belt, got her hand and wrist tangled in it, but didn't have time to fasten it around her. She held on tight, trying to keep herself from being thrown around.

When the car hit the guardrail, it felt as though her entire body took the impact. Her head smacked the side passenger window, making her see stars for a moment, then she felt the car sliding over the berm and very real terror scrabbled through the angry haze that had encompassed her.

If they rolled, she didn't know if she would survive. Only her tangled grip on the seat belt kept her from bouncing from one end of the car to the other.

Delbert wasn't so lucky.

Her thigh jammed against something sharp, and her elbow hit the dash. He landed against her. She screamed, as much out of dread as pain.

When the car came to a jolting stop, they were at an odd angle, with her passenger door against the ground.

Delbert O'Neil, his face covered in blood, slumped against her, pinning her down. She clenched her teeth as she tried to move.

Please let Reyes be okay. Let Jodi be safe.

Delbert moaned, but otherwise didn't move.

Her situation couldn't be more dire. How far had they traveled? Her head split with pain, thanks to how he'd clunked her before they'd wrecked. Her wrist burned and ached, likely from how she'd held the seat belt.

Pressing a hand to her heart, she felt the rapid *thump, thump, thump* of her terror, but she also knew she was alive—and she intended to stay that way.

Looking around, she realized she saw two of everything. She also felt like puking. That couldn't stop her, though. She had to move, right now, before Delbert came to.

If she passed out, who would send help for Reyes?

She assessed the situation as best she could and determined that first she had to get out from under his deadweight.

Easier said than done.

Little by little, she freed her trapped left arm and then her legs. Every small movement hurt, but she used the pain as an impetus. If she could escape, then she could get someone to go back to help Reyes and Jodi. That, as much as her own safety, spurred her to haste.

Getting out of the car required her climbing over Delbert. She literally held her breath and was thankful when he remained out.

As she was maneuvering, she spotted his gun jammed up between the dash and the badly cracked windshield. Getting it meant climbing over him again, but she couldn't leave him armed.

Unlike Reyes, she wasn't comfortable putting the thing in her pants, but the windows were shattered, so she tossed it out the driver's side where she'd have to exit. It landed on the snow-covered ground with a thud.

She was levering up and out, prayers on her lips, when suddenly

Reyes was there, scrambling down the ravine in a hazardous race, his face covered in blood, rage in his eyes.

Hurt, but alive, and the relief nearly did her in.

He slid in the snow, recovered, then bellowed her name.

Tears welled up, blurring her vision. Damn it, she'd held it together so far, and by God she wouldn't fall apart now.

"I'm okay," she said more softly, glancing back at Delbert, hoping Reyes hadn't roused him.

She screamed when she saw his eyes open. He stared right at her.

Reyes reached in, caught her under the arms, and easily lifted her out. Standing her behind him, he withdrew his own weapon and looked in at Delbert.

Whatever he saw took some of the tension from his body. "Should I fucking kill you now?"

Unable to help herself, Kennedy peered around Reyes.

Delbert tried a laugh that mixed with a groan. Blood and spit seeped from his lips. "Might as well, because I'm dead either way."

"I have his gun," Kennedy whispered, touching Reyes's arm. "I threw it out the window."

Giving up on Delbert for the moment, he turned to her, glanced over her body, and his mouth flattened. "Come here." Sweeping her up into his arms, he took a few steps until he reached a jutting, snow-covered rock. Carefully, he set her down and brushed back her hair with a shaking hand. "If his legs weren't already broken, I'd break them slowly and with pleasure."

"What?" Delbert had broken legs? "How do you know—"

"You didn't notice the bones?"

When she quailed, he muttered, "Never mind."

Dear God. *Delbert's bones were showing*? A convulsive gag shook her, making her head ache even more.

Keeping his voice soft, Reyes supported her. "Do you need to be sick?"

"No." If she puked, her head would likely roll right off her shoulders. "No, I'm okay."

He pressed a kiss to her forehead. "Where are you hurt, baby?"

She started to say, *Pretty much everywhere*, but he looked so stricken, she whispered instead, "You're bleeding."

"It's nothing. My face hit the pavement when they tried to run me over."

"Reyes." The tears suddenly overflowed. "I didn't know if you were—"

"I'm all right. Jodi is okay, too. I left her with Sterling. Cade is right behind us."

"Actually, I'm here now," Cade said.

Kennedy jumped, felt the startle everywhere, and scowled. "Where did you come from?"

Gently Cade tipped up her face, staring intently into her eyes. "Pretty sure you have a concussion."

She was pretty sure she did, too. "I think Delbert hit me with his gun. It feels like he knocked something loose. Didn't help that I made him wreck—"

"Made him?" Reyes asked, while nudging Cade aside.

Remembering how she'd attacked him, she started shivering uncontrollably. The cold wind didn't help, sending icy snow to continually pelt her face. Tears filled her eyes again, making her madder than hell—at herself. Her lips trembled, too, and her voice emerged in an agonized whisper. "I thought you were badly hurt. I wanted to get back to you, but he was driving away… I couldn't let him do that, so I started kicking and hitting him."

"Jesus," Reyes murmured. "He might have killed you."

"That was his intent anyway, right?"

Cade's gaze swept the area, then settled on the car. "So it is Delbert O'Neil?"

Reyes nodded. "He's banged up pretty badly. Broken legs, looks like a dislocated shoulder, too. Face is scratched to hell and back."

"The last was me," Kennedy said, wanting her due. "I also punched him in the nuts."

Both men stared at her.

"That's when he completely lost control of the car."

"That could do it." After pressing a kiss to her forehead, Reyes peeled off his flannel shirt and wrapped it around her, leaving him in only a thermal Henley.

"You'll get cold—"

"Shh, babe, let me do something, okay?" He bent his knees to look into her face. "You saved yourself. You realize that, right? The least I can do is give you my shirt."

Cade cleared his throat. "Want me to do the honors?"

Reyes cupped a hand to her cheek. "We have to question him, and fast. How about you go with Cade—"

"I want to hear, too." She deserved to hear. Damn it, she felt so wretched, but she had to know it all.

"You're cold."

"No colder than you," she insisted.

After a split second, Reyes nodded and then lifted her in his arms again. With Cade at his side, he walked over to the car. Cade lifted Delbert's gun, dusted the snow off it, and then leaned into the car.

Delbert's eyes were closed but they opened real fast when Cade jostled his foot with the muzzle of the gun, causing him to hiss out an agonized breath.

"So," Reyes said. "You and Rob Golly."

The weirdest thing happened.

Delbert's eyes flared, then he managed a sickly smile. "*Rob* Golly? That's what you think?"

"It's what we know," Cade said.

"You're wrong. Rob is dead."

Held in Reyes's arms, Kennedy felt a little warmer, and yet she still couldn't stop shaking. The violent tremors racked her whole body. "I thought he was dead," she admitted, unable to look away from Delbert's battered face. *She'd done that.* Well, she and the wreck, which she'd instigated, so—

"I suggest you start talking," Reyes growled, "or I'll make you talk, and I guarantee you won't like my methods."

"I only wanted her," Delbert murmured, staring at Kennedy.

Reyes tried to put her down then, his intent obvious. Kennedy held tight. God only knew what he'd do if he touched Delbert right now.

She didn't think she could stomach more exposed bones or blood.

That didn't stop Cade from reacting. He grabbed Delbert's leg just beneath a break. "Look at her again," he whispered, "and you'll regret it."

The pain must have been unbearable, because Delbert screamed around a string of rank curses.

"Cops will be here soon." Reyes hugged her a little tighter. "You've got one minute to tell me what you know, otherwise you'll be dead when the law arrives."

Kennedy stared at Reyes, whose gaze remained on Delbert. Would Reyes kill him? She honestly didn't know—and she didn't really care.

"Rob Golly's death is what started it all," Delbert babbled. Despite the cold, sweat dripped down his white face.

"Then where's the body?" Cade asked.

"His brother took it." Delbert's breathing became shallow. "Bet you didn't know about the brother, did you?" Blood bubbled out of his mouth. "He and Rob look enough alike to confuse anyone." Del struggled with a shaky breath and his eyes sank shut. In a rasping voice, he said, "He's insane. I knew if he got to Kennedy first, there'd be nothing left..." Grimacing, he paused. "He'll kill all of you now. He wants Jodi bad for what she did to his brother. He'll make her pay. You'll all pay." They could barely hear when he whispered, "Everyone you know will pay."

Cade stiffened.

"Go," Reyes whispered, and just like that, Cade was scaling the hill back to his SUV.

Near her ear, Reyes said, "Sterling could be at risk, even in the parking lot at the diner."

So much trouble she'd brought to all of them. Her head was pounding as she made herself nod.

He lowered her, then pulled her to his side as he stepped in close to the car. "Stay right next to me, and don't interfere."

"All right."

"Where is Golly?" Reyes asked.

Delbert didn't respond. He looked like he might not be able to. Mouth tight, Reyes snapped, "Answer me."

Delbert's eyes barely opened. "Motel."

"He's still there?"

"It's where I left him..." Head slumping to the side, he said no more.

His face was so white, Kennedy didn't know if he'd gone into shock or if he'd died. In the distance, she heard sirens.

Very softly, Reyes said, "Be glad she destroyed you, or I'd be taking you apart right now."

Surprised by that, she tried to figure out what to say. Reyes already had out his phone, and she knew who he'd called when he said, "Dad. Yeah, we're all okay." His attention moved over her with a worried frown. "Kennedy's banged up, probably a concussion... Yeah, I'll tell her."

"Tell me what?"

Briefly he covered the phone. "That you're going to need a lot of rest."

Right. She could seriously use that rest right now.

Reyes uncovered the phone and shifted his gaze to Delbert. "Pretty sure this prick just died on me and cops are almost here— What? Why is *he* coming?"

Wondering who "he" was, Kennedy hugged herself and waited, resisting the urge to collapse onto the ground.

Reyes groaned. "So it was you, not Madison? No, I'm not questioning you." He looked up the hill, prompting Kennedy to do the same. "They're here now. Later. Yeah, I will."

"Who's here?" She instinctively moved closer, pretty sure she'd already used all her reserves for dangerous situations.

"Detective Albertson."

Oh. That wasn't so bad. In fact, it reassured her a little—as long as the presence of a cop didn't get Reyes into trouble.

Sure enough, Crosby started down the hill, followed by two uniformed officers.

Reyes called up to him, "Ambulance here?"

"Yes." Using a skinny, barren tree branch for support, Crosby finished his descent. "Kennedy, are you okay?"

Leaning into Reyes, she nodded.

"She needs medical attention," Reyes said.

"Looks like you do, too." Crosby surveyed them both, then said to the officers, "Help her up the hill."

"She goes nowhere without me," Reyes stated.

Crosby accepted that, then moved to look in the car. "Jesus."

One of the officers removed his coat and held it out. Thanking him, Reyes tucked Kennedy into it and then said to Crosby, "A word?"

Scowling, Crosby moved away from the car as paramedics reached them.

Reyes, keeping Kennedy with him, stepped closer to Crosby so no one else would hear. "That's Delbert O'Neil, scumbag trafficker."

"O'Neil," Crosby murmured, and a heartbeat later, his gaze shot to Kennedy. "That's how you're involved?"

"Medical care first," Reyes insisted. Then he asked, "You can clean up this mess?"

That earned Reyes a snort. "I can follow the law, yes." His gaze again went to Kennedy, who stood there shivering despite the layers she now wore.

She was too damn miserable to care how much attention she drew.

Sympathetic, Crosby said, "Give me the bare bones first so I know what I'm working with."

"We'd just pulled into the diner. Soon as I stepped out, someone tried to run me over. While I was diving for cover, O'Neil cracked her in the head, stuffed her in his car and took off. I was right behind him, but when Kennedy came to, she attacked him and the car went off the road." He gestured at the wreck. "This is how I found them. You saw O'Neil, with the results of the wreck."

"You didn't touch him?"

"Wish I could take the credit, but no."

As if he knew Reyes had skipped a lot of pertinent info, specifically about Jodi, Crosby frowned.

Kennedy thought he'd say more, until he again looked at her.

His expression eased from doubt to concern. "We can talk after you're feeling better. I'll be along to the hospital shortly."

"Thank you," Kennedy said, glad for the reprieve. At the moment, all she wanted was to close her eyes...after she got warm.

"Thank Madison," Crosby said. "She clued me in enough that I'm giving you some leeway now, as your father requested. Don't abuse it."

"I'll be in touch." Reyes guided her toward the hill. "Can you walk, babe?"

"Yes," she said, though she wasn't sure if that was true.

"Good. The fewer people I have to trust, the better I like it." After waving off the paramedics who had started toward her, he casually asked, "Did you know my father is a doctor?"

"No." Yet she wasn't surprised. She'd already learned to never underestimate the McKenzie clan.

"He was a renowned surgeon, actually. He's retired now, but still one of the best."

Unsure what that meant, she asked, "Why are you telling me this now?"

He steered her toward his truck instead of the ambulance. "Because we aren't going to the hospital." He opened the door to get her inside. "That's what Dad really wanted me to explain to you."

"But Crosby—"

"Will figure it out soon enough."

HE HOPED DELBERT was dead. It would save him the trouble of hunting him down and torturing him to death, the cowardly worm. How dare he interfere? It was because of him that Jodi got away once again.

Oh, how he'd wanted to grab her. There'd been enough chaos in the parking lot, combined with the snowstorm, that it probably would have been easy for his men to accomplish.

That is, until the other big man had shown up. That one looked as if he chewed thugs for breakfast. He had to be related to the one watching Kennedy. The size and overall facial features were the same.

Perhaps he needed a bomb, something that would indiscriminately destroy them all.

Everyone except Jodi.

When she'd killed his brother, she'd sealed her own fate.

He would always remember finding his brother broken, stabbed and bleeding in that dank basement cell, murdered by a worthless tramp.

Yes, it would be better if Delbert was dead. Then he could put all his considerable concentration on Jodi.

CHAPTER FIFTEEN

NEVER IN HIS life had he been in such a killing rage.

Once his dad had started to examine Kennedy, he'd found severe bruising everywhere. Earlier, she'd stood there in the freezing snow allowing him to prioritize everything and everyone—except her.

"She'll be fine," Parrish said as he moved Reyes out of the way yet again.

Fine, although she continued to shiver uncontrollably, wore a perpetually pained expression on her face and had obviously taken a battering when the car crashed.

Walking around the exam table, Reyes tucked the blankets over the side of her that his father had finished checking. His heart hurt. His eyes burned.

He seriously wanted to kill some bastards.

And he wanted to comfort Kennedy.

The conflict of two such disparate emotions made him shake.

He took her hand in his. She looked so small and delicate on the hospital bed, wearing no more than a loose, sleeveless gown that tied in the back.

With her eyes mostly closed, Kennedy gave him a wan smile. "Other than my ears ringing, and the pain in my head, I really am okay. I was hardly aware of the bruises."

Hardly aware. That was her being brave again. "I'm so sorry, babe."

"Not your fault," she whispered. "In fact, I should be apologizing. I brought this whole mess into your lives."

Parrish spoke before Reyes could react to that nonsense. "She has a concussion for sure, and she's going to be incredibly sore as the aches and pains sink in, but I don't think there are any fractures." After gently prodding the worst of the bruises on her thigh, he stared down at Kennedy. "How did you hurt your leg?"

Her eyes sank shut. "I don't remember."

"Hmm." Parrish gently examined her wrist and forearm. "And this?"

"I tangled my hand in the seat belt when I realized we were going to wreck."

Ever so carefully, Parrish manipulated her fingers and then her hand. "No pain?"

"Nothing too bad. Mostly my skin."

"It's like mat burn," he explained, and he put a light wrapping over it. With that done, he covered the rest of her with the blanket, all the way to her chin, then pulled up a rolling stool and sat near her. "Can you tell me what you do remember?"

She frowned for a long moment. "I saw Reyes hurt. He'd left the rifle with me, so I was getting out of the car, thinking maybe I'd scare them…"

Parrish glared at Reyes, looking furious again. "Cade grabbed the rifle," Reyes explained. "My only thought at the time was getting to her."

Nodding, Parrish turned back to her.

"Delbert told me he'd have the others kill Reyes if I didn't drop the rifle, so I did." She briefly closed her eyes. "I didn't know how to use it anyway."

"You're going to learn," Reyes said. Soon as possible, he'd teach her a hundred different ways to better protect herself. Not that she'd need to, because he wasn't ever letting her out of his sight.

"I guess he hit me, because I woke up in the car and there was Delbert." She drew a shuddering breath. "I was so afraid."

It was torturous for Reyes, seeing her like this. Yet he understood the need to have all the facts. She'd get through them soon, and then he could hold her.

She opened her eyes a fraction. "I knew Reyes had been attacked and I didn't know if he was—" Her hold on his hand tightened.

"It's okay, babe." Reyes wished he could take the discomfort for her.

"It's not okay. Look at your head."

Of all the...

"It was a small cut," Parrish said. "No stitches needed, just a few wound-closing strips. He'll be fine."

She swallowed heavily, her eyes growing damp again.

Reyes leaned in to kiss her forehead. "It's okay, baby. Take your time."

"I knew I had to do something."

"To save yourself," Parrish said with a nod of approval. "And you did."

"I wasn't really thinking of me. Not then. I just... I knew I had to somehow send back help for Reyes." She winced. "I know what I did was stupid. I could have killed myself. When it was happening, though, I couldn't reason anything out. I just knew I had to fight."

Reyes lifted her hand to his mouth. He should have been there to fight for her; instead, he'd allowed himself to be taken by surprise.

"They must have been following Jodi." He kissed her bruised knuckles. "I should have realized."

Kennedy looked at him for a long time and then gifted him with a slight smile. "Despite what you think and what your father tells you, you can't prepare for every situation. You aren't psychic, and you aren't invincible."

"But I've been trained—"

"No," Parrish said. "She's right. Madison sent you after Jodi. Cade and I approved that plan. If you're in the wrong, we all are, but I prefer to agree with Kennedy. We can only be so prepared." He got up to pace. "Golly's brother apparently hired people to watch Jodi. We don't know why Delbert was on the scene."

"I know." Shivering, Kennedy shifted uncomfortably. "He said the other man was real trouble, and so he'd left. Something about not wanting to deal with him anymore because he was too crazy. Delbert called him certifiable."

"Hmm." Parrish lightly patted her shoulder. "Thank you for sharing that. If you remember anything else, let us know. Until then, the pain meds I gave you should be kicking in soon. You need plenty of rest."

"No problem." She closed her eyes again. "Soon as I warm up, I'm ready for a nap."

Parrish smiled, but Reyes couldn't. "We'll get you to bed in just a minute."

"When you feel better," Parrish said, "and I promise you will, stay off the phone and computer, and limit television. Reyes, you'll want to check on her every couple of hours, just to make sure she's responsive."

"We'll stay here tonight," Reyes told her.

"Here?" She blinked at him.

"Remember, I have my own suite. It'll be fine."

"But…" She glanced at Parrish, then lowered her voice even more. "I want to go home."

Home. Yeah, with Kennedy in it, his house was a home. The security was all there although the drive would be brutal for her. Just getting to his dad's had been grueling, especially with the window broken and freezing air blowing in. He hadn't seen an alternative, though.

"Here tonight," Reyes insisted, "then we'll reevaluate tomorrow. Okay?"

"You'll have privacy," Parrish assured her as he stood and walked around to Reyes, where he again checked his head.

"Ow, damn, Dad. Leave it alone."

Rolling his eyes, Parrish gave Kennedy a look. "Luckily he has a hard head, or he might've gotten more than a goose egg."

"It barely slowed me down," Reyes promised, to ease the frown of concern Kennedy now wore. "I've had enough injuries to know a serious one from a nuisance. Once I'd cleaned off the blood, anyone could see I wasn't badly hurt." Hell, the biggest ache he felt was in his heart.

A tap sounded at the exam room door, immediately followed by Cade, Sterling and Madison coming in.

Cade said, "I moved your truck into a garage bay so it wouldn't fill with snow. Tomorrow morning I'll take it to get the window fixed."

Normally Reyes would have insisted on doing that himself, but he wouldn't want to leave Kennedy while she was hurt. "Thanks."

"I brought Kennedy some clothes," Madison said. "A few T-shirts, sweatshirt and pajama pants, because she can roll those up. Sorry, but my jeans would be about a foot too long on her."

"And my butt would never fit," Kennedy said with a weak smile. "Thank you."

Sterling whistled softly as she got close. "Damn, girl. You look like you went a few rounds with a UFC champion. Your bruises have bruises." She gave an exaggerated wince. "Hurt much?"

"Mostly my head, but the meds are helping."

Sterling took Parrish's stool. "Did I ever tell you about the time I tried going out a narrow window face-first? I managed to escape a bad situation, but got a chunk of glass stuck in my thigh."

Lips parting in awe, Kennedy said, "No, but it sounds awful."

"It was. But hey, it led to Cade and me getting closer, so now it's a fond memory." Glancing at Reyes, Sterling nodded to the door, then started her story.

Ah, his opportunity to talk privately with his family. Making sure the blanket covered every part of Kennedy, he softly said, "I'll be right back."

Kennedy barely nodded. She was too enthralled with Sterling's gory tale.

Outside the exam room, he, Cade, Madison and Parrish huddled together, their voices necessarily low to keep Kennedy from hearing.

The last thing she needed right now was more to worry about.

"Do you know the bastard brother's name yet?" Now that Kennedy was safe, he could fully concentrate on forever removing the fuck as a threat.

"Of course I do," Madison replied. "He's Rand Golly, two years older than Rob was, putting him at forty-two. He has a long rap sheet, everything from drunk driving to felony assault, attempted kidnapping and arson. He got out of prison at the same time Jodi escaped. My guess is he went to see his brother right off, and found him dead."

Yeah, that could make a career criminal vindictive. Poor Jodi. The girl couldn't catch a break. What were the odds of escaping one abusive lunatic only to have another come after her? "She could benefit from one of Dad's programs."

"My thought exactly," Parrish said. "Kennedy will rest easier if she knows her friend is clear of danger. But first we need to eliminate the threat." He added to Madison, "I want eyes on that motel room every second of every hour. We need to know if Golly moves while we formulate our plans."

"Already done," Madison assured him. "I found a few cameras that give me great access. As long as he doesn't do something extra tricky like dig his way out, I'll see him. If he does go out, I'll be able to identify which car is his, then I can grab his plates. That'll give us even more info on him."

"Now that they're onto us," Cade said, "I don't want Sterling anywhere near there when I tag the cars."

"I don't want *you* there, either," Parrish countered. "We'll get by without the GPS."

Cade stiffened. "I can handle it."

"Don't be insulted." Madison patted Cade's shoulder. "I agree with Dad. From everything I've been able to uncover, Golly has a broad network behind him."

"His connections aren't the same as ours," Cade argued.

"Agreed. We'll have to cast a wider net now, and if there's even a tiny chance that you get spotted, the rest of the goons will go to ground."

"How many people are we talking?" Reyes asked.

I've found connections to twenty, including motel owners, diner owners, truckers and a few career criminal buddies that he probably met in prison. Nothing too high-tech, but I don't want to risk missing a step and losing any—" She glanced at Reyes, stalling.

"Women," Reyes said. It was a good bet that the sick bastard had an operation going. "Agreed."

"All the more reason for the GPS," Cade argued.

Obviously, Cade didn't want to concede the point. Reyes got that. They were take-charge guys who worked best when in action. "You're the patient one," Reyes said to his brother, "so imagine how I feel. If I can stand to wait while we sort this out, you damn sure can, too."

With that reasoning, Cade nodded.

Wanting to get back to Kennedy, Reyes asked, "Where's Jodi?"

"We put her in a nice suite at Dad's hotel. We dropped off additional clothes for her, stocked the small fridge and gave her unlimited use of movies and games."

"Meaning she has everything she'd need so there's no reason to leave the room." His father's hotel was another front. Yes, it served the legit purpose of renting rooms, but the entire upper floor was reserved for situations like this. It looked like nothing more than a five-star hotel, but boasted the same security they used in their homes. Jodi would be safe there. Still... "Kennedy won't be happy to know she's alone."

Cade shrugged. "Short of kidnapping her, there wasn't much I could do. The hotel seemed like the best bet."

Would Jodi stay put? He had no idea. "Pretty sure Kennedy will insist on seeing her tomorrow, so I'll want backup." If it was just him going, Reyes wouldn't worry, but with Kennedy? Too much had already happened. Never again would he relax his guard, not for any reason.

"No problem," Cade said. "Star will insist on going along."

Parrish folded his arms. "What's happening with the detective?"

Reyes rubbed the back of his neck. "He said Madison explained enough to give us some leeway." He glanced at his sister. "Though now that I ditched him at the site, he might rethink that."

Madison stared back defiantly. "Dad and I agree that he could be a valuable asset."

"Maybe." One way or another, cops were going to show on the scene of the wreck. At least Crosby was a cop he was familiar with. "I assume Delbert is no longer an issue?"

"Dead at the scene," Cade confirmed.

Although they might have gotten more info from him, Reyes chose to see his death as a blessing. It was one less person trying to get to Kennedy.

"I'll talk to Crosby again," Madison offered. "No worries."

Reyes stopped her from walking away. "How exactly did you clue him in?"

"I told him enough that he wouldn't detain you."

Cade's eyes narrowed. "Enough being how much?"

"Overall, I mentioned the task force and a general overview of

Dad's philanthropic work. Crosby was duly impressed, but now? I don't know what he'll think when he can't find either of them at the hospital."

Parrish considered things. "When I called him, it was just to say that there'd been an attempted kidnapping and it might involve Golly. That seemed incentive enough for him to jump onboard. But Madison is right. He'll want to be in control of things."

"Somehow, we need to string him along," Madison concluded. She smiled. "Leave it to me."

Becoming antsy, Reyes glanced at the exam room doors. He wanted to get back to Kennedy. "He'll have questions for me, but if you can put him off until tomorrow—"

"Impossible," Madison said. "He's a cop, Reyes, not a goon— he won't be easily manipulated. And as I keep telling you, he's on the up-and-up. His questions will be legit."

"Stick with the truth as much as you can," Parrish advised. "There were enough people in the diner to see the attack."

"And a few saw Kennedy taken," Cade said. "It'll all add up for a cop."

Madison gave a short laugh. "It's not like any of you to under-estimate someone as badly as you're underestimating Crosby." Turning, she lifted her hand in a wave. "Go get Kennedy settled. I'll see you later."

"She's taken with the cop," Reyes complained.

"Seems like," Cade agreed.

Parrish stared after her thoughtfully. Finally he asked, "Do you think Kennedy will want to join us for dinner?"

Knowing her as he did now, Reyes couldn't see her lingering in bed, no matter how much she wanted to or how she needed the rest. She seemed hell-bent on proving, more to herself than any-one else, that she wasn't a burden. "I'd bet yes."

"Then I better go confer with Bernard to let him know we'll all be in attendance." He clasped Reyes's shoulder. "You did great under the circumstances."

He didn't need false praise. "I fucked up."

Giving a small shake of his head, Parrish said, "I'm proud of you." He spoke next at Cade. "And you. You've both grown into very impressive men." He walked down the short hallway that headed to the stairs.

Stunned, Reyes glanced at Cade. "What the hell was that about?"

"No idea, except that having women around is softening him. My guess is that he looks at things differently when he sees us happily involved."

A disturbing thought. His dad, softened? No, he didn't even want to consider it. "I have to get back to Kennedy."

Cade gave him a long look. "You realize you're in love with her, right?"

He wasn't stupid. Figuring out what to do about it was the issue. "Come collect your wife, then I'll put Kennedy to bed."

Cade slowly smiled. "Be careful, brother, or you'll be softening, too."

Not likely. He was the hell-raiser sibling. The daredevil. The cocky jerk who got around.

But yeah, none of that seemed to matter a minute later when he found Kennedy drifting off to sleep while Sterling softly told another story.

Women had a miraculous effect on everyone.

In that moment, he felt pretty damned soft—in his head and in his heart.

MADISON SMILED AT CROSBY. Lord, the man was something to look at, even while scowling. They sat in her car in a deserted park where she'd arranged the meeting.

Yes, she could have handled things over the phone, but what was the fun in that? She'd told him a small fib, saying she was worried about others listening in, and so he'd agreed to the meeting.

"You're angry."

His scowl grew fiercer, making his dark-as-sin eyes glitter.

So sexy.

"Your brother is giving me the runaround. I expected to find him at the hospital or I never would have let him leave."

Ha! Clearly Crosby was underestimating Reyes, too. "I doubt that's true. You saw how badly hurt Kennedy was. She needed medical attention, so you wouldn't have delayed them. I'm even sure you realize why Reyes didn't go to the hospital, because you know how dangerous that route can be."

Frustrated, Crosby ran a hand over his sandy-brown hair, leaving it mussed.

Her fingers tingled with the need to smooth it back into place. "Where did he take her?"

"A secure facility where she can get care and rest without worrying that Golly might find her."

His gaze never wavered. "Where?" he repeated, more insistent this time.

She dodged that, saying, "In case you were wondering, Kennedy is badly bruised all over, especially one arm and her thigh." As far as diversions went, that worked well.

"Damn," Crosby muttered. "All I'd noticed was the lump on her head, and that was bad enough."

Madison liked how truly caring he was. It appeared to really bother him that Kennedy was injured. "By the way, Rob Golly is in fact dead."

He eyed her suspiciously. "You say that as if you're certain."

"Because I am. Brace yourself, Detective, but we've discovered that it wasn't Rob causing all this trouble. It's his brother, Rand."

Incredulous now, his eyes narrowed. "You and your family have an uncanny ability to discover things."

"Yes, I know. We're good. Modesty aside, though, I'm in charge of gathering info and I'm extremely proficient at what I do."

"Do you do it legally?"

Ah, he wanted to trip her up. Then what? She smiled at him. "If you have questions for Reyes, give me the number you want him to call and I'll see to it."

"I want to see him in person."

"Yes, but Kennedy is hurt, so he won't leave her side, and no— before you ask again—I can't tell you where."

His gaze searched hers, his indecision almost palpable. "She'll be all right?"

"Certainly, though she'll be sore for a while. Before he so conveniently perished, Delbert O'Neil struck Kennedy in the head with the butt of his gun. She was unconscious long enough for him to stuff her into his car and try to kidnap her."

"Thank God he slid on the ice or he might…" He stopped when Madison shook her head. "What?"

"It wasn't the weather conditions that caused the wreck. Kennedy attacked him. She was afraid Reyes was badly hurt and wanted to get back to him. From what I was told, she kicked him several times, then punched him in a place where no man wants to be punched."

He flinched. "And that caused the wreck?"

"You could drive under those conditions?"

Shrugging, he said, "If I had to."

That amused her and she grinned again. "My brothers also, though I doubt they'd let anything like that happen."

Crosby rubbed a hand over his face. "Tell your brother that I need Delbert's gun, and that I expect to be kept informed."

"I'll tell him, but Reyes will do as he pleases on that score." No reason to explain that they all avoided involving the law whenever possible.

Snow accumulated on the windows, making the interior of the car cozy and private, not that anyone was at the park today anyway. The heated seats kept her toasty warm, and Crosby's nearness kept her on sensual alert.

"You know what?" She tipped her head at him. "Why don't you tell me why this is personal for you?"

"No." Fed up, he allowed his anger to show again. "I've let you play your games. I jumped at your father's bidding. I even allowed your damned brother to leave the scene of a kidnapping. Enough, already. If you're not going to cooperate, then I'm done wasting my time." He reached for the door handle.

"Wait." Madison didn't want him to go yet, so she drew in a breath and admitted the one thing she could think of that might keep him interested and wouldn't compromise her family. "It's personal for me, and for my entire family, because we lost someone we loved to human trafficking."

Slowly Crosby sank back into his seat. "Who?"

"My mother."

Immediately his antagonism waned. "Damn, Madison. I'm sorry."

Now, why did his understanding make her throat feel too tight?

She'd lived with the loss of her mother for years now. "Dad took it especially hard." Skirting the issue of their vigilante work, she said, "That's why he funds the task force."

"To search for traffickers?"

"It's more than that, really." She didn't get to brag on her father very often, so she'd enjoy doing so now. "I know I glossed over this earlier, but Dad's involvement is actually pretty elaborate. You see, the task force he funds ensures that victims are represented legally. They get counseling and financial assistance, and they're offered access to recovery resources."

"Like?"

Getting into the explanations, Madison leaned closer. "Many victims have no idea what to do once they're saved. Some come from bad home lives so they can't get help there. Others fear retribution. They're lost and alone and still so afraid. Through the task force they're given safe housing, offers of education or employment, and enough financial aid to get back on their feet."

While she spoke, Crosby's gaze drifted over her face—and settled on her mouth. "Remarkable."

"I'm really proud of my family and all they offer, but I'm sure you can understand that for many victims, it's a very private endeavor."

"It's not the privacy issue that concerns me." His gaze finally lifted to clash with hers. "It's the possibility of illegal activity."

"You're accusing me?" *Why did she sound so breathless?*

"All of you, actually." His voice went deeper, rougher. "Now tell me what else you're up to," he insisted, and somehow it sounded sexually suggestive.

"You know what I'd rather do?"

His dark bedroom eyes narrowed.

Madison reached for him over the console. "I'd rather kiss you," she murmured, right before her fingers slid into his cool, silky hair and her mouth settled over his.

He went still for a heartbeat, and then those strong arms closed around her, pulling her nearer as he took over. Or tried to.

Being submissive wasn't really her thing, so she angled as close as she could get and deepened the kiss.

To her surprise, he laughed.

Insulted, she lifted her head and glared at him. "You're amused?"

Smiling, his gaze tender, he stroked two fingers along her cheek, then under her chin. "Yeah, you amuse me."

"That wasn't my intent."

"I know." He leaned in for a soft kiss. "My guess is you wanted to distract me. I'm tempted, but not quite that easy."

Of all the... She dropped back to her own seat, now glad that the console kept them apart. "You think the only reason I kissed you—"

"Yeah, that's what I think." His slight smile never wavered. "I wouldn't put anything past you or your family."

"Well." Her face heated with ire. "That's insulting."

"To me, as well."

"Most especially to you," she snapped. "For your information, I don't offer those type of personal favors for my family. I kissed you because I *wanted* to. But trust me, I won't make that mistake again."

"Good. Let's keep it simple, okay?" Lifting his hip, he drew out his wallet, found a card and handed it to her. "Have your brother call me within the hour. If anything else happens, I strongly advise you to let me know."

Madison sat there, fuming, turned on and, yes, still insulted as he opened the door and got out. The wind blew back his hair and his step wasn't as sure as usual thanks to the snow and ice.

Such a gorgeous man. So...scrumptious.

Such a dick.

And he thought she'd thrown herself at him for a distraction.

The truth was that she couldn't help herself. Early on he'd intrigued her. Meeting him in person had affected her dreams.

She wanted him. Terribly.

Maybe it was better he didn't know that. Sighing, Madison hit the wipers while also turning up the defroster. As soon as the windshield cleared, she spotted Crosby.

Waiting for her to leave. Concerned for her?

Or maybe he planned to follow her? Ha, let him try.

He stayed behind her to the entrance of the park, then they

each turned in different directions. Had he just been playing the gentleman?

Such a confusing man.

She didn't need him to protect her. No, she just needed him. Eventually she'd get her way. After all, she was a McKenzie through and through.

CHAPTER SIXTEEN

KENNEDY WOKE FEELING warm and comfortable in Madison's T-shirt and pajama pants. Beside her, Reyes sat against the head-board and perused his phone, the home screen reflecting in his hazel eyes.

She was snuggled against his side, part of the reason the chills had finally left her. A slight headache remained, but she could deal with that.

Loving him wouldn't be easy, not with the work he did. Valuable work, she realized, because without him Jodi wouldn't stand a chance. The police could only do so much when the law forced them to abide by a certain standard.

A standard Golly and his sick brother didn't deserve.

Suddenly Reyes looked down at her, said, "Hey," and set his phone aside. He smoothed back her hair, tipped up her chin and studied her face. "Your eyes aren't dilated anymore. That's a good sign."

"My headache is better, too." She struggled to sit up. "What time is it?"

"Almost seven."

"What?" She'd slept that long? She'd only meant to take a brief nap, not conk out for hours.

"You needed the rest, babe."

"Have you been here the entire time?"

"Did you think I'd budge?" He leaned forward to press a soft kiss to her lips, then an even softer kiss to her temple where Delbert had hit her. "You don't remember me waking you, to make sure you were okay?"

"No." She remembered crawling into his bed, but not much after that. She must have nodded off right away once she'd gotten warm.

"Are you hungry?" Reyes asked. "Bernard held dinner for us."

"Oh, no." The thought of his family waiting on her made her want to crawl back under the covers.

"Don't worry about it. It's only been half an hour. The food will be fine and no one is starving."

Using both hands, she shoved back her hair. "Is it okay for me to eat like this?" She held out the hem of Madison's shirt. "Delbert bled on my clothes."

"Bernard washed them, but yeah, they're stained. What you have on is fine. Cade and I will be in jeans. No biggie." He helped her out of the bed, then framed her face in his hands. "I found one of my flannel shirts for you to help keep you warm."

So considerate. Kennedy wrapped her arms around him and rested her face against his chest. "Thank you for taking care of me."

Tension stiffened his body. "If I'd taken better care of you, none of this would have happened."

"Even you can't predict every moment of every day."

He changed the subject, saying, "I'm so damn proud of you."

"Proud?" She leaned back to see him. "Why?"

"Why?" His expression was serious enough that it looked severe. "Damn, Kennedy. You were hurt and afraid, and still you kept your head and fought hard. Of course I'm proud."

"I caused a wreck." She still had the aches and pains to prove it.

"You disabled your kidnapper. That took a lot of guts. Most wrecks aren't fatal, especially when there's little traffic. It was a reasonable risk to take considering the alternative."

He made it sound premediated and deliberate, but she knew the truth. "I wasn't thinking clearly at all. I just...reacted."

"Instincts," he agreed, holding her closer, his heart beating a little harder. "You knew he couldn't get you alone."

She shivered, and it wasn't from cold. It was knowing what Delbert would have done to her if he'd succeeded.

So far she'd managed to keep those thoughts at bay.

"I'm sorry." He cupped a hand around her neck and gently rocked her side to side. "So damned sorry."

Kennedy wasn't entirely sure about his mood, and she didn't want to add to his burdens or put him on the spot, but the words just sort of slipped out, maybe because they needed to be said. Or because *she* needed to say them. "I'm here with you and we're both safe. I don't have to sleep alone, and I don't have to fear anyone." She knew Reyes wouldn't let her be hurt. "You're my own personal hero, Reyes."

"God love you, girl, you turn me inside out."

Her lips parted. What did that mean?

Before she could work up the courage to ask, he stepped back, grabbed the flannel shirt and helped her into it.

"Okay?"

The material was soft, and the shirt smelled like him. "Yes." Better than okay.

"I hope you're hungry."

She gave that quick thought and nodded. "Starved."

Smiling, he said, "Come on. Bernard loves nothing more than an enthusiastic eater."

She realized that was true when Bernard joined them for the meal in the formal dining room. Parrish sat at one end of the table, with Bernard at the other, and the siblings with Kennedy and Sterling on either side.

In deference to her injuries, the lights were kept low and everyone spoke in modulated, even tones.

It gave her the warm fuzzies to be treated so kindly. Not only that, they acted as if she were one of them. Not because she'd fended off Delbert, but because of Reyes. They saw her as his significant other.

And he wasn't objecting.

If anything, he'd doubled up on the attention he gave her, often reaching over to touch her, constantly watching her. She knew she must look wretched with the bruises and her mismatched, borrowed clothes, but clearly he didn't mind—and that made her not care, either.

Over a rib eye roast with buttery mashed potatoes and perfectly steamed vegetables, everyone caught her up on what had unfolded while she slept.

Reyes said, "I spoke with Crosby. He's pushy—"

"Like most cops," Cade added.

"—but he's all right." Reyes glanced at her. "He was real concerned for you. Wanted me to tell you he hopes you're okay, and if you need him for anything, just call."

"Why would I need him?"

Reyes, Cade and Madison all smiled.

"My thoughts exactly," Sterling said.

Parrish explained, "To his mind, the only real assistance, the *best* assistance, is an officer of the law. Dedicated cops have a difficult time accepting that their way isn't always the best way."

"He wanted to know where Golly is holed up," Madison added, keeping her gaze on her plate. "Reyes didn't tell him."

"Neither did you," Cade said. "I'm curious what the two of you discussed when you met at the park."

Parrish looked up. "You did what?"

Reyes scowled.

Sterling, who'd been mostly silent while she ate, looked up with a grin. "Sneaking out from under their eagle eyes, huh? Go you."

"My eagle eyes," Cade pointed out, "didn't miss it."

Madison affected a casual shrug. "I met with him, explained a few things, and got his number for Reyes to call. That's it." She quickly shifted the topic by saying to Kennedy, "By the way, we have everything worked out if you want to visit Jodi."

"I do." They'd already explained where Jodi was. Trying to imagine her friend in a fancy hotel left Kennedy boggled. Jodi couldn't like it. Still, according to Reyes, he'd spoken with her and she'd promised to stay put this time.

He claimed Jodi had agreed because she didn't want Kennedy stressed over it.

Kennedy didn't think that was the whole reason. The near miss had likely rattled her, too.

"When can we go?" she asked Reyes, knowing without asking that he'd accompany her there.

"Tomorrow is soon enough," Parrish answered before Reyes could. "I want you to continue resting tonight, and through the morning tomorrow. We'll reassess then."

She'd never before had such close medical care. She didn't mind being treated by Reyes's father—as long as the medical issues weren't anything embarrassing. "I feel much better, but thank you."

"Tomorrow," Parrish reiterated.

"In the meantime," Reyes said, "I don't want you to worry about Jodi. We have guards at the hotel." He reached over to cover her hand. "Even if she wanted to take off, they'd stall her long enough for us to get there."

They'd thought of everything, and it truly overwhelmed her with gratitude. Done eating, Kennedy addressed the table. "I can't thank you enough for all you've done." She smiled at Reyes, Cade and Sterling. "You've kept Jodi and me safe, and of course that's the biggie." Next she turned to Madison. "I'm in awe of your research ability, but your hospitality and kindness is appreciated, too. Thank you for loaning me your clothes."

Madison returned her smile. "My pleasure."

"And Bernard, the *food*. You are a man of many talents. I've never eaten so well."

"Hear! Hear!" Parrish said, lifting his glass of wine.

Bernard nodded regally as they all toasted him.

"Parrish." Kennedy had saved him for last, because for some reason her heart ached as she looked at him. This man had lost the woman he loved, and, instead of retreating from the world, he'd built something incredible to help others. "I owe you the most appreciation. This is all because of you. Because you cared enough to make helping others a priority." Her eyes grew damp, and for once she didn't care. She knew Parrish's relationship with his children was sometimes strained; she also knew he was the most amazing man she'd ever met. "Without you and all you've set up, I'd have no one to turn to. Jodi would be lost. We'd have had little hope at all. For us, the world would be a much uglier place."

Reyes pushed back his chair, and tugged her out of hers and over into his lap, where he hugged her. "She's right." He looked at his father, who appeared speechless. "I don't know any other man who could have accomplished what you have." He cupped Kennedy's bruised cheek. "Now more than ever, I appreciate what you've taught me."

"Agreed." With his arm around Sterling, Cade said, "If you hadn't groomed me for this job, I wouldn't have found Sterling. Thank you, Dad."

Madison grinned happily. "Here's to an amazing man who reared incredible children."

This time it was Bernard who cheered, "Hear! Hear!"

Parrish still looked flabbergasted, but he slowly smiled. "To family."

That earned another chorus of agreement. This time, Kennedy kept silent. Already, she loved this family so much. Pretty sure she always would.

Even if she wasn't a real part of it.

Not yet anyway, though she held out hope. Once they took care of Golly and she helped get Jodi settled, then she could figure out if she had a future with Reyes.

Anything less than a lifetime was unthinkable.

REYES WATCHED KENNEDY look around with interest. When he'd first brought her down to his suite of rooms, she'd been too zoned out to really pay attention. He'd guided her to the turned-down bed, then tucked her in. She'd given one big sigh and slowly drifted to sleep.

His heart had hurt then.

It hurt now.

Until he destroyed Golly and his entire network, he didn't expect the ache to let up.

"This is beautiful." Kennedy turned in a circle while looking at his living space with the couch and padded chair, a desk and PC, a bookcase and a TV on the wall. "It's like an upscale apartment."

"I didn't design it," Reyes admitted, "but I did weigh in on the choices. Same with Cade and Madison. In case of an emergency, Dad wanted us to have a place that was our own, but was also with him."

"Your father is an astounding man."

Seeing him through Kennedy's eyes, Reyes realized it was true. Funny how being reared a certain way made you overlook things. Yes, his dad could be as autocratic as a general, and he wasn't big on accepting anything less than 110 percent. But he was also supportive in ways Reyes hadn't realized until recently.

Everything he'd orchestrated, he'd done out of love.

Loving Kennedy changed things. When Reyes thought of his mother and the tragic way she'd ended her own life, he had an inkling of what his father might have gone through. How the hell had he recovered?

Not for a single day had he neglected his children. Instead, he'd given them all a new focus for their anger and grief.

It was a new focus for Parrish, as well. Without that, he might not have survived his pain. It took a strong man to forge on as his father had done. To use his grief as an impetus for good. To effect such remarkable change.

For numerous reasons, Reyes admired him greatly—now more than ever.

He snagged Kennedy's hand as she started toward the bedroom. Needing to hold her, he pulled her into his arms, breathing in the scent of her, absorbing her sweetness and insight. "Thank you."

Opening her hands on his back, she stroked him. "Reyes? Are you all right?"

"Yeah." As she'd said, she was with him. Of course he was okay. "Let me show you the rest of the place."

Though she continued to watch him with concern, she still appropriately appreciated the masculine design of the bathroom and bedroom.

"I have a dorm-sized fridge and a microwave, but I never use them since Bernard always has something good upstairs."

"Guess I'll need to go upstairs for coffee."

"Nah." He kissed her forehead, the bridge of her nose and, lastly, her mouth. "I'll fetch it for you whenever you want." To keep her from thanking him again, he asked, "Would you like a nice warm bath?"

Slowly she grinned. "The way you say that, I wonder if you have more than a good soak in mind."

"You, naked? The view alone will be worth it."

She laughed, the sound light and easy, proving she really was recovering.

"But, babe, you're hurt, so no hanky-panky." He lifted her bandaged wrist. "The water will sting."

"It'll be worth it."

"Come on." While she watched, he prepped the bath for her and set out fluffy towels. "What else do you need?"

"A way to put up my hair? Clothes to change into?"

"Will a rubber band do? Madison left more clothes, and Bernard washed your bra and panties, so that's covered."

Her face went hot, making him grin.

"What?" he teased. "I'm sure Bernard didn't mind."

"And if I mind?"

"Too late." Strange that he could be so concerned for her and also so damned turned on. "Do you need help getting undressed?"

She gave him a look. "No."

"Then I'll get your things for you."

When he returned a minute later, Kennedy was, indeed, naked, and Reyes began wondering if this was such a great idea after all. Just seeing her made him half-hard, but he wasn't about to—

"Stop it," she said, taking the band from him, flipping her hair forward and securing it.

He wouldn't mind seeing her do that a dozen more times—when she wasn't riddled with bruises. "Er, stop what?"

"Thinking of reasons why we can't enjoy each other." She sent him a look so sultry he had to lock his knees. "Just so you know, I need you."

"Kennedy—"

Her chin lifted. "I feel safer with you. Stronger, too. Being with you is like having everything good rolled up in pleasure. I want that, Reyes. I need to feel alive, and I need you close."

Damn, he couldn't breathe. Trying to soothe her, he whispered, "I'm not going to budge from your side, but I don't want to risk—"

"Did you miss the part where I said I *need* it?" Her lips trembled before she firmed them. "I need *you*."

Yeah, that did it. Whatever control he'd had was just blown to smithereens. He watched her gingerly step into the steamy water, favoring her injured leg. He was used to seeing bruises on himself. On Cade. But on Kennedy?

A light bruise spread out over her right shoulder blade. His dad wouldn't have seen that one, or the bruise on her left hip. Kennedy had been adamant that she only show so much, and she'd promised that nothing else was hurt.

He understood what she meant. There was *hurt*, and then there was *damaged*, like with an injury. On Kennedy, he couldn't seem to distinguish the two. Even the smallest scratch pained him.

He wanted to surround her with his strength, protect her against the world. And yeah, he wanted to hold her close, sink into her, ride her gently until they both forgot about the near miss.

Ruthlessly he blocked that thought. Just because Kennedy assumed she'd be up to sex, didn't mean she was.

She sighed as she reclined back, but when the water hit her abraded arm, she hissed a breath.

"Is it bad?"

"No, it just smarts." She gave him a smile. "I won't let you slide on sex, so stop looking for a way out."

What an incredible woman. "Now, how could I possibly deny you?"

"You can't." Sinking chin-deep into the water, she said, "Oh, this is nice."

"Warm enough?" Because now that she was naked and relaxed, he was seriously sweltering. After she nodded, he stripped off his shirt and knelt by the tub.

"There's room for two."

True. He'd deliberately chosen a roomy tub for those rare occasions when he wanted a hot soak to relieve stiff muscles. At the moment, it wasn't his muscles that were stiff, and he wouldn't crowd her for fear of bumping one of her sore spots. "How about I just enjoy you, instead?"

She eyed him. "Enjoy me how?"

"You stay just like that and let me take care of everything."

She considered that for a second, then smiled again. "Mmm, that sounds indulgent."

"For both of us." Reyes picked up the bar of unscented soap—the kind he used—and worked it into the washcloth until he had a nice lather. Leisurely, he bathed every inch of her, paying special attention to key places, until her breath was choppy and need left her skin rosy.

When he reached beneath the water to touch her, she groaned. Reyes couldn't look away from her face. He loved seeing her pleasure because it spiked his own. Right now her eyes were heavy, her cheeks flushed and her lips slightly parted.

"Relax your legs, babe."

Breathing faster, she said, "Maybe we should end the bath."

"Not yet." He pressed one finger into her and whispered again, "Relax your legs."

She swallowed heavily and gradually let her thighs fall open.

"That's it." Gently he stroked her, loving the heat of her body, the growing slickness. Her nipples, puckered tight, tempted him until he shifted to lean over her, licking first one, then the other. With a soft sound of need, she locked her hands around his neck and urged him to linger.

While he circled that nipple, playing with her, he withdrew his finger, then pressed in two. Her hips lifted.

"Easy, babe. I don't want to hurt you." No matter how he burned, he wouldn't forget that she'd been injured and was recovering. "Be as still as you can."

She groaned out a curse, making him smile.

"That's it," he praised her, when she relaxed again. He rewarded her by closing his mouth around her nipple, drawing gently first, then sucking harder as he moved his fingers inside her.

He felt her rising need in the way her body trembled, the rush of slippery moisture against his fingers and the sounds she made. Ever so lightly he drifted his thumb over her clitoris, again and again.

Though she locked her fingers in his hair, disregarding his instructions, he couldn't chide her over that—and wouldn't have anyway. She was so close to release that he doubted either of them could remember caution.

When the climax hit her, he nearly came, too. Water sloshed out of the tub, but who cared? Her body clenched around his fingers. He lifted his head to watch her expression tighten in honest reaction. So real. So beautiful.

Such a freaking turn-on.

As soon as she quieted, Reyes eased away from her and pulled the drain on the tub. His jeans were soaked so he shucked them off in record time, tossing them over the puddle on the floor. Catching Kennedy under the arms, he lifted her from the tub, set her on her feet and wrapped the fluffy towel around her before picking her up again.

She smiled, her eyes still closed, and let him have his way.

On the way to the bed, he said, "I will not hurt you."

"I know." She kissed his throat, her mouth open, her tongue hot. "I trust you, Reyes."

Lowering her to her feet, he gently dried her.

She laughed at his caution. "Take off your boxers."

Every day, in some new way, she astounded him. "Not yet." If he did, it'd be over.

Frowning, she poked his chest. "No more playing, Reyes." Then in a more plaintive voice, she said, "I need you *now*."

"Get in the bed."

"Bossy much?" She crawled in as she said that, stealing his breath in the process.

"Horny much, actually." He went to the nightstand to dig out a rubber, then sprawled out beside her. Reminding himself to use ultimate care, to utilize every ounce of gentleness he possessed, he took her mouth in a deep, wet, tongue-dueling kiss while palming her breasts. Every inch of her enticed him, her silky skin, her firm bottom, the taste of her, her scent.

He kissed her throat, down to her breasts, where he concentrated for a while on getting her back to the edge, then down to her ribs and her stomach. He kissed every bruise, every small scrape, and everywhere in between as he slowly progressed down her body.

Probably guessing his intent, she made small, desperate sounds of need.

Carefully parting her thighs, he looked at her, seeing her pink flesh swollen and wet. She definitely wanted him. Whatever pain she felt, it wasn't hindering her.

"Reyes?"

There were no words for all the things she made him feel. Without forewarning, he licked over her, into her, and didn't even mind when her hips lifted. Sex had a way of obliterating aches and worries, and given how Kennedy moved now, she wasn't feeling, either.

Lifting her thighs over his shoulders, he settled in to sate himself on her taste, licking her, prodding with his tongue, nibbling with his lips. Even when she quickly spiraled into another climax, he couldn't get enough. He closed his mouth over her clitoris and suckled until she cried out, her entire body straining.

Seconds ticked by, maybe even a full minute, and his senses returned in a startling rush. Damn it, he shouldn't have pushed her like that. He was supposed to be pampering her.

Dreading the discomfort he might see on her face, he rose up and found her resting boneless across his mattress, her thighs sprawled, her arms out and limp, eyes closed and cheeks damp.

"You're mine."

Her eyelids fluttered. "What?" she whispered.

No, he didn't want to get into explanations right now, not when he was strung so tight. He grabbed the condom and rolled it on. "If anything bothers you, if your head hurts—"

"Reyes." She smiled up at him. "Have you ever known me to be shy?"

"A little."

She pressed a warm kiss to his mouth. "Not with sex." She stroked a small, warm hand over his chest.

"The bruises—"

"What bruises?" she whispered, kissing him again, and this time her lips were open, her tongue bold.

Hell, he was a goner. Slowly he moved over her, giving her time to adjust her legs in whatever way was most comfortable for her. Gripping his shoulders, she hooked her uninjured leg over his hips.

Reyes slid one hand under her sexy behind, tilted her hips and pressed into her in one long, smooth thrust.

Heaven.

It was a good thing she'd already come twice because, after all that, he was on a hair trigger.

While he kept up an easy and steady rhythm, Kennedy seemed content to kiss him senseless while stroking his back. Just when he knew he couldn't hold back a moment longer, he pressed his face into her neck and growled a powerful release. And even then he was aware of her, of how precious she was to him, how delicate. And how strong.

She'd fought a kidnapper from her past who'd had the vilest of intent. She'd persevered through injuries and fear. And she'd stolen his heart, irrevocably.

Plus, she gave him the best sex he'd ever had.

"Somehow," she whispered near his ear, "it keeps getting better."

He couldn't yet speak, but he kissed her shoulder, then rolled to his back to relieve her of his weight. She should have been crying, or at least sleeping, after her ordeal.

Instead, Kennedy immediately snuggled into his side.

They rested like that for a bit until he thought to ask, "Did I hurt you?"

"Of course you didn't. You never would."

No, he wouldn't.

She yawned. "But I am crazy tired again."

He made himself man up, but it wasn't easy. "Give me two minutes." Leaving the bed, he disposed of the condom, cleaned up and found the pills his dad wanted her to take.

He carried her one with a bottle of water. At first he thought she was already asleep, until she opened her eyes. She'd removed the band from her hair and now it tumbled over the pillow. She rested one hand on her stomach and the other, palm up, by her head.

Liking the way she smiled, Reyes sat on the side of the bed and offered her the medicine. When that was done, he straightened the bedding, turned off the light and stretched out beside her. "I'll keep you warm, okay?"

"Yes."

Holding her close with one arm, he asked, "Why were you smiling?"

"I was just thinking how funny it was that today should have been one of the scariest since I escaped traffickers, but with you, it was also one of the nicest."

Damn, she knew how to level him.

I love you. The words burned in his throat, but saying them aloud would be a commitment. Before he did that, they had a lot to work out, most especially his career. He wanted her to know that one day he would comfortably retire. He wouldn't go into his old age fighting bad guys. He'd have money in the bank, a nice house... She wouldn't have to worry about growing old with him.

Her career was another matter. He was so damned proud of her, but he knew his limitations, and he couldn't imagine letting her go off on her own without protection. Not with her past, and not with his awareness of the dangers in the world.

Would she rebel against that?

He had dozens of concerns, but voicing them would start another long conversation when what she really needed was sleep.

When he realized her breathing had deepened, he knew she'd already nodded off.

They'd make it work, he told himself. He didn't know if Kennedy loved him, but she cared. She liked being with him. She loved the sex.

He could start there and build on the rest.

And with that thought, he drifted off to sleep, too.

CHAPTER SEVENTEEN

DURING THE LATE AFTERNOON, they headed over to see Jodi. Kennedy had insisted on seeing her friend, against protests from everyone except Reyes.

He, at least, knew her well enough to understand this was something she had to do. She wanted to be close to her, to hug her, to literally be there for her.

Parrish wanted her to wear dark sunglasses because of her concussion, though, honestly, the effects of it weren't nearly as bad today. Madison had given her a puffer coat to wear, so she wasn't cold. And with Cade and Sterling trailing them, she wasn't too nervous, either.

Reyes was in full-blown protector mode, meaning he constantly scanned their surroundings without talking much.

Little by little, Kennedy was starting to grasp the complexities of their operation and how they all worked together, complementing each other's efforts, giving physical and emotional support wherever needed.

That morning, before she'd even made it out of Reyes's suite, Cade had gotten the window on the truck fixed. Soon as she and Reyes had joined the others in the kitchen for a light breakfast, Madison presented new info she'd uncovered, specifically locating a few small-time thugs with a past association to Golly. They were still local, therefore it stood to reason that they might be working with Golly again.

They'd decided it was worth checking into, and another two hours were spent going over the names, records and current residences of each of them. It was a thorough discussion, with all possibilities covered.

The process had kept Kennedy enthralled.

Reyes's family was a unit, and she admired that.

Though Madison had her information perfectly organized, she didn't seem as chipper as usual. Kennedy would bet it had something to do with the detective, but since no one else mentioned Crosby, she didn't, either.

She'd sat beside Reyes, of course, and when Madison passed him full color images that she'd printed of the thugs, Kennedy was shocked to recognize one of them.

"It's him."

All eyes turned to her. "Him, who?" Reyes asked.

"The man who was on my balcony. Remember, I told you about him?"

"You're sure?"

"Yes." She'd never forget that face, not after the way he'd terrified her.

Briefly Reyes explained about the incident that took place before the fire. "The police thought it was an attempted break-in, but Kennedy never bought that."

"Not with the way he stood there smiling at me." The memory disturbed her all over again, and she muttered, "I had my gun, but was too frozen to do anything other than aim at him."

Sterling grinned. "Likely that was enough."

"Given you have a history with him, that almost guarantees he's tied to Golly," Parrish decreed. "Which also casts suspicion on any close associates of his."

"I'm on it," Madison had promised. "I'll have more by the end of the day."

Now in Reyes's truck with the afternoon sunlight reflecting through the newly replaced window, she was glad Parrish had provided the glasses. They served the dual purpose of protecting her eyes from the glare and shielding her tumultuous thoughts from his discerning gaze. Not that she wanted to keep anything from him, but with him so attuned to their surroundings, she didn't want to distract him, either.

As if he'd just read her mind, he asked, "Doing okay?" without glancing at her.

She accepted that nothing much got past Reyes. "Much better today, thank you."

"Headache?"

"Not too bad." She looked at the bruise on his forehead. "You?"

"A-okay, babe. Like Dad said, I have a hard head." He took an exit to an industrial area.

Kennedy saw numerous restaurants, stores and a convention center. A few miles down he pulled into his father's hotel, which really was swanky with elaborate grounds now glistening under the white snow.

Driving around a small, ornamental lake, Reyes parked in a private-access garage. Her tension grew as they entered through a heavy door with a biometric lock.

"You weren't kidding about the security."

"No one other than my family accesses this part of the garage or building." With his hand at the small of her back, he steered her into a private elevator. "Nervous?"

"Anxious about seeing Jodi," she admitted. With Reyes she felt comfortable sharing her worries, so as the elevator climbed, she didn't hold back. "She's unpredictable. I don't know how she's going to react to everything."

"We'll figure it out, I promise."

We. It truly felt like they were partners in this. Having Reyes at her side meant more than she could ever express to him. She'd gotten used to going it alone…and now she didn't have to.

He saw his generosity as no big deal. To Kennedy, it was the greatest gift she'd ever been given, and was far more than she'd ever dared to hope for.

"I don't want to startle her," Kennedy said, getting out her phone. "I told her I'd text when we were here." She sent the message as soon as they stepped out of the elevator. Then she gazed around in awe. They were in a big foyer of sorts that ran the length of a long hall. Windows at one end overlooked the parking lot and main road.

She saw only one door, meaning this entire space was for the suite they'd given Jodi? Remarkable.

When the door opened and Kennedy got a look at Jodi, her stomach plummeted.

Her friend looked like a shadow of herself. Had she slept at all? Eaten? Combed her hair? She'd been afraid of this, and now she was doubly glad she'd come to see her in person rather than just calling or doing a video chat.

"Hey," Jodi said, her tone so sullen it bordered on antagonistic.

At the moment, none of that mattered. Kennedy was so glad to see her, pugnacious attitude and all, she grabbed her up in a spontaneous hug.

Predictably, Jodi went stiff.

That didn't matter, either. "Oh, it's good to see you, to know that you weren't hurt in the scuffle." To know she hadn't found a way to sneak out on her own. Of course the McKenzies had all assured her on that score, but hearing it and seeing it were two different things.

Jodi huffed. "Would have been tough for me to get hurt when your ape was busy ripping them all apart."

"I didn't rip," Reyes jokingly protested. "I demolished. There's a difference."

Jodi pressed her back. "But you?" Her gaze moved all over Kennedy's face, and when she focused on her bruised temple, she flinched. "Damn, Kennedy, you look like—"

"Hell, I know." She briefly hugged her again. "Have you heard the whole story?" She wasn't sure how much Reyes or Cade had shared with Jodi.

"Ha! They didn't tell me much of anything except that you were okay and I had to follow orders."

"That pretty much covers it." Summarizing greatly, Kennedy shared what had happened.

"I'm glad Delbert died," Jodi said.

"Same, though I would have liked to have gotten hold of him first," Reyes admitted. "Far as I'm concerned, he got off easy." With a hand to the center of Kennedy's back, Reyes began urging them both inside. "Instead of jawing out here, how about we get comfortable?"

"It's your place," Jodi said, strolling into the suite. "You can come and go as you please."

"For now," Reyes replied, "it's yours. You don't have to worry about anyone showing up without an invite."

"You two did."

Surprised, Kennedy said, "I messaged you first." Then, because she understood Jodi's attitude was part of her defenses, she quietly asked, "You don't want to see me?"

"Sure I do. Just sayin' that it wasn't my choice to be here." She shot a resentful look at Reyes, then walked across a wide entry to a beautiful living room furnished with a cream velvet couch and two armchairs. She threw herself into a chair, looking much like a ticked-off teenager.

On one side of the room was a dining table with six chairs, and behind that a wet bar and kitchenette. On the other side, an arched doorway led to a bedroom and bathroom. Through the open doorways, Kennedy saw that both rooms looked mostly unused. The couch faced a wall of windows with an impressive view of the Rockies.

Every inch of the space had top-of-the-line finishes, giving it the look of a designer home.

Though she knew Jodi couldn't be comfortable here, Kennedy tried to encourage her by saying, "Wow, this is nice."

Jodi shrugged. "In a gilded-cage kind of way."

It almost embarrassed Kennedy for her friend to be so ungrateful. "Jodi," she chided, wishing for a way to reassure her.

Reyes stalked over to stand in front of Jodi. Arms crossed and feet braced apart, he *loomed*. Kennedy had never seen him do such a thing before.

Finally he asked, "Got a death wish, Jodi? Is that it?"

Losing her slouched position, Jodi straightened as much as she could with Reyes so close. "Maybe death would be easier than waiting for fate to screw me over again."

"Nah," Reyes said. "Girl, you have to know if Golly gets hold of you, it won't be an easy death."

Appalled by that bit of verbal reality, Kennedy gasped. "Reyes!"

Both he and Jodi ignored her.

"You might not put any value on your life, but Kennedy sure as hell does. Come to that, so do I."

"Ha!"

Reyes leaned down into her space and growled, "I'd like to rip Golly apart because of what he did to you."

Anger shot Jodi out of her chair. Reyes straightened but didn't back up, so she had to tip her head way back to glare at him. Given her short stature she barely reached Reyes's shoulders, and he weighed more than twice what she did, making it a ludicrous standoff.

Full of pain and suffering, Jodi growled, "You think I don't want that, too?" Her eyes turned red and liquid, her thin chest heaving. "Jesus, it's *all* I want. I'd gladly die if I could take that miserable bastard with me!"

"Well, you can't," Reyes said softly, laying his large hand on her narrow shoulder. "I'm sorry, so fucking sorry, Jodi, but Rob Golly is dead after all."

When Jodi would have lurched away in shock, Reyes held her still. Furious, she went on tiptoe to glare into his face. "Why would you be sorry about that? I wanted him dead! That's why I killed him."

He nodded. "You accomplished that much, and I swear, girl, I'm cheering for you."

"Then why...?" As if Jodi knew there was worse news to come, the tears spilled over and she started gulping breaths.

"Sadly, the danger doesn't end with him. But I know you're strong. You've already proven that a dozen times over. I know you're smart, too, so you'll listen to reason."

Giving one sharp, grave nod, she rasped, "Quit dragging it out. Let's hear it, already."

"What you need to know, what you have to understand, is that your life has value. Real, substantial value. Don't let Golly take that from you." He lifted his hand to briefly cup her cheek. "He's taken enough. Don't give him another damned thing."

Angrily she dashed away the tears and then, wonder of wonders, she said, "Okay."

"Thank you."

"Why are you thanking me?" she asked with another huff.

"Because Kennedy loves you, and I don't want to see her tormented by your stubbornness." He grinned a rascal's grin, dimple and all. "Now, how about we all sit down and talk this out?" Oh-so-gently, he led her to the couch where Kennedy sat.

Kennedy barely kept her smile contained. Every time she thought Reyes couldn't get more wonderful, he outdid her expectations.

"Fine." Jodi flopped back against the plush cushions and propped her feet on the glass coffee table. "Talk away. I'm listening."

With Kennedy on one side of her, and Reyes on the other, Jodi was boxed in—but she didn't get jittery about it like she usually would. Reyes had accomplished that much.

Kennedy half turned to face her. "Okay, so as Reyes said, the good news is that Rob Golly is dead after all."

"I thought the body wasn't there, though. How do you explain that?"

"Well..." It was so awful Kennedy hated to break the news to her. "It seems Rob has a brother. You probably never met him because he was in prison. Apparently, as soon as Rand got out he went to see Rob and found his body. I'm guessing it didn't take a sleuth to find out from Rob's friends that he'd had you, making you the most likely suspect."

Eyes wide in disbelief, Jodi stared at her, then laughed. "A brother? You know, I think Rob talked about him every so often. There was even a photo of them when they were younger." She laughed again, the sound rusty and mean, nowhere near humor. "I must have the rottenest luck ever. My life has been tainted from the day I was born. You'd be smart to stay away from me."

Kennedy sat forward in a rush. "I care about you, damn it!"

She fell a little more in love with Reyes when he raised his hand. "And me. I'll take it as a personal affront if anything happens to you, Jodi. So we're not going to let it."

"Terrific," Jodi said. "I have a plan."

Knowing the way Jodi thought, Kennedy groaned.

Reyes, being a little more diplomatic, said, "I'm open to ideas. Let's hear it."

"We use me as bait."

"No," Kennedy said.

"How?" Reyes asked at the same time. "Because losing you can't be part of the plan."

"You're a hotshot, right?" Jodi smirked. "You and that big, quiet bro of yours. And, hey, let's not forget the badass chick he's with."

"Er, that would be his wife," Reyes said, then conceded, "although she is pretty badass."

"So I'll trust you three to keep me safe. You can handle that, can't you?"

"Probably."

"No," Kennedy said again. "Out of the question."

Still slouched in her seat, Jodi swiveled her head around to smile at her. "You're my best friend," she said. "My only friend. You matter to me a lot, Kennedy. Always know that. But I can't do this. I can't sit around and wait to see what will happen. This place might be nice, but the waiting... It makes me feel like I'm back in that damned cellar, not knowing what will happen or when."

"Then we'll stay somewhere together."

Reyes went on the alert, but she couldn't let Jodi feel alone now. "If I'm with you—"

"I'd still feel like I was crawling out of my skin. It's the waiting, you know?" She gave a small, sad smile. "It's not so much my surroundings. Not anymore. It's that I'm not in control, and I flat out can't stand it."

"They're working on it," Kennedy tried to assure her, but Jodi was already shaking her head.

"Sorry, but I can either confront things head-on, or I can take off again. Those are the options I can live with. If I can get this over with sooner, while also having some really good backup, then hey, that's the route I'd prefer."

Desperate, Kennedy reached for her hand. "It's too risky."

Jodi slipped over to lean against Kennedy's shoulder in an uncharacteristic show of affection. "Sorry, girlfriend. Really. But it's not your decision."

Kennedy looked from Jodi's trusting expression—a sight seldom seen—to Reyes's enigmatic gaze. He was leaving it up to her, she understood that, but he wasn't objecting. "Reyes?"

He rubbed a hand over his face. "I wouldn't want to do any-thing unless you're okay with it."

"But?"

"I get what Jodi is saying."

Jodi grinned. "Damn, maybe I like you as a pal."

Before she could get too excited, Reyes added, "I'd need time to plan, so we're talking at least a few days." In a sterner tone, his frown aimed at Jodi, he said, "In the meantime, I'd expect you to stay put."

She crossed her heart. "No problem. I just need a light at the end of the tunnel."

Kennedy felt as though the air had been compressed out of her lungs. She didn't want to come off as a coward, but someone had to inject logic. "There's no conceivable way to plan for every possibility."

"No," Reyes agreed, "and that's something Jodi should con-sider."

Jodi hugged Kennedy's arm. "Don't be a pill, okay? I *need* to do this. And just think, if we pull this off, I'll be free."

Temper flaring, Kennedy demanded, "Free to do what? To con-tinue risking yourself? To continue chasing trouble?"

"Hiding from the world," Reyes added. "Living half a life, all in the shadows."

"Hey!" Sitting up in a huff, Jodi poked Reyes in the shoulder. "You're supposed to be on my side."

"I'm not taking sides, doll. But I have a solution that might please you both."

Kennedy really didn't want to hear it, but what choice did she have? She nodded.

Jodi shrugged. "Out with it."

"We need some assurances." Sitting forward, one elbow braced on his knee, Reyes pinned Jodi with serious intent. "We need your cooperation. We need you to want to make a better life for yourself."

"You want to take over? Be my boss?" She started to rise. "Screw that."

Kennedy caught her elbow. "Can't you at least hear him out?"

Jodi was resistant, then finally flopped back in her seat. "Sure. Whatever."

So. Damned. Stubborn.

And so hurt. It seemed Jodi was part anger, part open wound and part fear, with attitude holding it all together.

Reyes didn't let it bother him. "My father funds some great initiatives for helping women who've escaped trafficking. We can go over the nitty-gritty another time, but the gist of it is that we can set you up with legit employment that you'll enjoy, plus help you with a place to stay, any additional education or training you might need, and financial assistance to keep it going until—"

Already Jodi was back on her feet and angrily stalking away. "I don't take charity."

"Wouldn't be charity," Reyes said, "unless you choose it to be. A smart person would see it as an opportunity for a leg up. A way to improve her life. Plus, you could always pay it forward. The task force needs good people pitching in."

Kennedy stood. "Jodi, please. Can't you take that chip off your shoulder long enough to accept well-meaning help?"

She stood at the big windows looking out. "Then what? You'll be rid of me?"

Catching on to one of Jodi's worries, Kennedy softened her tone. "Then you'll have a regular job with days off. We can spend time together—lunches, a movie. Shopping."

"I don't shop."

"You'll shop with me," Kennedy insisted. "The point is, I want you in my life. I want a reliable relationship that's based on mutual respect and affection, not worry or fear."

In the smallest voice Kennedy had ever heard, Jodi whispered, "You can't respect me."

Reyes asked, "Why the hell not? I do. My brother does."

Turning in surprise, Jodi stared at him. "Don't bullshit me," she said without heat.

"Doubt I could." He came to stand by Kennedy. "Now quit being such a hard case and accept a friendly offering from people who care."

"Your pa doesn't know me, so how can he care?"

Kennedy spoke ahead of Reyes. "His father, who is a wonderful man, by the way, lost someone he loved to traffickers. Believe me, he cares—about me, about *you*, about every woman who's ever been in such a horrid situation. You're not the only one who wants to make a difference, Jodi."

Reyes smiled at her with pride. "So passionate. And one-hundred percent correct."

Jodi's eyes grew glassy again. "Okay, fine. I'll do it."

"Yes!" Reyes stepped forward and swept her into a hug, shocking poor Jodi senseless. He seemed to catch himself and quickly set her back, but when he saw her slow grin, he laughed. "You're a woman of your word, so I trust you won't forget this conversation."

"No, I won't." She gestured to the door. "Now go make plans, and keep me updated. The waiting is miserable."

Obviously, Jodi wanted some time alone to digest it all.

Instead, Reyes rubbed his hands together. "Let's get pizza first. I'll send someone out for it."

Jodi eyed him warily.

His smile never slipped. "We can stuff our faces and visit. Kennedy's feeling as cooped up as you are." He turned to her. "You'd like that, wouldn't you, babe?"

Her heart felt too big for her chest. "Very much so."

"There, you see? Surely you can suffer me long enough to eat?"

It took her a second, and then Jodi laughed, not a fake laugh, or one inspired by anger, but an honest, joyous expression. "You're nuts—but okay, sure. I haven't had much appetite, but suddenly I'm starved."

"There you go." He turned to Kennedy. "This'll be fun."

She was so overwhelmed, words stuck in her throat. The best she could manage was a nod. Reyes gave her a wink and went to the phone to call the lobby.

He'd won Jodi over so easily, just by being himself. Kennedy felt caught between a good laugh—and a hard cry.

She was afraid for Jodi yet ecstatic to see her so happy, madly in love with Reyes yet anxious about the future. It felt like she was on a wild roller-coaster ride of shifting emotional extremes—and she'd never been happier in her life.

With that realization came a new fear: If things ended with Reyes, then what? Would she be able to go back to her mundane existence of writing, speaking engagements and slogging through each day without enthusiasm?

If things ended, she'd be more devastated than ever before.

Thanks to Reyes's influence, she was a stronger person now—but was she strong enough to survive that particular heartache?

Before it came to that, she'd tell Reyes that she loved him and hope it made a difference.

For now, she'd just enjoy seeing the smiles of the two people most important to her.

"You're sure he's dead?" Rand asked. "He couldn't just be in the hospital?"

"He's dead, all right. The news interviewed some witnesses who saw the car go off the road. Said he was carried out of the ravine in a body bag."

"Did you check the local hospitals anyway?" He wouldn't leave anything to chance.

"Just like you told me. Couldn't find him anywhere. He's dead."

Rand smiled. Perfect. Delbert O'Neil had become a liability with his endless complaints and impatience. And that damned chain-smoking. The stench alone had been vile.

If Del hadn't taken off when he did, Rand would have enjoyed cutting his throat while he slept.

Pinning the small-time thug with a glare, Rand asked, "Any news on Jodi?"

"Her car was towed, that's all I know."

"Hmm." He rocked back and forth, thinking. The same behemoth who'd destroyed his men to protect Kennedy was likely protecting Jodi also. "Can you round up a few more guys?"

"How many?"

"Ten ought to do it." Added to the ten he already had, they could cover a lot of ground. "Offer them a hundred dollars a day to keep on the lookout for Jodi or Kennedy. You still have photos of them you can share?"

"Yeah, on my phone."

Rand tapped his fingertips together and prodded his tongue between his missing teeth. "Whoever spots one of them first will get a bonus of five hundred."

"Sweet deal. I'll get the word out right away." He turned to go.

Rand waited until he was out the door of the cabin before he turned to the remaining man. This guy was a little more reliable. "I need some supplies."

"Sure thing, boss."

He went down the list of necessary items. "Don't buy more than two things at any one store. Shop around in different places so you don't draw attention."

"Got it. Anything else?"

"Yes. Early evening, go by that construction site down the road and gather up anything that can be used for shrapnel. Nails, staples, broken glass. Even small chunks of rocks will do."

Eyes wider now, the guy said, "Uh, boss, are we building a bomb?"

"We?" Golly smirked. "Do you know how to build a fucking bomb?"

He shook his head fast.

"I do, so yes, *I'll* be building a bomb." It wasn't how he wanted to kill Jodi, but things were getting dicey now that Delbert O'Neil had screwed up the plans. He had to be prepared, just in case. "Get everything back to me tonight."

With that clear dismissal, Rand finally found himself alone in the cabin. He, too, was getting tired of being cooped up. Shouldn't be for too much longer, though. He'd either have his hands on Jodi, where he could enjoy his revenge, or he'd blow her into tiny bits. Either way, justice would be served.

He rocked a little harder as he imagined each scenario.

For two days, they worked on the details of the trap. It wasn't easy, but Reyes convinced Kennedy that it would be better for them to stay at his father's house for now. She'd reluctantly agreed.

And she'd withdrawn.

Reyes knew it was her worry about Jodi, and maybe about him, too, that kept her mostly quiet. Soon as they wrapped it up and ensured Jodi's safety, she'd relax again.

He hoped.

To keep up appearances, they went to the gym each day. Although he'd have preferred for her to stay at home, she refused, saying she felt safest with him.

A part of him relished her trust, and another part wondered if he was seeing the future laid out for him, how she'd always react to the danger inherent in his job. For himself, he wouldn't mind. It was kind of nice having a woman who cared.

Yet he hated the idea of her continuing to live on edge— because of him.

That second day at the gym, she went to his office to look over her manuscript while he continued dealing with the public. She couldn't resume her workouts yet, especially since his dad constantly warned her to take it easy.

If Parrish had his way, Kennedy would probably still be in bed. It was pretty remarkable how she pushed through, though. More from a sheer force of will to carry on rather than in a bullheaded way meant to prove anything to others.

A personality trait no doubt learned from her past.

With the colorful bruising on her face, Kennedy had gotten more than a few stares. She'd simply smiled and acted as if nothing had happened. So as far as he knew, no one had asked her about it. It helped that her warmer clothes covered her body, so the only mark showing was the one on her temple.

More than a little distracted with thoughts of Kennedy, Reyes almost did a double take when he heard one guy say to another, "Yeah, you just need to keep an eye out for either chick. You get paid by the day, and if you spot one of them, there's a nice bonus."

What were the odds? One guy was standing near the weight bench while another did some presses. They looked like many twentysomething guys who visited the gym, dressed in baggy sweatpants, dingy wifebeater undershirts and expensive gym shoes. Both had elaborate tats along their arms, and one had tats extending over his chest and neck. Stocking hats hid most of their hair, but judging by their brows, they both were dark.

Going for a casual vibe, Reyes whistled low as he started picking up discarded weights at the other benches to put them back on the rack, which got him close enough to glance at the small phone photo the standing guy showed to the one on the bench.

Jodi. Son of a bitch.

He didn't react as he listened a little more closely.

"No, I don't know the dude. Got the info from my buddy, Dub. You'll check in with him."

When he shared a phone number, Reyes committed it to memory long enough to get to the desk where Will, an employee, checked people in and answered the phone.

In his rush, Reyes rudely shouldered Will aside and grabbed up a paper and pen to jot down the number with the name. With that done, he murmured to Will, "Keep an eye on those guys by the benches. I'll be right back."

"Sure thing."

Will was a good worker who knew to keep his mouth shut and his eyes open. He had no real idea what Reyes did for a living other than running a gym, and he didn't ask. His loyalty had been tested numerous times already.

Reyes strolled to the office and handed the paper to Kennedy. "Call Madison and share this with her. Tell her I overheard a couple of knuckleheads talking about getting paid to look for you and Jodi."

Startled, Kennedy looked up. "What—"

"No time for questions, babe. I'll be back in a few. Stay here with the door locked. Got it?"

She nodded, stood quickly and followed him as far as the door, then closed and locked it behind him.

Thankfully, the men were still where Reyes had left them, and now they had a third man with them. He eavesdropped without hesitation.

"No shit? How many is he hiring?"

"Ten, I think, but I'm only supposed to round up five. So you in or what?"

"Yeah, sure. Where do I look?"

"We're supposed to spread out in this neighborhood, especially here around the gym." He glanced up Reyes.

Reyes nodded casually as he continued on by. When he reached the desk, in a low voice he asked Will, "You up for a side job? It's worth a day's pay."

Brows up, Will said, "Heck, yeah."

"When the kid in the gray hoodie leaves, see if you can spot his license plate number without being noticed."

"What if he's not driving?"

Yeah, that was a possibility. "See which direction he goes." Clapping him on the shoulder, Reyes said, "Thanks." He deliberately moved away from the men to the other side of the gym, where he had brief conversations with two women doing cardio, then a younger guy trying to bulk up his legs.

Though Reyes didn't stare at the men, he was aware of them the entire time.

When two of them finally left, including the one in the hoodie who been doling out info, Will moseyed out and, damn it, Reyes started to worry. If Will was too obvious, they might catch on to him and then he could get jumped later.

It was a fact that a lot of street toughs hung out at the gym. Reyes didn't discourage it. He owned the gym in this run-down section of town so that he could hear the word from the street.

So far, so good.

He was relieved to see Will cross the road to his truck, where he opened the door, got inside and rummaged in his glove box.

Good cover. He'd always appreciated Will as a smart kid, though he was probably twenty-two now.

A minute later he left the truck, locked the doors and jogged back inside. His nose and ears had already turned red from the cold, and he chafed his arms as he went to the desk, made a note and stuck it in the top drawer.

Smooth.

Holding up a candy bar that he'd brought out of the truck, he said, "Okay for me to take a break, boss?"

Will caught on quick, obviously. Appreciating how he covered his tracks, Reyes nodded.

Aware of the third man lingering inside and now watching them both, Reyes said, "No problem. I'll cover out here." Walking over to two regulars, Reyes took time to offer some instruction on a machine they were using incorrectly.

The third guy lost interest and left.

With the coast seemingly clear, the urge to check on Kennedy, to give the plate number to Madison, to follow after the knuckleheads all warred inside Reyes, but good training paid off, and he kept up the show of being nothing more than a fit gym owner interested in his clientele.

Good thing, too, because he spotted the gray hoodie goof peeking back in through the big front window.

Shame Golly had stooped to hiring scrawny troublemakers. Reyes would almost feel bad for schooling them on the error of their ways.

His issue now would be getting Kennedy out of the gym without them spotting her. He didn't doubt that at least one of them was already aware of her, but he'd prefer not to engage with them tonight. It'd be better if he could get her out of harm's way first.

Screw it. He went to the desk, picked up the landline and called Cade. His brother would be at the bar now, but he could work it out.

Making sure no one was near enough to listen in, and assuming the idiot peering in through the window couldn't read lips, Reyes explained the situation to Cade.

Of course Cade had a solution. He always did. "I can have Sterling pick her up at the back door. If you're ready to leave at the same time, you can follow behind them. Make sure Kennedy is wearing the sunglasses Dad gave her, and Sterling can bring a hat to stuff on her head."

In that moment, Reyes realized something interesting. He loved coordinating with his family.

For years he'd told himself that he did it because he'd been groomed for it, he was good at it, and it made a difference.

Now he knew it was more than that.

He thrived on this shit.

Cade would always be the older brother he looked up to, and Madison would always be the baby sister he adored.

Working with them was not only rewarding, it was special in a way few families ever experienced. They weren't just close, they routinely depended on each other. He knew his family would always have his back.

And because they understood that Kennedy was important to him, they had her back, too.

God, he was lucky—and until Kennedy, he'd never realized it. "Tell Sterling I appreciate it."

"She knows, but I'll tell her anyway."

They figured out a time for Sterling to arrive, and after Reyes disconnected, he grinned. Done playing, he went to the front door, opened it and said to hoodie-boy, "What's up, dude? You forget something?"

Like a deer in the headlights, the guy went blank. "What?"

"Saw you looking in. If you lost something, let me know. I'll look around."

Full of belligerence now, he said, "No, man. I ain't lost nothing. Can't a guy hang out?"

"Sure, no problem. It's warmer in here, though."

Lip curling, the guy turned and stalked away, going the opposite direction this time. So was he meeting someone? About a block down, he peered over his shoulder, and Reyes ducked back inside.

While he had a chance, he fetched the note Will had made and put it in his shoe. Once Will returned from his break, he thanked him again and finally went to Kennedy.

It really felt like things were coming together. Soon he'd remove all the obstacles, and then he'd tell Kennedy how he felt and ask her to stay with him.

Forever.

CHAPTER EIGHTEEN

"I WANT TO GO WITH YOU," Kennedy said, and he heard a frantic note in her voice.

"Not a good idea, babe." Reyes paused in the middle of sorting his gear to press a kiss to her mouth. God, he loved that mouth. Loved her ass, too, as well as that particular obstinate expression she was giving him now.

Her soft blond hair, her blue eyes. Her stubbornness and strength.

Hell, he loved every part of her, everything about her, all the things she made him feel and the ways she'd changed him. She'd become the center of his world and he didn't mind at all.

"Reyes—"

"Kennedy," he teased back. Even if she wasn't in a teasing mood, he sure as hell was.

The day had finally come to put the plan into action. It was made easier by Golly's watchdogs, who now haunted the gym and the streets around it.

The idea was that he'd stop in at the gym with Jodi, just long enough for them to spot her. Shortly after that, once the goons had a chance to notify Golly, he'd head out to a more remote area, where they could try their luck at ambushing him again. This time Reyes planned to be ready. He'd already chosen a nice high point where he and Jodi could wait them out.

He'd pick them off one by one without hesitation or a single moment of remorse.

For the other problems, meaning Golly's cohorts, Madison had found locations for them by using hoodie-boy's plates. The girl was a whiz at tracking. Hoodie-boy met with one person, and that led them to another person, and on it went.

He, Cade and Sterling would round up all of them. With Madison on watch, none of them would get away.

Once it was over, Kennedy would be free to choose whatever life she wanted. He planned to convince her to choose a life with him.

"You have it all covered," she insisted. "You said so yourself."

"True." It was as planned out as it could be. "But we have to split up. I'll be with Jodi. Cade and Sterling will get the other creeps. Madison will keep an eye on Golly at the motel, and bam, it'll be over."

"See? It's safe," Kennedy reiterated. "You know Jodi will be more comfortable if I'm there with her."

"There are too many things that can go wrong."

"Reyes." She slipped up against him, her arms around his neck. "If it's not safe for me, how is it safe for Jodi?"

I'm not in love with Jodi. Damn it, he was so close to having it all that he didn't want to blurt out a half-baked declaration now. He wanted to do it the right way.

The way Kennedy deserved.

He settled on saying, "Jodi knows how to shoot."

"I can shoot."

He gave her a level look. "Practicing a few times is not the same as using a gun in a high-pressure situation."

"So I'll be a lookout."

Damn it, he wanted to know she was tucked away some place safe, not out in the thick of it. Yes, he was confident of his ability, but shit happened. He couldn't bear it if it happened to her again. "Kennedy—"

"I'll get her geared up," Sterling said as she stepped through the open door of the suite. "Come on, Kennedy."

Smug, Kennedy blew him a kiss and hurried after his sister-in-law.

Reyes was right on her heels. "Now wait a damn minute."

She turned, a desperate expression on her face. "I swear I won't get in your way. I won't cry and I'll follow orders to the letter."

"Ah, hon..." He closed the space between them. "I'm not worried about any of that."

Sterling stood there, arms crossed. "She wants to be with you, you dolt."

"I *know* that."

Undeterred by his dark frown, Sterling continued, "I wouldn't let Cade leave me behind."

"You," he said, "aren't natural."

"Because I'm female? Well, look at you, being all sexist."

Cursing a blue streak wouldn't help anything, but Reyes did it anyway.

Kennedy touched his face. "I keep telling you. I feel safest when I'm with you."

He glared at Sterling, hoping she'd give them a private moment. She didn't budge. Frustrated enough to make his hair stand on end, Reyes stared at Kennedy a long minute. Best-laid plans and all that. His had just gone horribly awry. "If that's true," he said, feeling Sterling's smile as she listened in, "then maybe you should plan on staying with me."

"Yes! I knew you'd see reason." She started to go.

Reyes stopped her. "I didn't mean just today, babe." Watching her closely, he saw her eyes flare. "I mean after this is over."

"After?"

Let Sterling watch, he didn't care. Swooping in, he kissed Kennedy, taking his time, moving his mouth over hers, teasing his tongue along her lips and then into her mouth. She clung to him, and with a soft groan she reciprocated.

When he lifted his mouth, she looked dazed.

Reyes smoothed a hand over her hair, letting his thumb lightly brush the bruise on her temple. "Stay with me."

She bit her lips, then slowly smiled and nodded. "Of course I will. Thank y—"

Another kiss stopped her from thanking him.

"Ahem." Grinning, Sterling said, "Not that the show isn't great, but we're running low on time. So what's it to be? Want her in a vest and armed, or do you plan to lock her in a closet?"

Running a hand over his head, Reyes turned away, immediately paced back and cursed. "You'll stay right where I put you?"

Kennedy nodded.

"You swear you know how to shoot?"

"Adequately." She winced. "Can't promise I'll hit anything, but I can definitely return fire if necessary."

"You'll stay low, stay safe and—"

"Yes and yes." Grabbing him, Kennedy squeezed him tight. "I'll be right back. Don't you dare leave without me."

MADISON SAT IN THE LIBRARY, her laptop in front of her, watching all the players. Reyes, with Kennedy and Jodi, would reach the gym in the next fifteen minutes or so.

Cade and Sterling were at the back of an old house, slowly closing in on where two of Golly's cohorts had holed up.

Golly hadn't moved from the motel, though two men had come in to see him. It was sheer luck that a camera on the connected diner caught the front of his cabin. The picture was dim, but she made it out just fine.

When the two men left, she noted that one of them carried a heavy duffel bag. Suddenly she had a very bad feeling about things. She watched the men until they got into a car, then she wrote down the license plate number and did a quick, secure search.

Matthew Grimes.

With a name in hand, she extended her search and found that the guy had a long record, similar to Golly's, and lived locally. Why hadn't she known about him sooner? Was he someone newly brought into the schemes?

Her bad feeling grew.

Her dad walked in, and, being so attuned to his children, he immediately knew something was wrong.

"What is it?" Parrish asked, hurrying around the desk to look over her shoulder.

"I don't know." Madison skimmed all the players again. The car with the two men left in a hurry. Because her father encouraged

them to share misgivings—he was a big believer in instincts—
she laid out her thoughts.

"This is the first I've seen Grimes. Why would Golly need a
new hand at this point?" She looked at her father. "Unless his plan
of attack has changed?" A terrible thought, given everything was
already in the works. Both her brothers were out there, Sterling,
too, and now she felt like she hadn't judged the situation well at all.

Parrish, always methodical, stared at the screen for only a few
seconds before making a decision. "Call the detective. See if he
knows anything about Grimes."

Glad to have a valid reason to reach out to Crosby again, Madison lifted her phone and, with the number memorized, dialed him.
Knowing her father would want to listen in, she put the phone on
speaker and set it on the desk.

He didn't answer until the fifth ring, and he sounded harried.
"Detective Albertson."

Watching the screens, Madison saw the driver of the car take
an exit that would lead him to the general area of Reyes's gym.
Alarm bells went off in her head. In cases like this, she didn't believe in coincidences.

If the gym was his destination, and she'd bet it was, he'd arrive
within minutes of Reyes.

"It's Madison McKenzie."

Crosby missed a beat before saying, "Ms. McKenzie. I'm surprised to hear from you."

She rolled her eyes at his absurd deference. Whether he'd enjoyed it or not, she'd kissed him. He could certainly use her first
name. "You probably wouldn't have," she admitted, "not after that
insult you dealt me."

Her father's brows went up.

She shook her head at him, letting him know it wasn't anything
to concern him, then forged on. "The thing is, Crosby, I have a
situation and I'm hoping you can help me."

"Hang on one second."

She heard movement, then the sound of a car door closing, followed by the start of an engine.

"I was just on my way out. Crazy busy at the moment, but I
can talk while I drive."

"Thank you." She considered what to say, yet knew the outcome would be the same. "Now, I don't want you to get angry."

"That pretty much guarantees it right there," he growled. "What the hell are you up to now?"

He said that with so much accusation, she huffed. "Matthew Grimes. Do you know the name?"

Crosby surprised her with amped-up anger. "Damned right I know him. I'm headed to his last known location right now. How the hell do *you* know him?"

When Parrish gave her a nod, she confessed, "I'm keeping tabs on Golly. Grimes just left him."

"Jesus, Madison. You know where Golly is and didn't tell me?"

How could the man sound both hurt and frustrated by that when he'd made no effort to stay in touch with her? "We'll have to cover that later, Detective. Right now, I'm…concerned."

"As you should be. I knew Grimes hung with Golly so I've been keeping tabs on him. Last night the weasel went to six different stores buying up enough ingredients for several homemade bombs."

Madison caught her breath. *The duffel he'd been carrying.*

Leaning forward, hands flattened on the desk, Parrish spoke before Madison could. "He's headed toward my son's gym right now. How close are you?"

"Son of a bitch," Crosby exploded. "Your family has a lot of explaining to do when this is over."

"How close?" Parrish repeated in a hard demand.

"I'll call it in. Tell Reyes to clear everyone out of there."

"I'm organizing now. Don't make me regret reaching out to you."

Walking away, Parrish used his own phone to call Reyes.

Madison turned back to the phone. "Crosby?"

"Yeah?"

"Promise me you'll be careful."

He gave a gravelly laugh filled with affront. "Don't worry about me."

She'd worry if she wanted to. Irate, she glared at the phone. "Would it be too much to ask to be kept updated?"

Seconds ticked by, then he said evenly, "You haven't seen fit to give me your number."

Her heart skipped a beat. True, her calls came in as private, but she'd love for Crosby to have it. "I'll text it to you now." Why did it feel as if they'd just come to an understanding? "You'll contact me once you're at the gym?"

"I'm not going to the gym, but I'll let you know once it's been cleared."

"Then—"

"You're going to tell me what's going on," he stated, leaving no room for negotiation. "And you're going to tell me now."

REYES HAD JUST pulled up to the curb when his phone rang. It surprised him to see it was his dad calling, not Madison or Cade. Surprised him, and made him uneasy.

Making a quick decision, he pulled away from the curb and answered the call. "What's wrong?"

"Get away from the gym."

"Already doing that." He checked his mirrors, not yet spotting any trouble.

"Two men left Golly, headed your way," Parrish said, his explanation short and to the point. "Detective Albertson says the driver went shopping last night for the makings of a bomb."

"Damn." The ramifications settled in on Reyes. He had a gym full of innocents, and two women in the back seat of his truck.

"Albertson is on the way. I assume he'll alert other authorities." Parrish hesitated. "I want you to abort the plan. Given you three are the target, stay away from the gym. Divert to Golly's motel." His voice lowered. "Get the bastard."

"You'll get everyone out of the gym?"

"It'll be my next call. Albertson will clean up that mess."

Reyes tightened his hands on the wheel. "Got it."

"Watch your back."

"Always." Before explaining anything to Kennedy and Jodi, he backtracked by going two blocks down, then two blocks over. The women patiently stayed silent.

Once he was headed in the right direction, he laid out the situation for them.

Kennedy sat forward to touch his shoulder. "Someone will tell Cade?"

"Dad or Madison, but his plans won't alter. Cade is still on to close the net."

Nodding, she sat back again, quiet as she'd promised to be.

Jodi whispered, "This doesn't feel right. Golly doesn't want to blow me up. He doesn't want me dead at a distance."

Reyes tended to agree. "It's personal for him."

Jodi's voice grew urgent. "He's trying to catch us unaware."

Yup, exactly how Reyes saw it. "But we won't let him, right?"

"No, we won't." Kennedy took Jodi's hand. "Trust Reyes. He knows what he's doing."

Damn right, he did. "I don't think anyone spotted us, but I want you two to keep watch." Giving them something to do would make them feel more in control. "Tell me if you see anything suspicious."

With no real sign of nervousness, Kennedy said, "Will do."

Jodi remained silent. He could only imagine how she felt. The girl had been all set to use herself as bait, and now the plans were upside down. Shit happened. It wasn't the first time he'd had to adjust to changing conditions, but that didn't make it easy.

When he was near the motel, he called Madison hands-free on speaker. "All clear?" he asked.

"I haven't seen Golly move. But Reyes, I don't feel right about any of this."

"I know. Same." He glanced in the rearview mirror at Kennedy's set expression. She was doing her utmost not to look unnerved. Because he knew every business on the road, Reyes said, "I'm going to put them both in a restaurant."

"No!" Jodi said, immediately objecting.

Kennedy shushed her. "Let him do his thing, okay? He knows best."

Her confidence felt good.

Madison agreed with Jodi. "Golly might have contacts in every area business. I think you should keep them close."

He hesitated but knew she was right. Away from him, either of them could get grabbed. He'd die before he let that happen, so sticking close likely was the way to go. Deciding on a quick compromise, he asked, "Where should I park so that they'll be near, but not too close, and you'll have a constant view of my truck?"

"Three spots down from Golly's cabin is best. It's the third one from the office, and I believe the other two are empty."

"Huh. Wonder if Golly rented them to ensure his privacy."

"Makes sense."

Reyes parked beneath a security lamp. Though the night was dark, the lamp hadn't yet come on. Odds were it wouldn't. Not much in the motel seemed to be in good working order.

"Kennedy?" Madison said.

Leaning forward, Kennedy said, "I'm here."

"Why don't you get behind the wheel in case a hasty exit is necessary?"

She looked at Reyes, got his nod and agreed.

The parking lot was fairly quiet. In the office, Reyes could see a desk manager backlit by a lamp, and he appeared to be alone. Seeing the place up close, he was surprised it was even still in business. What had probably been nice cabins a decade ago were now more like hovels in need of serious repairs. The gravel lot had deep ruts and potholes, and an area that should have been grass was now snow-covered weeds.

"It's a dump," he said to Madison. "You sure it's legit?"

"A grandson inherited it, and it's gone downhill since then."

Shame.

Jodi snapped, "Can't we get on with it?"

"Getting there." Reyes studied the cabin. Curtains were drawn over grimy windows. His bad feeling escalated. "I'm not going to the front of the cabin. I'll circle around back and see if there's another way in."

While watching for any sign of attack, he opened the door and got out. Turning, he motioned to Kennedy to take over as driver. She quickly removed her coat and tossed it in the back seat, then slid behind the wheel.

Jodi, he noticed, had a Glock in her hand and a stark look of resolve on her face.

"Hey."

She glanced at him.

"No mishaps with the gun, okay?"

Nodding, she went back to studying the area, her uneasiness palpable.

Knowing he couldn't put it off any longer, he touched Kennedy's chin. "Lock up behind me. If anything happens, drive away. Do not try to play my protector."

Before agreeing, she said, "Swear to me you'll be okay."

"Course I will." He stole a fast kiss. "When this is over, you and I have plans to make."

Reyes's steps were silent as he moved in the shadows toward Golly's cabin. At the farthest side of the ramshackle structure he spotted a small, high window that he guessed to be in the bathroom. Around the corner, he saw a larger window and then the door. Tightly closed curtains kept him from having a view inside.

That in itself wasn't suspicious, yet tension prickled up his spine.

He backtracked to the small window. Aging cobwebs covered the sill, and a crack traveled upward from the bottom right corner. For most, the window would be too high to be accessible. His height and overall physical fitness served him well now. Catching the ledge with his fingertips, he levered himself up for a peek.

The room was dark and it took a moment for his eyesight to adjust. The bathroom door was shut, closing it off from the rest of the cabin. He was considering how he might enter through the window when a slight movement inside drew his gaze. He levered up a little higher for a better view.

Stunned, he realized that Golly, fully dressed, was stretched out flat in the narrow bathtub. Why would he... *Shit.*

Before the thought fully formed, he understood why everything felt off.

The front door was booby-trapped, likely with a bomb. Had he busted in, as he'd originally planned, he'd have been seriously wounded—and Kennedy and Jodi would be on their own.

Kennedy.

Silently he dropped back to his feet and, ducking low, went back to the front of the building. Gun in hand, he saw both women still in the truck, exactly as he'd instructed.

Beyond them, though, two shadows lurked.

No way would he let them get anywhere near Kennedy.

Flattening himself to the side of the building, he scanned the area, ensuring Golly didn't have more henchmen creeping around. He didn't see anyone else.

The men seemed to be waiting on something. Probably the explosion.

Picking up a rock, Reyes took aim and let it fly. It hit the man hunkering in the shadows closest to the truck. With a rank curse, he jerked around, giving up all attempts at stealth. So did the second guy.

Kennedy must have spotted them, because she put the truck in gear, prepared to move if needed. Damn, he was proud of her.

He waited, wanting the men to get just a little closer before he stepped out. Once they were within range, he'd have all the advantage he needed.

Then the unthinkable happened.

One of the men snarled, "Fuck it," and took aim at the truck, planning to shoot Kennedy and Jodi through the windows.

Terror put Reyes on autopilot. He stepped out with his gun in his hand, firing off a shot that sent the man stumbling back until he tripped over his feet and dropped. One more shot, and Reyes ensured he wouldn't be getting up.

The second man ran, disappearing into the darkness.

Furious that he'd allowed Kennedy to come along, Reyes started for the truck, his only thought to get her to safety.

The second man had already circled back, and now he shot at Reyes. Diving for the cover of the truck, Reyes barked, "Down!" to both women, then peered around the side of the truck.

He was a crack shot, better than good. It was the one aspect of their training where his ability trumped Cade's.

Reyes watched the darkness, spotted the target peeking out, squeezed his trigger and put one right through the bastard's head.

With all the gunfire, cops would now be on their way. Even if the desk manager hadn't called them, someone would have. It'd be best if he could—

The passenger side of the truck opened and Jodi stepped out.

Alarmed, Reyes straightened enough to see her. "Jodi!" If there were more men around, she'd be an easy hit. "What the hell are you—"

Grim faced, her jaw clenched, she lifted her Glock.

At first, Reyes thought she was aiming for him, but when she fired beyond him, he immediately turned to face the new threat.

The impact of her bullet propelled Rand Golly backward against the side of an empty cabin. He must have left through the back door and moved up the yards before stepping out to the lot. Pain twisted his face and he slumped, but didn't go down.

Jodi's bullet had hit him center mass, so there was only one explanation. A bulletproof vest. Still hurt like hell to get hit, yet it wasn't a killing blow.

Slowly Golly grinned at them...and showed the bomb in his hand.

"Get down," Golly ordered Jodi. She didn't move. Damn her, she actually took a step forward. "If I drop it, it explodes," he warned.

Curling her lip, Jodi stared at him. "An impact bomb? Really? How much reach does it have?" she asked in a dead voice. "Are you willing to kill yourself, too?"

"Yes," he hissed, his expression a morbid mix of pain and anticipation.

Kennedy, bless her practical, levelheaded heart, put the truck in Reverse and very slowly began backing away, enabling Reyes to keep pace with her. He wanted to reassure her, but he didn't dare take his gaze off Golly.

With an effort, Golly regained his feet, his twisted expression triumphant. "To avenge my brother, I'll kill all of you."

"Your brother," Jodi sneered, "was a smelly, disgusting, whiny little prick, and he sniveled like a bitch while I killed him."

Roaring, Golly straightened even more.

Sirens sounded in the distance. It was all going to hell fast.

"Jodi," Reyes said in his calmest, most even tone, despite the urgency humming through his veins. "Kennedy is going to be extremely pissed if you get hurt."

"Keep her safe," Jodi said.

Kennedy shoved open the passenger door and snapped, "Jodi, get your butt over here right now or I'll never forgive you!"

That command surprised both Reyes and Jodi.

Seeing the indecision on Jodi's face, Reyes promised her, "I've got it." When she reluctantly nodded, he said, "Now *run*."

Bolting away, Jodi sprinted for the truck. Reyes heard the truck door slam.

Golly, the bastard, tried to react in time, lifting his arm to throw the bomb—and Reyes shot him.

Deliberately, he didn't make it a killing shot.

No, he took out Golly's shoulder so that the bomb fell from his hand. A look of horror crossed his ugly face as he realized what had happened.

Satisfied, Reyes dove behind the truck.

Golly screamed a split second before the blast of sound, the rush of fire and the scattering of debris drowned him out.

Reyes heard the pellets hitting the truck, felt something sear his shoulder, and prayed Kennedy and Jodi weren't hurt.

Ears ringing, he slowly came to his feet and saw both women ducked down on their seats. Golly was on the ground, bleeding in multiple places. His sleeve was shredded—and so was his arm. It was probably the ragged, gaping hole in his neck that had killed him.

Doing a quick scan of the area, Reyes didn't spot any more threats. Other than the horrified desk manager, they were now alone.

The first sob alarmed him. Expecting the worst, Reyes jerked around and found Jodi with her face in her hands, her shoulders shaking while Kennedy tried to soothe her. She kept rubbing Jodi's back and twice hugged her.

She looked up and met his gaze, her smile sad, and gave Jodi another squeeze.

Jodi wasn't hurt, then. Likely it was an emotional overload now that the danger had ended.

Police swarmed into the lot from different entrances, lights flashing and sirens blaring.

And, damn it, Detective Albertson led the way.

Reyes set his gun aside, locked his hands behind his neck and waited.

There'd be no end of explanations to give, but the threat was now over and that's what really mattered.

Full of frowns, Crosby got out of his car and nodded toward Golly's body. "Rand Golly?"

"Yes." Reyes nodded to the other side of the lot, behind the truck. "Two other bodies in that direction. So you know, there are more weapons in my truck."

"I see." Crosby rubbed his face and said something to two of the officers. They headed for the bodies Reyes had indicated.

"I thought you were going to my gym."

"I sent others. Everything is fine there, and we now have several arrests."

Reyes had no idea what was going on, but at least his gym was safe. "I see." He frowned. "How is it you're here, Detective?"

Smile tight, Crosby said, "Your sister."

"No shit?" It wasn't like Madison to trust anyone other than family.

"I didn't give her a choice." As he approached, he took in the blood on Reyes's shoulder. "You're hurt?"

What bullshit. No one took choices from his sister. If Madison opted to share with Crosby, it was a strong indication of her trust...which meant Reyes could trust him also.

Slowly, watching Crosby in case he objected, Reyes lowered his arms. He, too, glanced at his shoulder. Blood soaked his shirt, but the pain was minimal. "Little shrapnel from the bomb. It'll be fine."

"Your brother rounded up several men, only he managed not to kill them."

"Cade is smooth like that."

Looking very much like a man in charge, Crosby took in the scene. "Golly had a bomb?"

"Threatening Jodi with it, yeah." He looked Crosby right in the eyes and said, "He planned a lot of damage. I had no choice but to shoot him."

"Your choice could have been to notify me."

He gave a noncommittal shrug. "Didn't know he had a bomb, or I might have." A *huge* lie. "Besides, my shot didn't kill him."

"No, it just caused him to drop the bomb, as you knew it would?"

Reyes said nothing. His methods had been efficient—he wouldn't apologize for them—and he wouldn't explain further, not until he spoke with Madison and got a handle on these new dynamics. A *cop.* What the hell was his sister thinking?

Lower, so the officers wouldn't hear, Crosby growled, "Do you realize the clusterfuck your family has created?"

He sure as hell wouldn't indict his family. "You wanted Golly." He jutted his chin in the direction of the body. "Well, there he is."

Reyes waited for Crosby to arrest him, and was still waiting when Kennedy left the truck and launched herself at him.

"She's obviously upset," Crosby grumbled. "Take care of her."

Smiling, Reyes slowly gathered Kennedy close. More and more it became apparent that Crosby had a very soft spot when it came to women.

An admirable trait.

While the cops did their thing, Reyes held Kennedy, thinking of all the things he wanted to say, but first he had to prioritize. "Is Jodi okay?"

She nodded against his chest, her hold tightening even more. "She will be, thanks to you."

"And you?" It wasn't easy but he set her back enough to tip up her chin. "I'm proud of you, Kennedy. Again." Pretty much always. "You did great, babe."

"I didn't do anything."

"Wrong. You had the foresight to back up the truck so I could use it as cover. You got Jodi's stubborn butt out of harm's way. You ducked when you needed." He pressed a kiss to her lips. "You were levelheaded and calm, and I'm *proud* of you."

Her lips trembling, she rested her forehead to his chest and mumbled something low.

"Hey, you okay?"

She took a solid step back so that his arms dropped to his sides. Her eyes widened when she saw the blood on his shoulder. "Oh, my God, you're hurt!"

"No, it's nothing."

Voice rising, she snapped, "Why is it never anything when *you're* hurt, but it's a big deal when I am?"

Wow, she'd been so calm up to that point that her agitated tone took him by surprise. Gently Reyes cupped her face. "Maybe because you mean so much to me?" He touched his mouth to hers again, lingering a few seconds this time. "Swear to God, Kennedy, it hurts me the most to see you hurt."

She hesitated, her gaze on his injury. "You promise it's not bad?"

"A tiny sting, that's all." He kissed her again. "As long as you're okay, I'm fine."

"Reyes." Releasing a long breath, she glanced around at the activity, then briefly at Jodi, who now stood beside Crosby, peering down at Golly.

Turning back to him, she gazed into his eyes and said, "I love you."

Reyes felt his face go blank. "Say again?"

"I love you. So damn much, and I know I always will." Her lips trembled. "Seeing you hurt devastates me, but I guess it's bound to happen again."

Holy shit, the lady had terrible timing. "You love me?" He had a difficult time grasping the words, coming out of the blue like they did.

Her chin lifted an inch. "I just thought you should know."

Of all the… Slowly he grinned. "Way to blindside me, babe."

"Sorry."

Reyes hugged her off her feet, turned her in a circle, then kissed her in front of gawking officers, a disgruntled detective and her smiling friend.

"Get a room," Jodi said, laughing.

Kennedy freed her mouth. "Oh, Reyes." She looked stunned. "Despite all this, Jodi just *laughed*."

"So she did." Jodi would be all right. The girl had a backbone of steel and a survivalist's instincts.

And she had Kennedy, the biggest asset of all.

When he realized Kennedy was shivering, he stepped to the truck, grabbed her coat and helped her into it. Then he led her over to Crosby, where the front desk manager was busy rattling off what he'd witnessed.

All in all, the dude made it sound like Golly was a lunatic and that Reyes had saved the day. Pretty accurate, really.

A cop quickly led the manager back to the office so they could talk.

Crosby looked at Reyes. "I'm guessing you know the drill."

"Arresting me after all?"

"No. But I need statements from all three of you." He gave an apologetic smile to Kennedy. "You can't keep her glued to your side."

"Wanna bet?"

Rubbing the back of his neck, Crosby said with insistence, "I gave you a few minutes, but now I need to sort this out."

Reyes was about to argue—because seriously, Kennedy wasn't going anywhere without him—when a sleek black car pulled into the lot. Recognizing it, Reyes breathed a sigh of relief. His dad had arrived.

"Now what?" Crosby grumbled.

Parrish McKenzie brought a whole lot of consequence with him. As he climbed out of the car, he looked like a stately senator and carried himself like a benevolent king. Better still, he had the instincts and ability of a warrior.

Content with how things were rolling out, Reyes said, "You can talk with Kennedy, but my dad will be with her." He bent to Kennedy's temple. "Everything is fine. I'll be back with you in just a few minutes."

Her gaze searched his, maybe because he hadn't yet returned her declaration. Soon, he promised himself. Very, very soon.

IT WAS FOUR in the morning when they finally got to bed, still at Parrish's house. Kennedy hoped she'd get a good long break now, because her system wasn't cut out for such constant cloak-and-dagger drama.

Reyes ended up with three stitches in his shoulder, and a mess of colorful bruising. *A tiny sting*, he'd said. Ha! The man had a small gouge taken out of his flesh. She supposed she'd have to accept that he wasn't one to complain.

He was usually too busy protecting, nurturing and being all-around awesome.

They'd found pieces of shrapnel from Golly's bomb scattered everywhere, including embedded in the side of Reyes's truck.

Recalling the awful shape of Golly's body, she knew she could have lost Reyes. He'd saved Jodi by risking himself, but he *had* survived. Given his personality and vocation, she'd have to focus on that.

Jodi was back at the hotel, where she'd stay for another week until a more permanent residence was ready for her, though she could now come and go as she pleased. They'd offered her alternatives, but she no longer minded the fancy suite—as long as it was temporary.

After her heartbreaking cry, she'd done an amazing about-face, looking forward to the future and, thankfully, glad to be alive. There was a new optimism about her, a zest to see what the next day would hold.

She'd be meeting with many people over the next week, including Reyes and her, to help her figure out the next steps. Kennedy was determined to make Jodi feel secure.

Just as Reyes had done for her.

Cade and Sterling had grabbed their targets without a hitch, which had led to information indicating a much larger trafficking network.

Parrish had made the decision to clue in Crosby so he could tie up all the loose ends. Kennedy discovered that the senior McKenzie had made allies with a few different people in the legal system—and some in political circles.

It seemed to her that Crosby had just been included in the hush-hush details of the McKenzie family enterprise. She knew Madison would be happy about that—if things progressed as she preferred. She'd put her money on Madison.

Now she and Reyes were stretched out in his bed, only one dim light breaking up the darkness. Tucked close to his side, Kennedy couldn't stop touching him. And kissing him. Though he kept smiling at her, he hadn't said anything about loving her.

She didn't mind. He'd had a lot on his plate dealing with Crosby, talking to his family and being very attentive to her. She didn't regret telling him she loved him, either. At that moment, she wasn't sure she could have held it in anyway. Honestly, she wanted to tell everyone, him, his family, Crosby...the whole world.

She, Kennedy Brooks, once an emotionally damaged woman forever trying to prove she was okay, disinterested in men, repelled by the idea of sex, now loved an alpha guy who epitomized danger—and she couldn't keep her hands off him.

Voice low and drowsy, Reyes said, "You beat me to the punch, you know."

"Hmm?" She loved his soft chest hair and the hard muscle beneath it. And his scent. Nuzzling against him, she breathed deeply, filling her head with that delicious smell.

"I wanted to do things right, not in the middle of chaos. Wasn't easy, but I was hanging on to my patience—then bam." He patted her backside. "You let me have it."

Smiling, Kennedy tucked her face under his chin. "Is this about me telling you I love you? Because I'm glad I did."

"I'm glad, too. Hell, *more* than glad." He fondly caressed one bottom cheek. "I love you, too, you know. I *more* than love you, actually. I want to marry you. Grow old with you. Maybe someday have little McKenzies with you."

The smile turned into a grin. "A rascal boy like you," she murmured, imagining it.

"Or a smart, strong girl like you." He kissed the top of her head.

"You really see me as strong?"

"I think you're the only one who doesn't see it. Your strength is quiet, steadfast, honorable and loyal."

He believed it, she knew...and she was starting to believe it, too.

"I want to share holidays with you, Kennedy, here at my dad's place, or even at your folks' place in Florida if you want. I will meet them, right?"

Filled with contentment, she nodded. "Yes."

"Good. So I want all that. Everything. From now until the end of time." He gave her a squeeze. "You love me enough to want that, too?"

"Yes." Teasing him, she said, "*More* than enough."

"Let's be clear here, okay? I'm the type of guy who's going to hover."

Was that supposed to be news to her? Playing along, she leaned up to look at him. "Meaning?"

"Meaning you go off on your own a lot, and I don't think I have the temperament to deal with that. How would you feel about me tagging along to play bodyguard?"

"Or sex servant?"

His slow grin warmed her. "Yeah, I can be a multipurpose kind of travel companion." More seriously, he asked, "You wouldn't mind that? I don't want you to feel smothered, but seriously, babe, I'd turn into an old man with gray hair if I was left behind to worry about you."

She kissed his chin. "I'll be happier keeping you near. But what if I have to travel and something comes up here? Your job isn't exactly nine-to-five."

"I know. And once you're scheduled, you couldn't just change things."

Clearly he'd given this a lot of thought. "Ideas?"

"Yeah. How would you feel about an actual bodyguard?" He rushed to add, "Only when I can't go along."

"Hmm." Having lived a life where she knew how easily things could go wrong, she actually liked the idea.

"Someone low-key," he promised, "who'd blend in and would still keep an eye on things. Someone you and I would research extensively."

"If I agree, will you agree to keep me informed of your jobs? To never keep any aspect of the danger from me?" She propped her elbows on his chest. "It'll be easier for me if I know what's going on."

Reyes trailed his fingertips down her spine. "Honestly, I never thought I'd enjoy talking shop with anyone outside the family, but with you it just comes naturally."

"That's a yes?"

"Ah, babe." He cupped her backside in both hands. "Right about now, I'd promise you anything if you'd just agree to marry me."

Giving him a thorough kiss, she murmured against his mouth, "Yes, I'll marry you."

He immediately relaxed. "Way to keep me in suspense."

"I love you, Reyes. More than I knew was possible."

"Same." This time his kiss was long and deep. "It'll be light soon. We should probably get some sleep?" He said it like a question, and judging by his wandering hands, sleep wasn't the number one thing on his mind. But as usual, he was a considerate, awesome, incredible man.

And he was all hers. "Who needs sleep?"

His hazel eyes immediately warmed. "Well, not me. But if you do—"

Kennedy straddled his hips. "I have a better idea."

"Hell, yeah, you do." He drew her close and kissed her in a way guaranteed to scorch her.

Yes, she was a little tired; she was also enormously happy, and she couldn't think of a better way to start their new life together than by making love to Reyes.

Now, tomorrow and always.

* * * * *

Keep reading for an excerpt of
Falling For The Rancher
by Tanya Michaels.
Find it in the
Cowboy By Heart: Anniversary Collection anthology,
out now!

Chapter One

It was surreal, staring at a photo of himself and feeling as if he were looking at a stranger. No, that wasn't exactly right, Jarrett Ross amended, studying the framed rodeo picture on the wall of his father's home office. The word *stranger* implied he didn't know the dark-haired cowboy, that he had no feelings about him one way or the other.

A wave of contempt hit him as he studied the cocky smile and silvery, carefree gaze. *Selfish SOB.* Six months ago, his only concerns had been which events to ride and which appreciative buckle-bunny to celebrate with after he won. A lot had changed since then.

Six months ago, Vicki wasn't in a wheelchair.

"Jarrett?"

He turned as Anne Ross entered the room. He'd been so mired in regret he'd almost forgotten he was waiting for his mother. Dread welled as she closed the door behind her. Did they need the privacy because there was more bad news to discuss? He wanted to sink into the leather chair behind the desk and bury his face in his hands. But he remained standing, braced for whatever life threw at them next.

"How did Dad's appointment go?" Jarrett hadn't been able to accompany his parents to the hospital this afternoon. There was too much to do at the Twisted R now that he was the only one working the ranch. But even without the countless tasks necessary to keep the place running, he would have stayed behind in case Vicki needed him—not that his sister voluntarily sought out his company these days.

"You know your father. He's a terrible patient." Anne rolled her eyes, but her attempt to lighten the situation didn't mask her concern. "Overall, the doctor says we're lucky. He's recovering as well as can be expected from the heart attack and the surgery. The thing is…"

Jarrett gripped the back of the chair, waiting for the other boot to drop.

His mother came forward and sat down in the chair across from him, the stress of the past few months plain on her face. Even more telling was the slump of her shoulders. She'd always had a ramrod-straight posture, whether sitting in a saddle or waltzing across a dance floor with her husband.

"I have to get your father off this ranch," she said bluntly. "I've been after him for years to slow down, to get away for a few days. I even tried to talk him into selling the place."

That revelation stunned Jarrett. He'd never realized his mom's complaints about the demands of ranch life were serious. He'd thought her occasional grumbling was generic and innocuous, like jokes about hating Mondays. People griped about it all the time, but no one actually suggested removing Monday from the calendar. It was impossible to imagine Gavin Ross anywhere but at the Twisted R. Not sure how to respond, he paced restlessly around the office. Despite the many hours he'd spent here over the past month, it still felt like trespassing. As if his father should be the one sitting behind the desk making the decisions that would affect the family.

"Your dad refuses to accept that he's not in his twenties anymore," his mom continued. "At the rate he's going, he'll work himself to death! And after the added stress of Vicki's accident…"

Guilt sliced through him. Was his dad's heart attack one more thing to trace back to that night in July? His mind echoed with the metallic jangling of the keys he'd tossed to his younger sister. He hadn't gone with her because a blonde named Tammy—or Taylor?—had been whispering in his ear, saying that as impressive as he'd been in eight seconds, she couldn't wait to see what magic he could work in an hour's time.

Jarrett pushed away the shameful memory. "So you and Dad want to take a few days of vacation?" he asked, leaning against the corner of the desk closest to her.

"A few weeks, actually. I haven't discussed it with him yet, but Dr. Wayne agrees that it's a good idea. My cousin has a very nice cabin near Lake Tahoe that she's been offering to let us use for years, and Dr. Wayne said he could give us the name of a good cardiologist in the area. Just in case."

When you were recovering from open-heart surgery, "just in case" wasn't nearly as casual as it sounded.

"Your father is mule-headed. Now that he's starting to feel a little better, he'll try to return to his usual workload. I can't let him do that. He may seem larger than life, but he's not invincible." Her gaze shifted downward. "And...without us as a buffer, Vicki would naturally turn to you for company and assistance."

The soft words were like a pitchfork to the gut. His sister, younger than him by almost seven years, had grown up idolizing Jarrett. Now his parents had to evacuate Texas just to force her to speak to him again.

"She's going to forgive you." Anne reached over to clasp his hand. "The drunk driver who plowed into the truck is to blame, not you."

He wanted to believe her, but it was his fault Vicki had been on the road. They'd had plans to grab a late dinner. Between his travel on the rodeo circuit and her being away for her freshman year of college, they'd barely seen each other since Christmas. But instead of catching up with his kid sister as promised, he'd ditched her in favor of getting laid. Vicki had been trapped amid twisted metal and broken glass when she should have been sitting in some restaurant booth, debating between chicken-fried steak and a rack of ribs. She'd always had a Texas-sized appetite, but her athletic hobbies kept her trim and fit.

Past tense. She no longer had much of an appetite. And although the doctors assured her that, with physical therapy, she would walk again, it would be a long damn time before she played softball or went to a dance club with her sorority sisters. She hadn't even been able to return to campus for the start of the new semester in August, another consequence that ate at him. Unlike Jarrett, who'd earned a degree with a combination of community-college courses and online classes, Vicki had been accepted into one of the best universities in the state. How much academic momentum was she losing?

Anne blamed Gavin's heart attack on years of working too hard and his stubborn insistence that "deep-fried" was a valid food group. But it was no coincidence that the man had collapsed during one of Vicki's multiple surgeries. The stress of his daughter's ordeal had nearly killed him.

"Jarrett." Anne's scolding tone was one he knew well from childhood. "I see you beating yourself up. You have to stop. If not for yourself, then for me."

"I'm fine," he lied. She was shouldering enough burden already without fretting over his well-being, too. "I was just processing the logistics of running the Twisted R while taking care of Vicki. I'll figure it out. You and Dad should definitely go."

"Thank you. Be sure to voice your support when he objects to the idea." She pursed her lips, considering. "We probably have a better shot at convincing him if you're *not* handling Vicki and the ranch by yourself. What if we found a part-time housekeeper who could act as her companion? Or, ideally, even someone with medical experience. My friend Pam's a retired nurse. I can ask her about home health care."

"Are we sure that's in the budget?" The mountain of medical bills was already high enough that Gavin had recently let go of their sole ranch hand after helping him find a job on another spread. Gavin insisted the Twisted R could function as a father-and-son operation if Jarrett was available to help full-time. No more rodeos for the foreseeable future.

Or ever. He hadn't competed since the night of Vicki's accident, and it was hard to imagine enjoying it again. Everything he'd loved—the adrenaline, the admiration of the spectators—seemed shallow in light of what his sister and dad had suffered.

"I'm not suggesting we hire a long-term employee," she said. "Just some help for a month or less. We have plenty of space. Maybe with Pam's help we can find someone temporarily willing to accept low pay in exchange for room and board. There could be someone young who needs the experience and a recommendation."

His mother made it sound almost reasonable, as if there were lots of people who would work practically for free and wanted to move in with a surly nineteen-year-old and a rodeo cowboy who'd taken early retirement. *What are the odds?*

Then again, they had to be due for some good luck.

"Okay," he agreed. "Call Pam and see what she says."

Meanwhile, he'd cross his fingers that his mom's friend knew someone who was truly desperate for a job.

"WHAT THE HELL do you mean I'm out of a job?" In her head, Sierra Bailey heard the familiar refrain of her mother's voice chiding her. Unladylike language was one of Muriel Bailey's pet peeves. *I just got fired. Screw "ladylike."*

Eileen Pearce, seated at the head of the conference table, sucked in a breath at Sierra's outburst. It was too bad Eileen and Muriel didn't live in the same city—the two women could get together for weekly coffee and commiserate about Sierra's behavior. "The board takes inappropriate relationships with patients very seriously, Ms. Bailey."

"There was no relationship!" Except, apparently, in Lloyd Carson's mind. Bodily contact between patient and physical therapist was a necessity, not an attempt at seduction. Sierra had never once thought of Lloyd in a sexual manner, but he'd apparently missed that memo. The man had unexpectedly kissed her during their last session. Which, in turn, led to his wife angrily demanding Sierra's head on a platter.

Taking a deep breath, Sierra battled her temper. "Patients become infatuated with medical professionals all the time. It's a form of misplaced gratitude and—"

"Yes, but in the year you've been with us, we've had multiple complaints about you. Granted, not of this nature, but your track record is flawed. Perhaps if you'd listened on previous occasions when I tried to impress upon you the importance of professional decorum..." Eileen paused with an expression of mock sympathy.

Comprehension dawned. This wasn't about Lloyd Carson and his romantic delusions. The board of directors had been looking for an excuse to get rid of Sierra. She felt foolish, not having seen the dismissal coming, but she truly believed she was good at her job.

Was she mouthy and abrasive? Occasionally.

All right, regularly. One might even argue, frequently. But sometimes PT patients needed a well-intentioned kick to the rear more than they needed to be coddled. *Lord knows I did.*

At twelve years old, Sierra had been a pampered rich girl whose parents treated her with a much different standard than her three rough-and-tumble brothers, as if she were fragile. Dr. Frederick Bailey and his wife, Muriel, had raised their sons with aspirations of global domination; they'd raised their daughter with the promise that she'd be a beautiful Houston debutante someday. No one had challenged her until the gruff physiotherapist who'd helped her after she'd been thrown from a horse.

He'd taught her to challenge herself, a lesson she still appreciated fifteen years later. The side effect was that she also tended to challenge authority, a habit the hospital's board of directors resented.

Given the barely concealed hostility in Eileen's icy blue gaze, it was a miracle Sierra had lasted this long. *You're partially to blame here, Bailey.* While she'd deny with every breath in her body that her conduct with Lloyd Carson had ever been flirtatious or unprofessional, Sierra could have been more of a team player. She could have made an effort to care about occupational politics.

As Eileen went over the legal details of the termination, Sierra's mind wandered to the future. Her savings account was skimpier than she'd like, but she was a trained specialist. She'd land on her feet. It was a point of pride that she'd been making her way for years, without asking her parents for money.

You'll find a new position. And when you do? Stay under the radar instead of racking up a file of grievances. In the interests of her career, Sierra could be detached and diplomatic.

Probably.

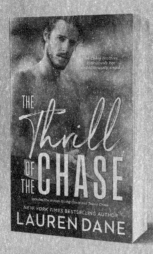 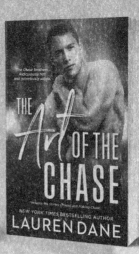

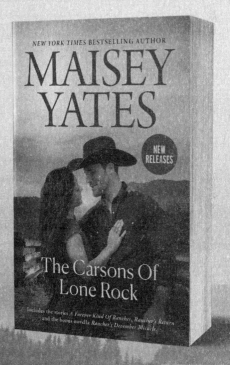

Subscribe and fall in love with a Mills & Boon series today!

You'll be among the first to read stories delivered to your door monthly and enjoy great savings.

MILLS & BOON

JOIN US

Sign up to our newsletter to stay up to date with...

- Exclusive member discount codes
- Competitions
- New release book information
- All the latest news on your favourite authors

> ## Plus...
> get $10 off your first order.
> *What's not to love?*

Sign up at **millsandboon.com.au/newsletter**